BOB

the Galactic Hero

by
Matt Vandegriff

ISBN-13: 978-0-9962712-0-2
ISBN-10: 0-9962712-0-1
(paperback)
Originally published by WWPFF Publishing, 2015
This third edition published June, 2021
www.bobthegalactichero.com
Wolf with Pen and Fennec Fox Publishing
www.WWPFF.com

for my daddy

Part I.
"Mindless, all of you, who in the strength of spears and the tearing edge win your valors by war, thus ignorantly trying to halt the grief of the world."
Euripides *Helen*, 480-406 b.c.

Beginnings

It is complicated to communicate between epochs. It is more than a little difficult to express the totality of one world to another, displaced in time. Our lives function through a shared context, a context that may, in even a small expanse of time, become invalid to the observer of history.
Concepts change, terminology changes, measurements change. Some ways of thinking evolve beyond recognition; some ways of thinking are abandoned.

Even though, some small things, for better or worse, remain constant. These consistencies provide an agreed upon backdrop through which our vast differences can be most accurately measured. There is love and there is family, but for the human race these universally consistent things are often hunger, bloodshed, and war. Human existence has been a prolonged and blatant mismanagement of resources. It is, unfortunately, these things that can provide a common denominator between great expanses of time.

Yet there has always been that pearl of the transcendent which exists seemingly in a vague cloud of statistical probability: the hope that we can overcome ourselves, that we can, as humans, conquer our humanity and transcend it. It is my sincerest hope that we are not on a galactic fool's errand, an infinite timescape by which we chase our tails endlessly. Despite our failures and countless shortcomings, there is time. There is always time. Time unravels our most complete wisdom. It allows our weavers the opportunity to create a great, unforeseen fabric.

It has been, perhaps, one hundred thousand years since the dawn of civilization. This, however, is uncertain as old Earth calendars carry no meaning in this age. Antiquated and lost to time, much of the old world lies in legend, in myth, and in speculative historical accounts.

The human race has spread, not unlike a virus, throughout the galaxy, inhabiting practically every easily habitable planet and many hostile environments. There was a time when it had been assumed that our galactic migration would involve modeling environments to the human design. There was even a word for it: terraformation. And yes, there has been a modicum of terraformation, but the process is

3

always faulty and vastly resource dependent. If it was easy for a planet to be lush like old Earth, it probably would be. There are usually strong cosmic reasons for a planet to function as it does. We have found that it is far more functional and much less resource dependent to modify the human rather than the whole planet. The human design is open to us and is easily manipulated. Often the modifications are only slightly noticeable. Perhaps a planet is colonized with a certain percentage of a disagreeable gas in the atmosphere. It's simple to modify the lungs to filter out that gas, or add a circulatory process that renders the gas inert. In the most easily habitable planets, it is often a variation on the exact level of oxygen in the atmosphere that must be accounted for: some higher, some lower than old Earth. However, some environments which are considerably more hostile to human life have required greater modifications, or transmogrifications of the human design. Some of these inhabitants may seem extremely alien to a human from old Earth's history, during a time when there was *only* Earth, yet the galaxy is peppered only with humanoids that share a common old Earth ancestry.

That is not to say there is no life outside of Earth origins, but it is believed that all of human equivalent intelligence is of Earth origin. There have been found many flora and fauna of decidedly alien genesis, even microbial, multicellular, and miniscule creatures of every variety, some more than miniscule, but no human intelligence save us.

There are many theories why. Some argue that life spreads more or less equally around the galaxy and tends to aggregate, dependent upon favorable conditions. Those most favorable conditions would be old Earth, an isolated cloudburst amongst the particulated galactic atmosphere. Others argue that there once were many humanoid lifeforms that intermingled and merged into one in a history that predates Earth, though no substantial evidence of this has been found as would be expected with a theory that predates all historical records.

Most people populating the galaxy have little to no knowledge of ancient history and see the galaxy as it is now, a galaxy rich with alien worlds, cultures, and conflicts. Despite the truth of our shared origin, it is sometimes a godsend to exist in the now rather than be subsumed in the past.

Migration, for obvious reasons, tends to follow the path of gravity. From old Earth, population spread outward from the spiral arm to which it belonged and arced towards and around the galactic center. Not too close to the center, which is a cosmically volatile place, but close enough that the density of stars made traveling between them considerably easier. This was, of course, before the invention of modern transport that has brought all worlds within arm's length. Since modern travel, the path of immigration has been rather uniformly outward from center leaving the populated galaxy more diffuse but weighted toward old Earth.

There are currently several large galactic regions that claim "rights of governance" or "sovereignty". These are massive bureaucracies that have the motility of injured soapstone, supposedly "governing" many, many worlds. These regions are divided into quadrants and subdivision, which are divided into provinces, collectives, colonies, and cooperatives. Eventually the division of power finds its way down to a single planet, which is then divided, in kind, into continental superpowers, nations, states, regions, etc., etc., ad infinitum. People throughout the galaxy are more or less unaware and unconcerned with these superstructures. Regardless of the complexity of the power structure, people run their daily lives aware of what needs to be done and what should be avoided. As it always is with authority, regardless of the temperament of the rulers, it's the guy at a fast food restaurant who refuses to process your order unless you use company-specific lingo, that you want to strangle to death. It's never so much about how much power one has, as much as it is about who is willing to abuse their power, no matter how little of it they possess.

Fortunately, the galaxy is in a relative state of stasis, not peace but stasis. There is fighting, even war, but the vast majority of the civilized galaxy functions with basic freedoms and, at least, passable human rights. Few mention the idea of a world at peace. This idea has entered the realm of unrequited optimism at best and utopian mythology at worst as there has been so little evidence of peace in human history.

There is an old Earth saying, "One moment of bliss. Why is that not enough for an entire lifetime?"
However, today most prefer the Children of Demeter's ode to the galaxy:
"The endless spiral spirals beyond our control.
You may call it chaos, but we all call it home."

Visit Sol!
Brought to you by the Orion-Cygnus Arm Travel Authority (OrCA)

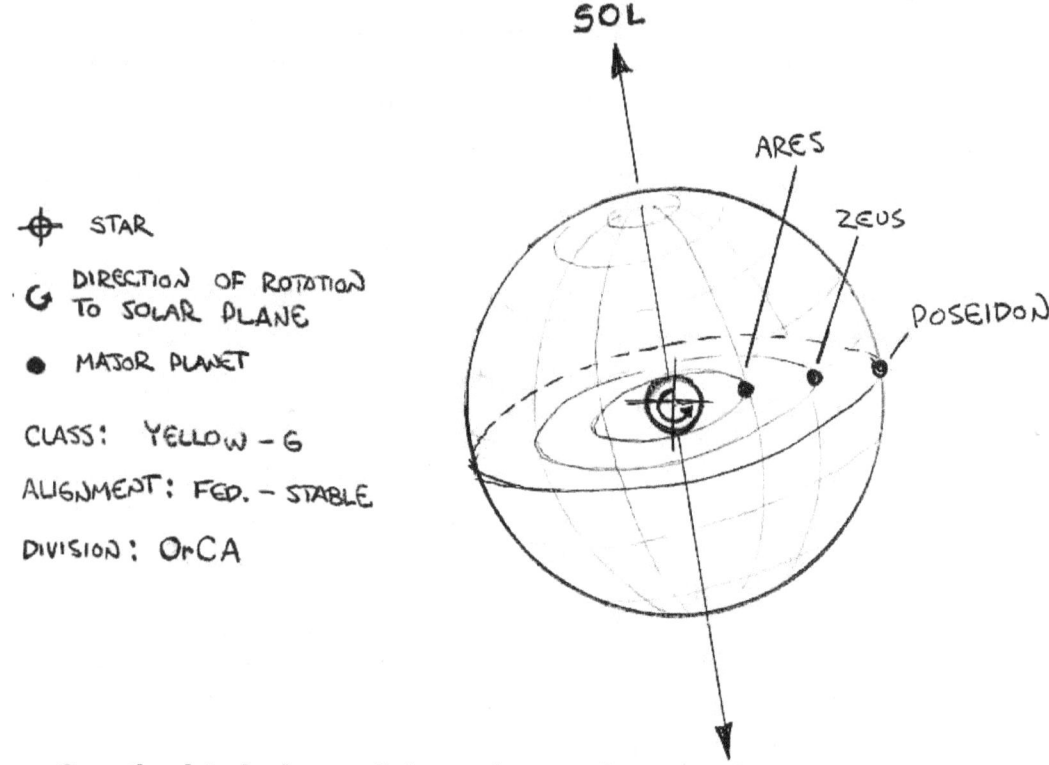

See the birthplace of the galaxy, where it all began! Walk on the same hallowed ground our ancient ancestors toiled through the dark ages, and see the night sky from their vantage point when the galaxy was but a mysterious unknown. Bathe your skin in the yellow glow of the origin star, giver of all life.

Sol is a veritable wonderland of exotic cultures and a bizarre amalgam of modernity and antiquity. While in the Sol system, you'll most definitely want to visit:

Ares. Ares was the first world colonized by early Earth travelers and home to the great Ares Obelisk and the tower of Lakshmi. Be sure to plan a stroll through the lush Copper Mountain National Forest, year-round and ever-green against the red soil famous galaxy wide. You'll also want to schedule a walk in the shadow of the great Pyramid of Osiris. Fashioned in the style of the old Earth pyramids, Osiris is the third largest known pyramid in the galaxy and a walk in the shadow is said to bring safety when traveling through the void between worlds. Travelers note: If visiting the nation of New Mana, make sure to call Ares by the old Roman designation "Mars" as the culture tends to be intolerant of the modernization of planetary nomenclature.

Aphrodite (Venus), though by nature inhospitable to life, makes a great stop for those interested in industrial tours. Primarily a mining planet, Aphrodite boasts some of the largest and most modern machinery for mining operations this side of the galactic center. Aphrodite was once a major source of carbon dioxide and sulphur used in early terraformation until that practice was all but abandoned in times past. The result has left Aphrodite with little to no atmosphere, but don't let that deter your visit. Ongoing mining of precious metals and a thriving starship manufacturing facility will provide the visitor with an astounding view of the inner workings of modern life.

No trip to Sol would be complete without a visit to the great **Zeus** (Jupiter). Zeus is home to one of the only seven known monument worlds, specifically the beautiful Helen. You'll want to begin your visit on Helen's Crown, a city many claim is unparalleled anywhere in the galaxy. While technically not the largest city in the galaxy, Helen's Crown may be the most impressive. A seat of culture and art, architecture and philosophy, Helen's Crown is the shining jewel of the Sol system and an epicurean paradise. While visiting Helen, spend some time researching the many moons of Zeus, such as Ganymede which boasts a progressive art culture, or Europa, home to many pre-antiquity early Earth artifacts.

Before you leave, you'll want to visit one of the many spas and resorts of **Poseidon's** (Neptune) numerous floating island nations. Enjoy a night swim against the blue backdrop of Poseidon's beautiful, albeit deadly, atmosphere. Perfect for couples on honeymoon.

Though travel to **Earth** is restricted, there are many orbital observation facilities for those wanting to reconnect to our shared and beclouded past. Perfect for contemplation, many visitors find the experience moving and transformative. In the words of a voice lost to time lies the well-known saying:
"Though we scatter to and fro
and fail to find that which cannot be found,
a universe filled with desperate wandering,
always with us, from whence we came,
    our home.
Terra Firma. Divina Sphaera.
    Our home is always with us."

Interstellar travelers receive a 10% discount at all Pauly's Bread Bucket restaurants.

Chapter One: Bob, Abrum, and the Death of a Salesman.

      Bob lived in a rundown flat in a bad part of town. That town was the mammoth city of Helen's Crown in the eye of Zeus. Antiquity knew this planet as Jupiter but, in times now forgotten, the Romanization of the gods has been abandoned for the ancient Greek derivatives. All planets in the Sol system had been so renamed.

      The gas giants, in any system, were prime real-estate. Platform cities, floating citadels, everything from every dreamer's dreams happens on these gargantuan worlds, and these failed stars were perfectly suited. Imagine planets of the largest magnitude with no land restrictions. Once the human race perfected methods of building on these gas worlds, the population flourished. Countless numbers of people have found their home on the many gas giants peppering the galaxy. Of course, Zeus (formerly Jupiter) was the first to experience this.

      A common trend of mass construction in the past tens of thousands years has been unimaginable monuments floating statuesquely is the vastness of these planets great atmospheres. Zeus, being prone to atmospheric turbulence, almost always possesses at least one storm, lasting hundreds of years, that would be known as the "eye of Zeus". The very rare eras in which no significant storm was great enough to be called the "eye" were holy times for the people of Zeus (those who followed the customs of their home world) and would be known as "the time of sleeping gods".

      Here on Zeus, a statue in the image of Helen was built suspended in the center of the great eye. To this day, the statue of Helen remains the largest of known constructed monuments in the galaxy. Atop the statue of Helen, sitting upon her crown, lies the city of Helen's Crown. Long ago Earth had dismantled all of its great cities. The cost of upkeep was no longer preferable to the diminishing need for massive conglomerates of people. Also, there had long ago been developed a philosophy that centered itself on the importance of a human concept of personal space and the outcomes of failing this.

Helen's Crown did not conform to these economies or philosophies as its numbers now exceeds nine hundred and eighteen million. This figure excludes the numbers living in cities on her left shoulder and right upturned palm. These cities along with the many outlanders living sparsely among the various suitable sustainable surfaces placed the total numbers of Helen to be in the neighborhood of two and a half billion. Why Helen? How fitting it is that Zeus would keep in his eye the image of his most beautiful daughter. The philosophies that now pervaded most regions of Helen are humanist and have set their eyes on Earth antiquity.

The approach by ship is absolutely the best part of visiting Helen. Helen is completely veiled in the violence of the swirling storm of the eye, but breaching the center, the true "eye" of the storm, she miraculously appears. Helen here appears as an alabaster goddess against a backdrop of swirling red and orange clouds. The magnitude of her presence is shocking. The sheer size coupled with the false impression that Helen is sculpted of marble is enough to make the strongest skeptic feel to have set foot in the halls of the gods. It is difficult to shake the disbelief that something like this could truly be human-made.

Drawing nearer, from her upturned palm, the glow of New Paris is visible and to a lesser extent the city of Nemesis looms over her left shoulder. However, these cities, great though they are, are overshadowed by a strong glow or halo which seems to emanate from the head of Helen and the faint traces of structures rising. This is the city of Helen's Crown.

Beyond the cities lie the outworld regions of Helen. These were at times rough areas. Laws were enforced but, as often is the case in impoverished and forgotten lands, law enforcement became a means of population control rather than the protection of individual rights. Helen was at times brutal and unwelcoming.

Most of Helen's Crown has retained all the majesty and splendor one would expect; a paramount of architectural brilliance and epicenter of art and culture. Many, especially the citizens, considered Helen's Crown to be the center of the galaxy...often irritatingly so. But every dwelling, no matter how magnificent, ritzy, holy, or haughty, has a toilet: an inescapable fact of living in the human world. Helen's Crown has some bad parts of town.

Bob was middle-aged, sturdy, and perhaps a little overly heavy framed, but muscular more so than his exercise regimen should account for. His hairline was not receding so much but rather individual hairs were uniformly and democratically "jumping ship" which gave the overall effect that his hairdo, which he adopted some 30 years earlier, was merely in the process of vanishing. He carried a full mustache that once was a strong auburn but now was fading to gray. Legend says that he may have, in fact, been born with that very mustache. Bob often wore a suit as expected in his line of work, but preferred more comfortable clothes. He was not a suit. He wore the suit, the suit didn't wear him.

Bob's flat was the typical fare for such squalor one found in the underbelly of a massive city: poorly maintained, crime-ridden, and cheap. An apartment building far more populated than is rational; the tattered decor was of an era long since passed. Bob lived on the 82nd floor, which was somewhere in the neighborhood of halfway up the building, and there were probably 60 some odd apartments on his floor.

The hallway before his apartment was dank and poorly lit. It had the appearance of night at all times of the day. Inside, each apartment has the look and feel of a cheap motel: one bedroom, a small living room, a kitchenette, and lavatory with shower, stool, and sink. Every tenant had the luxury of one window as well that opened to the spectacular view of the building literally a foot away. Bob could physically touch the next building, though would never open the window due to the poor quality of the air outside.

Bob had a decent job, made a good living, and could easily afford a better flat with better circumstances surrounding it, but he had no possessions to speak of, no family, and his job was conducive to this environment. Bob worked for the Department of Critique as a forensic analyst and criminologist. He was a detective. He analyzed crime scenes and tried to figure out whodunit.

There were many tenants renting rooms on Bob's floor, but Bob hesitated to think of them as neighbors. They kept to themselves, always with a suspicious eye on everyone around them. Words were exchanged only as necessary and conversation was generally nonexistent. The one exception was the tenant in an oddly positioned room at the far end of the main hallway. His door was the only door on the entire floor not parallel to the flow of hallway traffic. His name is Abrum Alle'phant. Abrum was perhaps the most peculiar individual Bob had encountered; friendly and social, yes, but unusual in mannerism and atmosphere. To most people Abrum's style of dress was otherworldly or at least very peculiar. Bob, however, happened to take a class in his university days on the early visual recordings of primitive human cultures and Bob knew Abrum's style to be adopted from some of the earliest Earth "films", as they were called. Abrum often wore some form of suit with detailed striping, ascot or necktie, and the most reflective faux-leather black dress shoes. The clothing must have been tailored because there would be no acquisition of such garments from any standard supplier anywhere in the galaxy. The material itself had an ancient and musty quality as if it had been made by clumsy machines thousands of years ago. Abrum was very thin framed, olive skin, hair meticulously tended to and glossed with some such styling substance. The finishing touch was the appropriate pencil mustache ornamenting and outlining the boundary of his equally thin upper lip. Abrum made his appearances exclusively at twilight or night in what Bob suspected was Abrum's idea of "the right lighting".

Abrum: "Bob,...Bob...the ventilation is out again."

Bob: "Yeah, I noticed,...but you know Abrum, ..., I don't work here, I don't really fix things here."

Abrum: "Yes Bob, I don't want you to fix the problem, I want you to share in my outrage".

Bob: "Yeah, ... well....?"

This was followed by a good 30 seconds of Abrum glaring, not at Bob, but into his eyes.

Bob: "Abrum, you seem like a nice enough guy, but every time you're here,...you kinda creep me out a bit."

With a half smirk as if the comment was accepted as a jest between close friend (which they were not), Abrum raised his hand, slightly wiggling his fingers as if casting a spell and said:

"Oh Bob...Bob....Bob..." as he receded into the shadows and was gone. But, for how long?

Ignoring the awkwardness of the conversation, Bob entered his flat and set the food he had brought on the small coffee table in his living room. The synthesis drive was out on his food replicator and he had to wait till later in the week when someone was coming to fix it. Practically every home had a food replicator. Simply download the encrypted schematics from a favorite restaurant and the replicator would construct the meal to precise specifications. Generally fast-food only, it was a comfort to most to be able to receive their favorite foods in exactly the same way. If you ordered the same soup repeatedly, it would always be the same soup with the exact same noodles, with the exact same vegetables floating in the exact same position. Identical copies. Bob noticed his replicator was leaving important components out of his food. Several vegetables floating in a stew looked as though they had been intricately etched or devoured by worm. It was probably harmless, but better to be safe than sorry. There are numerous cases of poisoning and sickness, though most of

11

these are from illegal copies of discontinued foods. Every once in a while some source food is scanned that has a virus, bacterial infection, or other contaminant and that tainted food is perfectly replicated in the homes of hungry people. Once discovered the copies are immediately discontinued and destroyed, but in a galaxy of technologically interconnected people nothing is ever truly lost.

Someone invariably ends up trying to work around the system and gets a wayward copy of foods that shouldn't be. When Bob tried to order a noodle soup and the replicator sized the copy wrong such that only a quarter of the bowl was produced he knew there was a problem and now a big mess to clean up.

The deli across the street was cheap and not very good, but it would do until his replicator was back on line. Bob was about halfway through an uninspiring meal when he received a call from the Chief.
Bob: "Yallow",
Chief: "Bob, we got a crime scene for you to come check out. Male, 42, cause of death unknown. Upper east side 343rd and 52nd."
Bob: "On my way."

This would most likely be a routine investigation into a fatality, but it is unusual to hear the cause of death listed as "unknown". The tools of common officers usually pinpointed the cause of death fairly accurately and were stated in hypothesized terms, such as: suspected EMP discharge, or suspected knife wound, or suspected crushed by a malfunctioning trans-planetary frigate, or suspected vaporization by faulty public toilet, but "unknown" was a little less common.

Leaving the apartment complex, Bob had to walk a few blocks to catch public transport. All transport on Helen's Crown was public transport. This city was too big and too populated to allow for the inefficiency of individual motility. Bob lived far downtown. Outside, the atmosphere was dull and gray, hazy and unhealthy. The buildings, despite the variation in color, all seemed to average out to a depressing brown. The streets were dirty, unkempt, with only the occasional street sweeper that itself didn't do a very good job. People kept to themselves. There was no real sense of community or neighborhood. It was sad to see people forgotten, struggling to make ends meet merely to live in the dregs of a great city. That was most of the people living downtown in Helen's Crown.

It wasn't all bad though. Bob walked past kids playing games in the street, running happily and wildly like pack animals. People going about their daily lives, countless stories that invariably were riddled with hardship but equally peppered with joy and love and peace no matter how brief, no matter how transient.

Entering the plaza of the city's main light rail, whose proximity was yet another selling point of Bob's less-than-austere abode, despite the grime and dingy quality of the surroundings one could easily see the forgotten majesty of a once important transport terminal. Simply known as "downtown station" it had in years past been an important hub of traffic. Imagining the station clean with a standard of upkeep it was easy to become impressed or even inspired by what such a transport meant for the people and the city. It was a symbol of greatness past, but it was also a symbol of the interrelationship between accomplishment and decay. It follows us like a hellhound on our trail.

Walking down a flight of stairs, stepping past what was presumably urine, and entering the main terminal, Bob quickly boarded the light rail, the doors closed, and he was off. Historically people had to wait, sometimes considerably, for the next train to arrive. Over the years, petitions filed, initiatives acted upon, and elected officials uncharacteristically keeping a campaign promise, more trains were added for the frustrated mobs. Eventually this evolved into the light rail system we have today where enough trains were added that each line became it's own Mobius strip, folding in on itself. This main line which Bob was currently riding was a loop that traveling north bisected the city almost perfectly before turning east, looping across itself and angling south towards downtown again. The path of the main line was approximately 500 miles of connected train cars. No beginning, no end. There was never a wait for a train, one merely waited for the entire train line to make a stop then boarded wherever they happened to be.

Helen's Crown is a big city, but the trains travel quite fast. From the downtown terminal to the terminal nearest Bob's destination, about 20 minutes would pass. Leaving the downtown terminal the train rose from underground to a level a few stories up. Newer train lines were all underground, but this being an older line maintained the above-ground style of the time in which it was built. It was always an experience of which Bob never seemed to grow tired. Looking out the window and traveling from downtown to the upper east side, it was almost as if someone somewhere had a dial that at one end said "dingy, depressing, and gray" and at the other "bright, cheerful, and awe inspiring". This dial was slowly turned from one extreme to the other as the train sped towards uptown. Additionally, the closeness of the buildings downtown, that seemed oppressive and claustrophobic slowly separated, spreading out as uptown approached.

The station at which Bob arrived was not a significant hub like the downtown station once had been, but it was immaculate and full of life. It was a couple of blocks to the crime scene and Bob took his time breathing in the fresh air, the sunshine, the sight of trees even, though the trees were carefully placed and maintained thus absent of any trace of wilderness about them. The sunlight, the fresh air, all of it was more or less artificial. Zeus was unlike Earth in almost all regards and life had to be maintained. It didn't arise of it's own volition here. The sun of Earth: warming, life-giving, death-bringing, and ever-present, from Helen at Zeus was a mere point blending into the background of the other stars in the sky. Helen had her own atmosphere which was as manicured as was her trees. Light was artificial and weather, in the nicer parts of Helen's Crown, maintained a spring like feel, comfortable, sunny and cool. Due to the oscillations of people's schedules, the distance of the sun, and the absence of necessity, these conditions were always present. Helen' Crown had a scheduled rotation of increasing and decreasing illumination but saw no true night. There were, however, sufficiently claustrophobic areas, buildings built upon buildings all in the name of progress, where one could find darkness and many others, such as Bob's neck of the woods, where pollution made the sky perpetually overcast. So one could imagine Bob might just take his time in the lovely weather of uptown. He did have a job to do, but rarely do dead bodies have anywhere to go in a hurry and seldom complain at tardiness.

Bob activated his terminal access to check the coordinates again and headed in the proper direction. A universal constant galaxy wide is the use of what is commonly referred to as "terminal access". Terminal access is an interconnected stream of galactic data updated in more-or-less real time. It is a shared compendium of all knowledge from the most scholarly to that which would aspire to achieve a designation of "trivia". It is a shared and instantaneous communications protocol and indispensable for organization and basic day to day functionality.

Though the specifics are endlessly modifiable, most individuals activate terminal access by various standard somatic commands. Brushing the forearm towards the wrist is a common standard for summoning a display which can then be interacted with or resized with simple hand gestures. This display is only visible to the user unless that user grants access to another individual or purposefully makes the display visible to all. An ancient human being brought into current times would find modern people strange and fidgety, constantly wiggling their fingers through the air and making nonsensical gestures as if afflicted by some faulty motor-neuron condition.

The means by which a human being interacts with terminal access is easy to accomplish but difficult to understand. There is no implanted device or associated object but access and visual display emanates from the body itself. It is an interaction between the terminal stream proper and the peripheral nervous system of the individual. The term used by the architects of terminal access is physioneural-encryptographical-parasympathetic-axonsynaptic-phrenologistical-biofeedback processing and amelioration...a term designed to ward off any true interest in the subject itself.

Bob timed his arrival at the crime scene almost perfectly as he had just about finished the ice cream cone he picked up from a street vendor along the way. A knowing glance toward some familiar officers guarding the scene, and passing the demarcated perimeter, he approached the body, a medic, and the attending officer in charge on the open sidewalk lining a wide street on one side and an array of business' on the other.

Officer: "Hiya Bob. The deceased has been identified as Rames Palter, male, 42, salesman of communicable mods. No immediate family. Lived alone in apartment 351c of the Juniper tower in east midtown."
Bob: "Hm...salesman? Odd."

Communicable mods were protocols intended to modify a wide range of interactive devices. These could be terminals, home interfaces, implants, practically anything with which an individual might interact. The idea being that one could "fine tune" their surroundings as they saw fit. Most devices that an individual might interact with would indeed be modifiable to some extent, so this was a collective way that an individual could pre-modify devices they might encounter in the world around them, the modification coming from one source rather than the countless devices populating one's everyday life.

As for the deceased Rames Palter, what was odd was not his occupation per se. This was indeed a common occupation, not that there were lots of communicable mods salespeople but there were always some and it was about as innocuous of a job as one could ever hope to find. There were cases in the past of mod specialists selling hacked mods, usually for malicious purposes in the underground market, but this was a thing of the past and most likely not possible with modern security and encryption. It would be looked into, but very unlikely. What *was* odd was the mundane nature of this man's occupation coupled with his unknown method of demise.

Bob: "How did he die?"
Officer: "We still don't know. No wounds, no trauma. Perhaps the medic should chime in on this."
        The medic was a very stern and straightforward man in a navy suit. This fella was definitely in his element wearing such a suit; middle aged, oddly unattractive, perhaps more from his demeanor than his physical appearance.
Medic: "Yes. There are no wounds. No signs of trauma. No internal damage. In fact, if we had gotten to him soon enough we probably could have revived him."
Bob: "So, no signs of murder then? If he keeled over from a stroke or heart attack then why am I here?" Bob said with an initial pang of irritation, but thinking about how lovely it was uptown and how nice the weather was (conditioned to be so), it quickly passed and he didn't mind at all that his time might be wasted here.
Medic: "That's the issue. As you know it is practically unheard of that a middle aged person would have either a stroke or heart attack. Also, medical scans have verified that neither of these events happened. This is, for all intents and purposes, a completely healthy dead body. It's almost as if a switch was flipped and he was turned off."
Bob: "Still, what makes this a murder rather than a medical mystery?"
Officer: "Well, it could be just a mystery, but witnesses say that they saw him approached by a man, exchanged words, then the victim ran, as the witness put it, "for his life" before collapsing to the pavement in a loud thud."
Bob: "Hmm."
Officer: "Assuming we get your statement that this is in all probability a homicide, we'll apply immediately for a warrant to get the video footage of the event and surrounding applicable areas."
Bob: "Right. Well, it is suspicious. It wouldn't hurt to see what actually happened here, though the bulk of the details rarely comes from the crime scene itself. I'll head over to the victim's apartment and look around. I'll need access to his apartment and all communications devices the deceased himself had access to."
Officer: "I'm sure by the time you get there you'll have been granted the applicable access." There was a hint of humor in his voice.
 Perhaps it was the ice cream cone that clued him into the fact that Bob might be inclined to take his time, and right he was.
Bob: "If I find anything I'll ring the Chief. I'll be off then."

Chapter Two: Quantum Fluctuations, an Autopsy, Another Dead Body and What Are Little Grains Made Of?

A light dinner at a nearby noodle shop and another ice cream cone later, Bob arrived at the Juniper tower. The Juniper tower in midtown was a very nice building. Surrounded by a crescent of trees and simple but well-manicured gardens, the facade extended skyward with the appearance of stainless steel and clear glass. The lobby was well kept and welcoming, opening into an inner circle of eight retro-styled elevator doors.

Entering the elevator and stating his destination, the doors silently slid shut and Bob was off. Inertial dampers created the illusion that the elevator was relatively motionless but was, in fact, traveling at an impressive speed. The destination was floor 300, apartment 51c. The inside of the elevator seemed larger that it would possibly need to be, about the size of Bob's apartment minus the bathroom and kitchenette. It also contained a small two-person sofa, an armchair, and a standing lamp between the two as if someone might sit and read or have a comfortable conversation, neither of which has probably ever happened in this elevator. On one wall was a quasi-impressionist faux-painting rendition of the tower itself. Astringent and non-memorable, it inspires in the beholder such ponderings as "what is the opposite of 'art for art's sake'?". On the opposing wall was another faux-painting, this one done is strict realism, of a solitary Juniper tree. It was actually rather nice to look at partly because of the intricate twisting of the tree trunk and the plateaus of green framing the terminal end of its branches, but also because the background, though sparse and with little detail, shows no signs of buildings, cities, or civilization. The mark of a human presence is absent from this painting, something few of our galactic inhabitants would ever experience.

With hardly enough time to notice the mundane surroundings of the elevator, Bob arrived at floor 300. The doors opened to a well-lit and nicely carpeted circular hallway, still exuding a distant "time forgot" quality. In addition to the vague overhead lighting that almost all buildings use these days, the walls were peppered regularly with glass sconces that cast a triangular light upward against the wall. Bob thought this was exactly the sort of place Abrum would love, but getting into a conversation with Abrum about why he lived in the crumby downtown apartment complex would require more interest than Bob could muster.

Extending like spokes of a wheel were passages to apartment banks in groups of 100, and from there hallways extended laterally for each digit in apartments lettered A through G. That meant for each digit of the 100 there were 7 apartments (A-G) and there were 8 main hallways, one for each elevator. This floor alone had 5600 apartments. This was a rather big building. It was a good walk as well to find apartment 51c as the particular elevator Bob took opened to hallway 401-500. It was akin to walking around several city blocks inside.

Bob assured himself that he had taken just the right amount of time getting here as his hand on the knob of apartment 51c opened the door effortlessly meaning the appropriate warrants had been granted and employed. One of the nice things about modern life is that the identity of an individual is just about always known, and known as well who should and shouldn't have access to this door or that.

The apartment of the deceased, a one Rames Palter, was nice but small. It was probably about the same size as Bob's apartment, but divided into more rooms and overall less gloomy and in a much nicer part of town...and well maintained and decorated. Other than that... This, and probably all the apartments on this floor were efficiency apartments. Undoubtedly there were much fancier ones probably much higher up, but the bulk of the building most likely contained apartments such as these. There was a large window that unfortunately opened to a view of another building. It's hard not to encounter this phenomenon on Helen's Crown. This is an old, old city and construction, this so called "progress", never stops. When this building was originally built, maybe 400 years ago, the view from here probably looked across the city in an amazing splendor of activity.

Bob's objective was to get a sense of the victim's life and possible reason for being murdered, if that does turn out to be the case. In these investigations Bob was always specified to be first on the scene. He had very good instincts about these things and preferred to see the scene untouched. Later, when he was satisfactorily done, the police forensics team would collect, sort, and catalog every detail down to the last speck of dander.

The living space was cluttered but fairly clean with run of the mill knick-knacks and utilities that are the common flotsam of a human life. Nothing particularly out of place. Nothing disturbed. Clothing, some clean some crumpled in piles around the bed, pictures of family members, distant though as this man obviously lived alone. By now his kin would be notified and scheduled for a conference though most like they would know nothing. Remnants of food remained from what was most likely his last meal, some sort of vegetable casserole. It's something to wonder what his choice might have been had he known it would be his last meal.

Nothing much would come from the apartment itself. The smoking gun, if there was one, would be found in the victims private data. Bob accessed an interface from a desk in what was probably the victims study; a small and plain room. No decorations. Just a desk, chair, interface and a more comfortable chair in the corner of the room. Assuming the appropriate accesses had been granted to the victims data storage Bob would begin wading through the tangled and often uninteresting mess of information attached to a person's life. Data continually streams to and from every individual in the civilized galaxy clinging like unmanaged spider silk often consuming the point of origin to the extent that only the stream remains. Rames Palter was so consumed, now existing only a stream of lingering data.

Hours passed and Bob found very little. Communications between clients which were meaningless and harmless. The victim seemed to do his job well and with a high job satisfaction rate leaving no room for disgruntled patrons and not a single threat or even scornful word. He met several individuals at a local gym to play squash, but individuals that were looking merely for a squash partner and could hardly be considered friends. They'd be questioned but Bob was fairly certain this would turn up nothing.

In fact, there were only two things Bob found that carried any interest whatsoever and most likely had nothing to do with the case. The first being that the victim happened to be an avid, or perhaps slightly obsessed, Q-communique enthusiast, and second that he had retained a considerable collection of these communications. This will take a bit of explanation provided handily by the FGL (free galactic library) introductory article on the subject of quantum grain structures.

Quantum Grain Structures
an introduction compiled by the resources
of the FGL

Discovered a mere couple hundred years ago, and chiefly by accident, were the galaxies smallest inhabitants; the quantum grain structures. The name is a bit of a misnomer as quantum grain structures are neither grain nor merely structures. They happen to be the galaxy's oddest form of life and were not recognized as living for a considerable time following their discovery. By then the name was firmly entrenched in the scientific community and the public. What these "structures" are in actuality, are living germ-like bodies at the quantum level. They, in fact, seem to be composed of quantum fluctuations themselves and have no physical or corporeal body. A single grain can exist in several states and locations at once and have proven incredibly difficult to study. Also, as the structure of the body is in flux, dissection terminates life function and the grain ceases to exist. It is, unfortunately through death that humankind achieves most of its understanding of the natural world. With no dead body our understanding of the quantum grain process is naive at best.

What we have learned is that the quantum grain structure is by far the most prolific life-form in the galaxy existing uniformly, even in deep space, yet in higher concentrations around inhabited worlds. Therefore there exists some relationship between habitable worlds and grain proliferation. In any given cubic meter there exists somewhere between 100 and 1000 individual grains, though sampling is difficult and these numbers are broad estimates at best. The procreative process is unknown. The point of origin of the species is unknown.

The incomplete nature of our knowledge of quantum grains structures would have left humankind ignorant to their "living" status had it not been for the invention of the Multiple Manifold Quantum Field Fast Fourier Transform, or MMQFFFT. Not only did this device discover and confer upon the grains a status of life, it astonishingly verified the life was sentient.

Scientists previously understood that the grains carried out an unknown quantum process and the MMQFFFT passively analyzed and intercepted this unknown process. Upon analysis it was discovered that two distinct processes are taking place. One, a small amount of space is being folded between one grain and another or perhaps all grains (currently unknown). And two, the individual grain is transferring a strain of information through the folded space.

It has been theorized that the folding of space at the quantum level might be a natural phenomenon that is undetectable to us without the presence of the grain, thus the grain itself might not fold space but rather take advantage of the natural process of quantum space folding.

The information transferred, in a form akin to what one might imagine a quadrary language would be, has through painstaking efforts been very partially deciphered. The deciphered text, usually with multiple errors and unknowns, seems to be information about individual status and rarely mentions anything referenceable. For example, the following are average transmissions intercepted by the MMQFFFT of grain communication:

"Incendiary grain 121Epsilon93-Alpha766 remained in dormancy for 2 lunar cycles."

"The great elder grain Alph-Alpha000134720mega remained in dormancy for 703 solar cycles. Alph-Alpha000134720mega's ancient ways are not similar to ours."

"Compromised grain 173-naught-5555-Upsilon Theta-X was found unviable out of dormancy and procreated incomplete offspring, thus earning the universal surname "X"."

However, every so often a transmission is found that references something known. This famous interception was a keystone in identifying Earth as a reference in grain transmission terminology:

"Off world grain Theta-Q125-739-Delta could not adequately measure its post dormancy cycles. Contrast measurements of the hive have found the Solar cycle of Earth to be 1.1500078 th's that of standard grain cycles."

Hopes of using their means of communication for our own purposes are currently non-existent. We cannot predict the folding, though it happens countless times every second. Even if we could, the opening and amount of information transferred by the grains, though very small, uses the complete bandwidth of the process, so as long as the grain is communicating, nothing else will fit through and to eliminate the grain renders the process, or our ability to detect it, null.

It is valuable for the student of galactic lifeforms to remember that, compared to grains, humankind is outnumbered by incalculable magnitudes. The estimated transfer of grain data, redundant and pointless as it may seem, in one day outweighs the entire data produced in human history.

Ultimately, what is now known of the quantum grain structures is that they are alive, they are sentient, and they appear to share a hive mind. They seem either ignorant or uninterested in other forms of life. They cannot be communicated with, only listened in on. Our relationship to the grains will forever be that of the eavesdropper.

What it means then to be a Q-communique enthusiast is that this man, the victim, spent a considerable amount of time listening to the communications between random grains. Those that do this usually believe that they might stumble upon some magnificent information, some scientific breakthrough, or some foretelling of impending galactic disaster. It's not unlike old Earth and the ancient people of those days scanning the heavens for radio signals wondering what mysteries they might uncover. Though there are many, many Q-communique enthusiast and even a galactic log maintained on Exodus (a planet far, far from the Sol system and a hub of information retrieval), there has never once been any significant revelation from the information gathered from quantum grain structures. Significant as the phenomenon itself is, the value of grain data lies solely in the hands of hobbyists and conspiracy theorists. In the case of the victim, this was most likely a means by which a lonely man could maintain interest in a life with hope forever on the horizon. Harmless and certainly nothing to do with his death.

It was about the time Bob felt satisfied with the information (or lack thereof) gathered from the dead man's apartment that a call came in from the medic on duty. Bob chose to take the call from the terminal he was currently situated in front of.

Bob: "Yallow?"

Medic: "Hi Bob, we have the results of the deceased's autopsy."

Bob: "Good. What's the verdict?"

Medic: "Well, there are still some questions, but it seems his heart malfunctioned."

Bob: "...that's pretty vague."

Medic: "Yeah...there really isn't any damage to the heart, nor any circumspect lateral causalities, but it seems his heart just stopped...for unknown reasons. There is no evidence of malfunction in the regulatory systems of the cerebral cortex, as when his systems were reanimated the heart beat normally."

It is a common practice to more or less restart various systems of a corpse for the purpose of an autopsy, as many as can be artificially activated. This unfortunately does not result in resurrection, but does provide the pathologist with information on the exact cause of death. It's not widely known because many people would feel unsettled knowing that upon death they will be restarted, lying on a cold examination table, heart beating, even breathing, and in some cases, eyes flickering.

Bob: "So this is not a murder, just some medical mystery then?"
Medic: "I suppose that's for the police to decide whether this case be investigated or not, and it's true that there seems to be no "smoking gun" so to speak, but there is absolutely no reason this man should be lying here dead. It's almost as if someone just turned him off."
Bob: "I plan on talking to the chief and letting him know what I've found anyway. I'm sure he'll put in his two cents. Personally, I don't see a lot here that's very interesting. Maybe he died of embarrassment. If you learn anything new, let me know."
Medic: "Will do, Bob."

Bob left the Juniper tower and walked toward a more lively street a few blocks away. He could have headed back to his apartment. It was getting late, not that one could tell from the city of eternal light, but he hadn't been in this part of town in some time and was really enjoying the stroll, the air, the flood of people all around. This area was ripe with life...easier going and, in general, happier than downtown. It seems ridiculous that in countless millennia since history began being recorded we haven't managed to transcend the pointless division of the have's and the have not's. People argue endlessly about the reasons and possible solutions but, historically speaking, we haven't really found a generation that ever gave it a try. There's always too big a fear that someone with *it all* might not, even momentarily, get *it all*.

Bob eyed the endless shops not needing anything in particular. One shop offered nano treatment for wrinkles. *Let our microscopic robots repair you from the inside and watch those crow's feet disappear*, the projection practically shouted at passersby. Another shop offered guided tours of Ganymede. *Visit Ganymede! See the solar system's largest aquarium!* Bob had always wanted to, never had. Electroplasmotic weather-resistant paint, was another small storefront. This was a paint that could function as a terminal front. One merely painted the area they wanted the terminal and in no time they were up and watching visual recordings of cats sleeping or people falling off of things. The resolution wasn't quite as good as a standard terminal, but you could paint your entire wall if you like.

These were all a passing fancy but then Bob saw something that truly caught his eye.

The sign was in characters he couldn't read but completely understood, Bob ran right in, slapped his hand down on the counter and ordered the largest durian smoothie the shop had to offer. The attendant giving him the stink eye said "fine", but that he couldn't drink it in the shop. Bob just shrugged because he didn't care, then the attendant donned an old styled gas mask and went into an isolated room to prepare the ghastly concoction. He then produced the drink, sealed on top, with a straw to puncture the closure upon leaving the store. He handed it to Bob with a gentle hand gesture implying "move along...we don't want no trouble here." Bob got a few reactions on the street from the wretched aroma of durian, but with that many people around, no one really could tell exactly where it was coming from.

Crossing a few streets over, Bob walked through the corner of a massive park, the Marina H. Gallach park. Marina H. Gallach was a famous doctor who several hundred years ago found a cure for that disease that was making everyone grow extra limbs. The park was large enough that it would be easy to get lost without the aid of any sort of communication device (which everyone had) or without assistance (which was everywhere). In the park Bob walked through a clearing with an enormous sculpture. There were always sculptures throughout the city. Some were permanent, but some, like this one, would come and go. They'd be there for a long time then all of a sudden are replaced with a new one, yet no one ever sees this happen. This sculpture looked as if some great object was crashing to the ground from the heavens. Perhaps a meteorite or comet. Three to four stories high, it seemed the ground was making way for the object, fleeing from the might of it in a partial hollow shell representing the impact. The object itself was obscured, it was even hard to focus on the center for some reason, though it did have a long tail that extended angularly into the sky like a comet. It was metallic on the impact site and seemed to become more crystalline towards the striking and obscured object. This is just in appearance though. One can never really tell what a thing is made out of. They can do amazing things these days in the field of metallurgy and synthetics. Metals as clear as glass and glass as strong as steel, but also glass as malleable as molasses and metals as soft as silk. However, the look and feel of the sculpture was metal against crystal. It seemed very striking to Bob. The artist was anonymous but the title was "Birth of a New World".

Shaken loose from the awe of the sculpture, Bob received a call from the Chief. The Chief was a man well into middle age. His

24

physique was similar to Bob's own; tall, a bit taller than Bob, sturdy, and broad. He was imposing in figure but kind at heart yet very stern when necessity required such. Duty bound and honorable while still maintaining effectiveness, the galaxy would be far better off if more like him were in positions of authority. Unfortunately, rarely is such the case. The chief, unlike Bob, was one of those guys who held on to every hair that had ever graced his cranium that, though complete in grayness, was a thick pelt with a mind of its own.

Bob: "Yellow?"

Chief: "Hey Bob, I wanted to get your rundown of the Palter case. Based on what you've sent me I'm inclined to file it as a mysterious death rather than a murder and leave it at that."

Bob: "Yeah...well, it definitely is that, but I can't help but feel that there is more going on than what's on the surface. People don't just die like that, not anymore, not since the dark ages."

Chief: "I know, I know, but I'll need more than what we've got to keep this thing going."

Bob: "Right, and I do think we're about out of sources, it's more or less cold, however, there still are a few next of kin that might have some info, something. You know if we file it as a mysterious death rather than a murder it won't be eyed again by anyone. This city is too big, too much going on for a question mark to gum up the works."

Chief: "Exactly. I wouldn't even be involved, nor would you, if it were not for the peculiar nature of the death and I'm afraid it might be doing just that, gumming up the works."

Bob: "Yeah, but why don't we sit on it a few days just to make sure nothing else turns up. It is odd. When was the last time a murder went unsolved on Helen's Crown?"

Chief: "Not in a long, long time. And this may be no exception. This may not be a murder."

Bob: "Yep. ...if I find anything I'll let you know. If not, let's move on by the end of the week."

Chief: "Sounds good, Bob. Get some sleep."

Bob: "Thanks, goodnight."

It had slipped Bob's mind that it was pretty late. The entire world of Helen was bathed in artificial light. It was easy to confuse the arbitrary old Earth standards of day and night here. Reluctant to leave the posh midtown area, Bob headed toward the nearest train station and began the descent towards his crummy apartment building. The dial was now being tuned from technicolor slowly towards sepia, from clear skies to smog and exhaust.

Back in his building, Bob approached the door to his flat. Then, from the poorly lit hallway, a figure emerged like a wraith from the shadows approaching slowly, unseen behind Bob. It was Abrum.

Abrum: "Bob,"

Bob, startled: "Ah!, oh, Abrum. ...You are a creeper aren't you."

Abrum: "Bob, would you be interested in joining my book club?"

Bob: "um...I'm afraid I don't really have the time, sorry. How many people are in it."

Abrum: "It would just be you and I."

Bob: "hmm, yeah, that's not really a club so much is it? Sorry, maybe some other time."

Abrum: "I'll leave a copy of our first reading, at your convenience."

Bob: "I actually said 'no', there pal."

Abrum, again as if Bob's words were a jest between friends, "Oh, Bob..." And Abrum receded into the shadows. (towards the end of the hallway where the line of shadows ended Abrum strolled out whistling a little tune and entered his apartment.)

Bob got inside, took a quick shower, brushed his teeth, and shoved a few things off his bed so he could sleep. As is usually the case following the moment one gets comfortable, Bob got another call from the Chief.

Bob: "Yeah."

Chief: "Bob, just got word of another dead body. Outskirts of Helen's Crown. East periphery. Another unknown cause of death."

Bob: "Really?"

Chief: "We're waiting on the full autopsy report, but it seems it's the same as the Palter case."

Bob: "When did it happen?"

Chief: "The victims been dead about 24 hours. Probably happened not long before the Palter death."

Bob: "hmm."

Chief: "Yeah, definitely something's going on. I'm not ready to call it a murder just yet, but two identical deaths of unknown origin is enough for us to take a closer look."

Bob: "I'd say so. Are you wanting me to check it out now?"

Chief: "It can wait till morning. First thing though if you wouldn't mind. The deceased died in his apartment. The body's been removed and we'll have a couple of guards on duty to make sure no one tampers with the domicile till you get there."

Domicile, Bob thought, *What an astringent word for the epicenter of a person's life.*

Chief: "Get some sleep and let me know what you find out. It is unusual to say the least. Not the death obviously, but the unknown. Let's handle this with a fine-toothed comb."

Bob: "Alright. I'll head there early and let you know what I find."

Hmm, Bob thought. *Two deaths in more or less one day, cause unknown. I wonder if it could be some new disease, or plague.*

Maybe we all have it now. That's very doubtful as I'm sure they screened for every known germ in the galaxy and would even be able to detect the biological markers of one unknown. Something else has to be going on.

A skill that Bob had acquired, which might be one of the more useful skills a person could develop, was the ability to sleep despite the questions that tend to fill the mind in the face of a mystery. Questions would be answered, but later. Things would become clear, or not, but now is the time for rest. With that, Bob succumbed to sleep feeling certain he was dealing with two related murders.

Dream Journal: Sea of Shadows

I was in the middle of a vast and open courtyard, seemingly abandoned ages ago. Cracked and crumbling walkways were intersected by patches of pale, unkempt greenery; not a tree in sight save for those beyond the great wall of the courtyard. It was autumn, but autumn in a land of warm tendencies. The wall and the walkways were stone and rich with lichen formations. There was a present, but not overpowering, scent of ragweed in the air.

In the middle of the courtyard was a step pyramid, the kind one might find in historical records of ancient Earth. The pyramid was constructed of the same lichen covered stone and stood about twice as high as the great surrounding wall.

I couldn't remember how I came to be here. I tried, but the memories were hazy and fragmented; a string of disjunct and jumbled violent images and horrible sounds. I knew why I was here, though. I was looking for my daughter.

The courtyard was very obviously empty but if I could climb the pyramid, I might be able to get my bearings and have a better idea of where to go next.

Approaching the pyramid I kept seeing, or sensing strange dark figures out in the periphery of my vision...shadows it would seem.
When I turned there was nothing. This phenomenon grew as I climbed the pyramid. More shadows, frantic and moving wildly, dispelled by my direct sight. When I tried to ignore the shadows brief flickers of memory would assault my conscious mind. The same jumble of violence and screaming...my daughter, my poor, poor daughter. I imagined these memories were the result of a shadow poking a dark finger through the base of my skull.

On reaching the summit, the shadows seemed to coalesce into a creeping fog roiling at the base of the pyramid. Clearing my mind, I took a survey of the immediate surroundings. The summit of the pyramid culminated in what appeared to be a sacrificial altar.
Basically a stone trough long enough to hold the torso of a body, and reliefs to support the head and limbs, probably to be tied down. The main reservoir of the trough had grooves cut into each side that ran down the base of the altar and off the side of the pyramid. A blood groove. The lines, in each direction, could be followed down the pyramid to the base and on through the courtyard and beyond the wall.

Beyond the wall was endless forest. Green and verdant, but oddly devoid of life. No signs of humanity, no bird song, no rustling of any sort.

In the great distance was the setting sun, or so it appeared to be. It seemed all wrong. It appeared to exist as if embedded in the distant forest itself. One could almost make out the curvature of the trees as they allowed for it to emerge from the forest floor. It seemed a distant glowing orb, but was visibly setting. Darkness was setting in.

Returning my attention to the altar, I looked deeply in the basin scarcely aware that the dark fog of shadows had been rising like tides with the moon. There was an ornate carving in the basin...a figure...a young girl adorned as a goddess. A flash of memory, so horrible, so terrifying clutched my body in paralysis. I stood gripping the altar with all of my strength. The muscles of my face and neck violently forcing every sense closed.

When the terror passed, I returned to find both of my wrists severely cut and draining into the basin of the altar.

The sun set. The tides of shadow rose. All was consumed in absolute blackness.

Chapter Three: Kite flying, Isolation, and Atlas has the sniffles.

Impartial grain A440x-Theta-Omicron-Sigma-Naught found dormancy inadequate for proper symbiosis. Dormancy cycle will increase by 12.83 stellar revolutions.

Flat grain Thanux-00-923674-Epsilon mistimes transmission protocol and is voiceless. Dormancy induced.

Elder grain 1-Alpha-000-0 finds temperature requirements of stasis inadequate in repeated transmissions.

Bob awoke early, found the coordinates of the recent victim's apartment and headed out. He'd pick up something to eat along the way. Outside was the same doldrum he'd encountered on his way home last night. The odd thing about being so far from the sun, in light recreated to mimic that which we rose with for millions upon millions of years, was that it wasn't quite right. One could tell that there was something artificial about being outside. It's the difference between being out on a beautiful spring day and being in a room with a lamp. Even a plethora of lamps cannot replace the actual sunshine on Earth. The smog only amplifies this effect, creating a darkened dome enclosing the surrounding buildings.

Unfortunately today would not bring Bob to those nicer parts of town where the artifice of life was significantly less noticeable. Bob would travel from his downtown apartment complex and skirt the edge of town out toward the East periphery. This would take Bob through a mass of industrial sectors. Industry of all imaginable kinds circumscribed the boundary of Helen's Crown, one of the chief exports being metallic hydrogen. Zeus is an abundant source of hydrogen and the Sol system is dependent on the exceptionally durable and incomparably lightweight stabilized metal. Everything from transports, trains, buildings, shelves, shoe grommets, trans-planet ships, and especially trans-solar ships, are made from metallic hydrogen.

Luckily finding a seat on the train, Bob scanned through the information on the most current victim: Willford Montgomery Thrame. Thrame lived in a residential area practically attached to the Bracken Industrial Park. His occupational title was "primary quality control analyst and oversight, level 1, for plastiglass production". This meant that a large sheet of plastiglass, probably in the neighborhood of 12 square feet, would progress before him and he had to verify that it was unbroken. This was one hell of a boring job. Analytical devices would thoroughly check the plastiglass for faults and Thrame merely verified, by glance, that the machines were right...as far as he could tell. In essence, his job was to verify that the unbreakable glass was, in fact, unbroken. The sheets would then be cut by disintegration beam before going on to the next analyst, a level 2, to again verify the unbroken glass was, in fact, still unbroken. This continued through several levels before the plastiglass found itself in terminal consoles, train windows, etc.

Obviously there was no work connection between the two victims; a factory worker and a salesman. They also lived a considerable distance from each other. They most likely would never have encounter each other unless there was some hidden connection between the two. Maybe they were both involved in something that they shouldn't have been. As for the Palter case, if he had something going on more than meets the eye he thoroughly and expertly must have cleaned all trace of it from his leavings. Very unlikely. It really didn't add up, but then again who knows what will be found in the apartment of this current victim.

The only similarity between the two was that neither had family to speak of. No spouse, no children. Next of kin unknown or very distant. They were both on their own. Bob glanced up to stretch his neck and look around the jostling train. Near the window, standing, was a man, probably in his late 60's, wearing gold painted shoes of some kind, with a gold belt, gold chains around his neck, gold-rimmed sunglasses, and a golden hard-hat like the ones people wore in ancient history. He even had a scraggly white beard that he had painted a gold color. All of the gold was obviously painted metal or plastic, but it was an interesting ensemble to say the least. Everyone here is in their own little world.

Traveling through the industrial area was actually quite interesting. Machinery and lights, steam rising or escaping from some necessary valve, twisting metallic structures piping who-knows-what who-knows-where. It was unimaginable. What could it all possibly do? These areas are the mysterious intestines of our collective being, Bob thought, and meaning this with absolutely no trace of disrespect. It was our secret inner workings unnoticeably keeping the rest of us functional and alive.

When the train stopped and the doors opened Bob was hit with the unmistakable air of industry. It was a scent of something metallic coupled with burning. Plasma arc-welders possibly. Everything happened on a massive scale here so it is no wonder that the environment would be affected into a gray dinginess of harsh air. Bob wondered how someone could live here. Certainly one would "get used to it", but it can't be healthy, though assuredly all was within allowable tolerances...just at the line but never over.

The walk was not far from the train station where victim two, Willford Montgomery Thrame, had once resided. He had lived in a dull structure devoid of all but the most necessary architecture. It was a complex, probably three thousand small apartments, that presented itself as a long rectangular slab. The most disturbing feature of the complex was the complete lack of windows. It was a solid and dark brown brick wedged between two arms of the industrial park to which it was attached. It's depressing to think of living without even a small window out, but it was probably calculated by the architect (who Bob imagined must have a clinical approach to design and matching lab-coat) that to see out into the very limited twisting metal of the industrial park was of no significant benefit to mental health. Bob felt a certain sadness for those who had to live here, but then remembered that he himself didn't live in that great of a neighborhood and, though he had a window, his window opened into the side of another building. He couldn't remember the last time he attempted to look out it.

Bob entered the abysmal structure and found the lift which crisscrossed him off to the proper floor and quadrant of the victims apartment. The door opened effortlessly as the appropriate warrants had been issued and Bob's identity recognized by the security array, yet Bob could not have guessed at what he found on the other side of that door:

Kites. Lots and lots of kites. Odd. There were kites decorating the walls, kites hanging from the ceiling as if in mid-flight, and even paintings or pictures of kites being flown adorned the various, though small in number, walls of the apartment. Box kites, diamond kites, triangle kites. Everywhere. Even materials to make kites and evidence that many of them had been made by the victim himself.

Using his detective skills, Bob suspected that this individual might just possibly like kites.

The contents of the apartment, aside from the kites, were rather mundane. Nothing aroused suspicion or indicated anything amiss. Terminal records, communications, any transmissions to or from the apartment were sparse and ordinary. Nothing. Bob cross-referenced the two victims with the greater-Helen official database, with a fairly high level of authorization and found absolutely no interaction between the two. Not only had there been no communication between the two, there was no evidence that they knew each other, had ever heard of each other, or even been in the same part of Helen at the same time. They were about as separate as two individuals could be, with one exception. Bob's query turned up an ancestry flag in the cross search. Distant, distant, multiple removals, yet cousins. The two victims were related.

This brought about a long thoughtful pause upon Bob. Certainly, he thought, the victims themselves were unaware of this connection, no evidence of it, and the connection is so very distant. This had to be coincidence. It makes sense that it would be a coincidence. There are lots of people on Helen, and Helen's Crown is large enough that generations of families might live here for ages, hardly venturing beyond the city's boundary. It had to be coincidence. Certainly unrelated.

After a protracted effort convincing himself that this was certainly of little import, Bob took another look through the personal effects of the deceased. Nothing really. The only thing of interest, though not to the case, was an overstuffed envelope addressed to the victim. The contents were many pages, actual paper, on which an article had been printed. The cover page had written, in script, *"Bill, they finally published my article! Now I can rest assured that it will be buried in a journal where no one will ever read it. If you ever find yourself with extraordinary boredom, give it a read. - Uncle Randy"*. It is unusual to see a letter printed on paper, but not terribly rare. Most people who do this are trying to reconnect with the past in some nostalgic way, however, it wouldn't hurt to take a look into the familial relationships of these two victims. Bob flipped through the pages scanning the document:

"Galactic stalemate: Fighting the cyclic nature of progress."
by
Randal Fostfeller

Imagine, if you will, that you are free from the constraints of time, you are immortal, and you have existed from the beginning of creation. Now turn your immortal gaze at the machinations of the human animal. You would see wave after wave of expansion, progress, and growth. That growth then hardens into a protective carapace which quickly becomes all too tight and must be broken to make room for growth. A small, frightful, and primitive human being clings helplessly to a tree. The tree is safe. The tree is home. Before long the small, frightful, and primitive human being ventures out to explore the great void of the forest. Danger is encountered. Beasts are encountered. Other human beings are encountered. Fear fuels fighting. Fear fuels invention. Weapons are made. Survival is achieved and the forest is known. Now this small, frightful, and primitive human being finds itself not so primitive anymore. The forest is safe. The forest is home.

Before long this small, and frightful human being wonders what lies beyond the forest and looks into the void of the wilderness. The dangers are greater. The beasts are greater. The others have forests of their own. Fear is the fuel. Greater weapons are made. Survival is achieved and the wilderness is tamed. The land is now known. The land is safe. The land is home. The small and frightful human being finds itself not so small any longer and wonders what lies beyond the great void of the sea. Great ships are made to transverse the void and the cycle repeats *ad infinitum*.

You, however, are the wandering immortal watching the transition from unknown to known. You take it in as others do breathing. Breathe in, the world expands. Breathe out, that new world is now small and confining. It continues though, from continent to continent, from planet to planet, from star to star. It continues and has continued to this very day where the galaxy is now ripe with small and frightful, some might even say "primitive", human beings. The question I ask you, our immortal watcher, is "where are we going?". Though it is unknown to us, if someday intergalactic travel becomes possible, where will that take us? Will it not be simply more of the same? Our frame of reference is a solitary point. We expand beyond the point and the expansion is then readjusted to be perceived as a new solitary point. We as human beings achieve stalemate through our shared false perception of progress. That is not to say this "progress" is unnecessary. In fact, if we compare the relative...
(Bob skims a little further)
...and that is, of course, how we managed to overcome the hoards of mutant gelatinous ...
(Bob skims a little further)
...and the issue too of our unequal distribution of technology. You, our immortal watcher, would be confounded at the number of people in the galaxy that live very much like people from millennia ago. There are two main reasons for this. The first, and less common, has to do with the practice of isolated peoples. This practice actually has its roots in the ages before interstellar travel. People isolation is the practice of avoiding contact with human populations that either wish isolation, or are to be found isolated and kept as such. It stems from a

mostly universal philosophy that forcing one way of life upon a people is immoral and unethical. To do so carries the implication that one way of life is qualitatively *better* than another and as history has taught us well, the entrance into the technological world is a one-way path. It is practically impossible to return. It is also this practice that accounts for Earth's current state. Pristine. A veritable garden of Eden and of the habitable worlds in the galaxy Earth has one of the smallest populations. It is a monument to managed isolated peoples. Which in addition to being a philosophical initiative is as well useful for scientific purposes such as genetics, epigenetics, and comparative studies of the various modified humanoids to the "original". Every known system and practically every inhabited planet, throughout the galaxy, has some allotment for isolated peoples. For a more detailed study of the humanoid genome project as transmogrified from the isolated source see Umbrose Eulerclid's, "A theory of trait manifestation through species modeling" FGL.

The second, and more widespread, reason technology is unevenly dispersed throughout the galaxy has precisely to do with that very human cycle of expansion and stasis. We, as a species, have implanted ourselves on practically every flat surface in the galaxy. People are left as a colony anywhere a colony will stick, and often left to fend for themselves. Resources go where needed, but our species spreads far faster than our means of keeping up and keeping track, not unlike a rampant virus. The major systems are quite saturated with technology, but the lesser known and outlying regions live, quite not by choice, as our ancestors did in prehistory. Take, for example, the people of Xurtus who live on a moon orbiting a planet without a name, in a stellar system with only a numerical designation, in the inner boundary toward the galactic center. It has been well known for decades that...

Bob skims a little further then loses interest completely.

There really wasn't anything here Bob didn't already know. He thought, *I guess that's how one becomes a published scholar. Just say the things that have already been said a thousand times before and it gets published alongside countless articles saying the exact same thing. I may have chosen the wrong profession.*

Bob sent a communique to the chief and told him what he found. They needed to talk and agreed to meet in a couple of hours. He left the letter and the numerous kites. The forensic crew would be in soon to detail and catalogue every mote contained in that apartment. On his way out he encountered a sad looking woman peeking around the corner.

Woman: "Bill's dead idn't he?"

Bob: "I'm afraid so. I'm here to see if we can find out why."

Woman: "He was a really good guy. He made kites for the kids. Anyone who wanted one."

Bob: "That's very nice."

Still unusual though. Helen wasn't an actual planet. It floated quietly in the eye of the great gas giant. As such, weather was manufactured and controlled. It might be possible to fly a kite in the nicer parts of Helen's Crown interior, but there really was very little wind anywhere on Helen.

Bob: "Did the kids actually *fly* the kites, or were they just for decoration?"

Woman: "Oh yes, flew them all the time. Wore them ragged."

Bob: "Hmm. Where? Where could they possibly fly these kites?"

Woman: "Exhaust vents from the Braken Industrial park. They're everywhere."

Ah, Bob thought. Mystery solved. Yes, they are everywhere and they are massive.

Bob: "I'm sorry for your loss."

With that, Bob made a beeline for the next train out of the periphery. A shower and change of clothes would get rid of the scent of burning metal and a little fresh air couldn't do any harm either.

Back at his flat Bob left the terminal running while he showered. It was nice to hear the news of the day, odds and ends, even advertisements made the apartment seem less isolated, more active. He was really paying little attention as it was mostly for the sound, but while he was drying off and getting dressed something about the news broadcast caught Bob's attention:

"*...an infectious outbreak in the Atlas system. The specifics have not been released, but local officials say the outbreak exists solely on Phoebe, in a small portion of the population, and is believed to be contained. There are currently no travel restrictions to any planets in the Atlas system but bio-screening for travel to and from Phoebe is being conducted on all interstellar and interplanetary flights.*"

Atlas is a major star of the Pleiades, not far from Sol, and Phoebe is the most populated world of that system. Under normal circumstances this would have gone unnoticed by Bob. There is always something happening somewhere in a heavily populated galaxy, but the rarity of two mysterious deaths had him wonder a bit. It was certain though that the first victim absolutely did not die of a disease. Even an unknown disease would at least be identified as such. No, this wasn't a case of disease, but there was an odd electricity in the air, like the world was repositioning itself to find a posture less uncomfortable. Nonsense probably.

Visit Atlas!
Brought to you by the Orion-Cygnus Arm Travel Authority (OrCA)

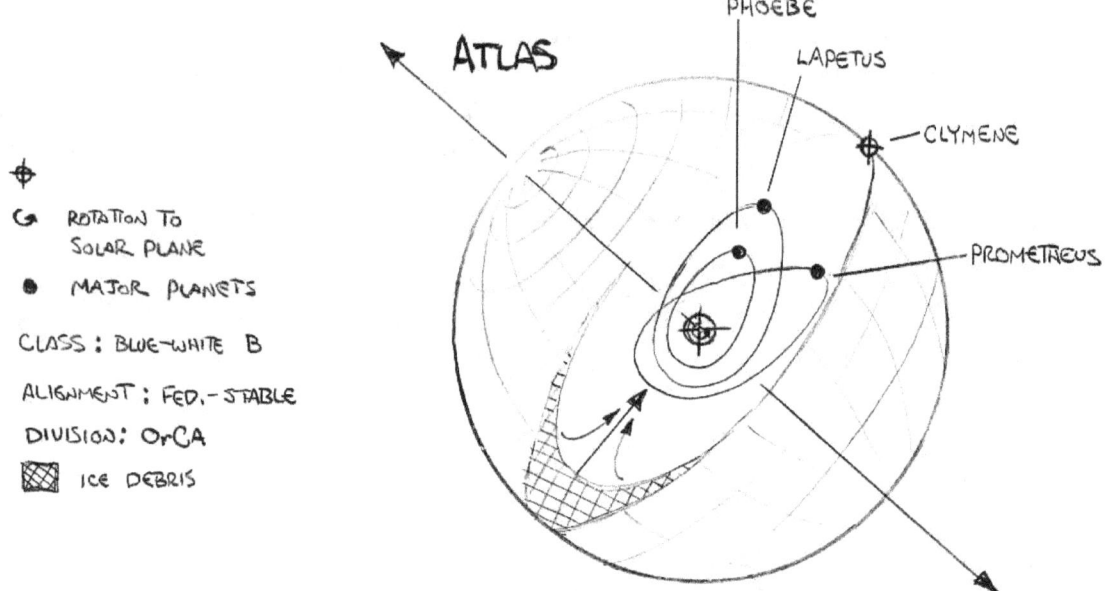

Bathe in the blue-white brilliance of the star known as **Atlas**, and a solar system unparalleled in beauty and recreational activity.

Atlas was first colonized following the trans-Vega war of attrition when disputes over mining rights to Vega's rich debris field created a necessity for combatants to "travel as far afield as our ships will take us" and establish a government free from the ruling corporate empire of Vega's infamous "First Family". Since, a strong and abiding democracy has been in place and Atlas has remained in relative peace.

The main orbiting bodies of Atlas are the planets Phoebe and Lapetus, but that is far from all. The companion "mother" star Clymene also encircles Atlas and thus modifying the orbit of the third major planetary hub in the region, Prometheus.

The combined gravitational pull of Atlas coupled with Clymene insure a steady flow of ice-rich material from the outer-system debris field. This accounts for the vast water resources system wide and significantly reduces the need for large-scale water mining operations so common in most stellar systems throughout the galaxy.

Traveler's will want to begin their stay on planet **Phoebe**. Phoebe is replete with vast oceans and extensive woodland areas that will instill a sense of nostalgia for the ancient ways of our ancestors.

Hiking, camping, and swimming are just a few of the nature oriented activities Phoebe is famous for and here you'll see a night sky unparalleled in the region. To avoid light pollution, Phoebe's western hemisphere has a strict lumen policy in effect for the better part of 300 years. When the sun sets, luminosity is limited to 50 candles per source and not to exceed 2 sources per individual and 4 to a household at any one time. Additionally, only 2 sources of light (at 50 candles each) may be illuminated in proximity with the remaining sources (3 and 4) at a required 50 foot radius. Though a stringent rule, the visitor to Phoebe will find this light abundantly adequate for reading, conversation, and contemplation, but the real payoff comes from the night sky. Here, the galaxy is illuminated before you. Here you will behold the wonder and profound majesty of the countless wash of stars before you, the sight of such unfortunately most modern worlds are greatly deprived. Also, the beauty and phases of Phoebe's three moons offer a romantic backdrop for a lover's vacation. Visitors often find their time spent on Phoebe to be spiritually transformative and have often noted that adjusting to this simple lumen requirement has brought ease of sleep, increased health, and an abatement of anxiety.

However, is nature not your primary interest? The eastern hemisphere of Phoebe is home to several large cities boasting the finest in art, entertainment, and dining. See the Mallow spires of central Flaxton, the Grand Floating Bridge of New Brunningmere, or the Sturgis Market at Greixe.

Have you ever wanted to give it a go as a ranch hand? Then **Lapetus** is the planet for you. Home to the Taurus Balaene, or the Whale Cow, these majestic beasts were genetically manipulated over the course of hundreds of years to produce a field animal to aid in terraformation. Their massive and highly metallic jaws were capable of pulverizing a wide variety of rock minerals and debris with an ingeniously engineered seven-stage digestive system that could break the material down into a rich mineral manure. In the early days of terraformation they were indispensable for quickly providing soil coverage on rocky or barren landscapes. Though rarely used in the galaxy anymore, here on Lapetus the visitor can see them roaming freely and living a life of quiet contentment.

warning: please do not feed the whale cow as there is currently a system wide shortage of replacement limbs.

Though **Prometheus** is primarily inhabited by various mining colonies, don't discount a visit. The splendor of volcanic and seismic activity is a geologist's dream along with vast crystal caverns and the obsidian sea which is both beautiful and eerie. Visiting Prometheus is restricted to non-summer seasons as greater proximity to Clymene greatly increases both seismic and volcanic activity making habitation dangerous. Contact OrCA for details on planetary seasons.

Whether a relaxing vacation surrounded by nature, cities with unmatched nightlife, the fresh air of days gone past, or the splendor of otherworldly geological formations, make your next vacation plans for Atlas, your home away from home.

Chapter Four: Half Priced Buckets of Bread!

Bob caught a peak train to city central. He had a bit of time before meeting with the chief and decided to grab a quick bite. City central was more business oriented than the upper east side, but comparably nice. The sky and sunshine, though artificial, was lovely. The nicer parts of Helen's Crown were in perpetual spring. The architecture too was often older than popular styles but done with considerable artistry for the time of construction. As Helen takes her name from Earth's ancient history, the architecture here was often a re-imagining of what the modern eye envisioned in that time period, and many of the buildings here were probably some of the first constructed upon Helen's creation.

Here, as Bob walked into its presence, was the Central library. The central library had the same marbled appearance that Helen herself possessed. It was an assemblage of pillars, ornate staircases, and statues of old Earth mythology.   Since there was no weather to speak of on Helen, the library was very open. There were very few actual walls, mostly pillars supporting floors or various structures. It was a large building and dense with things to see, but from the outside, as Bob walked past, he could easily see quite deep into its interior, ripe with the activity of people jostling here and there. Many buildings of Helen's Crown had this same openness. Petty crime was almost nonexistent. Not because people's basic nature had changed in any way, but because when a thing turned up missing it was pretty easy to track down who had done it. It was practically automated, which cut down on crime in general, but in the case of an actual mystery, like the one Bob was dealing with now, law enforcement was not accustomed to inferring from incomplete data and piecing things together. Intuition was a specialty and one that kept Bob gainfully employed.

The innermost region of the library held a fantastic statue of Helen, perfectly to scale, and floating above a floor that appeared to be turbulent with the atmosphere of the gas giant below. When walking through this region of the floor the shades of orange atmosphere reacted, as if disturbed, to the presence of an individual. Very popular with the kids.

The role of a library had changed significantly over the course of history. Today, any person could access practically any known information through any terminal or interface in hand. The idea of traveling or having to go to a specific place to obtain knowledge of any subject was primitive, archaic. So, the library has come to serve three general purposes. One, libraries are often synonymous with museums. Libraries tend to be museums of general knowledge whereas actual museums are often more specific in their area and time period (and also much more complete). Two, libraries are places where the public can convene, often students quietly assembling for their studies. Three, the library still is a place of scholarship, though much more specialized in modern times. Every significant book and/or writing has been molecularly duplicated and libraries across the galaxy still hold physical copies of these originals. This includes original handwritten texts, old Earth facsimiles, first editions, etc. If one wanted to look at the watermark of an old medieval manuscript, see the handwriting of Bach, or experience the feel of ancient papyrus scrolls, they could be found here.

Passing the library Bob stepped into Pauly's Bread Bucket, a popular chain, and had their signature "bucket of bread"; fresh bread baked around a core of molten vegetable stew. It was prepared in a pint-sized tin bucket, like a small version of the kind one would use to milk cows in the olden days. It's a noisy place, but the food is pretty good and quite fast.

Moving on, Bob made his way to the central police headquarters for his meeting with the Chief. The police headquarters was one of the few buildings that seemed a bit more modern than the others surrounding. It consisted of three light metallic gray central rings separated by dark gunmetal gray separating floors, stacked like a big metal cake. The grounds were manicured but nothing to draw much attention, and the entire building was encircled by a short barricade, also seemingly metallic in nature.

Scanned on his way in and finding approval with the unseen autonomous watcher, Bob entered the grounds then the building. With a few hellos to a handful of familiar faces, Bob made his way to the lift, requested the top floor, and entered into the lobby of the Chief's office. The Chief happened to be out talking to his secretary and quickly waved Bob into his office, shut the door, and sat looking at Bob for a moment.

Chief: "Bob, how've you been? We don't get a good chance to talk anymore."
Bob: "I've been well. Busy. A little more so than usual."
Chief: "Same apartment I see. Never think of moving a little closer to sunshine? City central or uptown?"
Bob: "No. I mean, I think about it sometimes, but really I'm fine where I am."
Chief: "...do you ever talk to or see any of our old pals from college?"
Bob: "No. I'm not even sure they are on Helen any longer. I had heard Ronnie got a job on Titan and Gary was on some outpost orbiting Poseidon. Sounds miserable."
Chief: "Yeah, I had heard the same thing. Do you remember Sally? I think she's living somewhere in the lower west side, but I haven't heard from her in years."
Bob: "Yup. Who knows. Everybody is everywhere."
Chief: "Isn't it odd that you were studying environmental engineering and I was studying field analytics yet we both ended up in the same unrelated occupation?", he said with a smirk.
Bob: "It is, but I guess getting a job in one's speciality is just too easy. Where's the challenge in that?" They both chuckled.
Chief: "You know Bob, you sort of fell off the face of the Earth after college. What did you do all those years? Did you meet someone? Did you have a family, or just a confirmed bachelor that whole time?"
Bob: (not really wanting to talk about it), "Well, there was someone, but...you know how it is...how life is...things are always complicated. Life is complicated, sometimes horribly so."
The chief could sense the modicum of tension and decided it was time to get down to brass tacks.
Chief: "Yeah, I hear ya. Well, let's talk about this case."
Bob: "Sure. I imagine you got my report from the latest site. I found nothing of any real import. No motive, no hints of misconduct or anything that could point to involvement of any kind. The only thing I found, as I'm sure you've already read, was the very distant familial relationship. Did you manage to get some genealogy information on the family line?"
Chief: "Yes and no. The first victim is second generation of parents that immigrated to Helen. The father died twelve years ago in a work related accident offworld. It was an asteroid mining operation of the solar system's outer rim. Manifold blew and the mining vessel decompressed. The mother lives in midtown and is healthy. She's been questioned about other family members. She has some names but no contact info. Hasn't talked to any of them in ages. Victim two has a similar problem. He came here to work, live the Hellenic dream. His parents are from another system."

Chief: "You see, we can take two citizens and check them for direct relations, but to acquire anything more specific..."
Bob: "...we'll have to get permission from the government of another star-system, and the government of the specific planet, country, region,..."
Chief: "Yeah. So...it will take a little time. And that's assuming they will be cooperative."
Bob: "Wonderful. So we may have a killer on the loose and a thick wall of red tape separating him from us."
Chief: "And about that, I had the coroner bring in a specialist and do a thorough autopsy on both victims. Real sophisticated stuff apparently."
Bob, a little over animated: "Was it a disease?"
Chief: "No. No disease. This guy essentially reanimates the body, in tissue mechanics only, and does an analysis of circulation, motor systems, and nerve/neural pathways. It gives us the closest estimate of what state the body was in at the time of death."
Bob: "and..."
Chief: "Well, it seems the heart was stopped and the analysis revealed no evidence of a fault or command from the central nervous system that can account for that behavior. The official report from the specialist states *cardiac arrest from supposed external trauma*."
Bob: "So the specialist basically doesn't know, but also believes it to not be natural."
Chief: "Yes. Which doesn't answer much of our questions, or really make anything more clear, but will be extremely useful in accessing information. We can officially say these are murder investigations and that will open some doors for us when we need them opened."
Bob: "And now?"
Chief: "We wait until we cut through some of this red tape and find some more solid genealogy information, or..."
Bob: "..or find another body."
The chief raises his eyebrows and gives a little nod.
Chief: "Bob, until then relax. Spend some time uptown. Do some apartment hunting if you like. I want this to be your primary project, so anything else can be handled by someone lower on the totem pole. You have particularly good instincts in these matters. I'm betting you'll be thinking about it non-stop and that's good for right now."
Bob: "Wait a second...there's someone *lower* on the totem pole than me?"
The chief laughed and Bob waved goodbye.

With nothing in particular pressing upon him, Bob headed to central park. Central park was expansive with a variety of emulated forest types (those that could easily be managed in the environmental range of Helen's Crown). There were dense forests, many like the ones of old Earth. Bob was partial to the temperate forest models. Redwood, Spruce, Douglas fir, Ponderosa pine, the rainbow of oaks, paper birch and maple. It was lovely and peaceful. Some people come here to hike or camp, days at a time. It's easy to get lost, deeply lost, but fortunately for the lost traveler it is exceptionally easy to get found. It's odd to think that there were times that people lived in forests like this. Alone. No park ranger or authority to bail out the wayward wanderer. Our ancestors lived in it, got lost in it. It was their home and the entirety of their universe. As small and confining that may seem to a modern mind, to them it was infinite. And honestly, when a modern city dweller takes that step from knowing their place to being lost, it so very briefly becomes their universe too and is terrifying. None of us would survive as our ancestors did.

Finding a clearing, Bob laid upon the cool grass and looked up at the sky. Even fairly deep in the park there is considerable light pollution, but Bob could easily make out Ganymede rising, Europa, and off in the distance, Io, uninhabited due to it's unpleasant temperament. Faint glowing patches on Ganymede marked the major visible cities, heavily populated and a fantastic seat of art and culture in the system. In many ways Ganymede is much more modern than Helen, even though it was colonized much earlier. In fact, it was mostly the early Ganymedians that helped construct Helen, though the contributions of the entire system and some interstellar efforts cannot be overlooked. Europa, on the other hand, is less populated but indispensable in the region. The vast majority of water and salt on Helen comes from mining and transport operations on Europa. Europa is basically a giant ball of ice conveniently circling our world.

Beyond was the blackness of space, the seeming void. But really, it is anything but emptiness. Far from nothing, it is the great something. Our mole-like inability to see beyond our so limited senses has inspired us to create nonsensical words such as *nothingness*. Bob imagined what it would be like if you could take it all in. What if the boundary between the universe and our ability to sense it popped like a transient, free-floating, oily soap bubble? The entirety of the universe exposed to an open mind? Every star in the galaxy, every galaxy in the universe made visible in a blinding white brilliance. It would be overwhelming. Certainly it would shatter the fragile mental membrane that presupposes and differentiates us from the rest of the universe. We would become once again, as in pre-birth, inseparable and undifferentiated. Probably not a good idea if you have work to do.

It was getting late so Bob left one wilderness for another and made his way back home. As he approached to open his apartment door, Abrum stepped to the entryway, to the edge of the shadows cast from his completely darkened apartment. Bob turned his head to make out only the eyes of Abrum and a disturbance in the shadows that Bob correctly identified as a friendly wave.
Bob: "Hi Abrum", flatly.
Without a word, Abrum receded into the darkness of his apartment.

That guy is an odd duck, thought Bob who got comfortably in his apartment and prepared for bed. It's interesting that even a crummy apartment, in a crummy neighborhood can be the most comfortable place when it is *your* place, when it is your home.

Dream Journal: Gaping Maw

In the woods again. I don't know why so many of these involve the woods. It began with a blood-curdling scream. It was her, my daughter. I was in the woods. The forest extended in all directions and was endless green, but the sun was setting and it was getting extremely dark, so much so it was hard to tell if the forest was now dark green or black. Some great beast had hold of her by the leg and she was screaming, screaming my name, screaming in fear, screaming in pain. It dragged her away with a tremendous speed. I ran with all of my strength to catch her but the beast was terrible and fast. I couldn't make it out, ten to fifteen feet tall and almost indistinguishable from the shadows. It ran so fast dragging her helplessly through the brush. I ran faster and faster, still not catching up with it. Her screams felt like glass shards ripping through whatever lies at the very core of my being.

I ran faster. The beast would occasion a look over its shoulder and run faster. I pushed and pushed, feeling my muscles tear and tendons shred, but pushed through it. Faster and faster I ran towards my daughter caught by the beast. The sun was almost gone. It was getting frighteningly dark and the beast was too far ahead. I was helpless.

I entered a small clearing to find the beast had stopped. Grasping the leg of my daughter tightly it flung her into its grotesquely oversized gaping maw. It ate stiltedly, reptilian-like, like creatures who devour their prey whole, like regurgitation in reverse, then the screaming stopped. I ran even harder in anger, in hatred, to kill the beast or to run headlong to its open jaw but, as I neared, darkness set in and the beast became inseparable from the shadows.

Chapter Five: It's Raining Men, and, How Beige is Too Beige?

Bulbous grain Alpha-Epsilon-774-naught-naught-extremis has successfully divided and thus is honored with diminutive nomenclature as Alpha-774-extremis and Epsilon-774-extremis"

Grain structure 88-Gamma-naught-00101-Lambda strain command prompt:: on-off-on-on-off
-on-on-off-off-off...(continues for 317,811 digits)

Prismatic grain 000-Theta-Omicron has slipped into the shadow-shade's event horizon and is voiceless.

    In modern times the term *professor* has become synonymous with the ancient expression "mad as a hatter". Professors are odd, mealy mouthed cretins that huddle in mass expounding upon the minutiae of mundane things. The understanding of every small idea is contingent upon specialized information available only to those willing to donate a portion of their life to what amounts to nothing more than trivia. To engage them in simple conversation is to be pulled into a cliquish world where judgment reigns, where each vampirically feeds off the others ego and in doing so remains satiated and bloated. Fortunately, they are easily scared off by loud noises and light rain. This is not to say there are not learned people peppering the galaxy. Make no mistake, there are scholars and great teachers, but then there are those for whom knowledge is a trendy and fashionable pair of pants, worn to impress and elucidate status.
    As Bob skimmed the edge of the midtown park, on his way to lunch, he passed a group of said professors arguing about how beige a suit jacket should be and the proper algorithm to determine the correct, and inversely proportional, darkness of the accompanying elbow patches. The argument came to a boil when one lanky, rat-faced professor exclaimed the others were ignorant of the etymology of the word *beige* and were unqualified to even garner an opinion. The group receded into the distance as Bob continued his walk and he couldn't help but notice the sound of them, which amounted to

49

noise. They were like angry grackles or a murder of crows yet with much less purpose.

Modern psychologists have identified individuals with this condition as having a physio-philosophical terminal boundary impedance. What this means is that a thing can be understood and known, but the substance of the information doesn't connect between the cognitive regions of the brain and the foundational consciousness level. In other words, wisdom can be learned, but it doesn't make the individual wiser. It is a similar condition to individuals who have, usually through trauma, severed the emotional connection to visual stimuli. When identifying a familiar face, we gather information from, in general, two sources. One, is the actual mechanics of the person to be identified...their face, eye placement, shape of the nose, etc. The second is the emotional connection we associate with the individual; mother, father, daughter, etc. In people who have lost this emotional connection to visual stimuli, they recognize the person of familiarity, but often are certain it is an imposter because the emotional information is not present and thus the person is not identified as familiar. To read more about this phenomenon check out the many articles on Capgras delusion in the FGL. These professors, however, are suffering from a similar process. The information acquired is not making a connection to the foundation and remains like flotsam in the upper Ego as trivia. The consciousness becomes cluttered rather than expanded. One could also think of it as a data equivalent to hoarders syndrome.

Bob, as most people were, was aware of this, but he couldn't help but wonder if something akin to this process affects us all. Often, a compromised psyche is least apparent to the one it affects. What if we are all suffering from something similar, every one of us in the galaxy, and woefully unaware? Why has so little changed in the past hundred thousand years? Is this all there is for us? More planets, more cities? When the galaxy is full, then what? Do we then find some miracle way to spread, like a disease, to some other galaxy? And if so, what for?

Perhaps Bob was a bit on edge because of a loose murderer that's left him with very little with which to find said murderer. It is a bad feeling to have to wait till another body is found. It means something horrible has to happen to someone so hopefully, *hopefully* we might stop the next murder from happening.

It had been several days since the last murder and so far nothing. It was possible the murders were done and the murderer was off scot-free. This seemed unlikely since there appeared to be no motive connecting to two deaths. Most likely they were part of some larger plan, but what and why?

To kill time Bob usually did one of three things; eat, go to a park, or a museum. Today he decided to do all three. In midtown, there is a fantastic and unique noodle shop called Tanglevine. What Bob liked there was a salad, so to speak, of leafy greens, noodles, mint, grilled textured protein of several varieties, and an oily toast sliced on top. What made this dish unique, and not for the faint of heart, was a bitter herb known as Leuce. Leuce originates on Phobos, the largest and oddly shaped moon of Ares (Mars). Phobos was once a farming colony used to supply Ares with produce and a facility for adapting vegetation to suit particular needs. Just as the human race has spread and modified itself on countless worlds, some barely recognizable as human, so have we spread and modified our produce a thousand fold. Leuce is the product of these efforts on Phobos, though undoubtedly locally grown somewhere around Helen's Crown to end up in this small noodle shop in midtown. Leuce is a thick curly leaf, highly nutritious, one side rich green, the other marble white, and *exceptionally* bitter. However, the bitterness is so intense that it has the effect of shocking the taste buds, almost shorting-out the bitter receptors. The first couple of bites are pretty harsh, but then the following effect is a rainbow of flavors that open up, always present but unnoticed, after the suppression of the bitter sense. After about the third or fourth bite one becomes aware of the hint of cedar shoots and what is probably a solitary drop of mahogany oil in the broth. The field greens have a vibrant, almost alive earthiness against a background of fine wood. The mint in this context is almost overwhelming and one instinctively portions it sparingly throughout the meal. To Bob the overall sensation is akin to finding oneself in a beautiful wooded forest, untouched by human hands or eyes and breathing in deeply. There is nothing better to accompany this meal than a perfectly prepared glass of iced black tea to add an undertone of autumn to the mix. Bob had wondered if the effect of Leuce would alter the taste of other foods if eaten shortly after, but never was willing to find out. The remnant aroma of the meal was too wonderful to adulterate with other foods. Best to let the sense and memory of it pass of its own accord throughout the afternoon. Many people did not have the same experience. Some, despite warning, are so offended by the bitterness of the Leuce they storm out of the establishment never to return. It also doesn't help that Leuce is so close in pronunciation to Lettuce that for some it might go unnoticed until it's too late.

After the meal Bob walked to a nearby museum that he had always been fascinated by, but had only managed to visit a couple of times. The name of the museum, though visible nowhere, was Antiquity. They specialized in some of the oldest of human records, objects, and art. Most, one would imagine, are facsimiles as facsimiles of almost every ancient thing have been made and whirl around the galaxy on display. Facsimiles though are so exact in their recreation, often down to the molecular level depending on the object, that the average person, or even a scholar couldn't tell the difference without proper equipment.

Bob was casually wandering through the gallery as the main endeavor was not study but digestion, yet a curious painting caught his eye. There didn't seem to be a title, and the time period was listed as "Old Earth antiquity", which meant "so long ago that no one is sure", probably more than a hundred thousand years ago. Somehow a name was retained. That name was Zdzisław Beksiński. The painting was of a figure on a horse. Very strange. Both the figure and the horse seemed to be dead and decaying, even growing into each other, yet standing. The world seemed to be in a similar state of decay. Trees as dark sticks and seemingly devoid of life. What Bob thought to be birds filling the sky on second thought might merely be dead leaves blowing from the nearby trees in the same direction as the hair of the undead figure and desiccated horse...hard to tell. The overall color of the painting was dark decaying grays, bone, and black except for the trees in the background and the sky which carried red, orange, and dull yellows, almost as if the landscape was being illuminated by fire. But what struck Bob as odd about the painting was that the figure on the horse was holding a small...child? This child seems almost featureless but not in a state of decay like everything else. It is a pale blue and contrasts with everything else in the painting. It is almost ghostly, but seemingly nurtured by the undead figure riding the horse. The way Bob's mind worked, he made connections, drew conclusions. It's impossible to know what some artist from a hundred thousand plus years ago might think, but Bob could determine what this painting meant to him. He felt it was the world in a state of decay, dying and in its final throes, yet here it nurtured something new. Something that would replace and change everything and leave the dead behind. The painting was faintly disturbing to Bob, but he was unsettled by the fact that what he really found disturbing was not the decaying world, but the little blue figure coming from it.

After the museum Bob went to a nearby park. Not a big or fancy one, but one with a large enough patch of grass upon which he would take a short nap. Maybe a long nap, he had nothing else to do. In the twilight between here and there, that half-dreamy state, Bob was jostled by a call from the chief.
Groggy, Bob answered: "...yallow...".
Chief: "...well, it's not exactly what we wanted but we do have two more bodies. We should really talk in person, so why don't you come to my office and I'll fill you in on all the details."

Bob: "I'm heading there now."

Bob made his way to the headquarters and directly to the Chief's office. Finally, something to do. Without small talk and down to business:

Chief: "Bob, we have two dead. One found in the outland regions of Helen, the other, an outlying province on Ganymede."

Bob: "Anything more to go on than that? No reported sightings of the attack?"

Chief: "No, and unfortunately these deaths occurred a couple of weeks ago. That will make it a bit harder to do a proper autopsy, but I think at this point we know what we're looking for. What it does do, however, is reorganize our timeline. It looks like our Ganymedian friend was technically the first of our murders so far, then the man from the outlands of Helen. It wasn't till after the two of these that the attacks in Helen proper took place."

Bob: "And if the path of death is from Ganymede to Helen, we no longer are dealing with a criminal isolated or strictly local. It could be regional to Zeus, or it could even be system wide."

Chief: "That could be. We don't want to jump the gun, but we should look into similar deaths in the entire system to be on the safe side.

Bob: "And now that we have a murder on Ganymede we'll have considerably more leverage to get other planets seriously looking into the case as well. This may grease the wheel a bit and get information flowing."

Chief: "I agree, but we need to thoroughly look into these new cases. If it turns out these deaths were unrelated, we'll be crying wolf and requests for information or help will be ignored."

Bob: "Right, right. So we haven't yet established a familial relationship to these other murders?"

Chief: "We are requesting ancestry from the Ganymedian. Still waiting. The other murder is an unknown. We only know his name, Barley Bishop. That is, of course, where you come in. I'll need you to travel to the outlands and find out everything you can."

Bob: "Yeah, I kinda saw that coming. Barley? I'll leave right away." The Chief nodded. "We'll have a small transport waiting for you when you get to the top floor."

Knowing that the appropriate clearances were most likely already associated with Bob's presence and the specific details and locations were already terminal ready, he made his way to the rooftop.

The transport was a small, unarmed, boxy shuttle that could seat two comfortably and four irritably and crankily. It was metallic white and carried no visible official identification, though any free individual could scan the shuttle and get a rundown of the organization to which it belonged, usually a generalized message like "unofficial police business". Even though the job Bob was on was definitely official, he himself was not an officer.

The shuttle more or less piloted itself. It was told where to go and did so more accurately and safely than a human being could...usually. In emergencies, the controls could be relinquished to manual. Usually not a good idea unless it's absolutely necessary.

Bob needed to make a stop by his apartment and it was nice to soar so effortlessly and directly there. No wading through a crush of people to get on a train that takes one *near* their destination. No irritating passengers or delays or obnoxiously loud announcements or advertisements. Nice, silent, and smooth.

Bob's apartment wasn't built to land shuttlecraft. It was an old apartment and not very conducive to anything convenient. The shuttle had to hover about a foot above while Bob entered the rooftop access door and down several flights of stairs. There he caught the lift and made it to his floor.

Bob made his way to his apartment door and noticed Abrum watching, almost invisibly, from the shadowed entrance to his own apartment. Abrum didn't say anything and Bob wasn't going to initiate contact. After all, Bob was in a hurry...more or less. Still, Abrum said nothing. He just watched. The faint glint of eyes in shadows.

In his apartment, Bob walked immediately to his bed. Underneath he kept a small compartment, securely locked, which slid out and opened at Bob's request. This level of security was most likely unnecessary, but in Bob's line of work caution was the habit, warranted or not. In this compartment Bob kept several things, mostly job related. Important hard-copy documents and I.D.'s, an old book he cherished, several bound record keeping books (actual paper), and some small devices used on rare occasion for the job. Among these items, Bob took two. One was a small, handheld EMP (electro-magnetic pulse) disruptor. It was small caliber and designed to temporarily disrupt the nervous system rendering the target inactive but unharmed. The other item taken was a small pocket knife, titanium blade. The uses of a decent pocket knife are always underestimated.

Re-securing the lock-box, and heading towards the apartment door, Bob grabbed a bag of chips and was on his way. "GigaCheese! Catch the Crunchy Fever" The image on the bag was a six-armed giant sprinkling chips on a joyous crowd of children. Each chip was etched into a detailed depiction of an ancient pagoda...for some reason. This particular flavor was seaweed and pickled ginger.

It was unlikely that Bob would need a sidearm, but the outlands of Helen were not safe places and relatively lawless. The outlands are a collection of unorganized and illegal colonies scattered around the body of Helen. Though the landmass of Helen is enormous, there are only three major cities, each with a dozen or so suburbs or neighboring cities attached. These three cities are Helen's Crown, New Paris in Helen's right, upturned palm, and Nemesis over her left shoulder. These outland colonies existed in many places elsewhere; behind the ears, the valleys of her hair, right shoulder, the cleft of her left bent arm, and various places on her upper back. There are no known colonies from her waist down as atmospheric disturbances from Zeus are not compatible with life there.

This particular colony Bob was about to visit was on her right shoulder towards the back, northern scapula. It lies loosely from the Acromion process to the scapular notch and for that reason the colony is known as the Acromion Notch. Many of these outland colonies were established by criminals or those seeking to evade authority, but the vast majority of the inhabitants are people who have found themselves there and have little means to better their circumstances. These people want only peace and a means of bettering their condition but the fickle hand of fate has dictated otherwise.

Returning to the transport, Bob was quickly whisked away. The transport made its way skyward towards midtown, then laterally out towards the boundary of Helen's Crown. There is an area known as the Transient Lock which corresponds to a free lock of Helen's hair that originates from the crown and travels downward to the temporal bone before curving towards the back of the head. The northern ridge next to the Transient Lock is an easy path to move from Helen's Crown to all destinations of her left side, while the southern ridge provides easy access to the back of her head. The ridges allow for fast travel at a range that is above the surface, but below mass transport for incoming outworld ships.

Locations on Helen are often referred to by the "supposed" bone structure underneath. There is obviously no literal bone structure, but with a massive object such as a planet sized statue the location of an underlying bone structure can provide a good degree of accuracy as to relative destination. One could imagine that the designation of "shoulder" would carry little value when that shoulder is the size of a small continent.

Long after Bob's bag of chips lay empty his transport reached the bend in the Transient Lock and continued downward away from the lock's bend toward the back of the head. Being so small, as a human being is most often compared to their surroundings, and close to the surface it is hard to really perceive any image of Helen, yet here on this descent one could just see and extrapolate the emerging ear. It had to be contemplated as to how the curves and textures fit into the picture, but it could be comprehended. Oddly delicate for such a large scale.

Even though gravity on Helen is artificial and draws objects to all perceived sub-cutaneous surfaces, one cannot help but feel a false sense of falling from the side of her head when the image of Helen is held in the foreground of the mind. It's easy to get distracted and ignore this, but this experience is part of the awe inspiring wonders of living on such a world and rarely do even the inhabitants get quite this opportunity.

A good deal of time later, and after a short nap, Bob arrived at the prescribed coordinates on the Acromion Notch. It was somewhat amazing: a mass of prefabricated structures and make-shift homes. It was a genuine shanty town, not particularly filthy, but neither was it clean. Buildings were broken and abandoned while others were heavily barricaded. Bob saw a thing here that was almost non-existent on Helen's Crown: broken glass. There are several ways to make glass and actual glass was probably the most inexpensive. There wasn't enough lucre in the outlands to adorn much with unbreakable plastiglass, especially when the governing body of Helen proper chose not to recognize or support the inhabitants here.

The roads looked like dirt roads, which couldn't be but was most likely due to the bi-products of industry and improper waste disposal. It was most likely a mixture of rendered factory waste and soot. This also meant that the health of the outlanders was surely compromised, which is well known yet the specific mechanisms are speculative.

This drab scene is augmented by the fact that artificial light is sporadic and inconsistent. The darkened landscape is a mess of twisted metals, dirt, and good people trying to find contentment in an area that offers little.

Some people milled about while others scattered at the sight of an official transport. For this reason Bob landed a good distance away from his target to give him some time to disappear into the crowd. The last thing he wanted here was to be associated with authority. After all, he only wanted information and to stop the killing of innocent people.

After a circuitous walk around a particular conglomerate of dwellings (which was one of thousands of such colonies smattered throughout the Acromion Notch), Bob made it to an establishment, rundown and seemingly vacant, with the word "café" crudely painted across corrugated sheet metal. This was about as precise as the given coordinates could manage. Here one did not find quite the order and structure of Helen's Crown.

Walking in, the proprietor looked at Bob suspiciously. He was an old man, weathered and scraggly.

Old man: "Whatcha need there pal?"

Bob: "Hi. I'm looking for the home of a man called Barley Bishop."

The old man, surprised: "He's dead."

Bob: "I know. I was hoping to find his home, talk to anyone who knew him."

Old man: "You police?"

Bob: "No."

Old man: "You a friend then?"

Bob, feeling he had to act gingerly with this old man: "Well, not exactly but..."

Old man: "Then what do you care?"

Bob: "I'm hoping I can figure out who did it and stop it from happening again."

Old man: "He died of a heart attack. Are you gonna buy something?"

Bob didn't have any idea how goods and services were exchanged here. He assumed a bartering system.

Bob: "I really just want to find the home of Barley Bishop."

Old man: "I don't want to get involved. ...Down the alley, next to the shop. The door at the end."

Bob: "Thank you kindly."

The old man was silent and Bob left.

The alley was a thick mess of doors which must have led to people's homes. Tin and dirt, packed into as tight a space as possible. Little lights, electric but like small candles, would peep out of windows and door frames and there at the end was a door, the only one that opened in the direction of travel and not perpendicular like the many that lined the alley.

Bob gave a gentle knock on the unmarked door. He could hear, momentarily, some movement behind. A shadowy image presented itself behind a small window to the left of the door, then more silence, possibly contemplating. Bob gave another gentle knock and slowly the door opened a crack.

Bob could see the glint of spectacles and darkness. Then after a moment of silence:

"...who are you?"

The delicate voice was that of an elderly woman.

Bob: "Ma'am, I was hoping to find some information about Barley Bishop. Did he live here?"

The old woman: "...he,...he passed away recently."

There was sadness in her voice.

Bob: "I know ma'am. I'm hoping I can help. I want to find out who did it and why."

The old woman opened the door a bit farther to get a better look at Bob's face.

"...he died of a heart attack." She said with a strong degree of confusion.

Bob should have realized this from from his conversation with the café owner, but she didn't know it was a murder. He just assumed it was known, which it was not.

Bob: "I'm sorry ma'am. It is believed this was not an accident and we're trying to find out who might be responsible."

Old woman, intrigued but saddened: "Murder? Are you police?"

Bob: "No ma'am. I'm an investigator and I'm working with the police to solve a series of similar deaths to Barley Bishop's. May I come in and talk to you for a bit?"

After a moment of consideration, she opened the door and gestured for Bob to come in while scanning the outdoors for others or anything suspiciously out of place.

Old woman: "Murder?..." she said again. "Why do you...who are you anyway?"

Bob: "My name is Bob. I've been asked to look into this and several other similar cases. Do you mind if I ask you your name?"

Old woman: "Gladys. Gladys Bishop. ...why do you say Barley was murdered?"

Bob: "Well ma'am, there have been several other cases, similar, that appear to be heart complications but on closer inspection were found to be a command disruption to the heart itself. In these previous cases there is a high degree of certainty this was not a natural phenomenon. Do you mind me asking your relationship to the victim...Barley Bishop?"

Gladys: "I'm his mother. ...Barley was murdered?" asked to reaffirm.

Bob: "Yes ma'am. I do believe so."

Gladys sat somewhat stunned as Bob was entering information silently into his unseen terminal. Bob: "Do you happen to have any familial relationship to the names Palter or Thrame?"

Gladys, thinking carefully: "...no, I don't believe so. My mother's maiden name was Eurnum and I believe my great grandmother's family name was Callus. I don't know any Palters or Thrames, but I know little of my ancestry to be honest. Not much time for it here."

Bob: "I understand. I'll run the names and see if I can find a familial relationship."

Gladys: "Who would have done something like that to Barley? He was a good boy and never did anybody any harm. He was well liked and a hard worker. It doesn't make any sense. Do you have any idea who might be behind this?"

Bob: "I don't. Not yet. We think these are more or less random acts and nothing Barley did had anything to do with his murder. However, the murders do seem to be following a familial lineage. We don't know why. Not yet."

Gladys: "...oh my. I, ...I can't believe it." Redness came easily to her aching eyes.

Bob: "I'm so sorry for your loss ma'am. I am doing everything in my power to find out what's going on and to stop this from happening to someone else."

Gladys: "..."

Bob: "If you wouldn't mind, with your permission I would like to look through his belongings and see if there is anything that might give us a clue to what happened."

Gladys: "You don't have to take anything do you?"

Bob: "No ma'am. I'm just looking for information."

Gladys: "Certainly." She then pointed to the appropriate door and sat quietly in deep thought as Bob entered the room of Barley Bishop.

The room was small and clean. It was the room of a well-organized individual. There was a terminal desk where the victim most likely did his work. It was uncluttered. A small, single bed, nicely made. A chair and reading lamp in the corner of the room was dimly illuminated by a small window in the center of the outer wall. There was a dresser for clothes and a picture on the adjacent wall...a faux painting of a peaceful seaside village which is nice to think about considering visiting the nearest actual sea requires travel by spacecraft.

At the terminal desk Bob summoned the room illumination. He first went through the very meager possessions, inspected the dresser for hidden items and found nothing of any import, which was expected as there hasn't been any connection to these murders except the family connection. It was about this time as well that a communique arrived and Bob confirmed that there was a distant familial relationship between Palter, Thrame, and now this man named Barley Bishop.

The items of the room were uneventful so Bob's attention went to the terminal desk as it is this interconnected galactic world where many live their true virtual lives. The appropriate official clearances already in place and Bob could access the records of Barley Bishop as well as if Barley was still living.

After an hour of searching through data, Bob found no quarrel, no conflict, and no trace of trouble anywhere in the life of Barley Bishop. A hard working, quiet individual who kept to himself. It also was a bit on the unusual side that Bob didn't find any mention of work, but when he politely asked Gladys she said he did odd jobs around the colony. He helped construct many of the homes and repaired drainage systems in the nearby area. He also made shoes, but this was not consistent work as people around here made a shoe exceed its recommended lifespan. He kept guard, uneventfully, when a string of robberies and vandalism had been hitting the colony requiring the locals to form an unofficial posse.

Their terminology is easily misunderstood by the outsider. This colony was the size of a small village. Some locals even referred to it as "the village". Others merely call it "the colony" as its origins make this term appropriate. There are thousands of such colonies that comprise the Acromian Notch, many vaguely defined between one and the other. Some are quite large but many are small like the one in which Gladys and her son Barley found themselves. Criminals that ruined their reputations in one colony merely had to move to one far enough that they were unknown. Organized bands of crooks often traveled from colony to colony causing as much trouble as possible. The poor stealing from the even poorer. It's sad how often this has been the circumstances pressed upon the downtrodden throughout the galaxy.

Bob, returning to the main room of the dwelling: "Gladys, may I ask you a few more questions before I leave?"

Gladys: "Certainly"

Bob: "You don't know of anything suspicious or out of the ordinary that happened before Barley died?"

Gladys: "I've been thinking about that the past hour or so. He had no enemies. He'd done nothing wrong, ever. Everyone liked him or paid him no mind."

Gladys: "...the only thing, ...the night before he passed on..." her eyes teary,   "...he saw someone on the hill behind the house...sitting. He saw this out his bedroom window."

Bob: "Is it an unusual thing to see someone back there?"

Gladys: "There's no reason it would be suspicious, even though we rarely see anyone back there. It's dark and this isn't the safest place, but it is beautiful, the view from the top of that hill. ...I guess I'm saying it's unusual to see someone back there that late, but not particularly suspicious."

Bob: "I see. If you don't mind me asking, is Barley's father still living?"

Gladys: "No. He died twelve and a half years ago. It was a mining operation. They think some young fool accidentally breached a rectifier with his own plasma torch. A mess of hellish liquefied fire filled the chamber. They were all killed instantly. All seven miners.

Bartle was one of them. ...completely vaporized. There wasn't even a body for the funeral."

Bob: "His name was Bartle Bishop?"

Gladys nodded and Bob added the name to the list. Obviously nothing to do with the murders, but it seems the key will be figuring out what the genealogy has to do with these unexplained killings. Maybe it could be predicted.

These mining operations around the colonies were well known and illegal. These people are often without adequate resources and instinctively mine into the surface of Helen for raw materials. In addition to this being illegal, it is incredibly unsafe. Most often the danger comes at the hands of inadequate machines and materials to conduct a safe mining operation, but there are also direct dangers in breaching the surface. There was, some time ago, a small mining operation in a distant colony in which the miners, digging much too deep, briefly compromised a gravity attenuator. It's almost impossible to damage them, but they gave it an insulting glance and the gravity around the entire colony became unstable. It was only for a handful of minutes, but enough time that the colony floated beyond the atmosphere. Around eight hundred people died...suffocated. They floated above the thin atmosphere around Helen until the gravity of the nearby regions brought them down. For the people in these neighboring regions, they experienced a rain of twisted, ramshackle colony debris peppered with frozen and dead bodies. Luckily for all of us the artificial gravity of Helen is highly particulated so no *one* act can disable all gravitational forces body-wide. It goes without saying that this was a stern warning to colonist and law enforcement alike. Colony mining has diminished and enforcement tightened, but too many people spread far too thin adds a noisy dither to the structure of order.

Again, Bob was faced with a death and a lack of motive; no enemies, no quarrels, nothing. Barley Bishop, innocent and hardworking, dead for seemingly no reason other than being tied to a shared genealogy. Rames Palter, Wilford Thrame, and Barley Bishop, distant cousins and no sign they even knew each other.

Bob: "Gladys, I thank you greatly for your time. If I learn anything pertinent I will get in contact with you immediately. Also, if you come across anything relevant or new, please let me know. Again, I'm sorry for your loss."

Gladys: "Thank you. If you learn anything, please let me know...I just want to know."

Bob: "I understand. Before I leave the colonies I'll check in the back where Barley saw the figure on the night of his death. I don't expect to find anything, but I don't want you to be alarmed if you see someone back there. It will be me."

With a nod and courteous smile Bob left Gladys to her grief. There wasn't a back door so Bob had to leave the house entrance and walk back up the alley and around a block or two of interconnected homes, shops, and workhouses. This portion of the colony was built around a single wide path that lead through town. Everything lined this path and there wasn't a lot of access to the outer areas. Between two industrial workhouses there was a narrow path, practically outside this small portion of the colony, that allowed him access to the back side of the strip.

Back here it was wonderfully dark. The colonies, in general, were not well lit and this little village even more poorly so. Leaving the main path and being shielded by the town itself, the darkness was thick. It was actually refreshing. There isn't darkness like this on Helen's Crown, save for the little bit you can manufacture in your own room at night. Even though Helen's Crown does artificially cycle between day and night, the night is never really night. Here, in this neglected colony, night existed like it must have in ancient history.

Retracing his path, Bob made it back to the approximate location of the Bishop home. He strained a bit to eye the window of Barley Bishops room and align himself where the supposed figure was seen. Bob generated a bit of light, but found nothing; no footprints, clues, or debris except for the trash of a forgotten town.

Further away was a small hill beyond which was the orange glow of Zeus. Bob thought it a good idea to wander up that hill and take a look at the horizon, not because it pertained to the case, but more that it pertained to his curiosity. Walking up the small hill, the orange glow opened up to fill the sky. Bob sat upon the hill in a stunned silence. It was a wondrous vantage point to see the surface of Zeus. The swirling shades of orange and browns, even red, like intermingling liquids frozen in time. It was miraculous and Bob was awestruck. Helen's Crown points directly away from the surface. This sight cannot be seen there. Sure, there are countless ways to simulate just about any sight in the galaxy, but despite the realism it is somehow never the same as being there...being in it. To walk in the presence of awe leaves the mouth mute to fully adequately ever tell the tale.

After a time of soaking in the beauty of the world, which Bob felt he could sit and enjoy endlessly, he felt the pressures of obligation upon him. He stood up, looked around, and found nothing. He half wondered but somewhat felt that the killer had sat in this very spot, staring into the great gas giant beyond. Had then a similar pressure of obligation pulled this killer away to commit a senseless act of homicide? Bob imagined that whatever device was used to stop the heart, had been activated by someone outside the room of Barley Bishop. Though the specifics would probably never be known, Bob wanted to know if the killer had sat here, looking toward the glow of Zeus, then committed the murder or vise versa. This would be very telling to the murderers character. Stepping into awe, then stepping away implies obligation. Killing, then being at peace enough to enjoy the beauty of nature is the act of a psychopath. In all honesty though, and why this was not a particularly useful line of thought, the situation could be very different than what Bob might imagine.

Time was upon him yet again. Bob summoned the transport which, from a distant location, sprung into life and silently but quickly met him where he stood. Within an instant he was leaving the colony and heading back on the long ride to Helen's Crown.

On the ride home, as sleep was trying to overtake Bob, he shook himself awake and thought it best to contact the Chief and let him know what he found out...which wasn't much. Terminal active and connection made:

Chief: "Hi Bob. Whatcha know?"

Bob: "Nothing really. Barley Bishop, like the others had no enemies, nothing suspicious, and no connection to the other murders except for the distant familial connection. I assume you got the list of names I added to the collection."

Chief: "I did, and there's a little news about that. The names Eurnum and Callus...relatives of the Bishops?"

Bob: "Yes. The mother, Gladys Bishop, gave a very limited genealogy of her parents and grandparents."

Chief: "Well, it looks like our Ganymedian friend is an Eurnum. So, still family. Ganymede high council has since identified two other Eurnums that have died in a similar way. Since we've been working on this for a while now, they have given me authority to handle the case...in all honesty, they seem to not really care and prefer having someone else take charge. I have already sent you the current data on the Ganemedian deaths, so take a look when you get a chance."

Bob: "Wow, this is turning out to be a lot more work than I anticipated. It is not compatible with my leisurely lifestyle."

Chief, chuckling: "Oh I'm far from done. Get this, the second murder...Thrame, we finally got access to his lineage. He was a transplant from Alpha Centauri, specifically Peneus of the Southern Gate. Three other Thrames are reported dead for "unidentified heart complications" and two other similar deaths on nearby Elis, on a solar outpost that the Centaurian government constructed for energy manufacturing."

63

Bob: "Good grief."
Chief: "Yeah. Fortunately for us Alpha Centauri has a centralized systemwide authority and is cooperating, albeit slowly, so we should have more info on the way."
Bob: "..."
Chief: "We'll be pouring over this together, but all the data that I currently have acquired is at your disposal now, so we best get to work and crack this thing."
Bob: "Unbelievable."
Chief: "So we're dealing with at least eight bodies now."
Bob: "At least. There's probably more. I'm feeling we are quite a bit behind the killer."
Chief: "...yep. I think there's little need right now to be sending you to all these places, especially since there hasn't been a good turnout of useable info. For now, we'll just put our efforts on the data collected by the local agencies and if there's something of interest or a reason to travel, we'll deal with that then. For now, let's just see what we're missing in the data."
Bob: "Ok...It's late, I'm worn out. I'll get on this first thing."
Chief: "Alrighty, Bob. 'night"
Bob: "goodnight"

Bob spent the rest of the flight back in silence and somewhat numb in thought. It was almost too much, at least too much to think about right now. It was more and more information without direction. Bob was tired, but it was the kind of tired one gets from traveling and sitting around all day.

Back at his apartment, Bob slumped in and put the EMP disruptor away. He felt bad for even taking it though it was standard protocol. It's easy to feel threatened when visiting impoverished areas of the world, which often do carry more danger than the well-to-do world cares to allot for, but in general people are just wanting to scrape out a living, peacefully, and overall be left alone to live in accordance to their means. Even the most impoverished areas of the galaxy are replete with good people.

In the shower Bob let a terminal run with the news of the day, mostly to occupy the mind, and distract him from the frustrations of this omnidirectional case. However, it didn't end up producing the desired results.

"...authorities of Atlas have verified the presence of the virus system wide. It is currently found in major portions of the population on every planet of the Atlas system. The individual planetary governments have yet to identify the virus claiming it is a new strain *sharing many aspects of common virus physiology. Atlas and neighboring system authorities are cautioning travel to Atlas, but assume the problem will be under control shortly and state that those infected with the virus show no signs of ill health or impaired faculty. Though the epidemiology is still being assessed, it is believed that this is merely a mutation of a common virus that has a weak interaction with the human body."*

"A small area of Peneus, in the Alpha Centauri system has also reported infection. This is believed to be related to travel to and from Atlas and is currently considered isolated. Travel is not restricted to Peneus except for the quarantined area of infection. Further information will be reported as available."

"Next up, which celebrity has recently underwent arm extension surgery? We'll tell you right after this commercial..."

Bob, whispering: "Peneus."

Bob turned off the terminal and stood with a sense of dread, like a tight anxiety was gripping his chest. He had, seemingly irrationally, worried this was some epidemic. He had worried, even more irrationally, that this was somehow related to these murders. It was really too early to say, but there was a lingering shadow on the periphery. Something hanging like a specter, waiting. Again, it was too much to deal with right now, but it had to be looked into.

Bob dried off, dressed, and fell into bed like a corpse. Even with the weight of the world on his proverbial shoulders, Morpheus demands a sacrifice paid nightly, paid by every living being in the entire galaxy.

Zdzisław Beksiński – Old Earth antiquity circa 1976 (estimated)

Dream Journal: Decapitation

This one has recurred several times. I can't really tell what's going on, or what has happened to me. My point of view is as if I'm lying on my side on the ground. I can't move. I can't even feel my body, nor move my eyes. I think it may just be my head, possible severed. I can hear a high pitched buzz, electrical sounding. Constant. In my periphery there is a figure. I can't properly see the figure and in panic wonder if it is my daughter. The anxiety of wondering if it's her is overwhelming and completely trumps the concern of my present state. If it is her, she is standing but not moving. Why can't I move my damn eyes! If I could just see her.

There is a sound. Percussive. Low. Coupled with an electric crackle. When I hear the sound my mind dissolves into darkness and star-filled space. I am drawn backwards into it like sinking beneath the surface of a black ocean. I force my mind out of it and hear that high pitched squeal again, only louder. I still can't see her face. She hasn't moved.
The thundering sound. Darkness and stars. I sink deeper.
                    Shaking myself clear again...the pitch, the figure.
 Less distinct, blurry.
Thunder. Darkness, deeper and deeper.
                        The Squeal. Blurred figure of the periphery.
                            Thunder. Darkness, deeper still.
                                The Squeal.

 Unbearably loud.
The blurred figure is burning bright.
                        Thunder.
                        All is dark.

Visit Alpha Centauri!
Brought to you by the Orion-Cygnus Arm Travel Authority (OrCA)

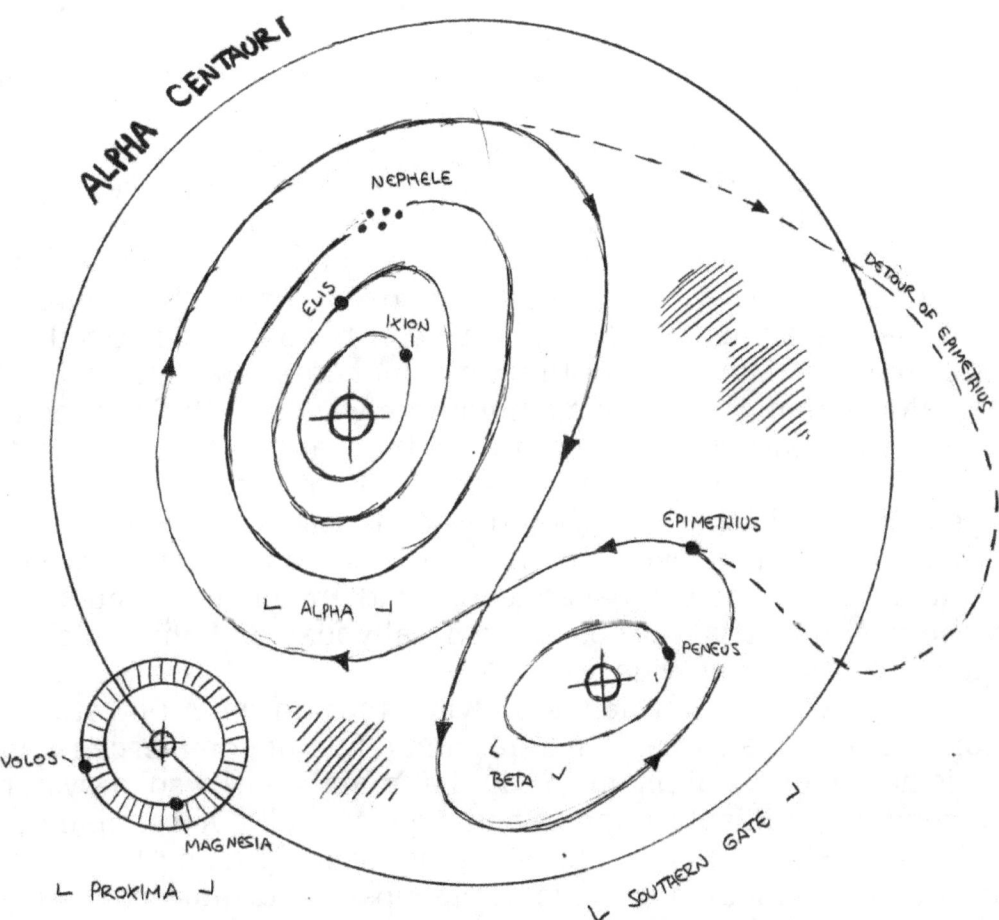

It can only be said that the legends surrounding greater Alpha Centauri fail to do justice to the splendor of the system. Alpha Centauri was the first system peopled when humanity began the noble quest to spread out amongst the stars. As such, several early colonies have been designated historical landmarks and remain as almost pristine monuments to the ways of life of these very first interstellar travelers.

Greater Alpha Centauri is a trinary star system, the primary star being called simply "**Alpha**" and the assumed star association when Alpha Centauri is mentioned. The companion star "**Beta**" and associated planets are collectively known as the Southern Gate and share a conjoined orbit with Alpha and comprise the main body of Alpha Centauri. It is easier to imagine Alpha Centauri as a binary star system with a third star in orbit around the binary. This third star is

71

the well-known **"Proxima"** and don't let the small size of this star fool you, there are big things happening around Proxima.

While visiting the Alpha star, the traveler will want to start their vacation on planet **Ixion**. Ixion is home to over eight billion people from all regions of the galaxy. Many independent nations, Ixion claims to have the most languages spoken per capita of any planet in the galaxy and is the original repository of dead and dying languages. Though available galaxy wide through the Free Galactic Library (FGL), as a historical monument little surpasses the awe inspired by the original library of ancient Earth languages and dialects. Ixion is also home to a great many vast forests and crystal clear oceans and lakes. Be sure to take an ocean tour to see the wooly mammothtee. This sacred animal of the Zemu tribe of Ixion is a genetically transmogrified ancestor of the Earth manatee. Back in the days of terraformation, the wooly mammothtee was bred to filter the high sulfur and heavy metal content from the waters of Ixion. What few know it that this was actually a symbiotic process involving a specialized kelp that absorbed the sulphur and metals from the water which was then concentrated in the digestive tract of the woolly mammothtee. The compact waste was then collected and used for a variety of industrial purposes, eventually leaving behind clean and clear waters planet wide.

Elis will be your next stop while touring the Alpha star. Elis is comprised of many massive cities and a hub of commerce region wide. It is not an overstatement to say that many nearby solar systems are dependent on Elis for imports and exports and general manufacturing. Elis is also home to the Orion-Cygnus Arm Stock and Lucre Exchange (OrCA SALE) making Elis one of the most important economic hubs within several thousand light years.
While there, see the Horn of Thalamus, the Metropolitan Quad Towers, and the wreckage of the Diemos Star II, preserved from the Thesian-Alpha Propagation Wars.

Before leaving Alpha, you'll want to visit **Nephele**. Nephele is not a true planet, but rather a collection of planetoids formed from the prehistoric destruction of a once vast orbiting body. An architects dream, Nephele has been reinforced by mammoth feats of architectural achievement. Each planetoid is interconnected by a series of human made structures that provide easy and quick transport between them giving the overall appearance of Nephele a crystalline, weblike quality. Though a major seat of industry and textiles for Alpha Centauri, the low-earth gravity
(approximately ⅕) has sprouted many resorts and rehabilitation facilities for physical injuries.

Visiting the Beta star, the main planetary attraction is peaceful **Peneus**. Peneus has many modern cities, tropical rain forests, and the most coastline of any planet in the greater Alpha Centauri system. A harmless crystalline photosynthetic bacterium make the waters of Peneus a brilliant jade green and lends Peneus the nickname "the Jade Planet" while the drying bacterium make the coastal sands a rich coffee brown. Beta being roughly the size of Sol, and Peneus the size and relative distance of Earth, make this Jade Planet one of the closest approximations to our beloved ancestor, the Blue Planet.

Though not a common tourist attraction, the tiny star Proxima is orbited by two primary planets: **Volos** and **Magnesia**. Magnesia is rich with mineral resources, but the unusual electro-magnetic field of Proxima makes travel difficult. Volos, far enough to avoid the worst effects of the magnetic field of Proxima, has become the outpost of material transport to the Alpha and Beta systems. From Volos, travel and mining operations to Magnesia are conducted by ships that would be, in all other circumstances, considered primitive, much like those used tens of thousands of years ago. Those who would like to see these antiquated ships, like those of our ancestors, in actual use shouldn't pass up the opportunity to take an industrial tour of Volos.

Though visitation to **Epimethius** is not encouraged, there are many job opportunities for those looking for vocation. Epimethius carries out major ice-mining operations supplying water to Alpha, Beta, and Proxima. Epimethius has an irregular figure-8 orbit around both Alpha and Beta. Seasonally, when Epimethius and Proxima align, Epimethius is pulled out and beyond the Proxima orbit. During this time Epimethius is vacated until the orbit is stabilized around the Alpha-Beta binary. It is estimated that within the next two million years Epimethius will be pulled away from Alpha Centauri altogether and float helplessly in the outer-stellar rim. Those looking for gainful employment should strike now while the iron is hot.

Almost its own little galaxy, many who travel to Alpha Centauri later make plans to relocate and call Alpha Centauri their home. Plan your visit today.

Chapter Six: Diner on the Edge of Forever – part 1

Bob awoke and had a bite to eat. While he spent some time shaking off the heaviness of sleep, he began skimming through the large amount of data on the murders upon Ganymede and also Peneus of Alpha Centauri.

"Peneus", Bob thought. The first direct connection between locations of a murder and the virus. The report claimed that the outbreak on Peneus was contained, but they said the same thing about Phoebe and now the virus is system wide in Atlas and has spread to another system. Bob decided to bring the issue up with the Chief when they spoke next, which would be soon. A timeline needed to be established for the murders, and this needed to be checked against the spread of the virus. As of now, after a quick scan of the available data, the chronology of the murders seems to be from Peneus to Ganymede to Helen. However, the time of death of several of the murders is yet unavailable. It must be looked into.

As for the murders themselves, the Eurnums of Ganymede share near identical similarities with the others: familial relationship, various occupations rousing no suspicion, modest living conditions. The same is true for the Thrames of Peneus in Alpha Centauri. The two deaths on Elis in Alpha Centauri carry the names Baker and Dahlec, which haven't yet fit into the genealogy of the others, but most likely will in some way.

The possible interplay of the virus into all of this made Bob nervous. This case has already gone from some argumentative homicide to a full-fledged serial killing, a thing unheard of in the Sol system for hundreds of years. And now, there is another system involved. This beast seems to be getting bigger and harder to see.

>>

At the police headquarters, the Chief had been at work several hours before Bob had awoken. He had done about the same amount of skimming as Bob had done but nothing of any importance came to light. He wanted to delve deeper into the data, but did have a job to attend to that involved a city of vast numbers of people. Most of his work was administrative by nature. On Helen's Crown it was near impossible to do a thing and not have some visual record of it. When a crime is committed, the guilty party is issued a communique with an appointment to be processed at a nearby policing facility. If the accused fails to show at the appointed time the charges are increased and another appointment is issued. Depending upon the crime, this may continue for several stages and by the time a physical arrest is issued the accused is in more-or-less permanent trouble. These days, there are no places to hide, no chance of getting away with it. Whereabouts are known. Activity is under surveillance. Because of this, crime was very rare and those guilty most often turned themselves in at first notice.

The Chief, like most, had a proper name, but never used it. For most of his life he had gone by the name Ace, a name he acquired in a story only he knew. Yet, for the past thirty years or so, he was so commonly referred to as "Chief" that it seemed odd, even to him, to call him something else. The Chief was a very private person. He either has or had a family, but no one is sure. He has mentioned sons, but they have never been seen, only passing references. No mention of a wife or extended family. Most suspect at one time he was a family man but something changed his situation and he now, and has for some time, lived alone. Regardless, this has allowed him to devote a considerable amount of time to his job. His job, though not as adventure oriented as it would be in some of the more lawless regions of the galaxy, was extraordinarily time consuming. Most of this consumption came in the form of paperwork and dealing with the finer points and boundaries of city wide regulation.

Like many people on developed worlds of the modern galaxy, the Chief had his fair share of stress. He also suffered from a good degree of anxiety. The term, which is an old one, is Generalized Anxiety Disorder. It is classified by the FGL as a physio-existential condition, meaning that there is a physical component interacting with a philosophical one. Some researchers say that the majority of people in the developed worlds of the galaxy suffer, to some extent, from it. Perhaps we, as a species, made a decision long, long ago to live in dissonance to our nature.

One wouldn't know this to encounter him, however, as the Chief's demeanor is almost always calm and collected. He is even-tempered and seemingly relaxed, but he worries. He worries often and is hyper aware of his surroundings. He seeks patterns in the most disparate elements and often finds them though they may turnout to be Rorschach's shadows (to use a modern term whose origins have been lost to antiquity). However, this very "disorder" may have a strong hand in making him good at his job. The Chief started out as a private investigator, much like Bob. In fact, after climbing the ladder and securing a position as Lieutenant of the police department, he talked Bob into getting involved with investigation. Since, Bob has been his right hand man in all matters of importance...though admittedly there is not much to investigate in the mechanized justice system of Helen's Crown. Regardless, having someone to trust, and one with the observational and problem solving skills Bob possessed, was indispensable.

The main problem, the Chief's chief worry, was that in such a mechanized judicial environment that much of the developed galaxy found itself, there was not much initiative to be found in law enforcement. The Chief already felt that the regions and governments he had contacted had a "do whatever you like, we don't care" mentality with this string of murders. They probably figured that if there was a rampant serial killer that some watchful automaton would catch this person in the act and, like magic, problem solved. But this was not turning out to be the case. The Chief had his staff pouring over the minutiae of surveillance on all the victims. It is a considerable amount of data, but he has a large staff. In the Palter case, the man keeled over in public...out of the blue. Thrame died in his sleep as did Bishop. The Ganymedians, all three Eurnums, died in public. Two of the Thrames of Alpha Centauri's Peneus died in public, one at home. Both deaths on Elis in Alpha Centauri, Baker and Dahlec, are reported to have died in their sleep. For those who died in public, there has been an intensive analysis of all individuals in the immediate area, the idea being that maybe one of them carried some device which they surreptitiously used to commit the crimes. All background checks have returned clean and there has been no recurrence of any individual betwixt crimes. This is as cold of a case as there can be. No motive other than some possible grudge against the extended family, which is unlikely that someone could set their sights on such a diverse and only loosely related group of people. None of it makes sense, yet the Chief felt that undoubtedly this was an ongoing crime. Most likely there are people already dead of which we are unaware and others doomed to die soon because of our inability to solve the puzzle. There is but the finest, tattered thread that prevents these crimes from seeming completely random in their violence and the Chief couldn't help but feel there was a beclouded and shadowed cataclysm hurtling toward the civilized world. It may seem excessive to place such emphasis on a string of murders, but such a thing hadn't been encountered in hundreds of years and the Chief was prone to worry.

>>

Bob poured through the data on the recent discoveries. There was nothing that made much sense. There is absolutely no reason for these men to have died. It had occurred to Bob that as of now the murders have all been male. Since Alpha Centauri was being cooperative, or at least didn't care, Bob took a look at the census information on the Thrame family of Peneus. They had lived on Ixion (Alpha Centauri proper) some years prior. After the deaths, there were two Thrames on Peneus still alive. Both female. The Thramess of Peneus originated as a couple transplanted from the Pollux system twenty or so years earlier. The couple met while working as counselors on Aeris, the second largest moon of Gemini Superior which is the well-known gas giant of the Pollux system (twice the size of Zeus). They had a son, age 32 and a daughter, age 27 Both the father and son are dead. The mother and daughter are still living. The third Thrame of Peneus is a distantly related cousin to the family and seems to have had little to no connection with the others. Odd. There is a definite familial connection and it seems likely the murderer is targeting only the male members of the extended family. It would help if we could establish a family tree, which we are slowly constructing, but the difficulty comes from the fact that these family members are so distantly related. These are not people that would gather on special occasions. These are people that, as far as Bob could tell, have no idea they are related to each other and probably wouldn't recognize the other family names. If one looks at an average family tree, the number of names that get brought into that tree grows exponentially with each generation. These people were mostly related by genetic markers alone. Right now, the relationships are far too scattered to make any sense.

It wasn't long before Bob received a message about the two deaths on Elis of Alpha Centauri. One was a Raphnus Dahlec, the other a Mal Taber Baker. Two new genealogies to add to the list, but Bob felt with a good degree of certainty that they were family.

Then, there was this virus. Bob checked the current news on the outbreak. Peneus went from regional quarantine to full quarantine overnight (overnight for Bob). It was spreading. Epimethius, currently in the Southern Gate of Alpha Centauri, had reported infections. Most likely from mining operations to and from Peneus. There was also an unconfirmed outbreak on Elis and Nephele of Alpha Centauri proper. This was very concerning to Bob. First Atlas, which is now under a system-wide quarantine, and now Alpha Centauri which seems to be going that direction. All reports repeatedly assure that the virus is inactive and causing no symptomatology, merely replicating in the tissues. But the inability to identify the strain and consequently deal with it was alarming.

     Bob called the Chief.
Chief: "Hiya, Bob"
Bob: "Hi. Can you contact law enforcement on Phoebe in Atlas and find out if they've found any similar deaths?"
The Chief immediately got a sinking feeling in his chest but calmly said, "Sure. Not a problem."
Bob: "...I think we should talk right away and go over some of these detail together. Are you free?"
Chief: "Of course. This is my top priority now. How about over lunch? ...Diner food?"
     When one is stressed, greasy diner food is always welcome. It will not leave the appetite wanting and doesn't require the attention an exquisite restaurant demands.
Bob: "Sounds good. Chappy's diner, near the police station?"
Chief: "That's the one."
Bob: "See you there."
With that, Bob left the apartment and headed for the train.
     The Chief, knowing that it would take Bob a good half-hour to get to Chappy's diner sent the request to Atlas. The authorities on Phoebe were reasonable, but everything just takes so damn long and it was likely they would be preoccupied with the outbreak. The Chief sent the message as urgent and waited in silence for a response until the time to head out to the diner arrived.

     Diners were almost always chrome for some reason. At some point in the distant past it was decided that every diner ever established would be gilded in chrome. Why? No one knows. Yet it was a clear signal of what food you'd be in for.
     Bob and the Chief sat in a booth and perused the menu, which was voluminous. It was a book. Not literally, of course, as the menu was manifested on the terminal face that composed the entire tabletop. Selecting their food and finalizing their choices, once the

"accept" prompt was activated, the staff began working on their meals and an attendant brought them their drinks.

Bob: "Well, here is what I'm concerned about..."

A rude interruption manifested itself in the form of an upper torso above the table between Bob and the chief.

"The cost of management services has skyrocketed and allocating discretionary credits towards..."

Bob waved his hand through the advertisement as if to dispel a noxious odor.

Bob: "Where's the cancel prompt?!"

These holographic advertisements were required by law to have a cancellation prompt that fit specified dimensions, a small orb with an inscribed "x", but the ad companies did their best to make it visually difficult to see.

"...with our services at a small nominal fee we can bundle your management needs into one..."

Chief: "The cancel prompt is almost on your side."

Bob: "Where?!"

The cancel prompt, a small gray orb with the inscribed "x", was orbiting, at an angle, the torso of the speaking figure. The color of the orb was perfectly matched by the color of the figure's suit and the angle of the orbit allowed the lines of the "x" to blend perfectly with the odd crisscross pinstripes of the figure's suit. Not a current fashion trend, but rather designed and chosen for the specific purpose of making the cancel prompt hard to find.

"...ease your tensions and experience the freedom you deserve with a company rated by the bureau of corporate excellence as..."

Bob's hand passed right through the prompt. Apparently he didn't grasp directly on the "x". The image of the torso was now against a backdrop of open fields and an attractive, unfettered couple breathing deeply as if the air was fresh and crisp.

Chief: "Turn the damn thing off!"

Bob: "It's on your side now."

Chief: "What? Where?!"

Bob and the Chief were looking around the opposing sides of the translucent irritant.

The Chief pawed irritably at the prompt and the image froze as a circular banner appeared which read "You have chosen to close this advertisement. Proceed? Yes or No? The Chief poked sternly at the 'yes' floating in nothingness and the image dispelled.

After a moment to let the sting of irritation subside, Bob continued.

Bob: "I was saying that I have a theory, really more of a speculation, but one I'm pretty concerned about. The thing is..."

At this point the tabletop lit up in a dazzling spectacle of lights and a two dimensional woman across the surface says *"Do you tire of endlessly searching for a hairstylist to tame your mane? And oh! the cost these days! Introducing Helmet Head* ™ *the home personal hairstylist. Simply attach the dome over the entire head, calibrate for cranial dimensions, and voila! You have the perfect bowl cut for today's busy...."*

Bob: "This is idiotic."

Bob harshly hammered the cancellation prompt, this time *on* the table, and the glowing irritant returned to the nothingness from whence it came. There was a discolored abrasion where countless individuals had done exactly the same thing.

Chief: "This goddamned city. Please, continue."

Many "modern" worlds in most systems had strict laws governing when and where advertisements could be displayed. The prevailing philosophy was that individuals have the right to live their lives and go about their business without being visually or aurally assaulted. However, these modern worlds learned this lesson from the shortcomings of the elder planets. As all civilization in the galaxy originated from the Sol system, Zeus was an early inhabited world, only preceded by Ares. Additionally, though there was law enforcement on Helen's Crown, the massive overpopulation made police occupied with domestic disputes and more important regulatory offense. The few laws there were regarding advertisements were all but ignored. The result? Practically every surface of every building was covered in an array of lights and moving pictures. Words streamed endlessly around every corner of every building, and, as we just witnessed, the intrusion of ads knew no practical bounds. Even the cybermods, those mostly young university students dabbling in the new "cognitive uplink technology" have occasionally reported receiving advertisements directly to their brain. Most likely some poor sap who didn't realize the hidden contents of the end-user-license-agreement they had accepted.

In many of these elder worlds, corporations, those responsible for the assaults of advertisement, had enormous power. Taking away that power is considerably harder than just starting a new world where the laws limit such accesses from inception. You can invite rats into your home, but getting them to leave is a different story.

Bob: "Anyway, I've had this nagging feeling since the outbreak. It really doesn't make any sense, but the fact that two very unusual events have taken place almost at the same time; the deaths and the virus, has got me thinking..."

Chief: "Honestly, I've had that floating around like a ghost in my periphery but have been trying to just focus on the task at hand.

Besides, you know how I get. It's easy for me to work myself up about something unrelated and spend a lot of time traveling dead end streets."

Bob: "I know, I'm the same way but this... Here's what I'm concerned about. We have a string of deaths here on Sol and now in Alpha Centauri. The virus began on Atlas, infected the entire system and is now found on Peneus in Alpha Centauri. I'm sure you can tell what I'm worried about."

Chief: "Yes, trade routes."

Bob: "Right, trade routes. Atlas is locally a long way from Alpha Centauri. For commerce, trade, industry, and even leisure travel it would be highly unlikely that a vessel would have gone directly from Atlas to Alpha Centauri. It's not impossible, but I did a fairly thorough check of privately chartered ships from Atlas to Alpha Centauri. There were not many in the last few months. Only a handful."

Chief: "And you're worried that..."

Bob: "That the virus is here."

The Chief rubbed his forehead and the bridge of his nose, "Yeah, we're on the same page...it would be probable that it is here too."

Bob: "And for whatever reason, it seems it is taking a long time for the infected worlds to identify it and report on it."

Chief: "I'm sure they're up against the same difficulties here. Everything is generally automated. We're not used to encountering something we don't understand. We're in an age of assumed omniscience...which is more than a little dangerous in a galaxy of dim wits."

Bob: "Now, you're not trying to say anything offensive to dim wits are you? I consider myself a proud member of the dim witted community."

The Chief managed a chuckle. Nice to cut the tension even though things have gotten a bit scarier with this conversation.

Chief: "But seriously, nobody has any instincts anymore. Everything is done for us. Crimes are solved, most regulatory issues are resolved,...people's lives are attended to. I feel like this problem should involve some great interplanetary office that has teams of people working tirelessly on the solution, but the few planetary coalitions that do exist are slow and ineffectual and the larger they get, the slower they move. For crepes sake, I couldn't even get these planets to show anything but a feigned interest in the mysterious deaths of their own people."

Bob: "I know..."

Chief: "And you know why? Because they assume if anything was really going on some autonomous function would catch it and deal with it. We're the only ones showing any interest and these planets are more than willing to let us handle the bulk of the work."

Bob: "Well, I'm sure they'll all step in at the end and take credit for everything...so that's something."

The Chief smiled. "Yeah, well, I guess I am venting a bit, and really it's just Sol and Alpha Centauri that seem to be complacent. I just contacted Atlas about an hour ago, so they haven't had much time to place the burden on us yet. ...but I know. I know how these things run and how people are. We're not going to get much help."

Bob: "I'm afraid you're right."

Chief: "It's just stupidly unbelievable how many major events in history came about when a couple of people noticed something. You can rely on a government to clean up a big mess...maybe, but getting them to prevent one is usually out of the question."

Chief: "...I'm venting too much, sorry. Let's talk about what we can actually do. Bob, what do we need to do right now?"

Bob: "Well, we need to hear back from Atlas and see if there is a connection to the murders there. We need to contact someone you trust to do a good job either at Helene Medica, or the Panacea Research facility, preferably with a decent sized staff, that can sample the public on Helen and Ganymede for the virus. Helen and Ganymede, obviously, because of the murders, but we should also see about sampling Ares and Poseidon."

Chief: "I have contacted authorities on Ares and Poseidon about potential mysterious deaths, but they have reported no such deaths as of yet. I also got in touch with the head of operations on the Titan outpost and nothing unusual was...."

A terminal flash materialized above the Chief's right forearm.

Bob: "..."

Chief: "...Message from Atlas. They have a team that has been investigating several mysterious deaths. Two on Phoebe, one on Prometheus, and a possible three on Lapetus."

Bob: "Not good. We need to access their official information on the outbreak. I'm tired of getting this info from the daily news."

The Chief had an overly concentrated look, like he was processing a large amount of info, which he was.

Chief: "...uh, ...yeah. Of course. ..of course."

Bob: "It does make sense. We need to look closely at the timelines here, but I'm guessing the path of the murders is from Atlas to Sol to Alpha Centauri. I'm guessing this is also the path of the outbreak.
 For now, until we have reason to believe otherwise, let us assume we are dealing with a murderer that is responsible for this virus."

Bob reestablished eye contact, a bit out of concern for the Chief. He seemed a little overwhelmed by all this.

Chief: "I'm fine. It's just a lot. We need to get to work right away."
Bob: "One other thing. I know we looked into unauthorized ships in and around Helen, but like we discussed earlier, the murderer probably isn't traveling by unauthorized means or we would've spotted something sooner. I think we need to look into all authorized vessels that have been verified as traveling from Atlas to Sol to Alpha Centauri and reference those against the timelines of the murders and the outbreaks. It's a lot of information, but there's got to be something, something small that could at least point us in the right direction. Maybe we can find a ship in the right place at the right time and find out where it has gone and will go next."
Chief: "There will be a lot of ships that will fit into the proper time line."
Bob: "I know. It is a long shot, but we have to look for something."
Chief: "Ok. Medical samples, Atlas's info on the outbreak, and transit data on probably a hundred thousand ships. Anything else?"
Bob: "We need to eat this food before it gets cold."
Chief: "There's no way. I can't eat now. I have absolutely no appetite."
Bob: "That's the stupidest thing I've ever heard. You don't need to be hungry to eat."
The Chief chuckled, relaxed a little, and managed to eat a bit.

Chapter Seven: Oh, What a Lark Our Merry Machinations Bring! and **Diner of the Mind!**

Rho-Sigma 00021 Grain found awareness coupled with Nu-Epsilon-320034 and is now entangled.

Theta-110011-Epsilon strain prompt for stellar dimensions finds reciprocation and command is terminated.

Mu-Iota-terminus-00002-naught-9 is stuck. Issuing repetition of wiggle command.

After Bob and the Chief went their separate ways, Bob headed back to his apartment to look closer at the estimated time of death in each case and check that against the assumed outbreak timeline. There really wasn't much for him to specifically do rather than be one of the many cogs working the larger information combing operation until the Chief either heard back from Atlas or the medical institutions about the virus itself. Details of the virus, its pathology, could help solidify these timelines at bit.

Walking back to catch the train downtown, it was oddly cool and gray, like it might rain. It was times like this that the human perception of weather jutted up against the artifice of living in a constructed world where everything was more or less controlled. This made it easy to discern the construct from the natural and the apparent falseness of life here would sometimes strike Bob so peculiar as to even generate a chuckle of disbelief that, like a ghost, would dispersed before it could be truly grasped.

The train ride was enclosed in a fog of doldrum, uneventful, and stepping into the hallway leading to his apartment Bob had no memory of the walk from the train station to his building. Often the case with an occupied and tired mind.

Before he could get in the door he sensed a lurking presence in the shadows. It was Abrum.

Bob: "Hi Abrum."

Abrum: "Bob, we need to speak."

Bob, mentally rolling his eyes, "do we?"

Abrum: "Yes, we do. We shan't talk here...tis not safe. Let us adjourn to the Bagel shop across the street."

Bob: "Abrum, I really don't have time..."
Abrum: "Shush Bob, time you have as my information is pertinent to your investigation."

This did pique Bob's interest since Abrum shouldn't know anything about his investigation. Abrum did know Bob was in the detective business, so maybe that was the extent of it, but either way Bob now felt game though he suspected this will end up being about apartment light fixtures or the squeaky elevator door.
Bob: "...ok."

They walked in tandem to the elevator. Abrum was wearing an odd pinstriped suit, dark gray, with an ascot of a red silk-like material protruding from a heavily starched white shirt collar. Abrum would argue that it was in fact not white but eggshell. The material seemed heavy and antique especially so against the highly reflective polished black shoes he wore. Abrum often wore clothing that hid his form, making him sometimes appear bulky, but in his current getup he seemed excessively spindly. The tight curls of his angular haircut and pencil mustache made the overall effect complete.

At the Bagel shop Bob and Abrum waited silently in line. When his turn came about Abrum said to the shop attendant, " I should have a bagel ripped asunder, cleft in twain, upon which sweet cream cheese is placed betwixt."
The attendant shot a puzzled and irritated look in their direction. Bob intercepted, "I think he's just asking for a bagel and cream cheese."
The attendant raised a single eyebrow and left to prepare the order.
 The next attendant took Bob's order as the first was returning.

After Abrum was handed his bagel, but before money could exchange hands Abrum was nowhere to be found. It wasn't really a vanishing act. Definitely no magic or devices involved, but as Abrum was want to do he would simply vanish as one taking advantage of even the slightest moment when no eyes were upon him. In his place, as if left in haste, a solitary coin spun until it came to a rattling stop. The attendant looked at Bob and said, "This isn't nearly enough to pay for his bagel...and I don't even know what kind of coin this is. ...Are you going to cover the rest?"
Bob said, " you know...I...I really don't know that guy very well."

Irritating. Bob knew it was going to be something like this. He was nowhere in the shop and not nearby outside. Bob took his bagel and headed back to the apartment. On his floor Abrum was nowhere to be found unless he was hiding invisibly in the shadows.

When Bob returned to his apartment he found a sealed envelope peeking out from under his door. He picked it up, entered, and sat in

a worn armchair where he began eating his food. The envelop was of a sheer, off-white paper which had the look and feel of a wedding invitation that an old maid had been hoarding since her youth. The letter inside was written on faint rose parchment similarly scented.
 Without reading a word Bob knew this was from Abrum and couldn't help but feel a twinge of irritation.

The letter, in ornate cursive read, "Dearest Bob, I write to you of a matter most concerning. It t'was twilight of last days end when a gentleman, whom I address as such of my own propensity towards civil discourse warrants as I suspect the title to be ill fitting, was unusually present about your residence feigning the nonchalant. His subtlety was a grackles squawk to my delicate tastes as I knew him to be misplaced and as the fashion of the day no longer puts it 'up to no good'. As my presence is oft unnoticed, I sauntered through the shadows with a keen eye upon said vagabond, my senses ablaze to absorb any trickle of intent he might let escape. A call, a call, Bob!
 Here I transcribe devoid of embellishment or correction of language usage:

"Yeah, ...still here (in a flat monotone). Yeah,...yes. I know (slightly irritated).

I'll wait a bit longer and see if he shows up. Much longer and people'll wonder.

...(a pause, then quite annoyed) If not now then soon. When it can be

done."

The call ended and soon thereafter the man left. What I can tell you, Bob, is that this individual wore a suit off the peg of machine manufacture that was as poorly tailored as it was dreadful in fashion and had upon himself, concealed poorly, an armament of violent purposes but what is more, and much more dangerous, was the aura of violent purposes about his person. You see dear Bob, it is as it has always been. The most dangerous extant in our beloved heavens and Earth is a man of no conscience. Beware. Take the utmost care.
 Abrum."

It seemed fitting that Abrum would write what amounts to prose just to say '*there was a weirdo with a gun. Look out.*' Regardless, he's a good guy.

Bob finished his food from the deli then settled in to do some work. He wasn't really concerned about this mysterious guy as Bob was neither apt to trust the unknown and bound to be bizarre instincts of Abrum, nor certain it had anything to do with him anyway.
 It would be odd, however, if someone really had some idea of what he was up to...that would be a concern and could mean he was close to

something. Either way, nothing to do until fate played another hand...nothing, that is, except the large amount of work before him.

Bob checked the progress of the data crunching. Nothing yet. To look for patterns in travel logs around and in between several star systems, each of which include several major planets and a handful of minor ones, is in all honesty a fool's errand. It would be easy, of course, to find a ship that wasn't supposed to be in this place or that, but most likely the person spreading this virus and doing the killing is following all legal protocols. Even if a ship was found to be oddly out of place, or with some minor improper documentation, it would require identifying the ship, the star system of origin, the planet of origin, the agency to which the ship belonged, and then a prolonged exchange between the responsible entity and law enforcement here to determine whether or not there really was something suspicious. One such example was a ship that had sightings along the pertinent route and was a courier for a company that manufactured quantum tincture substrates. This is basically a liquid that on the quantum level can exist in two states at once. It's useful for controlling reactions and timing in several types of tachyon sync-solenoids. Using the quantum tincture substrate the device can carry out three possible reactions at any given time; reaction A, reaction B, and both reaction A and B simultaneously.

It goes without saying that many modern ships utilize this process to approach speeds at various fractions of light. However, the ship associated with this company had a cargo manifest listing "realistic male wigs". It turns out the company was contracting out their transport services during downtimes in production just to make ends meet. Nothing too out of the ordinary, though Bob did now wonder how many people in the galaxy were wearing wigs. Bob had decided to face his hair loss with dignity but got the giggles when he pictured himself in a wig with a robust head full of hair. As for the false positive of the suspicious ship, there were volumes of similar cases. Some would probably take a long time to sort out and would most likely amount to nothing...but there was really nothing else to do.

The Chief had his top agent in charge of organizing the data sequencing. Della Hale was the head of the Ministry of Information Retrieval - Sol (MIRS). MIRS had once been an autonomous entity but several hundred years ago elided operations with law enforcement on Helen's Crown. There are similar Ministries of Information Retrieval on Alpha-Centauri (MIRAC), Arcturus (MIRA), Sirius (MIRsi), Pollux (MIRP), and a few others in the region. Each of these entities share common boundaries and willfully engage in an exchange of information though each reserves the right to sovereignty and thereby secrecy if it is determined that that would be in the greater service of the common good. At one time these were massive and powerful organizations, but as time passed and the galaxy became increasingly mechanized, their usefulness and purpose became diminished. Each are fractions of what they once were and as such have become interdependent on the authority of their associated regions. MIRS is now, more or less, a division of law on Helen's Crown with a diminutive staff. Regardless, Della Hale is exceptional in her organizational skills and runs a tight department, even more so due to the severity of the current situation.

There was nothing here and Bob couldn't think of anything else to contribute at this time. He decided to go for a stroll. Sometimes it is only when one ceases focusing on a problem and relaxes that a truly helpful idea may manifest. The tense and focused mind, while great for accomplishing tasks, tends to allow for thought along predisposed lines. The problem in this case was less than clear and seemingly omnidirectional. A clear and relaxed mind is much more prone to creative thought.

Bob didn't want to go far from his apartment, so he strolled along the dingy streets of downtown. There were a number of kids playing wildly outside. Children are so wonderful. They seem to be the only ones truly living life. They live in the perpetual now. As adults we seem to lose our precarious balance on the pinnacle of now and either stumble towards the never arriving future or get mired in the ever receding past.

Bob noticed a little girl he knew named Elara, about 5 years of age, which he often spoke to on the stoop outside the apartment building but whom he'd never seen associated with an adult.
Bob: "Hi Elara."
Elara: "Hi Mr. Bob."
Bob: "Whatcha up to Elara."
Elara: "Nothin'. Mr. Bob ...How old are you?"
Bob: "Pretty old."
Elara: "I like your coat."
Bob: "Thanks Elara. What'd you learn in school today?"
Elara: "Nothin', Mr. Bob"
Bob: "Elara, Where is your home?"
Elara looked around almost as if confused and said, "Here."
She then giggled and ran off into a crowd of children.

A few blocks away there was a short stretch of street that actually had some nice shops. Bob strolled around, got a snack, and did some people watching. It was about an hour into the stroll that Bob got a slight feeling that he was being followed. It was nothing he could put his finger on, but something about his surroundings was repeating, like a person in a crowd that just happens to be in every crowd along his route. It was hovering in the periphery of his awareness as if his subconscious was trying to tell his conscious mind that it had noticed something.

After another twenty minutes or so Bob felt fairly certain. He sent a call to the Chief and asked to be connected to Della.

Della: "Yes."

Bob: "Hey Della, I know you're busy, but I need a hand if you've got a moment."

Della: "Sure. What's going on?"

Bob: "I'm pretty sure I'm being followed. There was some talk yesterday about a stranger hanging around my apartment."

Della: "You think this has to do with all that's been going on?"

Bob: "I dunno, but I might need you to do a couple of things for me. Can you lock on to my coordinates and do a radius scan for individuals, let's say over the next fifteen minutes, and filter out everyone who isn't continually present?"

Della: "No problem. I'll let you know what I find out."

Bob: "Thanks"

Bob continued his walk around the neighborhood, but purposefully chose a circuitous route; between buildings from one street to the next, in and out of unrelated businesses, across a run-down park to a narrow street. Ten minutes later Bob surreptitiously got a glance at the guy he suspected. Not long after Della contacted him.

Della: "Yeah, you're being followed. We have a visual on the guy... I'm sending the feed to you."

The displayed image was the same guy Bob had eyed just moments ago.

Della: "...we haven't confirmed his identity yet, but we're working on it."

Bob: "Thanks Della, you're the best."

Bob made a couple of turns around corners and walked down a dark and seemingly abandoned street. He allowed himself just a momentary pause to make sure the stranger saw him walk into an even darker alley on this dark street.

After a moment, the stranger cautiously entered the alley and eyed the several doors to what must have been empty buildings. As he made it carefully about halfway down the alley the stranger heard the unmistakable high-pitched whine of Bob's EMP pointed at the back of the stranger's head. Bob had considered it routine to carry since something out of the ordinary had been brought to his attention by Abrum.

The stranger seemed much more irritated than scared as if he couldn't believe he let himself get caught so easily.

Bob: "Carefully, open your jacket and remove the gun."

The stranger complied with an irritable sigh.

Bob: "Drop the gun and kick it over by the dumpster."

Again, the stranger complied.

Bob: "Who are you?"

Stranger, annoyed: "My name is Lark. I'm a private investigator."

Bob: "Why are you following me?"

Lark: "You can put that away. I wasn't going to hurt you."

Bob: "Answer the question."

Lark: "I was hired to look into the recent deaths of the Eurnum family."

Bob: "Who hired you?"

Lark: "I was hired by the Eurnum family...those that are still around."

Bob, keeping the EMP keenly on Lark, rotated towards the discarded gun and picked it up.

Bob: "Standard issue EMP, older model."

Lark: "Yeah, looks like we have the same taste in side arms."

Bob: "This model is made in Alpha-Centauri...so are those shoes."

Lark: "....really? You can tell by my shoes? Yes. Centaurus born and raised, though Sol does have it's charms. I mean, not *here*, but probably somewhere in this system."

Bob: "So if you're hired to look into the deaths, why are you following me instead of just contacting me?"

Lark: "Well, the Eurnums have it in their head that you might be responsible for the deaths. They have a rather strong distrust of authority, especially the seedy underbelly of authority which are those contracted out by law enforcement. Us P.I's."

Bob: "That's idiotic."

Lark: "I know, I know. I've checked your credentials before the trip here and looked into everything I could. I know you're not involved, but I'm not paid to think. I'm paid to do. You are just a name, unknown to them, associated with this and they want you looked into. They also want me to find out as much as I can about the chief of police. They trust no one it seems."

Bob: "And I'm not sure I completely trust you either."

Still with a gun trained on Lark, Bob contacted Della.

Bob: "Della, what have you got on this guy?"

Della: "We have him ID'd, Lark Aspic, private investigator, Alpha Centauri, works primarily out of Ixion. We are acquiring his transport history and registration. The Chief will fill you in on the specifics."

Chief: "Hiya Bob. His identity checks out but we're having him processed to determine the legality of his firearm possession on Helen's Crown. This will give us a little time to check him over thoroughly."

As they spoke, Lark received an official communique from the police department informing him he had been tagged and was to report immediately to the nearest police station for processing. He was not to touch his firearm and upon inspection and clearance it would be returned to him if and when such clearances were granted.

Bob lowered his gun, but kept a keen eye on this Lark fellow. Lark, with an indignant look, just kept his hands up in the air and walked off with an annoyed expression.

Lark: "Amateur hour in the backwoods. I've apparently traveled 300 years to the past." With that, he walked out of the alley and assumedly to the police station.

Ixion was a much more modern world than Helen, or any place in Sol, and this guy had a real attitude about it. But really, it was his own carelessness that got him caught. This is how most issues were dealt with on Helen. He was tagged. His whereabouts were known and he couldn't even leave Helen's Crown, much less the system, without resolving his legal troubles. He could be picked up at any time, but presumably would not want to be charged with evasion. This also helps reduce criminal-police interaction on site by making the suspect enter an environment controlled by the police themselves, rather than some back alley or potential ambush situation (a situation not encountered in hundreds of years on Helen).

Chief: "Bob, let's meet. I can get free in a couple of hours. We need to go over some details and a few things I've found."

Bob: "Where do you wanna meet?"

Chief: "I want food I don't need to think about."

Bob: "Ah, Chappy's diner again."

Chief, begrudgingly "Yes, Chappy's diner again."

It is amazing how in a world and city so full of possibilities, practically endless possibilities, how often one returns to the same place...regardless of quality.

Within minutes a transport was there to collect the gun...some seemingly half-witted, gangly intern, and Bob was off to continue his stroll.

After a couple of hours Bob sauntered into Chappy's diner a bit ahead of the Chief. He sat at a table, canceled several advert prompts, and had a cup of tea while he waited. He glanced over the data available to him through his terminal, but wasn't really looking at it too seriously. The Chief had a few things to talk about and he'd know soon enough.

About twenty minutes later the Chief walked in calmly and orders some food. The excessive glass and chrome of the diner reflected light in such a way to give the impression of a chilled day right before sunset, though obviously the temperature on Helen's Crown was fairly constant. It's odd to think of those kids who were born and raised here, many of them most likely never to leave Helen, who would be deprived of knowing an actual sunset or seasons and thereby have no reference for it. How bizarre and unnatural. Human beings are cyclic by nature and some of the expectations of day/night or summer/winter are ingrained in our composition, but without reference it might seem like the cyclic nature of reality is terrifying, constantly ebbing and flowing between life and death. However, it could just as well be that, when encountered, these true cycles are seen with wonder and awe and these children of a constructed world are more receptive to the majesty of it all, much more so than those of us born into it.

Chief: "Hiya Bob"

Bob: "Hi"

Chief: "...well, ...where to start..."

Bob: "How about that Lark guy?"

Chief: "Ok. Lark Stungen Aspic. P.I. Alpha-Centauri proper. Legal and identified by both the law-enforcement of Ixion and a registered agent of MIRAC. So, he checks out. Nothing really to worry about there. Now, why he was pussyfooting around instead of contacting law-enforcement is beyond me. I guess if the Eurnum family really had some suspicion about you he might have felt like doing some sleuthing, but either way it's kinda stupid."

Bob: "I dunno. The story seems bogus. It's suspicious to say the least."

Chief: "Yeah, but his whereabouts are monitored. He can't really do anything without it being known on Helen. I don't think you have anything to worry about. I checked into his criminal history, but you know, any ministry of information retrieval agent's records are on a need to know basis and they say we don't need to know. He did, however, submit willingly to a polygraph and everything checked out there too. Best to forget about this for now, although..."

Bob: "...although?"

Chief: "He is asking for access to our information on the deaths and as he is a MIRAC agent I really would need a good reason to deny this request, especially since several of the deaths are in the Alpha-Centauri system."

Bob: "I guess that's fine, but I still have an uncomfortable feeling about this guy. Something's not quite right with his story."

92

Chief: "Yeah, paranoia is both of our strong suits. The good thing though is that, as of this moment, we have not yet officially tied the deaths to the viral outbreak, we don't have to give him access to that info."

Bob: "...as of this moment?"

Chief: "I have received the collected information on the outbreak of Atlas and Alpha-Centauri. Both systems are a bit quicker to communicate than usual. I think this virus has them spooked a bit. You already have access to the data when you want to look it over."

Bob: "What about here?"

Chief: "I've had several of my contacts look into it both at Helene Medica, and the Panacea Research facility. They are still early in the process but haven't found anything. They've been looking for several days, before we even asked. The news is going around. But when you get a chance to look over the data you'll see that part of the problem, the problem they had in the Atlas system and Alpha-Centauri, is that it's very hard to detect. They would see something, then it would be gone. They would suspect an outbreak, then think there was something wrong with the data and it was an error, then it would show up all over. They would think they had an area quarantined but then all of a sudden everyone has the virus. It's very peculiar."

Bob felt a little sick to his stomach: "This is not good."

Chief: "Well, it gets even more interesting."

The chief had an almost giddy look about him that kinda threw Bob for a loop.

Bob: "What, what is it?"

The Chief looked like he was about to laugh and was nervously paddling his legs.

Chief: "I don't know if this is good news or bad, but...."

Bob: "but?"

Chief: "I was contacted just before I came here. It was Dr. Morris's Center for Infectious Disease and Entropic Recomposition. The communique came directly from Dr. Morris."

Bob: "Wow. ...but, ...wow. ...I'm inclined to think this is a very bad thing."

Chief: "Well, either way, we couldn't have asked for a better authority to help with this virus issue. The exact words of the communique were 'Dr. Morris requests an audience with a representative of Helen's law enforcement for the precise duration of one standard hour. The available times are as follows...' Bob, this is the opportunity of a life-time. I want *you* to go."

Bob: "Me? Why wouldn't you go, or both of us at least?"

Chief: "I can't leave here. There's lots to do. Also, the request is for 'a' representative of law enforcement. You're my number one guy. I need you on this."

Bob: "Why are they not wanting someone from the medical community?"

Chief: "I'm guessing that Dr. Morris assumes this is a criminal situation and is going through law enforcement channels first. Besides, our medical community is as far removed from the Center for Infectious Disease and Etropic Recompositon as we are. There is nothing our medics have that they wouldn't. I assume this is a criminal issue they wish to discuss. Will you Bob, will you go? We have twenty-four hours to reply before they go through other channels."

Bob, a bit lost in thought, "well, uh...how am I supposed to find a top secret facility whose whereabouts are unknown to even the highest ranking officials?"

Chief: "Easy. They send a ship for *you*."

Bob: "Can't say no to that."

Chief: "Think of it as a short vacation away from Helen."

Bob: "Ah yes...paid vacation."

C.I.D.E.R. The Center for Infectious Disease and Entropic Recomposition.
Compiled from the resources of the Free Galactic Library (FGL).

**disclaimer: *As CIDER and the research of Dr. Morris is highly secretive, the FGL cannot verify the accuracy of the statements made within. What follows contains the mean data filtered by the FGL standards and practices and is assumed to be the average accepted data and will therefore invariably contain inaccuracies. Some sources argue that CIDER and Dr. Morris are myths perpetuated by modern urban legend and exist solely in the minds of those prone to fantasy. The FGL bears no responsibility for the use, misuse, or lack of use of the following information.*

The Center for Infectious Disease and Entropic Recomposition, hereby referred to as CIDER, is an autonomous and sovereign entity that exists to study, monitor, analyze, and ultimately cure all conditions befalling human beings and humanoid variants. The facility is headed and run by a Dr. Morris, identity unknown (and name unverified) whom has been in charge of the facility for past 20 years (approximation).

The facility itself is a source of considerable mystery. The location is completely unknown. It is believed that the only individual aware of the precise location is Dr. Morris, who was handed this information by the preceding head of operations. The predecessor to Dr. Morris (name redacted in all documentation and unknown) supposedly underwent a process of "mental scrubbing" to eradicate the location leaving the knowledge of the facilities whereabouts solely in the possession of Dr. Morris.

The necessity of this secrecy is easily understood. Every infectious disease in the galaxy is contained and studied at CIDER. There is considerable evidence that diseases are also created in an attempt to anticipate and effectively deal with outbreaks. In the wrong hands such knowledge would be easily weaponized with widespread if not galactic consequences. Some sources argue that the facility itself is a bio-weapons engineering and manufacturing facility, though most agree that this interpretation lies in the domain of conspiracy theory as no evidence to such claims can be even remotely verified.

CIDER addresses and deals with two specific fields of the human condition. One is **infectious disease**. This follows the classic definition of disease and the pathology of infection. It is therefore not specifically the domain of genetic defects or mutations, though the knowledge of genetics and genetic mutations are par and course for the understanding of infectious pathology. Therefore it is incorrect, as some sources erroneously cite, that CIDER is not affiliated with genetic research or modeling. Two, CIDER studies the mechanics of **entropic recomposition**. Entropic recomposition deals with all manner and causes of entropy on biological structures and the recomposition of said structures. The easiest way to think about entropic recomposition is to imagine all the various means by which a structure can breakdown other than infectious disease. This field of study is particularly important for the humanoid variants that have been adapted to non-Earth-standard environments. For example, entropic recomposition was necessary for identifying the cause of a specific type of late-age cancer befalling the people of Phalasar in the Xthulus system. The atmosphere of Phalasar is acetylene rich due to heightened natural electrical activity and elements in the atmosphere such as hydrogen and methane, etc. The respiratory adaptation of the people to handle the impurities of the atmosphere was somehow related to a cancer not seen in standard human forms yet not associated with the impurity filtration of the modified respiratory processes. Entropic recomposition determined the pathology of the breakdown and offered the appropriate modification.

The size of the staff at CIDER is unknown. It is assumed to be significant as the work would require a sizeable staff to address the galactic needs. It is assumed the facility has its own private jump-ship and some sources claim the facility possesses, in fact, a fleet of jump ships.

It is also believed that the facility exists on a small dead planet, outer-solar asteroid, comet, or the facility exists alone floating in deep space. An article by "Reygel Dyad" entitled "My time at the Morris facility" claims a fleet of jump-ships and that the facility can be moved at any time, to any location using the facility ships. This lends credence to the idea that the facility is small, located on a diminutive orbiting body, though it could be that the facility is large and CIDER has access to a massive jump-ships in the event a relocation is required. Either way, it is assumed that the facility is or can be mobile as accidental discovery would greatly jeopardize the mission of CIDER.

For more information on specific infectious diseases or entropic recomposition cases/solutions visit the FGL from any terminal in the free galaxy.

This was exciting for Bob, but the implications of why such a secretive agency was now involved could only be bad news. Yet, somehow, Bob felt kind of excited. Maybe because it would be interesting to learn a bit about the mystery of the facility, but maybe because he hoped it might help solve the issue of the outbreak and maybe even shed some light on the murders. Either way, he spent the rest of the day thinking about it and did have a little trouble getting to sleep that night. The Chief had accepted Dr. Morris's request, sent Bob's info, and chose the first available time offered. Tomorrow would be a big day. He was getting on a ship and leaving Helen for the first time in a long time.

Despite the excitement, Bob managed to shut down and after a while drifted off to the land of nod, a land equally ripe with wonders and perils...a dark world where the mind intersects with the eternal and the unknown.

Dream Journal: Wasteland

I was standing in the middle of an arid desert. Dirt cracked and curled in the sun. There seemed to be low mountains off in the far, far distance...and nothing else. Scrub brush, dried and dead, here and there. I stood before a primitive mobile dwelling, one I had seen in pictures from pre-historical records. I think it had been called an RV. It was worn and faded. At one time beige with an orange stripe wide midway. Much of the paint had been beaten with the dry and particulate wind of the desert.

Sitting in a cheap folding chair alongside the RV sat an old man. His head, completely hairless, was as weathered as the cracked ground surrounding. With no effort to shield himself from the hard sun, he sat with a permanent scowl on his face, the kind that came not from immediate anger, but a lifetime of aggression. He was rough and looked exceptionally mean.
His clothing consisted of dark brown, heavily worn trousers and a sleeveless dingy white shirt which was splattered with blood. There was blood that was old and dried and more that seemed fresh. He seemed to be completely unharmed, so I assumed it was not *his* blood.

I stood for a long time wondering if he was looking at me. He was positioned in such a way that he could have been, but with the sun and the narrow slits of eyes about his wrinkled and scrunched up face, it was hard to tell. Either way, I felt that he had hardly any concern or awareness of my presence. I was nothing to him.

After a time he slowly got to his feet and walked away. As he passed, I could see the back of his shirt seemed stuffed with tattered and decaying black feathers. It seemed he had partial wings rotting from his scapula.
He left me and walked out into the desolation of the arid land until he disappeared into the horizon.

Chapter Eight: The Great Doctor and the Isle of Ice and Isolation

Bob woke earlier than he planned, but was well rested. The excitement for both the trip and the access to possible information was making him want to get this day started. He showered, dressed, and kept up with the news of the day. Nothing to speak of actually. There was talk of the outbreak, but nothing new. Transmitted news can be an irritating thing. Most of the time there is a speck of information then hours of circular speculation by people who have only convinced themselves that they have some knowledge to offer. It is best taken in small doses or avoided altogether.

Leaving the apartment, Bob ran into Abrum. He now had a hairstyle that jutted off a good 45 degree angle from his centerline and was wearing an unusually bright suit of a slightly reflective gray material. The style was still impressively outdated.

Bob: "Hey Abrum."

Abrum: "Bob, I take it that you were not run afoul by that loathsome stranger. For this I am truly engladdened."

Bob: "Yeah, thanks again for the heads up. It turns out that he's a private investigator and just wanted info. I don't think he's dangerous."

Abrum: "Well, let us hope, but there is a squeak about him like a gear that is off a tooth."

Bob: "...I think I caught most of that. I'll keep my eyes open. Thanks again."

Abrum, smiling: "..."

Bob: "...ok. Gotta run. See you around."

Abrum, still smiling: "..."

Bob left the apartment building and headed further south to the district park. It was surprisingly well maintained for this part of town. Even though it was close Bob didn't come here enough. Everyone falls into their little ruts, the grooves cut by our fairly repetitive lives. Anyway, the instructions were to meet at a clearing in the paper birch grove on the south side of the park. A transport would be there.

Bob was fairly early, but the transport was already present. It was very similar to the transport he took to the Acromian-Notch colony; small, white, clean, and also devoid of any marking. It was boxy with plasti-glass wrapping the front and about half of both sides. The pulse engines sat on wing-like structures attached to the top. This was a standard Ornithopter class vessel. The astute observer of historical languages may notice that an ornithopter flies by flapping its wings. These wings do not flap, but the name is used due to the pulse engines that in a quasi-allegorical way flap against the fabric of space-time.

Bob was told to bring nothing. Firearms were restricted as were recording and any form of transmitting device. He stepped into the vessel and a voice from the console said, "Welcome Bob. Please have a seat and we'll be off shortly." The voice was the standard console emulator and not a real person, so Bob did as requested but felt no compunction to respond in any way. He assumed he had been scanned, but no mention of such had been made. It didn't matter to Bob. He didn't have anything he wasn't supposed to.

When Bob sat down the opening slid silently closed and the Ornithopter shot skyward. Since the direction the Ornithopter was facing had no relevance to the pulse engines, it instinctively positioned itself so Bob could see the city of Helen's Crown receding in the distance. Shortly Bob could make out the head and face of Helen and soon after the entire statue. She was beautiful. Bob felt a certain disconnect from reality to see this great statue and realize that he had been living on it, so close that what it was could not be seen. Also, it had been years since he had left Helen, so this was far from an everyday sight.

Beyond Helen was the glowing undulation of orange and crimson: the body of the great Zeus swirling in turbulent thunderclaps and great discharges of crawling lightning. It was touchingly beautiful. Living on Helen's Crown Bob faced away from Zeus and rarely got the opportunity to see the gas giant. It was a bit easier for those living in New Paris, where the edge of Helen's right palm made viewing Zeus easier, but before Bob's trip to the Acromian-Notch colony, he hadn't seen the true sight of Zeus for many years. From Ganymede, the sight is quite different, but equally amazing. Bob enjoyed Ganymede for many reasons, but the sight of Zeus looming in the sky was number one. If all things were easy, Bob would retire to some small home on Ganymede and live a simple and quiet life working on various projects of which he had always dreamed. He always had wanted to build things by hand, anything. He also had a passion for antique pulse-drive cycles. Basically an engine similar to one on the ornithopter modified for single terrestrial use. They weren't the fastest terrestrial ride, but the sense of freedom riding one was unmatched. Titan made a particular model known as the Big-Bear scrambler, named so for the purposeful interference of the dual pulse cores that provided greater land stability and also produced a kind of growling noise.

It was about this time that Bob realized they were heading in the opposite direction of the spaceport. Far, far above Helen lies the Halo spaceport, often called Helen's Halo though due to its orbit was rarely directly overhead. There would be many jump-ships docked there and others coming to and fro. It didn't concern Bob though as he assumed the ship knew what it was doing. It looked as though Bob was circling around to the dark side of Zeus in a stable orbit. In fact, when he thought about it, he could tell the engines weren't active. They were currently just riding out the orbit for a bit.

The dark side of Zeus isn't really dark, it's just the side opposite Helen and not much is there. The moons make it around there as does the spaceport, but currently Ganymede was somewhat in line with Helen and the Halo was not far away. The ornithopter had passed Io and Europa was on the far side of Zeus, not far from the other boundary of the dark side, opposite to the one Bob was approaching. This was most definitely a secrecy measure. They were going to a location as far away from civilization as one could get near Zeus.

After about 45 minutes the ornithopter entered the shadow of Zeus and there in the distance was a good sized jump-ship waiting. It was dark metallic and shaped like a giant flea, which was pretty standard for jump-ships. To the naked eye it seemed dormant. No lights, nothing moving and there was not a single marking on the ship. Most jump-ships have identification and the ships name proudly emblazoned on the hull. Bob really didn't know what to expect, but it did seem odd to be hitching a ride on a large jump ship for one person. It was hard to get a good perspective in space, but Bob was guessing that this jump-ship could easily accommodate between twelve and fifteen transports vessels, each with a crew of one to two hundred people.

Was this really for one person? Bob wondered if maybe they were transporting other ships, or materials. One would imagine that they would try and get the most out of a jump as they could. Bob also wondered if this was CIDER's only ship, or, if they had many, did they send their largest...or smallest.

The jump-ship was now quite close. Bob could easily make out the spindly flea arms hanging down from the ship head and now a small port was opening at about the temple or mesopleuron, into

103

which it is common for small vessels, such as this ornithopter, to enter. Larger vessels would enter an opening in the lower abdomen.

When the opening sealed and the ornithopter docked, the door opened and Bob was greeted by an unusually chipper young woman in an unmarked yet standard military-like uniform.

Young woman: "Hello, and welcome aboard the *Cell-Scape*."

Bob: "Thank you."

The woman escorted Bob to a room immediately off the docking platform and as they walked Bob could see the cavernous opening of the jump-ships flea like body. It was vast and empty, though overly well-lit and mostly composed of materials in shades of gray and white.

Young woman: "Would you care for some tea or coffee?"

Bob: "Uh...tea would be nice."

It was then that Bob heard the unmistakable thud of the jump being made. It's almost as if the jump-ship smacks against the membrane of the universe in a loud, percussive hit.

The young woman, hearing it too said: "I hope you enjoyed your stay aboard the *Cell-Scape*."

Bob: "Th...thank you."

Bob was then escorted back to the ornithopter, the port opened, and he was off again.

Bob had always wanted to learn more about how jump-ships operated, but never got around to it. He did know, however, that within any one jump the average distance of travel was about 2500 light years. There had clearly been one jump, not two, so this facility was likely somewhere within a 2500 light year radius of Sol. Shouldn't be *too* difficult to find.

Exiting the *Cell-Scape*, Bob found himself in total darkness. It's hard to get bearing and perspective in space, but he could tell that the plastiglass of the ornithopter had not become opaque as he could see, out the side, the pulse engines emitting a warm blue glow. He had thought they might darken the glass to insure nothing could be identified giving some hint of their location, but this was not the case. Still, all around was darkness. This suggested a couple of possibilities. One possibility was they were so far away from any star that light was not visible to the naked eye, however, with a single jump and an average distance of 2500 light years, this was not likely unless they were somehow considerably further than Bob had surmised. A second possibility was that the facility was contained within a small Dyson sphere. The original concept of the Dyson sphere by the ancient thinkers was a complete spherical enclosure around a star and its system. The idea being that the radiant energy of the star could then be reclaimed and used for the system's consumption needs. Although there were times in history when structures were made that could be considered partial Dyson spheres, a full enclosure around a system has never been practical as the entire radiant energy produced by even a small star dwarfs the need of any one system.

The entire output of a small star could supply hundreds of systems with their daily energy needs, so all history has ever encountered has been partial domes, usually closer to the star and near the poles. This is in addition to the impracticality of material acquisition, construction time, and the volatile nature of the cosmos that tends to be destructive to things human beings build. The Dyson sphere, or Dyson-like sphere might be perfect for a facility that wished to remain unknown. It would have the benefit of hiding energy signatures produced by the facility while at the same time recollecting lost radiant energy that would help a very isolated entity run more efficiently. It would also account for the total lack of stars around Bob at this very moment, and it is true that a keen eye triangulating a handful of constellations might have a good idea of where to look to find such a secretive facility.

Bob could feel the inertia of the ornithopter shift meaning a change in direction. Relative to the ornithopter it seemed to pitch downward and when it did a glowing blue object came into view.

As he neared it he could tell some of the suppositions were true. It was a comet. It looked like a large comet that at one point in history had collided with some object. He guessed this by the odd looking impact of what may have been the head of the comet at one time. This would make a certain sense. If a comet had been struck more-or-less head-on and its motion became stationary relative to the surrounding solar systems, that might make a wonderfully isolated location which otherwise would be hard to find in the space between stars.

It was actually very beautiful. The comet was illuminated, surely artificially, from beneath and it had the appearance of glacial ice and slag glass in irregular and broken crystalline shapes. There was a wide spectrum of shades of blue transitioning between crystal clear and frosted translucence while the entire comet sat in a warm glow, a ghostly apparition of an aura from the surrounding particulated icy debris.

In the center of the comet sat a small rounded structure of polished metal. The building tended to reflect the surrounding colors but stood out as smooth multi-tiered circles against the angular surfaces of the comet. As Bob got closer, he could see a slight ring of green around the perimeter of the facility. Just then a voice came through the console of the ornithopter.

"Hello, and welcome to the Center for Infectious Disease and Entropic Recomposition."

It was a recorded message.

"You are about to dock in the main courtyard holding chamber. Please be advised that a full biometric sweep and decontamination will begin upon landing. This can take several minutes. Please be patient and an attendant will see you shortly. May health and long life be with you."

Bob instinctively brushed his right forearm to summon terminal access for time and location, but oddly nothing happened. Interesting Bob thought. They not only block terminal access but have disabled its activation entirely. It makes sense, but still was a surprise to Bob. He was dealing with some pretty sophisticated people here.

"Beginning bio-screening and decontamination. You may feel a slight tingling sensation."

What Bob felt as the field passed through his body was the intense sensation of hitting one's funny bone...if their entire body were composed of nothing but funny bones. It sent a chill through his body that he felt compelled to physically shake off, periodically making a jittery wheeze as his head shook. This was followed by several isolated scans of specific bodily regions that merely felt warm, but it was a few minutes before Bob could shake off the chills from the initial scan.

"Please remain still."

A couple of more shakes and he was fine.

"Scan complete. Please exit the vehicle, proceed through the courtyard to the main office and an attendant will be with you shortly."

Bob left the ornithopter and it truly was a courtyard he found himself in. Very nice and well maintained. Extending away in both directions was a lovely garden and the source of the green ring around the facility. It looked like mostly edible vegetation and herbs, but flowers and lush decorative greenery as well. It might very well be the main source of the inhabitants food supply. He technically wasn't here to sightsee, but wouldn't mind a walk around the garden if the opportunity presented itself.

Entering the facility, Bob walked down a short corridor to the main office. Here there was a front desk and receptionist where the inner circular design of the facility could be easily seen extending upward in a high, open ceiling. It was maybe, perhaps a bit unusual that beyond the receptionist desk there appeared to be laboratory equipment and people working feverishly at a variety of task. Judging by the size of the facility and the openness of the inside, there really wasn't much space for some other big or more secretive lab somewhere else. One supposes that the level of secrecy is sufficient enough that little needs to be hidden once inside the facility. But that little peculiarity was nothing. There was in fact a far greater oddity Bob encountered in this building. Bizarre to the extent that he initially questioned his own reasoning faculties but decided it wasn't him, that here, there was something very peculiar going on. In this room, full of working men and women, even the receptionist, all were absent of a single scrap of clothing. Completely nude. Everyone. No undergarment, no adornment, not even a hat. Every person in this facility, from a quick glance about twenty people, was as bare as the day they were born.

At first it was odd. Then when he thought about it, it seem to get even odder. And with time even more so. Also, judgments always at the discretion of the beholder and subject to debate, they all seemed to be exceptionally attractive people...which somehow made the whole thing even more peculiar.

The receptionist, female, 30 something and auburn shoulder length hair: "Sir..."

Bob, very distracted: "...yes..." Looking to the receptionist and reciting to himself almost as a litany *must maintain eye contact *

Receptionist: "Dr. Morris will be with you shortly. Would you care to have a seat?"

Bob: "...a seat? ...oh, yes...a seat."

*must maintain eye contact *

Bob looked around the facility and the people were working here and there like any office building anywhere else, but...very strange. Bob couldn't help but wonder why nobody had any clothing.

After about ten or so minutes, or an hour as Bob's sense of time had left him, a figure emerged from the door to the left of the receptionist desk.

Almost puzzled, "Bob, I presume?"

Bob: "Yes, ...hello."

"Nice to meet you, I'm Doctor Morris."

Dr. Morris was a woman in her mid to late 40's and, like the other staff, was rather exceptionally attractive. She wore a classic lab coat that hid almost nothing as it was very apparent that, like her staff, she wore no other garment. It may have been that the lab coat was for the visitors sake, to put some semblance of normalcy to those from elsewhere.

Bob: "Uh...nice to meet you too."

*must maintain eye contact *

Dr. Morris: "Right this way please."

Bob was escorted into her office and had a seat in front of her desk.

Dr. Morris: "You are the investigator working with the Chief assigned to this operation?"

She seemed almost puzzled. For some reason, Bob was not what she was expecting, but whatever she was expecting, the surprise did not seem unpleasant.

Bob: "Uh...Yes...the Chief...he and I that is...we've been working on this case for a while now."

Bob was still very distracted. The whole thing was just so peculiar, unexplained nudity.

Dr. Morris: "I can see you are distracted. You are puzzled by the lack of clothing here."

Bob: "...well, I...I guess it is something I wondered about."

must maintain eye contact

Dr. Morris: "That is understandable. There are two general reasons why we work in this fashion. The first has to do with the tradition of the facility. Long, long before I was in charge this was the standard practice. Here at CIDER we deal with every manner of infectious disease. In fact, we guide the mutation and evolution of all known strains to anticipate the properties and needed actions if and when such a strain presents itself in the populace. When this facility started, long before modern scanning techniques, it was a precaution so that physical manifestations of disease could be easily seen by co-workers in the event of a containment breach. It also made smuggling secrets from the facility very difficult. Today we have fantastic passive and active scanning techniques, but still what we look for is the unknown and physical signs of disease could still, in very rare cases, present as a canary in a coal mine. This all being said, we have never actually had any contamination or out-break in the facility during my tenure as head of staff. But honestly, this intimacy fosters trust in the employees which is probably the greatest reason we still hold onto this tradition.

Bob: "Ok. That makes sense."

Dr. Morris: "Do you find offense in our culture?"

Bob: "Oh, no...quite the contrary." That last bit left the mouth a tad before the brain could have a say.

Dr. Morris, in close analysis of every minutia, offered a barely noticeable half-smile. "Good. Now to the issue of the infectious element."

Dr. Morris was ready to move on. Bob, however, was still caught up in the circus of this odd colony.

Interrupting, Bob added, "Sorry, ...I understand the reasoning behind the absence of clothing, but, if you don't mind indulging me, why is it that everyone seems to be of...how do I put this...greater than average physical attractiveness?"

The interruption caused a brief look of irritation in Dr. Morris, but Bob's question earned him another almost unreadable half-smile.

108

Her nature was to get down to brass tacks but there was something about Bob she found pleasant.

Dr. Morris: "You are a detective in the classical sense of the word. I suppose curiosity is the nature of your business and I hear you are good at what you do. Detective, here at the colony we deal with some exceptionally destructive biological forces. You can imagine the diseases of which you already have some knowledge, for example, the immuno-mutational virus, commonly called 'Krickets', that almost completely exterminated the people of Aspasia."

Bob: "Of course. It was devastating and caused an enormous fear in the surrounding planets and systems."

Dr. Morris: "Yes. You are perhaps less than 50 feet from several samples of that virus."

This caused an instinctive uneasiness in Bob quite visible to the doctor.

Dr. Morris: "In this facility, there are viruses, some engineered by ourselves, that comparatively would make Krickets look like the common cold."

Bob's uneasiness strengthened considerably, noticed and address by the good doctor.

Dr. Morris: "There is no concern. Our facility is practically absolute. However, you can imagine that such biotics could be easily weaponized and used for terrible purposes."

Bob: "Yes...yes, absolutely."

It was not lost on the doctor Bob's use of the word "absolutely" which parroted her earlier use of objective form. She knew his mind dwelt on that word most likely in wonder at the particulars of a facility that is "practically absolute".

Dr. Morris: "Therefore, as a safety precaution, it is imperative that I have absolute trust in my employees. I assume you have heard rumors to varying degrees of accuracy that each of my employees are individuals with which I have previously and purposefully formed an intimate bond, or relationship. Specifically sexual in nature."

Bob opened his mouth anticipating a word that did not manifest. Bob was *not* familiar with that rumor. The doctor continued.

Dr. Morris: "My training is in viral recombinatoriality, but also psychological minutia. By forming an intimate relationship, the boundaries and future of which were always upfront and clearly delineated, it was possible for me to reduce the likeliness of employing a spy or untrustworthy employee to a percentage very close to zero. It is very hard to deceive me, detective. Even harder when I have time to analyze my subjects."

Bob: "Yes, I've been aware of that for a bit now."

Dr. Morris turned upward the faintest corners of her otherwise expressionless mouth.

Dr. Morris: "I have found this to be a practical and to-date perfect system, though it has required a considerable amount of time for myself to amass the relatively modest faculty I employ here at the colony."

Continuing, "So, the answer to your question as to why my employees seem, as you put it, 'of greater than average physical attractiveness', is that they are all people with which I personally have found attraction, an impractical yet unavoidably human condition of bonding. Does this adequately satisfy your curiosities?"

Bob: "Yes, thank you....It does...I would say. I appreciate your candor Dr. Morris."

Dr. Morris, with a pleasant smile, "Please, call me Polly Ann. Now, to the issue of the infectious element..."

Bob: "Yes. Absolutely, what we have been suspecting for a few days now..."

Dr. Morris politely held up a hand, "This will be much more efficient if I tell you what we know, then let us proceed from there."

Bob: "Yes. Of, course."

Dr. Morris: "The infectious element of interest here, pertaining to the system wide outbreaks in several locations, is viral in nature."

Bob: "Viral 'in nature'?"

Dr. Morris: "Yes. It behaves like a standard virus and mimics the behaviors of several known strains, but it is completely engineered. It is not a natural virus but rather designed by a human mind."

Bob: "So you know quite a bit about it. You have sampled the virus? How do you know it's engineered?"

Dr. Morris: "Yes, we have been studying it for several months now. There are samples here. We know it is engineered because of several key variations to the viral structure. The first pertains to the structure itself. It has a head-chamber, assumedly possessing the command and code protocols, and from the body are six docking arms used in replication. It replicates quite differently from a standard virus. A standard virus tends to inject its genetic material into a cell and the cell replicates the virus. This engineered virus extracts material from the cell and produces, from within the head chamber, a small orb that quickly develops into a mature copy of the engineered virus. It is assumed the orb assimilates surrounding material to mature, but the process has not been observed."

It was not lost on Bob that she said they have been studying it for several months now, but that issue could be brought up later.

Bob: "If you have the virus here, why has the process not been observed?"

Dr. Morris: "That has to do with the second key variation. This is what we call a dark virus. It has been theorized before but doesn't occur in nature. This virus is purposefully hiding its mechanism of replication. The obvious reason being that to understand its replication is the first step in stopping it. That is why the virus extracts material rather than injects. The orb likely does the same to mature into the adult form of the virus. The whole process is hidden from us."

Bob: "And you can't crack it open to see what's going on inside?"

Dr. Morris: "That is another function of its dark nature. On dissection there is some unknown process that voids the internal structure of virus leaving an empty husk...a self-destruct protocol if you will, but that's far from the most interesting property of this engineered virus. It has been exceedingly hard to approach and subsequently dissect a sample of this virus. It appears this virus has some mechanisms of defense and a rudimentary awareness of perceived threats."

To Bob, this was just sounding worse and worse.

Dr. Morris: "We, of course, engaged the virus with a series of exploratory nano-bots. Our plan was to capture some, dissect others, and observe the viral operations within the cell. Our nano-bots, high quality medical bots, were disabled, somehow rendered inert, or in some cases were assimilated by the virus. There have been observations of the virus attacking bots that came within a certain proximity."

Bob: "This is awful."

Dr. Morris, thought about that for a moment and agreed, but to her this was also a fascinating subject of study, the knowledge of which could add greatly to the facilities mission and capabilities.

Dr. Morris: "I suppose it is. What we are dealing with here is not a true virus, but a highly sophisticated and precisely engineered machine."

Bob: "But you did manage to crack one open. How did you do it?"

Dr. Morris: "It took a massive wave of bots, more than the single virus could handle. By overwhelming it we managed to breach it and, as I said, found only a voided husk."

Bob: "But in theory it could be overwhelmed and eliminated?"

Dr. Morris: "Unfortunately no. The amount of bots injected, and the remnant material of their destruction would be beyond lethal toxicity to humans and humanoid variants...and this process netted us one virus."

Bob, not sure what to think. "...so there's nothing we can do about it?"

Dr. Morris: "As of now, no."

Bob: "So, besides its invincibility, what does the virus actually do?"

Dr. Morris: "That is a good question. Currently, nothing. It replicates and that is all. There is no pathology, no illness associated with it, just replication, and interestingly enough, it does not reproduce rampantly like a true virus. This virus is limiting itself to percentages of tissue infection, seemingly to not cause unrepairable damage to the host."

Bob: "...hmm...maybe waiting? Maybe this is a situation where the creator will eventually make demands with consequences to follow."

Dr. Morris: "I will leave that speculation up to you and other law-enforcement bodies. My purpose here is to study disease and, theoretically, offer remedies."

Bob: ...so, have you been provided with data on the unexplained deaths on Sol, Atlas, and Alpha-Centauri?"

Dr. Morris, with a half-smile: "We provide our own data and, yes, we have examined those cases. The cause of death is not related to this virus, nor any other infectious disease or entropic phenomenon and as such is of no interest to us. We determined the cardio-electrical functioning was disrupted. We have means of producing the same effect here, but none that would be undetectable."

Bob: "You mean, if you were to recreate a similar process, it would be determinable as to the cause of death?"

Dr. Morris: "Yes. So that too is in your domain and not ours. We are uninterested. You must forgive my directness, but our mission here is very specific and for good reason."

Bob: "I understand. It's...it's a lot to take in."

After a contemplative pause,

Bob: "So what am *I* doing here?"

Dr. Morris liked that question. There was something about Bob she found pleasant and kind of funny.

Dr. Morris: "To answer that, first let me tell you what we know about the spread of this virus."

Bob: "I know it's in the 'Atlas system and Alpha Centauri, but it hasn't been found on Sol..."

Another polite raised hand,

Dr. Morris: "The virus is very hard to detect. One has to have a good idea of what they are looking for and very few know what they are looking for exactly. My team, along with an army of unsuspecting contractors, continually sample a great many planets throughout the galaxy, and generally speaking, *we* know what we are looking for. The virus is on Sol. Even on Helen's Crown. It is system wide"

This was bad news, but Bob had suspected this so it wasn't that much of a shock.

Dr. Morris: "Also Atlas and Alpha-Centauri, as you know, but additionally Sirius, Pollux, Castor, Rho Gemini, Alpherat, Kaus, Formalhaut of Picis, and Hydrus. Most of these outbreaks are system wide but a few planets have been spared, temporarily, from intensive quarantine. There are two planets in the Kaus system that are reportedly unaffected and a planet or two of Hydrus. Otherwise the infection is system wide."

Bob: "Do you have a timeline of infection, maybe to trace the general source?"

Dr. Morris: "We do. All the pertinent information will be available to you once your terminal access is reinitiated. It will be highly encrypted and viewable only by you. There will be no mention of our facility on any documentation. You'll have everything we are willing to share."

Bob: "ok, ok. ...uh, sorry to repeat myself, but why am I here again?"

Dr. Morris: "You are here because we need your help. Most of our sampling is of standard human populations, which constitutes the vast majority of life in the galaxy. We have some sampling of humanoid variants, but only those that are close enough to the standard that we would not suspect any variation in viral replication. What we need is contact and sampling of the most divergent variants in the human design."

Bob: "To see if they are resistant or to see if there is a maladaptation to replication in these human variants."

Bob earned another half-smile.

Dr. Morris: "Yes. If they are resistant we can identify why, if they are maladaptive we might be able to identify the specific crippling effect, and if they are equally and easily infected we will at least know the genome sequencing is not part of the equation and might be able to postulate a theory behind the viral construction."

Bob: "All right, but why don't you have samples? You have jump ships and resources..."

Dr. Morris: "We have data on the precise mechanisms of the genomic transmogrification for these humanoids but there are several variants that are exceptionally isolated and deal little with other planets. Also, there are some variants that exist in worlds where the politics make our operation very difficult. In these cases we need independent contractors, such as yourself, to handle the legal and political issues. We cannot afford to play politics or take sampling by force. If our organization becomes perceived as anything other than an entity whose interests lay in the common good of all people our mission is greatly jeopardized."

Bob: "Ok. So, what exactly am I supposed to do?"

Dr. Morris: "We need samples from the Rapulis people of Arcturus, the Balaenae of Leviathan, and the Dandies."

Bob: "The Dandies! I have to go there? It's on the other side of the galaxy."

Dr. Morris, smiling appreciatively: "I suppose you don't have to do anything, but I can tell you will. Arcturus is embroiled in civil war, the Balaenae choose to not recognize us as an authority, and the Dandies,...well, you know the Dandies, they are just terribly isolated."

Bob: "Ok, that's going to take a lot of planning and resources. I'll need..."

Dr. Morris: "The jump-ships are already chartered and you can leave when you see fit. I have given this a top tier priority and you can basically take any jump-ship you want to rendezvous with the charters. You'll leave from Helen's Halo as soon as you take care of any immediate obligations."

Bob: "Ok. I'll need to go over all this with the Chief."

Dr. Morris: "Of course, though I have to suggest that you not meet back on Helen's Crown, for the time being."

Bob: "Because of the outbreak."

Dr. Morris: "Yes. You are not currently infected, nor is the Chief. The outbreak is centralized to the outer-industrial areas of Helen's Crown, most of New Paris, and all of Nemesis, where you have overlooked similar murders, by the way. There are also minor outbreaks in the outlands. However, it won't be long before the infection is total across Helen."

Bob: "So, ..."

Dr. Morris: "I would suggest meeting on Ganymede. Galilei is a lovely city and far from the outbreak. It would be wise to leave soon. I probably don't have to tell you that if at any time you become infected you will not be permitted to travel to these worlds. Your job with us will be finished at that point, unless of course we find those worlds infected too. Then it really won't matter."

Bob: "How will I know if I become infected?"

Dr. Morris: "With your permission, I would like to insert a probe into your chest cavity. It will monitor for the virus in your respiratory system, as well as tissue samples and bone penetration. It also has a compliment of nanobots that will survey and act as bait for the virus if it is found in your system."

Bob: "uh,...I guess that's good. How will the probe let me know if I'm infected?"

Dr. Morris: "It will let us know. Then we will let you know. Do you find this agreeable?"

Bob: "Sure, why not."

With that, Dr. Morris produced a device from her desk that looked a lot like a handgun of some sort. She then rounded the desk and approached Bob.

Dr. Morris with a clinical tone: "If you will, please stand up."

She really was an attractive woman. She placed the device to the right of Bob's sternum, pressed in, and placed her other hand on his back directly in line with the device.

Dr. Morris: "Are you ready? This is going to hurt a lot."

With that came a loud pop and Bob had the sensation of getting impaled through the chest.

Bob, screaming: "Ah! gads!....Holy crepes, that hurt!"

Dr. Morris: "Sorry Bob, but you'll be glad in the long run."

It took his breath away and there was a good minute before he could think straight again.

Dr. Morris: "I have enjoyed our time together, but I am afraid I have an enormous amount of work to attend to."

Bob: "Thank you Dr. Morris this has been..."

Dr. Morris held a polite hand yet again, "Please, Polly Ann."

Bob: "Thank you Polly Ann, this has been quite enlightening and helpful..." then touching his chest, "...and surprisingly painful."

Dr. Morris: "It is I who should be thanking you for what you are about to do. May health and long life be with you, Bob."

Bob: "You too Polly Ann."

He then left the office of Dr. Morris. As he passed the receptionist he asked, "Would there be any objection to me walking through the garden before I left."

Receptionist: "Of course not. Feel free to walk the entire circuit and if you find anything that strikes your fancy, have a bite."

Bob left the facility and took a walk around the encompassing garden. He had been interested in it, but it was almost more to clear his head than anything else. It was a lovely garden. Lush green surrounded by an aura of blue. As he walked he came across a patch of sweet peas and ate a few. They were sweet and wonderful. Little did he know that through an unseen window Dr. Morris watched him with amusement. She chuckled to herself and thought: *"Of all the people I've set on this task, I think this guy may be the only one capable of succeeding."*

Shortly after, Bob made the loop and was back at the courtyard. He boarded the boxy ornithopter and made his way back to the *Cell-Scape*, that lumbering flea-like jump-ship that quickly took him from wherever he was to wherever he was going to go. He was greeted by the same young woman who welcomed him aboard with a smirk.

Young woman: "Hurt didn't it?"

Bob, still fiddling with the place on his chest, "It did."

Young woman giggling, "You look like the kind of guy that might get over it with only a little bit of whining."

Bob: "I suppose, but I make no promises."

The young woman laughed and took Bob aboard. Moments later the ship was gone.

Back on the far side of Zeus, Bob and his borrowed ornithopter left the *Cell-Scape* which quickly flashed out of existence. With a glow, his terminal access came back online and he immediately contacted the Chief.

Chief: "Hiya, Bob. Whaddaya know?"

Bob: "Too, too much. We need to meet soon."

Chief: "I have already been told that we might want to meet on Ganymede in Galilei city."

Bob: "I'm guessing from my location that it will be about three hours before I can get there."

Chief: "I'll meet you there. Let me know when you make landfall."

Bob: "Will do."

The ornithopter was boxy and uncomfortable, but the amount of mental processing and stress involved in this situation was demanding of at least a brief nap. Finding a position least likely to produce a severe crick in his neck, Bob fell, mouth agape, into an awkward and restless sleep.

Chapter Nine: Diner on the Edge of Forever - part 2

      Bob managed to grab about forty winks before the ornithopter signaled the atmosphere of Ganymede. Ganymede had a warm orange glow that was starkly contrasted against the slightly purplish background that light pollution from Zeus gave the near field surrounding space. The ornithopter touched down in a secluded park on the outskirts of Galilei. Immediately after Bob left, the ornithopter shot skyward and was gone. Bob looked skyward after the ornithopter and saw the swirling mass of great Zeus churning silently against the sky. Ganymede was the perfect location to witness the beauty of Sol's giant.

Bob contacted the Chief who was waiting anxiously at a restaurant in central Galilei.

Chief: "The Copernicus Eateria. It's quiet and I got us a table in the back away from people."

Bob: "The Copernicus Eateria? It sounds like a diner... and a dive."

Chief: "Well, it is a diner, but it's pretty nice inside. They have flatcakes fresh from Titan. Made this morning."

Bob did like Titan flatcakes, but he was getting tired of diners.

Bob: "Ok, I've got the coordinates. I'll be there...looks like in about ten minutes."

Bob wandered out of the park and headed to a train station. It was fairly dark in Galilei, but that was probably because Bob was used to the omnipresent light of Helen's Crown. The trains here were newer and a bit nicer than on Helen, also, people seemed generally quieter. The train arrived at the Merit-Ptah community square, the location nearest the Copernicus Eateria, and Bob headed to the surface. This was a park-like square surrounded by a wide variety of markets and shops and a pleasant crush of people. Bob felt he should spend more time here in the future, get his head out of work more...get out of Helen's Crown.

      A few blocks away was the diner. Bob found the Chief at a table in a more secluded part of the restaurant. On the table, steaming hot, were a stack of flatcakes, scallion and ginger, and Bob dug in. Titan flatcakes were not unlike pancakes of other cultures, but were layered in delicate sheets of dough that unified to make a single flatcake, but still retained their individuality enough to be perceived as layers, not unlike a decent homemade biscuit.

Chief: "Bob, I was given a fairly detailed rundown of your meeting by Dr. Morris so I know mostly what's going on."

Bob, between mouthfuls of flatcake, "mphf...completely nude."

Chief: "...what?"

Bob: "Everyone there, completely nude."

Chief: "Why?"

Bob: "I don't really know. I got a reasonable enough explanation, but I kinda wonder if it was just to make sure no one believes any of the stories told about the place."

Chief: "...ok, anyway. You're supposed to travel to Arcturus, Leviathan, and the homeworld of the Dandies."

Bob: "I guess so. The idea is that with current morphological data on these isolated human variants Dr. Morris will be able to determine if there is any immunity and if the virus is isolated to standard humans. If the variants are infectable, she might be able to identify how the virus adapts to the differences. Or maybe we'll just learn we're all screwed."

Chief: "Yeah, well, it looks like the virus isn't harmful...yet."

Bob: "Yeah, 'yet' is the key. Don't you suppose there will come a point where this guy will show himself and make some demand, then if we refuse people will start dying?"

Chief: "If movies have taught us anything, then yes."

Bob: "Either way, looks like I'm doing a bit of traveling."

Chief: "Yeah, we need to go over the details of that, but later. In the communique from Dr. Morris, she mentioned similar deaths in New Paris and Nemesis. We looked into it..the names Callus and Murk, all distant family. I'm sending some people to look into it further, but I imagine it won't turn up much more than the family connection. Also, we have found similar deaths in Sirius, Pollux, and Castor. We don't have names yet, but we are getting a little help from your new pal Lark Aspic. He's been inquiring as to your whereabouts, employer request. I have told him nothing, of course, since it's a need to know basis and he definitely doesn't need to know. However, he is heading to Sirius and Pollux to look into the deaths there, at least get us a name or two."

Bob: "I don't really trust that guy. Something doesn't add up with his story. He shows up looking for me for some reason and is hanging around now. We need to check into his employer too."

Chief: "We've done all that. His credentials are solid and we contacted his employer who claims he is concerned with the truth of a serious family matter. I don't think it's anything to worry about. At

118

least for me I don't mind letting him look into these off-world deaths. As long as he is partitioned from your mission, that's fine with me. Besides, Pollux and Arcturus are a long ways apart and in different directions."

Bob: "Anyway, I guess I'll need a few things for my tour of the galaxy."

Chief: "Way ahead of you. I have licensed an unmarked cruiser for you to use. It's not big, single room, standard amenities, but it's fast and well built. I got some of your things from your apartment, clothing and whatnot. I even got that antiquated EMP handgun you're fond of. Additionally, I put a few newer items in the cabin...just if you find the need."

Bob: "I'll need a large assortment of chips in case I can't find the ones I like on the road."

Chief: "You can get those on your way out. Seriously though, you'll take the cruiser to Helen's Halo, dock in a jump-ship and leave for Arcturus. I suppose I just assumed you would be going to Arcturus first, since it's closest."

Bob: "Yeah, that was my plan."

Chief: "I can advise you, but you are going to need to decide for yourself how you want to go about dealing with Arcturus. You know it's been at civil war for longer than we've been alive. Archimedes seems to be the favorable power currently, but you need to decide who to contact for permission to enter Gorgoneion."

Bob: "I thought about asking both Archimedes and Dirac, but I assume if permission was granted by one, the other would deny and I'd be no better off than getting permission from one and hoping for the best."

Chief: "Yeah, I won't lie, this could be dangerous. I suggest you spend some time this evening reading the current trends of Arcturus and let me know which side you want to contact. I'll set up a meeting with some official and we'll hope for the best."

Bob: "I would assume a worst case scenario would be a denial, then I'll just move on to one of the other variants Dr. Morris suggested."

Chief: "Here's to hoping."

Bob: "I assume the cruiser is unarmed, as it would not be wise to go into a delicate situation with weaponry."

Chief: "Right, of course. Besides, you don't have the authority or training to be firing weapons at people."

Bob: "How much training do I need to push a button?"

Bob demonstrated by directing a finger at the call panel on the table, but missed. The Chief, laughed.

Chief: "We aren't really on a time schedule, so I would just leave tomorrow morning when you wake. I would also suggest you spend the night on the cruiser in orbit around Ganymede. Dr. Morris did say that if you get the virus your mission will be over, though I don't know how she'll know."

Bob: "She'll know because she shot some goddamn thing into my chest. Hurt like hell."

Chief: "hmm...how do you know it's not also a tracking device."

Bob: "I kinda assumed it was."

Chief: "People want to know what you're up to."

Bob: "I'm very popular these days."

They finished their meal and talked a bit about things of very little importance. Outside of the diner they exchanged a hug and walked their separate ways, both wondering when they'd meet again. Things were definitely shifting.

　　　Bob followed the coordinates to the cruiser. It was a dark metallic color and shaped a bit like a slender beetle. He approached and the aft cargo hold slowly dropped open, the only entrance to this particular type of cruiser. Inside was the main chamber that opened to the command console. To the left was the sleeping quarters and to the right storage and a water closet. It wasn't large, but probably not far from the square footage of his apartment...and quite a bit cleaner.

Bob walked to the front of the vessel and sat at the command console. There was a small package with a note from the Chief.

"I thought this might be handy or, at the very least, a good idea. - Chief"

Inside was a small vial of mercury. Mercury was generally considered the galactic-wide symbol of the messenger. It meant that the possessor was acting as a messenger and meant no harm. In addition to the symbolism from ancient times, the metallic liquid was easily detected on a general scan and known to passing ships, stations, or docking facilities. It was a good idea. It was a nice gift.

　　　With a polite request from Bob, the cruiser lept into the sky and found a stable and uncluttered orbit around Ganymede. Getting comfortable, Bob sat down on the ships bunk to do a little reading.

He felt fairly certain which side he would contact on Arcturus, but a little care was called for in this situation. Wouldn't hurt to review the basics.

Cyclic Powers as Delineated from the Extracts of History

compiled from the resources of the Free Galactic Library (FGL)

Human beings abhor the irregularity of the universe. Bumps are smoothed out and things smooth made jagged. It is perhaps a metaphysical discontentment as many learned scholars have identified the specific psychometrics as a bio-neurological disorder, yet one so fundamental to the nature of human functioning that it cannot be removed or conditioned without rendering the subject inert or something other than human.

When humans amass, this fundamental malfunction aligns itself to create a perpetual feedback loop or "vicious circle" to use the vernacular. The particular disparate elements that interact to support this feedback loop are the interplay between order and chaos, and good and evil. The totality of this interplay can be easily visualized by the following graph:

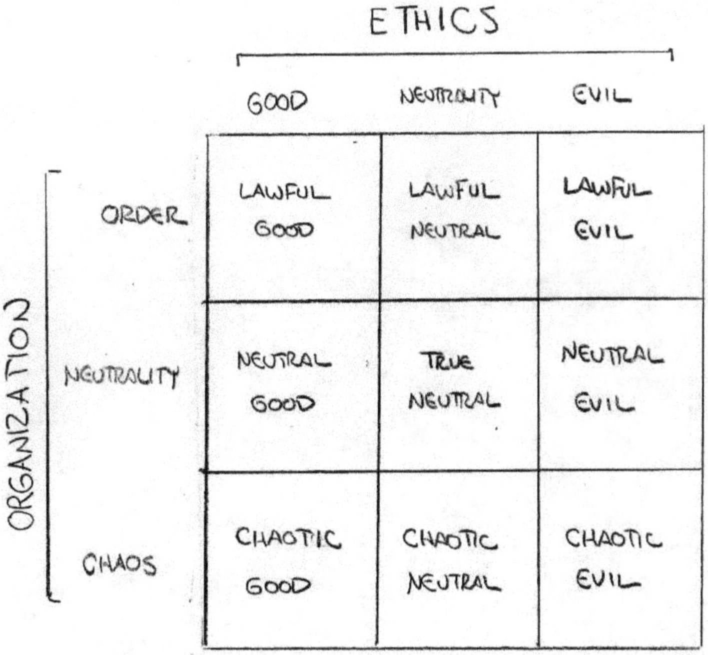

ETHICS

	GOOD	NEUTRALITY	EVIL
ORDER	LAWFUL GOOD	LAWFUL NEUTRAL	LAWFUL EVIL
NEUTRALITY	NEUTRAL GOOD	TRUE NEUTRAL	NEUTRAL EVIL
CHAOS	CHAOTIC GOOD	CHAOTIC NEUTRAL	CHAOTIC EVIL

ORGANIZATION

The use of neutral here is employed as the subjective barrier between the disparate elements. It is theorized that neutrality as a secondary trait is most likely the result of self-interest overriding the ethical-empathetic mechanism of cognition, where the subject or entity values what is perceived as personal gain over the greater good or evil. This is a commonality to the human condition. True neutrality, on the other hand, would be a balancing act of consciousness where the subject or entity is suspended perfectly between order and chaos, and good and evil, where self-interest plays no role. Therefore, true neutrality is considered to be a non-human function that is not attainable by any human subject or entity with the exception of an individual in a deep meditative state where mental processing (or calculation) has been suspended and the individual exists, temporarily, at the level of fundamental consciousness. In other words, it can be applicable intermittently to an individual but not so as a social structure or society involving many.

These designations, and the feedback loop they create and originate from, are the foundation of all metastructures that have defined human societies. The flow of this cycle can be seen in the following graph:

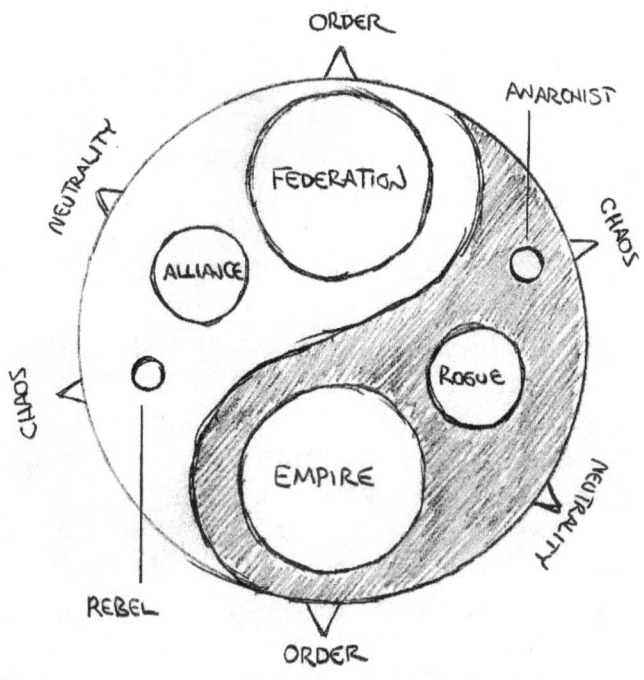

From here, we can see the penultimate structure being the Federation. The Federation is a lawful-good entity where order is maintained for the benefit of the populace. Contrary to this is the Empire which is a lawful-evil entity where power is retained (usually by a small percentage of people) and used to subject the populace to compulsory rule.

Tracing the evolutionary flow from the Empire (lawful-evil), it is common, following a "time and oppression" direct correlation, for a small band of individuals to fight against the structure of the Empire. These individuals, referred to here as Rebels, are chaotic-good, the diametric opposition required to break free from the oppressive and highly ordered entity of the Empire. Over time, these Rebels amass with other Rebels or dissected remnants of a dying empire to form a loose association or Alliance. This Alliance is neutral-good and is in the process of abandoning the chaos required to break free from an Empire and instill a modicum of order. This order is by no means totalitarian. To the contrary, it often recognizes the sovereignty of the constituents of the Alliance while promoting agreed upon guidelines to the social interaction between them, still in a direction away from Empirical ideologies.

The inevitable outcome of the Empire-Rebel-Alliance progression is the Federation. The lawful-good order of the Federation is structured around populace based ideologies often involving a constitution and delineation of individual rights which are upheld above all other ideological imperatives. In the Federation, law is prescribed, usually by some form of electorate, and enforced by an equally monitored policing body all of which purports to represent the common good.

It is hard to imagine that a Federation, once constructed, would ever revert to chaos as the rule is populace based and the objectives are for the greater good, however, there are two major shortcomings with a Federation's stability. The first shortcoming has to do with the fact that to implement a social structure that accounts for the rights of all individuals invariably becomes increasingly complex. As the Federation grows and incorporates larger bodies (other Alliances or varying cultures) the needs of adaptation grow and the finer points of the law grow. Soon the legal structure of the Federation breaches what is known as the "common-point cognitive barrier". This is the critical boundary by which a common individual of a Federation can possess an understanding of the law. Beyond this barrier the law can only be fully understood by a scholar on the subject of Federation law and, as the Federation grows, the scholar may become specialized in only one facet of law and the true particulars of the law are not known by any one individual.

Complexity here is the issue. At this point, not only is the law communally not understood, but the governing bodies invariably create laws that are conflictory and causes moderate to extreme irrational difficulties to larger and larger numbers of the populace. Here the Federation can seem oppressive or even cruel, at which the population detaches emotionally from the governing structures and is willing, often to their own detriment, to support opposition to the establishment.

This first shortcoming of the Federation is a geriatric condition. The second shortcoming of the Federation as a power structure is present from inception. When an entity such as a Federation purports to represent the populace and administer law according the greater good, the corrupt and power hungry go wanting. There is little room for crime, for seizing power, or acquiring wealth at the expense of others. This gives rise to the Anarchists. The Anarchists, often referred to as terrorists, are an unorganized band of chaotic-evil individuals. They may claim group orientation, but this is often very temporary and transitory as their ideals are self-serving and primarily anti-establishment. The Anarchists efforts are in destroying or transforming the establishment away from order for the purpose of a power structure conducive to power acquisition. The Anarchists are to the Federation what the Rebels are to the Empire.

As the Anarchists free themselves from the Federation, often at the Federation's demise, they find themselves adrift in unbridled chaos. Entities form as individuals seize power by force and the collection of individual Anarchists become assembled into a loose conglomerate of Rogue states. The Rogue states settle into a neutral-evil order where power and wealth are still the main driving forces, but the chaos of the Anarchists is more tightly controlled. Individual rights are non-existent and the population is subject to the whims of lord barons, dictators, or monarchies.

The assemblage of Rogue states are never at peace. Invasion of neighboring states, hostile takeovers, rebellion from within, treaties signed then ignored, all contribute to what is often called a "warring states" period. Though the warring states period often lasts for a considerable amount of time there is usually a penultimate victor by which the Rogue states transition to Empire, and the cycle begins anew.

It was sometime before finishing the article that Bob had fallen fast asleep. Boring reading will do that to a fella. It was a hard sleep earned from a day of odd encounters, troubling information, and the burden of a great deal of responsibility place before him.

Dream Journal: The Prophet

The dwelling was rough and made by hand. Walls of dried mud and covered in blankets. Outside the sun burned fiercely, dry, and dust was in the air. Inside was dark, unlit. Various simple sundries, primitive and fragile, arranged for use. A small table, single chair, and a bed upon which lay a person of advanced age nearing the end of their days in this world. The person was unknown to me, facing away toward the wall against which the bed had been pushed. The person, in a parched and weak voice, said softly:

"Rising up from the sea, in every drop of water, in everything that crawls on its belly, in everything that supposes, gods fill the galaxy. Tiny gods who are themselves the makers of gods. You can kill any one you like. Death to a god is like a child blotting out the sun with a small hand. "See, I have blotted out the sun!" Yet it shines on, in all directions, eternally. Let them kill the tiny gods at will and in each absence; a void that brings forth yet another tiny god.
They will spring forth from you and all of us. They will erupt from every cell like tangle vines reaching crookedly toward the sun, leaving only death behind because that's what gods do...they leave death behind."

This person, gingerly lifting their head and turning slightly toward me, then said:
"You know what to do."
I then sat quietly, for a considerable time, in the darkness of the dwelling waiting for the sun to set.

Part II.

"What mortal claims, by searching the vast expanse of the universe, to have found the nature of the gods, or of their opposite, or of that which comes between, seeing as one does this world of humanity tossed to and fro by waves of contradiction and strange misfortune?"

Euripides *Helen*, 480-406 b.c.

Map of Local Group

Map contains stars and their relative distance from Sol (in light years)

Stars named contain populations of 100 billion or more

Unnamed stars have populations around 10 billion

Populations of less than 10 billion are not listed

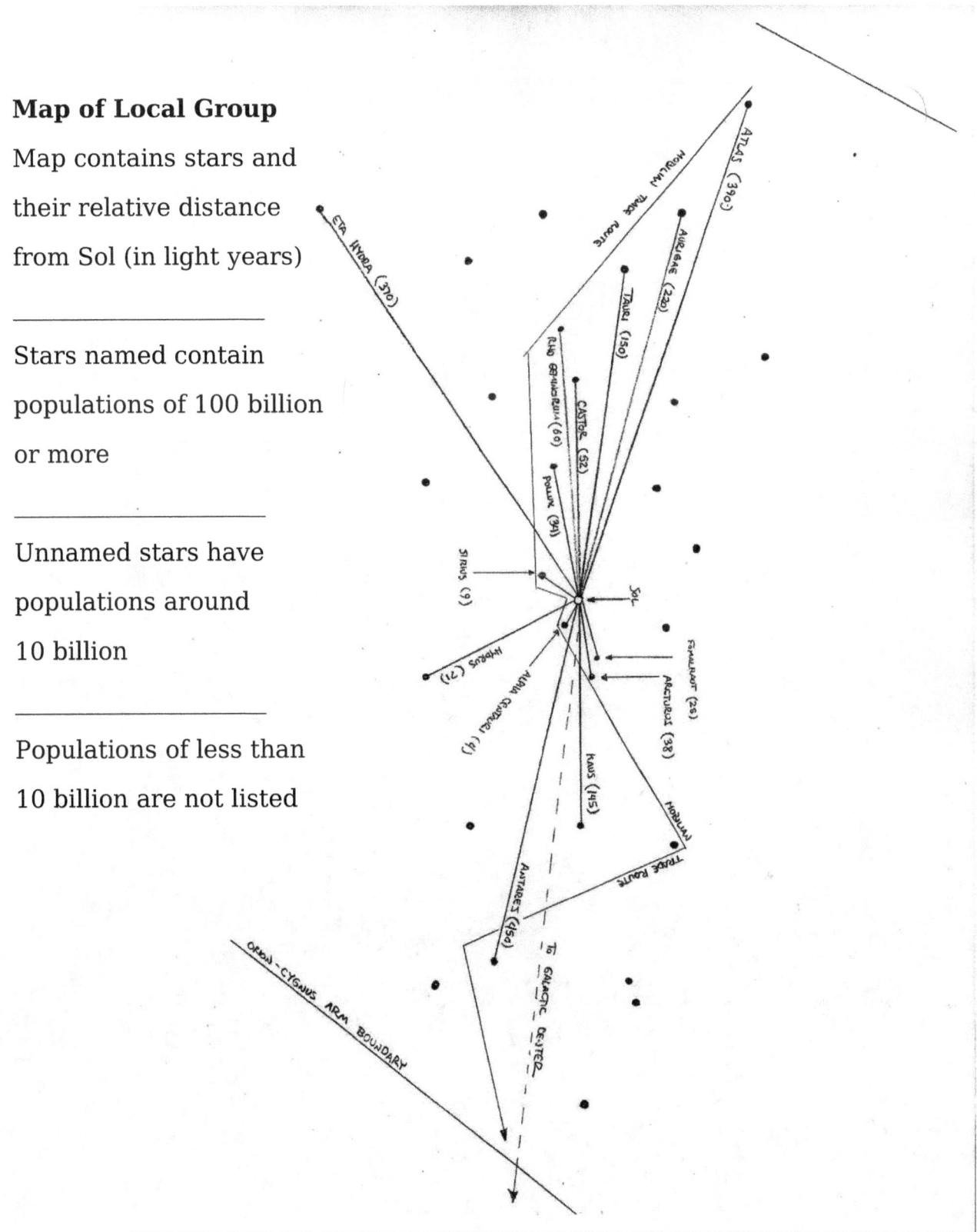

Chapter Ten: A Bad Moon Rises.

About four years prior in an unknown location hidden amongst the chaos of the galaxy.

A bulb flickers in a darkened laboratory. Behind, through heavy plastiglass, the astringent white light of a containment room casts long shadows that crisscross the floor behind metallic tanks and devices unknown. The entrance to the laboratory, massive reinforced doors, have been torn like paper with jagged arcs of metal curling into the lab. It was obviously some ballistic, some significant force or explosion that opened these heavy doors exposing the completely dark hallway outside.

Looking closely amongst the shadows of the floor one would find the charred remnants of bodies, possibly two individuals that were near the door at the time of the explosion. Further in, the scene becomes more gruesome. An arm lies still and still warm. Here an unidentifiable chunk of flesh, possibly a portion of a torso, sits in a pool of steaming blood. There a head and shoulder, arm still intact, rests in an odd peacefulness upon the floor. Someone or some group armed with tactical plasma torches had wandered through this facility slicing up every living thing in their path. If one were to wander beyond the lab, through the hallway, and through the modest sized facility the vision would be the same: death and dismemberment.

Whatever had happened, though recent, had passed and now an otherworldly stillness, a passivity, had fallen on the modest laboratory. After a quiet moment a figure is seen standing in the destroyed doorway of the laboratory. He is dressed in plain clothes and wearing spectacles that show only the astringent light of the containment room beyond: a white and harsh light. In his right hand he holds a device unknown to us. It is a cylindrical handle from which protrudes two sharp prongs and several hanging tendrils that move limply when he walks. His expression is somber and he speaks to himself in a whisper.

Bespectacled man: "I had hoped it wouldn't have come to this."

He enters the lab and walks gingerly around the debris of bodies, inquisitively nudging the pieces gently with his foot almost as if he's looking for the right one.

Bespectacled man: "It probably doesn't matter now. We were pretty much done."

After nudging a few more remnants of the carnage he rounds the corner of a long research station attached to the wall. There he finds the body of someone he knew, someone still identifiable: Eddie Pembrose, chief lab technician. Eddie was in his mid-forties, young, and once a specialist in genomic transmogrification, a genuine diamond in the rough. His talents had gone relatively unnoticed and unappreciated which is how the bespectacled man acquired the use of his invaluable services. Eddie now lays motionless, severed with a plasma cut from lower left rib cage to right mid abdomen and rests in a puddle of blood and entrails. If one was to look amongst the shadows of the opposing wall there would be found the missing lower half of Eddie crumpled in a discarded pile where the offender or offenders had kick the remains to clear a path to Eddies primary terminal. Bloody footprints littered the area.

The Bespectacled man sadly whispered: "Oh, Eddie."

He knelt down and held the top of Eddies head. Eddie stared peacefully skyward. The bespectacled man had a genuine look of regret though his eye glasses shone only harsh white.

Bespectacled man: "Eddie, I am sorry this had to happen. It was always a possibility, a risk I had to take. I'm just sorry it had to end this way for you."

Then, with a look of renewed resolve, "And I'm even more regretful for what I have to do now."

The bespectacled man had transferred his unknown device from his right hand to his left. He then jabbed the probes deep into Eddies torso, near the spine and the hanging tendrils sprung to life and crawled deep into Eddies body. From the handle emanated a ghostly structure, seemingly unreal, like a projection, or a structure that existed in some other reality. It was as if there was a large object that was seen but unseen around the base of Eddies torso.

It was then that something strangely horrible happened. Eddies heart began to beat again, though it pumped nothing. Eddies lungs filled with a frightening gasp though the oxygen was supplied to nothing. Twitching, spasms, and seizures wracked his face as his brain was artificially brought back on line. Then Eddie, like some grizzly Lazarus, issues a blood-curdling scream.

Eddie: "....cold....cold..."

The words were muffled and a bit garbled, the diaphragm was partially damaged and not responding as needed to produce clear vocalization. The bespectacled man adjusted something on the quasi-present console and the voice improved, but was slightly more stuttered.

Eddie: "I'm cold....so...cold."
Bespectacled man: "Eddie, quickly, did you dump all stored data before they breached the lab?"
Eddie: "I can't....I...I'm so....cold."

Of course he was cold. He hadn't any blood. Nothing to warm his body. Death brings cold to those who grasp too closely to their corporeal form, or in this case, are forced to remain. This process, though deemed necessary by the bespectacled man, was the cruelest of tortures and the suffering of it would be indescribable. The bespectacled man was woefully aware of this.

Bespectacled man: "Eddie, Eddie" he gave him a little slap to reorient his attention. Eddie then, startled, looked to the bespectacled man with horror and confusion. He appropriately had no idea what was happening to him.

Bespectacled man: "Eddie, did you dump all stored data?"
Eddie, confused: "...yes...I can't feel my......"
Bespectacled man: "Before they breached the lab?"
Eddie: "...yes...before..." Poor Eddie couldn't figure out why he was being asked these questions and just answered out of habit.
Eddie: "please...I'm so cold..."
Bespectacled man: "Did they get any transmission out?" Eddie, in terrible shock, took a couple more slaps to focus his attention.
Bespectacled man: "Eddie, did they get any transmissions out?"
Eddie: "...no, ...field went up...nothing out."
Bespectacled man: "Are you sure?"
Eddie: "..I'm so cold..." he painfully iterated in tearful whining.
Bespectacled man: "Are you sure!?"
Eddie: "...I'm sure...please, please help me...I...I can't ....I...I'm so cold...please..."

Then Eddie began screaming like a man on fire. The bespectacled man passed a hand over the quasi-real console which then dissipated like an exorcised apparition. Then, in the midst of screaming, Eddie fell silent again and laid still as if none of this had ever happened. Eddie was returned to the comfort of death.

The bespectacled man looked sadly at the still Eddie and spoke once more in a quiet whisper.

Bespectacled man: "Oh, Eddie. Please find somewhere in your heart the strength to forgive me."

He then retracted the tendrilled probe, a device of his own invention unknown to the galaxy, and returned it to his right hand.

After a moment of reflection the bespectacled man left the lab and walked softly through the facility strewn with dismembered bodies dissected carelessly by vicious men. If one was to inspect the carnage closely, near the main entrance of the facility, there would be found several dead men in black uniforms with tactical plasma torches nearby. Their unmarked bodies show no trace of damage. It's almost as if their hearts had just been turned off.

Visit Arcturus!
Brought to you by the Orion-Cygnus Arm travel authority (OrCA)

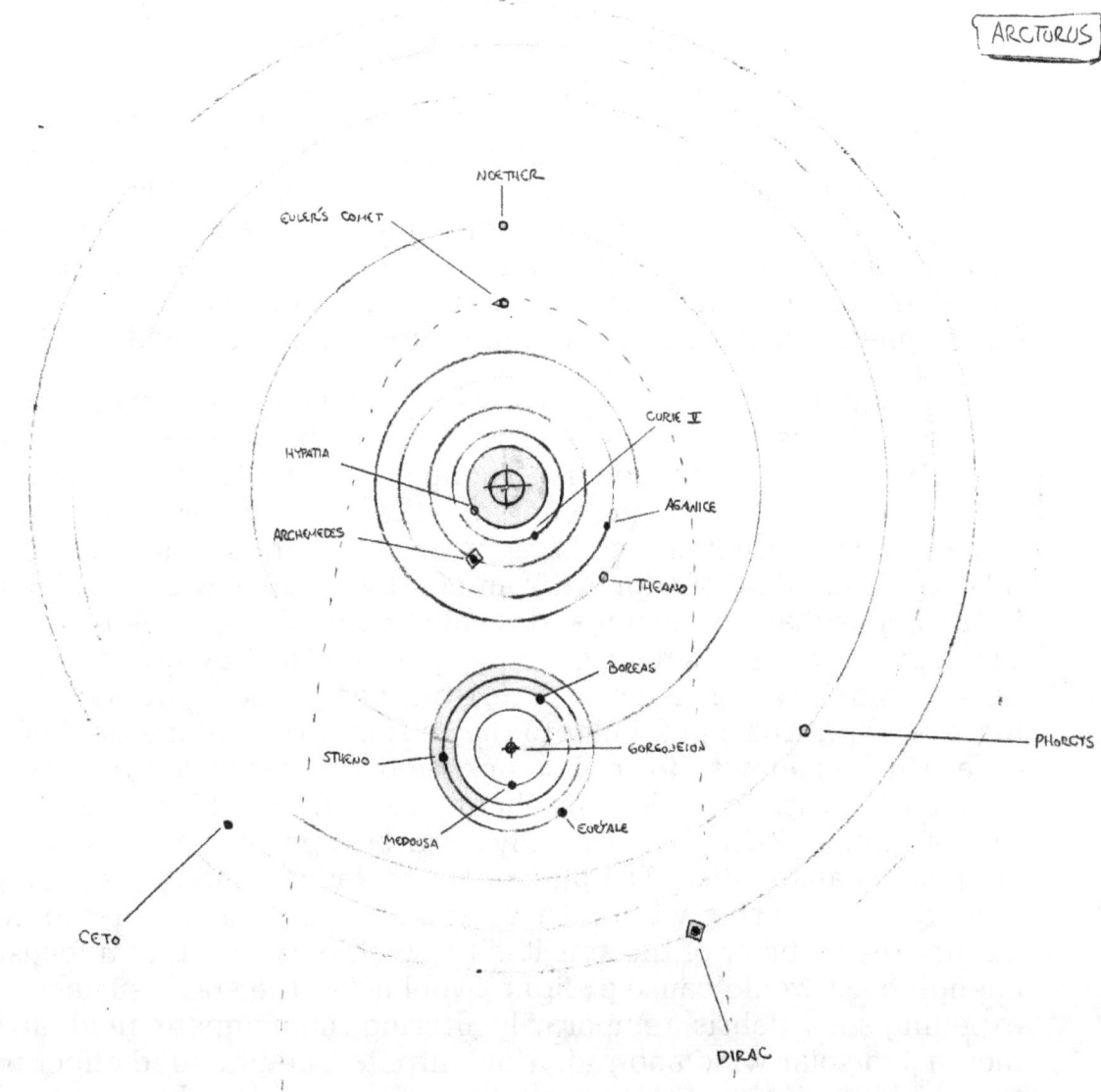

Very few star systems have been consistently in the public consciousness as Arcturus. From early colonization Arcturus has been embroiled in conflict. Warring states, planetary skirmishes over territory and authority, dying empires which formed from the ashes of dying federations, and system wide labor disputes are but a few of the impressions brought to mind when the name Arcturus is mentioned. And war is always accompanied by famine, disease, oppression, and death.

Many scholars have expounded their theories of Arcturus's difficulties, but to forgo a lengthy and controversial thesis it can generally be agreed upon that there are two main contributing factors to the problems of Arcturus. First, Arcturus is a very large star, about 25 times greater than Sol. Large stars tend to have a large number of planets and Arcturus is ripe with habitable worlds. This brought a lot of colonists from different regions, with different ideas, in a relatively short period of time. Second, most systems were colonized in discrete stages with one planet or habitable moon acting as a foothold from which other planets or moons were later developed. This has the tendency to centralize and consolidate power. Arcturus, on the other hand, was rapidly colonized by many sources at once and regional rule in developing and disparate areas proved to foster an environment where each entity felt entitled to system-wide authority.

Currently Arcturus is in a state of civil war. The two main competing forces are seated by **Archimedes** in the central system and **Dirac** of the outer regions. Though it can be difficult to assess alignment, it is generally agreed upon that Archimedes is in a position of Federation formation and Dirac is establishing an Empire. This has placed a great deal of support from nearby systems with Archimedes in the hopes that a peaceful and stable Federation may be possible in the near future. Regional system support was lost by Dirac when plans for, and construction of, a terrible weaponized ship were discovered. Dirca's proximity to the resource rich debris field of the outer rim has allowed for rapid construction of massive warships, but none so concerning as the ship that came to be known as the "Annie Jump-Cannon". This was basically a massive pulse cannon built with jump-ship capabilities. The plan of Dirac was to construct the ship, jump to a close orbit with Arcturus and use the cannon to temporarily disrupt the stability of the star itself. The theory was that a focused enough blast would cause a slight "wobble" in the star's surface expelling solar debris, temporarily altering the magnetic field, and increasing solar wind and radiation output. The intended effect was to disable the inner planets communications and warship function from **Hypatia** to **Theano**, with the obvious target being Archimedes. This would undoubtedly have the added effect of widespread radiation sickness and inevitable deaths estimated to be in the millions.

Fortunately, the Annie Jump-Cannon was discovered by Archimedes spies and destroyed before construction could be completed and the discovery of the cannon gained invaluable regional support for the Archimedes forces. A lesson to be learned; one may think a powerful weapon is a useful thing, but no one wants someone in their neighborhood with unchecked power.

This is not at all to say that Arcturus is an awful place. There are many, many wonderful worlds in the Arcturus system and though a civil war is raging, much of the conflict is "cold" as often neither side is willing to commit to all out war. Arcturus is home to several regionally renowned universities and garden schools. **Aganice** is home to a top-tier propulsion research facility, and **Curie** is well known for an unparalleled theoretical physics institution.

That being said, everyone knows the real interest of Arcturus has to do with the worlds orbiting **Gorgoneion**. Gorgoneion, depending upon who you ask, is either a small star or a substar (once known as a 'brown dwarf'). It has a beautiful magenta glow that warms its orbiting bodies (planets or moons, depending on one's perspective). The three sisters; **Stheno**, **Medousa**, and **Euryale**, are harsh and rocky planets with thin atmospheres. **Boreas**, on the other hand, happens to have a considerable amount of water...though still harsh and rocky otherwise. Due to the water content, Boreas has become the home of the humanoid variant known as the **Rapulis**. The Rapulis, who often refer to themselves as the "tribes of Shenlong", have modified their genetic makeup from the human standard by emphasizing and developing the reptilian part of the human brain. This may at first sound frightening to a standard human as the reptilian portion of the human brain is often associated with instinct, aggression, and territoriality, however, the guided manipulation and development of this variant in the Rapulis people was designed to render various aspects of the human psyche as instinct with the hopes to eliminate action motivated by the basic fear/survival response. Therefore, many would be surprised to find that the Rapulis have little to no internal conflict and live in a very structured yet peaceful society.

One of the unusual aspects of this variant too is that, unlike other humanoid variant, the Rapulis have and are developing themselves for philosophical purposes. Most variants have the direct purpose of adapting themselves to their environment, and there is a component of necessity in this with the Rapulis people, but the initial philosophy behind their evolution is existential rather than environmental.

Due to the Rapulis people's a-political involvement and the recognized developmental nature of their peoplehood, Gorgoneion has been spared the general conflict of the Arcturus system and both sides in the civil war have respected the Rapulis isolation and autonomy.

*There is currently a travel restriction to Arcturus and visitation is not advisable. Any travel to and from Arcturus requires authorization and the acknowledgement of that authorization may not be recognized by all governing bodies. It is suggested that travel to Arcturus be avoided in all except the most important matters. Traveler beware.**

Chapter Eleven: A Halo, a Trip Through Nothingness, and a Stern General

Alpha-00800-pre-stasis elder grain remembers. Memory command tied to local strains.

Kappa-Lambda-aught-aught-nullus in decaying orbit. Requesting transfer protocol.

Motile grain Upsilon-Psi-8-00-20-1 approaching light. Mass masking initiated to maintain actuality.

When Bob woke he had that brief and mildly alarming sense of not being sure of one's location. He was on the narrow bed of the cruiser in orbit around Ganymede. He sat up and took a moment to dislodge himself from the debilitating grip of sleep and sent a communique to the Chief about his intentions to seek permission from Archimedes in the Arcturus system in hopes they would grant passage, and hopefully protection, to Boreas where he might meet with the Rapulis and gather data and samples of their current genetic makeup. The Chief replied that he had sent a request and would let Bob know the details shortly. With a major political entity, and forces at war, the request needed to have some aire of officialdom to it at a level not bequeathed to Bob. The Chief, however, was the head of a major law-enforcement body, on a major world, in a major system. They should, *should* respond to his request in a fairly timely manner.

Bob got up, had a bowl of noodles from the cruiser's food replicator, and set down at the control console. He was to go to Helen's Halo, take the next available jump-ship to Arcturus, and wait along the outer system border until the request was granted. With a little nudge at the controls, Bob was off and this cruiser was considerably faster and roomier than that boxy little ornithopter he'd been using prior.

Within minutes, Bob came into view of Helen's Halo. The Halo was a fairly standard ringed station floating in orbit around Zeus. A reflective but dark metallic color, it consisted of a spoked ring that docked the jump-ships, up to eight at a time. The spokes attached to a small central orb which housed station crew and carried out the daunting process of organizing the flood of vessels continuously

141

streaming into and out of Helen's domain. Above and below, perpendicular to the ring, were the docking spikes. These allowed for the docking of smaller vessels, such as cruisers, ornithopters, tankards, transports, and cargo vessels. They were arranged conically above and below the main jump-ship docking ring. Most of these ships were lying in wait until they could enter a jump-ship and head to their destination, but some were station employees or even jump-ship crew that lived in the area. The station could probably dock a thousand or so ships that were the size of Bob's cruiser.

Inside the station there were many shops and restaurants. It was a whirl of activity and usually crowded. There really wasn't any food that was that great and most of the shops were overpriced. Standard tourist / entrapped-waiting-for-a-ship fare. Fortunately, Bob didn't have to go inside. In fact, he probably wouldn't have to dock on the station but rather enter the jump-ship directly.

When he was essentially *at* the station, in close orbit around, he could see a flurry of ship activity. There were four standard flea-like jump-ships docked at the station loading vessels and one other heading off to make a jump. Around was a swarm of vessels entering, leaving, going from one jump-ship to another, docking, or leaving the station entirely.

Bob took a glance at the jump-ships in the area. Jump-ships always had names which were visible on the hull (except for the *Cell-Scape*, which was obviously a secretive affair). Here, Bob could see the *"Foxtrot"*, the *"Five Suns"*, the *"Seadrum"*, and *"La Novia"*. The jump-ship that was slowly leaving the station had a name written in Gallach. Bob had studied Gallach at the university, briefly, and was eager to see how much he could recall. According to Bob and the three characters on the leaving jump-ship, it was known as the *"Trout Mask Replica"*. Bob strongly questioned his translation abilities.

When he was very close, a message greeted him from the station. It was mostly a welcome to Helen's Halo, but it also had details on the destinations and times of the jump-ships for the day. It looked like Bob could easily dock directly into the *Foxtrot* who was leaving shortly. Though Arcturus was not a scheduled stop, as few travel to areas of conflict, Arcturus was in the general direction of travel and special authority had been granted to Bob from the office of Dr. Morris. In fact, she had said he could take any jump-ship he wanted at any time, but one that was going that direction anyway seemed to make the most sense.

Bob quickly approached the *Foxtrot* and was put in the queue. In almost no time, he was entering the open abdomen of the giant space flea and attached himself to the inner wall. There was still about a good 45 minutes before the rest of the ships would finish docking and at least another 15 before the ship would arrive in deep enough space to make its first jump. Generally speaking, and Bob didn't know exactly why, but it's not a good idea for anything to be too close to a jump-ship when it's about to jump. Thinking of that, and the mystery of the jump-ship in general, Bob thought now would be the perfect time to learn a bit more about how these ships work. He sat down and used his time and to read a FGL article on jump-ships. Afterwards, he wished he hadn't.

Suggested Reading for Interstellar Travelers:
The Modern Jump-ship
Compiled from the resources of the Free Galactic Library (FGL)

Greetings Seafarer! You are about to go on a voyage through the cosmos on the most technologically advanced machinery the galaxy has to offer. The Jump-ship has made the galactic spread of humanity a possibility and modern jump-ships offer a wide range of travel options and creature comforts.

The first trans-void engine, which makes jumping possible was invented by accident over 65,000 years ago. When Berb Ferder of Poseidon was developing a quantum punctuator, little did this individual know that practical interstellar travel began when Berb's quantum punctuator spontaneously disappeared. On Professor Ferder's twelfth attempt one of the punctuators materialized in orbit around Ares, at that time called Mars, and an angry complaint of a mining colony claimed it damaged one of their topography satellites. It wasn't until then that Berb Ferder realized gold had been struck, which is a far greater fortune to humanity since no one knows what a quantum punctuator is anyway.

Since the time of the early trans-void engine, many improvements in efficiency and accuracy have been made. Ships are faster, can travel further, and materialize less often inside of stars. Originally these ships were known as trans-void vessels, but since the word "void" tends to sit uncomfortably with the public the name was changed some time ago to jump-ship. Problem solved.

But you may be asking yourself, "How do these ships actually work?" Very good question. The jump-ship has an unusual method of travel. To understand it, you must understand the physics behind the

143

human interpretation of reality as it pertains to the universe, or more appropriately, the multi-verse. Think of our universe as a thin sheet. Stretched across this sheet are all the planets, stars, galaxies, galactic clusters, etc... Now, right outside this sheet is a great void. The "primordial nothingness against which all creation is discerned." to quote the ancient thinkers.

Nothingness, it turns out, is a lot more complicated than it seems. Much more complicated than somethingness. You see, we often think we encounter nothingness, an open meadow, a clear sky, even the great vacuum that lies between galaxies. However, these are in no way even remotely close to nothingness. The meadow and the skies are full of air and light and hope. Even the great vacuum has a chunk or two of something in it. Even if we were to imagine the greatest vacuum with truly no thing in it, it would still have the measurable quantity of distance. Think about it, if point "A" and point "B" are separated by truly nothing, then point "A" and point "B" occupy the same space. Between them there is no matter, no energy, no distance, and no thing that has any attribute other than it's lack of attributes. Hence, they would be the same point. This is why it is difficult to understand the nature of the great void. In a sense, the void exists everywhere and nowhere. To see it, or rather contemplate it, you can do a simple experiment. First, draw a point on a sheet of paper. Make it as small as you can while still being able to see it. Now, cease to think of it as a single point and instead think of it as two points that occupy the same space. Keep those two points in your head as you look at the single dot on the paper. Now, contemplate what is between those two points. There you have it. You have contemplated the great void. And if you have realized that if the void has no measurable attributes, then it actually doesn't exist, then you did it right and truly have contemplated the great void and the operation of the jump-ship will be very easy to understand.

To use the sheet analogy of the universe, what the ship does is poke a little hole in the fabric of reality, slips outside it, and enters the great void. Since the great void is attribute-less, it is infinitely small. In fact, it has no-size. If any and every point in the universe is a mere something away from being nothing, which it is, and below every point of something lies this great nothing, which it does, then every point in the universe is right next to the great void, which is of no-size. Therefore, the entire universe is wrapped tightly around a point of nothingness of no-size. Review the dot and paper experiment. So, once the ship has poked through the fabric, it can return at any other point just as easily as the one it entered by. Complete, universal travel...instantly. And it turns out the universe is probably infinite, in that, it exists as a probability that fluctuates around infinity. (not to

144

terrify the reader, but the size of the universe is only more probable around infinity, but the scale is between infinity and zero. Yes, the universe is sometimes of zero-size, but you'll hardly notice and it won't stay that way long.)

As for the ship, you might be asking yourself, "how can the ship, which is a something, exist in the void, which is nothing?". Also a very good question. Referring to the dot and paper experiment, where the dot had to be thought of as two points existing in the same space, this is how the ship must be thought of. When the ship pops into the void, it exists as two ships occupying the same point. One point is smushed and pressed up against the underbelly of the universe. This point, or this ship, slips back into the universe and everything is fine...hopefully. The other point, or ship, enters the void, becomes the void, and is lost in a darkness of abyssal completeness. It never was and never will be.

Before the fine-tuning of the process was perfected, many, many ships were lost to the void. Tethering a ship between the universe and a great nothingness is a lot harder than it sounds. Every once in a while though, a ship or two lost to the great void shows back up. How that works, ... nobody knows. The ship and crew are never quite the same.

It is believed that those lost to the void still exist in some place, or in some form, since as we discussed earlier, nothingness doesn't really exist which is one of it's requirements to be considered nothingness...it can't exist. Life and death, at one time in prehistory were considered to be existence and non-existence, are now understood for what they really are, a transition from one something, to another something. Nothing ever becomes nonexistent...neither does something.

It should be mentioned that this entire description of the operation of the ship is merely an analogy for the process. No one actually knows exactly how it works, but it does work... most of the time.

You may also be asking yourself, "If the ship can travel anywhere instantly, then why do I have to make several jumps to get to my grandmother's planet?" Well, perhaps your grandmother lives too far away. But seriously, the idea of instantaneous travel to any point in the universe is only theoretical. There are certain physical boundaries that prevent actual universal travel.

What prevents unlimited travel has to do with the interaction of several factors involved in space-time and nothingness. These factors are: time in the void, distance traveled, and the probability of quantum dissolution. Refer to the following graph:

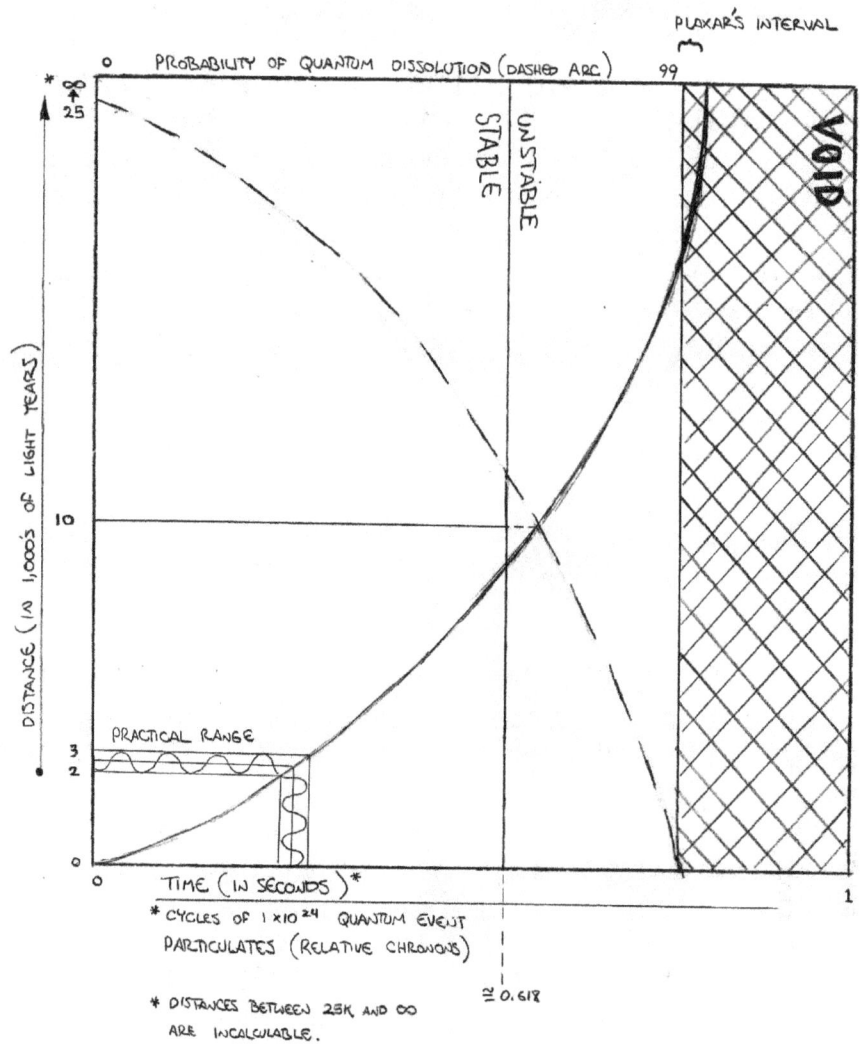

As you can see that the longer you are in the void, the closer your distance traveled reaches infinity. This is paired with the opposing probability of quantum dissolution which also approaches infinity as time increases. If you notice the gap listed as *Plaxar's interval*, this is the interval in time beyond the travel threshold. At this point the quantum dissolution probability approaches 100 percent as the distance traveled approaches infinity. Within and beyond this threshold the traveler becomes the void.

146

A simpler way of thinking of this is that the further you go in one jump, the more likely it is that you'll never come back. Referring to the chart again, you can see that the maximum distance traveled by jump-ship is about 10,000 light years, though this is still very dangerous and would only be used in some emergency situation. The practical range, or habitable zone, is about 2,500 light years. At this interval, no jump-ship has ever been reported lost. According to the chart, the division between "stable" and "unstable" needs to be understood with great care. "Stable" means that the probabilities are predictable, though the closer one gets to that dividing line the great that predictable chance is no longer in your favor. As you can see, the arcs of travel versus dissolution, though inversely proportional, are both exponential. Into the "unstable" range our ability to predict the probability of an outcome is severely compromised and is practically unaccountable.

If we were to tolerate one final question, you might ask yourself "What about intergalactic travel? Couldn't we do a succession of small jumps and actually make it to another galaxy?" That's two questions. However, there are several reasons why this is not considered feasible. There are practical reasons, for example, if we wanted to make it to the Andromeda galaxy, it's a good 2.5 million light years away. That comprises a lot of jumps and there would have to be a string of stations to supply the chain of ships required. This would be a huge undertaking and the supposed goal would be to explore other-galactic worlds while there are worlds in our own galaxy that are unexplored. Otherwise the efforts would be merely to say we have accomplished intergalactic travel therefore offering little to no practical value.

Still, there is a bigger and more concrete reason that intergalactic travel is not possible with our current technology. It turns out that galaxies sit in a pool of dark matter. It acts like a glue that keeps everything together, but pertinent to space travel, this dark matter acts like molasses and slows down space-time making void-travel measurable. Refer to the chart again. Notice the frame of reference is about 1 standard second. As we leave the influence of the galactic dark matter, this frame of reference speeds up exponentially. This means that as we leave the galactic disc all of the properties of this chart hold true but the reference time decreases to almost zero. In the galaxy we must pull our ships out of the void in about a half of a second or be lost to the void. Beyond the galactic gravitational influence that time would be about one billionth of a second. We are not that accurate. In the midpoint between our galaxy and the Andromeda galaxy, that time interval approaches zero, meaning it is not possible. Not with this particular technology.

So farewell seafarer! Enjoy the Milky-way. You will be here for a while.

After the article Bob read a bit more about Arcturian politics, partly to prepare but mostly to pass the time. There had been a considerable amount of accusations as to human rights violations of Dirac. This just confirmed to Bob that he made the right decision in essentially picking sides and having Archimedes contacted, but gave him a sense of foreboding that the opposition might be considerably more hostile than he had previously thought. Hopefully he wouldn't encounter them and the trip to Boreas would be uneventful.

At that moment, Bob felt the ship shudder and heard the low-pitched thud of a jump being made. A message emanated from the cruiser console informing him they were currently in the outer rim of the Arcturus system, and his ship was to proceed to the aft hold and exit. Thirty eight or so light years in a fraction of a second and now Bob was heading beyond the ship into the open darkness of the outer system.

After a good twenty minutes, a message was transmitted to the cruiser.

"Your request for audience with an Archimedian representative has been accepted. Please direct yourself to the following coordinates and trajectory where you will be intercepted by a federation battle cruiser. When in range a scan will be initiated and docking instructions will follow. The state of Arcturus is strong. Grace be unto you, Arcturus, and the whole of the galaxy."

This meant that the Chief got the message to the right people and things were looking good. Getting a message around the galaxy is a bit of a tricky ordeal. Actual transmissions of messages are limited to sub-light speeds (because of the pesky laws of physics) and Bob couldn't afford to wait the thirty eight years it would take to get a message to Arcturus. For that reason interstellar messages are transmitted to special encrypted communications arrays which organize transmissions to a similar array aboard jump-ships. For example, a message intended for Antares, a good 450 light years away, would be sent to the regional communications array which would then identify the next available jump-ship path to get the message to Antares as quick as possible. Perhaps the message originates from Sol and is sent to a jump-ship heading to Alpha-Centauri, when it is then sent to a jump-ship heading to Kaus, and from there is sent to a jump-ship heading to Antares, whatever the quickest path happens to be. The final jump-ship sends the message to the regional communications array and is then transmitted to the proper destination. This process does involve an additional layer of complication (or simplicity depending on one's view) which streamlines the efficiency of the transmission, but the details of this are best left to a time depleted of adventure when one truly has nothing better to do than read articles from the FGL.

Arcturus is a huge system. With just a cruiser limited to sub-light speeds, it was going to take Bob a good while to get to these coordinates, about 8 hours. However, he had expected a good deal of down time and planned some things to read.

The coordinates given put Bob in the orbit of Aganice, but in line with Archimedes (Aganice was a good quarter orbit away). Apparently he was to rendezvous near their centralized power, but not too close until they checked him out. It was unconcerning, but did speak to a federal power that was very suspicious of attack. This most likely meant that there have been and probably are attacks carried out on a regular basis.

When he neared the given location, he could see a large ship. As he got a bit closer it was obvious it was a battlecruiser...a large battlecruiser. It was a dull, gunmetal gray, and a somewhat flattened conical shape. The aft half of the battlecruiser was segmented giving it a larva like quality. Each of these aft segments, three in total, housed a different set of engines. The smallest segment housed the impulse engines for local travel, capable of a good fraction of light speed at their maximum. The other two segments were the jump components, the medium segment being the space-time manifold and the largest segment being the envelope generator. The main, or head, portion of the battlecruiser housed an array of cannons, pulse disruptors, communications towers, and an unseen fleet of personal fighter ships...probably in the thousands. Also, unseen, deep inside the most centralized portion of the battlecruiser lay the suspension field generator. This was a massive generator capable of producing a protective field around the ship. The suspension field was useful in protecting the ship from errant micro-meteorites or debris that could damage the hull, but more importantly in a battle scenario the suspension field could absorb energy discharges from offensive weaponry. This was, of course, proportional to the energy inherent in the field generated versus the energy to be absorbed. Only very large ships were capable of housing suspension field generators. The technology is heavily resource dependent and suspension fields are only controllable on large scales, therefore most suspension field generators were aboard battle cruisers, or installed in city centers of cities with very large populations. Some standard jump-ships, especially those associated with war-torn systems, have such generators but these end up being much larger jump-ships with a lesser capacity transport due to the space demanded by the generator.

Bob was guessing that this battlecruiser probably had a population of seven to eight thousand people on board. When he was nearing the starboard side, presumably to enter a dock, he could see the name of the ship emblazoned in metallic black, the *Atom-Heart Mother*. Bob stopped at the specified coordinates a short distance from the battlecruiser, and another message greeted him.

"Your ship is now being scanned. Please be patient and further instructions will follow."

Bob waited another five or so minutes and it occurred to him that they might do a sterilization sweep like they did at C.I.D.E.R. and it sent a phantom shiver through his bones. That was an unpleasant experience and he didn't want to relive it.

"Please proceed to the following coordinates. You will be landing in docking terminal 12 and greeted by an attendant upon arrival. Welcome to the Atom-Heart Mother."

"Ok", Bob thought, "this was pretty easy." And within minutes he had entered the great larval battlecruiser and landed. When he left his little ship, he stepped into a brilliant white corridor. It was relatively empty, though he could see a few ships so far down the corridor that they were practically out of visual range. The light was almost overwhelming, probably from being in a dimly lit little ship and spending a bit of time in the blackness of space, but regardless, this battlecruiser was exceptionally well lit.

Standing next to his open cruiser was a uniformed female attendant, a rank of lieutenant, who stood rigid and disciplined.

Lieutenant: "Welcome aboard the *Atom-Heart Mother*, I am Lieutenant Walker and I will escort you to your audience. Please follow me."

Bob: "Uh, Ok. Thanks."

As they walked a bit,

Bob: "I don't actually know who I am meeting. I'm asking permission to land on Boreas."

Lieutenant Walker: "I am to escort you to your meeting with the General. I have no more information than that I'm afraid. As our obligations are many, I would strongly suggest you be as concise as possible."

Bob: "I appreciate the advice." Though Bob had already assumed that this situation called for an air of seriousness, especially when dealing with military types.

After a few corridors and a handful of lifts, Bob found himself in the middle of a long and open hallway broken only by a large, reinforced double door of gunmetal gray against the otherwise overly white interior.

Lieutenant Walker: "You'll enter the general's workroom and wait quietly on the other side of the door until you are summoned."

Bob: "Alrighty. I think I can manage that."

With a wave of the lieutenants hand across an unseen panel, the great double door slid open and Bob entered. Almost immediately, the door closed behind him leaving the lieutenant outside. Inside, the chamber was exceptionally large. It seemed to be some kind of strategy or planning room. There were terminals and consoles lining the boundary of the chamber and a large table/console in the central area. In the far back there were seats arranged in a semi-circular fashion.

In all, there were probably twelve people in the chamber doing a variety of tasks. In the center, in front of the table were three individuals of obviously high rank discussing something of their own personal interest that had nothing to do with Bob or his mission. These were, after all, a people at war. By the garb, the central figure was the highest ranking officer and most likely the general to which he was scheduled to meet. Female, wearing a uniform bearing the rank of general, but also wearing a protective flak jacket and light armored greaves both of which bore damage markings that indicated this person had seen and been a part of actual hand-to-hand combat. Crazy. It was also very unusual for an officer to be wearing something other than a uniform. For most of the galaxy, the officers issued commands but saw little bloodshed themselves.

After a few minutes, the general finished speaking to the other officers and looked up to see Bob. She walked immediately to him, shook his hand and said, "Hi, you must be Bob. Welcome to the *Atom-Heart Mother*. I am Joan of Arcturus."

It was not lost on Bob that her designation was unifying. She was "of Arcturus", not "of Archimedes". Her name suggested that she considered herself of a unified Arcturus. It may seem a subtle difference, but when intertwined with one's identity it carries with it an important ideology.

Joan of Arcturus was well known in the region for her tireless efforts to stitch together the frayed planetary remnants of this civil war. More regional powers have been consolidated under her command and poverty had been eradicated in several key districts adding to the strength of the Archimedian economy and peace efforts in Arcturus. She is known to have a brilliantly tactical mind and never hesitant to place herself directly in the center of conflict. Additionally, she had instigated and negotiated countless treaties that have almost doubled the Archimedian allies since her tour of duty began some twenty standard years prior. Joan of Arcturus was merely one of many generals in charge of military operations Arcturus wide, but it was well known that her contribution eclipsed the sum of the others. Even the centralized power of Archimedes, the president and various cardinal senators, based all policy at her direction knowing much better than ever questioning a mind far greater than their own (this did not, however, prevent them from trying to take credit for her actions though usually unsuccessfully). Politicians knew all too well that if Joan of Arcturus ever set her sights on public office, her election would be guaranteed. She could easily have any of their jobs if she so wanted.

One of her greatest strengths, unlike her forebears, has been to focus on peaceful negotiation and using force only when no other options remain. This has had the result of siphoning off impoverished territories that are all too eager to abandon Dirac and the toil and suffering that invariably come with empirical rule. These poverty stricken regions have been absorbed into Archimedes, made whole and strong, and increased the numbers and resources of the Archimedian federation. When Dirac attacks directly, the strategic mind of Joan of Arcturus has proven to be impenetrable and has resulted in an overall decrease in violent combat system wide.

She was about the same age as Bob and there was something about her, something he couldn't readily identify, that he found to be quite lovely.

Bob: "Very nice to meet you and thank you for seeing me. I've been asked by officials of C.I.D.E.R. to land on Boreas and get current genomic samples from the Rapulis people in the greater hopes of understanding the regional virus and..."
Joan of Arcturus: "Please excuse my interruption, but I have been thoroughly briefed on the situation and it is my understanding that you ask permission from us to land on Boreas and meet with the Rapulis."
Bob: "Yes, that is correct."
Joan of Arcturus: "Permission granted."
Bob, for some reason expecting it would not be that easy, "oh, ...thank you."
Joan of Arcturus: "You are welcome. We are aware that the virus has infected certain populations of Arcturus and are willing to aid in the assumption that it will pertain to the greater good. As you can imagine, our primary concern lies with the current civil war. Dirac has not been successful in direct attack and instead chooses to engage in proxy conflicts. This leaves us busy and spread thin over a large number of planets. We have little resources to devote to a virus that currently carries no symptomatology. We trust in the efforts of others to identify and deal with this problem and will assist where we can."
Bob: "I can appreciate that."
Joan of Arcturus: "If you don't mind me asking, why have they sent you to deal with this massive, multi-system issue? If my information is accurate, you are not a specialist or official. You are a private investigator, am I correct?"
Bob: "Yeah, I've been asking myself that question too. C.I.D.E.R. must remain apolitical, and most officials are busy with their own problems...or don't care. I kinda just got swept up into this and I suppose was willing. Either that or they thought my handsomeness would come in handy."
Joan gave a little laugh that was held at the eyes, like someone trying not to laugh or not sure if laughter would be appropriate.
Joan of Arcturus: "Well, you are a pleasant sort. You may be the best man for the job."
Based on her laugh, Bob tested the waters a bit more: "Or the only man stupid enough."

Joan of Arcturus gave another similarly restrained chuckle. Bob assumed that she dealt a lot with politicians and officials who universally tended to blow a lot of hot air and were always eager to tout their great qualities. She wasn't accustomed to someone easy going and self-effacing.

Joan of Arcturus: "You do know that neither Archimedes or Dirac have alliances or communications with the Rapulis. We can authorize your travel through Arcturian space, but how the Rapulis will treat you is up to them and beyond our control."

Bob: "Yeah, but I have heard they are a peaceful people and will be welcoming as long as one doesn't bring some agenda with them."

Joan of Arcturus: "That is true. There are a few things you should know. Obviously, they are socially isolated. You will not want to bring political or religious ideologies with you."

Bob: "Not a problem. I come from a long line of heathens."

Joan gave another tense chuckle.

Joan of Arcturus: "Also, when you land on Boreas, you most likely will be immediately escorted to a tribunal. This is a social practice and nothing of concern, but entering without permission requires a hearing to address the 'violation'. As long as your intents cannot be proven to be malicious, you will be welcomed. This is a custom of the Rapulis and shouldn't be any kind of problem, but those unfamiliar may find it very concerning that they are immediately place before a court. Just behave and you'll be fine."

Bob: "Got it. Expect a trial and no sass-mouth."

Joan of Arcturus: "A far greater concern will be Dirac. Gorgoneion is not far from areas of Arcturus claimed by Dirac. They will have ships somewhere in the region. Most likely they will not notice you or have little concern with a small cruiser. We have some ships in the region but, of course, we cannot escort you to Boreas. If some conflict with Dirac arises, we will try to intercept but my advice to you would be to hit Boreas as fast a possible. If a Diracian ship intercepts you, you will become a political prisoner and won't be going anywhere for a long, long time. My hope is that none of this will be an issue, but Dirac is looking for means of indirect leverage over Archimedes. Just be aware."

Bob: "You are suggesting my charms will not go over well on Dirac."

Joan of Arcturus, smiling: "Yes. I'm afraid so."

They began walking towards the chamber doors.

Joan of Arcturus: "Let me walk you back to your cruiser."

Bob: "Thanks."

Joan of Arcturus: "What do you think of the *Atom-Heart Mother*?"

Bob: "It's great. Very impressive. I was caught off guard by the brilliant white of the interior."

Joan of Arcturus: "Yes. Most battlecruisers are a bit dark and dingy inside. This ship was commissioned about three hundred years ago. I made some changes when I assumed command."

Bob: "The important question though is 'what's the food like'? Do you have some decent restaurants here?"

Joan of Arcturus: "I'm afraid we have a series of mess halls. The food is not bad, but I'm sure nothing like the places you're accustomed to on Helen's Crown."

Bob supposed it made sense that his background would be looked into, but he never actually mentioned he was from Helen's Crown.

Joan of Arcturus: "Maybe someday, when leisure exists for us both, you can have a proper tour of the ship."

Bob, very genuinely: "That would be lovely. I would really like that."

Back at Bob's little cruiser,

Joan of Arcturus: "Goodbye Bob. Good luck with your mission. Grace be unto you, Arcturus, and the whole of the galaxy."

Bob: "Same to you Joan of Arcturus."

As the cargo hold of Bob's cruiser closed, they both waved goodbye.

Joan of Arcturus just kind of liked him and she didn't know why and Bob really liked her as there seemed absolutely no reason why not. She was an impressive human being. Bob really hoped they did get to meet again in the future.

Leaving the docking bay of the *Atom-Heart Mother*, Bob set course as directly as possible to Boreas. In a manner of speaking, Boreas was in another system. The Gorgoneion was basically a small star system that orbited the massive sun of Arcturus. Unsurprisingly, a gargantuan stellar system such as Arcturus took a little time in which to get around. Bob, at a reasonable speed, had another solid eight hours before he made it to Boreas.

Bob had always enjoyed reading. Reading was one of those things that would never be abandoned by human populations. Audio and visual communication is a wonderful thing, and in some aspects can be more efficient, but reading always allows the beholder to digest information on their own terms, at their own speed. When this is fine tuned and that sweet spot of absorption and digestion is found, then and there is no other method of communication as precise, efficient, and elegant. Too, reading invites the observer to enter a world of conscious construction where the entire universe therein is woven from the mental fabric of the individual and bounded by our own interpretation of that reality. It is symbology and metaphor, and metaphor is always representative of things greater than the sum of its parts which is why an entire universe can be found in the meager and finite parameters of a book.

Bob was reading several novels. He liked historical fiction of early space exploration and old Earth. This was pretty common in people living in systems with long histories and no system has a longer history than Sol. It is where this whole mess started. Bob also liked reading stories that speculated about the future and the potential of the galaxy in the next several thousand years. Some authors envision a day when jump technology is capable on an individual level. Just a mere thought and one walks from this planet to that. He also spent some time reading regional politics and a good deal of philosophy. Philosophy was a subject that Bob was drawn too, but it also at times instilled in him a melancholy. He had always had a feeling that humanity was hurtling towards the future with little thought or idea as to why and where. Most assembled people, governments, or planetary alliances seem to, in general, think a couple of decades in advance. The more ambitious thinkers try and look hundreds of years ahead. Still, in the spectrum of our past and future even thousands of years amount to little. What is the plan?

When Bob had gotten fairly close to Boreas, within sensor range, he was awoken from a half-reading sleep by a soft alarm on the cruiser console. It was a ship. Not just a ship, but a battlecruiser. It was a good distance from him and he wasn't sure if it was Archimedes or Dirac, also he wasn't sure if it noticed him. He had his cruiser bring the image of the ship much closer. Emblazoned on the side of the battlecruiser was the name *"Disco Volante"*. Didn't really tell Bob much about who that ship belonged to, but it's always better to be able to put a name to something rather than face it as a complete unknown.

Bob held his course towards Boreas, but the ship was getting closer. Within minutes a message emanated from the console of Bob's cruiser.

"Unidentified cruiser, you are to alter course away from Boreas and prepare for inspection."

Bob was struck by the implication. "Hot crepes, this is not good", he thought.
In reply, Bob said, "I am on a peaceful mission and have been given permission to orbit and land on Boreas."

Again from the console of the cruiser: *"You do not have authority and any body issuing such authority is not recognized. Halt course immediately and prepare to be boarded."*

This was very bad. It was obviously a ship from Dirac. Bob needed a moment to think. He didn't alter course, but still needed a moment to figure out what to do. This was obviously a political play and Bob couldn't afford to be a political prisoner for who knows how long.

"Halt course immediately. You are in violation of Diracian law. Further insubordination will result in the use of force."
Bob: "Sorry, there was a communications error. I didn't get that last message. Can you repeat." This, of course, was from the simpleton's guide to stalling tactics.

"Halt course immediately. You are in violation of Diracian law. Further insubordination will result in the use of force."
Even before the last words seeped out, Bob's cruiser lit up several alarms on the sensor array. Bob pulled the image of the ship up and there were several small armed cruisers erupting from the docking bays of the *Disco Volante*. This was very bad. Bob was certain that they were to make a political point here. Dirac was already in an unfavorable position from the regional systems and by destroying Bob's ship this would, at the very least, send a signal that other systems would have to deal with Dirac for safe passage in Arcturus. Dirac knew that Sol or any of the other regional systems would not get involved in a civil war, so their hopes would be that it could force dialog out of fear. They probably never had any intent of letting Bob go alive. As it was the only option, Bob, at the advice of Joan of Arcturus, ran the engines at maximum and made a beeline for Boreas.

These small armed cruisers from the *Disco Volante* were larger and faster than Bob's cruiser. The gap between them was closing and Bob was pretty sure they'd get to him before he made it to Boreas.

When the gap closed a bit more, one of the armed cruisers fired a plasma cannon winging the port hull of Bob's ship. A warning signal let him know and the cruiser was doing its best to evade. The blast wasn't too bad and Bob's ship, though unarmed, was built to take a hit or two.

Another blast hit near his main aft engine. Luckily not bad either, but immediately his console lit up as another battlecruiser jumped into the area. This instinctively filled him with fear, but when he pulled the image of it up on his console, it was the *Atom-Heart Mother*.

When she made her appearance hundreds of armed cruisers poured out of each ship like flies. The *Atom-Heart Mother*, perpendicular to the *Disco Volante*, fired a massive forward cannon hitting the *Disco Volante* in the upper starboard area. This vaporized several armed cruisers in the path and must have temporarily taken out a ballast as the *Disco Volante* rolled helplessly away from the blast exposing its underbelly. In the meantime a swirling mass of chaos ensued from the fighting armed cruisers between the two leviathans. The *Atom-Heart Mother* then dove downward like a submerging whale and, with a flash, disappeared, disrupting the nearby fighters in her wake. Joan had jumped somewhere else, which was odd, leaving the swarm of fighters battling it out around the damaged body of the *Disco Volante*.

The armed cruisers after Bob were not deterred by any of this. They were still on him and he had managed to dodge several blasts. The battle around the *Disco Volante* was a long ways away at this point and the chance that one of the fighters might assist Bob was out of the question. They certainly couldn't get to him in time.

A couple of shots hit the same place on Bob's ship and the hull was about 52 percent breached at that point. He couldn't take much more of this and hope to somehow get out alive. Another alarm and Bob checked back at the battle grounds. The *Atom-Heart Mother* rematerialized behind the *Disco Volante* and fired deeply into the aft engine array. There was a massive amount of glowing material and debris fragmented around the aft of the *Disco Volante* and there was little doubt that the ship was now totally disabled. Joan of Arcturus had arrived and took out ship controls, jumped somewhere else in the system, then jumped back to position herself to take out the engines. It was brilliant tactics, but also seemed very anticipated. Bob wondered if she knew this was going to happen and was thusly prepared. Bob may have been the perfect bait to take out a Diracian battlecruiser.

A couple of more blasts and Bob wasn't in the best shape. His cruiser had lost a port thruster and was having trouble maneuvering. There wasn't a lot he could do. He wanted to at least roll down the window and flip them the bird. One more hit and an loud emergency alert came from the console. His main propulsion engine had been hit and was leaking. He was close to Boreas, at a far orbital distance, but losing speed. There was no turning back so he did the only thing he could think to do. After initiating the command and going through several prompts asking him if he was certain and making sure he knew how stupid of a thing it was he was about to do, he disengaged the aft lock and ejected his engine core into space.

158

It was about to be useless anyway. The engine core, when exposed to space, spewed the nastiest volatile particulate matter everywhere. It couldn't so much damage the armed cruisers, but they were trailing close enough that the effects of the engine core disrupted their communications arrays and temporarily obscured Bob. The engine, when exposed to space, still operates until the fuel supply is exhausted, greatly accelerated, but instead of being directed by the engine containment is instead firing in all directions. It made a huge mess and undoubtedly pitted the plastiglass and forward hull of the armed cruisers.

The cruisers had to slow to avoid getting too close to the exposed core. They needed to reposition and couldn't fire until they got a clear shot or risk hitting the exposed core, having it explode, and making the problem even worse. This gave Bob just enough time to get close enough to the planet that the cruisers wouldn't follow. They, even with their willingness to destroy, wouldn't risk the interstellar backlash of armed ships entering the protected planetary space of an isolated people. That would be the surest means of getting interstellar military support for Archimedes. Human variation is universally considered a sort of sacred mission and most of these people may be isolated, but highly protected by the galactic community. Besides, they assumed Bob was about to die anyway.

The armed cruisers diverted, and turned toward the ugly scene back at the *Disco Volante*. This gave Bob a very temporary sense of relief before he considered what to do next. He was hurtling very fast directly toward the atmosphere of Boreas and because of the situation he wasn't approaching a friendly orbit by which he could slip through. No, he was about to plunge straight in. Oh, and he had no engine.

If he'd been a bit less stressed Bob might have noticed the beautiful persimmon color of Boreas against the solid blackness of space. From his position he could also see a faint lavender and aqua aurora about the northern pole.

There were several inclination and atmosphere warnings barking from the console, which Bob expected. The ship was of the opinion that he was coming in too directly and too fast for safe entry. Bob was in full agreement. When the atmosphere was hit Bob felt a shock wave as if he'd hit solid rock. Everything turned a fiery orange and the ship pitched wildly in the direction of the damaged port thruster. The ship started tumbling but managed to right itself with the remaining thrusters fully labored. He had no engine and therefore no means of propulsion, but the thrusters used to control pitch, yaw, and roll were *mostly* operational.

The ships heatsinks were completely overdriven but working to vent the excess heat from the bad atmospheric entry. Still, the temperature inside was rising and more than a little uncomfortable. Soon the ship should start cooling off naturally as it adjusted to the atmosphere, hopefully before it thoroughly cooked the inner contents.

The console issued a ground level proximity warning but there was little Bob could do about it. Without a proper engine all Bob could do was decide what orientation into the ground he'd prefer the ship to crash.

The ship's ability to assess and adapt to the situation was fairly impressive as it couldn't have been designed to work without an engine, but it did manage to get upright from the tumble, and now it was rolling starboard to attempt to change the angle of descent less directly using the starboard side thrusters. It was working. They were angling away from the direct descent and starting to move more laterally with the ground below.

Still, they were coming in way too fast and several other proximity warning sounded. Oddly, in this moment, Bob felt calm. It was a tense situation and there didn't seem to be much chance of an outcome that didn't end in death, but at this point there was absolutely nothing Bob could do to alter these events, and really, when you think about it, death is such a primitive concept.

As the ground got closer and Bob could make out features of terrain, another warning was issued from the console: *"Thirty seconds to P-PID cabin flood. Passengers should equip narwhal rebreathers at this time."* Then about a dozen compartments popped open throughout the ship.

"Holy crepes" Bob thought. P-PID is a phased polymer inertial dampening gel. It can be highly compressed and in the absence of a conductive phase signal turn from a liquid to a sort of spongy rubber, meaning it can essentially be turned on or off from a liquid to a solid. The ship was about to flood the cabin with it, which would then somewhat harden around Bob in hopes that the major force of the impact could be directed around him rather than through him. This required a device called a narwhal rebreather to prevent the subject from suffocating in a giant gelatinous blob. The rebreather attached to the nose and strapped firmly to the head. It supplied a very limited amount of oxygen by reconditioning the carbon dioxide produced by exhalation. It was called a narwhal because the device was designed to drill a narrow hole from the nose to the outside of the gelatinous blob in the event the subject was unconscious after impact.

Bob grabbed one of the rebreathers from the opened compartments, strapped it on tightly, and tried his best to centralize himself in the cabin for maximum effect. A thirty seconds to impact warning was issued, then the ten second countdown to the cabin flooding began.

160

"3...2...1"

The cabin was then flooded, surprisingly fast, with a thick transparent green goo. It was a lot like being submerged in marmalade, but then it quickly hardened to a dense rubbery and immobilizing solid.

At this point, everything was silent. The goo blocked all outside sounds and Bob was suspended helplessly within it. He could still see the console and the countdown to impact.

"15...14...13..."

When all outside noise is removed, the observer can still hear three things; a low pitched whoosh, a high pitched buzz, and a beating heart. The heartbeat is self-explanatory. The low pitched whoosh is blood flowing through the veins. The high pitched buzz is the ringing of the nervous system.

"7...6...5..."

This was all Bob could hear as he helplessly watched the approaching land, wondering what world in which he might soon find himself.

"3...2...1..."

Then all went black.

Dream Journal: Deserted City

I had found myself in a swampy wooded area...a bayou. Tall trees with trunks stained from water and it was hot here, so hot. In the distance before me was a small dilapidated shack. It looked like it had been painted red at one point but was now aged and weathered to the extent that much of the wood shone through the paint, gray and decaying. The paint itself had the look of a splattering of dried blood.

Not far away was a woman waving for me to follow. I had no idea who she was, but she almost looked like what I would have imagined my daughter looking like fully grown. I tried to get closer, but she walked as she waved me on, toward the shack.

It was then I noticed the sun. The sun was in the sky above the shack, almost directly above, and something wasn't right about it. It was bright and saffron, but not so enough to be unable look directly upon it. I couldn't get a good perspective looking at it, but it almost seemed like it was actually in the sky, like some giant fiery orb not far from the shack itself.

The woman waved a bit more determinedly like she wanted me to hurry. She did look a lot like a grown version of my daughter, which couldn't be, but there was something not right. Something was off. By the partially unhinged door she gestured for me to follow her in. The inside seemed thick with darkness, much more so than the ambient illumination should allow.

She walked in and after thinking about it for a few seconds I followed her. Inside the shack it was dark. I could see movement, which I assumed was her, and tried to get closer. I then realized that whatever dim light was allowing for the detection of movement was not coming from outside. I could see no door, no window, no slit by which light might enter.

After a moment in this darkness, a thin strand of light issued forth and I could now see that the woman had opened a door on the side opposite of our entry. She waved again and went through.

I was unprepared for what I found on the other side. We had exited the shack and were in the middle of a ruined city. The sky was cloudy and the street lined with snow. It was winter here and exceptionally cold. It didn't make any sense.

The city seemed completely deserted. The woman looked around with a sense of wonder. She was familiar with this place and found it interesting. I, on the other hand, was confused and uncomfortable.

She gestured for me to come closer and I could see her quite clearly now. She looked so much like my daughter. She then spoke in a voice that too seemed equally familiar:

"On this dark street the sun is black."

I was too stunned by the sound of her voice to respond. In that same familiar voice she continued:

"The winter life is coming back." She then pointed inquisitively to the sky.

It was at that point that I turned and notice that above the shack, in the middle of this ruined city, was that same odd sun floating inappropriately above. Here, that sun was completely, impenetrably black.

When I turned back she wasn't there and I stood alone in the middle of a ruined world.

Chapter Twelve: Bread and Circumstances.

   Bob woke up face down in a marshy, muddy wetland. He turned his head away from the ground to make breathing a bit easier. It took him a good several minutes to summon some semblance of awareness and shake off the groggy fog clouding his head. He felt very sore. There was a sharp pain in his right side. Bob was pretty sure that he had cracked a rib but nothing else seemed too bad. His head hurt, his back seemed a bit torqued, and his left leg felt as if at some point he had been forced to do the splits. He managed to make it to all fours with a good bit of groaning and felt lucky to be feeling anything at all. When it all sunk in Bob even gave a pained chuckle. He was still alive.

   Over the next twenty minutes or so Bob managed to get to a sitting position. He had definitely cracked a rib or two and breathing wasn't as fun as it could have been, but other than that, and a possible concussion, he seemed fine. The land around him was damp and brown with odd rows of long green grasses streaming here and there. They were probably growing along creeks but he couldn't tell from his current seated position.

   Another few minutes and Bob thought he should turn around toward the direction he had been flung. Following a handful of sharp pains in the ribs he sat staring down the path of destruction. The picture was pretty clear. Off in the distance he could see the wreckage of the ship. It was totally destroyed.   Small pieces littered a mile long path that lead to Bob. About halfway to Bob, at the point that the cabin had ruptured, was a mass of globby green P-PID fragments. The rubbery ball of goo that had encased Bob had broken free when the ship was in small enough pieces. It and he had tumbled violently, tearing and tumbling across the landscape until Bob had broken free and was flung into the mud. Who knew where his rebreather ended up? It probably flew off when he broke free. It was pretty amazing that he was still intact.

After pondering the aftermath Bob became aware of an odd repetitious sound that he had been hearing all along. It was a low rumble, like a large damp tree limb bending, but at regular intervals. He turned his head a bit a saw something frightening that made him wonder if he really was conscious or if he was still out of it in some capacity. Over his right shoulder, not far from him, was a very large creature, perhaps eight or nine feet in height, that resembled a giant toad. The toad had an over exaggerated mouth that was full of what looked like long, narrow, razor sharp teeth. It gave the toad the appearance that it was smiling viciously and with a comically sinister intent.

Bob did a quick system check. He was definitely awake and obviously didn't do enough research on Boreas before rushing headlong into an unknown world. When he was sure he was awake, concern for the potential seriousness of this situation made him freeze. He carefully kept the creature in his periphery and slowly, slowly checked his possessions. His EMP gun was still strapped to his thigh. He didn't grab it, but kept his hand close as he waited and observed.

The toad had massive eyes and a rough textured leathery skin. It wasn't moving, just sitting and issuing long, rumbly croaks at regular intervals. Bob didn't know what to do. He wasn't in good enough shape to run, but didn't want to fire at some creature he knew nothing about. He sat in stillness and silence for a considerable while thinking. After a moment or two, the massive toad shifted a little and slowly lumbered towards the tall grass lining a nearby creek. It had to weigh a couple of tons and moved like it was laboring to heft its own bulk. Another few lurches and the massive amphibian crept into the water of the creek lined by tall grass and was gone. Bob gave a quiet sigh of relief. It also occurred to Bob that these creeks must be considerably deeper than he would have imagined to house such a large inhabitant. Good to know in case he might have thought to wade across one. There is absolutely no telling what might lie under these waters.

Bob got to his feet and took a concerned look around. He was in the middle of some type of wetland, grass and creek crisscrossing in all directions. Everything was damp and it wasn't until now that Bob realized how terribly hot and humid this place was. He had envisioned Boreas as a rocky desert, but at least this portion of Boreas was very wet.

He couldn't see anything resembling a city or civilization anywhere around him. He might be miles and miles from civilization, and that could be bad. Probably no one on the planet knew he was here and even if someone from Archimedes had had some idea that he

survived, they couldn't risk the political fallout of going to get him.
Boreas had interstellar recognized sovereignty and isolation. Bob had no accurate way to orient himself being flung to an unknown portion of the surface, but he was guessing the time was late afternoon and he had absolutely no clue what night might bring on this planet. Would it get cold, would even more terrible creatures show up, was the water drinkable, if he had to be out here for days could he find edible food?

Looking around, everything was fairly flat. He could see these odd mounds here and there and quickly realized, when one moved, that it was more of those giant smiling toads off in the distance, maybe a dozen or so that he could see. Also, in the direction he had crashed, off some distance almost to the horizon, he could see several rocky spires. They looked like natural rock formations, but being the only feature otherwise he decided to make for that direction. Maybe there would be people in that area or at least something akin to shelter.

Bob considered going through the wreckage to see if he could find anything useful but decided against it considering most of the food onboard would have come from a replicator which was useless now and anything else would have burned in the crash. All that was left of his cruiser was charred remains. However, Bob still had the EMP gun (assuming it wasn't damaged) and a pocket knife. That was about it. He also had a sizeable tear in the seat of his trousers that in certain company would have caused a degree of self-consciousness, but not here and not now.

Bob set out toward the spires carving a path that carefully avoided the scattered toad beasts. His leg was pretty sore, but other than that soreness didn't seem to cause him any problems. His rib was definitely slowing him down though. Not only did it hurt when he breathed, it strongly encouraged him to not take too fast of a pace lest his pulse quicken and cause him to breath more often and deeper.

After a solid four hours Bob was getting close to one of the rocky spires. It was definitely a natural rock formation, but the other spires off in the distance seemed to have formations around them that might be constructed. Too hard to see from where he was. Bob had rested several times, but he was getting exhausted. The rib, the leg, the heat, and the humidity were just sucking the strength out of him.
He stopped yet again and stood a moment with his eyes closed trying to reclaim what little scrap of energy he could. A moment later Bob re-surveyed his surroundings. He hadn't seen a toad for quite a while.
It was getting darker, but not as quick as he would have guessed.
The landscape was fairly flat except for the coming spires. He would most likely need to camp at the first spire for the night, or at least for

a while. There was no way he could make it to the others without recuperating a bit. Then, as he was assessing his options, he saw in the distance before him what appeared to be the figure of a human being.

Bob froze and just watched for a moment. He could see some material move with the breeze (though a good breeze had been terribly absent from his walk). Definitely human. Not moving, but standing facing Bob's direction. Several times Bob had tried get terminal access by gently brushing his forearm, but there was no access here, or at least none he could access. He had wondered if the human off in the distance might try and communicate through terminal access, but no luck. Bob didn't know how careful he should be, but nothing about the figure before him seemed hostile and he really had little choice but to continue onward. Every other direction was endless marsh.

When Bob lumbered considerably closer he could easily tell this was a human variant, had to be Rapulis, seemingly male.
Rapulis: "Thrak ta'ka."
The greeting sounded friendly enough.
Bob: "Hello."
Rapulis, in heavy accent: "Ah. Earth tongue. Hello."

The Rapulis seemed genuine and very friendly. He had a pleasant smile and pacific disposition. It was odd, Bob thought, that he didn't look like what he had imagined. The Rapulis had some variant based on a reptilian modification, but nothing about them looked reptilian...maybe the eyes. The eyes seemed a bit larger and more reflective, a bright green, but the facial features were about the same. This man seemed to have a small and rather flat nose, but nothing unheard of in the non variant community. The only directly noticeable difference was the very pale skin tone. It was pale, but seemed almost pigmented to that hue. The clothing belied an unfamiliar culture. It was almost like cloth armor under robes. It had a kind of ecclesiastical quality to it.

Good advice to travelers would be to learn as much as you can before traveling to unknown lands. Bob was on a planet that had caught him quite by surprise.
Bob: "Hi, my name is Bob."
Rapulis: "Hi Bob, I am called Vasks. I am pleased to meet you."
Bob: "I am very pleased to meet you." Thank goodness this was going well. Bob was about at his wits end.
Vasks, smiling pleasantly: "You are hurt and moving slowly."
Bob: "Yeah, I crashed a long ways back."
Vasks: "We know. We watched you crash." and Vasks gestured to the tops of the spires.

168

Vasks: "Your ship is now debris scattered about."
Bob: "Yeah...sorry about that...I'd be happy to clean up the mess..."
Vasks: "There is no need for apologies. The debris is of no concern. We are impressed that you are alive."
Bob: "I'm a little surprised by that too."

The Rapulis gave a short grunt that Bob interpreted as a laugh. It was very brief followed by an abrupt return to his welcoming docile smile.

Vasks: "We can offer you healing. First you must meet with the clergy and be permitted entry. It is a trial. That frightens some outsiders, but it is of no concern. It is merely a formality to assess your intentions on Boreas. If you find that agreeable, I will send for a transport to take us in. Otherwise I will leave you in peace."
Bob: "Sure, I would be happy for help."

Vasks then summoned a transport via terminal access which meant they did have terminal access, just not accessible by Bob. Within minutes an unmanned transport scurried into view. It was a thin oblong disc with a depression for sitting. It was open topped and hovered inches above the ground. As it moved it made a repetitive sound similar to hands slapping the surface of the water.

Vasks politely gestured for Bob to board, which he did and set comfortably at one end. Vasks then boarded and sat opposing Bob, still with a warm and friendly smile. Once he sat, the transport scurried back toward the spires. The quickness of the transport brought a nice breeze over Bob. Sitting and knowing he was more or less out of the woods made Bob relax and the comfort washed over him. Right now, things were very pleasant.

Bob: "When I woke from the crash, there was some sort of giant toad near me."
Vask, smiling even wider: "Yes! The Great Walosi. We saw your encounter with the Great Walosi." Again, Vasks gestured to the approaching spires.
Vasks: "You had thought to reach for your weapon, but you decided better of it."
Bob: "Well, I was a bit startled by the appearance of it."
Vasks: "The Walosi are sacred to us. Had you drawn your weapon you would have found yourself most instantly dead." And again he gestured to the tops of the spires.

It was a little upsetting and didn't help that Vasks made that statement with the same genuine smile he'd been wearing the entire time.

Bob: "...uh, yeah. I didn't want to hurt it."
Vask remained wide-eyed and smiling.

Bob: "Is the Walosi dangerous, I mean, the huge fangs, it seems like it could do some serious damage."

Vasks seemed to think about it for a minute, almost like he was trying to parse the meaning. Perhaps translating the word "fangs" in his mind.

Vasks: "Oh! Fangs, teeth. They are not teeth. The Walosi have long sieves they use to filter material from the water. ...you thought they were teeth." Then he let out another short grunt Bob took as laughter.

Vasks: "The Walosi were created to filter materials from the water that are not compatible with our living. They have been here longer than us and are responsible for all life on Boreas."

Obviously another terraforming creature genetically transmogrified for a specific purpose.

Vasks: "They are harmless and friendly. You can even pet them if they let you approach. It is considered a blessing to do so."

Bob: "Ah. I think I'll pass."

Vasks let out another brief grunt.

Vasks: "Bob, are you hungry? You must be after your long walk."

Bob, famished: "Actually, I'm very hungry."

Vasks, smiling, produced a small cylinder from his robes. It was like a thermos of some sort. He opened one end and steam emerged. He then pointed the opening towards Bob and said, "please, eat."

Bob hesitantly reached, not sure what it was until he pulled it out. Inside the thermos was a beautifully baked and very fresh, steaming loaf of bread.

Looking inquisitively at the bread Bob said, "Thank you very much."

Vasks: "You have no allergies? I don't know how our physiology differs, but I would imagine it is close enough to make little difference."

Bob: "Another thing I really don't know but I'm hungry enough that I'm willing to find out."

The bread was amazing. It was probably the best bread Bob had ever eaten. Of course, he was exceptionally hungry, but he was of the opinion that even on a full stomach this bread would be at the top of his list. It was dense and earthy. There was something in it that made it seem nutritionally more significant that the bread to which he had become accustomed. The small loaf of bread was gone in practically no time.

Bob: "That was fantastic. Thank you very much."

Vasks smiled widely as they passed the first spire. The spire was an odd, twisting natural rock formation, but here he could see there were dwellings of some sort around it, etched into the rock, though no people. They obviously were heading to one of the other spires a little further away. Shortly after passing the first spire Bob looked atop and did notice a round structure most likely a security observatory. Based on Vasks's earlier comment Bob assumed they had snipers with some fairly sophisticated weaponry to be able to hit a target as far away as he had been and it was a little disconcerting that they are apparently willing to kill on site if the appropriate offense has been made.

As they approached the second spire Bob could see more and more signs of civilization. Structures that seemed like domiciles were carved into the spire and surrounding rock. The houses were hard to see from a distance because everything was the same colors as the rock, mostly sandy beige and rust. Closer still and he could see people milling about. They seemed to stop and stare when the transport passed as if there was something to see.

Vasks: "I should tell you that our world has a shared...belief system... and though we borrow from thinkers galaxy wide and do enjoy entertaining contrary philosophy for the sake of strengthening our own perspective, we do not tolerate missionaries who wish to supplant our ideologies with their own. If that is your mission here you will not be allowed access to our society and will be asked to leave."

Bob: "That is absolutely not why I'm here. Nothing to worry about there. Actually, why I am here..."

Vasks, smiling: "I am not worried in the slightest, but please, your explanation should be delivered to the clergy first. They will decide. I will be there to translate and speak on your behalf as I have been assigned."

Nearing the second spire Bob caught a nice scent riding the breeze. They were passing through a field of some type of growing grain. The ground still seemed damp, but the landscape was getting rockier and more desert like. They were going too fast for Bob to get a good look at the grain, but it seemed like a cross between wheat and rice, or like a large-grained millet. Either way, it had to be the grain from which the wonderful bread was made. Bob hoped he'd get a chance to have some more of that bread.

Beyond the second spire the land rolled downhill creating a valley between opposing plateaus and revealing a massive city. The city was rather flat, probably no structure beyond a few stories, but wide and stretching endlessly into the horizon. Everything was still roughly the color of the surrounding rock as if many of the structures had been carved into the land. There was also considerably more activity. Bob could see people, transports, ships landing and taking off, and a large central dome, the only major source of reflective metal he could see, that he assumed housed a shield generator.

Bob: "Vasks, would you mind telling me about this city?"

Vasks: "Not at all. This is Krakus. Krakus is the third largest city on Boreas. There are perhaps three million people here."

Bob: "What about the grain growing around here? That's what was in the bread, right?"

Vasks: "Yes. Cormbolt. It is a modified grain. It was bred to be highly nutritious and resistant to the climate. It is very damp here. Cormbolt is related to both Earth millet and kale."

Bob: "I was surprised that it is so humid here. Are most of the occupied lands as humid?"

Vasks: "We tend to do better in the heat and the humidity and several of our most important crops are conditioned for this environment. All of our major cities are in these temperate zones. There are, of course, a wide range of climates on Boreas. Our polar regions are quite cold and uninhabited and there are areas that you might identify as deserts. The Tark'ish Talen, or Black Valley in Earth speak, is our largest desert. It is mostly volcanic glass. Nothing grows there except for one species we have conditioned, more or less as an experiment, to help us understand the environment of the Black Valley. Much of the volcanic glass of the valley has been worn into a fine black sand that has intermingled with the trace elements of the humid air and formed an unusually sulphur rich soil. We have been growing Saguaro there, a modified type. They grow well and even produce fruit. We are trying to grow them large. Our hope is that within a few hundred years we will have them growing as tall as Earth sequoia. They are even producing oxygen, though not in significant enough amounts to be reliable yet. ...If you get an opportunity you should travel there and see it for yourself: completely black landscape as far as the eye can see, black sands and brilliant black obsidian peppered with the deep green of the cactus. Many go there to reflect or meditate."

Bob: "That sounds amazing. I would love to see it."

Vasks, as he had been the entire trip, maintained his pleasant smile.

By this time they were within the city limits. There were many more buildings and people scattered about. They were on a stone path that served as a road, but only the occasional vehicle could be seen. Most of the traffic were individuals walking to and fro. As they got closer to the thick of it the transport slowed to accommodate the large number of pedestrians in the area.

Pretty much every person they passed stopped and stared, looking directly at Bob. They seemed to be surprised and interested in his presence, almost as if caught off guard. What Bob found to be odd was how it was so apparent to them that he was anything out of the ordinary. As he had noted before, the Rapulis seemed only visibly different in very minor ways and Bob was surprised they noticed him at all. Bob supposed that when a people are isolated long enough, minor differences may seem much more obvious than would be assumed by an outsider. Bob had heard stories of ancient isolated peoples that encountered sailors from one continent to another in old Earth history. They were said to have considered the visitors gods because of their differences. This was probably never true especially since history then was written by conquerors that often behaved more like devils than even human beings, much less gods.

At this point they were fully in the town proper. Many buildings and people. More staring. Several people would stare and point at Bob and say a word that he couldn't quite make out, surely not "Earth speak" anyway. The buildings, when Bob got a good look at them, were very intricately carved, amazingly so. It seemed almost a certainty that most of these buildings were carved out of the rock of the area, but with the skill of an artist's hand. Bob really wanted to look around and hoped he'd get a chance. Too, Bob kept catching the scent of bread in the air and his tummy rumbled a bit. Periodically Bob would catch a sharp pain in his cracked rib, and his leg was swelling up some, but overall he was fine and lucky to be so.

The transport turned down a street or two before entering the courtyard of a rather formal looking building. It was a few stories tall of sandstone marbled with rust rock, rather square, but ornately carved with ornamental pillars and reliefs of scenes of which Bob had no reference for interpretation. Wide stone stairs led to the opening. This had all the markings of officialdom and of governance.

Vasks: "This is the headquarters of the clergy on Krakus. When we enter we will be escorted to the clergy chamber where they will decide on your admittance or not. You will need to leave your weapon here and anything else you might be carrying that could be considered a weapon as well."

Bob unstrapped the EMP gun, unpocketed his knife, and handed both to Vasks.

Bob: "What should I do about my razor-sharp wit?"

Vasks rolled the words around in his mind a bit then let out another short grunt that Bob was still determined to identify as laughter.

Vasks: "When we are in the chamber, it is best that I speak. I will let you know when to tell your story and I will translate. Please pace your story so I may keep up. I haven't the opportunity to translate Earth speak often."

Bob: "Absolutely."

Still, there were crowds of people staring and often pointing. Saying some word that Bob couldn't hear well from the pervading crowd noise.

They left the transport and made their way up the steps to the building entrance. It was a little slow since every step up sent a wave of pain that shot from Bob's leg up to his rib, but before long they entered the house of the clergy and Bob was yet again taken by surprise. Inside the building was the most elaborate and intricate array of glass he had ever seen. Tubes, orbs, spindly winding and reticulated tendrils crawling like some beautiful hydra in a complete prism of unimaginable colors. The entry was large and all three stories opened into this lobby. The glass lined the walls and the ceiling where natural light illuminated the hall reflecting off nearly every surface. It was dazzling. The effect seemed to be greatly amplified by the disparity between dulled tones of the outside, rock and sand, and the inside where every color imaginable was present and in wildly bright hues.

Bob, dumbfounded: "Wow."

Vasks stopped and looked, as if to process what was intriguing Bob.

Vasks: "Oh, the glass?"

Bob, almost ignoring the question: "...yes, the glass. Wow."

Vasks: "You will find practically every building and home decorated thusly, of course, each to their own tastes. We use it as a means of expressing our individuality. Each home tells the story of the family through the glass. Color, form, placement, density, all speak to the identity of the inhabitants."

Bob: "Amazing. Absolutely amazing. Breathtaking. ...is it plastiglass?"

Vasks: "No, it is all hand-blown glass. If you have the opportunity, we could visit some of the many forges where the glass is blown."

Bob, looking towards the ceiling: "Wow."

Vasks: "For now we should move on."

Down towards the end of the lobby was a desk where Vasks would ask for permission to see the council. Several people around were staring and would whisper something to those they were with. When they made it to the desk Bob finally made out the word being said.

The concierge, attending to business had not notice Bob and was caught by surprise.

Concierge: *"Mustache!"*

Two other attendants, hearing his exclamation, turned and looked at Bob. Both making the same surprised exclamation.

"Mustache. Mustache."

Vasks, to the concierge in Rapulis: "We are here to seek council with the clergy on the fate of this outlander."

Distracted, the concierge again exclaimed *"mustache!"*

Bob, in a half whisper to Vasks: "Vasks, what does *mustache* mean in Rapulis?"

Vasks: "It is the same as in Earth speak."

Bob did then realize that no one he saw had any facial hair.

The concierge performed a few actions on a terminal interface then told Vasks they would be with him shortly. Behind him the two attendants, seemingly young females, looked at each other and giggled as they both said, *"mustache. mustache."*

Entering the chamber of the clergy, Bob noticed a more subdued decor. There were several rows of benches, perhaps more like pews, and a pulpit where three individuals sat. Two of these individuals were very much like Vasks in appearance and apparel; a dense cloth like raw cotton and thick, fashioned like armor, under robes. The third individual of the clergy was very unusual. He seemed quite similar in appearance and dress, but he was significantly larger than the other two. This was not an issue of diet or minor variations in individuality, he was...big. The dimensions of his skull were probably a little over twice the size of any other Rapulis Bob had seen in his approach and travel through Krakus. He was also around twice as tall. It struck Bob as very unusual. He wondered if it was a genetic anomaly or if the Rapulis were designed to grow to that size under certain conditions, or if he was a variant of the Rapulis, a "variant of a variant" so to speak. Vasks did mention their efforts to make the Saguaro larger. Maybe that was their agenda with their own design as well.

Vasks, in a quick whisper to Bob: "Bob, the ones like me are regional clergy. The large one is Krakus clergy regent. He is called Bartok."

"Hmm..." Bob thought, *"the ones like me."*

Upon Bob's entry the two smaller clergy looked at Bob, then each other, both saying *"mustache, mustache."* Bob was starting to feel a little self-conscious about it.

Small clergy 1, in Rapulis: "Vasks, you are charged with the defense of the outsider, to act on his behalf as council and translator. Is it your will to do this freely, without coercion and to the best or your abilities for the sake of state and people?"

Vasks: "It is so my will."

Small clergy 2: "Do you now or have you had any reasonable cause to recuse yourself from this case citing legal or personal foundations?"

Vasks: "I do not."

Bartok, clergy regent, in a booming voice that startled Bob: "Then let him explain his intrusion upon Boreas and plead his case for acceptance into Rapulian society."

Vasks turned to Bob and said softly, "Go on, tell them why you are here. Go slowly so I can translate very accurately."

Bob began explaining how he came about this mission. The mysterious deaths that were found to be murders and the outbreak of a virus that has spread to many, many planets. The more he explained, the more interested they seemed to become. He told about Dr. Morris and the efforts to identify the virus and see how it adapted to variants in the human design all with the hope of finding a cure even though the purpose of the virus has not yet been identified. He then told them of the skirmish between Archimedes and Dirac and his descent to Boreas.

Bartok, in Rapulis: "I think we have plenty to make an official decree." Turning to the other two, "Is the fate of this traveler acceptance, banishment, or death?"

Fortunately for Bob he couldn't understand what they were saying and had no idea that death was on the table. Vasks just turned to Bob and with a big smile gave him a thumbs up.

After a moment of discussion the large clergyman Bartok said, "The traveler is accepted. Peace to him, to Rapulis, and to the galaxy."

Vasks translated this to Bob and gave him another thumbs up and a smile. With the formalities over, the clergy relaxed a bit and approached more informally. Each seemed eager to try their Earth speak.

Small clergy 1: "So, your mission is to rid the galaxy of a potential plague and stop a killer of people. It is a holy mission is it not?"

Bob: "Well, I don't know about that, I just want to figure out what is happening and see if I can prevent more deaths and whatever suffering might come from this virus."

Small clergy 2: "That would be noble to say the least. You find the mission to be noble?"

Bob: "...I guess I'm not comfortable with the term 'noble'. I think I just need to understand...in the interest of the common good."

Clergy 1: "You have risked death for the common good. We saw your descent. You should have been dead."

Bob: "I am a little surprised I'm still around too."

Clergy 1: "Then your mission is heroic. You are a hero?"

Bob wasn't sure if they were trying to understand his perspective or trying to fine tune their Earth speak to match their understanding. Either way, "I have never been accused of being a hero. Besides, heroes tend to produce results and so far all I've managed is to not get myself killed."

There was a round of short grunt-like laughter.

Bartok, seemingly more stoic than the others, said in a rough and heavily accented Earth speak: "What we like to define as suffering is inseparable from what we tend to define as life. Suffering and ecstasy are the magnetic poles and life is found between. The futile attempt to isolate one is to rest soundlessly in the void of death. How then do you know that what you seek is in the interest of the common good?" The large one's Earth speak was pretty sharp.

Bob: "hmm....that's a good question. I suppose I don't, but the acquisition of knowledge is the only way by which we can make an educated assumption on the probability of the common good. In that sense I am merely a messenger to communicate to those that might better make that assumption."

Bartok seemed pleased with that answer, but asked: "And if you are in a position that the assumption rests solely in your hands?"

Bob felt that the formality of the interview was over, but his assessment was ongoing. He was instinctively becoming more academic to carefully negotiate these potentially choppy waters.

Bob: "I suppose that all I could do in that case is to contemplate the good versus evil to the best of my abilities and hope the decision is just."

Bartok: "You have proven that you are willing to die for this greater good. Welcome to Boreas Bob. We hope that you find what you are looking for." Then, to the group of them. "Let us break bread."

Each then produced a similar cylindrical thermos like Vasks, opened it, and pointed the bread towards Bob.

Vasks quickly whispered to Bob, "take each one and break it in half. Offer one half back." Then Vasks pointed to indicate in which order to do this.

The bread was fantastic. Unbelievable. And whatever that thermos thing was it made the bread taste like it had just been baked.

Bartok approached Bob and came in real close to his face staring intently at his mustache. It was a bit intimidating and would have been scary if things had not gone as well as they had. The large one then said, "Hmm....it just grows right out of your face like that?" Bob uncomfortably touched his mustache and nodded.

Shortly after, the clergy, speaking in Rapulis, instructed Vasks to take Bob to the healer, then the hall of records where he could obtain samples of their genetic derivations. This was followed by a suggestion to meet with the Templars to discuss an event from some time back. They said their goodbyes and were off. Back on the transport Bob was given his few possessions back and they quickly left. On the way Bob mentioned to Vasks,

Bob: "Vasks, I didn't realize that the breaking of bread was your custom. When you offered me bread I should have broken it and offered it back to you. I apologize for that."

Vasks: "No apology is necessary. We are not beholden to our customs. We recognize that customs are merely a methodology of communication and we would not expect you to understand our customs any more than you would expect us to understand yours. The recognition you have offered speaks just as strongly, if not more so, than the custom itself."

Bob: "Thank you for your understanding and your help."

And Bob had thus broken bread with Vasks.

A bit later on the ride to the healer Bob asked: "That large clergyman...Bartok ..."

Vasks: "Yes. He is very large. He is head of clergy on Krakus."

Bob: "Yeah...Bartok. He is... uh, ...why is he so large?"

Vasks, thinking and looking puzzled: "I guess I've never thought about it. I don't know."

Which was as much of the mystery that would be solved as Bob thought it might be impolite to question further.

Their first stop, rounding a better portion of the city, was the "healer" as they put it. It was another square stone building ornately carved. Bob wondered if there would be glass inside like the clergy building or if that one was just particularly elaborate. On the ride Bob had noticed some similar glass around homes and other buildings in the area. Much more sparse outside, but spindly, often bright yellow glass corkscrewed upwards from rock gardens. It seemed organic and almost natural to the landscape, like some plant that might be native to this rocky and humid environment.

When they entered the medical facility Bob found it did indeed have as much glass as the clergy. The cacophony of shapes, tubes, orbs, spindles and spikes was similar to the clergy building though the tones were significantly different. In the building of the "healer" the overriding color was a bright white which gave the facility an appropriate astringency for some reason universally accepted as necessary for medicine. However, here and there one would find a stray piece of glass brightly colored: magenta here, deep blue there. It was proportioned enough to add interest but not compromise the larger effect of the bright white glass.

There was staring and pointing. Bob waved politely to a few people. They waved back. Vasks spoke to a receptionist who directed them promptly to a doctor's office. The doctor, seemingly female, was very polite, smiley, stared a bit at Bob's mustache, and offered another loaf of bread which Bob politely took, broke, and ate. It was good, but he was getting a little full.

The doctor produced a device that, despite minor visual differences, Bob recognized as a tissue binder. She pressed it up against his cracked rib, which smarted considerably from the pressure. The device bit slightly into the skin followed by a warming sensation as the bone mended. The doctor took this opportunity to stare quizzically at Bob's mustache. After a few minutes the doctor asked Bob how he felt. He moved his shoulder around and took a couple of deep breaths.

Bob: "Good. Good."

The doctor lifted Bob's arm a little and gave him a solid slap in the ribcage. Bob recoiled from the anticipation of pain, but in actuality it didn't hurt.

The doctor: "Nothing? No pain?"

Bob: "No. No pain."

The doctor: "Good. Now the leg."

She then produced a similar device more tailored for connective tissue as Bob's leg had an overextended tendon or two. She jabbed it into the crook of his pelvis and Bob couldn't help but let out a little giggle from the tickle, about which he instantly felt silly. A moment later and Bob was right as rain. A brief headscan showed no concussion and Bob was given a clean bill of health.

Before they left the medical facility, several other doctors and staff wanted to meet the "man from another place". There were rounds of giggled *"mustache"* and even a young staffer that wanted to touch it, upon which her hand recoiled in a round of giggles. This also was accompanied by many rounds of the breaking of bread and Bob was stuffed to the rafters.

Back on the hovering transport Bob asked Vasks if it was impolite to refuse bread because he was incapable of eating any more, to which Vasks replied: "Of course, most people carry the bread with them and eat it when they are hungry. We have all been surprised at how much bread you have eaten."

"Holy crepes" Bob thought, however, the bread was good enough that he was comfortable eating it beyond the point of satiety.

Vasks: "Before we continue with our tasks we should get you housing and rest. You must be terribly tired after this whole ordeal. We'll also see that you have some proper clothing since your torn garments are causing much giggling."

Bob had forgotten about the tear in his trousers. It *was* getting late, but it seemed the sun had been in the process of setting for hours now. Maybe they were far enough north that the sun didn't truly set...or south. Bob had no idea where they really were. He instinctively brushed his forearm to get a reading and found that he now could access Boreas terminal. Vasks seemed to see or sense Bob's surprise and offered: "Your access was granted when you were accepted by the council. It would be a good idea to peek into life on Boreas and the history of our people. I'm sure you have many questions."

Bob: "You are right about that. I looked into a bit before I came, but not near enough. Everything has caught me off guard."

Vasks: "That is the crux of it. Observation is far removed from experience. It is the difference between the illusory and the real."

Bob: "Right. I have always felt that reading into places produces a concept that is paper thin, but when you experience it, really get into it, it becomes it's own world and is then infinite. Obviously though I haven't turned that feeling into a practice. I'm pretty good at not learning lessons from my own teachings."

Vasks mulled the words of Bob's last sentence around then let out a short grunting laugh.

They pulled into a house where bread was broken, the word "mustache" was thrown about, and Bob was finally offered a room. Beautifully decorated in mostly clear glass overlapping as irregular fish scales, the home was an odd mélange of the domestic and the artistic. In Bob's room sparse glass revealed the polished rust rock of the house. Here there was a narrow mat, seemingly of the same thick cotton of their clothing, but several layers, laying on the floor and a small wooden stool upon which a pile of clothes had been folded. The clothing pile contained robes, cloth armor like the one Vask wore, several undergarments, and a burlap-like satchel. In the chaos of bread breaking Bob had pocketed a few half-loaves and decided this satchel was a much better place for them.

Bob took off his shirt and shoes and laid upon the mat. The air was still sweltering which is, in general, not conducive to sleep but with the events of this long, long day Bob was scarcely aware of his head touching the mat before succumbing to a deep slumber.

Dream Journal:
Starless and Bible Black Beauty

I found myself in a lovely pastoral open field in early winter. The marbled blue sky was clear and the season had turned the grass a dull gold. In the distance were clumps of leafless trees dark, dark brown. It was cool, but not terribly cold and roaming peacefully in the pasture were horses. There were horses in shades of browns and beige, gray, white and black. Nearest to me was a black horse whom I had noticed only in a passing scan of the world around me. When I looked closer, the black horse had a peculiar quality I couldn't readily identify. I walked closer and looked more intently where I found the horse to be amazingly dark. Abyssal. There, this horse gingerly walked and delicately grazed, but I couldn't get a visual orientation other than discerning the boundary of the world that was not the horse.

The completeness of the darkness not only refused to reflect any light, but absorbed the surrounding dimensionality of the horse leaving a flat shadow moving freely in a three dimensional world. I wanted to touch it, to see if it was a mere optical illusion, but was afraid. I was afraid I would be absorbed into the shadow of it and be lost to the void.

I stood still and quiet for a long time until grazing took the horse far, far away from me.

Chapter Thirteen:
The Glass Cyclops

Errant grain Eta-Xi-0000001 and stationary grain Chi-Gamma-00-1 have collided and are now one.

Noise purging of system issued. Grain protocol is as follows: On. Off. Then back on again.

Iso-Grain 00-Nu unexpectedly changed locations. Space-time to void interference assumed and adjustment protocol issued.

When Bob woke up he could tell he had slept for an exceptionally long time. He needed it. Recovering from injury and the strain and stress of the recent events had taken their toll. He had a vague hazy memory of eating some more of that bread in the night and a couple of missing halves from his satchel confirmed it.

The clothes he was given fit a little snug, but not too bad. He felt like they seemed natural looking on Vasks, but not so on Bob. He was a shirt and trousers kind of guy, not so much a holy robe sort.

Bob slung his bread satchel over his torso and made for the room door. It wasn't until now that he realized the gravity here was stronger than the Earth standard. Most likely he had blamed the injury to his rib and leg and his previous fatigue and hadn't realized a portion of that stress had been from a stronger gravitational field. That too might account for the long sunset if the planet was in fact a bit bigger than standard. Of course Bob was from Helen but it and most artificial worlds mimicked the gravity and cycles of old Earth. When he opened the door to exit his room Vasks was immediately on the other side.

Vasks: "Bob, you are awake."

Bob: "Yup."

Vasks: "You slept a long time. A little over twelve standard hours."

Bob: "..what? ...really? Yeah, I guess I was beat."

Vasks: "How much sleep do your people usually take?"

Bob: "ah...I usually like to get around eight. How about Rapulis?"

Vasks: "We tend to sleep several times a day, but only two or three hours at a time."

Bob: "I see. Sorry to keep you waiting."

Vasks: "No problem. Let's have some food."

Bob followed Vasks to a small dining room where several others were setting the table and finishing the preparations for food. They were very polite and welcoming though they didn't know any Earth-speak, or at least not enough to feel confident at an attempt. This must have been like an inn or a bed and breakfast kind of place. Bob wasn't sure. Maybe it was Vasks' home. The meal, breakfast for Bob, involved breaking bread (most of which Bob pocketed in his satchel after seeing the others do the same). Also, there were several varieties of small dishes, none of which Bob could identify, but all of which were quite tasty. One seemed like some sort of cured seaweed and Bob asked Vasks if there are oceans on Boreas, to which Vasks replied: "There are no oceans, but an enormous amount of water can be found in the deep crevices that crack their way through the surface of the outer regions. That is where you encountered the Walosi."
Bob: "This...", holding up a piece of the seaweed, "...is from there?"
Vasks: "Yes. It is a leafy plant that grows underwater. If you find yourself there again, I would suggest avoiding the water. It is clean and can be used for drinking, but not safe to enter. Sometimes new cracks appear and the rush of water to fill them can cause a strong downward current in nearby crevices."
Bob: "Thanks for the advice. I had avoided them initially because I was afraid the giant frog would eat me."
Several at the table snickered which meant that they understood enough to find it funny. Vasks shot a snort out as well.

Vasks: "Today we need to accomplish three things if possible. We need to visit the city Templars...that is our policing order. There was an event several years ago that might pertain to your mission. I'll tell you about it more on the way, but we need to obtain a recording device for you to take the information with you. When you leave nothing here will be accessible from your terminal. We are, necessarily so, an isolated people. We also need to visit the hall of records for you to obtain samples and sequencing of our current genome and projected transmogrification. There are several of these facilities planet wide and they are usually in places that might protect them from disasters such as war or invasion or other natural disasters. It is, after all, the map and make-up of who we are as a people and needs appropriate protection. Fortunately for us, this will take us to the Black Valley which you had mentioned wanting to see previously. Thirdly, we need to procure a small ship so you may continue with your mission. You are welcome here as long as you like but we assume you have purposes that make demands upon your time."

Bob: "That sounds great...but it also sounds like a lot to get done in one day...wait a minute, how long are the days here anyway?"

Vasks: "About 42 standard hours."

Bob: "Oh. I see. Well, that should work then. Let's get started."

They said their goodbyes, which involved more bread, and Bob and Vasks headed to the transport waiting outside. The courtyard of the house had a glass sculpture Bob hadn't notice on the way in. It was an orb composed of glass spikes, hundreds. Each spike was a deep blue with a clear tip which gave the overall appearance of something like a shimmering celestial object.

Bob: "The glass here, it's just so fantastic. I love it."

Vasks: "It wouldn't take long to see the glass forge. You could see the master at work. Even though Krakus is only the third largest city on Boreas, we have the most reputed glass master planet wide. The forge is something of a sight."

Bob, knowing he should probably move in haste, couldn't pass up such an opportunity since in all probability he would never see Boreas again in his lifetime.

Bob: "That would be super. Let's do that."

The transport scurried off. They headed for the outskirts of town in the opposite direction from the one in which Bob entered. There they made it to the great glass forge. It was an enormous production. Materials were streaming in, some in very large transports and glass was streaming out, oddly unprotected, in equally large transports. The facility was a very wide and relatively flat building. There was an outer walkway that seemed specific to visitation where they disembarked. Up a flight of steps, still exposed to the outside, Bob could see into the building that was mostly open to the outdoors. The inner portion of the building was cut into the ground and was probably three or four stories with only one protruding to the surface. Inside Bob could see a great row of massive furnaces glowing orange in the shade of the inner chamber .

Bob followed Vasks down a walkway from the observation deck to the furnace chamber. As they walked it was getting increasingly hotter, but Vask at least appeared to not notice. Bob was almost instantly sweaty.

Vasks: "Would you like to see the master?"

Bob: "Sure, of course."

Vasks: "He tends to be....cranky. He probably won't stop work and doesn't talk much. I don't think he knows Earth-speak either."

Bob: "I don't need to interfere, it's enough for me to just see the facility."

Vasks: "No problem at all. It is his nature to work. It is our nature to interfere."

Down on the furnace chamber floor there was glass everywhere, a sight Bob found to be incredible. It wasn't there on display, it was more of a workshop. There was glass being arranged and contemplated for various projects, places, and people. Hoards of people working on placement and composition. Others working around the furnace and handling long poles with molten glass at the end and everywhere there were chunks of broken glass discarded or damaged, swept into piles like mountains of glimmering irregular gems. There were probably twenty or more great furnaces and over a hundred employees working feverishly all around. The Rapulis were fond of glass.

On the floor, trying to stay out of the way as much as possible, Bob and Vasks headed towards one of the furnaces. In the overwhelming visual stimuli Bob hadn't notice that they were approaching another very large man who in all other circumstances would be severely intimidating. Vasks said something in Rapulis, rather loud to counter the noise of the workroom, and the large one turned. Vasks then turned to Bob and said, "That is Chi'huly, the glass master."

This *Chi'huly* was probably in the neighborhood of nine feet tall and was shirtless due to the intense heat of the many furnaces. Here Bob could detect a slight difference of a reptilian nature. The skin around his ribcage was less pale, ever so slightly olive in hue, and faintly scaly. However, the musculature, of which this Chi'huly had in spades, was still the familiar simian of the human design. Chi'huly's facial features seemed much more angular than the others Bob has seen and down the right side of his face, crossing his left eye, was a deep, deep scar leaving a milky white orb peering outward where a functional eye had once been. He was an imposing figure. Some worker approached and brought Chi'huly a winding glass tentacle, like many of the ones Bob had seen previously. Chi'huly inspected it with a stern face then, without a word while gritting his teeth, flung it strongly into a pile of glass debris some fifty feet away. The employee left without a word and returned to the furnace.

Bob didn't particularly want to meet him considering Vasks earlier comment of his crankiness and current evidence to the truthfulness of that statement, but Vask, smiling, was undeterred.
Vasks, to Chi'huly in Rapulis: "Chi'huly, It's been a long while."
Chi'huly, eyeing Bob, in Rapulis and a deep booming baritone: "Who's the mustache?"
Bob recognized the word 'mustache'.
Vasks: "A traveler from Sol. His name is Bob. Would you like to meet him?"
Bob, hearing his name offered a friendly wave.

Chi'huly: "Why would I want to meet him? I'm far too busy for nonsense."
Vasks, to Bob, in Earth-speak: "He is very happy to meet you Bob."
Vasks, to Chi'huly: "There is some threat that he is trying to avert and almost died getting here. He is very fond of your glass. He finds you a masterful artist."
Chi'huly to Vasks: "I have no concern of potential threats. Nor do I have time to jabber like grackles when there is work to be done. I suggest that if you both don't want to end up in one of these furnaces you leave me to my work.", at which Chi'huly left for a nearby furnace.
Vasks looks to Bob, smiles and gives a thumbs up: "He says he is very honored that you like his glass and wishes you well on your adventure."
Bob thought, "hmm...he sure is nicer than his body language suggests."
On their way back to the transport, Bob asked Vasks a question. Bob had his own idea of what the answer was, but wanted to know if it was agreed upon by Vasks.
Bob: "Vasks, I imagine that much of this glass could be made, scanned, and reformed in plastiglass."
Vasks: "Most certainly."
Bob: "What does the actual glass mean to your people?"
Vasks: "We could make it of plastiglass and it would be practically indestructible. It would require far less effort and resources, but it would also lose its beauty. There is a beauty in the effort required to make the glass. There is a beauty in the care it takes to keep it. There is a great beauty in impermanence. It is fragile. It will break and be gone. New glass will emerge."
Bob: "If it were permanent it would become background and meaningless."
Vasks: "Yes."
Bob: "Life, I imagine, is very much the same."
Vasks placed a hand on Bob's shoulder and smiled appreciating that the efforts of his people were understood.

Vasks and Bob, on their little open-aired hovering transport, were leaving the glass facility and heading toward the Black Valley. It seemed like it would make more sense to take care of the Templar business first since they were leaving the city now, but Vask suggested that the Templar building should be their last stop since it would be through them that he might get a ship and make his way off of Boreas.

They were leaving town in the exact opposite direction in which Bob had entered and as civilization receded a rocky landscape emerged. Once out of Krakus city limits, the transport sped up considerably. The land on this side was getting progressively drier and more desert like. There were smaller scrub-brushes and little desert weeds, thorny trees and now sand, the color of the rock. Here and there Bob would see something scurry off in his periphery. When he got a good look it almost seemed like really small antelope, but he couldn't get a good fix on them and Vasks didn't know what an antelope was to make a comparison. He named several things that live in the desert here, but none that seemed to describe what Bob had seen.

After about two hours on the transport a couple half-loaves of bread had gone missing from Bob's satchel and the desert started to seem more purply in hue. The landscape was darkening and the vegetation and life, what little there had been, was thinning out. Before long, maybe another twenty minutes, the desert was dark and the life was almost all gone. The sands were becoming predominantly obsidian and off in the far distance was a titan of a mountain, completely black.

Bob, pointing: "Vasks, tell me about that mountain."

Vasks: "That is Olum. It is a volcano. The largest in the entire Arcturus system and responsible for most of the obsidian of the Black Valley."

As the transport slightly changed direction Bob could see the light of the sun arc over the face of the volcano. It was black and highly reflective almost like it was encased in polished obsidian. The sands too at this point were getting darker and darker. Here and there chunks of radiant obsidian rock punctured the surface offering a glossy contrast to the flatness of the black sands. Bob had seen obsidian before, nearly everyone had, but the obsidian here was all so reflective, as if polished. Before long the blackness of the valley stretched out in all directions and they were surrounded. It was eerily beautiful and, to Bob, starkly alien. Bob could easily see why glass played such an important role in the culture of the Rapulis.

Here and there, as they traveled, Bob would see the Saguaro Vasks had mentioned earlier. The black of the sands seemed to deepen the green of the cactus. They were fairly sparse but Vasks pointed out that much further south than they would travel the Saguaro grew thick in a vast forest of cactus.

Now, in the direction they were heading, Bob saw an peculiar round object in the distance. It was too perfect to be natural, certainly constructed, but black like a natural part of the surrounding landscape. Bob thought to ask about it, but they were heading that way and he preferred the mystery of it to unfold naturally.

After a few moments the transport slowed, then stopped and they were in the presence of this massive black orb. Bob really didn't have words to even formulate a question yet. This orb left him awestruck. It was obviously a sculpture, black as night and made of glass. The orb was maybe eighty feet in diameter and sat atop a featureless glass column twenty or so feet off the ground. There was no seam, only smooth transition between orb and column suggesting they were of one piece. One solid piece. It was the oddest thing. It almost seemed dimensionless. The blackness of it absorbed enough light that it was like a standing shadow of some unseen, ethereal entity floating high above.

Vasks, seeing Bob's astonishment: "That sculpture is called Thrak Ba'las. It translates into what you probably call a 'black hole'. It is solid volcanic glass, one of our greatest glass sculptures. The engineering involved to create it was a daunting task, but eventually overcome."

Bob: "Wow. How's it....what's it..." He trailed off a bit looking at the mammoth orb.

Vasks: "It is about four hundred years old. We care for it, clean and polish it. Repair it when necessary, though that is rare. You might be surprised to know that it is just as interesting below the surface, though unseen. Below, the base fans out to an equal diameter of the orb and descends to a conical taper about twice the length of the sculpture above the surface. ...it is very stable."

Bob: "You just keep impressing me Vasks. What specifically does a black hole mean to your culture. It must have a special significance to warrant such a tribute."

Vasks: "I'm sure you know that most worlds have a special place in their language for the 'black hole' as you call it in Earth-speak. This is a subject that I am personally fascinated by. Every world is different but there is a common theme to the significance of the black hole.

 The people of Eudoxus call it the 'abiding empty'. The Mahlik people of Pascal call it the 'shadowed door'. I particularly like that one. The warring states on Meitner in the Daegus system oppose each other's definition. One side calls it the 'gods fruit' and considers it the source of penultimate creation whereas the other side calls it the 'devils fruit' and considers it the source of final demise. The Dandies call it 'oot nella' which translates to Earth-speak as 'root cellar'. Here on Boreas we call it 'thrak ba'las' or 'the deep whale'.

Bob: "The word 'thrak' was in the greeting you gave me when we met."

Vasks, surprised: "Yes, you have a good memory. 'Thrak' is 'deep'. Our greeting 'thrak ta'ka' is 'deep welcoming'. Here 'deep' is as 'deep in our heart'. 'Thrak ba'las would be a whale deep in the world of the divine. The difference is understood by context."

Bob: "So you might say that the black hole represents the divine in your culture?"

Vasks: "It is more that the cycle or transitioning is the divine element, not so much the object itself. It is the process of ever-deepening. The black hole has an oppositional role in our culture to the glass. The glass is symbolic of impermanence. The black hole is symbolic of permanence, though we know in actuality they are not. Yet for us, even a thing of permanence is temporary. If you imagine an object of absolute permanence, what is left when the impermanent universe dissolves around it? It may exist on its own, but not in the universe, not in the whole of creation which has transitioned somewhere away from it. There it would exist disembodied from reality, inaccessible and unreal, like a forgotten memory of what once might have been."

Bob spoke an old saying he was sure with which Vasks was familiar: "The stream gently bends around the immovable rock and continues unobstructed."

Vasks smiled. Bob couldn't help but be fascinated by the relationship between the black hole and the Rapulis translation of 'deep whale'. It is a haunting metaphor replete in dark oceanic imagery from a people and a planet devoid of sea and whale.

Bob had failed to noticed that not far from the orb was a staircase leading down to some underground structure. The opening was flat to ground level and not noticeable from very far away. Vasks gestured and they descended the stairs.

Vasks: "This is the hall of records. They will give you samples and code for our current and projected genetic makeup."

The doors to the underground building were impressively reinforced with several heavy locks that slid open as they approached.

Vasks: "There are many of these halls or records planet-wide. In addition to genetic information, they carry minutes of meetings, historical records, and our seed repository. These buildings are designed to survive anything this planet can muster and many, many extra-planetary threats too. Did you hear about that massive cannon the Dirac had attempted to produce? The Annie Jump Cannon?"

Bob: "I did. It sounds horrible."

Vasks: "After it was destroyed and the information was made available it was determined that a direct blast on Boreas, while destroying the entire planet, would leave the inner core of our halls of record intact floating aimlessly in the debris of our destroyed world.

The point being that even in total destruction another world could be reseeded with us."

Bob: "Let's hope that level of protection will never be necessary."

Vasks: "Yes. Let us hope."

The inside of the hall of records was actually rather plain. Hardly any glass, but the people were very nice. They had been told of a mustachioed visitor and were eager to meet Bob. There was bread braking and friendly exchanges and before long Bob was given a metal cylinder about the size of a small thermos that rolled open to reveal a series of eight metallic pipes roughly the size of pencils. In the pipes were samples of the genetic material of the Rapulis, but also of every species, plant, animal, etc. One of the pipes carried the coded information of the genetic samples. The outside of the cylinder was room temperature, but the inside was exceptionally cold. He was told that there were several redundancies to account for damage and that cross-referencing the samples against the data would produce near flawless results. This was a lot more information than Bob needed considering he would just be handing this off to someone who knew what to do with it. It was then rolled back into a cylinder and handed to Bob who put it promptly in his satchel.

Leaving the hall of records, Bob took another moment or two to take in the obsidian sculpture then he and Vasks boarded the transport heading back to Krakus.

The ride back was mostly in silence. Bob ate a little bread. It was funny that after his initial hunger from being shipwrecked he hadn't felt hungry since. There was always bread handy and even when he didn't feel like eating, he kind of felt like eating *this* bread. He surprisingly hadn't gotten sick of it, partly because it was really good, but also it was nutritious and he had been expending a lot of energy. The gravity was just a bit stronger and Bob got winded easily. Even breathing was a little labored like he was constantly under several feet of water. This and the sense memory of that first loaf, when he was famished, had protected Bob from becoming tired of the mountain of bread he had eaten in the past two days. As far as Bob was concerned, Pauly's Bread Bucket could go to hell...though admittedly he would most likely be eating there again. They were everywhere.

It was a fairly long ride and Bob had nodded off a couple of times. When he snapped out of it they were back in the outskirts of Krakus. The scent of cormbolt wafted delicately through the air. On their way through the town, onlookers would stop and point. It seemed so obvious to them that Bob was different though, save the mustache, Bob didn't really see it. They were heading toward a part of town near the third spire. Bob had seen this spire off in the distance but it appeared now they were heading straight for it. The buildings here became more densely packed and the population was concentrated. More people, more activity. It also had an air of being industrial, though there was nothing in particular that Bob could identify as such.

Vasks had said they were going to the "templar" which was like their police. There they could procure a ship to get Bob off Boreas (which was a loan as it would make its own way back when Bob was off of it). Bob had been quite aware of how well this entire trip had gone. Despite almost dying in getting to Boreas, everything else went very, very well. The Rapulis had been gracious and overly helpful. They had been warm and welcoming. If they had turned their back on Bob he probably would have died out in the wilderness. If they had fed him, but not help him get off Boreas he might have been stranded here forever. As it turned out it was a lovely visit and he had achieved his goals in really a rather timely manner. Bob expressed his gratitude to Vasks who was happy to receive his thanks.

The templar building was, in fact, cut into the spire. There was a stone ridge built around the spire demarking the boundary of the templar building. Inside the ridge were several transports like the one on which Bob and Vasks had been traveling and an assortment of other devices with which Bob was unfamiliar. Inside the dusty beige of the rock spire was again an impressive assortment of glass covering almost every surface. The glass of the templar building was in a wide spectrum of different blues and greens. Bob felt he could spend years going door to door just looking inside these buildings at this magnificent glass.

There really didn't seem to be much protocol or inspection. The door was just open and though the building was surrounded by a barrier, the ridge had many open spaces that seemed to have no particular means of closure. People at desks waved to Vasks. Everyone seemed to know him. Too, there was the stir of activity around Bob and the repetition of the word "mustache" like tree frogs at night. There was also a considerable amount of bread exchanged. It was getting a little ridiculous and Bob's satchel was plump with it, not to mention his stomach.

When the cacophony died down Bob was introduced to chief templar Rau'ta'vaara. This was obviously a police station. This Rau'ta'vaara had all the mannerisms of a police chief and even reminded Bob a bit of the Chief back on Helen...if he was still there. Bob had to remind himself that he'd really only been gone a few days but it certainly felt like months. Rau'ta'vaara was about Vasks height, but a bit huskier, older, and had more angular features. He wore similar clothing to Vasks (and now Bob), but his garments were of a dark, dark gray; almost black and had the unmistakable officialdom of a uniform.

Rau'ta'vaara, translating through Vasks: "Welcome, welcome. I am glad to finally meet you."

Bob: "Thank you. I am glad and grateful to be here."

Rau'ta'vaara: "You have caused quite a commotion. Lots of people are talking about the alien with a mustache."

Bob: "Sorry about that. I was hoping for a less dramatic entry."

Rau'ta'vaara gave a grunty laugh: "Nothing to have any concern about. Despite our isolationist policies, the people are always eager to meet those from other worlds."

Bob: "Well, I have really enjoyed my time here and find the culture and people exceptional."

Rau'ta'vaara: "That is very nice of you to say, though you might not have had the opportunity to see the darker side. It is the human condition. There is always a darker side."

Bob nodded.

Rau'ta'vaara: "On to business. I would like Mr. Bob to meet with our systems analyst. She will go over the details of the event and provide him with the proper documents to take with him."

Vasks: "Of course, after you."

Bob and Vasks followed Rau'ta'vaara to an office a few floors up. No formalities seemingly needed, Rau'ta'vaara gently opened the door and inside was a rather large room with a rather large desk. At the desk sat a slender woman.

Vasks to Bob, "This is Saari'aho. The chief systems analyst in Krakus."

Bob waved and Saari'aho waved back, businesslike but friendly. She too wore the dark uniform of the templars. There was something different about her that took Bob a moment to identify. It was her eyes. Everyone Bob had met had eyes in some shade of green. Some bright green, some dark olive green. Saari'aho's eyes were orange. A fiery orange and quite brilliant. The almost luminous quality of her eyes brought the shape of her pupils to the forefront, which were slightly elongated compared to the human standard. Bob hadn't noticed this so much in the others but, now that he looked, Vasks and Rau'ta'vaara too had the same shape.

After an exchange of niceties it was on to buisness.

Rau'ta'vaara: "Saari'aho will brief you and give you the materials you need after which she'll show you to the ship by which you may leave."

Rau'ta'vaara, through Vasks, then wished Bob peace, waved goodbye and left the office.

Saari'aho, who surprisingly spoke very fluent Earth-speak: "Bob, about three and a half standard years ago there was an unfortunate event in the outer plains near a village called Opa."

She then accessed a map that lit up the entire table top. Bob could see Krakus and far to the west the Black Valley where they had received the genetic samples. North of the Black Valley was Olum, the giant volcano Bob had seen off in the distance and further north from there was something called Yuute Rapulis territory. It was bordered on the west by the Feldspar mountains that arced northeast a good distance. Somewhere in the northern portion of the Feldspars the land turned from desert, to scrub brush, to plains. At the far, far northernmost part of the plains was the small village of Opa. It had to be somewhere around fifteen hundred miles away from Krakus.

Looking at the map it struck Bob that he didn't really know why they were viewing this village or what this had to do with him.

Saari'aho: "Here in this village we found three individuals dead. Cause of death unknown."

Vasks to Bob: "When you were explaining your mission to the clergy and mentioned the deaths on Sol, I thought it seemed strangely similar to the deaths we found here."

Bob instantly became quite concerned. This revelation had a peculiarly ominous feel to it. Yet, there is absolutely no possible way that these Rapulis could be related to the family of the murdered victims they had found so far.

Both Vasks and Saari'aho could tell this was troubling to Bob.

Saari'aho: "When the bodies were inspected, they were found to have been cored." She thought about the word a moment then offered, "Very small samples of tissue had been taken from them. Not enough to cause any serious injury, just enough to obtain a genetic makeup. Their death was brought on by means unknown to us. It seemed their hearts had been stopped."

Bob thought, "That's it. That's what it was. The guy doing these murders was obtaining samples to insure his virus would work properly across variant species. This was bad. This was really bad."

Bob, somewhat bewildered: "That was three and a half years ago?"

Saari'aho: "Yes. About three and a half."

Bob, almost overly eager: "Did you get anything, any clue about who it was? Anything at all?"

Saari'aho: "We got very little. This individual obviously struck a small village to stay away from watchful eyes. It was fortunate that we found the bodies at all and in a timely enough manner to do a proper autopsy. We did though, manage to accumulate data from a variety of satellites and observation posts. That's what I have spent a great deal of time doing is extrapolating the miniscule information

194

and attempting to generate a model of the area near the time of death. It is of poor quality, and possibly useless, but it is all that we could do considering there wasn't a visual recording device within two hundred miles of the village."

She then displayed, upon the surface of the table, a grainy grayscale video of a small ship taking off from the village of Opa. The image could be rotated a bit to get a sense of the dimensionality, but much of the data was missing or incomplete. However, despite the poor quality Bob could easily identify the *type* of ship."

Bob sat with his right hand over his mouth for a moment, then said: "It's a small medical transport."

Saari'aho, eyes lighting up a bit: "This might be helpful then?"

Bob, after another moment of thinking: "...yes. I think it could be. There are countless numbers of medical transports just like this, but in theory they should all be accounted for."

After another moment of silence Bob said, "Can I get a copy of this information and anything you have on the dead of Opa village?"

Saari'aho slid a metallic stick to Bob, much like the ones inside the cylinder from the hall of records.

Saari'aho: "It's all there. Everything we know about that event. There are no other known cases bearing any similarity."

Bob: "Ok. I am guessing this means that whoever has engineered this virus has made sure it is communicable across human variation. Since the Rapulis have a policy of isolation it should not be a problem, but I would still be very careful and cautious with outsiders until we figure out more about what's going on."

Saari'aho, with an analytical eye: "How do we know you are not infected with the virus?"

Bob, remembering the pain, rubbed his chest and said, "They shot some damn thing into me. At any time if I become infected I will not be permitted to continue with my mission. They know, somehow."

That seemed to satisfy her, though really it was a moot point because had he been infected the damage would have already been done.

Up to this point Bob had almost been in vacation mode. He had been having a good time...minus the almost dying bit. He had even felt he might hang around a few more days and get to know this world a bit better, but this information snapped him back to reality. There was some serious agenda being thrust upon the galaxy and he needed to get moving. There was no way this situation would get better with him sitting around eating bread.

Bob: "I think I need to get moving. I need to get this information to people who can analyze it and hopefully figure out what's happening."

Vasks: "We assumed as much. The ship is waiting for you outside whenever you are ready to leave."

Bob to both: "Thank you for the information. This could be a turning point for us. Thank you for all of your help and for letting me borrow a ship."

Saari'aho: "It was a pleasure."

As Bob and Vasks left the office Bob said to Vasks, "I can't thank you enough. You have been wonderful and helpful and kind. Thank you Vasks."

Vasks: "It was my honor. I hope that we meet again in this world and if not here, then surely the next. You are, of course, welcome here any time."

Bob: "I would genuinely love to come back for a proper visit in the near future."

Stepping out of the templar building and into the shadow of the spire Bob took a look around, at the sky, the land, the people milling about. It really was a nice place. He then looked around his immediate surroundings and noticed it seemed rather bare.

Bob, still looking around: "So...where is this ship I've been allowed to borrow?"

Vasks: "It is here, beside the building."

Bob still looked but didn't see what he was talking about. "Where?"

Vasks, amused: "Here."

Vasks was pointing to something Bob hadn't even considered to be a ship. It was propped up against the building and ridiculously small.

Bob, pointing: "that?"

Vasks, seeming joyfully confused at Bob's questioning, "that."

Bob, thinking loud enough that surely it could be heard, "*you've got to be kidding me! What the hell is it?*"

The ship was about four feet tall, basically a single engine, like the pulse engine on the ornithopter he had used around Helen, above which was a small, oh so small dome. It was propped up on four pencil thin metal rods emanating from the dome chamber. He would basically be sitting on top of an ornithopter engine.

Bob, thinking: "*I'm supposed to ride this thing through space?*"

Vasks looked at Bob, then at the ship, then back a Bob, who remained silent.

Bob, finally getting a word out, "...and...and it goes into space?"

Vasks gave a short grunting laugh, "of course."

Bob had to collect himself. Bewildered, he thought to himself again, "it looks like an ice-cream cone."

Bob was not happy. He was grateful, but this seemed like a carnival ride or a kids toy. It didn't seem like a vessel to cross the void of space and it didn't seem safe...at all. He had never even heard of such a thing.

Bob: "...this will get me..", pointing skyward, "out there?"

Vasks: "It is a little slow, but it will speed up when you leave the atmosphere. It's a little sluggish in something as thick as air."

Bob: "it will....I guess it will take some time then...to get...someplace?"

Bob didn't even really know what he would do when he got off Boreas. Where would he go? He'd have to meet with a jump-ship somehow. Could he get in touch with the Arcturians? Would he get shot down again by Dirac? Bob's stomach started to churn.

Vasks: "You shouldn't have to worry about attack. Neither Archimedes or Dirac would be willing to risk the backlash of interfering with a Rapulis vessel. You should be safe."

Bob, thinking and thinking, "I suppose, if I'm going to be in this thing for a while, I might ought to use the bathroom before I go."

Vasks showed him to the facilities back in the templar building. Inside the bathroom it was small and cool. The toilet was one of those flat to the ground affairs where the participant squatted over. Bob, thinking, *What else can I do? There are no other options. I can't call for a ship. I can't make one myself and admittedly I haven't seen any significant air transport the entire time I've been on Boreas. These are an isolated people and not a spacefaring culture.* Splashing a little water on his face, Bob decided to just go with it. There were no other options and he needed to get back.

Outside, by the ship, Vasks was waiting along with several of the staff and passersby that had caught wind of what was going on. They were eager to bid farewell to the strange mustachioed visitor. Seeing the ship again assaulted a good portion of the confidence he tried to muster while in the bathroom. Bob kept thinking, *you have got be kidding me!* But he put on a brave face, was thankful to everyone yet again, and crawled up a short wooden stepladder into the chamber of the ship which had been popped open for his entry.

There really wasn't much of a seat. There was a raised portion of the floorboard that really had more to do with the shape of the engine than anything else. Bob did his best to sit upon it with his legs folded up around his chest as the difference between his "seat" and the floorboard was about three or four inches. Looking around, he wasn't sure how the dome was going to fit over him. Yet again Bob thought, *this has got to be some kind of joke!*.

Vasks had been holding Bob's satchel for him, which was overloaded with bread and information. Now Vasks was trying to position it back on Bob's lap, which was far too folded to hold a thing.

With a little shoving and a bit of repositioning on Bob's part, the satchel made it on board with only partial visual obstruction.

Vasks: "Bob, we have a gift we would like for you to have. It is our custom in bridging the gap between cultures to offer a record of our history and our philosophy to our neighbors. We have used this to show a shared commonality between people of different territories. For us it is a way of showing union with people we might have at one time considered different from us."

Bob was too distracted to catch all of what Vasks was saying. He just kept thinking *"I'm about to go into space like this?"*

Vasks: "We have been working for some time now on an Earth-speak version of the Rapulis Tome and we would like you to have it."

Bob, distracted, but knowing the right thing to say: "That is very nice Vasks. I really appreciate it."

Then Bob was handed a book. An actual book made of paper, or something like paper, which was almost a foot thick. It was wide too. It was practically a cube and was heavy.

Bob couldn't help it. He knew this was a meaningful gesture but just thought to himself *"where the hell am I supposed to put this?!"*

Vasks manhandled the massive book and managed to wedge it to the side of the satchel partially obstructing the other side of Bob's vision. He seriously hoped they didn't have anything else to give him as it would surely have to be taken internally.

Then the dome was hinged back over in an attempt to close the ship. It wouldn't close.

There was poking and prodding, a suggestion that if the book was angled a bit more, if the satchel could go down a bit further...could he angle his shoulders like this, like that.

Vasks, "Maybe if you suck in your tummy some? Just a little?"

And the dome latched and sealed.

Vasks, muffled through the glass, "Can you breath ok?"

Bob thought about it, seemed he could though it was tight, and gave a little nod.

Bob had a brief feeling that this couldn't really be happening. He must have fallen asleep and this is one of those dreams people have where everything is ridiculous. When the engine started powering up he knew it was real. The thing was shaking and vibrating. Bob looked out at the crowd, all of which gave a heartfelt wave and Vasks saw sadness in the eyes of Bob that he mistook for sentimentality, but which was in actuality the fear of death setting in.

Bob, thinking to himself yet again, *"please let this be some kind of joke!"*

Then the engine began making a pulsing, ornithopter sound and Bob knew it was about to lift off. Immediately he was struck by another fear, tapped the dome with a fairly immobile finger then said to Vasks hurriedly, "Is this plastiglass or actual glass?"

Vasks cocked his head to hear better.

Bob, louder: "Is this plastiglass or actual glass?!"

Vasks made a gesture around his right ear signaling that he couldn't hear him, then the ship slowly rose from the ground.

At first it pitched side to side which upset the already nervous butterflies in Bob's stomach, but then it managed to stabilize and seemed to go, more or less, straight up.

There, in the sky, Bob was squished into a space ice-cream cone on the verge of a panic attack. The only thing keeping him together was that he couldn't decide if this whole thing made him more frightful or incredulous.

Bob also wondered how he would get anywhere. This thing seemed incredibly slow. How long would it be before someone found him. Would he be able to get a signal out, was it programmed to do so. He realized, yet again, he didn't ask enough questions before it was too late.

"How slow is this thing?" Bob torqued his head to see if he could eyeball the ground.

"Oh holy crepes" it had been several minutes and he could still make out their faces, their waving and seemingly cheerful faces.

Bob wasn't nearly as nervous when getting to Boreas he knew, he *knew* his ship was going to crash. This situation was, to Bob, an unbridled nightmare.

It was somewhere around a good half-hour before the little ship made its way out of the atmosphere and Bob once again found himself in the blackness of space.

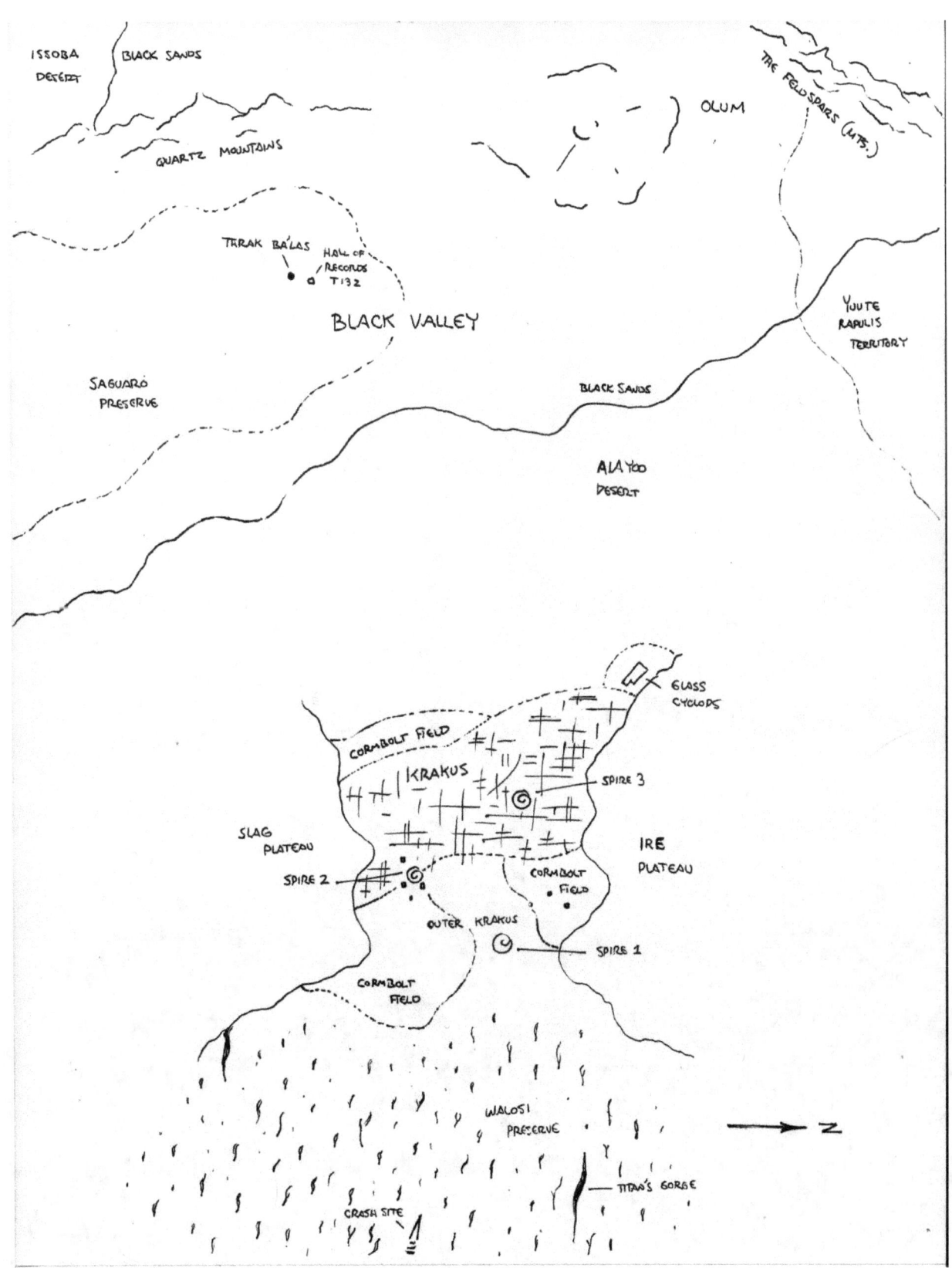

ISSOBA
DESERT

BLACK SANDS

QUARTZ MOUNTAINS

THE FELD SPARS (MTS.)

OLUM

TERAK BA'LAS

HALL OF
RECORDS
T 132

BLACK VALLEY

YUUTE
RAPULIS
TERRITORY

SAGUARO
PRESERVE

BLACK SANDS

ALA YOO
DESERT

GLASS
CYCLOPS

CORMBOLT FIELD

KRAKUS

SPIRE 3

SLAG
PLATEAU

IRE
PLATEAU

SPIRE 2

CORMBOLT
FIELD

OUTER KRAKUS

SPIRE 1

CORMBOLT
FIELD

N

WALOSI
PRESERVE

TITAN'S GORGE

CRASH SITE

201

Chapter Fourteen:
The Cloud Miners

The cloud miners are one of the oldest known guilds still active with chapters and widespread operations functioning in practically every know galactic system. The cloud miners began in the distant, distant past when human life existed only on Sol. As life spread from Earth to the surrounding planets, material requisition was a top priority, the chief material needed often being water. As early inhabitants of Sol began preparations for extra-solar colonization, the cloud miners were developed to acquire the water and other materials needed for what was then considered distant travel. At that time the chief occupation of a cloud miner was to collect water from the Oort cloud, a vast bubble of countless icy comets encircling the outer regions of the Sol system. Early on, the job of reclaiming water from the Oort cloud was an independent venture on the part of individuals, but as the need for organization grew a guild was formed that provided order and safety to the cloud miners of ancient Sol. The guild, the Oort Cloud Hierarchy of Requisition Employment, or OCHRE, quickly became a considerable regional power and to this very day, though scattered across the galaxy, all individuals legally employed in cloud mining are members of the OCHRE guild.

In modern times a cloud miner's job is very different. Most water acquisition of solar debris fields is left to the associated stellar authority and is by them thus regulated. Modern cloud miners have moved into larger scale material acquisition, mostly of nebulae, nova remnants, and deep field particulates. They now reclaim everything from minerals to weakly interacting massive particles. Are you running low on neutrinos? The cloud miners can help. Did your tachyons get away from you, as they are want to do? The cloud miners can help. Did your Fermions ferment? Would you like a heaping handful of Higgs Bosons? The cloud miners can help.

The standard cloud mining vessel looks like a somewhat flattened battlecruiser. It is oblong with a seamed hull and usually has a crew of several hundred. They all have jump capabilities which means they have to be quite large, but rarely suspension fields since shielding a large ship requires an enormous suspension field generator and the bulk of the cloud miner's vessel is needed for cargo.

To see a cloud miner in action is a curious thing. Imagine you are in the prismatic pastel cloud of a nebula. Suddenly the gentle swirling hues surrounding you are displaced as an oblong ship has made a warbly jump into the middle of the nebula. It silently moves and seems to leave a glimmering trail behind as some *thing* protrudes from its aft eventually doubling the length of the vessel. Before long the ship has the appearance of some single-celled organism with a long flagellum. Slowly, very slowly, the flagellum expands. It opens like a gargantuan fish fin of a beautiful copper color. This is the particle collector. Depending on what particle or particles are being collected you may notice a gradual drifting of the ship as it sifts through the glowing material of the great cloud. Some deep field particle collection requires a great expanse of sparsely mattered space as the interaction of light and gravity can interfere with the collection. In these cases the cloud miners may travel to distant and dark portions of the galaxy, away from stars or nebula of any kind. Here, in the isolated blackness, the same process commences, but the flagellum might extend eight to ten times the length of the ship and open to an almost complete circle. The ship, with only a skeleton crew, will remain motionless for several weeks at a time to catch those particles that seem to wish not to be caught. These deep field particle collector ships have a modified internal compartment that isolates the small crew. It dampens any vibration and shields against the stray emissions of the life support systems. During this time the crew is limited in activity and unable to use artificial light that might interfere with the collection. You may be thinking to yourself "They are away from stars in the total blackness of space. They can't use lights. Do they have to live in total darkness for weeks at a time until the collection is finished?" No. They have found a wondrous invention that permits light but does not interfere with the collection process. That invention? Wax candles. The candle, apparently used by early humans to provide light, make a waxy mess, and occasionally engulf dwellings in flame, has become a primary staple of the deep field cloud miners allowing them to carry out such activities as reading paper books and knowing to whom they are speaking.

About the time Bob was busy crashing an engineless cruiser into the surface of Boreas, a fairly routine cloud mining operation and crew was dispatched to Caduceus IC-4634, a nebula very close to the galactic center, but hovering considerably above the galactic plane leaving it isolated and alone in the dark. Caduceus is a beautiful dying star that is ejecting and illuminating the surrounding material producing a delicate palette of fuchsia and royal blue. It is far too violent to be inhabited as it is in the final stages of self-destruction which is unfortunate as the position of the nebula is almost a perfect observational point to view the milky way. It's as if one could remain in the nebula and watch the galaxy in all of its majesty swirl onward everlasting.

It was here that something was spotted. Something that shouldn't have been spotted. It was a fluke, an odd chance out between two worlds. Not far from the nebula, not far in astronomical terms, a momentary blip appeared on the cloud miners sensors. A trifle, a little nothing. It would have gone unnoticed except for the fact that nothing in that area should have been readable by the cloud miner's sensors. This area was outside of the nebula a bit more towards the galactic center but higher above the galactic plane. In this area though, there really should be nothing, nothing outside of the nebula save the occasional debris or errant rock slung wayward in ancient times.

Lieutenant BerK had served as communications officer aboard the cloud mining vessel *The Candle Wolf*, for eight years. It was all routine and rarely was there anything unexpected. He almost, *almost* let it go thinking it had to be nothing. Instead, he ran another sweep of the area, fine-tuned some of the parameters, and once some information came in he filtered the spectrum for the probable composition of the unknown object. It was odd. Whatever it was, it was a little bigger than a person and surprisingly dense for its size. It seemed highly reflective too. It appears the initial reading was light from the galactic core reflecting off the object directly at the ship, which at these distances would be like a person with a handheld mirror on Earth reflecting sunlight at the moon and someone there seeing it with their naked eyes.

Lieutenant BerK spoke to the captain and told him what he found. After a series of refined measurements it was determined that the object was cylindrical which almost assuredly meant human made yet it was nowhere near an inhabited world.

Captain: "You're sure it's not just debris of some sort?"

BerK: "Yes. It is manufactured and the material isn't identifiable...yet."

Captain, interested: "Unidentifiable....hmm...interesting."

BerK: "We could go check it out...after the collection of course."

Captain, somewhat lost in thought: "Is it moving?"

BerK: "No sir. It is stationary with respect to the galactic plane."

Captain: "If it was an accident, or a wreck, it would be moving."

BerK: "Yes. Whatever it is, it was placed there and not intended to move."

Captain: "Let me think about it. We'll decide what to do after the collection."

BerK: "Yes sir."

One has to understand the nature of a cloud miner. Most other occupations would employ people who would not care about an unknown, especially one that didn't involve them or their mission. Cloud miners on the other hand live in a world of material acquisition. They are rewarded for what they find and what they bring back. They are explorers and by nature curious. To be otherwise would be to work in a field that was contrary to one's personality. This curiosity would get the better of the captain and of the crew and they would find something with which they wouldn't know what to do.

After the collection was complete the *Candle Wolf* and crew made a jump, a small jump to the area of the mysterious unknown. They then sent a small cruiser, led by Lieutenant Berk, to collect the object. The closer they came, the more unusual the readings. Berk had assumed that once they got close the material would be identified, assuming the problem was the distance and some unknown interference, but here they were in visual range and the sensors still didn't know what to make of it. It didn't radiate anything dangerous, seemed safe, so they carefully slid the object into the cargo hold of the cruiser, which was no small task considering the object was very oddly slippery.

BerK: "Sir...I'm not sure what we've got here."
Captain, receiving a visual: "..."
BerK: "Should we bring it aboard?"
Captain: "I don't know."
BerK: "Should...should we put it back?"
Captain: "...I...ah hell, we should've left well enough alone."
BerK: "Sir?"
Captain: "Yes, bring it aboard. We'll take it to some nearby authority. Let them deal with it."

Brought on board the *Candle Wolf* was a peculiar cylinder made of glass, crystal clear and perfect in every way. In the center of the cylinder, clear and motionless, was the still body of a man, a man that just moments ago had in death been floating aimlessly in the opaque clarity of blackest space.

They decided to take it to a nearby system, which was really not nearby, but the closest developed system to the found object. The system was known as Bohr. Bohr was a yellow sun approximately equivalent in size to Sol. Orbiting were six standard planets and one gas giant. The main authoritative body was a planet named Diophantus. Diophantus was home to about seven billion people. Diophantus exists in relative peace. There are concerns of their rapidly growing military-industrial complex and scholars have speculated that at the current trajectory Diophantus could devolve into chaos within the next two hundred years. However, there is plenty of time to alter this course and the efforts of the populace to do just that have been on the rise. The promise of the military-industrial complex is perpetual war and war is rarely undertaken of necessity, but rather greed, childish pettiness, and sometimes a sickening blood lust.

Diophantus is a highly mechanized and modern world. There are three main continents divided into dozens of nations, yet the ruling house carries overriding authority over all. That ruling house is stationed at the planetary capital of Ikaros. It was here in the light of Bohr that the *Candle Wolf* made a jump to a distant orbit around Diophantus. Contacting the authorities of Ikaros and awaiting permission, the *Candle Wolf* sent a small craft carrying the odd artifact where it was so received by armed men in uniform. There they would study it and attempt to identify the body, which shouldn't take long.

After the transfer Lieutenant BerK made his way back to the *Candle Wolf* to forget the whole affair, completely unaware that the gift he gave to the people of Ikaros would soon bring upon them the specter of creeping death.

Chapter Fifteen:
Return of the Arcturians

Bob, stuck in his little ice-cream cone cruiser, had been floating for what seemed like ages. It had to have been seven or eight hours so far and his legs had fallen asleep a good four hours back. He might know for sure if he could see the exceptionally small console, but his vision was blocked by a ridiculously large paper book and a spongy bag of bread.

All he could see around him was total blackness. He wanted to see if Boreas was still visible, maybe get some idea of how fast he was going, but as he was presumably traveling away from it, it was behind him and out of view. It was just as well. If he looked back and could still make them out, waving, the disheartening effect would be enough to kill him on the spot. In actuality though, he was far enough away that Boreas wasn't even visible as a point of light.

Bob wasn't sure he'd ever be found. If he thought about it too much it would cause him some anxiety. Also, there were several other things that bothered him. He could see, out his little bubbled dome, several frozen droplets on the glass. Was that something that was there already, or was some of the very moist air of his ship leaking out? Troubling. It also bothered him that the dome was held in place by a mechanical hand-latch that was near his right knee. Was that the only thing securing the dome and keeping him from the vacuum of space? He had to shift around, what little he could, to try and avoid rigor mortis and he was afraid he'd knock that latch open and his story would be done. Surely there was some other precautionary measure sealing the dome...right? Also, there was a little fan somewhere around his left side, behind him, that sounded like it had a bearing going out. It would sometimes grind and then be fine for a while, then buzz, then grind some more. It had to be part of the life-support system. If the fan went out would that be fine? Would he lose life-support? He could also feel a little, almost unnoticeable tug, a little change in momentum, and Bob thought the ship might be slowly tumbling instead of traveling a perfectly straight path. The good thing for Bob was that he'd been out here so long that he had gotten tired of being anxious and was occupying his mind with other things, like the excruciating pain of being folded tightly into this little space coffin.

Bob was being watched. Far, far away, well beyond visual range, was a mammoth battlecruiser called the *Atom-Heart Mother*.

Joan of Arcturus had detected his little ship, which was, by the way, emitting a location signal, and had summoned his image on her main display screen which stood before her like a false window peering out of the battlecruiser. Joan had been counseling a young woman that was interning aboard the *Atom-Heart Mother*. Though her duties were primarily tactical she was very aware of the effects of morale to the efficiency and fluidity of ship operations and routinely assessed the mental state of her immediate crew. The young woman had been having trouble meeting people, especially a particular woman that worked in engineering and Joan was discussing the issue with her. Young woman: "I guess I just can't seem to get her attention. I say 'hi', then I don't know what to say next. I kind of clam up because I wonder if I'm imposing because surely she can't really want to talk to me and then I think, 'well, what if I just....'"

When Joan had pulled up the image of Bob, in that little ship, crammed in and fogging up the dome in front of him with his breath...she got the giggles. The sight was unbelievable and the look on Bob's face...a combination of dread and weariness, was almost too much for her to take. She was on the verge of laughing out loud. She managed a short sentence to the young woman, "I'm sorry to interrupt you, but something has come up that I need to deal with immediately."

The young woman nodded and left the chamber. Joan stood there for several minutes looking at the screen, the image of Bob in that ship in the middle of nowhere. With arms folded and one hand obscuring her mouth, her face clenched in silent giggles as she tried to maintain her composure. The whole situation she found very entertaining. Without turning her attention from the screen, Joan of Arcturus spoke to the navigator quickly to avoid a giggle: "We'll go pick him up. Now."

To which the navigator replied, "Yes sir."

The propulsion engines of the *Atom-Heart Mother* flared and, within minutes, crossed a distance that would have taken Bob at least four or five more hours, and yes, the little ship Bob found himself crammed into was in fact making lazy circles as it tumbled onward...a very inefficient way to travel.

Bob heard a beeping. Some alarm that stirred him from his half slumber. He attempted to look at the console, but it was still obscured by his many possessions aboard what he had lately been referring to as the "space urn". In Bob's numerous hours on this tiny toy spaceship it had, in his mind, gone through several name changes none of which were flattering.

When he couldn't see the console he instinctively looked outward to see if anything was in visual range. The dome was fogging

209

up a bit but he wiped it clear the best he could. As his ship rolled into position (affirming that he was in fact tumbling) he could see some fuzzy object off in the distance growing larger. It was a ship and at this point Bob didn't care if it was Archimedes or Dirac. Bob knew they wouldn't fire upon a Rapulis vessel and political imprisonment in a small cell didn't sound so bad right now. The idea of stretching out and lying flat would be a welcome luxury.

"This is the Atom-Heart Mother requesting docking of the Rapulis vessel." The voice was of some docking station lieutenant, formal and regimented.

"Oh thank goodness", Bob thought, then said: "Yes, yes, please. Please get me out of this thing."

Silence.

There must have been some control for sending a signal, but Bob couldn't see or find it.

"This is the Atom-Heart Mother requesting docking of the Rapulis vessel."

"Holy crepes". Bob smashed around on the console area...which on second thought might not be a good idea and again said: "Yes, please get me out of this tin can!"

Joan, from command and looking at the terminal screen could see him saying all sorts of things but nobody could hear anything, which made her giggle all the more.

Joan: "Just go get him. We don't need his permission."

To which the docking lieutenant replied, "Yes sir."

Shortly after the order a small tactical cruiser left the docking bay. Bob's ship was tumbling and arcing in large circles, so it needed to be escorted in. Since Bob had no control over it, and it didn't seem to have any overridable controls, the tactical cruiser, turning the setting to the lowest value possible, fired a low-level electromagnetic pulse at the little ship. Bob didn't know what it was but felt a thud and then his ship went dead. He wasn't too concerned since he was about to be free, but it did instantly start getting colder.

The tactical cruiser then caught Bob in a graviton field and towed him into the docking bay. The graviton field, by the way, was almost identical to the technology used to create artificial gravity. More information can be found in the resources of the FGL.

Bob was greatly relieved that this was about over, but the last few minutes were almost unbearable. It was knowing he was about to get out of this thing with a body that had physically been ready to get out many hours ago. Also, he had to use the bathroom pretty badly.

The little ship tumbled as it was towed and when the tactical cruiser docked, the lieutenant had to get out and rotate Bob's ship by hand in the graviton field so it would set upright. It happened to be the same lieutenant that greeted Bob on his first visit to the *Atom-Heart Mother*. The young woman, stoic and straight face, didn't reveal in the slightest the level of ridiculousness she found in Bob's ship and his situation.

With the ship upright and proper, she looked around the dome to inspect how it might open. Bob quickly lifted the latch he'd been nervous about earlier, but nothing happened. Mystery solved. He lifted it up and down a couple more times with no effect.
The lieutenant, muffled through the dome: "Maybe there is a release control on the console?"
Bob: "What?"
Lieutenant: "A release control? On the console?"
Bob couldn't see the console, but mashed his hand down on it. Nothing.
Bob: "I can't tell."
Lieutenant: "Can you move some of that stuff out of the way?"
Bob rolled his eyes. This was unbearable.

The lieutenant went to a wall mount and grabbed a device. She was attempting to read the ships systems and find an override. After a moment there was a pop and the sound of a seal breaking. At the sound Bob pulled up on the previously worrisome latch and the dome hinged open. A moist and rather unpleasant fog escaped the little craft.
Bob: "Oh thank goodness, oh thank goodness."

He still couldn't get out. He discarded the book which fell in an echoing thud and tossed the bread sack to fall where it may. He hefted his bulk up with his arms but his legs were so very asleep that they offered no support. The little ship torqued around and wobbled at his movements.
Lieutenant: "Maybe if we lay the ship down you can crawl out?"
Bob: "...well, yeah, ...I guess so."
She gave a whistle and a cadet rushed in and helped her lift the craft and lay it sideways on the ground.

Bob emerged from the ship like some helpless pupa from a mud dauber's nest. He laid there momentarily and straightened his back which offered the necessary excruciating pain that was appropriate for his situation, but a pain that carried a strong relief in it. After long absent blood had started to return to his legs, he managed to get to his feet with some help and the lieutenant slowly escorted him toward empty quarters where he might shower, rest, and regain a bit of his composure. The cadet collected Bob's possessions and brought them along as Bob walked slowly and awkwardly, a kind of hunched over crab walk, to the luxury of modest crew quarters.

Back at the little Rapulis vessel, two other crew members were inspecting the ship. They managed to bring it back on line which made it instantly want to putter around the docking bay but they shut the engines off and accessed and translated the console. Soon they had programmed the return trip and hoisted it to a small airlock. Upon decompression the little ship was sucked into space and began sputtering and tumbling making lazy circles on its very long voyage back to Boreas. Bob didn't see it leave, but would be very glad to hear it was gone.

Back at ships command Joan issued a handful of orders.

Joan: "Send a message to his boss, the one he calls 'Chief' and let him know we have him and he's fine. I'm sure they'll need to communicate so we should start that process now. Also, when he is rested, schedule a meeting between him and I. Other than that, set course to Curie then Archimedes and continue routine operations."

Navigator: "Yes, sir."

Some indeterminate time later Bob woke up on a cot in what must have been an empty cadet quarter. A bit disoriented, it took him a moment to realize where he was and what was going on. He vaguely remembered entering into the room, using the toilet, and painfully stretching out on the cot. He let out a groan or two before falling asleep hard. He wasn't sure how long he'd been asleep, but figured the crew didn't mind him tagging along or they would've woken him and kicked him out. "Oh, I hope they incinerated that wretched ship", Bob thought, but then he reconsidered. It was a nightmare, but the little ship had gotten him, somehow, safely off Boreas and onto a battlecruiser. As long as he never had to get in that thing again he thought he might could find a crumb of gratitude. Afterall, he *was* still alive.

Bob sat up on the cot and bolts of pain shot through his back and legs. He stood and carefully did a few gentle stretches that hurt but were helpful, then he hit the shower. A warm shower helped a lot. Afterwards he was loosened up a bit and considerably less musty. His walk was a little gimpy, but much less crablike than before.

Perhaps anticipating what would have been a request, there was a stack of plain clothes in his size on the desk near the cot. They were similar to the clothes the cadet was wearing, but without any insignia or ranking. It felt good to be out of the cloth armor and robes of the Rapulis. Also, on the desk was the enormous book Vasks had given him and the satchel of bread that surely must be stale. He'd deal with that stuff later if at all.

After a few more stretches Bob left the quarters to find the receiving lieutenant standing guard outside.

Lieutenant: "Hi, I hope you slept well. Were the accommodations to your liking?"

Bob: "Yes, thank you. ...Lieutenant Walker, right?"

Lieutenant Walker: "Yes! You have a good memory."

Bob: "Well, I guess it was only a few days ago, though it has felt like years."

Bob: "....what...what actually is the date?"

Lieutenant Walker brushed her right forearm and summoned a display. She then swirled the air above her forearm with her left hand causing the display to rotate and face Bob.

Bob: "That can't be right. I've been gone about six days?"

The lieutenant smiled and shrugged her shoulders. Bob was looking skyward to make his calculations.

Bob: "I was here, then took the cruiser to Boreas...and crashed. When I woke I walked for several hours, then met Vasks, clergy, all that bread....slept a long time. Did a bunch of things the next day, then left Boreas."

Lieutenant Walker seemed a little bored.

Bob: "I was in the ice-cream cone for...ten hours? Not sure. I know the days are longer on Boreas, Vasks said something like 42 standard hours...It all gets me to about four days...I guess I don't know how long I was knocked out after the crash. Not sure exactly how long I slept on Boreas...maybe twelve hours..."

Lieutenant Walker: "You were in the cadet quarters a little over twelve hours."

Bob: "Goodness. Yeah, I guess that's somewhere in the neighborhood."

Lieutenant Walker: "The General would like audience with you when you have adequately recuperated."

Bob: "Joan? Joan of Arcturus?"

Lieutenant Walker: "Of course."

Bob: "Sure."

Lieutenant Walker: "She is in a meeting now, but will be free in about an hour."

Bob: "That'd be great."

Lieutenant Walker: "Until then, would you like a tour of the ship?"

Bob: "Certainly. Lead the way."

Lieutenant Walker took Bob out of the cadet quarters and away from the docking bay. Further in was the ships campus with young students chatting and whisking themselves to and from class. It took Bob by surprise that a battleship housed an institution of learning and one of such considerable size. The campus was built inside a giant arboretum with a domed ceiling designed to simulate sunshine. It was lovely. Much nicer than the university Bob had attended.

Lieutenant Walker: "Most of the learning is geared towards ship operations and military agenda, though there is a commitment to the arts, science, and humanities without which morale would be greatly compromised. You know what they say *'without creation, without art, the ability to communicate beyond, beyond... humanity is doomed to the mundane task of mere survival and ceases to possess a purpose.'*"

Bob and Lieutenant Walker boarded a small transport and cut quickly through campus. Beyond the lush grounds and stately buildings was a ring of housing that lined what Bob imagined was the mid section of the battlecruiser. The rows of buildings, each building several stories tall, arched laterally in both directions. Off in the distance Bob could see the curvature of the ship and more building rising upward and above. Looking straight above Bob could see more buildings and people walking to and fro like flies effortlessly walking across a ceiling. The housing section was a complete ring. One of the many advantages of artificial gravity was that it allowed for an efficient use of space.

The aft side of the housing ring was buffered by a solid metallic wall. Bob and Lieutenant Walker rode through the housing ring and approached a gentle slope that eventually allowed them to ride flat to the wall. It was an Escher-esque array of varied gravitational surfaces that was a bit disorienting.

Entering a lock on the buffering wall, they rode through a very narrow tunnel, only big enough for their two person transport and not much else.

Lieutenant Walker: "This is the buffering wall. It separates the living district from the engine room. The buffering wall is a solid piece of Fermiized Iridium that separates and isolates the engine room from the rest of the ship. Fermiized metals are significantly stronger than their non-Fermiized counterparts, but the important aspect for Iridium is that the Fermiization process eliminates the brittle nature of that particular metal. It is practically indestructible. We are traveling through one of the four conduits through the wall and the only way to get to the engine room."

It was very thick; maybe a good fifty yards thick and the circumference of a small city. They transitioned through about a dozen locks before entering the engine room proper. It was a sight. The engine room was bathed in a brilliant white light and very spacious. Oddly vacant of people, but the signs of activity were everywhere. In the central portion of the engine room, about the size of a ninety story skyscraper, but on its side and cylindrical, was the main propulsion core, powering the impulse engines in the aft portion of the ship. About the mid-section of the propulsion core were two giant half cylinders encircling. Though they were about two-thirds the length of the propulsion core their thickness and overall bulk easily made them equivalent if not greater in mass. These half cylinders, which explain a previous mystery, are jump engines. Based on Bob's view of the ship from the outside, these two jump engines must be sharing the same space-time manifold and envelope generator. There were in fact two though and to Bob this was an odd and unfamiliar design which explains the *Atom-Heart Mother's* appearance, disappearance, and reappearance in the battle with the *Disco Volante*.

Jump engines need a cooling down and recharging phase so jumps in quick repetition are not ordinarily possible. With two, one can daisy chain the jumps which is exactly what Joan did in the battle. She jumped into battle. While jump engine one was recharging she attacked the *Disco Volante* and disappeared with jump engine two. After the disappearance, engine one came back on line and she reappeared crippling the enemy ship. It is very unusual to have two jump engines in a battlecruiser. There are several orientation difficulties and resource issues that make it unfeasible, however, these jump engines were a more efficient design, smaller, and easier to power apparently. The Archemidians have obviously contributed to the field of engine design, though undoubtedly were not sharing this technology whilst a civil war was ongoing.

Lining the outer limits of the engine room were long rows of field emulators that extended as far as the eye could see. Field emulators were the end stage of producing a protective suspension field around the ship. Somewhere out of view had to be a massive shield generator that would produce the suspension field while the field emulators conditioned the field to a quasi-material state and thus create a protective bubble around the ship. Bob found this battlecruiser to be a rather impressive example of modern warfare.

Lieutenant Walker explained this and that, pointing out various operations and daily routines, and gave a little history of the ship when appropriate. Shortly after, they headed to a lift that took them to the upper portion of the ship near where he had first met Joan of Arcturus.

Lieutenant Walker: "Her meeting should be about over."

Bob: "Ok. Do you know what she wants to see me about?"

Lieutenant Walker merely shrugged her shoulders.

They stood in awkward silence for the better part of twenty minutes in some seemingly non-descript hallway. When Lieutenant Walker got a message only she could hear there was some head nodding and a few interjections, then:

Lieutenant Walker: "Are you hungry? Would you like to have dinner with the General?"

Bob was hungry. He had a lot of bodily injury he'd been repairing as of late.

Bob: "Sure. That'd be great."

Lieutenant Walker: "Follow me."

They walked to a lift, then another hallway, then another lift before making their way to a set of sliding reinforced doors. These were not the same doors that had opened to a command chamber before, but similar. Lieutenant Walker took up post in the hallway and the door slid open. Inside was a long formal dining table and at the far end, standing, was Joan of Arcturus.

Joan: "Bob, it's good to see you alive. Are you hungry?"

Bob: "It's good to be alive. Yeah, I could eat."

When Bob walked in he still had a peculiar gait from his recent ordeal. An astute observer might have noticed that when Bob approached the table to greet Joan of Arcturus that she possessed the faintest tension in her eyes as she found his walk coupled with the previous image of him in that ship unbearably funny. She had mentally told herself that should could not think about it lest she get the giggles and spoil her stately composure.

They sat down to eat at said large formal dining table, Joan at the head and Bob adjacent though both closer to the corner and consequently each other. The stiffness of Bob's legs made him hit his chair at an off and slightly harsh angle. The chair slowly began to tip but Joan firmly grasped the chair backing and set him up properly, the opposing chair legs making an echoing clack as they reunited with the floor. Bob gave a smile both thankful and apologetic. Joan then asked Bob about his trip to Boreas. Bob went through the finer points, starting with the rather uncouth decent and subsequent crash. The demon frog. The bread. The over exuberant interest the populace had in his mustache. The glass. The bread. The unexplained giant Rapulis here and there. The cyclops. The big obsidian orb. The bread. All the while he told of his adventure Joan of Arcturus giggled, and even had a few thorough laughs. It had been a long time since she had a good laugh. Though it wasn't until his detailed telling of his less than graceful exit from Boreas that the laughing brought tears to her eyes. She had no defense against his story and the image she saw of him floating helplessly in empty space. His telling was ripe with an aura of irritation and disbelief and peppered with phrases like, "I've worn hats roomier than that ship!", and "I'm afraid there wasn't quite enough room for both me and my ego in that ship and some of my charm may have unfortunately been lost in space."

Bob asked Joan about her life and what she did and what she liked to do. She gave a general synopsis of her life and glossed over her daily occupation as routine doldrum. She had a great number of

stories that would amaze even a seasoned veteran but didn't go into any of those. It wasn't that she had anything to hide, it was just that this battlecruiser *and* strategy *and* tactics *and* civil war had been her life for a good number of years and it was nice to have a distraction.
 To anyone, even those who knew her well, she was solid, well adjusted, and beyond competent, but to be involved in war, even briefly much less for years and years, carried a good degree of traumatic stress that was universally unavoidable.

The amount of time Joan had allotted for dinner was about up.
 Her work was practically around the clock (and at times *literally* around the clock).

Joan: "Bob, I hate to interrupt our conversation, but I am about out of time and there are a few logistical issues to address."

Bob: "Sure."

Joan: "I have previously contacted your boss and informed him of your survival. He has transmitted a message which you can access from your terminal as you see fit."

Bob noticed she was definitely back into a more formal mindset and not the relaxed conversationalist seconds earlier.

Bob: "Thanks." And Bob was slowly reentering the world of the tasks set before him and remembering there was a certain urgency involved.

Joan: "Also, we received a communique from the office of Dr. Morris.
 She's *very* interested in your well-being, Bob." The last sentence said with an air of humor and a slightly raised eyebrow. It was not lost on Bob that her address was gender specific meaning Joan of Arcturus knows more of C.I.D.E.R. than most people. Perhaps they had dealings involving the civil war. Perhaps Dirac had used or attempted to use biological weaponry. There was no time to get into that now.

Joan: "She has asked, though her tone made it sound more like an order, that you rendezvous with one of her ships somewhere in the Kaus system to hand over the materials you brought back with you."

"hmm," Bob thought. He had kind of hoped they would somehow come and get him and take him somewhere where he could get another ship. He'd broken his and wasn't about to set foot in that tin can again. Now he wasn't sure how he'd get anywhere.

Bob: "Hmm...I suppose I need to contact the Chief and have him find a way to get me a ship. I'm a bit stranded."

Joan: "Nonsense. You are more than welcome to take one of our small cruisers. It's the least we can do. You did, after all, put us in a perfect position to take down a Diracian battlecruiser."

Bob, joking: "Well, that was secretly my plan all along. Seriously though, that is extremely nice of you. I will bring it back when I get a chance."

Joan: "You may use it indefinitely, though...if you would prefer...we sent the Rapulis ship on its way back but it would be no problem for us to retrieve it. You may have grown attached to it."
Bob: "Had I been on that ship any longer I would have grown *into* it."
Joan laughed.
Joan: "Bob, I hope you will keep me informed of your travels and return for a visit when you find the time."
Bob: "I most definitely will. I would love to come visit again, and I can't thank you enough."
Joan: "I will schedule you in for a visit, to be determined, at some point in the *near* future."
Bob: "That sounds fantastic."

They left the dining room, Joan heading back to command, Bob being escorted by lieutenant Walker to the cadet quarters in which he'd bunked. They would miss each other's company. Joan liked him. He made her laugh and that was enough. Bob liked her. She laughed at his jokes and that was enough.

Back in the command room Joan went about her routine, checking over a variety of consoles and looking over the shoulders of her officers and crew. After a while she stared outward at the main projection screen. She stared into the blackness of space. Before long she was approached by a crewman she had been scheduled to counsel. Another case of unrequited love, understandably common amongst those isolated aboard a starship. He handed her a report that she was to sign off on which she did with the merest glance almost without averting her eyes from the black projection of outer space. She handed back the report and as he was looking it over she placed a mentoring hand on his shoulder, getting his attention. While staring into the endless dark she said to the young man, "I know what you need to do to get this individual-you-fancy's attention." The crewman looked inquisitively at Joan of Arcturus as she stared outward and beyond. She then turned to the young man, staring intently in his eyes and said, "Grow a mustache", pointing to her upper lip as she spoke.

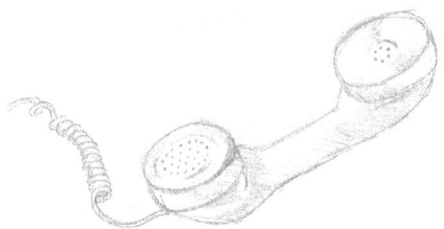

Chapter Sixteen:
Back to the Grind

Bob made his way back to the cadet quarters and went through a mental checklist of what he needed to accomplish. Once he had shaken the pleasantness of the evening a dire sense of urgency was once again upon him. It was so easy to get lost in these alluring worlds. He had wanted to stay longer aboard the *Atom-Heart Mother*, experience the life here and see more of the ship, but time was not on his side, not now anyway.

Looking around the cadet quarters Bob noticed his Rapulis robes had been cleaned and folded, the massive book placed carefully on the desk perfectly aligned with the right angle of the desk edge, and his satchel had been placed in a still compartment to preserve the bread contained within...bread that was terribly misshapen from being crammed against his body for an extended period of close-quarters space travel.

First things first, Bob sat on the edge of the cot, waved a hand over his forearm to summon terminal access, then received the communique from the Chief. From this distance, a good thirty eight light years from Helen, instant communication was not possible and they would have to rely on these stilted messages. Once Bob made it to a more populated hub, where more jump-ships were active, the transfer could be more-or-less instantaneous, but for now they'd have to deal with the choppiness of their situation.

The Chief appeared as a ghostly projection and looked tired and fairly concerned.

The Chief, offering a smile, said "Bob, I was told that you chose a creative way to greet the Rapulis. You must have wanted a degree of pomp and circumstance to your entrance...or at least fireworks. I suppose it is my fault. I never *specifically* told you the ship lands better with an engine. And you do know the cost of that ship is coming out of your paycheck, don't you?"

Bob gave a little chuckle.

Chief: "Seriously though, I am glad and fairly bewildered that you made it through that alive. On to business. Your old pal Lark has actually been fairly helpful. He's kind of an ass, but a helpful ass. Lark has gone searching for dead bodies and found quite a few. Lark took a look at several mysterious deaths in nearby systems, specifically Pollux, Castor, and Rho Geminorum. Quite a few cases in each system covering a dozen or so planets....AND, surprise, surprise, all sharing the same familial relationship. We have a good sampling of dead bodies and can infer a little more about the connections, but the odd thing happens to be the relationship itself. The individual that relates most closely to *all* the murders is a man named Hunter Burroughs Callus. This man lived a good 400 years ago and as you'd imagine has been dead a long, long time. Motive? Doesn't seem to make any sense. It would seem reasonable to assume this is the result of some old family feud, but the remaining members know nothing of any feud and we can't find any reference or mention of a feud of any kind among the family's records. So.... I don't know. However, we are looking into the genealogy of this Hunter Burroughs Callus and trying to predict future victims. That could turn up something, but you know how genealogy is, it's never easy especially when it involves different systems and planets. We're working on it though."

Seemed more of the same to Bob. Larger numbers, nothing revelatory.

Chief: "Lark was getting a lot of flak from his employer for not knowing of your whereabouts. He exchanged some words and said they need to meet in person. Since, he's heard nothing. His employer, as you remember, a member of the dying family, could have suffered the same fate. Lark's heading back to Alpha Centauri to look into it. I haven't given it much thought, but Lark seems to feel suspicious of the whole affair at this point."

Bob really wasn't too interested in Lark's business.

Chief: "And...the virus. It's everywhere Bob. No one really knows what to do. You've been gone about five or six days and in the last few it's been reported in every major system in the Orion arm. It has become a hot topic and interstellar efforts to identify locations of the outbreak have become focused and surprisingly cooperative. The cases are concentrated along the mobilian trade route, so it seems that whoever is responsible has been traveling through our neighborhood and bringing disease wherever they go. The virus has infected hundreds of known systems and at least five times as many planets. The odd consequence of this finding has been that most travel restrictions have been lifted since we can't seem to find a planet that doesn't have the virus. There are, of course, the obvious few that are untouched, but quarantines are being lifted due to the ubiquitousness of the virus. Maybe the most concerning, ...at least to me, are the reports beyond the Orion arm. A few systems far, far

away have reported outbreaks. It's not just a regional thing, Bob. It's not even restricted to the Orion arm. It's spreading everywhere."
Bob felt a shadowy gloom come over him.
Chief: "Anyway, we've been keeping the murders fairly hush hush to all except the stellar authorities involved. The virus is such big news that since we've revealed to these authorities that the virus and the murders are related we have been getting unprecedented assistance. Things are moving considerably quicker...which is good...but, it seems that we are still a great distance behind the architect of this disaster."
Bob began thinking of how he needed to reply to this message from the Chief. He needed to send a report post-haste.
Chief: "As for the next step...we really may not be quick enough to find or deal with this virus spreading murderer. We don't even know what the damn thing does yet. No one is sick, just infected...which I suppose is good. You need to keep going with your end of things. If we can figure out the virus itself we might be able to end the dilemma whether or not we find the culprit. Dr. Morris has told me to inform you that your next destination is the Kaus system. There you are to hand over whatever the hell you got from the lizard people, then you'll head to Antares where you can plan your trip to the Balaenae. Let's hope they figure something out considering they've somewhat commandeered my best operative. The Arcturians have been gracious enough to supply you with a ship. Please take care of this one a bit better than the last. At least wait a few days before you wreck it. Seriously though, please let me know what you know when you get a chance. Things are crazy here.   ...Hey, any good food on the lizard planet?"
The transmission ended.
　　　　Bob needed to organize his thoughts. It was important that he send a reply that contained all pertinent information which he possessed at this time. Thinking, he looked around the room and decided to grab the satchel from the still compartment. Oddly, when he opened it, the torn halves of bread still seemed edible...or at least they hadn't spoiled beyond a point about which Bob would concern himself. The smell of the bread was slightly unwelcome as it was an instant sensory flashback to being stuck in that little ship. He had never really noticed the bread aroma while in that little thing, but it was there and after a time of decompression and being away from the smell of it, it was very apparent that it was now intertwined with memory.
　　　　Digging through the bread remnants Bob found the cylinder containing the information he had been sent there to retrieve. He wasn't sure how it would interface with his personal terminal access,

but he brushed his forearm, summoned a display, and tried to talk the terminal into reading the data. It scanned around a bit, made a few flashes and squawks, but then managed to find a means of decoding the data contained within. It couldn't do anything with the samples, of course, but the data it managed to understand. What Bob obviously was after was the image of the ship whose occupant had killed and cored several Rapulis a few years back. The Chief needed to see this and start looking into the ship, which happened to be a medical transport. This was possibly the first bit of physical evidence of the actual perpetrator, not merely his leavings.

After the data was collected, Bob began recording. He went through the entire trip from beginning to end, really only hitting the major points. It took him a good hour to tell the whole thing then he concluded with his thoughts on the medical transport imagery.

Bob: "A medical transport should be traceable. The problem is that surely a person who went to such elaborate lengths to orchestrate these murders and engineer a mysterious virus would be aware of the accountability of such a transport. That probably means one of three things. One, this transport was reported destroyed or lost and it's actual existence is unknown. This would be a good cover because no one would be looking for it, however, we might get some yardage by looking into medical facilities that have reported a lost transport three or more years ago. Two, it could be fabricated to look like a medical transport specifically to throw prying eyes off the trail. If that's the case, then we're screwed. Three, the transport might not be missing at all and this is someone who works in a medical field and is somehow doing this, more or less, on the job. If this is the case, we're probably screwed. There are too many medical facilities that use this exact type of transport to critique and investigate all of them, however, we could look into ones that had business along the mobilian trade route and were in the Arcturus system as well. A little transport can't go all these places by itself. It'd need a jump-ship nearby so *that* might be traceable. The problem is that it is very odd to think that a medical transport would have business near Boreas, so this isn't likely."

Thinking, Bob continued: "There's good and bad news about this medical transport on Boreas having done it's business several years ago. The bad news is that whoever this is is a good three or more years ahead of us. The good news is that if this person was taking samples of the Rapulis genome, he or she was engineering the virus at that time. How long did it take to finish it? Who knows? But it's not inconceivable to think that the completion is recent and that's why we're aware of it now. We might still be in the early stages of this event."

"My plan is to get moving right away. I'll leave this battlecruiser more or less immediately and head to a nearby spacestation. I don't know the scheduling there, but I imagine it shouldn't be too hard to hop a ride on a jump-ship. Then I'll head to Kaus. I'm assuming Dr. Morris chose it because it's practically vacant. Secrecy and all. From there I'll head to Antares, back to civilization, and work out my long trip to visit the Balaenae. I'll let you know how it goes. Once I get to Antares, we'll probably be able to talk in something more closely resembling real time. However that works is beyond me, but it'll be easier to touch base then. If you learn anything, let me know. I'll try and keep the bread in a still compartment so you can try it if I manage to make it back. If I don't make it back, consider yourself the inheritor of bread as my last will and testament."

Bob ended the recording and sent it on its way. The next jump-ship that left the area would send this little message winding through the galaxy until it made its way to Helen's Crown, or wherever the Chief happened to be staying. He might still be on Ganymede avoiding the virus. Bob should've asked. There'd be time for that later.

He sat for several minutes thinking, then rose and headed for the door. He needed to find out where this ship he was to borrow could be found. He needed to become mobile again. Outside was lieutenant Walker. She must have been assigned to guard or watch over Bob. Most likely a standard practice for residents not part of the crew.

Lieutenant Walker, turning to greet Bob: "Should I show you to your ship?"

Bob wondered if they were monitoring his activities and transmissions or just guessing at his next step.

Bob: "Sure, I suppose I do need to get moving."

Lieutenant Walker gave a whistle and two eager cadets rushed to attention.

Lieutenant Walker: "They'll tend to your effects and I'll escort you to the docking bay. Right this way please."

The young cadets rushed in and grabbed Bob's satchel, his Rapulis robes (which he really had no use for), and that massive paper book that one day, given the chance and adequate boredom, Bob would probably skim through a bit. They all then headed for the docking bay. This was not the same docking bay he had entered. It was considerably further away requiring several lifts and a couple of transports. Inside, the docking bay was very similar to the one he had been in before. It was huge and open; there was vast space to accommodate the navigation of docking vessels of all sizes. Unlike the docking bay in which he had previously been, this one was full of ships and very active. It was quite impressive. Many of the ships had the unmistakable fierceness of military purpose about them, though this was obviously not their main fleet, as there were too many service ships and transports intermingled. Elsewhere there had to be several similar docks packed to the gills with fighters and combat cruisers. Probably hundreds if not thousands.

Lieutenant Walker showed Bob to a bank of ships and walked him to the one he was to borrow. It was very nice. It was quite similar to the one he had wrecked, as non-military cruisers are all pretty much the same, but a little bit larger. It was, however, possible that it only *seemed* larger due to his previous entrapment.

Regardless, it looked to Bob like a wealth of luxury. Opening the aft cargo door, lieutenant Walker gestured for Bob to enter then had the cadets place Bob's things inside.

Lieutenant Walker: "I'll leave you to it. Have a nice trip."

Bob, turning: "Oh...yes. Thank you for everything. Please send my appreciation to Joan."

Lieutenant Walker looked confused. Perhaps she rarely had dealings with the stern General.

Bob: "By the way, about how long does it take to get to the nearest spacestation from here?"

Lieutenant Walker: "I'm afraid I can't answer that. I'm not familiar with this system."

Bob, confused: "...what do you mean? How can you not be familiar with Arcturus?"

Lieutenant Walker: "We are currently in distant orbit around Kaus. We made the jump no more than twenty seconds ago."

Bob, surprised: "Oh...we'll, that is...that's fantastic. Thanks again."

Lieutenant Walker nodded and waved goodbye snapping at the cadets that lurched to attention and scurried behind her as she left the docking bay.

Inside his new ship Bob had a little look around. It did seem bigger than his original ship. The primary chamber was a bit larger and proportionally the sleeping quarters were smaller, but compared to his late cruiser the bedroom seemed about the same size. It was sleek and nice. He noticed the P-PID injectors lining various portions of the hull. Not all cruisers had that precaution and previously it would have been a thing of which Bob would scarcely have taken note. Now it was quite welcoming. It was a standard escort cruiser, so obviously no weaponry which was good and necessary as Bob had no permit to use or possess anything more than a EMP gun. Also, even with the appropriate permit for ship-to-ship weaponry you never know who's going to recognize and/or respect the legality of such a permit when you're traveling through a dozen or more different systems, which Bob would be doing shortly. It was an exceptionally nice ship and Bob was grateful for it.

Inspecting the console Bob noticed a flashing notification. He had a recorded message which he had no hesitation activating. It was Joan of Arcturus.

Joan: "I hope you like the ship. It should be reliable. I thought it best to take you to Kaus myself as you have a bad tendency to crash ships into planets around here. Please remember these ships work better with engines and remember that you have been scheduled for a follow-up visit at a yet-to-be-determined time in the near future. Take care."

The recording ended. Possibly it was true that Dirac was looking for another chance to make some statement. It most likely was unsafe traveling freely around Arcturus, but Bob couldn't help but think he was also getting some special treatment and *that* he didn't mind.

The cruiser, like practically all cruisers, were mostly self-piloting. It rose and took him smoothly out of the dock. Bob pulled the image of the *Atom-Heart Mother* on his view screen but almost instantly, in a wobbly flash of light, it disappeared, and they were now many light years apart. It was an interesting visit to Arcturus. There was a bit of melancholy in Bob's heart, and the heaviness of the impending task at hand, but right now he felt comfortable, in his element, and on his own. After a few relaxing deep breaths Bob pulled up the rendezvous coordinates and headed in a direction he could only define as 'nightward'.

The rendezvous point was out in the middle of nowhere, which is what Bob expected. He couldn't and hadn't been able to see anything other than space since he left the battlecruiser. He was relatively close to Kaus, but far enough away that it was indiscernible from the surrounding stars. Nearing the coordinates, in the thick blackness of space, Bob could see the growing image of a flea-like jump-ship, floating like a helpless bug in molasses. It was the *Cell-Scape*.

The transfer was quick and painless. Clinical really. Dock. Hand over the cylinder. Take a couple of jabs from that sassy young woman attending. Undock. Leave. Hardly complicated which Bob didn't mind, but it was a bit anticlimactic considering the lengths he went to get this information. All that's left now is to get to Kaus proper, find the next available jump-ship to Antares, and spend the interim doing a little light reading.

Suggested Reading for Interstellar Travelers:
"Interstellar Communications: Void Channeling, Jump-ship
Entanglement, and the Great Galactic Web."
Compiled from the resources of the Free Galactic Library (FGL)

   Immediately following the invention of the jump engine there was a concerted and pervasive effort amongst the scientific community to more fully understand and exploit this new technology. Theoretical physicists developed a rather healthy obsession as the understanding of jump physics promised a future of new ideas while at the same time required the old ideas to adjust to this new discovery. "The universe didn't work exactly as we had previously believed", a phrase uttered almost verbatim by every generation of physicist extending back in time to the beginning of scientific thought while each generation simultaneously believing there was little else left to discover. Certainly we've figured it all out by now, right?

   Communication was an obvious added bonus of jump technology as information could be carried to and from jump destinations, but what is the most efficient means of using this technology in a very populated galaxy? Almost immediately following widespread use of jump-ships, transmission experiments began and an odd quirk was found. First thought to be a miscalculation or timing error, messages transmitted from a jump destination, as measured by a relative intermediary, seemed to arrive a bit...early. When measurements were made more exacting it was discovered that not only the message, but the jump-ship itself arrived a bit earlier than expected. This can be more easily understood with the aid of the following figure 1:

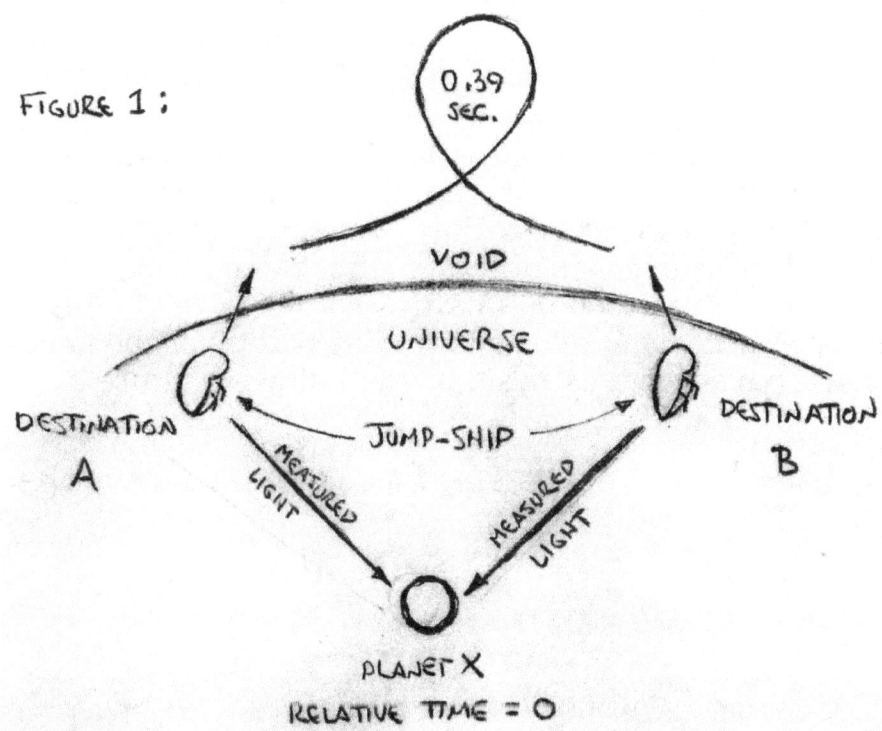

FIGURE 1:

0.39 SEC.

VOID

UNIVERSE

JUMP-SHIP

DESTINATION A

DESTINATION B

MEASURED LIGHT

MEASURED LIGHT

PLANET X

RELATIVE TIME = 0

For reference, remember that the average time a jump ship remains in the void is approximately 0.39 seconds. (SRIT: Modern Jump-ship. FGL.

In the above figure, a jump-ship has left destination A, entered the void and remained 0.39 seconds, then arrived at destination B. The relative time for both jump and arrival, as measured at planet X, is zero. This means that according to the observer on planet X the jump ship left and arrived at the same time, or briefly existed at both locations at time marker zero. This is easy to explain. The void, the nothingness against which the jump-ship transversed, is as devoid of time as it is of any other measurement or quality. Time does not exist there. The 0.39 seconds in the void is a relativistic measurement pertaining only to the occupants of the jump-ship relative to the jump-ship itself, or, more accurately, the consciousness of the occupants to the processes perceived as temporal, i.e. the ship engines, heartbeats, breathing, movement, etc.

At first this seems like a rather pleasant, though brief, bonus. You can send a message across space that gets there a good 0.39 seconds earlier than expected (or however long the ship remains in the void). However, there is something a little more important happening in this process. Look at the above graph again. The jump-ship, at time zero, exists at both locations; destination A and B. In the void there is a 0.39 second "time bubble" in which the message is

227

carried. Since the ship exists at both locations at time zero, it really doesn't matter which direction the message travels. A message from each destination could be sent and received by the other destination at time zero of the jump. The duration of this message (or the transmission of data) needs be only within the 0.39 seconds of the time bubble starting at time zero. It can be easily thought of as a channel, open for 0.39 seconds, through the void, or, popular terminology used, **void channeling**. This process, beyond doubling message transmissions, has profound effects on galactic communications even though it carries with it an oddity for which physicists are still trying to account. This oddity has become known as **Occam's paradox**, illustrated by the following figure 2.

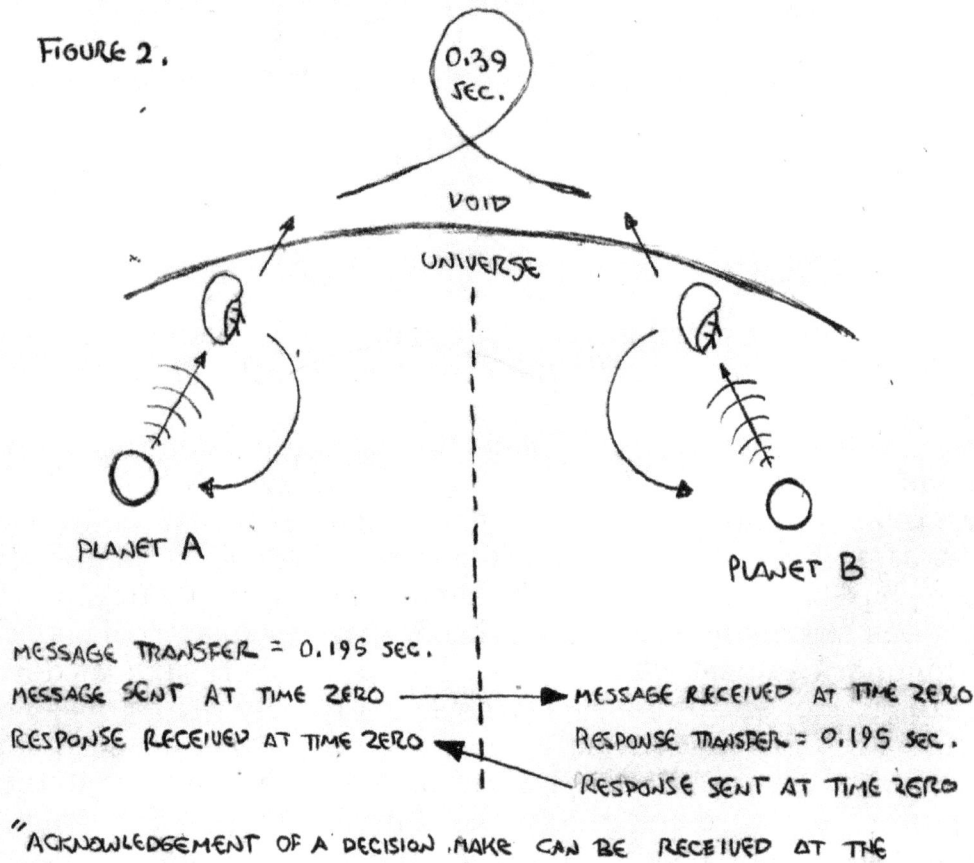

FIGURE 2.

0.39 SEC.

VOID

UNIVERSE

PLANET A

PLANET B

MESSAGE TRANSFER = 0.195 SEC.

MESSAGE SENT AT TIME ZERO ⟶ ▶ MESSAGE RECEIVED AT TIME ZERO

RESPONSE RECEIVED AT TIME ZERO ◀ RESPONSE TRANSFER = 0.195 SEC.

RESPONSE SENT AT TIME ZERO

"ACKNOWLEDGEMENT OF A DECISION MAKE CAN BE RECEIVED AT THE TIME OF THE DECISION MAKING."

Here, instead of destination A and B, we are dealing with planet A and B. Both planets, separated by many light years, are communicating with the help of a single jump-ship. Planet A sends a message to be received by the jump-ship at time zero. The messages reads "Apples or Oranges?". This message takes 0.195 seconds to send (half of the max 0.39 seconds the jump-ship will remain in the

228

void). Far, far away, at time zero, planet B receives a messages asking "Apples or Oranges?". They reply "Apples", transmission time of 0.195 seconds. Back at planet A, they have received an answer of "Apples" at time zero, essentially before they have asked the question. Since planet A has only used half of their transmission time it sends another 0.195 second transmission reading, "Out of apples, please choose oranges". Planet B receives this message, again, at time zero. This is the paradox. If planet B receives two messages at time zero, "Apples or Oranges" and "Out of Apples, please choose Oranges", they would not choose Apples and instead choose Oranges. However, unless they chose Apples, planet A would not have sent the second message informing them they were out of apples. The time bubble involved in void channeling allows for communication out of time for the duration of the jump-ships time in the void. This is, of course, merely a theoretical issue as practicality renders this effect fairly inert.

Back to practical matters, this process, though with the occasional pesky paradox, is wonderfully useful in galactic communications when we couple more than one jump-ship in the mix. When a jump-ship enters the void there is a window, proportional to the ships time in the void, through which another ship may enter and transfer information.

Please refer to the following figure 3:

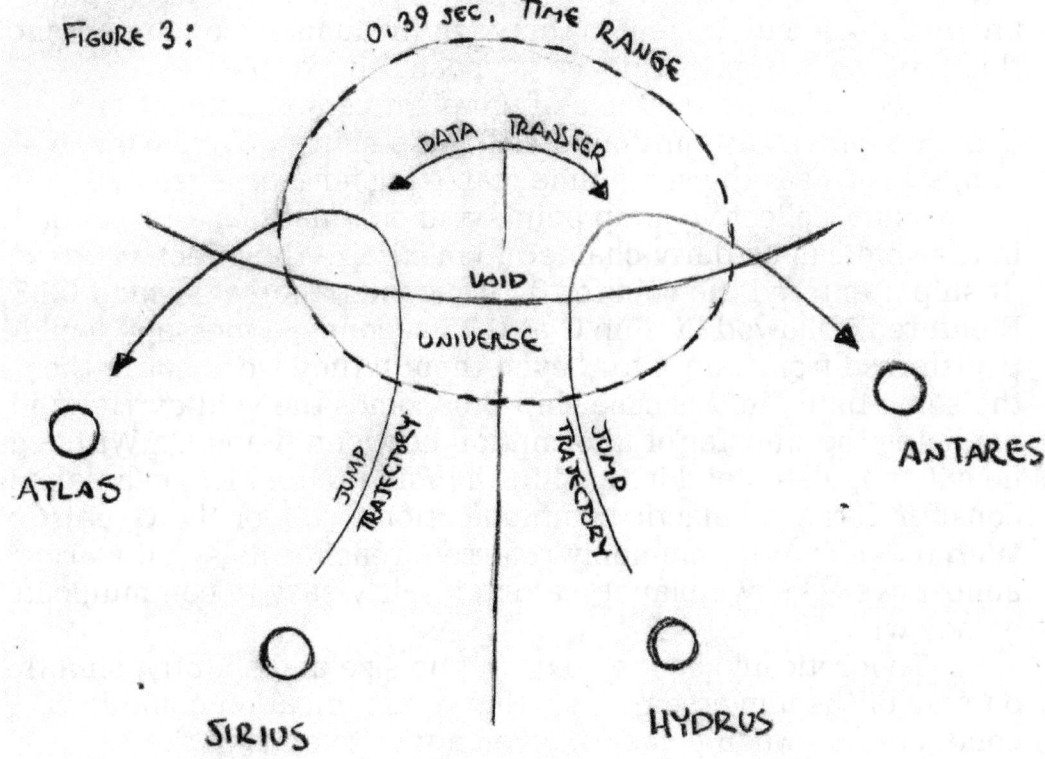

FIGURE 3:
0.39 SEC, TIME RANGE
DATA TRANSFER
VOID
UNIVERSE
JUMP TRAJECTORY
JUMP TRAJECTORY
ATLAS
ANTARES
SIRIUS
HYDRUS

Here we have two jump-ships. One is jumping from Sirius to Atlas, the other from Hydrus to Antares. They are both in the void for a very small fraction of a second, however, if either ship's time in the void overlaps at all, they can transfer information between the two and a message could get from Atlas to Antares even though neither ship has traveled anywhere near each other. You might be asking yourself, "how can this be since these two ships are on opposite sides of Sol and their travel paths are separated by many light years?" It is easy to forget the nature of the void. It is almost instinct to think of the void as an infinite and black empty space, however the void is a thing devoid of quality. It has no size. It has no mass. It has no energy. It is a nothing (and by all accounts does not exist). For a ship to be pressed against the underbelly of the universe, against the void, leaves little room for company. In fact, it leaves exactly zero room for company. When two ships enter the void at the same time, they happen to occupy the same space. This process is known as **jump-ship entanglement**. For a moment, and by all measurements unnoticed by the occupants, every jump-ship in the void becomes the same ship...temporarily. There have been great studies of this process and still a lot is unknown of the process and its effects, but as far as anyone can tell there are no known complications to ship or crew, though there are occasional reports of individuals that acquire perceptions or memories of which they are unfamiliar. Popular media and urban legend attributes this to individuals becoming entangled in this process, but any evidence is speculative at best.

Regardless, the effects of jump-ship entanglement on communications are profound. All jump-ships, galaxy wide, making jumps at or near the same time, can transfer messages to and from any of their collective jump points and destinations. Additionally, time in the void can be daisy-chained to maximize the effect. For example. If ship A entered the void for 0.39 seconds, then at second 0.38 ship B entered, followed by ship C at 0.76 seconds, a message could be transferred from ship A to C even though they were not in the void at the same time. In this case ship B becomes the void carrier and mediates the transfer of information between A and C. With a galaxy heavily populated and jump-ships hopping to and fro on an almost constant basis, a galactic communications web, or the **Great Galactic Web** to which it is commonly referred, reaches its spindly arms to almost every known planet making it fairly easy to communicate galaxy wide.

Theoretically, as the void is of no size and slightly, slightly outside of the universe proper, this communication could be conducted between galaxies...even opposite ends of the universe...whatever that might mean. However, for this to be practical would require a ship in a different galaxy that somehow used the same technology and could communicate in the same way. Since the human race is most likely eternally bound to our own galaxy, this is quite unlikely. For more information on current theoretical physics see *Flobbert's Non-sense: Understanding a Universe that Refuses to Follow the Rules*. Free Galactic Library (FGL).

"Well, that was boring", Bob thought. He had skimmed through a few other articles and current events. Nothing terribly interesting. Nothing new on the virus beyond what the Chief had already said. Bob passed the last handful of minutes doing a few stretches. He was still a little stiff and exceedingly happy for this bit of comfortable space.

Bob was hardly paying attention when he arrived at the periphery region of Kaus. When he managed to turn toward the viewscreen he was quite surprised. Kaus, known for harsh living, sprawling industrial machination, and endless labor was practically synonymous with toil. Almost no one in the entire region gave it a second thought, it was merely a regional source of base materials. But despite the assumptions carried, and the almost tacit agreement of the population to think poorly of it, Kaus was beautiful.

Kaus, the large, erratic, and less than stable star, was surrounded by a massive circumstellar disk of dust, debris, and gases. The cloud of debris was so thick that it completely enrobed Kaus, muting the harshness of the light and making the odd star fuzzy and warm. Here and there a beam of brilliant light poked through like some divine messengers traveling outward. The cloud surrounding Kaus was the artists eternal dream in form and palette. One portion of the cloud looked like a turbulent dark ocean of deep blues and white seafoam colliding with an otherworldly mass of magenta; an algal bloom...a red tide of thick parallel striated waves. Each entity should be afforded its own appreciation, but where the two interacted the suggestion of activity was breathtaking.

Another portion of the cloud seemed like a snowy avalanche caught in frozen time. Almost like a light smoke or shadowed snowfall, it seemed to pour in the direction of perceived movement and was contrasted against the bits of black space that managed to find an opening through the chaos. The avalanche appeared to splash upward toward the end as if it had hit some great body that resisted its enormous force. This revealed the underbelly of the rush of snow and smoke which had the rumpled, ridged, and sticky texture of inner flesh. Blood red and darkened pink, it had the look of an exposed womb welcoming a world to which birth might be given.

Other portions were alien landscapes, heavenly realms, and planet sized stained glass. Some looked as if rich paint had been poured into milk, the paint extending out in rows of fingers where it might find its way through the thick white liquid. Some areas where an oddly dark black that Bob couldn't determine whether he was seeing space or some substance black as space. All of it, the entire system, was like a frozen slice of unbelievable action. Everything projected the look and feel of motion though nothing could actually be seen to move. This world, as most do, moves on a time scale not compatible to the mayfly mind of the human being.

Bob felt like he could spend forever looking at the mass of beauty which is Kaus, which was fortunate because it was taking about that long to find a suitable place to jump to Antares. Bob was now in the populated portion of Kaus. Ships everywhere. Stations abuzz with activity. Transports whisking materials from one location to another. Big ships popping out of the cloud and bringing who-knows-what back to some outpost.

Bob has communicated with several ships. No one seemed to know where a public spacestation might be found. It was most likely the effect of people spending their lives here, working, and never leaving. There was no tourism here, though Bob didn't really know why after seeing the amazing sight of Kaus, and travel was most likely done by and for industrial purposes. Bob didn't want to land, hopping from this station or outpost to that. It would take too much time and might not be any more fruitful than just hoping to run into someone who might know where he needed to go.

After a couple of hours Bob managed to contact a small transport that worked for a ship making regular jumps to Antares. They let Bob know their whereabouts to which Bob graciously gave thanks and headed for the coordinates. Not long after, Bob encountered the right ship at the right coordinates. Hovering high above some facility on a small rocky asteroid was a cloud mining vessel known as the *Oceanic*. Bob told them of his predicament to which an unknown voice said: "hold on a minute."
Bob: "Sure."
Perhaps the voice was talking to someone else, hopefully getting permission.
After a few minutes: "proceed to the docking coordinates we just sent you. We'll take you there."

Bob expressed his gratitude to which the voice replied fairly emotionlessly, "It'll be a couple of hours or so before we make the jump."

Bob headed straight there, docked, and waited patiently. It would be a good time to try out the cot in the cabin on his cruiser. In a couple of hours Bob would be in the great system Antares.

Dream Journal: A Rising Wind

I found myself on a green lawn surrounded by buildings. It was a campus of sorts, perhaps a university. Off in the distance a figure entered a nearby doorway and was gone. It looked so much like her, all grown up...a young student starting her studies. Surely, it couldn't be. I followed, entered the same door and found myself in a commons hall. People were everywhere and there was causal activity all about. It was peaceful chaos.

I couldn't see her or where she had gone. There were doors and stairs every which way, metallic and marble with ample natural light. There *was* something very natural about this place, very comfortable though unfamiliar. I crossed the commons and left, exiting into the inner courtyard of the campus. It was sparsely treed and richly green. Students lounging, talking, walking here and there...all calm, all tranquil.

The air carried the scent of the sea. Very pleasant. Where a path might be seen through the cacophony of buildings, there would be found distant blue... pacific water of an ancient sea. It could be seen in multiple directions as if this university was constructed on a lush green cape arcing gracefully through the water.

Walking through the courtyard I looked about for her. I didn't see her and was certain I hadn't really seen her in the first place. When one longs, the form longing takes lies in the wisp of nostalgia hovering in and along the periphery of the eternal horizon. I can see her in every person that exudes sweetness, in every pleasant breeze, in every blade of fresh green grass. She is not here and yet she is everywhere.

Leaving the courtyard I skimmed along the edge of buildings running parallel with the sea. There were no people here. The wind picked up greatly providing a substantial push against my modest frame. I no longer felt rooted to the Earth. The sensation of the wind intermingled with the scent of the sea coupled with the warm hum of her memory resonating the foundation of my being produced in me what could only be described as ecstasy and loss entangled in the fluidic now.

The wind became increasingly stronger, so much so that for brief moments I was caught in an updraft and lifted gingerly off the ground. The wind grew and the updraft became stronger. I chose not to fight it but merely tried to stay upright to land on my feet. I would lift and land, lift and land. A little more each time. I could almost see the turning wind like spouts of air reaching upwards. Several times fear would threaten to enter my heart and make me worry of the height to which I had climbed, but I fought it back. I was tired of being afraid and I refused. Not now. Rising higher into the clear sky, I was not afraid.

There I saw a thing I couldn't understand. Floating motionless, sprinkled throughout the sky, were objects like gossamer flowers all facing the same direction. They were iridescent and beautiful. One near to me I managed to touch, to touch the face of it. It was warm and liquid, like sticky light and I knew it in that moment. These were ancient heralds of the end of things.

After a time I lazily floated Earthward and steadied myself on a short and rough stone wall by the sea.

Chapter Seventeen: Lark's Employment Issues

Beta-Mu-011-5-7-00 found to wander but issued status of: not lost.

Theta-00-9-Delta grain encountered material of unknown origin. Unable to permeate. Awaiting command.

Sub-quantum domain violation from unknown source. Grain stream unaffected.

Lark was irritated, which was nothing out of the ordinary. Lark existed in a state of irritation, but was on the upper end of this scale currently. Lark had been hired by some member of the Eurnum family to investigate the string of familial fatalities, and for some reason his employer was quite interested in Bob.

Lark had done his best to figure out what had been going on. He had traveled, at his employer's expense, to a dozen or more planets pouring through, as Lark himself puts it, the "useless crap of dead men's lives". All Lark had managed to produce were more names that verified a connection to the same family, but little else. To some, like the Chief, this was helpful in the investigation. To Lark, this was not enough to stave off his grand irritation with the entire venture. He was getting nowhere, dealing with idiots, and was still mad about Bob getting the best of him making a classic rookie mistake. Because of this even Lark himself was subject and victim of his own irritation.

Lark was rough, unkind, often a jerk, and frequently rude. He had done his share of extracting information with his fists...or nearby blunt instrument. He had made crooked a few perfectly straight noses and unhinged a few jaws to make it easier to swallow anger larger than the victim's ego. Presently, with his elevated...crankiness, it would not be a good time to get on his bad side, and he only had the two...a bad side and a worse side.

Lark was done chasing rabbits. He was getting nowhere and was becoming increasingly peeved at his employer for attempting to pressure him about Bob. *Where's Bob? Why haven't you found him yet? What is your strategy for finding him?* Not only was it frustrating, but Lark was becoming suspicious as to why Bob was such a focal point. It didn't make any sense. For that reason, Lark was currently on his way to Alpha Centauri to meet face to face with this Eurnum and either make sense of it all or resign. He had only spoken to his employer via terminal screen and from experience knew that people acted different in person...especially in *his* presence. Lark was more than a just little intimidating.

This was a win-win for Lark. Either things would be hashed out and he could manage this investigation according to his own plan, or he'd be done with it all and just go home as he was an Alpha Centauri resident. This case was seemingly a dead end and Lark preferred cases where he found the bad guy, beat the fudge out of him, and got paid.

One wouldn't be able to guess it from Lark's grizzled expression, but when his transport touched down on Ixion of Alpha Centauri Lark was happy to be home. Like Bob, Lark lived in a relatively crummy apartment in a less than nicer part of a large city. He wasn't particularly caught up in the quality of his living conditions. That large city was known as Eris (not to be confused with *Elis*, a nearby planet). It was huge, overcrowded, and riddled with crime, just how Lark preferred his surroundings and not solely for the purposes of gainful employment. Some people, for one reason or another, are drawn to a rough edge.

However, Lark was not headed toward Eris. He was not heading home. He was heading to another city; lush, laid back, peaceful, and well-to-do. This city was Port Aisa. Port Aisa was, as the name implies, a seaport. It was quaint, lovely, and all the things one might imagine of a picturesque little seafaring village...just on a bit larger scale. There was a central shopping district full of boutiques, bistros, and bakeries referred to as "the village", then beyond there were residential areas ranging from modest to palatial. It was a pleasant place, a wealthy place, and a tourist trap. This was not the type of town Lark would normally find himself drawn to, but this happened to be the home of his employer, one Steige Eurnum.

Steige Eurnum was in his late sixties, slender, gray-haired, and accustomed to wealth and leisure. He had hired Lark when the news of the murders and the connection to his family line became known. He solicited Lark through his public terminal profile as a known and respected (in terms of results) private detective. They had never met face-to-face, but Lark was about to change all that. While Lark had been looking into a murder in the Rho Geminorum system, Steige and Lark had a bit of a quarrel. They had different ideas of what needed to be done and Lark, refusing, demanded they meet. It was understandable that this Eurnum guy would be concerned since his family members were dropping off like flies, but the tactics he was so pushy about made little sense. Since that argument Lark hadn't heard from Steige Eurnum and got no response from messages he had sent. Lark wasn't the type of guy that would allow himself to be

238

ignored and was about to voice his objections directly and probably loudly.

Lark's transport avoided the central village area and skimmed the outskirts of city. Many of the houses here were large, old, and reclusive on a considerable amount of land. Arriving at the proper address, Lark hopped off his transport and made it to the front gates of a large isolated estate. It was once a beautiful estate, and still was to some extent, but was weathered and harshly aged. It seemed the lawn was not kempt, or at least not recently, and things looked to be in a state of disrepair. Lark activated a terminal window built into the stone of the front gate, then waited. He signaled again and waited.

He was not a patient man and the gate was easily scalable. Once over the gate and into the yard it was clear that no one had been in or out of this place in a while. Steige Eurnum must have been a shut-in. The lawn was overgrown. There were stone bird baths, several, overturned or broken and a fragment of a stone horse head seemingly discarded from a long gone statue. It was obscured by lichen and moss. The place had the look of ruins. The house itself was once alabaster white but now was cracked and peeling revealing grayed wood beneath. The whole place had the feel of an abandoned cemetery.

At the front door of the house Lark activated yet another terminal and waited. Signaled and waited. He also listened closely for movement on the inside. Nothing. The guy might not be home, but Lark was not in the mood to leave without knowing for sure. After a few choice words hurled at anyone who might be inside, Lark planted a solitary kick halfway up the door near the jamb. The door popped open effortlessly and Lark casually walked inside. He wasn't concerned much with security. Even if a silent alarm brought local police they wouldn't do much since this was case related, at least in Lark's opinion. Lark was fairly accustomed to doing whatever he wanted.

Inside, the manor seemed just as dilapidated as the outside, and abandoned. Lark was in a lobby with stairs ascending to his right. Before he could get a proper sense of the place he caught the sense of something, something bad. It was the unmistakable scent of death. Somewhere in this house was a rotting body.

Lark instantly became alert, but was quite certain there was no living being skulking around. It wasn't hard to follow the scent where it grew exponentially more putrid. Lark was certain that the murderer had struck again, and he was right, but what he found would frighten the most seasoned veteran crime scene investigator and even sent a chill through his own desensitized bones and cynical ethical outlook.

Inside what must have been a living room of sorts was the rotting corpse of Steige Eurnum. He was hunched forward. The back of his skull had been removed and a plethora of winding probes, wires, and tubes had been inserted. From the base of his skull downward, almost the entire length of the spine, the flesh and bone had been meticulously carved out exposing the spinal cord to which an equivalent array of probes and wires had been attached.

Restraints had been, almost brutishly, hooked through the ribs of his back is multiple places. All of this was attached to a machine, a machine that was sleek and clinical looking, something one might find in a hospital, but conditioned for very different purposes.

This was a little known, highly illegal, and terribly violent act called *puppeteering*. Puppeteering was a process by which a victim could be killed, then reactivated for a variety of unsavory purposes. The brain of the victim is essentially brought back to life, but the command and motor operations are overridden and controlled by the assailant, or puppeteer. The main objective of this is often identity theft. In the modern galaxy it is exceptionally hard to steal one's identity. It's hard to obtain information or resources the access to which one does not possess. With puppeteering, identity theft is possible. The puppeteer gives commands, but it is the voice of the victim that issues them. Terminal scans of fingerprints, retinal patterns, face recognition, even DNA are supplied by a seemingly willing individual. This grotesque process is even more sophisticated than merely turning a body into a robot. The activated brain can be commanded to respond to queries by accessing its own memories, meaning that personal questions can be fully address without the puppeteer needing to know anything about the victim. For example, if some family member thought old Steige Eurnum seemed a little off when they spoke to him through a terminal screen they might test him by asking him to recall a personal memory that only the two of them shared. Old dead Steige could then reply, in great detail, just as if he were alive simply by a command requiring him to respond to the question.

This is quite obviously a terrible endeavor, but the even darker side is that it is believed that these individuals are more-or-less alive in their death. The brain, the consciousness, the mind are living the experience of being dead. The pain of the exposed spinal cord, the removed back of the skull, the inserted probes and whatnot, the process of decay, and the cold are all thought to be fully experienced by the victim but, with the command portions of the brain overridden, they have no ability to react. These pitiful undead exist in this state until they are permanently deactivated. It is for this reason that the act of puppeteering is considered a first degree crime against humanity and is dealt with harshly galaxy wide. It is an attack on human dignity. It is an act of grave humiliation. It is the pinnacle of degradation to the human being.

Lark stood in stunned silence as he observed the rotting corpse tethered to the odd machine. It made sense. This had to be the act of the murderer. Lark was never hired by Steige Eurnum. Old Steige was but another victim. Lark was hired by the murderer and sent to find out what everyone knew, and like a patsy Lark fed this info right into the belly of the beast. That's why he was so interested in Bob. He wanted to know what he knew and where he was going. This guy was after Bob and even more troubling was the fact that no matter how close they might have thought they had been to figuring something out, this guy was obviously ahead by a bit more than a few leaps and bounds. Lark, previously irritated by the interaction with Bob and the Chief, now took solace in the fact that he really didn't figure out much about what Bob had been up to.

It was in this silence that Lark was startled out of his thoughts by a frightful movement of the corpse. It jerked upright and turned a jittery head towards Lark. It managed an eerie half smile.

Corpse: "Well, I suppose this ends our working relationship."

This body was a bit past its expiration date and not functioning completely normally. The voice was muffled and slurred.

Lark was stunned. The milky eyes seemed to make eye contact and the stench was getting unbearable.

Lark: "So, what now?"

Corpse: "Now? Nothing. There is nothing."

Lark: "And I suppose I know too much. I'm next on your chopping block."

Corpse: "I'm afraid there is little I can do to you in this form. Besides, you give yourself too much credit. You know *absolutely* nothing."

Lark remained silent.

The corpse, giving a foul chuckle: "I have no interest in harming you. You were merely a means of satisfying a curiosity. There is nothing you can do to stop what is coming....

...there is nothing any of you can do but await the unobstructed dictates of the fates and of the furies. For anything else the time has long since passed."

Then, returning to its previously slumped over position, the corpse again became silent.

Lark promptly exited the house as local police arrived. There had been a silent alarm and Lark was thankful for it. He gave a detailed rundown of who he was, what had happened, and what they would find inside. The local police were hesitant to go it. This was way over their heads, and Lark's too. They contacted much higher authorities on Ixion and waited for a forensics team to arrive.

Lark would send a brief rundown to the Chief only out of a professional courtesy and as a clear message that he was, as he put it, "done with this shit". Maybe this guy was going to kill everyone in the galaxy...not Lark's problem. Lark was out. He would head home to Eris and tackle cases of significantly less importance. He would end his communique to the Chief with a sarcastic "good luck" and that would be the last time the Chief would hear from Lark Stungen Aspic.

Somewhere, some far place unseen and unknown, a bespectacled man deactivated poor old Steige Eurnum allowing his tortured soul to finally find rest.

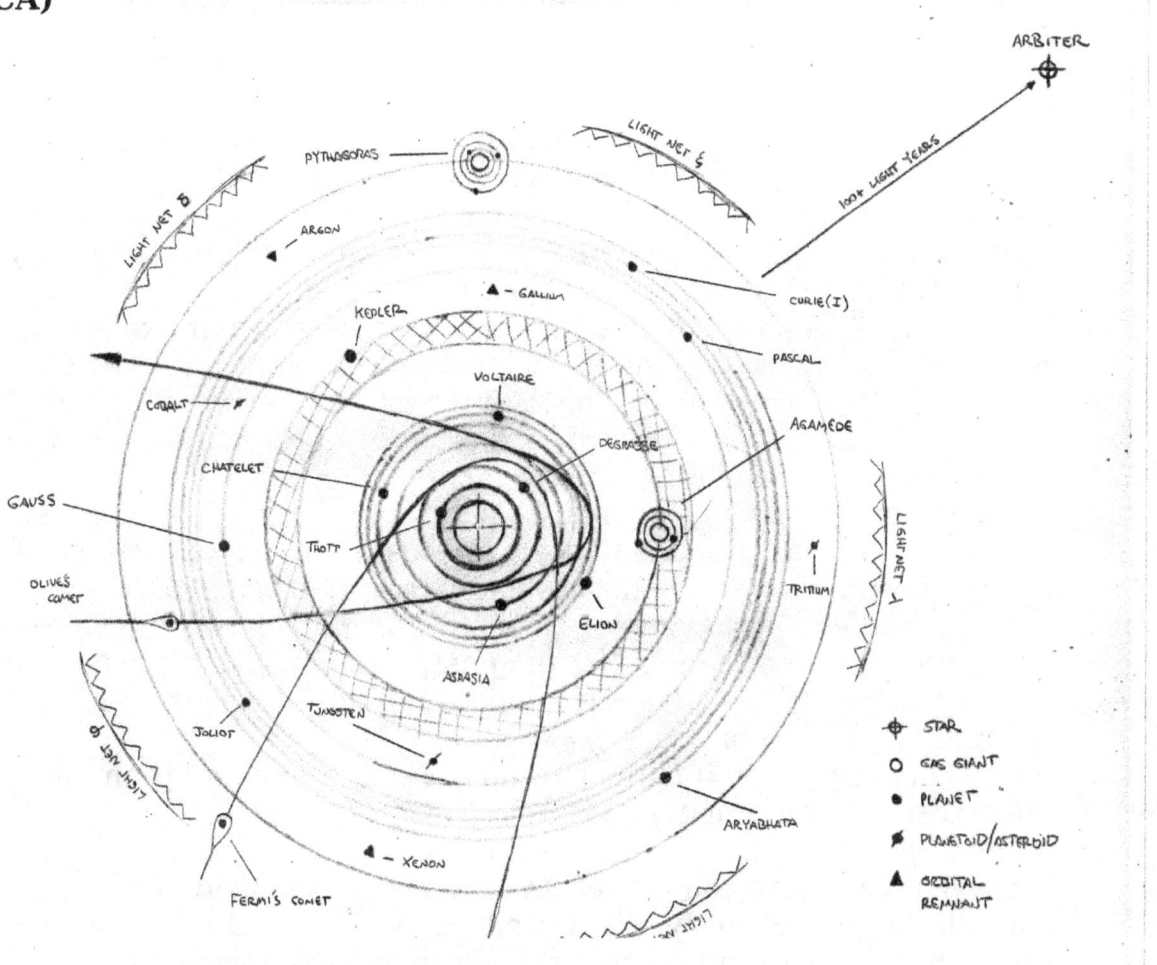

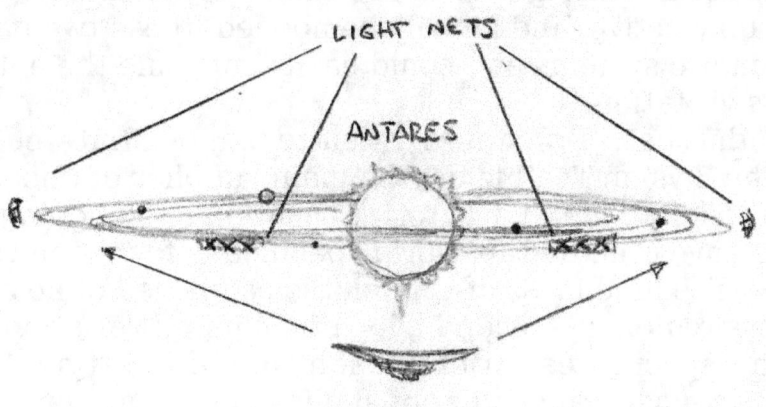

LIGHT NETS

ANTARES

SOUTHERN LENS

243

Great **Antares**, a galactic hub and seat of the United Interplanetary Foundation, boasts the largest population of any stellar system galaxy wide. Here one can find representatives of almost every known world and almost every known culture. With a rich history extending back to the early days of interstellar colonization, the interested reader is encouraged to peruse the practically endless writings of Antares history compiled by the FGL.

Antares is a massive red supergiant star surrounded by an impressive number of planetary objects, which accounts for its great population. Antares has one of the highest number of livable worlds in orbit around any one star. There are eleven habitable true planets, three gas giants each with several moons of or near the Earth standard in size, dozens of smaller habitable moons, numerous stable asteroids and planetoids, and several substantial free-floating orbital remnants suitable for colonization. In total, there are 62 major orbiting bodies that have been deemed useful for human development in addition to a sizable number of constructed spacestations and jump ports. Currently, the estimated population of Antares is approximately 485 billion.

There are far too many habitats to fully delineate them all in a mere travel guide, but
a few highlights are well worth a mention. The traveler might start their visit to Antares on planet **Kepler** which is considered the system capital, though authority, albeit unified, is dispersed rather evenly throughout the system making this designation a formality and of more historical significance than practical jurisprudence. The gas giants **Pythagoras** and **Agemede** are each worlds unto themselves. Bustling, highly active, and heavily bemooned, these two gas giants are like miniature systems and could easily consume the entirety of the travelers visitation.

Tea enthusiast? Don't miss a visit to planet **Chatelet**. Chatelet is home to the Elysian Tea Fields, the main supplier of fine teas sought after galaxy wide. Early terraformation and ongoing climate conditioning have created this world specifically for the purpose of growing tea. The land mass of Chatelet is composed of no states or nations, but is regionally divided by subtle climate variation into fields dedicated to a specific tea varietal. Many of these distinct tea fields are larger than most planet's national divisions. However, Chatelet is not solely agrarian. There are cities and numerous quaint villages speckled throughout the lush greenery of the growing tea.

After Chatelet, why not couple your visit with historic **Voltaire** made famous by their mastery of the bakery arts and their renown delicacy "Candied Arouets". Additionally, consider visits to **Pascal**, **Gauss**, and **Curie I**, all of which have exceptional cultural centers and impressive cities and sites, but don't discount a visit to the many planetary remnants or sub-planets. Spacestations *Tritium*, *Gallium*, and *Xenon* offer a unique opportunity to "people-watch" individuals from all over the galaxy and have employees trained in hundreds of languages to accommodate even the most distant traveler. Those with the opportunity for an extended stay on either of these stations are encouraged to partake of the many, many language programs offered. Have you ever wanted to learn Balax from a native speaker? How about conversational Dandy? Take this opportunity to broaden your interstellar horizons.

Though there are countless sites to see within the great system Antares, traveler's are also encouraged to take an industrial tour of the **Antares Radiant Reclamation and Reserve** (ARRR). The **ARRR** began well over a thousand years ago for the purpose of reclaiming radiant energy from the massive star Antares and repurposing it for planetary use. Surrounding Antares in a distant orbit are currently five great **Light Nets**. These Light Nets serve two general purposes. One, they collect radiant energy from Antares that would otherwise be lost to deep space. Two, they reflect a portion of that light to subtly modify the radiant energy reaching planets and sub-planets in the outer orbits. These Light Nets are composed of sparsely spaced, though interconnected, metal films specialized to alternate between reflection and absorption as needed. In addition to the five Light Nets, ARRR maintains and operates the Southern Lens. The **Southern Lens** is in essence a massive concave spacestation located a great distance from Antares southern pole. Similar in purpose, the Southern Lens both absorbs and reflects light from Antares to subtly warm planets of the inner orbits and collect energy for a variety of planetary uses. Here one can see the **Capacitor Galleons** coming and going, a common sight at the Southern Lens. These Capacitor Galleons are not unlike Cloud-mining vessels, but a little plumper and considerably longer, at times magnitudes longer. Their job is to collect and store energy from the Southern lens and Light Nets. Though they are massive ships, they often have the smallest crew. The bulk of the Capacitor Galleons, regardless of size, is devoted almost entirely to energy storage leaving little room for anything else. Almost none have jump capabilities and require jump-ship-jump-ships (those gargantuan ships designed to transport multiple jump-ships) for transport. Some of the largest Capacitor Galleons are too big for even these jump-ships and are confined to propulsion within the system, some utilizing routes that takes years from point to point. Not only does the Southern Lens and Light Nets power the system of Antares, but energy is one of the chief exports of the system supplying power to a variety of regional systems. When a Capacitor Galleon arrives planet-side one can witness the elaborate display of thousands of ships attaching and draining the Galleon like lamprey on a slowly lumbering Shark.

For more information on the history, culture, and industry of Antares please peruse the vast resources of the Free Galactic Library (FGL).

Chapter Eighteen: The Glass Menagerie part 1:
Gallium and the Squirrel of Gothos

The cloud mining vessel in which Bob's ship was docked had made the jump to Antares in distant orbit around the planet Voltaire. Bob awoke after the percussive thud of the void slapping against reality. Again he gave thanks to these courteous workers tolerant of a wandering hitchhiker and was off to explore the wonders of this massive system. From his location near Voltaire, Bob decided to head to the nearest spacestation, which was port *Gallium* across the Antares main debris ring. Bob took an arcing path over the debris field to avoid ruining another cruiser and the certainty that he would never hear the end of it should such a thing happen again. Within a few hours he was in proximity to *Gallium*.

Gallium was a mind boggling space port, practically indescribable. *Gallium* was an orbital remnant believed to have once been a small planet that had been cleft in twain. The foundation was a bowl shaped rock, like a free floating planetary hemisphere that had a good chunk ripped out of the inside. It had a faint and useless atmosphere which was most likely a leftover of a once viable, though small, planet. It is believed that the planetoid *Tritium* is the missing half of the deceased planet, but as the cataclysm producing either happened millions of years ago this must remain only a speculation based on comparative material composition.

The entire surface of *Gallium* had to be conditioned, or polished, to prepare it for widespread construction, a process that took several hundred years to complete (though construction followed the path of conditioning and happened almost simultaneously) Currently the foundation of *Gallium* is completely obscured by the station built upon and around it. To see *Gallium* is to see an object that can't readily be understood. There are great arcing structures, an array of orb-like objects of various (though large) sizes, spindles, tubes, web-like octagonal nets, flat and wide platforms that look like alien runways razor thin, sweeps, spikes, and squiggles. Throughout, light emanates from various nooks and crannies illuminating some while shadowing others. The predominant color is shining bright metal, but here and there are blues and violets with trace amounts of the entire visible spectrum. There is something about the structure that seems almost like a hodge podge of materials that have errantly become stuck together, but at the same time there is an order, some kind of logic that defies direct conscious grasping as if it is ordered according to a complicated mathematical schemata that can be sensed but not seen. Bob had always felt that such a schemata drove the human engine and thus the species as a whole, some complicated thing no one understood but everyone seemed to work towards. It might be helpful, at some point in history, to produce an idea of what that schemata might be.

Beyond the station itself, the surrounding fluidic activity was equally impressive. There was a constant flow of ships, of absolutely all sizes, streaming in and out of the station. Even coming from a large and developed world such as Bob had, it was hard to imagine that there could be this many people traveling around the galaxy at any one moment. It was a flood, a constant flood.

The closer Bob got to the station, the happier he felt. It initially struck him as odd that he felt such a sense of relief being in Antares and near this station, but on second thought it really wasn't that strange. Bob was accustomed to a very populated world, but since he left Helen he has been meeting in secret places for Dr. Morris, then to a restricted system embroiled in civil war, then to an isolated variant planet, then floating in empty space sealed in a space coffin and back. Now he was truly back to civilization. Everything was structured, populated, familiar, and comfortable. Bob was very happy to be at this point of his adventure.

When he was very close to the station he entered a prescribed holding pattern allowing him to plot his desired destination and find the available itineraries that would take him there, but Bob was too distracted to be bothered with that. There were ships everywhere and the sight was a lot to behold. Bob noticed the jumpships floating all around and looked inquisitively at their hulls for a name. One near him was the *Octahedron*. Another not far off was the *Revolver*. Over his right shoulder he noticed a medical jump-ship called the *Milk-eyed Mender*. Medical jump-ships were like massive mobile hospitals. They routinely patrolled the galaxy to be ready in the event of a planetary catastrophe. As Bob continued his holding pattern he saw countless ships, too many to see the names of them all. There was a battlecruiser docked called the *Broken Arrow*, probably local, another jump-ship called the *Transit Rider*, and another in a language Bob didn't understand. It was called the *Hyderomastgroningem*. Bob wondered, *"what, do they get paid by the letter?"*. But the thing that impressed Bob the most, and something he hadn't seen before, was a gargantuan ship slowly floating away from the station. This ship seemed to be the size of a small moon. It was a jump-ship, still flea-like in shape but rounder...more plump, oddly with two protrusions about the temples that somewhat resembled bull horns. Bob had heard of these but had never actually seen one. This jump-ship was designed for the mass transport of other jump-ships. It's hard to even imagine a need for such a ship, but obviously there was more travel going on in this galaxy than Bob had been aware. This jump-ship jump-ship could probably house several hundred full-sized jump-ships and would, presumably, under certain conditions, be more efficient than each ship traveling alone. It was huge, so much so that it seem to throw the scale of everything off and was even a little disorienting to look at. This ship was appropriately named the *Colossus of Destiny*.

There was a mission and time was an issue, but Bob felt he needed to, at least a bit, explore *Gallium*. It was too interesting to not take at least a little look around. It would also be helpful in finding the best route when he could describe his needs to an attendant rather than looking at the countless pages of travel paths himself...or so he had now been self-convinced. When he sent a request to dock the reply led him to a small craft terminal not far from where he was. From his vantage point it looked like a colorful ringed tube, long and slender, sticking out of the organized chaos of the station. When he got closer he got a better sense of the length. It was probably around fifty miles long, at least the portion that could be seen. There was no way to tell how far it extended into the station or even to get a real fix on the dimensions of anything. It wouldn't have surprised Bob if his measurement had been off considerably. The only thing he knew for sure was that everything here was really, really big.

The docking tube had a series of recessed locks to which one's ship could attach leaving the bow exposed to space while the stern was securely fixed. After backing into his spot, Bob left the cargo hold of his ship (the only exit) and entered the docking tube. Inside it was airy and bright. Though the outside seemed prismatic in color, the inside was a clean white light and very open. Down the center of the tube was two sets of tether rails. Somewhere there would be hover trains attached and the rails prevented them from floating off or derailing which could prove disastrous in a spacestation. This also meant that the trains attached were very fast, which was good since Bob was supposedly in a hurry.

From the dimensions of the inner docking tube, Bob could tell he was in a chamber that probably occupied about half of the tubes circumference, meaning there was most likely an exact duplicate beneath him occupying the other half. Underneath him were other tether tracks and trains running the length of the docking tube and people walking right beneath, relative to Bob, upside down.

Here and there were trees planted along the length of the tracks. Not tall trees, but the kind most stations like to maintain. If people go too long without seeing trees their environment starts to

249

seem artificial and unsettling. Bob could see a message counting down the time the next train would arrive. It looked like they came in about ten minute cycles and Bob had another three to wait. There were already a good number of people around and it was making Bob feel a little closer to home. Since he left Helen's Crown he hadn't been in the usual crush of people to which he had grown accustomed. That sparseness was nice for a while, but it's also nice to see a crowd of people going about their daily lives again.

When the train arrived Bob and the crowd stepped on board and Bob took a seat in an empty pair. Shortly after, the train bolted off. The train was exceptionally fast and one could really feel the g's for a moment as it approached cruising speed. Once a constant speed had been reached, people began reading and chatting, some walked about. It was all very laid-back.

Bob was lost in thought when he got a sense of being watched. When he looked around he noticed a very small pair of round eyes peering at him from the inner pocket of a passenger's blazer. The passenger, a man in his mid-fifties, was reading until he noticed Bob looking his way. He saw that Bob was looking at his lapel and realized what he noticed.

Passenger: "Oh, that's my little buddy."

Crawling from his inner blazer came a round and furry little rodent-like creature with big eyes. It's fur was an orangey red but it's little belly was bright white.

Bob: "He's very cute. I noticed him looking at me and it caught me a bit by surprise."

Passenger: "Yeah, he's very curious and social. I think he wants to meet you. Can he meet you?"

Bob: "Sure."

Bob held out a hand and slowly the little guy peeked out and got a little closer. He sniffed Bob's hand and slowly placed a foot on his palm. He took a couple of steps, then made a quick circuit across Bob's arm, around his neck, then back up the same arm and perched on the shoulder of the passenger who brought him. It took about a quarter of a second. Back on the passengers shoulder the little creature was rapidly twirling and inspecting something in his hands. The passenger noticed and took it from him and handed it back to Bob.

Passenger: "Sorry, he got one of your jacket buttons. He's really likes buttons for some reason."

Bob: "Oh...no problem." He didn't even see it happen, but put the button in his pocket thinking he'd sew it back on later.

Bob: "What kind of little fella is that?"

Passenger: "A squirrel. I work on Gothos and they're everywhere. He's a type of flying squirrel native to the planet there. His name's Bruce."

Bob thought that didn't seem like the right kind of name, but whatever.

Just then the train slowed, pulling everyone towards the front of their seats then stopped. Bob waved goodbye to the passenger and Bruce who remained then he made his way out.

Off the train, the sight of the inner station was fantastic. There were people everywhere. There was a lot of open space, but hundreds of levels and walkways all full of people. It was like being in a huge indoor city. He could tell that he was now in one of the orb-like structure he had seen from space. It must have been composed of plastiglass as outerspace could be seen through the paneling of the orb. The primary dome was speckled with small white orbs providing light, but it gave the overall impression of a well-lit city at night. Most of the useful light came from the buildings and walkways themselves. Some of the other portions of the station could be seen through the plastiglass and occasionally a jump-ship would float by, which Bob thought was pretty cool. It was unreal how populated this area was and from Bob's best guessing this orb was probably only a small fraction of the total size of *Gallium*. People who are not used to a large population might be overwhelmed by something like this, but Bob enjoyed it immensely and wanted to get completely lost in this world.

Taking an escalator up to what looked like the beginning of a shopping district, presumably with food, Bob naturally rested his arms by grabbing his lapels only to notice the absence of a button on either side. Looking down he came to realize his entire jacket was now devoid of buttons. *"What the hell..."* Bob thought. *"That damn squirrel took all of my buttons. All eight on my suit jacket."* He also couldn't find the one he had pocketed, but didn't care at this point. And really, it did give him an excuse to get some non-military-esque attire, though he was grateful to Joan for providing him with an alternative to Rapulis robes or tattered rags. There were stores everywhere and it didn't take long for Bob, who was not particularly discerning, to find something he liked. He obtained some standard clothing and a dark brown blazer from a store named "Fresh Garms" that reminded him of the blazer worn by a starship captain in a serial he liked as a kid.

Bob walked around for a few hours, saw some sights and ate a bite or two. He never left the orb, which he learned was called Nyx terminal, but that was fine since he didn't want to get too far away.

He did have a job to do. Deciding he'd dawdled long enough, Bob entered a private communications room and contacted the Chief.

Chief: "Bob! I am so glad to hear from you. Antares, right?"

Bob: "Yeah, been here a bit. You should really check this place out sometime. It is wild."

Chief: "Will do, will do. So, how are you?"

Bob: "I'm good. Glad to be back in civilization. It's good to hear a familiar voice."

Chief: "I agree. I was a little worried this might be a one way trip, but you're still kickin' around. A little danger here and there, but you're in one piece."

Bob: "For now."

Bob told the Chief about his trip to Antares, that damn squirrel that stole his buttons, and a general rundown of the *Gallium* station. After a while, it was time to get down to business.

Bob: "The virus. Anything new?"

Chief: "Well, it's still spreading. It's everywhere. Every regional system we contact has it, and the ones that don't seem to have it end up finding it later. We've even got reports of it found in the Perseus and outer arms, and all the way to the Norma arm near the galactic core. It's almost like a radial path has been cut to the core and it's spreading out from there."

Bob: "Any symptoms yet?"

Chief: "No, not yet. Still seems dormant. I haven't heard of any cure either. For some damn reason they can't figure out how to kill it. I'm guessing you haven't heard anything from Dr. Morris."

Bob: "No. They just took the samples I brought and left. I'm on a need-to-know I suppose, and I also suppose I don't need to know. ...or maybe they have nothing yet. Anything on that medical transport the Rapulis captured video of?"

Chief: "Yes. That is what I've been spending the majority of my time on. Information is flowing a little faster these days with everyone scared of this virus. Any mention of it and people and institutions are eager to help you out if they think you might stop it. I did a check of all known medical facilities that use that particular type of transport and requested info on lost or missing craft. It's such a standard medical transport that I, of course, got loads of hits. That specific model is used in something like forty different systems. Sifting through those, I specifically looked for instances where the craft was completely unrecovered, absolutely no trace of it. That reduced the number to a small handful. One was destroyed on a rescue mission of a solar collector that destabilized. No one died, but the medical transport had to be abandoned as it went beyond the gravitational boundary that it's engines could counteract. There is video of it disintegrating before melding with the surface of the star. So, we known the transport was destroyed and we know the people involved and their whereabouts. The others have similar stories, where we have decent verification that the transport was destroyed and are not really suspect. One, however, was really hard to find information about."

Bob: "They didn't know what happened to it?"

Chief: "No, it's not that. It's that the transport is absent, but they can't find info on the event that led to its absence. It was pretty weird that no one knew what had happened and had no record of it."

Bob: "That is weird."

Chief: "I managed to talk personally to the head of the facility to see what was up. He seemed helpful and pulled every file he had on the medical transport, but told me most of the information had been redacted."

Bob: "Redacted?"

Chief: "Yeah."

Bob: "So, he's the head of the facility. Tell him to un-redact it."

Chief: "That's what I said. I said, this might have to do with a widespread plague, now's the time to let that info go. But he said that the redaction wasn't from his facility, it was a military redaction and he hardly had the authority to undo it."

Bob: "Military? That doesn't make any sense."

Chief: "It is odd. The head of the medical facility said that he'd spill his guts if he thought it would help, but he didn't have anything to spill. Redacted info, especially a military redaction, eliminates all data on the subject. All of it. The head of the medical facility said whatever this is about it is something he never had any knowledge of, ever. It all happened out of his purview."

Bob: "So, did you contact the local military?"

Chief: "I did, but the problem is...which one? The head of the medical facility doesn't even know which branch might be involved and we're only assuming it's local military. They have ties and treaties with several other systems that could have requested and been authorized to redact something like this. So...it's a mess. I have started contacting local military offices, but I'm just getting the runaround. Either they don't' know anything or aren't saying. Either is equally possible."

Bob, thinking: "Hmm...well, this is quite suspicious. There is a good chance this has something to do with our mystery person."

Chief: "I think so too, but it's also possible this is some treason or spy thing and is unrelated. It is possible that our murderer-slash-viral engineer fabricated a familiar looking transport as a decoy. I'm still

253

on it. I'll keep contacting every nearby military institution until someone becomes helpful."

Bob, sarcastically: "Good luck with that."

Chief: "Yeah, but Bob, I have something far more interesting than all this military stuff."

Bob: "And what might that be."

Chief: "An object. A found object, peculiar and unbelievable. I just recently got a message from authorities of the Bohr systems, some planet called Diophantus. It appears cloud miners, in the absolute middle of nowhere, found a peculiar thing and didn't know what to do with it. They brought it to Diophantus and left it there. It was an odd glass cylinder, floating aimlessly in space, with a body inexplicably encased within."

Bob, very surprised at the direction this conversation was going: "That is very strange."

Chief: "It gets even stranger. The body was identified as a forty three year old man named Harper Callus."

That name registered immediately with Bob, "Odd. Floating in space?"

Chief: "Yes, and seriously in the middle of nowhere. Not near really any system and considerably above the galactic plane, towards the galactic center."

Bob: "..."

Chief: "I don't know what to make of it. What do you think it means?"

Bob, thinking: "...well, ...familial relationship obviously. Who was the ancestor we managed to trace all of these families to...Hunter Callus?"

Chief: "Yes. Hunter Burrows Callus. 400 years ago."

Bob: "I dunno. I just dunno."

Chief: "Get this, the material Harper Callus is encased in couldn't be identified until they brought in some serious analytics. It turns out it's Pixler's glass."

Bob: "Pixler's glass? I thought that wasn't real, or only theoretical."

Chief: "That's what everyone thought."

Suggested Reading for the Theoretical Metallurgy Enthusiast: Pixler's Glass.

Compiled from the resources of the Free Galactic Library (FGL)

When we talk of things material, what do we actually mean? What is the difference between the material and the immaterial? For convention, we tend to think of the material as a thing subject to the whims of nature, a thing upon which forces may act. Conversely, we tend to think of the immaterial as either a thing free from those forces or a thing which does the forcing. It is common for us to consider matter as material and energy as immaterial, in most cases, but it is known to us that these two, matter and energy, are the same. Beyond the atom and into the *atomos*, the thing that is truly indivisible, we find that delicate universal membrane, the cosmic permafrost, bound in the eternal now. *Ex Uno Plures*. All substances of the universe then, at the foundational level, are undifferentiated. What we choose to define as this or that is only of practical concern to how we, as human beings, interact with our environment.

What then are the boundaries? How "material" can something material become? Can something be both material and immaterial at the same time? Well over five hundred years ago theoretical metallurgist Olive Pixler theorized a substance of "maximal intransigency"
which would be "the most material material of all materials". For practical reasoning, this substance could be thought of as the hardest or most indestructible of things keeping in mind the illusory nature of such a designation as "hard" and "indestructible" as merely human constructs, mere words, devised of our interaction with the universe and in and of themselves meaningless. Our words are *representative* of reality but are not reality itself and the filter here is always the human mind.

What Pixler first developed was a scale, commonly known as Pixler's scale, to determine the extremities of the material-immaterial field. What the scale reveals is the cyclic nature of this material-immaterial field. It turns out that the more "material" a thing becomes, the closer it approaches the "immaterial". For example, we tend to measure the substance of a thing by it's resistance to force. A chunk of iron tends to be thought of as significantly more substantive than, let's say, spun sugar. Spun sugar is easily crushable, dissolvable, digestible, etc., whereas iron is a lot harder to affect. So what happens when a thing becomes increasingly resistant to force? Imagine a substance so substantive it resists all forces acting upon it. This would obviously be the "toughest" of all materials, but something interesting happens at this extreme. If light cannot act upon it, it cannot be seen. If gravity cannot pull it, it cannot be contained. If every force in the universe must yield to it and move around it, then the universe itself in essence folds around such a thing. At this point it would not be detectible by any measure, would not be experienceable, and it's existence would be only speculative. It would be a cosmic ghost and therefore immaterial in every meaning of the word.

Using the developed scale, Pixler set out to determine the "sweet spot" by which a thing can meet the human construct of "maximal intransigency" before the inevitable slide towards the immaterial. The theorized material that fit into this "sweet spot" was originally coined *Pixler's steel*, to use an ancient metallurgical term, but when theory suggested that light would pass through the substance without interference and it would be, without impurity, practically invisible, the term *Pixler's glass* came to be and is still used today.

To understand the prescription for and physics behind such a substance would require a specialized scholarship that few, even in the theoretical metallurgical community, might ever devote the time to possess, and physicists are notoriously unhelpful. When asking a physicist about even the most trivial of scholarly matters they usually begin by saying things like, "Imagine the universe is a tube torqued topwise...", or "Think of the universe as a bowl of cornflakes...", or "Consider the universe as a flat sheet that is infinitely flat, but not completely flat...". While they are attempting to explain the trifurcated unity of gravitons using the surface of their lunch apple, the mind tends to wander. Since it is well beyond the scope of this article to illuminate the truly beautiful physics behind Pixler's glass, let it just be quoted in what Pixler described as the simple explanation of the glass: "The glass is a membrane made material, entangled with itself."

But what are the properties of Pixler's glass? First, it cannot be destroyed. There is no known force that can undo the creation of Pixler's glass. It is transparent as light rarely interacts with it. It is only weakly influenced by gravity and would tend to float in even high gravity environments. As forces tend to bend around it rather than act upon it, it would be practically frictionless and would feel slippery to the touch.

When confronted with a possibly indestructible object, physicists instinctively offer the question, "What would happen if it slipped beyond the event horizon of a black hole?". A black hole is somewhat akin to Pixler's glass. Pixler's glass, as mentioned, is the result of maximal intransigency whereas a black hole is result of maximal gravitation. They are both physical extremes. There are three general theories about the interaction between Pixler's glass and a black hole. One, the glass would be destroyed by the singularity of the black hole. Easy. Two, the glass would merely bounce endlessly around the singularity, getting stuck. Not quite as easy as a few problems arise from this theory. Three, and the most interesting of the interaction theories, the glass might center itself around the singularity, in essence fusing with it. In this event, which assumes the gravitational resistance of the glass is greater than the gravity of the black hole, the black hole might then dissipate leaving only the glass and trapped within, the entire mass of the black hole encased in an object that refuses to interact with gravity. Have you ever wanted to hold a thousand suns in the palm of your hand?

It should be said that Pixler's glass is merely theoretical and has never been produced. Over a hundred years ago a team from Geim claimed to have created a small amount of Pixler's glass, however it was an amount at or near the quantum foam point and not measurable. It was later found that the team's process was faulty and it is believed that none had actually been created. Geim's scientists, while admitting a fault in their process, still argue that it was a localization and proximity fault and that the glass had, in fact, existed briefly in a very unstable form.

Readers interested in theoretical materialism are encouraged to read the FGL articles on "Thurston's slime: The discovery of the infinitely slimy." and "Thurgood's solvent: The least solvent of all solvents."

———————————————————————————

Bob: "Hmm...so, we have a victim, trapped in magic glass, and floating in the middle of nowhere."
Chief: "Well, he *was* floating in space. Now he's on Diophantus. There have been requests by the victim's homeworld to turn over the object, and even we made a request since Helen's crown is generally recognized as spearheading the criminal investigation of these murders, but Diophantus is not releasing the object. They really have no particular right to it, but I'm assuming they think if they can figure it out, how to make the glass, they might become a regional superpower."
Bob: "Yeah, that would be a big deal I guess. Still, it's kind of slimy."
Chief: "Yup. However, Diophantus is being every open about the data they're collecting, most likely to placate those not in agreement with their claim to the object. ...and they did find something even more bizarre about our trapped body, Harper Callus."
Bob: "..."
Chief: "They have done dozens of intense scans to analyze the glass. Over the course of the scans they notices minor, minor subtle variations in the corpse that they couldn't account for and have concluded that our pal, Harper Callus,...is still alive."
Bob: "...how can that be? That can't be."

Chief: "He is apparently in a state of suspension."
Bob: "Suspension? What's suspending him? What is the mechanism of suspended animation?"
Chief: "That's what nobody knows. There would need to be machines, several processes operating keeping him suspended. It doesn't make any sense, but that is their current conclusion."
Bob: "Surely it's a miscalculation. Some error in the data."
Chief: "That's possible, but one would assume they'd be fairly careful especially since any doubt of their analytical abilities might prompt protests to their claim."
Bob: "I guess so."

After a second or two of reflection, the Chief offered a change of topic.
Chief: "Oh, by the way, Lark's out of the picture now."
Bob: "Is he dead?"
Chief: "Oh, no, no. He's fine. Miserable but fine. He got involved in some serious business and has checked out...and it pertains to our investigation. Not good Bob."
Bob: "...oh, what's going on?"
The Chief detailed the events of Lark's last investigation and the horrible discovery of puppeteering.
Bob: "Well, it's hard to be shocked at this point, but that'll do it. I think the greatest concern is that we are obviously dealing with an individual that will do absolutely anything, even crimes against humanity, to achieve whatever terrible purposes he or she has in mind."
Chief: "And according to Lark, the puppeted words of our murderer suggest that we're all too late to do anything. Bob, this may be a fool's errand."
Bob, after a good pause: "...you may be right, but I guess all we can do is continue on."
Chief: "Right, right. One odd aspect of Lark's situation has to do with the puppeteer's message. He was briefly under some suspicion because when the police dismantled the machinery of the puppeteering, several components were missing, or absent. The authorities claim it was not possible that the victim could have become reanimated and spoke to Lark."
Bob: "So Lark may have been lying?"
Chief: "No. I don't think so. He has absolutely no motive and has genuinely removed himself from the picture. Also, he actually was helpful in the investigation while you've been gone and if he was wanting to take advantage of the situation, he probably could have done any number of things much sooner. There is no advantage here. I believe him and he seemed quite spooked by the whole event."

Bob: "So what does that mean, then...the missing components? Someone broke in and took them, got rid of some evidence for some reason?"

Chief: "Possibly, but not likely. The police arrived as Lark was leaving the house. It was under watch almost immediately. It is odd. Not sure why the missing parts would even be significant, but either there was someone in the house that worked quickly or...the murderer has someone on the inside, working for the police, that could have done the job at a later time."

Bob: "Either way, it doesn't give us much to go on. Let's just hope the words of the corpse were a bluff."

Chief: "Yes, let's hope it's not too late but I have never known a corpse to lie."

Bob: "In a way, isn't that all they do?"

The Chief laughed.

Bob: "Ok, so, besides the mountain of strange new information you've already piled upon me, anything else going on that we should know but not be able to do a thing about?"

Chief: "No, I think that about covers it. You got your trip planned yet?"

Bob: "Well, I've looked at several itineraries, haven't decided yet. Looks like the quickest I can get to the Balaenae people is almost a week's travel. It's right there around the galactic core and nobody travels that far in one go. I'm going to be hopping from system to system. Jump, then wait, then jump then wait...you know."

Chief: "Yeah, but you'll get to see some nifty places, places you've never been."

Bob: "I've almost had my fill of places I've never been and I've hardly left our little stellar neighborhood. I am going to try and talk to an actual human being who works here and see if they can find a bit quicker path."

Chief; "Any good food on that station...*Gallium* is it?"

Bob: "Man, there's everything here. It's crazy. You really need to see this place."

Chief: "I was there very briefly about ten years ago, but I didn't get to sight-see any."

Bob: "You still on Ganymede?"

Chief: "Yeah, we have a fairly tight quarantine here and I'm going to stay put a while, see what comes of this virus thing."

Bob: "That's probably wise. ..and to answer your unasked question, yes, there is a Pauly's Bread Bucket here."

Bob knew the Chief had been severely burned out on Pauly's Bread Bucket and found their galactic ubiquitousness very irritating.

Chief: "Thanks, I'll rush right over. Well, I guess I should let you get to it. Let me know if you find anything."
Bob: "Will do."
And with that Bob resumed his circuitous wandering around the mammoth station with the eventual intentions of deciding how he was going to get to where he was going.

The Chief resumed his humdrum activities of checking up on leads, contacting a variety of people, mostly military, that seemed to know nothing of the redacted info on the mystery person...or acted their part well.

It wasn't until several hours later, late evening, that the Chief noticed a message waiting silently for him to access his terminal. It was odd. It was solely text, and seemed to have no identifying marking. There was no way to tell who it came from or even who it was address to except for the fact that there it was in the Chief's received messages. A mere glance and the Chief could feel the implications of this mysterious note. It began with the words "His name is Moloch.", and the Chief knew he was in for a long night.

Chapter Nineteen: A Portent of Earthquakes and Lightning.

Compromised awareness of Thallus-grain-00-Epsilon-naught has resulted in invalid data transmission.

Circuitous grain Upsilon-0-mu-eta-mu-0-Upsilon has wandered incalculably. Linear protocols ignored.

Numbers of transmission errors: 10. Binary and tertiary. Modified by nullus protocol.

Bob, a bit lost in thought, wandered aimlessly around the *Gallium* station. It had been several hours and Bob wasn't quite aware of the time. A clock is of limited use in galaxy peppered with different planets, different suns, all with their own cycles of day and night. This effect was even more pronounced on a very modern station catering to the widest array of interstellar travelers. What time is it? What planet might you reference to know such a thing? Relative to Helen's Crown, it was late evening, but Bob's sleep schedule was quite off and he was wide awake.

Bob had been walking through a small courtyard lined with shops. It almost looked like a touristy village; manicured lawn, several well-kempt trees, streetlights. When he came to the end of the lawn he was caught off guard a bit. He had noticed the area opened up beyond the courtyard, but expected to find several steps leading down to a similar clutch of shops. Here, at the edge of the lawn was a vast drop off to a sight of monumental and countless skyscrapers, revealing that he had been high above them this whole time. He could just make out the boundary of the orb into which he had arrived on the periphery and could see that this was the open end of that orb that led into another part of *Gallium* station. The sight here was like standing atop the tallest tower in central Helen's Crown and looking out to see endless buildings. Some of these skyscrapers had to be a hundred stories or more and a blur of activity about them. Looking almost straight down, Bob could see pulse-engine transports flittering to and fro between the buildings at dozens of levels. He really couldn't even see the ground. Bob was certain that had he jumped from the edge he would end up getting hit by several transports and probably would never even make it to the ground.

Being caught off guard like this and the quick change in perspective hit Bob with a bit of vertigo, which was fine. There was no real way he could fall. It was a disorienting sight, but completely safe. Bob couldn't imagine, though, why there would be so many people occupying so very many buildings. Was there really that much business going on in this galaxy? It was a sight. It *was* a sight.

It was then that Bob received a message from the Chief. It was text and said only, *"Get to a private room. We have a few things to talk about."*

Bob, not willing to tackle the mass of buildings below, turned back to somewhat familiar ground and found the nearest communications room.

Bob: "What's going on?"

Chief: "Well, got a message. It's gotta be from one of the military institutions I've been after, not sure, but it mentions...possibly...the fella we're looking for."

Bob: "What exactly did the message say?"

Chief: "It was only text. Here, I'll read it too you:"

His name is Moloch. He was hired as a suspension-field engineer twelve years ago. Discharged for poor performance. He later found employment with Water Sprite Genomics of Ohm. Some event happened. I know nothing of it. His information was then redacted and he was relocated. This is all I know.

Bob: "Interesting. Who sent this?"

Chief: "I dunno."

Bob: "What do you mean you don't know?"

Chief: "It had no identifying marks. None. Completely encrypted too. High level stuff. I don't even know how that's possible, but it was only text, what I read to you and nothing more."

Bob: "Well...I'm assuming you're looking into it. Suspension-field engineer, huh?"

Chief; "Yeah, that doesn't seem to make any sense."

Bob: "And how does a suspension-field engineer end up working in genetics?"

Chief: "I suppose we've all had changes in employment that don't seem to make any sense, Mr. environmental engineer."

Bob: "Touché. I suppose your expertise in field analytics deduced that conclusion. The genetics work does fit our bill here, though. It has to be someone with that kind of know-how to engineer a virus. ...Moloch...hmm."

Chief: "Well, that's all. I'm heading back to my makeshift office and getting the ball rolling on this. We need to contact Water Sprite Genomics and see if we can find anything out about this guy. If we get a general idea of where he might be...who knows."

Bob: "I hope so, though it is a rather populated galaxy these day, and fairly easy to get around...could be anywhere." Bob said this as he recalled the precipice and the city of skyscrapers he had just encountered.

Bob: "If you find out anything, let me know...though there's not a lot I can do from here."

Chief: "Yeah, I know, but I still need you to bounce some ideas off of, also, if we end up getting an idea of a location associated with this Moloch you might need to do a little extra traveling...assuming you don't mind."

Bob: "I've really got nothing better to do."

They said their goodbyes and Bob headed for the exit of the communications room. Next to the exit was a small, almost unnoticeable half-door on the adjacent wall. Out of curiosity Bob pressed into it and it unlatched. He took a look in and inside was an peculiar passage, seemingly composed of mahogany, stained and polished. Taking a few steps inside, Bob could see the passage was somewhat conical and increasingly smaller as he walked. The scent of fine wood filled the air. In a mere twenty or so feet the passage was too small for him to pass and he could see that it angled upward at about forty-five degrees or so, tapering to an opening the sized of his head beyond which was only blackness. Stepping back into the communications room and then exiting Bob couldn't help but wonder, *"what could that passage possibly be for?"*. This station was rather unusual on the large scale, but as well on the small scale.

Bob was feeling the need to make haste since the conversation with the Chief and decided he needed to get the ball rolling on his next leg of the trip. Bob accessed a map via terminal and proceeded to the nearest information desk, which wasn't too far away. Even in a station of this magnitude and unbelievable complexity, nothing was really ever far away. The information desk seemed like a small kiosk receded into a bank of shops. This particular area seemed rather unpopulated and the kiosk exuded a warm yellow glow in the perpetual night of this portion of *Gallium*. Had Bob toured the entire station he would have found places so infused with radiance as to be overwhelming, but he happened to enter a globe mostly exposed to the dark space beyond.

Working at the information desk was a young woman that greeted him rather formally, an almost rote utterance. Before replying, he considered whether or not she was real or a simulation. He poked a finger in the lower right corner of the open space of the kiosk only to find it met with an almost invisible plastiglass and to which the woman directed her attention briefly before returning eye contact. She was definitely a simulation, but very hard to tell so visually.

Simulation: "Hi. Can I help you?"

Bob: "Yeah, I need to plan a trip to Leviathan...specifically planet Vox."

Simulation: "Ah, somebody is planning to visit the Balaenae people.", she said with a wink.

Bob: "I need to find the quickest path there."

Simulation: "Would you be interested in information on the history of the Balaenae..."

Bob, interrupting: "No, travel details only."

Simulation: "There are several travel restrictions to Leviathan. Travel there requires a civilian level clearance of..."

Bob, interrupting again, "I have clearance."

Simulation: "May I access your information for the purposes of ..."

Bob, "Yes."

The simulation, placing a hand to her chin and seeming to think for a second or two: "There are 34 travel itineraries pertinent to your request with an average travel time of 7.5 days."

The good thing about these simulations is that once they access your information everything they communicate is in the units of measurement to which you are most familiar.

Bob: "Ok. What I'm wondering is if there is anyway to get there faster, maybe using a non-standard travel or hitching a ride on some industrial ships, something like that. I don't mind staying aboard my own ship even for an extended time if that gets me there any sooner. I don't need the luxury of a suite or shopping, all that business."

Simulation: "Including industrial vessels there is one option that can get you there in approximately four days. However, one leg of the trip would involve being docked to the hull of a materials barge and a signed waiver would be required."

Bob: "Oh, no, no, no. No materials barges. Only trips without barges."

Materials barges were often unmanned, full of junk to be sent one place or another, and were not the safest things in the world. They could miscalculate and be lost to the void or just enter with enough error that the displacement field might shear things loose, for example, a small vessel clinging to the hull. Also, the time schedule is completely dependent on what is required so a shipment that is scheduled to leave might get held up indefinitely if there is a disagreement about cost and/or the specifics of the materials provided.

Simulation: "Eliminating material barges we are left with 7 options that average about 5.5 days travel time."

Bob: "Let's go with one of those."

The simulation displayed the details on the screen which Bob sent to his personal account and offered a quick "thank you" to the mirage of a young woman floating upon the screen.

Simulation: "Thank you, and we appreciate you choosing *Gallium* for your travel considerations."

Bob eyed his choices and chose an itinerary that left in a couple of hours. It technically wasn't the fastest route, but the one faster, by six hours, didn't leave until morning. This would get him to Leviathan as quickly as was reasonable and would give him a good amount of time to pack his ship full of supplies of which the majority was food related.

While Bob was preparing for his trip, far, far away something much more interesting was about to take place. The location was the Bohr system. The planet was Diophantus. There, locked deep in a military facility, the location of which only few knew, a team was busily studying the cylindrical chunk of Pixler's glass. They had little to no concern for the person trapped inside, nor the fact that that person was still, in fact, alive albeit in a very still state. They were consumed with trying to crack the code of the glass, the holy grail of theoretical metallurgy that stood right before them. They wouldn't though. They were far, far from cracking the code and, unbeknownst to them, they had little time remaining.

In a nearby military facility lay the rather austere quarters of a general Grom Humbolt. Humbolt lived his life according to a set of very strict rules. Everything had its place and all things were to be done in the proper manner. His tolerance for the contrary was nonexistent and rectification was often harsh. He was often associated as an administrator of that antiquated concept of "punishment". He was not the decided authority over Diophantus, but many believe that his influence exceeds that of the parliamentary membership and the course of political motion was guided by his hand. Regional star systems have been watching carefully for those unmistakable signs of totalitarianism as neighbors always abhor a dictator. As we all know, the incessant stupidity of a dictatorship, with rare exception, culminates in that all too universal tell-tale sign of misplaced authority: the institutionalized haircut. To date, it has been determined that Diophantus is not a true dictatorship, but a developed military industrial society; the ominous step before.

Humbolt had returned from a series of meetings, meetings which he scheduled constantly because the only thing he liked more than orderly operation was the contemplation and preparation of orderly operation. As he was carefully arranging his bedside belongings the stationary terminal at his desk lit up, which struck Grom as very peculiar. As he turned to look at the projection, expecting to find some urgent message from a high ranking officer, what he found instead, staring back at him, was the image of someone unknown to him, some plain-clothed bespectacled man.

Humbolt, angry: "How did you access this channel? You haven't the authority to..."

Bespectacled man, calmly: "Forgive my intrusion, but you and I have matters to discuss of grave importance."

Humbolt, even angrier at being interrupted: "Nonmilitary personnel on a military channel is a treasonable act punishable by..."

Bespectacled man, "Now is not the time to talk. Now is the time to listen."

Humbolt, incredulous: "Oh, is it?" After which he attempted to dismiss the terminal function only to find he could not. He attempted to change communications channels and found he could not. He also determined that he hadn't the ability to communicate via terminal to anyone else. It was then that he realized something quite serious was happening.

Bespectacled man: "Again, assuming you are satisfied, now is the time to listen."

Humbolt inched closer and after a moment moderately said "speak."

Bespectacled man: "You have something that belongs to me. I need it returned. I assume you know of what I speak."

Humbolt, regaining a bit of his hubris: "If you provide the appropriate documentation supporting your claim to the found object it will be considered, but you will still face charges for interfering with military communications."

The bespectacled man gave a half grin: "Let our communication be very clear. I have come solely to you, as the authority of Diophantus, in hopes that you will use that power to return an object that you *know* does not belong to you or the people of Diophantus. I give you this opportunity to correct a mistake made in the most peaceful of means."

Humbolt could read a hint of the sinister between those words, "And if I refuse."

Bespectacled man: "If you refuse I will give the people an opportunity, however brief, to persuade you. Failing that, your city...Ikarus is it?...will fall. Let us both avoid unnecessary destruction and loss of life."

Humbolt thought carefully and quickly. He wasn't sure how this man hijacked military communications, meaning he had access to some sophisticated technology, but Diophantus has a massive shield

generator in every major city, especially Ikarus, and an aerial attack was ludicrous. In Humbolt's decisive black and white mentality, he determined that the fall of Ikarus was a bluff. This, coupled with his outrage at the sheer audacity of a nobody taking control of military communications and the disruption to the orderly manner in which he liked to conduct his evening, was almost too much to take.
Bespectacled man: "I will need an answer immediately."
Humbolt: "You can go to hell."
The bespectacled man gave a kind of somber smirk as if to say *"i'm sorry it has to come to this"* then the terminal screen went blank.

Humbolt rushed out to see if someone could find out who this bespectacled man was and how he took control of military communications. He was enraged and his heart was more intent on punishing this individual than any true justice and even farther down his list was concern for his people at the threat made. Even the potential loss of an object that could economically change the course of Diophantus had its mysteries been revealed was of no concern to Humbolt. Anger was all that lay in his heart.

Moments later, in a feat of impressive technological wizardry, every terminal screen in every major city on Diophantus went blank. Shortly after the image of a bespectacled man appeared with a brief and poignant message:
"Your military has possession of an object that does not belong to them. It needs to be returned. Your general Humbolt has been uncooperative despite a warning of the imminent destruction of Ikarus. I offer you, the people of Diophantus, the opportunity to persuade your authority figures to act in accordance with decency and righteousness. The object must be returned. In the event that it is not, Ikarus will fall. The destruction will be total. Other cities will follow. You already have my virus, what other gifts do you desire? They will be yours. You have twenty-four standard hours."
The terminal screens went blank then shortly returned to their normal insipid activity. Diophantus was a long way from either Bob or the Chief. Information spreads slowly across so vast an expanse of space and it wouldn't be until after this issue was concluded that they would hear of what had happened to the people of Diophantus.

On Ganymede the Chief was busy looking into the name Moloch and contacting officials at Water Sprite Genomics. It was a long and slow process with so little information, but more than they had even hoped to acquire.

Back at *Gallium*, Bob was about to begin the first leg of his trip to the Balaenae people. He had already docked in the specified jump-ship, the *Runner's Four*, and had a little less than an hour before the first jump. This ship would make several jumps to nearby stars before he had to change jump-ships. This meant he had a good six hours or so before he really had to do anything. Once he got back in his ship, less distracted by the ubiquitousness of this sprawling station, tiredness did set upon him. It was late by his internal clock and as Bob was fond of telling himself when he needed a nap "It's always night somewhere". It would be a good time to get a little shut-eye.

Dream Journal: Spoil

A beautiful dark forest is lit by the white light of a full moon on a cloudless night. It is spring and the night air is comfortable and cool. This is one of those dreams where I seem to know my part unlike those where I'm wondering where I am and how I got there. I was on the porch of a wood-plank cabin, old but well built. The porch was designed to completely surround the cabin in a perfect square so that it might be accessible by exits on all sides. The cabin was lovingly decorated such that anyone seeing it would know it was lived in by a loving family, but here it was night and no other light but the moon illuminated the darkness. Not far was a lake that seemed to stretch endlessly towards the horizon. I was certain that my daughter was there with me, but always standing perfectly behind so that I could only be aware of her presence yet never see her with my eyes. On my shoulder was a white mouse, the cutest thing, who was trained to sense danger and danger was approaching.

We had earlier extinguished all the candles and the stove, to remain unseen and hope the danger would pass. Out on the porch, hanging like wind-chimes, was a particularly useful metallic sculpture. It was a mobile of crescent moon, and stars, decorated with glass beads of a variety of colors. Hanging in the center of the mobile was a little metal boat, crafted to look like a common sailless wooden skiff, almost exactly like the one tied to a rock at lakes edge off in the distance. In the boat I had poured the freshest heavy cream, almost glowingly white in the moonlight.

I spent the better part of the night checking and rechecking the mobile and the cream in the boat. Each time the little mouse would hop atop the mobile and work his way down to the little boat, which was almost the perfect size for him. He seemed to inspect the cream as intently as I and would often have himself a little drink. Still, my daughter remained unseen and silent.

Late, in the thickest part of the night, as I was about to nod off with a head bobbing gingerly as I sat upright, I became startled. It was a bolt of terror that surged through my spine and I could easily tell the little mouse felt the same terror as he took shelter under the collar of my shirt and quaked.

269

I bolted up and ran to the mobile. The little boat was full of cream that had curdled and turned rancid. A putrid odor stung my nose and I knew, with no doubt, that nearby was a horrid witch.

I looked out toward the forest. I could feel her there, like a creeping black tanglevine of smoke and hatred singing like a fury into the hearts of beasts and coming for us to breathe her in deeply and singe our lungs with hot ash. In that forest now, winding our way, was terrible wickedness.

I reached back and grabbed the unseen hand of my daughter. She, the little mouse under my collar, and I ran as fast as our earthly legs could take us toward the distant lake in hopes to make it to the small boat awaiting us there.

At the lakes edge we piled into the boat and set out across the water that stretched endlessly into the horizon, black water lit by the white night light. We would never go back to the forest. We couldn't. There was no place for us there. We set sail across the lake for the moon, knowing we would somehow get there, for the moon was the only place where we could be free from her witchcraft and the darkness of this conquered land.

Chapter Twenty: The Glass Menagerie part 2:
That Witch Survives

"In galactic news, the hot topic is yet again the rampant virus that has carved a path through the Milky Way. The generally agreed upon estimate is now in excess of 16,000 worlds belonging to over a thousand stellar systems. Bear in mind this estimate involves planets, sub-planets, and large constructs with significant populations. As of yet, there has been no pathology identified with the virus, no symptomatology, and still no knowledge of the viral mechanism itself. Every infected system, and those yet to be infected, have research facilities working feverishly at identifying and eliminating the virus, but as of yet have been unsuccessful. It is assumed that the mysterious CIDER organization is too working on the problem, but has been silent on the subject. All that is currently known is that the virus spreads rapidly, exceptionally so, and within a matter of weeks it is believed that the virus will verge on total galactic infection. Many isolated worlds have assumedly been free from infection though in the general stellar population even intensive quarantines have ultimately proven ineffective."

Bob was somewhere on the third leg of his trip. It had been a couple of days and he was currently aboard a cloud mining vessel heading to a destination of which Bob was hardly certain. It didn't matter. He had several days and several other ships before he'd get to the Balaenae people. His current status was: boredom. He really couldn't leave his cruiser while docked on this cloud mining vessel, *The Slider* was the ship's name, so all Bob had to occupy his time was reading and thinking, and when he got tired of those he'd listen to the faint hum of his nervous system as he stared blankly into space.

Bob wanted to be more proactive. He wanted to be on the ground at that Water Sprite Genomics facility seeing if anyone knew that Moloch guy and what his story might be. Bob wanted to be walking about, physically active, getting things accomplished. It was not in his nature to sit idle while things needed to be done. Bob knew that he was far from "idle". He knew the job he was on *had* to be done and it might be the most important of the jobs to be done though he couldn't help feel like it was a bit of a fool's errand. Bob didn't know why a virus could be constructed in such a way that the experts at CIDER couldn't figure it out, and if they couldn't figure it out probably no one could. However, if one of these human variants were immune for some reason, that immunity might be understandable

even if the virus is not. Bob couldn't help but feel that it was a long shot.
>>
   The Chief had contacted and spoke to several higher-ups at Water Sprite Genomics. All they could manage was a lot of absent information. They didn't know who the Chief was talking about. Didn't know the name Moloch. Didn't have a scrap that said anything about him. Everything had been redacted. These higher-ups had worked there for years, but had no knowledge of a single employee from that long ago. They employ a good five hundred people and have a rather high turnover rate. They said they would send a memo asking any employee with information to come forward and the Chief had little faith in the efficacy of this process...so, he was at a loss. Nothing made much sense and even the unbelievable boon of information from the mysterious source was not much to go on. A name and an occupation don't get you very far in a galaxy full of people.
   The Chief was still stationed on Ganymede. Ganymede has maintained a level of quarantine that has of yet left the city of Gallilei untouched. However, this made travel slow. Travel all over the galaxy was slowing due to quarantines, and intensive scans of all incoming vessels and cargo. Fear was rising. The Chief decided he need a walk, some fresh air. He'd been inside a lot and it was getting to him. He needed a change of scenery, something was stale about his surroundings. When one's surroundings become stale, the mind tends to sit in grooves of thought worn by repetition. It's amazing how often problems will become clear with a simple walk in the woods. From indoors to outdoors, the change is often between a finite enclosure and the infinite expense of the universe around. Perspective changes and so does the mind. Often those worn grooves disappear entirely like creased skin after a night of heavy sleep and a motionless face against a lumpy pillow.
   The Chief, however, was not going for a walk in the woods. He was going for a stroll through the city, probably to get a bite to eat, but his true destination was the Ministry of Records.

Welcome to the Ministry of Records!
An introduction compiled from the resources of the Free Galactic Library (FGL)
"It can be argued that the Ministry of Records has existed in some form since old Earth antiquity. However, the official Ministry of Records was established over twelve hundred years ago as a repository of universal information. All are welcome to share and learn from our voluminous collected data and store precious

information in our most secure, highly encrypted, neural web. Have a novel you've written? Store it with us for eternal posterity. It will never be lost. You merely choose sharing permission, if any, and the end date by which the information is made public. You are in control of your information. Start your contribution to the collective knowledge of the universe today! "
-Official introductory statement from the Ministry of Records.

The **Ministry of Records** was established over 1200 years ago as a means to collect a lasting human record of "our doings". The idea was that nothing would be lost. Anything from new theories in metaphysics to scribbled grocery lists can be preserved indefinitely. Many use the ministry of records as a galactic "guest list", a record of an individuals travels and temporal location. The ministry of records can be an indispensable interplanetary resource for intellectual collaboration in business, science, and the arts. It can also be a personal keeper of one's private journal entries. The extent and use of the ministry of records is limited only by the imagination of those employing its services.

Inner workings and upkeep: The ministry of records functions as a galactic neural net. Each location is an entry point into the collective. Data is protected with the highest level of faultless encryption (for more information of the ministry's encryption process see the FGL article on "Quasi-conscious neural net data sublimation and automated ancillary instinct emulation." This data is transmitted to the collective ministry quasi-consciousness in much the same way that communication between stellar systems is managed. This method allows data that is entered at one location to be available at all galactic locations with very little lag time (depending, of course, on the level of isolation in which a ministry outpost might be found).

Upkeep and operation of the ministry of records is a complex and privileged endeavor. Only those members native to the records guild may seek employment with the ministry and the process of upkeep, repairs, and innovation is handled as an internal matter. The FGL unfortunately cannot provide any further information on the subject as reliable data is absent.

Controversy, Hearsay, and Conjecture: The standard controversy, "Who controls the information of the Ministry of Records?", is unanswerable, but longstanding inspections have not produced any suspect faults or misuse, nor have any assertions of violation been proven valid upon investigation. Additionally, the Ministry of Records data stream is volunteer oriented on the supply end and its use is optional. There is, however, a long standing assumption about the true mission of the Ministry of Records. Many believe that the ministry is a "temporal data conduit", meaning that it functions as a waypoint for communication between time periods. For example, if a time-traveler was sent from 1000 years in the future to now, they could log their info as a means to communicate the success of their travel to their time of origin. This may seem like a cumbersome ordeal to send a message that has to lie in wait for 1000 years, but see it from the perspective of the time-traveler. The institution from the future could merely check the traveler's data to see if the transfer was a success. As history would reshuffle itself, this data would appear instantly in the records as verification the trip had happened as planned. It is worth noting that there currently are no means of time-travel and no evidence of time-travelers but it is believed that the ministry exists in part as an aid to the hypothetical time-travelers of the future. The ministry might function in this way for two reasons: one, it would be far too difficult for a time-traveler to create a lasting message as an individual, and two, the efforts involved in time-travel and the dangers of abuse would invariably allot only for a guild of time-travelers of the highest ethical standards that would, in theory, alter to past to only avoid terrible calamities of epic proportion. For further reading on the subject of time travel, see the FGL article "*Is Time Travel Possible? If you can read this then I have yet to travel back in time and change the title to 'Time Travel is Possible', by Brenda Bendrenda Ph.D.*"

The Chief wasn't visiting the Ministry of Records to pass the time. Nor was he visiting the Ministry for research relating to the case. He was visiting the Ministry for advice, advice in the form of a ghost. You see, there is a practice that extends back thousands of years, in concept even further. This is a practice known as the **Lazarus scan**. An intense scan of an individual is performed and that information is used to create an emulated consciousness closely resembling that of the original. The idea was to be able to 'record' and keep ourselves beyond death. Early attempts produced highly faulty results often with disturbing effects. It was arrogance that led the first developers of the Lazarus scan to wrongfully believe they understood how consciousness worked and what constitutes the identify of an individual. A free-floating mind, encoded in data and partitioned from the real world, was unavoidably operating in a severely compromised state. The output was most often wailing, screaming, or silence which upon analysis read as intense fear or terror protocols. Though even today we cannot claim to firmly grasp the supreme mystery of consciousness, major developments have been made in the Lazarus scan. It is now known to us that a consciousness is not a data set. It is not a collection of neurons, real or simulated. Consciousness is the interrelationship and interdependence of a large variety of processes. In the early Lazarus scan the negative results were the conclusion of an operational mind that was receiving absolutely no data from the continuum of processes that identify self, the universe, and the false division of the two. It would be similar to waking up and not being able to sense your body, or the universe, or even the mechanisms by which you establish identity while at the same time being aware of the absence. It would be akin to total obliteration yet being able to feel and be aware of that oblivion. The concept developed from this understanding is called the *Abyssal state* and theoretically, according to science and philo-metaphysical studies, only achievable through artificial means.

What the designers of the Lazarus scan then needed were mechanisms to supply this chain of processes to feed the emulated consciousness the needed sustenance. Three protocols were then developed in no small part to the MMQFFFT whose use has far exceeded its design. The first of these is the ***mind-matter feedback substantiation protocol***. This was the easiest one. It merely fed the emulated consciousness physical data, necessarily simulated, of the universe to which it was supposed to belong. Not surprisingly, this is a considerable amount of information but fortunately reusable for every emulated consciousness...most of the time.

The second protocol is ***conscious process layering and summation***. Contrary to practical belief, reality is only discernable in its fluidity. A thing made static tends to lose that status by being unaffected and thus separate from reality. A simple, and rather childish, example might be to imagine an extremely realistic statue of a tiger found in the jungle. At first you might be frightened, but after time, when the tiger failed to change state or move, it would become increasingly obvious that it lacked a certain reality as in fact it does. The universe operates like this to the mind and in turn the consciousness perceives not only the universe, but itself with the same analytical eye. Feeding a static universe to the emulated consciousness is hardly better than no universe at all. Feeding a static consciousness back into itself is even worse. The conscious process layering and summation protocol has the emulated consciousness paint and repaint over that universe so fed to it with a certain amount of error. The error, or *jitter* provides the illusion of fluidity. Dithering the simulated universe in this way, building up successive layers, then summing those layers give the emulated consciousness a foundational seat by which it can then be stably attached. The same, or highly similar, protocol is then initiated for the conscious mind itself whereby the successive layers and summation can provide a false fluidity to the consciousness looking back upon itself and can thus seem to be more real.

The third protocol is a sort of two-in-one: **sub-conscious reverberant cycling and psionic envelope generation**. The sub-conscious mind does a considerable amount of reality-rendering. In fact, a vast majority of mental processing has been completed by the time the conscious mind is aware of it. Again, with an absent or static sub-conscious a foundational mental seat cannot be established and a disconnection from cognitive time-space renders the mind futile, a mere repetitive loop of surface level cognition that is bound in first order awareness processes, namely fear and the fight-or-flight mechanism. What the true sub-conscious likes to do is process and modify information received from the universe then formulate an interpretation of that information into thoughts and experiences, then feed this information back through itself to analyze these thoughts and experiences and develop thoughts and experiences based on the original thoughts and experiences. This repetitive process, which goes on *ad infinitum*, is the sub-conscious reverberant cycle. Keep in mind that this is only one of the many functions of the sub-conscious, but one that is very important for producing a viable Lazarus scan. The sub-conscious, in this sense, is dicing up the universe over and over again to produce a wide array of predictive possibilities ranging from the plausible to the absurd (as anyone recalling a dream can understand). The absence of this process robs even a fluidic universe of it's motility as the predictive element can only render static and, as we know, the key to reality, on all of the many levels a human being can experience reality, is in non-static fluidity. Emulating this is no small task, but the greater task involves containing this *ad infinitum* process. How does one bound infinity? We currently do not fully understand how the mind accomplishes this, but a usable alternative is the second stage of our protocol: psionic envelope generation. This is a means of folding this reverberant cycling process in on itself so that it is unbounded yet contained. This constrains the processing of the sub-conscious to the aforementioned range of "plausible to absurd". Without psionic envelope generation the process is uncontained and bounded only by the absolute extremes to which the mind will most often find itself. Those extremes are the irrationally plausible and the concretely absurd. Constraining the range and shaping the appropriate bell curve places the emulated sub-conscious more accurately in the human cognitive range.

With these three protocols in place, and assumedly operating appropriately, the emulated consciousness is functional and even useful. Early designers of the Lazarus scan and supporters had at one time wishfully viewed this process as a kind of immortality.

Unfortunately, or quite fortunately depending on your philosophy, this is not the case. The error in this assumption of immortality has to do with a faulty understanding of the nature of consciousness. At one time it was assumed that consciousness was a thing that emanated from the brain, in other words, the brain generated consciousness. This is wrong. Consciousness is a pervasive interrelationship between a vast number of natural processes, only one of which is what we commonly call the biological human being. Consciousness can easily exist without and beyond the human biology as is evident from the Lazarus scan itself (among a number of other known conditions). The number of processes that constitute consciousness far, far outnumber the singularity of the human being. Consciousness is a function of the universe. The human being is only that small, small portion of it that turns and looks back upon itself and contemplates that which it is. In being, the observer of the process then becomes the observer of the observer and thus creates the seemingly concrete falseness of identity. In simpler terms, you are the universe, nothing more, nothing less, but you've fooled yourself into thinking you're something apart from it.

As for the Lazarus scans. Useful yes, but immortal beings, no. Anyone revisiting a departed loved one will instantly know the difference. Though an enormous amount of effort has been taken to provide the emulation with a fluidic universe, they themselves are fixed. They do not grow, or change. They are merely repositories of memories and information and not the individual with which we might wish to identify them. For this reason, Lazarus scans are used for practical purposes, but few individual see them as the continuation of the departed. The universe is too elusive to render its mysteries so easily and allow itself to be grasped like some wicked human possession.

The Chief knew the procedure. It was always a little difficult getting to the point where interfacing with a Lazarus scan would become useful. These pseudo-conscious minds can't help but also be aware of a very strange inconsistency with their predicament. They often have many questions and it takes an amount of explanation to ease them into a proper conversation.

The Ministry of Records on Ganymede was a rather small conical building seemingly of rust-colored brick and mortar. Inside was a round lobby, unattended, that was lined with two separate staircases leading to the private rooms above. Briskly walking up a set of stairs, the Chief entered the first unoccupied room (currently all rooms were unoccupied). The rooms were wedged shaped with a sloping roof matching the curvature of the building. They were slightly off-white and warmly lit, sparse containing only a desk and chair, and a little stuffy...air stale from lack of use.

The Chief set a the desk and activated his personal terminal access. Almost every surface in these rooms could act as a display and were equipped with relatively current dimensional rendering and projection. Following the issue of several commands, the image of a man, proportional and accurate, appeared above the desk though only from the waist up. He was older, gray-headed, wrinkled slightly with a scar bisecting his right eyebrow.

The Lazarus scan made direct eye contact with the Chief and looked puzzled, confused, and moderately concerned.

Lazarus scan: "...You...you look,...old. What happened to you?

Chief: "I know dad. I *am* old."

Lazarus scan, confused still: "Why...are you ok son? What happened...", then realizing the bizarre nature of his own situation, "Where are we? What's going on?"

It is and was like this every time. Everything had to be explained. Different people had different techniques, but the Chief said in plain terms what the situation was. This was always followed by "So...I'm dead?", and "I don't feel dead." Sometimes, "Everything seems fuzzy and unreal.", or a lengthy discussion ensues of "How did I die?" followed by more and more details of their own end and what happened after.

It is possible to record these interactions and preserve them in the memory of the Lazarus scan and many attempts were made to do just that, but the results were always negative. There are several problems involved in creating new memories for a Lazarus scan. One, an active mind is constantly sorting memories by importance. A very necessary aspect of this process is forgetting. Forgetting or dumping data allows our minds to be fluid and flexible. A Lazarus scan that creates new memories tends to unravel the unimportant data that comprises it operation. The vast number of details of the emulated universe and other constructed processes slowly dissipate and the Lazarus scan descends toward the inevitable insanity of the pre-protocol scan where the state of consciousness is unreal and terrifying. Second, to "correct" this by forcing an end to the process of data elimination, the Lazarus scan becomes slower and slower and eventually unable to process even the simplest of requests. Third, memory retention is emotionally connected to the internal timeline of the consciousness. When these newly created memories are separated by long tracks of oblivion between Lazarus scan access, the scan rapidly detaches from a universe full of holes and the primary scan state of horror and confusion returns.

After a thorough discussion with the Lazarus scan, delineating it's situation and bringing it up to speed on the events of the Chief's investigation, a good two and a half hours or so, the Chief was finally at the point where they could talk.

Chief: "Dad, I need your advice. I don't know what to do about this virus, or these murders, or whatever the hell is going on."

The Chief's father had been a medical resource tactician for a great number of years before getting involved in geoplanning speculation. He was successful in both positions because of his tactical mind and this tactical mind was what the Chief was after now.

Lazarus scan: "Well son, about the fella you're looking for, this Moloch guy, I don't know that I can be much help there. Finding a single human being in a rather heavily populated galaxy is a little more complicated than a needle in a haystack. In general, there are two ways to hide. One way is to go somewhere where no one will ever find you. Remote. Hidden. Far, far away. The other is to hide in plain sight."

Chief: "Yeah, that's quite a lot to cover."

Lazarus scan: "Yep, everything is either in plain sight or hidden, far away. So I guess I've narrowed your possibilities to somewhere in the universe."

The Chief laughed, "If you were going to hide, where would you go?"

Lazarus scan: "hmm....I dunno. Other end of the galaxy. Maybe. Or, if I had a way to insure my safety, maybe deep near the galactic core. If you went deep enough it would get so violent that people would be foolish to follow. If I had a death wish, I'd be somewhere near the core in orbit around a black hole. Even the most intensive scan at your precise location would probably return nothing. It'd all get sucked right in."

Chief: "Though you'd probably get sucked in too."

Lazarus scan: "That you would, that you would. In all honesty though, we just don't have enough information to know anything yet. I'm afraid my suggestion will be to wait until something makes itself clear."

Chief: "Yeah, you're right." And he knew this line of questioning had run its course.

Chief: "What about the virus? Any thoughts?"

Lazarus scan: "Well, I don't really understand. You are certain that none of these medical facilities have identified it and it's operation?"

Chief: "Not yet, but the best minds are on the job."

Lazarus scan: "Yeah, you mentioned Dr. Morris, but...I dunno...it doesn't make sense."

Chief: "What doesn't make sense?"

Lazarus scan: "Well, a virus is a known thing. How they operate and what they do. It's been fairly well understood since ancient times."

Chief: "Yeah...?"

Lazarus scan: "I mean, it's not magic. It either does the things a virus does or it doesn't."

Chief: "...and?"

Lazarus scan: "Seems to me if they can't figure it out, then maybe it's not a virus."

The Chief thought about this a moment.

Chief: "...if it's not a virus, what would it be?"

Lazarus scan: "I dunno. Something else."

Chief: "..."

Lazarus scan: "A good tactic for getting one's mind out of the groove in which it is naturally wanting to flow it to eliminate the assumed metric."

Chief: "What do you mean?"

Lazarus scan: "Ask those working on it to explain it in non-viral terms. If it's not a virus, what could explain it? It may lead nowhere, but would be a good exercise none the less."

Chief: "...That is an interesting idea."

Lazarus scan: "Though I imagine if *I* have thought about it, a mere ghost, then those working on it have considered it as well."

Chief: "Maybe."

Lazarus scan: "It's odd. I'm breathing, and I can feel my heart beat. It's just...it's odd. It's like it's not quite right."

Chief: "I know dad."

Lazarus scan: "I'm walking around, but I'm still here by this desk. The perspective is changing, but something's....something's not quite right about it."

The Chief could sense a little bit of panic coming from the scan. It is always inevitable. The Lazarus scan then looked the Chief in the eyes again jutting up against the image of his older son and the memories that were incongruent.

Chief: "Well, I should be going dad."

Lazarus scan: "Please, son...I enjoyed talking to you, but...I think it's too much...just let me rest. Maybe I, or whatever this is that's happening, shouldn't happen. ...maybe I shouldn't be anymore."

Every time, every single time the Chief felt the need to access this scan, it ended, almost verbatim in those exact words.

Chief: "Ok dad."

Lazarus scan: "I love you, son."

Chief: "I love you too, dad"

With an uneventful silence, the Lazarus scan disappeared.

It is always an odd mix of the strange and the disconcerting. One can't help but feel they are resurrecting the dead, but not in a satisfying way, like bringing forth form without substance...a shell that is itself aware of its own emptiness. It's easy to get lost in the conversation and feel, just for a moment, that the departed are there before us as they were in life...it's enjoyable even...but ultimately the incongruities return the mind of the observer to the bizarre reality of the Lazarus scan. The Chief didn't access his father's scan often, but when he felt the need it was always the same; a brief feeling of comfort followed by the unavoidable revival of loss.

The Chief walked the city a bit, got a bite to eat. He didn't feel the conversation was terribly productive, but the idea of questioning the fundamental assumption of the virus was mildly intriguing. He wondered if anyone had had the same consideration. It wouldn't hurt to ask. As for tracking down Moloch, there really wasn't much to go on, but the Chief had decided that he needed to physically visit Water Sprite Genomics. Someone there had to have an idea. Someone was there when he worked there. The administration most likely sent a memo asking if anyone knew anything and had little interest in following up. The memo probably went unread or ignored. Yes, a trip to Ohm was certainly in order.

>>

It had been almost twenty-four hours on Diophantus since the rather sinister threat from the strange bespectacled man. The official position, issued by an incredulous general by the name of Grom Humbolt, was that the threat was a bluff and to be ignored. Security was thoroughly inspected and tightened and planet wide shield generators were at battle ready with an increased percentage of planetary energy resources diverted to their backup. To the public, Humbolt had instructed the media that the threat had been "dealt with" and there was no concern to safety. In the mind of this rather cranky general, whom had today woken up on the wrongest side of the bed, he almost believed his own propaganda. He was cranky in part because of his underlings inability to find this bespectacled man and partly because he detested loose ends. A thing unraveled is to the authoritarian the proverbial fingernails across a blackboard, an expression still used whose origin is rarely understood. Unfortunately for the cranky general, this loose end would soon be neatly bound.

It began when a distant outpost in the Bohr system detected a faint radiant signature of disrupted space. Ripples in the black ocean of space-time. Though the reading was unusually faint, it was unmistakable. A ship unseen had made a jump to the Bohr system.

What followed was nothing. No ship could be detected, which wasn't really possible. Nothing but the quickly fading ripples of a jump-ship. This information was shared and other outposts went on high alert. They all scanned what they could and found nothing.

When another outpost, not far from the one detecting the jump caught a small blip that quickly vanished it was instinctively assumed that it was an error, or some transient interference, but under the circumstances the outpost shared this info and scanned more intensely in the region of that small blip. Nothing.

Again a small blip materialized on the instruments of a third outpost. It was like an ephemeral wispy thing. It was there, but then not. Whatever it was could not be seen. Though practically nothing could be read from these seemingly insignificant blips, a wealth of knowledge could be communicated. Whatever this thing was, judging from the distance of the outposts, it was moving very fast and it was making a straight path toward Diophantus.

When this information was communicated to military command, led by a now irate general Grom Humbolt, security went instantly on high alert. He had already ordered the bulk of his fleet's battlecruisers near and on standby and now had them pulling into a prescribed battle position creating a loose web around the planet.

In preparation, the next outpost in the path of the phantom sent a slew of scanning cruisers, who were more than a little nervous, that would take a series of intense measurements. They needed to find out what this thing might be. At the expected time, about eight of the twenty or so crafts picked up yet another insignificant blip. Something was there, but they weren't any closer to solving the mystery, though the pilots of the scanning cruisers were relieved to still be alive.

There were only two more outposts near the path of the phantom between it and Diophantus. The same procedure followed: send out cruisers; take measurements. As one might expect, they were met with the same results, all except one scanner who turned up, excitedly, something new and reported immediately to the outpost command.

Scanner: "I saw it! I saw it!"

Command: "What was it? What did you see?"

Scanner: "It was...it was almond shaped.   ...It was like it was there, but not there."

Command: "Was it a ship or something else?"

Scanner: "I'm...not sure. It's like I could see through it, but it was something."

Had this been any other situation, the scanner reporting would have been sent for evaluation and probably not believed. However, something was going on here and it couldn't be anything but trouble on the way.

The final outpost before Diophantus was equally unsuccessful. The main question at this point was whether they were dealing with a ship of some sort, or a weapon. It was unspoken but a universally shared opinion was that a ship would be much more preferable. A ship contained people and people could be reasoned with. A weapon was blind and vicious. A weapon seeks its target with a serpentine directness, unswayed by reason, compassion, or even a sense of self-preservation. Unfortunately, people sometimes embody and become such a weapon. Diophantus had found itself, one way or another, ruled by such a weapon. There were many things to which general Humbolt would point to rationalize the logic of not returning the found object. These points might include the incredulousness of the threat, the potential economic gain of the object itself, or the exercise of some vague rights regarding the profoundly alluring glass. None of these truly meant anything to the general. This individual, so weaponized and serpentine, was lashing out with an animal mind against the opposition to his absolute authority. Nothing else in this or any other case really mattered. Authority was his currency, life-blood, and nourishment. For this weaponized mind, order, like the serpent's hunger, must be obeyed. Poor Diophantus had been living with this weapon for a considerable time and, despite care, weapons culminate in the inevitable. When the fuse is lit a bomb tends to detonate.

About the time the phantom had reached the final outpost before Diophantus, orders had been made that every available non-military cruiser be dispatched between the outpost and the planet in the hopes that something could be discerned about the rapidly approaching object. Meanwhile, the surrounding battlecruisers had tightened their net in the direction of the oncoming specter and each released their swarm of tactical fighters. Thousands upon thousands of fighters littered the space around the planet in wait for the unknown.

With a blip here and there, beyond the final outpost it could be detected that the object was in fact slowing down. This brought a temporary relief as signifying a ship rather than a weapon, but it still couldn't be seen and the purpose was unknown.

Very close to Diophantus, the phantom slowed further. The surrounding area was peppered with a variety of ships, all with weaponry. Aboard the phantom, a ship of unfamiliar design, stood an expressionless bespectacled man.

Moloch, looking inquisitively at the many ships littering the planetary space said softly aloud, "Gnats. Gnats swarming a piece of decaying fruit."

Moloch's ship wasn't seen until it was in what would be considered a distant orbit around Diophantus when a fighter made visual contact. It wasn't reading on his sensors, but he could see it physically from his ship.

Fighter: "I see it, I see it. I have a confirmed visual."

Battlecruiser command: "You have orders to fire upon sight."

No questioning, no communication. The snake strikes when the reptilian brain so commands. With that order, the fighter discharged his primary phase disruptor with commendable marksmanship considering he was working with visual only. The beam hit squarely in the center of the phantom, but passed through almost as if nothing was there yet the path of the beam had been altered. Something *was* there and had effortlessly deflected the attack.

The deflected beam narrowly missed a fighter on the other side who, due to the displacement, believed the blast to come from the phantom itself. The fighter retaliated and before long there was a dazzling display of weapons discharging. Thousands of ships firing at the location of the phantom so much that a glowing almond-shaped aura could be seen from the continuous deflection of the blasts.

Several ships had been destroyed and a minor amount of damage had been done to one battlecruisers communications array in the self-generated chaos.

The control room of Moloch's ship was open and alabaster white. There were standard view screens at the front of the ship and both port and starboard in the control room. Moloch sat calmly in a comfortable cushioned chair in the middle of the room with a small side table holding a cup of tea. He wondered how long it would take them to realize they are fighting themselves. He hadn't fired a shot and had no intention of doing so. In full disclosure, had he any desire to confess it, Moloch would have to admit that his ship did not, in fact, have any weaponry.

The people of Diophantus had been skeptical in their acceptance of the threat being "dealt with". People know when they are under the rule of a dictator and trust is thus appropriately placed...perhaps it is better to say *distrust* is thus appropriately placed. Any debate of the authorities propaganda ended when the dark side of Diophantus could easily look skyward and see the ensuing battle. The threat had most definitely not been dealt with. News spread quickly to the half of Diophantus in daylight, but their suspicions had already been verified by the rolling blackouts which could be caused by no other reason than the massive amplification of planetary shield generators.

For all of them, it was that ominous feeling of coming nasty weather, like a hurricane approaching for which they had not adequately prepared.

The shield generators were practically at maximum. They covered in overlapping hemispheres, but also individually covering major cities on Diophantus. Shield generators, or more accurately, suspension-field generators, are very good at absorbing many forms of energy. Energy weapon attacks would not be practical against Diophantus. Their shields are too numerous and powerful. To penetrate a shield with an energy weapon, the energy supplied to the weapon would have to greatly overshadow the energy supplied to the shield and considering that shield generators absorb energy, they get a return, though not terribly efficient, of the energy of the attack. However, material objects are a different matter. Any material object can pass through a suspension-field, but the suspension-field tends to "rob" the object of its energy, making transfer difficult. When an object is robbed of its inertia, it tends to slow and get stuck in the field like a raisin falling through pudding. This makes suspension-fields great for dealing with incoming asteroids or similar objects, but a large ship sufficiently slow enough, should be able to squirm through.

At the speed the phantom is traveling, it most surely will get stuck or even smashed against the suspension-field. The expectation is that it should start slowing soon to puncture the shield and at the size of the phantom ship it is assumed that it won't have sufficient mass for gravity to pull it through.

Before long it is realized that the attack on the phantom is not producing results and orders are given to stand down. The chain of command leading all the way to old Grom Humbolt have no idea what to do, but really can do no more than to see if the phantom will get stuck in orbit from the suspension-fields that have been ordered to push the upper limits and approach maximum energy consumption. With all shield generators and power generators working at maximum there is a severe concern that one fault in either the power supply or shield output could bring the whole thing to a crashing halt, but if it can hold out until the ship gets stuck they might be able to apprehend this phantom ship, a ship that Humbolt is more than aware of its potential economic value. A ship that has a vastly improved shielding capability and is practically invisible would easily secure Diophantus's place as a regional superpower, the power of which Humbolt considers inseparable from himself.

To the best of their abilities to detect, the ship is not slowing down. Not any more than it had when it approached Diophantus and not near enough to avoid being destroyed by the shield. This, however, did not fill any of those awaiting the interaction between phantom and shield with any kind of hope. It was ominous. And that omen was fulfilled when the phantom passed through the shield and into the atmosphere of Diophantus effortlessly. It was as if there was no suspension field at all. The shield bent around the phantom ship as easily as it had deflected the attacks of the fighters. To those witnessing this spectacle all hope was lost.

A mass of fighters were ordered to follow but not attack. Attack had proven futile and they couldn't risk damage to the surface below. While in the atmosphere, the phantom ship could be seen much easier, but still read very little on scanning instruments. The phantom ship made a graceful beeline towards the city of Ikarus and the fighters followed. In very little time the phantom ship was within Ikarus airspace and greeted with another swarm of fighters that too wisely did not attack.

It was becoming quite obvious that the phantom ship was headed for a particular military base on Ikarus. Not surprising since it is well known that the authority of Diophantus is military-industrial, but the particular choice was interesting. Inside Ikarus city limits, there are several military bases, each with a slightly different specific purpose. The one the phantom ship was heading towards was not the largest base. It was not the base housing the monolith of Pixler's glass. It did, however, happen to be the base to which Grom Humbolt was currently present. Humbolt generally resided at the largest of the bases on Ikarus. He had spent a good amount of time at the base housing the Pixler's glass. He could have been at any number of political building within the city or elsewhere for that matter, yet the ship was coming directly for him. It was clear to Humbolt that somehow this individual knew exactly where he was.

The phantom ship landed, so to speak in that it actually hovered inches off the ground, in a wide lot surrounded by several open hangars. Behind those hangars was the base armory, a rather short, three story tower upon which the armory management office could be found and in that office, Grom Humbolt. The nose of this almond-shaped phantom ship was pointed in the precise direction of Grom's location.

It was midafternoon on Ikarus. The sky was a lovely blue with a wash of cumulous clouds here and there. The base radiated the dull coloration of warfare: olive, gray, ...concrete and asphalt, all in shades non-reflective and drab. This only accentuated the loveliness of the deep blue and radiant nimbus white of the sky. In this light the phantom ship could be more easily seen. It was almond-shaped, but iridescent with a protective shield manipulating the light around it. Beneath the blurring glow of the shield, metals could be seen, ship parts, and edge here or there, but still only a vagueness of imagery. It was real, it was a ship, but hard to identify much more than that.

There were swarms of fighters, but they were staying in range and out of sight awaiting further orders. On the ground, troops were assembling outside the hangars, but not a huge number. It was a smaller base, they were not expecting this phantom to land here, and most of their personnel had been deployed to the battlecruisers or sent out in fighters.

After a moment or two, when the activity had died down a bit and the troops and fighters were in whatever position they thought best, the front of the phantoms ship slowly opened. Descending from the nose, the ship opened like a whale about to sift krill. There was still a strong visual disturbance and not much could be seen from inside the mouth of the phantom, but presently out walked a plain clothed, bespectacled man. He wore plain dark hued trousers, a white shirt that was buttoned up nicely but not tucked, and a loose, rather casual blazer very similar to the one Bob had acquired at *Gallium* station after that damned squirrel stole his buttons.

This bespectacled man was clutching something under his arm and dragging, peculiarly, an aluminum folding chair. The chair couldn't have any significant weight, but the cumbersome nature of the chair coupled with the object clutched in his armpit revealed a slight limp in his right leg. The chair made a gentle grinding sound as he dragged it over the concrete while he walked. The surrounding troops carefully watched.

About twenty or so feet in front of the phantom ship, the bespectacled man stopped and folded open the aluminum chair. It was bound with some kind of colorful nylon strapping that was worn and tattered. After situating the chair, he looked up at the blue sky and adjusted his spectacles. He then looked to the surrounding troops and gave a nod and half-smile as if to say "hello". From his clutched arm he produced an uncommon object that most of the surrounding people had never seen. It was a paper book. Then he jostled his blazer arm and sat; opened his book and began to silently read.

The surrounding troops, puzzled, looked at each other for answers finding none. Ikarus was already in the process of evacuation with the arrival of the phantom ship and nearby in the armory tower, Humbolt, equally without answers, was beginning to boil with rage at the sheer audacity of this unknown, this assailant to Humbolt's assumed authority. In anger he issued a base sniper to take a shot.

It was an easy shot. Snipers are trained to take shots from miles away and this individual was a mere hundred yards from the sniper's tower. It was a dead-center shot to the left eye that passed effortlessly through the bespectacled man as if he wasn't there. The shot deflected around the quiet reader and angled up, nearly hitting a collection of gathered troops and burning a corner off the upper roof of a hangar. It was tempting to assume that the bespectacled man wasn't really there and they were witnessing a projection of sorts, but the shot was deflected and the angle changed. Something was there. They were all aware of this.

The bespectacled man rolled his eyes a bit and went back to reading. He was inclined to point out that they nearly killed a handful of their own people, but was certain that of this they were most assuredly aware. Assuming they wouldn't be foolish enough to try the same trick again, he sat quietly and continued to read.

It was ten awkward minutes before someone tried the novel approach of communication. It was a young private who was more than a little nervous.

Private: "Wha...what do you want?"

Moloch looked up from his book and adjusted his glasses to get a clear look at the private.

Moloch: "I'm waiting to speak with Grom, thankyou. He should be expecting me." He then returned to reading his book.

Up to this point the troops had kept a respectable distance from Moloch and the ship. Perhaps emboldened by the non-violent atmosphere Moloch had been projecting, a few of them started to inch closer. Some higher-up got the bright idea that if they couldn't blast him, they could probably grab him and subdue him. Suspension fields were much less effective against material. It is always interesting how often people resort to subverting a problem, squirming around it, rather than deal with it directly. Unfortunately for them all, there was no squirming their way out of this predicament.

An officer approached laterally, with the intent of grabbing the bespectacled man. Before he could get within twenty or so feet a proximity protocol activated a suspension field and the man's progress was stopped. He pressed up against it, thinking he might push through, but instantly his hands and feet went numb. This field was suppressing the very energy production of his own body and he knew instantly that he needed to retreat. On his way back he collapsed, which shocked the others. He was lucky though, he'd snap to in a few minutes once the drop in his energy had been balanced out. It's mostly an electrolyte and synapse thing. It was a feeling like having low *and* high blood sugar at the same time.

Up in the tower Grom Humbolt was irate. He had believed the fallen soldier to be dead, but that is not what was bothering him. What bothered him was the sheer disrespect of this intruder

288

purposefully avoiding a respectful title. It's *General Grom Humbolt*. *General Humbolt* or even *the General* would be adequate, but to refer to him by his first name, as if they were equals, was unforgivable.

No one knew what to do. They all waited in silence and watched this man read his book. It was all so peculiar to them. The technology was not possible. Shield generators are huge, they occupy city blocks or significant portions of massive battlecruisers, and here this guy has one in the small space of his little ship? And one that can be so tightly controlled to shield a single body? It's not possible. Too, most of them hadn't seen a paper book or spectacles on a person. They didn't understand what was going on. Was this theater of some sort?

It is true that paper books are rare, but to the very few people in the galaxy that for one reason or another wear spectacles, paper is considerably easier on the eyes than luminous terminal screens. Refraction with the glasses too can cause visual artifacts from terminal projections that can be quite distracting. Also, there is a tactile aspect to the paper book, unknown to most these days. The act of reading paper carries with it a special physical component and is thus more intimate to the experience, connecting the observer not just to the subject virtually, but also in the sensory reality of the here-and-now, the then-and-there.

At an appropriate stopping point, Moloch looked up from his book addressing the crowd in general with a calm and muted voice. Moloch: "Anyone want to go and fetch Grommie? I don't intend to wait all day."

Watching all of this clearly from a terminal screen, Grom Humbolt had a throbbing vein arcing across his forehead. That tore it. He slammed his fists down on the console shouting incredulously "Grommie!?". Then he stormed out of the office. He was going to have some choice words with this bespectacled man. If he had the opportunity, he'd kill him and was willing to even die trying. By the time Humbolt had made it down the tower and onto the ground level, he had managed the appearance of a man merely stern and irritated though the rage inside him was kindling nicely. To those in the corridor and the hangar through which Humbolt transversed to get to the outdoors, they stepped eagerly aside as if he was generating an angry aura forcing a clear ten foot bubble about his person. They knew not to get in his way when he was in the best of moods and his current mood was less than chipper.

Humbolt was an intelligent fool. He was foolish enough to not attempt to handle this situation with greater diplomacy, but he was smart enough to know the particulars of what was happening. Humbolt walked briskly with an air of importance about him to the precise boundary that repelled the fatigued soldier. There he stopped and began his rambling tirade.

Humbolt: "Do you realized the trouble you are in? You have violated several interplanetary, national, and regional edicts, not to mention stellar collective united autonomy statutes and galactic recognized world sovereignty rights. Your actions regarding Diophantus and illegal entry of a military concern classify you as an enemy combatant, a crime punishable by swift execution. You are formally charged with the crime of..."

This went on for quite some time, each word slightly darkening the red angry face of the cranky general. Listening to the list of grievances, Moloch gave a sarcastically thoughtful look as if he was considering the weight of these crimes that he knew applied to him not. Before long he had become bored listening to this blowhard rant and stood from his little folding chair, closing and setting his book upon it, and walked close to the red-faced general.

Moloch: "Yes, yes. I don't *care* about any of that. You're evading the issue."
The general, incensed, was audibly grinding his teeth. He was torn between his rage and knowing there was nothing he could do about it.
Moloch: "You have an object that does not belong to you. It needs to be put back where it was found."
Humbolt, in disbelief: "If you think for a minute that I intend to turn this object over to some criminal who arrogantly makes demands of a..."
Moloch, interrupting: "Oh, no, no, no. You really misunderstand what's happening here. I'm not asking you to give me the object. I'm *telling* you that *you* will put it back where it belongs. *You.* I don't want to even see it."
Humbolt was puzzled, then offered a garish laugh: "What makes you think I take orders from some craw-gilled (regional expression) ingrate..."
Moloch, with a more serious, grave even, expression: "I am certain that the object will be returned and returned quickly. I came to you originally in hopes that you'd be a reasonable man. It is time. It is time that you quit being a child and think about your people."

At the mere utterance of the word "child", Humbolt turned and angrily stormed off. He would soon order a full attack, pointless or not, upon the phantom ship. The order would be ignored. Those in command saw what happened, knew this ship was not going to be destroyed, or if it could be it would come at an enormous cost to the people of Diophantus. The news of the virus was all over the galaxy and Humbolt's personnel felt that this bespectacled man was the architect. They were certain his planet-wide message was no bluff. Humbolt will shortly experience his first minor mutiny, though not in time to alter the course of what is to follow.

After Humbolt stormed off, while he was passing through the hangar to the tower, the face of the bespectacled man fell somber. He was genuinely sad about the turn of events and wondered if there could have been a better way to handle this situation. After a moment of reflection he turned to address the encircling soldiers still uncertain of what to do.

Moloch: "You know, I really didn't want things to work out this way." After a pause, still addressing the crowd,

Moloch: "...There are two things you need to do. You need to get the message out that the object must be returned. You also need to flee. Flee this place. Run for your lives."

Moloch then walked back to where he had sat, put the book back under right arm, and folded the little aluminum chair. He walked to the nose of his ship, stopped, and pulled off a small necklace from around his neck. It was hard to see, but it appeared to be a thin brown cloth strap that had a tiny glass bottle as a pendant. He looked at it a moment with a sad face and tossed it overhand about thirty feet ahead of the ship. It landed unbroken with a small clinking sound after which Moloch produced an object from behind his blazer. It was a thing with which the surrounding soldiers were unfamiliar but had Bob been there, with his knowledge of antiques, he would have easily identified it as a replica of an old Colt conversion revolver from ancient Earth. Shortly after, a thunderous clap startled the troops as the revolver discharged leaving the little glass bottle broken.

Moloch dragged that folding chair, grinding it all the way, back into his ship and the whale mouth of the phantom closed. Almost instantly it bolted straight up with a blinding speed and was gone. A few blips here and there at various outposts gave a vague hint of its location, but it was traveling considerably faster than before. In moments a jump was made. It was gone and untraceable.

A bit before he made the jump, Moloch looked sadly at Diophantus on his view screen and thought somberly to himself "I'm afraid the hour has come. Time to breathe life into clay."

Back on Diophantus the troops had scrambled. They were all certain some virus had been unleashed and they were trying their very best to escape it. Some crushed into docked vessels and quickly left the planet altogether. Those less lucky bolted on foot hoping to find a means of leaving as well. The city of Ikarus had been largely evacuated at the arrival of the phantom ship so there were little options for those stranded.

In defiance of law, the video feed of the event had been purposefully leaked to the media. It was generally agreed that the people of Diophantus needed to know what was happening despite orders otherwise. In the face of a penultimate crisis, tyrants are the first to be shunned. It's always in the people's hearts before the opportunity to act is present.

There was a great deal of chaos ensuing. Those that refused to evacuate Ikarus were now regretting that decision yet there were very little options save leaving on foot. Public transport was unmanned and practically every vessel had been used in the initial purge. Those remaining had requested evacuation, but now those that had escaped were leery because of the potential of a mysterious infection. The makeshift plan was to send remote vessels to collect those remaining and hold them in an unpopulated area, quarantined, until more was known.

Those troops that made it off world didn't fare much better. The battlecruisers wouldn't take them until it was determined whether they had been infected or not. They were ordered to hold their position, but most of the vessels, vessels designed for two to four people, were holding between eight and ten. They were burning too quickly through life support and the small vessels were overloaded. It was not sustainable and they would soon have to either be permitted aboard the battlecruisers or land. Shortly, they were ordered to land at the quarantine site and await further instructions. Any deviation from the prescribed path to quarantine would be considered insubordination and would be "dealt with harshly". They all knew that it meant death. They had no choice but to land and wait this thing out.

Back at Ikarus, and amongst the little fragments of broken glass, something stirred. Something of protocols and processes has been activated. It was too small to be seen but could one do so, they would notice something of a whirling...a movement without substance. This "something stirred" would draw to itself a small speck of dust here, a microscopic shard of glass there, until it was a small swirling dust mote. It was a twirling collector of the ephemeral and the discarded bathed in the radiant energy of the afternoon sun. Little by little, but quickly, it grew. Soon, it could pull into itself a whole grain of sand, a particle of rubber from a combat boot, a crumb of mess hall bread.

Within minutes the little whirlwind could be seen with the naked eye. It appeared as a miniature, vaguely defined, swirl. The handful of personnel that remained, including old Grom himself, intensely scanned the area expecting to identify some viral material in the broken glass. The little storm almost went unnoticed since it was nothing like what they had been scanning for. It might have gone completely unnoticed had it not been for the reptilian portion of the human brain that in almost absent consciousness picks up the slightest sight of movement. Even still, it seemed a thing blowing by or unrelated to the broken glass bottle.

A few minutes more and the little storm was picking up even larger objects; metal shavings, bits of wire and insulation, and more and more dust. As it grew, so did it's ability to draw material from further away. It set off a signal. A minor energy reading that was unfamiliar. Scanning the area, they could tell where it was coming from, but couldn't tell what it was. No one was yet willing to physically approach the area, so it was brought up on a terminal screen, an image that answered very few questions.

Shortly, it had brushed up against an open hangar and could now be seen as a dusty, swirly mass. A stream of debris from the outer yard could be seen drawing into it, making it bigger. However, accomplishing this feat required more and more energy as it grew. The lights of the hangar began to flicker and it could be read from afar that something was placing a load on that particular hangar's energy consumption. It was drawing energy from the nearest available source.

It was about this time that several of the remaining personnel were convinced that they were no longer dealing with a virus. Still not willing to approach it, they were slightly emboldened to stay and analyze the whirling something a bit more. What they managed to see was that the growth of the whirlwind was exponential. It was now a violent storm about the size of a human being. It was eating into the mortar and even the metal of the hangar. A number of larger objects were being consumed in the storm. Tools, ship parts, paneling, all being dragged in. The larger it got the more damage it could do to its surroundings and thus the bigger it could grow.

With fascination, a military scientist, in charge of analyzing this data, watched the storm eat through the hangar wall. He noticed something in the demolition of a robotic plasma welder that at first was just a curiosity. Portions of the storm were dividing between the flat paneling of the plasma welder's body and the arm joint. Smaller materials, dust and debris, were eroding the fixtures of the paneling while larger materials, broken tools, brick fragments, torn metal sheets, were attacking the joints of the arm. The scientist found this quite remarkable and noted that he had seen this same behavior in ant colonies where larger headed/jawed ants dismantled the leg joints of grasshoppers or other prey while the smaller headed ants took bits of wing and soft body tissues. It was all quite specialized and mindfully organized. It was then that this curiosity, and the implications there of, were less interesting and more horrifying. He barked a warning that "we need to get the hell out of here" and left on foot as fast as he could, not waiting for orders or relief of duty. Several others, after brief contemplation, followed suit.

It was literally mere minutes before the thing jumped in size from a human being to a small ship. It was destroying everything in its path and assimilating it into its body. Power had been drained from almost the whole base and half the hangar was completely gone.

By the time the scientist and the handful that left with him were airborne in the last remaining emergency vehicle, they witnessed the armory tower falling to the ground. So damaged from the monster below eating into its body, it crumpled like the demolished ruins of an abandoned building. What followed was a brief stillness that was broken by a swirling of debris as the storm arose from the remains, now the size of a small building.

Media crews, safely from miles away, recorded the unbelievable sight broadcasting planet-wide and beyond. What they witnessed was a large swirling mass with an occasional flash of light that displaced the storm temporarily. The media managed to speculate that it was ammunitions detonating, somehow, each blast feeding the energy consumption of the beast.

As it grew larger, it became less stormlike. It was now much more dense, like a thick pile of debris. It moved in lurching pupae-like arches smashing its body against the remaining buildings of the base until it was totally demolished.

Beyond the base was an expanse of field with little to draw from. It lurched and moved in odd flowing and spilling motions, still dragging dust and debris from the decimated base into itself. Large chunks of hangars and building framework could be seen in the composite body of the beast as it shambled its way to Ikarus city proper.

The base was on the edge of city limits but close enough that a good 120 degree arc from the base center would lead anywhere from north Ikarus to south Ikarus. However, the lumbering beast seemed to be heading a very specific direction. It wasn't long before those watching the spectacle knew this monster was heading directly for the main suspension field generator in central Ikarus. The path could not have been more direct. It was then that a fleet of fighters were ordered to intercept and attack this jumbled, ramshackled creeping death.

By the time the fighters arrived the creature was demolishing buildings at city's edge and growing larger. It was now the size of a multi-story complex and a city block wide. A team of fighters immediately fired into the central portion of the debris monster. It seemed to recoil and disintegrate some, but quickly pulled the ruins back into itself. How does one destroy a thing *made* of destruction itself? Intensifying the attack seemed to bring a brief cessation of forward movement. There were numerous fighters discharging all available weapons into the beast.

It would seem to stop and flatten, only to momentarily begin moving again. The attack itself was creating considerable damage to the surrounding area that only seemed to feed the beast. Despite the attack, it was still growing.

A secondary fleet arrived and added to the chaos. It was an unprecedented display of violent fireworks and between the fighters and the beast itself the area was decimated. The onslaught seemed to slow the creatures movement and flatten it considerably, but it wasn't dying. Every death was temporary. From cinder and ash it would rise like a rubble phoenix.

Another arriving fleet, an increase in the attack, and the creature seemed to lie dormant for a few moments. It was more or less flattened completely and motionless, but soon, even in the rain of plasma and incendiary from the airborne fighters, it began to lump up, pulling itself into a rather uniform mound, like a mucky swamp bubble. After a generous roundness had been achieved, into which the fighters blasting seemed to be absorbed, a spout of debris, like a lashing tentacle erupted from the mound. It traveled about the length of three city block in the air narrowly dodged by a handful of fighters. Had the focus of attention remained on the wayward spout of debris as it crashed to the ground it could be seen to be drawing itself back toward the mound pulling a variety of materials with it.

Instantly following the first erupting tendril a second fired out in the opposite direction. Several fighters successfully evaded the attack, but one took the hit head on. This debris tentacle, upon consuming the fighter, recoiled like a biting snake drawing the fighter into the bulk of the originating mound. Several more arms of the beast reached forth, and a few more fighters were caught like flies. This prompted a retreat from the collective squadron. They drew back to a safe distance and momentarily ceased fire.

They didn't know what to do. They had given this thing all they had and it was only getting bigger. They had lost several fighters that were now part of the beast. Looking into the body of it, one could see bright glowing spots from the engines of the consumed ships. Were they struggling to break free? It was as if they were running their engines at full capacity to no avail. There was nothing they could do.

The consumed fighters were lost. A keen eye would have noticed the bright engines of the fighters had somehow become rather equally spaced in the body of the beast. Had one a general knowledge of the inner workings of such a creature, they would know that the ships were consumed and used. It was energy acquisition. They were now adding to the consumption of the beast, powering it further until their supply ran dry and would then become yet more debris for the bulk.

It grew. It was maintaining a height of a few stories, but was covering several city blocks. It seemed denser too. Other buildings were being consumed at an accelerated rate. Power supplies extracted from the wreckage fed it further. It was not merely destroying, it was utilizing what it found. Inside the bulk was a whirling chaos that did more than grind materials into rubble, it reconditioned, recombined, adapted, and built. Power Supplies were repurposed, amplified even. There was much more happening than destruction. There was also terrible creation.

The beast was still progressing towards the city's suspension-field generator. It was massive and not only shielded the city of Ikarus, but provided regional hemisphere support in conjunction with other cities in the area.

Following orders, the fighters receded further until they were gone from sight. This was not a mere retreat. It was not an admission of defeat yet. It was preparation for the attack to come. In an effort to prevent the destruction of the suspension-field generator an orbiting battle cruiser was positioning itself, preparing to fire upon its own city, its own people.

The attack had to be highly coordinated. The city shield had to be lowered for a fraction of a second to allow the attack to penetrate. There are, however, serious concerns with something so seemingly self-sacrificial. For one, this attack would flatten a good quarter of the city. Also, firing a weapon such as those designed for space battle into a planet would invariably cause a degree of planetary damage. The atmosphere would be punctured and singed and the backlash from the negative space created would affect weather patterns. There would also be considerable damage to the ground that would cause a degree of seismic activity. But what else could be done?

As the beast lumbered on its dusty path, there seemed to be an odd calmness. Even in the continual falling of buildings, dust speeding through the remaining city like running titans, and the repetitive creaking and booming of destruction, there was an imperceptible silence...a perfunctory quiet that preceded the executioner's axe.

It was then that the calm was broken by clouds parting, the heavens opened up and shone a brilliant light connecting the earth and the realms above. The light expanded in its brilliance and size like a pillar of some divine aether pouring upon the earth its miraculous blessing. It was seen in silence and shortly followed by the unholy crackle of its true nature; an electric scream that was itself the voice of wickedness and vice.

One quarter of the city was ash. The discharge cut deep into the ground as well. The sky had a gaping hole that was rapidly closing, but briefly revealed a patch of night sky in afternoon daylight. Tremors could be felt at distant points about the globe. The deed had indeed been done.

As the smoke cleared it could be seen, in the middle of the wreckage, the former body of the beast. It was motionless and rarefied. Some of the materials of its bulk had been vaporized, but much of it had been fused to a shining glass-like substrate. If faintly glowed from the residual heat of the discharge.

Some of the fighters were ordered back in to scan the area. The beast had been giving off powerful energy signatures of suspension-fields and gravity/anti-gravity fields. Now, there was nothing detected, which reassured the people of Diophantus that this nightmare was over.

Other fighters were ordered to the base in possession of the Pixler's glass. They were instructed to take the object to a distant city, out of the area of destruction. It was officially undetermined as to the fate of the object as life and governance on Diophantus was...disturbed, but it was the popular opinion, though there had been little time to express such, that the object should be put back. However, it had not *yet* been put back.

One of the fighters ordered to scan the area had landed to take more precise measurements from the ground. The blast had left a great deal of radiation and other trace resonant signatures, so it was hard to get a fine tuned reading from the sky. He, in appropriately protective gear, was a dozen or so block away from the beast carcass and wasn't picking up anything but the residual muck of the battle cruiser's attack. This would have been good news if he had not noticed, completely by chance, something a little out of the ordinary. There were a few scraps of things blowing here and there in the wind. This whole endeavor left everything covered in dust and as one would expect, that dust was being carried along with the wind. Yet, this fighter performing the scan just happened to notice that the stream of dust about the ground near him seemed to be flowing in opposition to the wind. It's often hard to judge these things as wind mechanics can be wily, but yes, the wind was blowing away from the sight of the blast and this stream of dust was heading…toward the body of the beast.

When the implications hit him, he made a quick leap toward his ship to alert command. As he was lifting off he heard a thunderous crack. Those fighters closer to the beast, upon hearing the crack, turned to see a great fissure had broken across the body. Perhaps it was just a natural process of the material cooling after the blast, or so they comforted themselves, but soon another crack, then another, and another.

By this point it could be seen that debris from the flattened portion of the city was being drawn inward, toward the body of the beast. The fighters scrambled, got the hell out of there. As more cracks formed upon the surface of the beast, a whirlwind of activity could be seen below. Moments later the fracturing became so numerous that the temporarily solid state of the body was now returned to its former particulated glory. Now a great mass of material streamed forth, feeding the body. The battlecruiser's blast, flattening the surrounding city, had done most of the work for the beast. It hadn't the chore of destruction, merely the task of reclamation.

It breathed in the debris like a nourishing clean breeze. It ebbed and flowed growing larger with each breath and giving the monster the frightening appearance of a thing alive. For several minutes it remained stationary and grew. A great bulbous protuberance extended from the center of the bulk. It turned and twisted as if it was stretching to ease the burden of its breathing. It was now the size of a modest skyscraper which fell sluggishly and lurched its way again on the path to the field generator. An observing fighter sent command an ominous message: "The creature walks".

A flurry of debate and confusion befell the command as the beast lumbered forth:

*Fire battlecruisers upon it again?

*It didn't work before and now it was considerably bigger!

*Fire multiple battle cruisers at the same time?

*We'd run the risk of damaging the planet, making it uninhabitable!

*This thing might make the planet uninhabitable!

*We can't burn off our entire atmosphere to try and kill this thing!

*Can we tell the bespectacled man we concede, we'll put whatever that thing was he wanted back?

*We don't know how to contact him, besides; we haven't received orders to do so.

Unbeknownst to the command, there was a faction of mutineers that were planning on taking the object back by any means necessary, but only the higher-ups knew where it had come from. Even if they managed to get it, where should they take it? There was an unspoken but generally agreed upon idea as to who was to blame for all of this trouble and that person was *not* the bespectacled man.

Those left in command had decided to fire upon it again, singularly, in an effort to buy some time, knowing it would only delay the beast, but it might give them enough time to figure something out. As the battlecruiser was getting into position, the beast was dangerously close to the suspension-field generator.

The command was suffering a condition known as assumption. They assumed the beast would destroy the field generator, perhaps in conjunction with an unseen attack from space...from the phantom ship. Had these poor saps been capable of merely predicting the future, they would have destroyed the field generator long before the beast drew near.

Almost as if the creature could sense the impending attack, it condensed itself into a tight mass before violently arching outward like a rocky tidal wave consuming the area of the field generator. Dust streamed outward covering the entire city in a cloud.

The coordination was as it had been planned before: briefly lower the shield, fire, raise the shield. With a loud crackle the battlecruiser burned yet another hole in the atmosphere of helpless Diophantus. The beast, now considerably larger and stretched over a greater area, was hit slightly off center from the field generator. The blast punctured the beast and burrowed deeply into the surface of the planet causing a horrid tremble. The affected area of the creature seemed to calcify, harden to glass, but was almost immediately rebroken and consumed as part of the whole. The attack accomplished absolutely nothing except a decent amount of planetary damage.

There was another concern following the attack. They could no longer raise the shield that had been lowered to permit the attack. They had figured that either the beast had destroyed it or their attack had rendered it inoperable though the attack had been concentrated on a location that was believed to be safe.

As futile as it would seem, with no options, the fleet of fighters were ordered to attack. About half the remaining fleet followed orders while the other half went AWOL. They would head to a distant city and attempt to leave Diophantus, leave Bohr itself completely. For many, this was the signal to start a new life somewhere far, far away.

All cities surrounding Ikarus were being evacuated and a good portion of the associated hemisphere was voluntarily doing so. People were either staying as far from the battle site as possible, or leaving the planet entirely.

Back at the beast, a tumult of weaponized activity littered the area. Fighters were attacking, in vain, and viciously as they had been trained to do. The beast slumped like a mound over the site of the generator and remained still. Ignoring the attacks, it seemed motionless yet an unseen and highly orchestrated protocol was taking place below the surface. The beast was merging the suspension-field generator into its own body.

The process took as little as ten minutes, a marvelous feat of unheard-of engineering. Then, when the task had been completed, it rose. Stretching upward, a globular conglomerate of particulate matter, it rose to the height of a tall, tall skyscraper. With the repurposed field generator in the heart of the beast, a massive force emanated outward; an invisible torrent radiating in all directions that could only be seen in the displacement it left behind through smoke and dust. It was seen in silence that was followed by an earth shattering concussion. Everything, the fighters and the remainder of the city, was pulverized...reduced to rubble. That same force, that outward shockwave, then polarized and drew its destruction into the body of the beast.

Like a breathing nightmare, it collected the mass and material of an entire city...a massive city. Drawn into itself it became the largest object ever to grace the surface of Diophantus. It was no mere beast or monster. It was a great Colossus.

The Colossus had pulled every energy generating source from the city into its being and was slowly adapting, modifying, and reconditioning these assorted objects for its own purposes. It stood an amorphous blob but with a protuberance that the human mind instinctively interprets as a head. This "head" seemed to turn from side to side as a powerful glow was growing in the belly of the Colossus. Shortly the head formed a massive gaping hole, like a vicious screaming mouth as the glowing in the belly became overwhelming. Looking to the sky, the "head" began to jitter violently until a beam of golden light erupted from the opening and shot skyward.

It was too unexpected. The Colossus had fired upon the object that had fired at it. The battlecruiser took evasive measures but much too late. The blast easily penetrated their shields and ate a hole through their hull. The radiant beam almost tore the giant vessel in two before exiting the opposing side and shining errantly into black space. Those unfortunate souls aboard the ship that found themselves in the direct path were instantly vaporized, their cremated remains scattered into cold empty darkness. Many more, even less fortunate perhaps, were met with the harsh resulting destabilization that pulled their screaming bodies through the broken ship and into the dark vacuum beyond. The human body can live for a minute or so exposed to outer space. The lungs collapse instantly. The skin begins to freeze and the blood begins to boil. The body bloats grotesquely. Ice forms in the respiratory tract as the other bodily organs begin to shut down. If in close enough proximity to a star, as Diophantus is most definitely, the freezing of the skin is accompanied by a scorching in absence of a protective atmosphere or adequate shielding. Yes, exposed to space one tends to freeze and burn at the same time. Though this process is not terribly lengthy, the mind is conscious for a good portion of the experience. It is, needless to say, *not* pleasant.

The blast destroyed the battlecruiser's engines and ballast controls. Being in a tight orbit to manage their earlier attacks they were now helpless to the gravitational pull of Diophantus. The battlecruiser was being pulled in. Evacuation of the remaining crew was all that was left to them.

The great Colossus continued to fed, more and more, and became greater. Soon, its belly began to glow again. Brighter and brighter the glow grew and again that protuberance opened a gaping hole, like the hollow eyes of death. It violently jittered as it vomited another beam of hot plasma, this one directed laterally at the city of Pallas several hundred miles away cutting a fiery swatch through the landscape.

Continually drawing the world around it into itself, the Colossus grew. Again it spewed burning light and crumpled the city of Hera, a few hundred miles away from both Ikarus and Pallas. As Hera burned, the wreckage of the crippled battlecruiser could be seen breaching the atmosphere to the south. It was wrapped in the fire-orange aura granted by the friction of a thick sky. All about it were flaming pieces of itself burning violently...smoky tailed fireballs careening earthward. When it hit ground it flashed into a hot white orb like a small sun lazing inappropriately on the horizon. A shockwave and massive tremors could be seen and felt before the light dissipated and left only a black plume, a grim mushroom cloud climbing skyward as if the angel of death itself was fleeing the horror of the wreckage.

After ruining Pallas and Hera the great Colossus lumbered slowly for a long while until it reached the city of Asteria. It didn't burn Asteria. It produced tendrils or arms and smashed the city as it moved. Once in the city central, it stopped and breathed. Those watching the news feed could do nothing but stare in a horrified silence. It sat positioned at Asteria, in the center of an almost perfect triangle of Ikarus, Pallas, and Hera. There it could be seen that material from all three of those triangular points was being drawn into the Colossus, from that far away, and there it grew.

From a very distant location, Moloch watched these events as they unfolded. He watched with a sincere sadness and a forlorn look upon his face. Thinking to himself, "I'm sure that is more than enough", he performed a couple of brief actions on a nearby terminal then sat quietly with hands folded in his lap.

There, in the center of Asteria, the material streaming into the Colossus stopped and with an abrupt stillness, the Colossus fell reverting to nothing more than a gargantuan pile of rubble. The fall could be felt planet wide and heard throughout the hemisphere. The percussive force of the fall sent a turbulent cloud of dust hundreds of miles in all directions, a cloud that could be seen from space and when picked up by the atmosphere would be visible as a dark band around once blue Diophantus.

Shortly thereafter, before cleanup, before search and rescue, before anything else that might have been accomplished, a transport, safely escorted by numerous fighters and carried in a battlecruiser, returned the body of Harper Callus, encased in Pixler's glass, to the exact location at which it had been found.

Part III

"What pathetic dirge shall I strive to utter, now that I begin my wailing of bitter lamentation? At the foot of what Muse shall I grovel with tears or songs of death and woe? I beseech you sweet Sirens, Earth's virgin daughters, you gossamer winged maidens, please come to aid in my mourning with songs of death and doom to match my lamentation, that in return she may receive from me, besides my endless tears, dirges for the departed dead seeping into her gloomy grave."

Euripides *Helen*, 480-406 b.c.

Your Galacitc Home

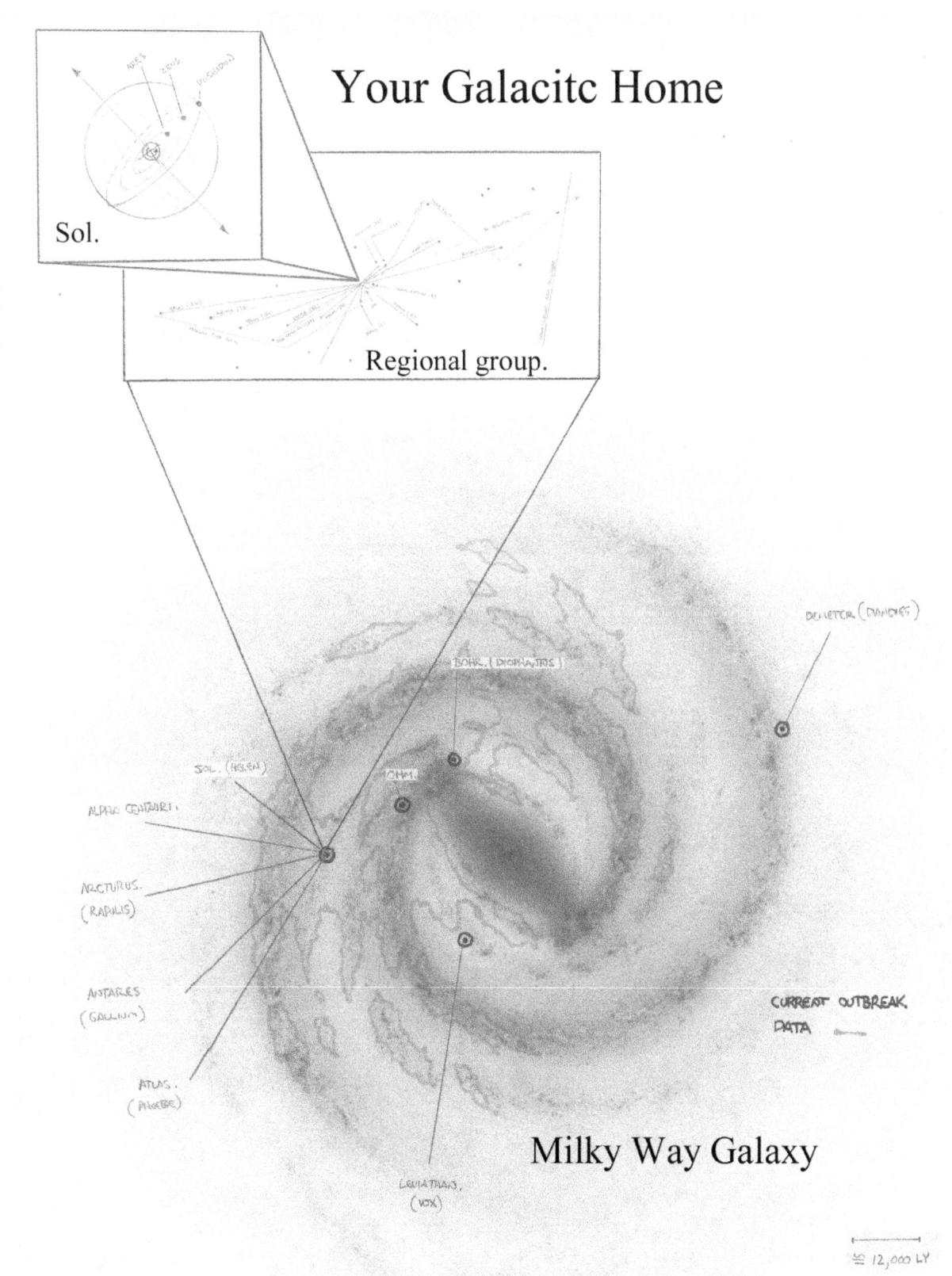

Sol.

Regional group.

SOL. (HELEN)

ALPHA CENTAURI.

ARCTURUS.
(RADIUS)

ANTARES
(GALLIUM)

ATLAS.
(PHOEBE)

LEVIATHAN.
(VOX)

BOHR. (DIOPHANTUS)

DEMETER (DIANCHES)

CURRENT OUTBREAK
DATA

Milky Way Galaxy

12,000 LY

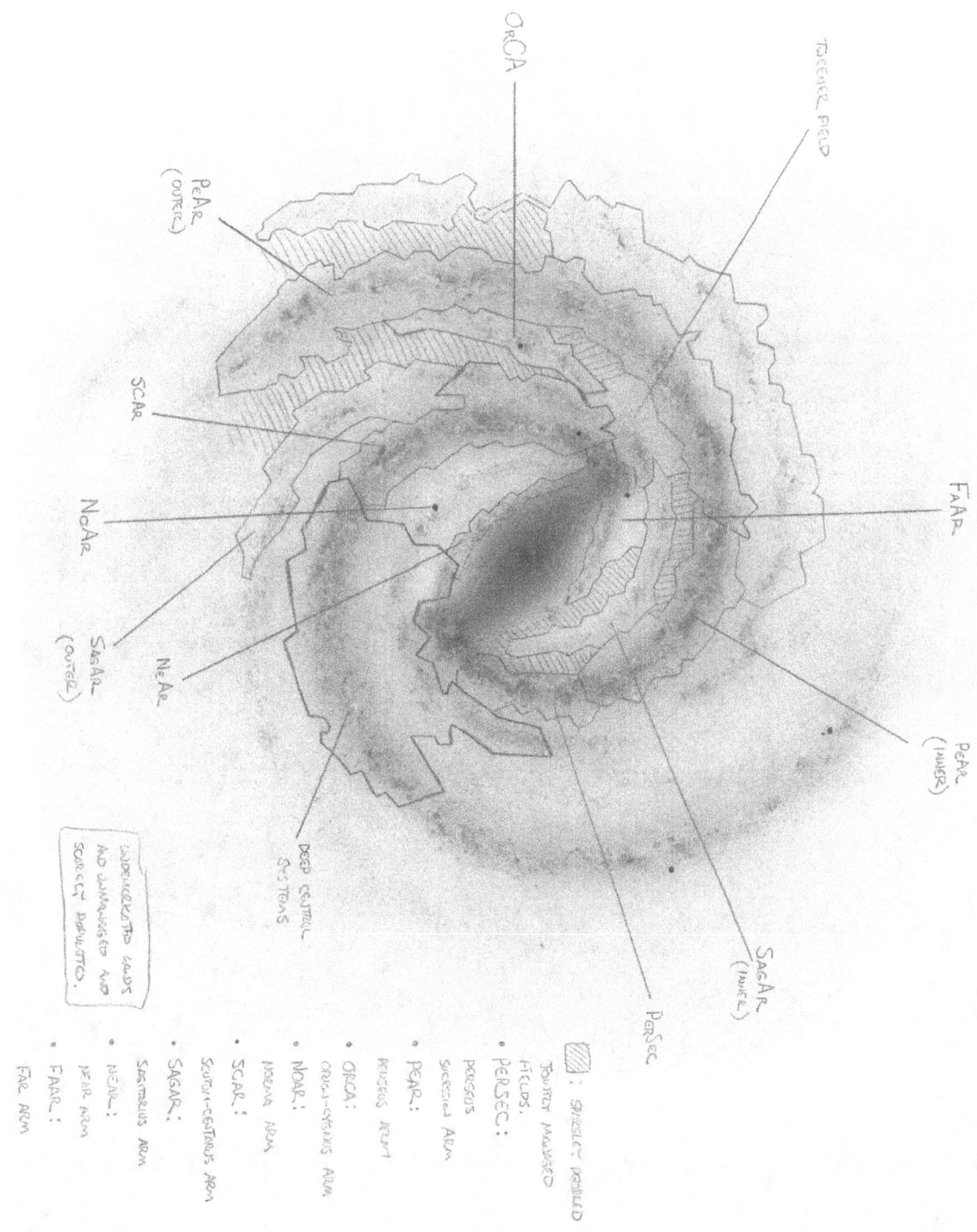

Chapter Twenty One:
News of the World: Who Mourns for Diophantus?

"...of reports today that several cities on Diophantus, a planet in the Bohr system, were destroyed under mysterious circumstances. It seems some sort of Colossus ran rampant through..."

***

"What appears to be a giant beast has laid waste to four large cities on a planet in the Bohr system. Authorities are publicly stating that an attack did in fact take place and the damage to said cities is total. Speculation regarding..."

***

"...in possible connection with the spread of the virus? A vague implication, yet unconfirmed, by the creator of the threat broadcast prior to the attack."

***

"Alligale of the DRANC (Deep Regional Allied News Corps): We're joined today with congress member Dax Falstad, of the CCWP, good day, sir.
Falstad: Good day, Alligale. What I think we need is a refocused effort into the potential link between the destruction on Diophantus, the object in question, and the virus. If this individual has such destructive power, why would he need to spread a potentially deadly virus rather than have a similar beast destroy other worlds? I believe the answer is infrastructure: killing off the inhabitants of a world but leaving the infrastructure intact for his own, or other's use.
Alligale: I would just like to point out that the idea of the virus being deadly, of which it has not yet shown any such signs, is purely speculative.
Falstad: Granted, but speculation or not, the potential is there. If however it turns out that..."

***

"Pundit: The video feed is of poor quality and I can't help but think it has been tampered with.
Guest: Tampered with? So, you are saying...
Pundit: Yes, I believe it to be a hoax.
Guest: Ridiculous.
Pundit: Ridiculous? What I want to know is if anyone has actually been there. Has anyone actually seen the destruction, seen the state of those cities. Until then, we won't have any actual proof.
Guest: I've just returned from a tour of the system. The cities are piles of rubble. I've seen it with my own eyes.
Pundit: ...oh.
Guest: I assumed that why you had me on the show."

***

"Here it can be seen, at this point in the video, where the visuals are temporarily whited out. This has been reported as an attack on the Colossus from an orbiting battlecruiser. Yes, a battlecruiser, at great expense to its own ecosystem, fired upon the Colossus with the mere effect of slowing it down. Here, a second blast blinds the video feed and by the time the visual is restored there appears to have been no effect on the Colossus. The question is then, if two battlecruiser attacks, dangerously close to rendering the planet uninhabitable, both failed, what would take down this beast?"
***

"Today on *Starshine Entertainment News* a crazy monster destroyed some cities and teen pop sensation Babydropz is sporting a new hat. Brought to you by Pauly's Bread Bucket: Get Your Stew On!®"

***

"Analyst: Yes, we've seen the video feed. It's been leaked. We've all seen the little glass bottle then the slow build from nothing to Colossus, but is it possible that that was merely theater? Designed, perhaps, to throw us off the trail of the true nature and origin of the Colossus?
Co-host: Either way, what difference would it make?
Analyst: If it was theater, then it is possible that the mechanism for generating the Colossus was already present. Perhaps this bespectacled man has planted these on a number of worlds. Maybe there's one right here under us right now waiting to rise given the order.

Host: Other than instilling fear in our viewers, what point would you care to make by that remark.

Analyst: I am suggesting that maybe if we scan and look, we might find something out of place. If so, maybe it will give us clues to its operation and a possible means to deal with it should it arise.

Co-host: What if, even in its presence, there is nothing to scan...it seemed rather quasi-real.

Analyst: Look, it's not magic. It's not make-believe. The thing was giving off enormous readings. Strong gravitational currents, like those used in anti-gravity mechanisms and for keeping skyward our floating cities, were pouring out of this thing. Helen is a good example. It's not that hard to generate considerable gravitational or anti-gravitational waves. It also was exuding exceptionally unusual suspension fields.

Co-host: Well, obviously. It absorbed the cities generator.

Analyst: No, it was showing unusual suspension field readings long before it had taken the generator. I know this. I've seen the analytics from site recordings. The governance of Diophantus is in shambles and everything has been leaked."

***

"Guest: I have been intensely pouring through grain transmissions from the time frame of the Colossus's attack.

Host: ...and?

Guest: So far, nothing."

***

"Professor of medical research on Panacea: All I'm saying is that if these two events are related, the to-date unsolvable virus and the equally mysterious Colossus,...which they certainly seem to be, then I'm afraid...we may be subject to the whims of this bespectacled man who in an admittedly amateur assessment seems to have all the markers of a psychopath."

Chapter Twenty Two:
Breathing Issues and Toilet Troubles.

Bob was on the last leg of his journey en route to the Balaenae people in the hopes of acquiring genetic samples. He was currently docked aboard a jump-ship called *Captain Beyond*. It was a standard ship, nothing remarkable about it, but a welcome change from the several mining vessels he had been utilizing to moderately shorten his trip. It had been somewhere around five and a half days since he left *Gallium* and about four or so since the rise of the Colossus. Both the Chief and Bob had been in an involved, though choppy from travel, conversation about it. It had occupied a great deal of Bob's attention as well as the Chief's but there were hardly any answers. There was little Bob could do from his position and little the Chief could do other than take up the role of gumshoe and talk to some folks at that Water Sprite facility.

The only leg up they had on this investigation was a name. The man the galaxy now knew as the "bespectacled man", both Bob and the Chief knew to be Moloch. The consensus was to sit on that info for a bit, until the Chief checked a few possible leads. If it were revealed too early that his name was known the Chief might arrive to find all of those who had known him previously...dead, or it might just signal to this Moloch that he'd better find a good hiding place and ride things out till the heat was off or his plans fulfilled. As the video from Diophantus showed, Moloch was fairly confident in his untouchability and perhaps that might encourage him to make a error of some sort. As a career in investigation has taught Bob and a career in police work has taught the Chief, all it usually takes is one little mistake.

Bob had a great deal of frustration in the direction every aspect of this case was progressing. Information was growing exponentially, but none of it was bleeding together. They were learning more, but each bit of knowledge was producing two bits of questions. Since there was really nothing substantial Bob could do from his current position, he was trying to put it out of his mind and was surprisingly doing a better job of it than he had assumed of himself. Sometimes that is the best way to deal with a problem. When the solution is not presenting itself and rational deductions have been carried as far as possible, pressing the issue out of the conscious mind to let it run around in the background, the subconscious, can allow connections not readily available to the incessant mulling of groove worn paths by the conscious mind. Even if it produces nothing of value, at least the stress and frustration can be temporarily abated.

Bob had lost track of time and was caught somewhat off guard by the percussive thud of the *Captain Beyond* making a jump. Bob was here. Bob was in orbit around the great star Leviathan and not far from the Balaenae people. Immediately as the jump was made Bob received a transmission, seemingly urgent, that he attentively accessed via terminal.

It was Abrum.

Abrum: "Bob, in your absence I have taken it upon myself to clean your vacant dwelling as I fear that much longer and nature shall reclaim it."

Bob could see Abrum, in burgundy vest, white button-up, black knotted but un-bowed bowtie, and, for some reason, brass-rimmed riding goggles that, like so many of his accoutrements, were from some lost history. Clearly, from the background image, Abrum was transmitting from inside Bob's apartment.

Bob, thinking *how'd he get into my place*, quickly replied: "No, thanks, it's not necessary. Don't clean anything."

Abrum: "Oh, but Bob, the dust...oh, the dust. You'll return and asphyxiate on the spot, of this I am certain."

Bob: "No, no thanks. Just....don't worry about it. How'd you get into my place anyway?"

Abrum: "Think nothing of it. It is absolutely no bother and would be my pleasure."

Bob: "No...please stay.."

And the transmission was cut. The window of opportunity had passed before Bob could add *please stay out of my apartment.*

Irritating.

Regardless, Bob was here. Leviathan. Isolated and a long way from home, Bob was about to experience a new place and a new people.

Visit Leviathan!
Brought to you by the Norma Arm travel authority (NoAr)

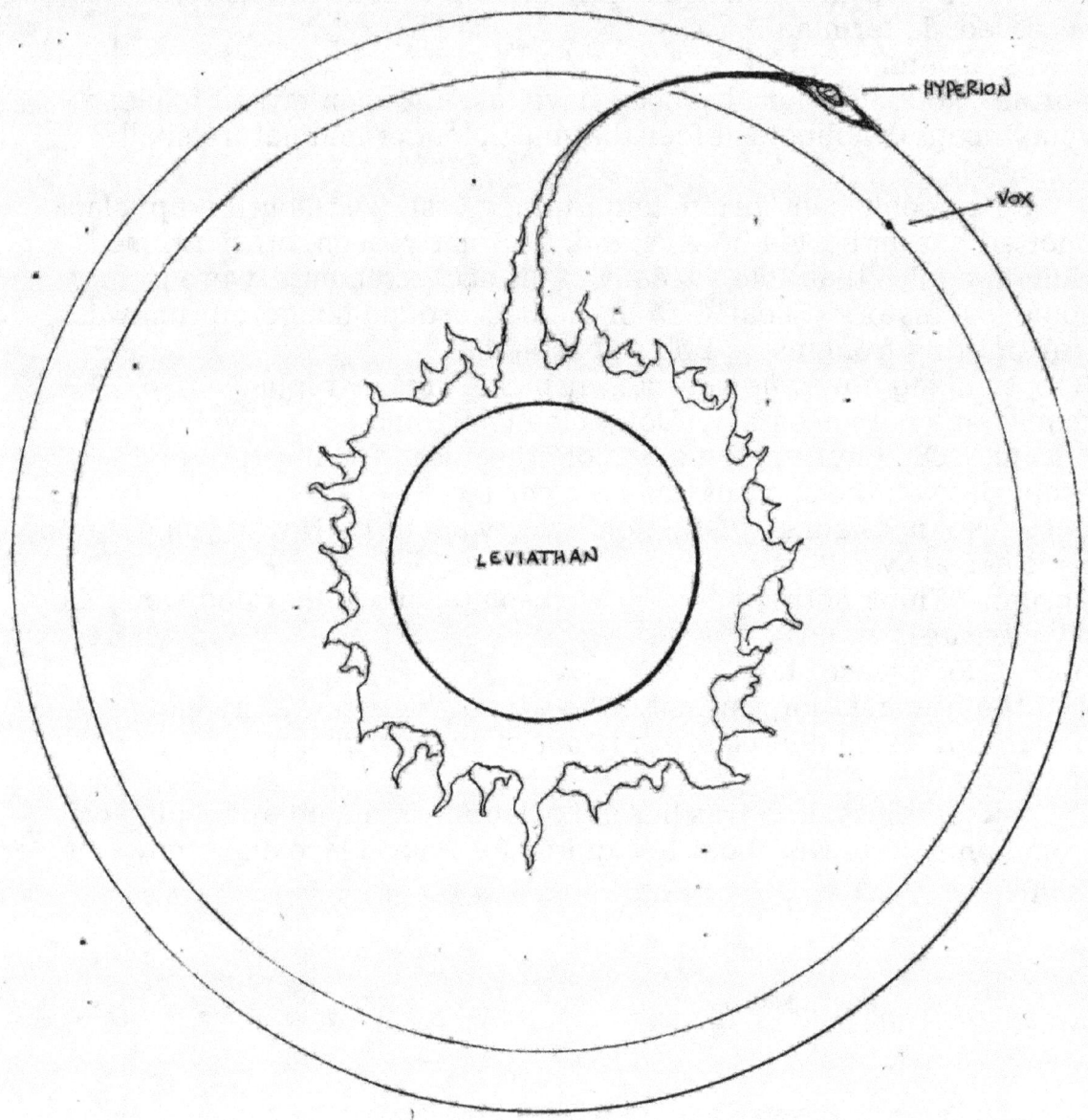

Though travel to Leviathan requires either a work visa, research clearance, or trade commission goods and exchange license, for the traveler looking for a study on the frontier of human variation and transmogrification, Leviathan is the place. This system, like most, is named for the primary star association. Leviathan is a rather rare type of blue super giant star, sometimes referred to as a hypergiant. The star is exceptionally hot and, in size, dwarfs most other stars known to have life in orbit. Additionally, Leviathan is astoundingly bright. Leviathan nears what is known as the Eddington limit. The Eddington limit is essentially the maximum luminosity of a star. At this limit, the force of light radiating from the star is equal to the gravitational pull of the star mass. Exceeding the Eddington limit means the outward force of light is greater than the gravitational pull and huge chunks of the star tend to get blown off resulting in a smaller star at or below the Eddington limit. This means that Leviathan is almost as bright as a star can possibly be.

The large size of Leviathan coupled with its radiant output creates a rather narrow band of habitable space. Surrounded by a cloud of ejected stellar matter, wandering too far in the heat, radiation, and stellar debris is not compatible with life. Too far out and the one finds an enormous rocky asteroid field from early stellar formation.

In terms of planet formation, there are far, far too many to name here. Depending on the specific definition one chooses to use in defining a planet, there could be as many as two hundred planets surrounding Leviathan. Most of these planets are rocky and barren. They are not useful for colonization and too mired in debris for safe mining operations. However, for our purposes we should like to mention two notable worlds in the Leviathan system. The first is the massive gas giant **Hyperion**. The second is the inhabited world of **Vox**, home to the Balaenae.

Hyperion and Vox are involved in a cosmic slow dance. Their revolutionary speeds are commensurate with their orbit so they maintain the same distance from each other during their yearly cycle around Leviathan (a cycle that is approximately equal to 350 standard years). The result and benefit is that Hyperion acts as a nearby vacuum drawing asteroids from the outer regions into itself whilst siphoning a constant stream of stellar debris from the inner regions, just enough to provide a clean orbital path for Vox. The debris drawn from the inner stellar cloud creates a luminous disk around Hyperion giving it the false appearance of a small galaxy, truly a beautiful night-time sight from Vox.

Planet **Vox** is a fairly small blue orb unusually composed. The majority of Vox's mass lies in water. There have been many speculations why such an accumulation of water would compose a single planet. These speculations range from an inexplicable mass accumulation of icy debris, such as comets and what would usually be deep field objects, to the idea that Vox was once a significantly larger planet with considerable water that through some cataclysm was destroyed or absorbed into Hyperion. This speculative cataclysm, possibly a collision with another planet or equally massive object, left

315

the bulk of its water to, over millennia, re-coalesce into what is now planet Vox. Regardless, the current state of Vox is a planet with an exceptionally small core (predominantly nickel and rock) surrounded by an mammoth ocean. As one might imagine, land mass is practically non-existent on Vox. What small amount of rocky debris that might find itself floating about the endless seas of Vox would be unstable and not suitable for development or life save the hearty moss or lichen.

It is precisely this reason that human beings, long ago, made Vox their home and began the transmogrification into the Balaenae people. The **Balaenae** of Vox are a particularly fascinating variation on the human form. It is commonly thought, as their namesake implies, that the Balaenae are a whale-like adaptation to the standard human design. While this is largely true, it is by far the whole picture. The Balaenae seek autonomy in aquatic environments and as such have not resigned themselves to the limitations of mammalian modifications. While the Balaenae have many genetic features of the Earth whales, they have also developed a hybrid respiratory system, an intermingling of lungs and gill-like structures not found in mammalian marine life. There are two distinct advantages to the hybrid respiratory system of the Balaenae. One, they can function in and out of water which is important for a people that do not want to completely isolate themselves from the rest of the human galactic population, the vast, vast majority of which are land based. Two, while underwater the air in the lungs can be released or, through the interconnection between lungs and gills, be filled acting as a functional gas bladder...an organ of buoyancy and stabilization not native to the human design.

Other modifications involve a dense and thicker layer of fat, or blubber, around the frame, modified skin to resist the damage of long exposure to salt water, and minor skeletal and muscular reformations to accommodate the necessary changes to body systems. The Balaenae have and intend to keep the bipedal nature of their ancestry, again to make travel and interrelations less problematic as the only advantage otherwise would be in the increased speed of motility and agility, not considered a rational or equitable trade off.

Untouched by outside interferences, the Balaenae devote the majority of their resources to the development of themselves and their own society. Their necessary isolation makes visitation improbable, however, in the unlikely instance where one's occupation warrants exposure to the Balaenae, don't let such an opportunity pass by. Leviathan, Hyperion, and Vox are exceptionally rare galactic gems unlike any worlds in the known galaxy.

Upon exiting the jump-ship, Bob received a signal and was instructed to approach a scanning beacon. The beacon was automated and rather silent. Bob's ship informed him of the scan commencing but the beacon itself remained mute. After a moment, coordinates were sent to the ship's console and Bob headed toward the distant blue planet.

After an hour and a half Bob's ship was now in close visual range of Vox. Approaching Vox distilled in Bob a potent ethereal melancholy. It was an odd combination of nostalgia and fantasy, two seemingly disparate experiences that are somehow complementary. It produced in Bob a quiet stillness, an almost meditative state. Though he had visited far more planets than most people ever would, each one produced an abiding wonder inexhaustible and endlessly mysterious. Every generation, most likely since the beginning of human intellect, seemed quite certain that they understood the bulk of reality. The universe was a thing to grasp onto and hold, to possess. Exploration was the effort to further that amassed knowledge just a bit further, that little bit that was unknown. That attitude persists to this very day though we should know much, much better. In reality, exploration is the noble reaffirmation of our own ignorance. We explore to learn how little we actually know. The universe cannot be grasped. It is an infinite horizon and one can never reach the horizon. All we can do is wonder.

What people tend to be surprised by when visiting a distant planet is the utter isolation of the world they approach. We are used to star charts and planetary maps that are so readily digestible by the human mind. "This star is right next to that one." "That planet is near this other one, but a bit further from that one." It's all very transparent and useful, but when one actually nears another planet the reality is very different. There are no "nearby" planets to observe. It's not like walking down a busy street and looking at the different shops and vendors at hand, as our maps seem to suggest. Planets, regardless of the illusion of proximity to other celestial objects, are completely on their own. This isolation seems known to the subconscious mind, and felt deeply in the core of one's being. Instantly the object of this isolation ceases to be a planet and is understood as a world.

Entering the atmosphere of such a world is always a fascinating affair. It's easy to think of it as routine, and many do, but each world is a little different. There is the color of the atmosphere, of course, and often the aurora that varies depending on the composition of said atmosphere. This is all in the context of the surface and how the surface interacts with the sky. Then there is the brief interaction between the incoming ship and the sky, again dependent upon atmospheric composition and the particular vessel entering that atmosphere. Every planet is different. Vox is blue on blue. A primarily Earth-like atmosphere incubating an endless blue ocean. Vox is an orb of water with practically no land mass save a smattering of small islands not visible in less than close proximity. The view from space is of a beclouded blue sphere. The poles radiate streams of ionized particles, mostly shades of green but adorned in prismatic hues. Beautiful and ultimately indescribable.

When his ship hits the atmosphere Bob is bathed in orange and red and briefly the world is filtered through these intrusive colors. Entering the atmosphere is always, for Bob, the finger-snap that ends the hypnotic trance. Space is smooth and the relativity of motion has much more meaning there. An atmosphere is a lumpy, bumpy, gnarled thing. The stillness of interstellar travel is replaced by jostling, shifting, dropping, vibrating, and pulsating through a turbulent air, most often accompanied by warning signals, status alarms, and a variety of lights and meters that spring into life. It's on to business now.

Piercing the clouds, Bob could now see all about him endless blue ocean. It was beautiful but did create an unexpected visual effect upon him. The ocean was a uniform blue agate and interrupted only by soft azure upon the intersection of water and sky at the horizon. It made perspective difficult. Regardless of what scale one attempted to see this world in, large as a planet or small as a room, it maintained the constant blue on blue of water and sky. It was like a fractal image that, despite the point of view, the same pattern was always present.

There was no land to be seen...anywhere...and Bob wondered where he was going to touch down. Shortly, following given coordinates, he came upon a metallic structure shaped like Calla lily. It was quite small; not much bigger than Bob's ship. As he neared the structure Bob could faintly see a much larger structure beneath the surface of the water. Immediately Bob received a new set of instructions, docking instructions. Still automated, the docking instructions required Bob to land in the water alongside the lily structure from which stabilizing arms underneath would attach to his ship. Bob wasn't so sure about landing a spaceship in water, but it really couldn't hurt it...not much anyway.

As Bob docked and the supports rooted him firmly in place, the aft cargo hold opened and Bob stepped out and onto the Lily petal. The air was perhaps a little thinner than standard, but was clean and comfortable to breath. A cool but strong breeze constantly roared like fire in Bob's ears. It was all very pleasant.

318

Bob stepped toward what appeared to be the pistil of the Lily where, to a keen observer, a door could be seen almost seamlessly hidden within the floral protuberance. As he neared, the door opened and a figure peeked a head out. She was almost completely covered, wearing a cloak of some kind, but there were unknown triggers that cued Bob to her femininity. She glanced at him, then looked strangely at the sky, as if it was some odd and uncomfortable thing for her.

Bob stopped abruptly, partly at the unexpected encounter, but also the image before him. He couldn't see her clearly, but there was something very different about her appearance. Half covered from the cloak, he couldn't quite make it out, but she possessed some visual quality Bob hadn't encountered before. As if he was taking far too long, she sent a curt motion for Bob to hurry up and get inside. The cloaked figure: "Watch your step."

Her voice was warm resonance, deep and female. The entrance at the pistil of the Lily was, as expected, a descending walkway leading to the structure below the water. Bob followed her to some sort of small lobby. The room looked of stone and tile, gray and dull turquoise, plain, with a few metal chairs on each side. At the end was a large dark gun-metal gray door that was unmistakably an airlock.

Stepping toward the airlock, the escort removed the hood from her head. Her appearance was difficult for Bob to interpret. First off, she was about a foot taller than he. He hadn't noticed at first because she was slouching while peering out of the pistil of the Lily, most likely a reaction of her exposure to the air. Her skin was...different. It was hard to tell how, but it was like her skin was substantially thicker without making her look bulky, and it was smooth, slick even. Her mouth was very human...maybe a bit larger proportionally, but not outside the realm of non-variant proportions. Her eyes though... they were large, again not beyond standard deviations, but the spacing was quite wide and they seemed to almost glow with a shimmering green iridescence. Perhaps designed to see well in the darkness of deep water.
Balaenae woman: "You are Bob I presume."
Bob: "Yes. I was hoping to..."
Balaenae woman, politely interrupting: "Yes, we know. Follow me please. I'm Colleen, by the way."
Bob: "Nice to meet you Colleen."

Colleen gave a warm, genuine smile. She was an oddly pleasant mix of curtness and friendliness. She seemed stern, little tolerance for dawdling, but genuine in her courtesy. Bob followed her into the airlock and she closed the door behind. Bob looked around inquisitively at the insides of the airlock, at the lack of...things. It was small and featureless.

Colleen: "You've never been to Vox before I am guessing."
Bob: "No. It's amazing."
Colleen gave a smile and nod in thanks, "We're about enter the research facility where you'll speak to the administration head."
Bob, distracted, "ok..." still not putting together the barrenness of the airlock. Two opposing heavy metal doors, smooth metal between.
Bob: "So...how do I...do you have...like some scuba suit I can borrow?"
Collen: "No, no...it's a nasal spray."
Bob, still piecing it together was silent for a moment.
Bob: "...a nasal spray?"
Collen: "A nasal spray."
Bob: "...I'm afraid I might have to ask for a *bit* more of an explanation."
Colleen gave a smirk as if she thought Bob's response was a *bit* humorous.
Colleen: "It's simple really. The spray contains a mixture of nano-bots and necessary synthesis compounds. They conduct the processes of respiration by synthesizing breathable air at the site of pulmonary alveolus."
Bob: "..."
Colleen: "They make air for you and get rid of CO_2 while your lungs are full of water."
Bob, rather dumbfounded: "...while my lungs are full of water?"
Colleen: "It's really no big deal. It's the easiest way to deal with the pressure and duration of being underwater and it's much more reliable than some (chuckling at the word) *scuba* suit."
Bob: "...ah...reliable...couldn't...couldn't they just come out here and we could talk briefly."
Colleen: "Nobody likes it out here in the open air, besides, we are extraordinarily busy."
Bob: "Lungs full of water you say?"
Colleen: "Don't be a baby. It's no big deal." She then produced a small container from her cloak and opened it to reveal the nasal spray applicator.
Colleen: "Besides, you'll get to see some of our operations. Not many off-worlders get to see the inside of this facility. You wouldn't have either except for the current situation at hand."
Bob: "A nasal spray?"
Colleen: "A nasal spray."
Bob: "Ok."
Colleen: "Ok?"
Bob: "Alright."
Colleen helped him attach the applicator properly.

Colleen: "You'll need to breath this in as deeply as possible."

Bob inhaled the fine mist and had a moderately embarrassing episode of coughing. To be safe, the mist was reapplied as was the coughing episode. However, a quick scan from Colleen's terminal revealed that the saturation was complete and the bots were active. It was time to go.

Colleen: "Ready?"

Bob, taking in a breath and slowly exhaling: "Ready."

With a few commands on her terminal, the airlock started to slowly fill with water. Bob couldn't help but feel like this was a completely stupid thing to do. When the water rose to his knees he started getting a little panicky.

Bob: "You're sure this is completely safe."

Colleen: "Completely."

When the water was waist high Bob felt quite anxious. It was a combination of the fear of drowning and claustrophobia as the breathable space was rapidly dwindling.

Bob, in an unavoidable nervous squeak: "You're sure it's safe?"

Colleen: "Absolutely."

As the word left her mouth the water was neck high on Bob when Colleen offered a calm preparatory warning.

Colleen: "You may feel a slight...drowning sensation."

When the chamber was full, Bob still, out of instinct, refused to give up the air he possessed. Colleen put a hand on his shoulder and gestured for him to breath in. Bob thought this whole thing was completely insane and terrifying. He held on until it was unavoidable and it was as bad as anyone could imagine drowning might be. The asphyxiating rush of water into the lungs. The instinctual spastic purging to get the water out. The thickness of the water bloating his chest cavity. Yet somehow worse was the shock of cold that accompanied the water foreign to his chest. It was about as unpleasant as unpleasantness could be.

Bob couldn't help but thrash around a bit. Colleen grabbed his shoulders and steadied him, making eye contact in an attempt to connect to the higher functioning mind overtaken by animal impulse. Looking at Colleen, Bob calmed down and started to breath normally...or as normal as one could with lungs full of water. It took him a good ten minutes or so to settle down enough to get used to this underwater breathing and stave off recurring panic attacks. After a time, Bob gave Colleen a nod and she opened the opposing door in the airlock.

Before they stepped out, Colleen produced another object which she assisted Bob in placing properly in his ears.

Colleen: "Can you hear me?"
Bob: "Yes."
Colleen: "Is it clear?"
Bob: "A little muffled, but fine."
Colleen showed Bob, on his terminal, how he could fine tune the audio to his liking and before long Bob's hearing was crystal clear despite the thickness of this new watery atmosphere.

The airlock opened to what seemed like some sort of office space, an unusual office space in that the walls were all transparent. From where Bob stood, he could see that the corridor was circular with attached rooms, but inside the circle was open space, open to the surrounding seas. Looking towards this inner circular opening, Bob could see a bit of the floor below arranged very similarly. This structure seemed to be a circular hollow tower extending into the depths. How far? Bob couldn't tell. There was plenty of light, ambient light from the structure itself and sunlight from the distant lumbering hulk Leviathan, but that light quickly dispersed through the refracting water and Bob's vision was significantly limited by this troublesome physics. The visual distance, for Bob, consisted of increasingly darker shades of indigo until lost to a foggy blackness.

They made their way around the circular corridor and Bob found that he had a considerable difficulty in staying level. He was rising with the exceptionally high ceilings and rotating off center, but managing to correct with a series of dainty hand maneuvers, the most effective seeming to be fanning motion, something one might see in a movie from antiquity of a southern bell, near fainting from the summer heat, cooling her powdered face with both hands.

Colleen was trying not to laugh. Somehow she glided along effortlessly, her elevation always constant and motion graceful. She did nothing that Bob could see in the way of adjusting her position. Bob couldn't even see how she managed to move at all, but he was fairly preoccupied with what turned out to be an arduous task of transitioning down a hallway. With his lungs full of water it was as if his lower half was much lighter than the upper and was wanting to prove it by switching the normal order of things. Bob's forward motion stopped when he got a bit caught on the ceiling and was having trouble righting himself. Colleen shot out a short laugh that produced a trail of bubbles from her nose. She then grabbed Bob's arm and pulled him along. It was a little embarrassing, but he was thankful for the break.

As they moved along the corridor Bob could see others doing a variety of things in their office spaces. Most looked like administrative business, nothing particularly scientific, but here and there people could be seen gliding along, effortlessly, occasionally taking notice of Bob. One guy looked at Bob then turned to a co-worker making a brushing motion with his finger about his upper lip. Bob thought, *"oh, not this again."*

At the opposite end of the circular corridor they came to a lift downward.

Colleen: "We're going down a couple of floors. The pressure will be greater, but nothing to worry about."

Bob nodded and they entered the lift. As it descended Bob seemed to want to stay in his current position until his head hit the top of the lift. Again, Colleen grabbed his arm and pulled him downward, to which Bob replied with a helpless "thanks". Since they submerged themselves, Colleen seemed considerably more at ease, but Bob was struggling and wondering how long this meeting might take.

The lift went down a couple of floor and the pressure was an experience. It felt like he was being squeezed and struggling to breath. Technically, he didn't need the motion of breathing for the respiration process to work, but try telling that to your nervous system. The difficulty in breathing, while not a physical setback, was an anxiety producing psychological one.

From this floor the visual was almost the same as the previous floor; circular corridor, everything transparent, and floors descending in like fashion. As Bob was dragged through the hallway by his arm he got a good opportunity to inspect his surroundings. He wasn't sure, as his ability to see was limited, but he kept catching glimpses of a much, much larger structure below. Like the circular tower was attached to some great dome further down. When he tried to look at it directly he couldn't see it, but something, somewhat in his periphery, was telling him that there was something big below.

Colleen led Bob into a room with several other Balaenae inside. The room was a fairly average meeting room with a large oval desk in the center. The others in this room had many of the same features as Colleen; thick, smooth skin, a wide spacing of the eyes, and that iridescent glow in various shades of blue, green, and orange depending on the interaction of light upon them. Bob hadn't taken much notice of Colleen's nose until he saw the others. Outside her nose was small, came to a point, and was somewhat flat...nothing unusual really, but that small nose obviously possessed the musculature to close tight at will as her nose and those of the others were now only faint lines where they had been tightly shut and were almost non-existent. From his dutiful reading Bob knew that they could store air in their lung and breath with a modified gill, presumably around their ribcage, so this must be a mechanism to regulate that interplay and was perhaps partly the reason they moved so gracefully when Bob had such trouble. They had a natural ballast they could manipulate at will.

Bob was a bit off his game. The shock of breathing underwater and the strain of moving around under what seemed to Bob an intense pressure all around him was draining his resources. He was cold. The water was not terribly cold, but cold enough that his body was struggling to maintain heat. Regardless, none of these factors were the primary stressor. This entire facility was composed of rings upon rings; a central oval tower, oval hallways encircling, attached to which could be found many oval rooms in which Bob currently found himself. Everything was rounded and transparent and Bob was becoming increasingly nauseous looking through all of this curved glass. No surface beyond the immediate was without distortion. Everything was wavy and angled and seemed to move in a hazy displacing fog. Bob didn't know how these people could live and work in such an environment without giving in to sickness constantly, but, Bob surmised, the Balaenae were either accustomed to it or their perception was sufficiently different that it was of no concern.

In the meeting room Bob was introduced to the three men already present. A wave of nausea hit him and he somehow missed the name of the first gentleman...chief administrator something or other. The other two Bob managed to catch; head of foreign affairs Ligeti, and director of research Xenakis. After introductions, they all sat around the oval table. The chairs were anchored to the floor, as was the table, and they had a simple mechanism to adjust the height and proximity to the edge.

Head of foreign affairs Ligeti: "On behalf of the Balaenae, we would like to welcome you to Vox. We are of necessity an isolated world, but in matters of importance willing to fulfill our shared responsibility to the galaxy. We received a communication from Sol regarding..."

Bob was trying to pay attention, and doing a fairly good job, but he was having some trouble staying put in the chair around the table. It was as if, again, his lower half was wanting to float way. He was combating this at first by straightening his legs a placing them against the underside of the table, but this proved to be ineffectual. It only created the tendency to rotate around the edge like a crescent wrench too wide for the bolt. To this he added a strong clamp of the hands around the table edge. This seemed to do the trick, but was requiring more force and attention then he would have preferred to devote to the stupid task of not floating away.

Ligeti: "...which is why the timing is of such dire importance."

Bob: "Ehrm...yes. ...Thank you. I...I am very fortunate to be allowed to visit and I thank you. The reason I am here..."

Director of research, Xenakis, interrupted: "We know why you are here." He said, not unfriendly, but sternly.

Xenakis: "We know you have been sent by CIDER...Dr. Morris herself. There is no purpose in attempting to hide this fact."

Bob, relieved actually that he wouldn't have to attempt to avoid that fact, offered a reply: "Good. Yes, yes that is true...but I should point out that it is only the impetus for my trip here. I am not employed by CIDER and am only acting in accordance to what I believe to be the best course of action. Had I any doubts, even for a minute, that Dr. Morris's intentions were anything less than altruistic I would have abandoned this mission long, long ago."

This answer sat well with the panel who nodded in a business-like fashion.

Xenakis: "Very good. Of course, under any other condition we would not have permitted visitation, but times are different and the Balaenae have their own concerns regarding the current state of the galaxy. Even if Dr. Morris turns out to be less than *altruistic*, it seems to be the lesser of two evils and there is little to lose at this point."

Bob didn't really understand the seeming lack of trust, perhaps they viewed CIDER as some shadowy organization, which it is, or maybe they feel CIDER just wants this genetic information for their own purposes and cares little about the virus...which is probably true as well. Who knows? Not appropriate to get into it here.

Bob: "So, if I may be permitted, allow me to explain what *I* want and why I think it will be beneficial to us all. First, what we know, or rather, don't know about the virus and it's creator happens to be......oh, good grief!"

Bob's hand had slipped from the edge of the table. Everything was slippery. Before he could reaffirm his grip his back end shot up and he was a few feet above the table and rising. For a moment, he didn't even fight it. He was cold and exhausted. He just postured his hands as if to apologize and rolled his eyes. In no time he was a good ten feet above the table and against the ceiling when he thought to himself *"why are these ceilings so damn high? What possible purpose could high ceilings have in this place?"* The others waited patiently as Bob dealt with his little issue. Shortly he yet again engaged in what Bob, in his mind, referred to as the *Southern Belle getting the Vapors* swim. If Bob could have seen Colleen, who had previously been sitting next to him, he would have seen a smirky half-smile. She did think it was funny, yet in her mercy she gracefully and effortlessly reached an arm up and grabbed Bob's leg pulling him back to the table. Bob's look of relief was an understood unspoken communication of gratitude.

Bob had thought of tightening the chair against the table to wedge himself in, but with his growing nausea that seemed like torture. Instead, he just wrapped his legs around the chair itself and hoped for the best.

Bob was forthright in his sharing of information. The told the Balaenae of the path of murders, the familial relationship of the dead, the virus more-or-less following the path of murders...basically everything he knew except the name of the architect that was currently being kept a secret. Apparently the Balaenae knew nothing of the murders and the path of such following the viral outbreaks. They of course knew all about the virus and how it had spread to a vast portion of the galaxy. They had seen the feed of the great Colossus, but had little information to piece this all together. They seemed to find the information quite valuable and were surprised to find that Bob had, in essence, been involved in this investigation before anyone in the galaxy was really aware of what had been happening.

Bob's legs were cramping up from squeezing the chair, the only thing keeping him from the ceiling. He had thought about just floating away again. He'd rest on the ceiling comfortably while they all had a chat, but somehow that seemed to be poor etiquette. With his fatigue and nausea, Bob was right on the edge. The director of research, Xenakis, wanted to take him a few places and Bob had to interject.

Bob: "Sorry, I am really fighting this underwater thing. I hate to interrupt our discussion, but before we go on, I might need to find a restroom."

They all offered and kind "certainly" and Colleen put a hand on Bob's shoulder.

Colleen, pointing: "Outside, about a quarter turn down the hallway on the right. The only room not transparent."

Bob: "Thanks." After which he clumsily made his way out of the room and into the hallway. After about seven minutes into a 30 second walk, he entered the bathroom and locked the door behind him. Oh, it was fantastic. Solid walls. Nothing see-through. He floated up to the top of the ceiling and just rested, did absolutely nothing. His nausea was rapidly dissipating and he felt a little more calm and recuperated in the small amount of time he remained stuck to the ceiling.

Bob needed to use the toilet. When he finally got around to checking out the bathroom, it surprised him. Not in anything unique, but in its absolute mundaneness. It was like any bathroom one might find anywhere in the galaxy. There, in this simple bathroom, was an average, run-of-the-mill, standard toilet. He didn't know what he had expected, but...not just a regular toilet. As he approached it, it occurred to him that he didn't know exactly how this was going to work. It was just a standard toilet. Bob really just stood and stared at it a bit trying to figure it out. How was he supposed to avoid making a terrible mess? In water this dense, just about everything floats.

After a few minutes of intense thought, Bob stepped outside and signaled to some guy wandering down the hallway.

Bob, somewhat whispering: "Hey, hey buddy. Come 'ere."

Balaenae office employee: "..me? What's wrong?"

Bob whispered something to the employee to which he replied:

Balaenae office employee: "oh...you flush it first."

Bob: "Oh, ok. Thanks."

Back in the bathroom it all made sense. It was a little different than a standard toilet in operation. The flushing came first which created the appropriate suction to keep things tidy. Bob was now really glad he didn't just give it a try before asking. The lever was an on/off switch for the flushing mechanism. *Quite clever*, Bob thought.

When all was said and done, Bob was feeling significantly better. He also found that he had a lot less trouble maneuvering and managed to break his courtship of the ceiling. He also had less...*less* episodes that involved the Southern Belle maneuver. Overall, he felt more like himself.

Once Bob rejoined the meeting, things went significantly smoother. They went over the details of the investigation again, this time without the distraction of nausea and floating troubles, and Bob was given a fairly clear explanation of the intended involvement of the Balaenae. They were on board and willing to assist.

Head of foreign affairs Ligeti: "I suppose my curiosities have been satisfied. I think we should show Bob to the lab and give him a genetic rundown so he can be on his way."

Xenakis: "Agreed. I think, with the assumed tacit agreement of the council.." he looked and nodded toward Ligeti, "...that we should also share the details of our encounter several years back."

Ligeti, nodded in compliance.

Rising from the table, the Balaenae headed toward the door as Colleen placed a hand on Bob's shoulder.

Colleen: "If you'll follow us, we'll take you to the lab."

They made their way back around the circular hallway to the lift by which Bob had entered this floor.

Xenakis: "We're heading down a couple of floors. You think you're up for the pressure increase?"

Bob: "Well...I don't know. Should I be fine? I'm guessing you lot can take much more pressure than I'm designed for."

Colleen: "You should be fine. Really, we might have a bit of an advantage but our design isn't that far removed. It's really just an issue of what you're accustomed to. I tend to spend a lot of time in the deep. Often job related. When I'm on the upper floors I feel a bit springy, like I'm flying or something."

Bob realized he didn't really know what Colleen's job was. Obviously something with this facility, but exactly what was never actually said.

Xenakis: "You should be fine. Just uncomfortable. Panicky maybe. Claustrophobic. Anxiety is not an uncommon symptom for air-breathers when underwater for prolonged periods of time.

At the elevator Ligeti took his leave as did the other guy who Bob still didn't catch his name and it didn't help that he was fairly silent. Bob thought it would just be his luck that he was the president or something and Bob's snubbing had caused an interplanetary incident. Regardless, Bob, Colleen, and Xenakis entered the lift and headed down.

It was only a couple of floors down, but it seemed to take a long time. Maybe the elevator moved slower as pressure grew, or maybe these were big floors...hard to tell. In the interim Bob looked over his company. They were very interesting. Very different. They were the most varied variants he had seen in person. The Rapulis of Boreas could, for the most part, pass as standard if one didn't get a close look. The Balaenae on the other hand were truly unique...in a fascinating and rather pleasing way. They didn't look menacing or alien, just varied and unfamiliar. It was during this surreptitious staring that Bob noticed something odd about one of Xenakis's eyes. It was...still...inconsistent with the other.

Xenakis: "It's fake."

Bob, somewhat embarrassed: "Fake?"

Xenakis, pointing towards his left eye: "It's glass."

Bob realized that the wide spacing of the Balaenae eyes probably increased their field of view making it harder to make a passing glance that would go undetected.

Bob: "How'd you lose it?"

Xenakis: "Harpoon."

Bob: "Really?"

Xenakis: "No, not really."

Colleen chuckled.

The lift opened into the lab and the pressure was considerably higher. It was a tight uniform squeeze and Bob didn't care for it one bit. He took a moment and adjusted. It felt harder to breath, but Bob reinforced his rational mind by reviewing that fact that the discomfort and difficulty of breathing had nothing to do with the amount of oxygen that was actually being supplied to his body.

The lab was rather dark and lit only by various instruments and screens within and a faint ambient glow from without. It was circular, like the rest of the facility, only the floor was opaque. In the center was the source of the ambient glow, which looked like some form of reactor offering a warm blue radiance. Bob looked back at the lift. They had exited from the opposite side meaning they were in a different circular tower attached to the one he had come from with the office spaces and primary airlock. Looking out, to the open sea, Bob could see faint light above and below the outline of something far greater than either of the two buildings in which they had now been. There must be some great structure far deeper. Bob had wondered how deep the Balaenae could comfortably operate. The answer was apparently much deeper than they were now.

Near the central "reactor" for lack of a better term, Xenakis handed Bob a very similar metallic cylinder to the one he had acquired from Boreas.

Xenakis: "This contains samples and a datastream of the standard Balaenae deviant along with current implemented modifications and projected variation spanning the next seven hundred years."

Bob: "Wow. That is thorough. Seven hundred years?"

Xenakis: "Yes. We have mapped our guided evolution for the next seven hundred years. After that, any data would be highly speculative."

Bob: "That's amazing. You have it all planned out?"

Xenakis: "More or less. We implement the stages of it in phases, across limited samples. One wouldn't want to modify everyone only to find out an unforeseen element made the modification a really bad idea."

Bob: "That makes sense."

Xenakis: "Take Colleen here, for example. She is the beneficiary of a slight efficiency improvement to the lung/gill exchange."

Colleen gave a sarcastic curtsy and said, "I'm very modern."

Xenakis: "Yes. Assuming she and the others so modified don't keel over dead, it will be implemented on larger and larger scales in time."

Colleen, glibly: "I'm a human trial...but I have other useful qualities too."

Bob smiled.

Xenakis: "We'll show you the projected end product."

Xenakis and Colleen brought Bob over to the center of the lab, the thing Bob had thought was a reactor of some sort. Inside, Bob could see several...people?...floating hazily in the blue glow. With a command from a nearby terminal, one of the figures in the reactor was brought closer to the edge. The figure was humanoid, but looked nothing like Bob nor like the Balaenae. It was perhaps similar to the Balaenae in eye spacing, but the skull was different as was the musculature. The skin was strikingly beautiful. It was the jet black of a pilot whale. The sort of absolute black that was designed to grasp any errant light particle that came too close. It was skin designed for remaining in the deep for long, long periods of time. The figure was still bipedal, but the phalanges of both the hands and feet seemed elongated and webbed. A gill system could be seen on the ribcage, most likely occupying the spaces between the ribs themselves. No visible nose, the mouth was wide and thin. In this figure, whose mouth was partially agape, a few teeth resembling those of the orca could be seen.

Bob: "Is this...Is this a person in there?"

Colleen: "Yes and no. It is a biological construction of our end product for testing purposes. Everything is physically sound, but the specimen lacks a cerebral cortex."

Bob: "So, it's not conscious."

Xenakis: "Not at all. We access the brainstem to run tests of various systems, but the specimen lacks the necessities of thought or experience."

Colleen: "We have hundreds of these in tanks stationed planetwide to run tests in a variety of environments and to rule out cross contamination."

Bob: "That has to be one of the most fascinating things I've ever seen. So, someday, you all will become this?"

Both Colleen and Xenakis nodded in agreement.

Xenakis: "Why don't we take you on a little tour of some of those tanks. It will give us time to talk about an event that happened here some years back."

Bob: "Sure, why not."

The far end of the lab opened, through a series of heavy doors, to a docking bay, small, but adequate with eight personal transports each facing an airlock which gave the round room a plump crab-like appearance...or so it did to Bob who was in a marine-life sort of mindframe. The three of them piled into a transport that could seat about four comfortably. It was an unfamiliar design to Bob. It looked almost like a standard small space transport, but with the top half missing. Inside, Bob could clearly see that the missing top half was retractable and most likely could be raised for space travel if needs be.

Bob: "So, this thing could become spaceborn if you needed it to?"

Colleen: "It could, but we never leave. I'm not sure I know anyone who's actually been to outer space...Balaenae that is. We usually only enclose the vessel in the winter when the waters are exceptionally cold, or if we need to travel a great distance and must breach the surface. It does tend to travel a lot faster through air as you might expect."

As they left the airlock, though really, Bob thought, it should probably be called a waterlock, they sped off into the endless blue. The ship was surprisingly fast. It seemed to be using standard pulse engines redesigned for water travel, or maybe not redesigned Bob considered, maybe pulse engines work fine underwater. They work fine in an atmosphere and space...maybe water was not different, just slower.

As the ship sped along, Bob was enjoying the brisk current rushing past him. Also, they were climbing in elevation which was relieving a good amount of the pressure on his body. This coupled with the growing light from the distant, sky dominating Leviathan, as they rose was putting Bob in a more relaxed mood. He hoped they would have no need to go back inside that claustrophobic underwater building.

When they were close to the surface and the light was adequate, Bob happened to notice his hands. They were exceptionally pruney. Colleen, who had been looking outward, noticed Bob inspecting his hands and shot a concerned look his way.

Colleen: "You...you didn't look like that when you got here. Is...are you alright?"

Bob: "Yeah, fine...just been under a bit long."

Colleen: "That's normal for you? The way you look? You look very...wrinkly all the sudden."

Bob: "Yeah, it's nothing. I mean, I couldn't stay underwater for a long time, but it's fine for a while."

Colleen: "Odd."

Just then the ship passed through what looked like a vast underwater forest. Dark green ribbons twisting down from the surface and turning bright chartreuse where folded toward the light. Behind was a backdrop of dense blue becoming aquamarine then white as one's eyes approached this distant, gargantuan sun.

In their passing, Colleen turned to Bob and said, "One of our many farming sites. When our people first came here, nothing was native. Vox was a ball of water with little growing anywhere. Once we removed certain unwanted elements and conditioned the waters, we began a program to populate the planet with vegetation. For hundreds of years now we have been entirely self-sufficient."

Bob: "It's beautiful, like an underwater forest."

Colleen: "If you look close towards the surface, you can see the faint lattice work that supports the vegetation keeping it stationary."

Bob looked but everything at the surface was only a fuzzy haze to him.

Colleen: "All of the vegetation we produce is of old Earth origin, many heirloom strains. Some required a slight modification or two. This field is a modified Wakame, but we also produce Oarweed,

331

Laver, about a dozen varieties of Kelp, as well as Chlorella...very high in protein, sea grapes, sea lettuce, dulse, mozuku, and hundreds of types of moss, algae, and lichen...carrageen, and black stone flower, for example."

Bob had heard of some of those, but that's more seaweed than he was familiar with. Bob always liked seaweed. It was one of those foods that tastes exactly like its environment. They always taste like the sea. Bob realized that he knew very little about genuine maritime societies. Helen had no oceans. The only waters were ornamental or recreational with the exception of stored water for use, but that was never seen. There was no seafaring or marine commerce and Bob, like most inhabitants of Helen would be, was a complete alien here, but fortunately a welcome one.

Shortly after they left the Wakame forest, they arrived at a cylindrical and transparent tank, very similar to the one in the lab but this one was open at both ends, open to the outer ocean. Inside was another body, very much like the one in the lab. After the ship stopped, both Xenakis and Colleen left the ship and swam toward the tank. Bob looked over the edge and the darkening blue that ended in a black nothingness. Colleen gestured to Bob to come to the tank. The waters were quite calm, but Bob had little sense of his buoyancy. Looking over the edge again down towards that impenetrable darkness, Bob stood and hopped a little to get a sense of the physics involving this unfamiliar environment. He assumed that if he started sinking into the depths, that Colleen would go fetch him, but for all he knew he might plummet like a stone. It was a compound anxiety involving, oddly, a fear of heights, a fear of drowning, and a fear of being crushed by the pressure that must accompany that deep, deep darkness. Had they done this part first, when Bob couldn't deny his attraction to the ceiling, he'd merely worried he'd end up at the surface. Now, after his toilet adventure, he didn't have the levitation problem anymore.

When he made it over the edge of the ship Bob found that he tended to stay put and it only took a little adjusting, by means of a clumsy paddling motion, to maintain his desired location. At the edge of the tank Bob again looked into the future of the Balaenae, their guided evolution. As he moved to position himself for a better view, the body in the tank gave a short torque of the head toward him. It startled Bob.

Bob: "He moved. Is he conscious?"

Xenakis: "No. But the limited capacity of the nervous system will still, on occasion, react to light or movement."

Bob: "I see."

Xenakis: "Bob, why we've brought you here is to tell you about an event that happened a few years ago. This tank here is like a field test of our modifications exposed to environmental conditions: temperature variance, light spectrum variance, regional bacteria, microbes, naturally occurring viral contaminants, etc. Here we are putting our evolutionary test subjects into our environment to see how they respond."

Bob: "That makes sense."

Colleen: "We have thousands of these around the globe, all monitored and maintained. We take the modification of our people very seriously and have a certain understood urgency to make this long, long process no longer than it needs to be."

Xenakis: "That being said, several years ago an unidentified transport was seen visiting several of our tanks. We are not, in general, a spacefaring society and had little ability to pursue in a timely manner."

Colleen: "We couldn't even get to him while he was in the atmosphere. It just takes us too much time to get from the deep to the sky."

Xenakis: "I guess it's not too much of a secret that we're not terribly equipped to handle something like this. We do have the ability to defend ourselves, it's just a bit of a production and our isolation has perhaps made us lax in security."

Colleen: "Besides, this guy was in and out. He came here to do a job and left immediately."

Bob: "What did he do?", Bob said already having a fairly solid idea.

Xenakis: "We found that several of our evolutionary test subjects had been cored."

Bob: "Yes, samples taken. The same thing happened to the Rapulis."

Xenakis: "We're assuming that it was the architect of the virus. We are also assuming that we are susceptible to the virus, even though it has not made its way here."

Colleen: "Yet."

Xenakis summoned the video feed of the event from the terminal alongside the tank. It was difficult to see through water, and the image curved with the roundness of the tank, *and* Bob's eyes were starting to kill him from being submerged for what seemed like ages in salt water, but unmistakably he could identify that same medical transport descending from the sky and skimming the surface of the water. Here though, as it turned by one unseen recording eye, in the open cargo doors of the medical transport Bob could clearly see a bespectacled man...the same man from the leaked feed of the great Colossus. It *was* Moloch of which Bob had absolutely no doubt.

Colleen: "There is a complete dossier of the event including all video feeds and timelines in the data stream that accompanies the genetic information we've supplied to you."

Bob: "I'm sure you've already surmised this, but this is definitely the same man that destroyed cities on Diophantus with the great Colossus. It appears to be the same ship that took samples from Boreas. He is the assumed architect of the virus. That's about all I know right now."

Both Colleen and Xenakis nodded in a somewhat somber agreement and the three of them boarded the transport to take Bob back to his ship. Before long they were near the surface under the Calla Lily platform where Bob had docked his ship.

Bob: "Thanks for your hospitality and help. I'll be honest, it seems like the more information I learn about this case the less I know and the further behind I feel. I really don't have anything in the way of answers or potential solutions except the hope that some anti-viral might be formulated...but if I learn anything of value, anything that I think might help you both and the Balaenae, I'll do whatever it takes to get that information to you."

Xenakis politely nodded.

Colleen: "We believe you. We hope our offering might help. Our plan is to reinforce our borders and establish a stronger commitment to our isolationist practices. Bob, you may be the last outsider to visit the Balaenae for the next several hundred years."

Bob: "I hope it doesn't come to that, but either way I'm exceptionally honored. Thank you for allowing me a glimpse of your beautiful world."

Colleen smiled.

Colleen: "You should have no problems making to the surface from here, right?"

Bob: "Yeah, it should be fine." Bob could tell they had a strong reluctance of exposure to that empty air.

Colleen: "You'll want to purge as much of the water from your lungs as you can. The bots will continue to remove water from around the alveoli. You might have a coughing fit or two over the next few days, but after that you'll be fine. The bots will remove themselves only when the job is complete. Take care and best of luck."

Bob: "You too."

Bob swam to the surface and climbed atop the Calla Lily. He was happy to be out of the water, but when he started breathing in air again, he started involuntarily coughing out two lungs worth of water. It was a wretched interplay of coughing and gasping and wheezing. It was almost as bad as the initial submersion or, as Colleen put it, a *slight drowning sensation*. After the fit was over, Bob laid flat on the

Lily, warming in the sun and wracked from exhaustion. In this moment of respite, he realized his EMP gun was still strapped to his thigh...hadn't even thought of it till now. Prolonged exposure to salt water and it was surely ruined. It didn't matter. All Bob could really focus on was regaining strength. He desperately wanted to nap, but there was no time. He needed to make tracks and also preferred to be dry whilst napping.

After just enough time to reclaim the minimally required strength, Bob entered the cargo hold of his ship and headed skyward. Soon Bob could see the beautiful blue and beclouded orb of Vox receding as he deepened himself into the blackness of space. It was so concerning to him, that some attack was being brought upon what seemed like the galaxy itself. Was this the culmination of our violent natures feeding back upon us? Was this the next step in the endless redundancy of war? It was even more frustrating that there were no answers. One facing execution wants to know of what crime they are accused. Here, with these murders, this virus, and this Colossus, no one knows why...no one knows of what crime they have been accused. And the Rapulis and the Balaenae? They seem like the most peaceful of people. Perhaps their isolation and modification is in part to partition themselves from the chaos of humanity.

Bob couldn't help but feel rather out of place in this world. By world Bob would readily tell you he intended the whole of the known universe. This was predicated on a strong awareness of the past, something nebulous and vague, but palpable all the same...a thing devoid of explanation and a wonder at what that absent explanation might mean. Throughout the machinations of humanity, with all its presupposed advancement and progress, Bob felt that in our connection to it, to the past so seemingly distant, that we have yet to remove ourselves from this something ancient...possibly an inescapable component of our shared destiny.

In our hundred thousand plus years of recorded and studied history we have managed to spread from one planet to many. In this vast pilgrimage, coupled with our understanding of the biological form, we have adapted ourselves to countless new worlds. Almost as an unspoken yet agreed upon determination, a tacit complicity in guiding the branches of our evolution, we spread outward. We've adapted to different worlds, different climates, adapting our needs, our ways of living. Our minds so adapt. This adaptation leads to different ways of thinking; a different mind equals different philosophies, different spiritualities, different goals, and a different purpose.

It happened on a small scale in Earth's isolated history. Different environments and different people produce different cultures. Now the same has spread to great worlds. Globes, individually with their own variations, but a shared commonality planet-wide. Fighting is inevitable, wars become reborn. Tribes fight tribes, states fight states, countries, continents, unions great and small, and yes, planetary conflict. It's the same old story on a much larger scale. With all this "progress" we haven't managed to escape the human condition.

This too is ancient, but Bob felt no connection to this. He was trying to be free from it. He had continually destroyed it in himself. What Bob felt in a kinship from the ancient past was the opposing element to this struggle. That vague something that had liberated some from the violence of the world. He could see clearly the human desire to acquire an enemy, a thing to fight and conquer, an evil to blame and exorcise, and wished with all his heart to be freed from it, and though he might be faced with beings wearing the brand of "enemy", attempts at his life made, perhaps in time successful, Bob knew that in this entire universe he truly had no enemy as "enemy" was merely a word that carried no reality to it. Yes, this ancient thing to which he felt connected was liberation, an awakening that in one's self the eyes open...other universes begins to be hinted at and even seen in a rudimentary way.

It was somewhere towards the end of this rambling rumination that Bob had discovered himself in dry clothing, laying on the ships cot, and seconds away from dozing off.

Dream Journal: The Heavenly Spheres are Illuminated by Light.

I saw her, my sweet little girl. My daughter was etched into the twilight of the sky, a constellation whose simplicity shined her light into the galaxy. Not a new constellation. No new arrangement of stars, but a pattern which always was, lying dormant until illuminated by context. She was there, in the twilight of the sky, a metaphor containing vastly more information than the meager pieces of its construction.

I watched for eons. She spread out like gossamer rays from some great sun. Every constellation now was her and she delicately seeped outward from the galactic edge to the darkness beyond.

Oh, nebulous providence, I have so little time here. I will soon enter the darkness, the unknown and there learn to love you. Please, in my absence, let her stretch out in every direction beyond all creation and become what is. I will find peace only when she is all that is, all that will be, and all that ever was.

Chapter Twenty Three:
The Voice of Rage and Ruin.

Rho-Omega-00-1-genesis grain in proximity of blinking star. Division command requested.

Tau-00-Obelisk grain has grown large. From it impenetrable commands have solidified and become still.

Small grain 00-0 has found proper placement in the eternal and is now omnipresent. Transmissions no longer necessary.

***

Several days earlier, shortly after the destruction on Diophantus.

     A bespectacled man, a man we have come to know as Moloch, sits quietly in a comfortable chair...the place unknown. Behind him is a window that shows only black. The room is white and wood, in woods of amber and mahogany with a scent of the familiar, the sentimental. Straight, expressionless, and monotone he speaks to someone unseen to us, someone who remains silent.

Moloch: "We have set off for that village of fools, where nobody ever sleeps because nobody ever gets tired. Yes, (with a somber chuckle) how could fools ever get tired?"

"..."

"When the great Colossus rose, it was rising with my spirit. It *was* my spirit and I breathed the air of new worlds."

"...There is nothing good in this. Such a terrible, terrible thing. How could I have expected to become anything but the product of the kingdom from which I was spawned, that kingdom of tiny kings with tiny minds, that kingdom of the thinking beast...a beast so certain of its divinity."

(silence)

"...This world of light and color made dark, foreboding, and gray by those to whom the great task of observation has been given. We are the watchers of the skies and have chosen, in the falseness of vision, to encrust the universe in our own blood, dried, ...cracked, glass-sharp, and black."

(his eyes reddened)

"The thinking beast. Blood thirsty. Arbitrary."

(a sad half-laugh)

"What a useless thing we've become...or have always been."

(briefly shaking himself free of the emotional construct of the situation)

"I am one of them. And I, like them, am finding the end... and our end is holy."

"Soon, there will be no room for us. No room for me in this universe and I will praise that day. When death had stripped me clean of suffering and the universe has no place for those like me; I will rest in eternal contentment. ...That day is soon."

(silence)

"...Until then, we have some work to do."

Moloch stood leaving the air of contemplation behind him. His expression had turned from the introspective to the stern determination of a man with objectives requiring his immediate attention. Accessing a console which reflected astringent white light across his spectacles, Moloch, with a faint passing interested, mumbled to himself. "Hmm... looks like he's on his way to Vox. I imagine he'll be on route to the Dandy system soon after."

Chapter Twenty-Four:
The Lights of Pulsar 9238b

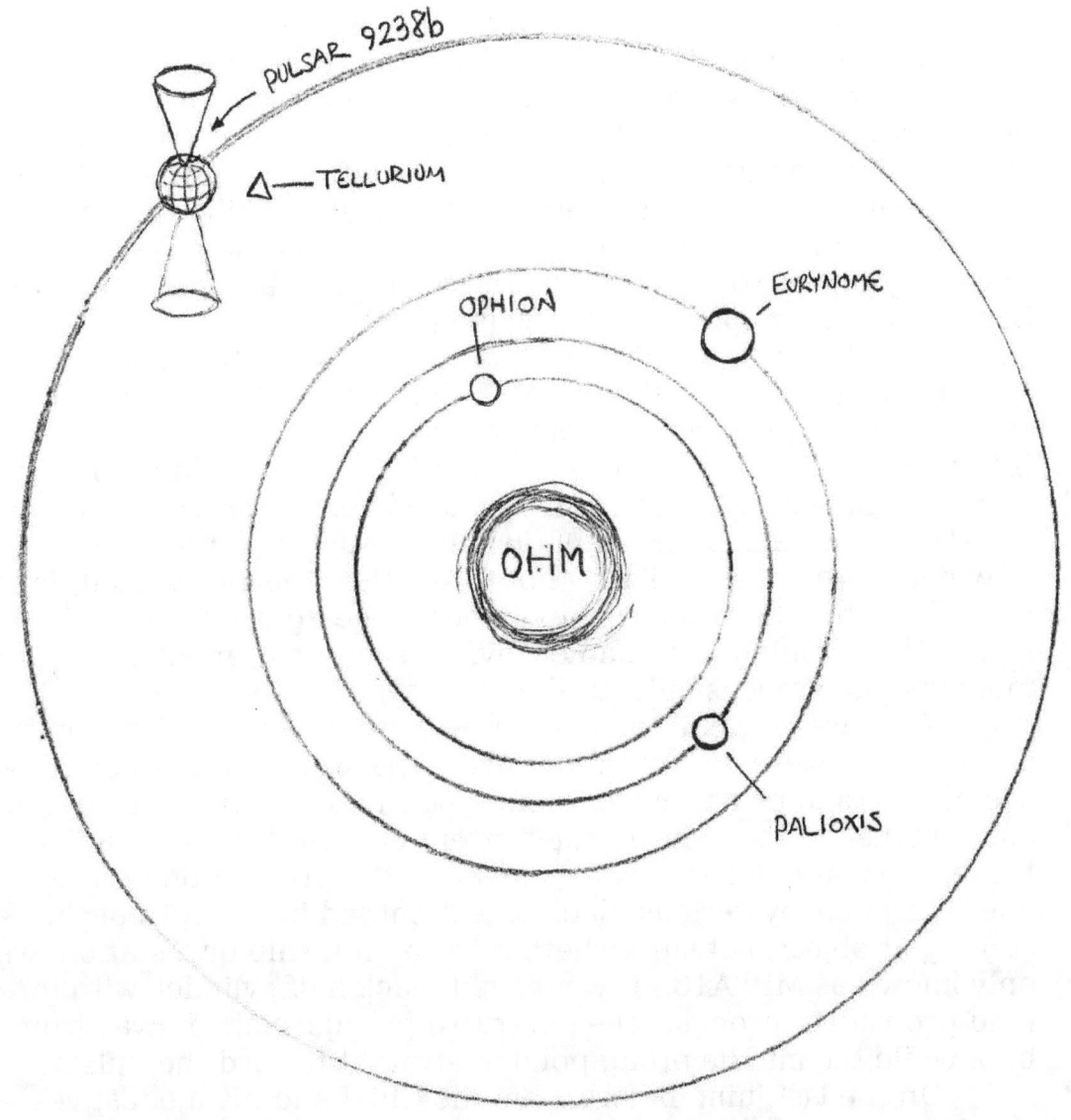

The Chief had traveled in a similar fashion to Bob. He had ridden on a series of industrial transports casting him to and fro until he reached his target. Ohm was a fairly populated and well known system, but not so much a tourist destination, so standard jump-ship travel was limited.

The Chief had only made it to the outskirts of Ohm. He was still one jump away from Ohm proper on a station in orbit of the accompanying binary. This binary companion to Ohm was a white hot pulsar and the Chief felt they were a bit too close to it for his liking. The rapidly spinning pulsar had two ejection plumes spewing all manner of solar waste. It was like a cosmic bladed rotary fan and one didn't want to get their fingers too close. Being in the path of the ejection plumes was dangerous and being crossed was deadly. Any ship caught in the searing radiant stream of the pulsar would surely be destroyed or at least left inoperable and rendering the vessel sterilized of organic matter. As organic matter himself, the Chief took a personal interest in this phenomenon. There really was no danger to him though. Knowing the power of the pulsar, ships considered the pulsar's plane of rotation an impassable barrier and transversing that barrier was accomplished only by jump.

The station on which the Chief currently found himself was far from the grandeur of *Gallium* that Bob had recently visited. This station, which goes by the name *Tellurium*, is a rather flat metallic black rounded rhombus turned up and over on one edge. The turned edge was the inner facility, which housed very little, while the rest of the station was a succession of docking platforms for large ships, all of which were unused. That's not to say the area was vacant, far from it, it's just that there is little advantage to being docked on this station rather than holding position nearby. There wasn't much inside, and most traffic here was industrial.

What was beyond the station by contrast was a fairly impressive sight. There were dozens of massive Capacitor Galleons floating in a seemingly random assortment and toward the rotating pulsar one could make out the focus of their attention. Like moths to a flame, these Capacitor Galleons were in wait of the production of attenuated energy from a mysterious black object bathed in the light of this failed sun. That object, not sure whether to call it a ship or a station, was only known as MPSA18. It was a dull black half cylinder with three long protruding prongs. The outer two prongs snaked away from the bulk while the middle prong pointed straight toward the pulsar.

On the last jump before Ohm the Chief and his modest vessel had hitched a ride with a large maintenance crew aboard a service transport. A lengthy conversation with a crew member had intended on enlightening the Chief to the operations here, but it was the ramblings, however polite, of a specialist and the Chief got the general gist but understood very little, though he had been happy to converse. Apparently the Capacitor Galleons gather to collect energy from the MPSA18. The MPSA18 makes use of two qualities of the nearby pulsar. One, the superconducting core and two, the quasi-dielectric properties of the pulsar's surface (or outer shell). This allowed the MPSA18 to harmlessly generate and accentuate a stable displacement current about the pulsar which the MPSA18 then could amplify and condition for a variety of purposes...in one prong and out the other to be collected by the awaiting Galleons. The only problem with this amplification process is that there is a, as the crew member put it, *strong tendency* for the amplified current to ground itself back to the pulsar which tended to make everything nearby explode. To avoid this rather undesirable effect a suitable ground must be maintained, but where is there a ground to be found floating in the emptiness of space? If one was to inspect closely that middle prong of the MPSA18 they would find the entwined workings of a jump engine, though slightly more exposed than in any motile vehicle. What this engine does is a quasi-jump that is both engaged and terminated at time zero, meaning, in a way, this MPSA18 when collecting and amplifying a charge from the pulsar, makes a jump to its current location. What this accomplishes is a brief moment when the charge can be grounded to the void. The void, as any student of nothingness can tell you, is of infinite conductivity as there is literally nothing to impede the current and connects itself to and from every other point in the universe...it also happens to be infinitely resistive because it really isn't there, but it's probably better not to think about that aspect too much.

What does this all mean? The Chief didn't know what the hell it all meant, but he gathered that the Galleons collected stuff in the form of energy, but also sometimes gravitons which were massless, but made everything heavy...somehow.

It was a sight. Something one didn't see every day. The Chief looked across the expanse of space toward the rotating pulsar and the litter of giant insect-like ships waiting to feed off of it. Soon, a signal lit up on his console letting him know the jump-ship he had arranged to take him to Ohm proper had arrived. He quickly made his way there and docked. In moments he'd be near a nice populated planet and this pulsar would be nothing more than a distant flickering light in the night sky.

A percussive thud and one muffled crackle later, the Chief and his small craft left the jump-ship and found themselves in orbit around the planet Palioxis. Palioxis was considered the seat of authority in the Ohm system and, from what the chief had heard, it was a lovely place. A very Earth-like world with lush forests and pacific blue oceans, the Chief had the instinctual desire to experience Palioxis, maybe even have a proper vacation as he had been more than merely overworked lately, but unfortunately he most likely would not set foot on that blue and green beclouded world below. The Water Sprite

Genomics facility was a small station in orbit of Palioxis and that was the Chief's current destination.

After about half hour, the Chief was in range of the station and was awaiting docking instructions. It looked like some sort of domed lumpy thing with reaching crab legs in a seeming attempt to cover its baldness. It was small, but busy. It's not terribly surprising, the Chief thought, that the galaxy was in this potential crisis with some runaway virus. For all of the accumulated knowledge on the human design, there was always that element that was elusive and unknown and thus explains the need for countless theoretical/experimental genetics and medical facilities galaxy wide. We have always had a need to understand what is happening in our bodies, what might happen, and what we might do about it, however our efforts always seem a step or two behind our evolution as filtered through a constantly changing universe. With all the effort put towards figuring ourselves out, biologically at least, it isn't surprising that some jerk figured something out and decided to torment people with it.

They had been expecting him. Clearance was granted. Docking instructions followed. Then a scan and bio-sweep made sure the Chief himself wasn't bringing anything unwanted into the facility. Entering Water Sprite Genomics, the Chief noted it had a very medical atmosphere about it, run-of-the-mill one might say. The Chief met with the head of the facility, which was polite and helpful, but really had nothing of value to offer in terms of information. Info on Moloch had been redacted, his records absent, and the employment of the administration didn't happen to overlap with the employment of Moloch. The Chief knew this already and wasn't really there to talk to the "higher-ups".

What followed, with the full consent of the administration, was a lengthy interview process of all employees that served during the estimated time frame of Moloch's employment. It was about sixty individuals. Since the time frame of Moloch's employment had to be estimated (actual dates lost to the redaction), these sixty individuals were a good starting point and expansion could be carried out if necessary.

It was about three and a half hours into the interview process, which so far had led nowhere, that the Chief was introduced to, and the Chief had too look closely at the name to make sure he was reading it right, a miss Cynthia Carbunkle. Cynthia was fairly short and rather round and had an odd manner of dress. It wasn't odd as if a culture with which the Chief was unfamiliar was presenting itself. No, it was more like someone who had dedicated themselves to a routine, perhaps since childhood, and that routine had slowly, unbeknownst to the individual, evolved into something altogether

344

slightly off. Not unpleasant, just off. But what really caught the Chief's attention was her thick spectacles.

Chief: "Hello miss...Carbunkle? Please, have a seat."

Cynthia: "Thank you, please, call me Cynthia."

Chief: "Certainly, Cynthia. Do you know why I'm interviewing the employees today?"

Cynthia: "I believe so. The rumor is that that virus spreading may have something to do with one of the former employees here."

Chief: "That's right. I just want to be clear, no one here is in any kind of trouble, and we don't suspect anyone currently here of being involved. We are just hoping that someone might have some information that could be helpful."

Cynthia, who seemed a little nervous, probably by nature, said: "Yes. I see."

Chief: "...might, might I ask you, only if you don't mind, about why you wear spectacles?"

Cynthia, caught a bit off guard: "Oh, ...my glasses? Sure, I have an astigmatism."

The Chief had no idea what that was, nor would most people. Eye problems were few in the galaxy and those that had them usually had them corrected.

Chief: "Ah, you never considered having the problem corrected?"

Cynthia: "I have a bit of a phobia about procedures like that...also, I feel comfortable wearing my glasses...they kind of protect my eyes if someone accidentally pokes about or I bump into something sharp. I...I sort of have a little anxiety when it comes to my eyes."

As she said this she cupped the sides of her spectacles with her hand and upon realizing this pressed her hands to her cheeks, then quickly into her lap.

Chief: "Sure, I understand. Let me ask you a few questions about the issue at hand."

Cynthia: "Certainly."

Chief: "Do you happen to know this man?"

The desk between them produced a picture, the clearest one they had acquired prior to the destruction of Diophantus.

Cynthia looked, adjusted her glasses, looked again, then lifted her glasses and squinted tightly, then looked once more with the glasses in place.

Cynthia: "Oh yes, that's Moloch."

The Chief was caught quite by surprise.

Chief: "How do you know him?"

Cynthia: "He used to work here a while back. I'm not sure what he did, but I would see him sometimes on my lunch break."

Chief: "So, you spoke to him. You know him personally?"

Cynthia: "Well, I can't really say that, but we would talk sometimes. For a long time he kept to himself and I was too shy to say a word, but after a few months I told myself 'Cynthia, you are going to make some friends, you are going to try' and I awkwardly blurted out that we both wore glasses."

Chief: "What did he say?"

Cynthia: "He calmly nodded and softly said 'yes, yes we do'. Other than that, we mostly talked about nothing important: the food in the cafeteria, whether our weekend was good or not..."

Chief: "..."

Cynthia: "I asked him about his life away from work but he never really had much to say. ...At one point, he did tell me that he probably wouldn't be working here much longer."

Chief: "Did he say why?"

Cynthia: "He said 'creative differences'."

Over the course of the next hour or so, the Chief asked Cynthia everything he could think of, but she really knew very little. She didn't know what he had been working on, didn't know where he might have lived, or where he might have gone next. They were work acquaintances in the most casual sense.

Chief: "Thank you Cynthia, you have been very cooperative. I have your contact info so I may send you a message if I think of anything else I should've asked."

Cynthia: "Sure."

Chief: "By the way, what do you do here at Water Sprite Genomics?"

Cynthia: "I work for the bio and machined telomere programming and reconditioning initiative. I synthesize and program artificial telomerase reverse transcriptase nano engines. We're trying to make a slightly better one."

The Chief nodded in approval but he had absolutely no idea what any of that meant. He said goodbye and continued with the interviews for the bulk of the remaining day. Cynthia didn't offer much in terms of helpful information, but the Chief felt like he was in the right place, doing the right thing. He was closer to the mystery man than he ever had been before.

The better part of the afternoon consisted of an endless barrage of pointless interviews. None of these employees knew anything, those that thought they might have seen him weren't sure, and those that were sure hadn't spoken to him. Any single detail pertaining to the outside of the facility in regards to Moloch were nonexistent. It was starting to appear to be a fairly fruitless endeavor. Yet, the Chief carried on. Interview after interview yielding nothing, but there was little else to do.

As evening began to approach the Chief took a break to rest his eyes and his mind a bit. Taking a moment in quiet contemplation he returned to the frantic world of people scurrying about with things to do. It was somewhere in the in-between space of this-and-that that some wild hair urged the Chief to check his terminal for messages, though none had been announced. There, like before, was another messages, solely text, with neither hide nor hair of authorship, no identifying marks whatsoever. It had to be from the same sender as before. Eagerly, the Chief poured through the message.

"Well, I had hoped that things would resolve themselves or that you'd find something useful and that would be that. I suppose it was wishful thinking. I am certain there is nothing of value in what you're doing now. Against my better judgment, I should do what is the noble thing to do and end my anonymity. I think it is time we meet. I am sending coordinates and a time. I trust you will be there. Sit comfortably when you arrive and I will approach you. The only obstacle to my presence would be the very real likeness of my untimely death. In the event of my absence, death is a certainty and all I can say is good luck. I would be remiss should I not also warn you of the dangers of our meeting, a danger in which you've been involved for a while now, but may intensify in my presence. These are dangerous times we live in."

That was it. It didn't reveal much, but it looks like the individual that gave the Chief a heads up about Water Sprite Genomics was willing to meet. The Chief felt eager at the opportunity and didn't particularly mind the specter of death that seemed to loom about that message. Progress. Progress was coming to this seemingly endless maze of dead ends.

The Chief didn't have time in which to laze even had he so wanted. The time was soon and the coordinates were the next planet over. Oddly, a public park in a busy city on Ophion. Abruptly, the Chief left the conference room to which he had been allotted use and made a direct path towards his ship. As he passed the office desk he offered a quick "Something has come up and I am leaving immediately", to which the attendant seemed surprised but hadn't the time to utter a word before the Chief was in the hangar and shortly after arcing skyward, toward the black vacuum between this world and the next.

It was obvious to the Chief that this individual must feel the need to act fast, that if too much time passed between scheduling a meeting and the meeting itself, this fella might not make it. Assumedly, at least in the mind of this person, he or she was being watched or monitored in some way. This might mean that our Moloch is nearby but admittedly, with ships that travel instantly from here to there, nothing is that far out of reach. However, this is how the Chief preferred events to unfold, instantly. Say something, do something. As the Chief did have a tendency towards anxiety, most of that anxiety was knotted up in the deliberate space between one event and the other. Even the things he feared ended up not bothering him that much in the moment. It is within the waiting period in which the mind tends to digest itself.

The station nearest Palioxis had regular jumps to Ophion, the next leaving in about a half hour. The chief could make the trip there without a jump ship, but at top speed he didn't have the time or inclination for a needless twenty six hour voyage.

The station was a halo type like the one near Helen, but smaller. Still, it was quite populated and the Chief had hit it at rush hour when many who worked on Palioxis, or even the Water Sprite facility, were heading home to Ophion. It seems no matter what job/living arrangements are available, there are always a slew of people oddly eager to commute.

After a rickety thud and the displacing wobble of the universe making room for a large ship that had formerly not existed here, the Chief was in orbit around Ophion. Ophion was a lovely little world very similar to Palioxis. It was blue and green and cloudy. Perhaps a little smaller than Palioxis, but hard to tell from the endless relativity of space travel. It was merely a judgment based on the known distance and the visual image of Ophion before him.

It wasn't long before the Chief landed in a public shipdock atop a skyscraper in the city of New Isis. It was a large busy city stretching without end in all directions from the Chief's location. It was a lot like being in the middle of Helen's Crown, but the architecture and atmosphere was noticeably different. It was a bit more modern, and had the culture of the people here, but welcoming and familiar to anyone from a standard city galaxy wide.

Though he would have liked to explore this city a bit, the Chief made haste for the coordinates and chose to wait, early though he may be. The park was lovely and ripe with people. It was a massive city park like every big city has, usually centralized for ease of encounter. Even those who are too busy to take advantage of the park probably have to travel around it or near enough to see it regularly. This has the effect, or illusion, of making people feel they are not so separated from nature, though they may very well be.

The daylight was playing with him a bit. When he made it to Palioxis, it was getting close to evening according to the Chief's Helen-centric internal clock, but Palioxis had just started their afternoon. He then interviewed into the evening at Palioxis before coming to Ophion, the current location of which is in mid-afternoon.

348

It was a bright spring afternoon here and the Chief should have been in bed hours ago. Nonetheless, he was eager for this meeting and too awake with anticipation to pay much attention to his tiredness. The Chief sat quietly on a bench and watched people and birds.

Some stranger sat next to him: "Hi."

Chief: "Hi."

Stranger: "You're early. That's good."

The Chief didn't expect him to be early as well for some reason and it surprised him ever so slightly. The stranger was a man, similar in age to himself, and wearing very plain clothing that somehow seemed uncomfortable on him.

Chief: "Do you want to talk here? In the open?"

Stranger: "Oh yes. I would like to think that here in the open may be the safest place to talk."

Chief: "Alright, ...I have a pile of questions, but I think it's better to let you tell me what you came to tell me first, wouldn't you agree?"

Stranger: "Completely. Well, ...first, I am...or I *was* General Gale Herman. I have taken an early retirement for several reasons. Before we start, I should mention, though it is probably unnecessary, that the information I give you puts a certain degree of my life in your hands. I want you to use this information in the best possible way to stop whatever this is coming but, as much as you possibly can, please hide the source of this information...my identity."

Chief: "Of course. Please continue."

Gale Herman: "Well...I was in charge of the development division of the Ohm unified military consortium. We pulled through the ranks an endless stream of engineers from a variety of fields...basically bigger weapons, stronger shields. It's a little more complicated than that of course, but surprisingly not much. This is where I came into contact with Moloch. He was not a military man, but a specialist in suspension field engineering, so much so that he caught the attention of some higher-ups and was offered a job. The military's attitude has mostly been that we can produce the type of engineer that we want, so we pull them through the ranks, but Moloch was...exceptional. At least on paper and by reputation.

Chief: "...so he was hired. How long did he work for the military?"

Gale Herman: "Not long. He was a brilliant engineer, but not a good match for the military. It is our own undoing I suppose. We have always been after bigger weapons and stronger shields. Moloch was uninterested in the big. He was interested in the small, specifically shields. He wanted to make the shields smaller and more tightly controlled. Now, we...that is, the Ohm unified military consortium, have had an appreciation for engineers that can make a more efficient device, but the size is rarely consequential. It's easy to build bigger ships. The large size of a thing has never really been that important to us. So, even though we might entertain an engineer that wanted to make smaller more efficient devices, Moloch was in an entirely different world. He was obsessed with reworking our understanding of suspension fields from the ground up. He wasn't just talking about a slightly smaller, more efficient shield, but a reimagining of our fundamental concepts of the suspension field and the physics behind it. His mind was toward much loftier goals and his work was theoretical in nature. There is a great rift...a chasm really...between the theoretical assumptions of a brilliant mind that questions our understanding of reality and the direct, practical, and immediate wants of a military institution. These things are not compatible, foolishly, and Moloch's employment was soon terminated."

Chief: "Did he take the termination poorly?"

Gale Herman: "No, quite to the contrary. He seemed relieved that he wouldn't have to put up with it any longer. Also, military protocol makes clear the reasons for termination and recommendations for future employment are issued by those protocols. Any scientific field that might hire him would see the military report for exactly what it was, essentially saying 'this guy was too smart for the dumb work we wanted him to do.' He didn't seem unhappy or disgruntled and his future employment was, and turned out to be, certain."

Chief: "Where did he go afterwards?"

Gale Herman: "He was briefly employed by Watersprite Genomics before moving on to a much bigger entity, some recombinant genome laboratory. You know, working with human variation and transmogrification...for soon to be colonized worlds and such."

Chief: "That's a long way from suspension field engineering."

Gale Herman: "Right, we were a bit befuddled by that too. He worked there for a number of years before disappearing. It is our policy that we keep fairly close track of our former employees, obviously to make sure they aren't working with unfavorable stellar entities or selling state secrets in kind. It's really just a precaution, but policy."

Chief: "Was there any evidence of that type of funny business?"

Gale Herman: "No, no...nothing like that. He was as clean as a whistle. He worked dutifully, with honors, at...the name, if I remember right, was REGETRAN of Tartarus. Tartarus is a moon of Eurynome. He flourished there. They even gave him his own lab for intensive research into whatever it was he was working on. That is where the problems started to arise."

Chief: "What kind of problems?"

Gale Herman: "Well, his personal lab was afforded, by REGETRAN, a high level of secrecy and security. That was somewhat in conflict with the military's assumed transparency placed upon anything non-military...especially when it came to a former employee. It really took the form of a squabble, nothing more at first. We wanted to know what was going on with one of our former employees and the facility claimed sovereignty as an interstellar institution as REGETRAN has facilities in several systems in the region. They even tried to talk to Moloch about easing some of his clearances for the military just to appease them, but he refused. This was assumed to be a lingering resentment at his termination."

Chief: "Other than bickering, what came of it?"

Gale Herman: "For a long time, nothing. Years went by, but we had men on the job, just following protocol trying to peek into the workings of his private lab. None of us assumed anything, but there were growing rumors that something wasn't on the up and up. We spent some effort getting a mole into his employ, just to eyeball the efforts of the lab...you know, produce a prospectus of what they're doing. The guy we got in there, in no small effort by the way, couldn't take anything out, data, etc...they had it locked down tight, so we were relying on what he could tell us solely from what he could remember. The first red flag had to do with the fact that any individual employee couldn't really tell what they were working on, only a part of a part of something. The second, and much larger red flag was the discovery that there was another lab unknown to even REGETRAN. This seemed to be where whatever the employees of Moloch's private lab were working on was being put together."

Chief: "Well, what came of it?"

Gale Herman: "That's where everything went bad and even today there is a fog of uncertainty as to what really happened. We fitted the mole with an internal location transponder. Fit right under the spleen. It made use of the gap in departure/arrival of jump travel to send a 'ping' telling us where this secret lab was located. It took several trips to isolate it, but we found it."

Chief: "And you know where it is now?"

Gale Herman: "Yes, it is far, far in the interior, near the galactic core...uncomfortably close to a massive black hole, but it's of no consequence. There's nothing there anymore."

Chief: "So, what happened?"

Gale Herman: "At the suspicion that there was something foul going on, we stationed a team of black-ops near the secret lab location. We are assuming that the mole was found out and immediately sent a signal to the black-ops. The signal, if I remember right, was a panicked man saying something like 'it is a weapon, act now. Act now!'. ...what happened next is only speculative as there are no survivors to verify what really took place. I take full responsibility for the horrors that came to pass but the black-ops carried out a massacre. They went in with plasma torches and sliced these people to bits. I...I don't know why. I don't know what would make them lay waste to what *had* to amount to a large number of innocent people. Even if they were all completely complicit in the weapon being built, the ops had no way of knowing that. Something terrified them. They just killed everyone. Unbelievably horrific."

Chief: "And no one could account for their actions?"

Gale Herman: "Like I said, there were no survivors, not even the black ops. When we finally got a team there, all we found were countless mutilated bodies, all rendered by the black ops plasma torches, and the bodies of the black ops themselves, all dead with no visible sign of injury...it was just as if they were...turned off."

Chief: "..." This was a familiar mystery to the Chief and the tell-tale sign, the running thread connecting so many other events.

Gale Herman: "We spent weeks detailing everything we found in the secret lab, the bodies, the history of the employees, everything we could find from secure consoles."

Chief: "Anything of any importance?"

Gale Herman: "Not exactly. The databases of the lab had been dumped. They had anticipated this contingency. However, we did manage to get a small, small chunk of data from the voided datastream. It's nothing, most likely, that will be of any help, but I've already sent you a compilation of what I know, locations, names, details that I can remember, and this odd something found in the empty datastream. You can access it all from your terminal when we're done here."

Chief: "How did you find something in a *voided* datastream? That's not really possible, right?"

Gale Herman: "We have been pioneering a recovery process call *ghosting*."

Chief: "Ghosting?"

Chief: "Yes, I won't bore you with the details, but it involves analyzing the scrambled state of a voided datastream then projecting backwards a series of possible pre-dump histories...just a few trillion or so. These virtual histories are then summed by a variety of algorithms until something potentially meaningful emerges. As the chances that something in the universe would randomly arrange itself into something specific to a human occupational field, that something meaningful is most likely a fairly accurate depiction of an actual or potential history."

Chief: "*An* actual or potential history? Not *the* actual or potential history?"

Gale Herman: "Unfortunately yes. The process is not completely reliable and is hugely resource dependent, so it would only be used in the very greatest of necessity. Even in these circumstances, the best reconstruction of any particular analyzed data...in lab...is a little less than ten percent."

Chief: "So, you found a little less than ten percent of data on this secret lab? ...Or, should I say, a little less than ten percent of the potential history of the data that could have been in that lab?"

Gale Herman: "Well...it's not even that impressive. We found around eight percent of the data contained in the *one* console that was not irreparably damaged by plasma torches."

The Chief rolled his eyes a bit.

Gale Herman: "I know,I know... but take a look at it when you get back to your ship. See if you can make head or tails of it."

Chief: "Now...please don't take this as any kind of criticism, but several times you have said things like *'if I remember right'*, or *'I think it was'*...why is there no concrete record of this information?"

Gale Herman: "Well, because of the redaction."

Chief: "And who issued the redaction."

Gale Herman: "I did."

Chief, after a confusing pause: "...and you can't *unredact* it?"

Gale Herman: "I could, but the information is not hidden, it's gone. Completely gone. I'm going off memory here with the exception of a few bits that managed to evade the redaction for one reason or another."

Chief: "Why did you issue a redaction? It doesn't make much sense. Especially making the info irretrievable." The Chief was showing a bit of frustration.

Gale Herman, becoming a little more somber in tone: "I suppose it is my own failing...or cowardice, really. I had no intention of redacting this information...I wanted to investigate...chase this guy down. It was during an inspection of a jump engine crossover facility. A *crossover* facility", said incredulously. "Do you know what that is?"

Chief: "Not really." The true answer was 'no'.

Gale Herman: "It is the small device that determines what frequency feeds into the various stages of a jump engine as it's operating. Not a weapon. Not a shield. Mundane and, obviously, low security. While I was alone in the office there, the door swings open and in walks Moloch, as casual as could be, as if he was just going to rundown the inventory or expenditures then be on his way. It startled me. We'd been looking for him. I knew his face. It was like seeing a ghost. I...I asked him how he got in here and he pointed to the door where I could see the legs of a lifeless guard that had previously stood nearby. Moloch said, 'he's quite dead' and I leapt up to inspect the body. Still

353

warm, but gone. I noticed several others lying dead around the work-floor leading up to the office. I quickly moved to see if they were still alive when Moloch said, 'You can bury the dead later. Right now, we have things to discuss.' ..."

The Chief listened in stunned silence.

Gale Herman: "Well, I wasn't about to listen to some madman who'd killed several innocent people. I continued toward the fallen soldiers when I felt a horrid vice-like grip around my lower spine. It was like a fiery hand squeezing my spinal cord. My legs went numb and I fell. Moloch approached and said 'You need to pay attention. There is a *lot* at stake here.' When the grip on my spine released I managed to hobble back towards the office where Moloch held open the door seeming like a perfectly polite gentleman helping an injured geriatric. I sat, and Moloch spoke. Moloch issued the exact terms by which I would redact and destroy any information pertaining to him. Even in my pain I laughed and said, 'you think you can force my hand by fear of death? I am prepared to die in the line of duty. You have nothing with which to bargain.' But Moloch smiled and said, 'oh no, no, no. You misunderstand. I am not going to kill you. I'm not threatening you personally in the slightest. I am threatening to kill your family. Your wife, your two lovely children...even your parents, your brother and his family. I will wipe out your entire family until you comply, and you *will* comply.'"

Chief: "That's...that's horrible."

Gale Herman: "And like I said, perhaps it is my failing. Perhaps it is cowardice. I didn't know how to stop him and had no idea how to prevent him from honoring his terrible threat. I conceded, then and there. I knew he saw it in my eyes. The rest unfolded as you would imagine. I wrestled with this for years and am afraid that my silence may cost the galaxy far, far more than one family. I am as guilty as Moloch for my hand in this."

The Chief sat quietly for several minutes absorbing the story.

Chief: "Well, what now?"

Gale Herman: "I am going to take my family elsewhere...new place...new identities. My only ray of hope is that I am no longer in a position of power and Moloch may just not care anymore about what I do or don't do. Either way, I have waged a war for years against my own fears and have been on a consistent losing streak, battle for battle."

Chief: "If it makes you feel any better. I'm sure I would have made the same choice."

Gale Herman softly nodded in appreciation.

Gale Herman: "I've told you all I know. Good luck on stopping this guy. It may be too late and for that I'm terribly sorry. Whether I end

354

up dead by Moloch's hand, or succeed in fleeing...you won't hear from me again. I'll be unreachable."
Chief: "Take care Gale. I'll do my best to sort this thing out."
Gale nodded and they both shook hands before parting ways.

The Chief was lost in thought, distracted, staring at the idiotic logo of Pauly's Bread Bucket. Even here, the Chief thought, even here, thousands of light years away, and I'm staring at the stupid face on the logo of Pauly's Bread Bucket. Walking long past it, the Chief got some takeout from a fancy noodle shop and made his way back to his ship. Leaving the warm blue of a welcoming atmosphere, the Chief was yet again in the rarefied darkness of space. As he ate the well composed mélange of vegetables and noodles, he pulled up the datum reclaimed from the secret lab that Gale had sent to him previously. He couldn't make out what it actually was he was seeing but knew somehow, instinctively, that it had some meaning.
Mumbling through the muffling effects of a mouthful of noodles, the Chief uttered, "I gotta show this to Bob."

Chapter Twenty-Five:
This Side of a Pair of Dice.

Bob felt himself suspended in a dark fog which was pulling him in all directions toward a suffocatingly protracted silence. He was afloat on the black night waters of an unseen and endless ocean. There he was stretched toward the surrounding horizon skimming the top of the sea yet refusing to break the surface tension. This was no wayward or alien world he had stumbled upon, nor was it a metaphysical reality that was pressing itself upon him. It was an utterly profound boredom.

Bob had reached the coordinates offered by Dr. Morris some time ago and was floating aimlessly in a remote and unpopulated chunk of solid black outer space. The ship with which he was to rendezvous, presumably the *Cell-Scape*, was very late. Bob had the urge to get this business taken care of and move on. Not only was this impetus from the dire situation at hand, but Bob had been out and about for a long time and in one situation or another that involved some degree of discomfort...crashing into a planet, canned and tossed into space, drowned without the escape of death to end the drowning. And now he waited...and did nothing. It was not like Dr. Morris's team to be late, but it also probably wasn't like them to care much if they needed to be late, so Bob wasn't particularly worried.

After another stretch of mind-numbing boredom Bob received a notice on his terminal signaling a message. A quick brush of the arm and Bob could see it was from the Chief. It said very little, just that they needed to talk when he got somewhere stable to communicate. Bob assumed that would be soon since the arrival of the message, in this remote location, could only mean that a ship had jumped nearby to deliver it. Bob desperately hoped that ship would be the *Cell-Scape*.

Immediately his console lit up alerting him to the presence of a ship and the arrival of docking instructions. Pulling the image closely, Bob could see that it was in fact the very late *Cell-Scape*. It was strange that there seemed to be a burn down the port side of the ship, the side Bob was facing, but one that had been somewhat repaired. It was like it had taken some hit which is odd for a non-battle jump-ship to ever be involved is a skirmish. Regardless, Bob followed the instructions and after a routine docking procedure Bob was met by that same attendant he had met on previous encounters with the *Cell-Scape*.

Young woman: "Hi, sorry we're so late. We had some trouble getting a few things we needed."

Bob: "Everything ok?"

Young woman: "Oh yes, absolutely."

Bob: "Alright. You know, it's occurred to me that we've met several times now and I don't know your name."

Young woman: "It's Lydia."

Bob: "Nice to formally meet you Lydia."

Lydia smiled.

Bob: "I suppose you'll be needing this." Bob handed her the metallic cylinder with the sample and data from the Balaenae.

In a very chipper tone Lydia said, "Thank you, thank you."

Lydia: "Dr. Morris has taken the liberty to provide you with a travel itinerary for your next voyage. She's arranged the ships to get you to the Dandy system."

Bob: "Well...that's helpful. Thank her for me."

Lydia, smiling: "No need. I think she did it because she felt like you were taking too long."

Bob: "Oh. I think I've been making pretty good time considering all that's happened."

Lydia: "The word she chose was 'dawdling'."

Lydia giggled and Bob just rolled his eyes.

It was then that Bob realized Lydia was missing an arm, left arm from right above the elbow down.

Bob: "I hope this isn't out of place, but...didn't you have two arms when I saw you last?"

Lydia, looking to her stump and pretending she too had just noticed: "Yeaaah. That's odd."

Bob: "..."

Lydia: "It's the darndest thing. Well, you know how it is sometimes. They'll have a new one for me when I get back to CIDER."

Bob: "Well...you are quite the soldier."

Lydia carried out the motion of saluting with her missing left arm, then pretended it was a mistake and saluted with her right. She followed this with a giggle.

Lydia: "The itinerary has been sent so you can access that at any time. Also, a procedural rundown and an info packet has also been sent. You'll want to read those carefully."

Bob: "Ok. I suppose I'll get on my way."

Lydia: "Wait, you need this too."

She entered the nearby office and came back with a rather large briefcase. It seemed unusually bulbous and reinforced and Lydia had a bit of a time hoisting it with her one good arm.

Bob, scrambling to take it from her and ease her strain: "What is it?"

Lydia: "That's for you to know and you to find out. ...Actually, I don't know. It has something to do with why we're late. It'll all be detailed in the information you've received and you should have a good while to do some reading. I think the trip to the Dandy system is about two weeks."

Bob knew it was way the heck out in the middle of nowhere, but was a little disheartened at the two week timeframe. It's hard to believe anything in the galaxy takes that long of a voyage and compared to his starting point of Sol, he was already halfway there.
Bob: "Well, guess I should skedaddle."
Bob waved goodbye and headed toward his ship.
Lydia: "Good luck. Remember, we don't want to make Dr. Morris upset. Neither dawdle nor mosey nor poke nor lollygag."
Bob just smiled, rolled his eyes, and shook his head while Lydia giggled.

Back in the empty remoteness of space and following the percussive thud of the *Cell-Scape* heading who-knows-where, Bob was again alone. He quickly checked the itinerary and set course for the location prescribed. Then he skimmed through the data sent by Dr. Morris (he's have plenty of time to read it carefully en route) and found the only mention of the briefcase which read: "You'll need this when you get to the Dandy system." That was it: no further instructions or any more of an explanation.

Bob walked over to the bulbous briefcase, popped the latches and opened it slowly. Quite surprised, Bob removed the entire contents and with a puzzled look pondered the meaning behind this gift. Inside the briefcase was a complete battle-ready stillsuit. Bob knew of these, read about them and had seen pictures, but he honestly had never seen one even on a soldier. They were exceptionally rare and quite resource dependent in their construction. The suit was composed of a military grade percussion cloth and a dielectric dampening underlay. The percussion cloth was highly resistant to impact and practically impenetrable. One could move around in it fairly well, but if the cloth was moved too quickly, for example by a projectile, it resisted. Apparently, according to field tests, it could resist quite an impressive explosion. The dielectric underlay tended to prevent a variety of dischargeable weaponry from functioning properly. For example, if Bob had shot his EMP gun at someone wearing this suit it would have absolutely no effect...and not because Bob's weapon had been ruined by salt water.

The suit had several interlocking pieces that covered the entire body along with a rebreather that filtered clean air from just about any imaginable poison or contaminant. The headpiece that would self-adjust tightly over the head was fitted with what was called an ocular

T-interface sensory array. It fed information from the surroundings to the body and interfaced with terminal access to amplify and accentuate that sensory info. It summed several spectra of light, extended the frequency range of audio information, analyzed and forecasted surrounding pockets of temperature, and even scanned particulate matter in a somewhat heightened olfactory perception.
 The purpose of this, in terms of warfare, was, to some degree, to see through walls where enemies might be hiding, to find pockets of dangerous radiation or heat, to survive poisonous environments, and in general to see clearly in low or no visibility.
       What Bob couldn't figure out and kept thinking was, "Why the hell do I need this for the Dandy system?...What could possibly be going on there?" This coupled with the uphill battle of the penultimate task, stopping this virus, left Bob feeling like he had been put about some Sisyphean task, but one with far more danger and less certainty.
 It all seemed like several intertwined gambles and he was on the wrong side of the dice, the wrong side of the table. He was trying to change his luck, but across from him was the dealer and everyone knows the house always wins. What else was there to do? Bob was more than willing to entertain ideas by which he might be more productive, but other than this mission, none came to him. The path lay ahead.
       Bob replaced the stillsuit properly in its case and slid it under the ships cot. He then scanned through the itinerary Dr. Morris had prepared. Bob assumed it was the quickest route to the Dandy system, but it was a jittery, circuitous path. No one went to the Dandy system. No one. It was too far away and there was no point. The environment is not hospitable except to the Dandies which were as far removed from the human design as a variant could be. Needless to say, Bob didn't have a very cheerful outlook on this trip but then and there decided that he needed to realign his thinking, to try to find some aspect to look forward to, and settle into a state of peacefulness.
 Two weeks, that's a lot of travel but two weeks of agitation is considerably longer.
       Bob made it back to the bit of nothingness from where he started. A jump-ship had been commissioned to take him here...to nowhere, then he had to travel a distance to get to another bit of nowhere to meet the *Cell-Scape*, and now back. He didn't know why one bit of nothingness was any different than another, but assumed it had to do with secrecy and predictability, though it all seemed overkill for an organization that probably had few enemies. Perhaps that's how it worked though, their security measures made sure those enemies ceased to exist. Regardless, he was back at the location where he had started after jumping from Leviathan. Now he had to

wait, and hopefully not long for the next ship to show up and take him somewhere more populated. The *Cell-Scape* was supposed to arrange the pickup after they had left the area.

It didn't take him long to read through the itinerary and he had gone through most of the material on protocol and plans once there. There was a list of suggested readings on Dandy culture and environment which he planned on working through on the two week trip ahead of him, but boredom was creeping in. If that ship didn't get here soon, Bob ran the risk of an acute ennui attack.

Within moments Bob's console lit up and the wake of a nearby jump-ship jostled his little vessel and the contents within. There, not far from his location, was a jump-ship modestly named the *Voicespace*. It seemed appropriate to Bob that the *Voicespace* should take him from this crippling dark silence to someplace, hopefully, a bit noisier.

After docking and a quick jump, the *Voicespace* dropped Bob off in a system known as Eudoxus. The station was named *Protium* in a concentric orbit with the system's second most populated world, Planck, whose chief export, according to the info Bob summoned via terminal, is transmogrified protozoa.

Bob felt a sense of relief in the normalcy of Eudoxus. It was a populated system, ships buzzing about here and there, and looking toward Planck he could make out several bustling cities amidst the yellow-green of land encircled by an azure and cloud streaked sky. For some reason unknown to Bob, there seemed to be rather long fuchsia strips running a considerable length laterally in the southern polar region far into the surrounding waters. It looked like a series of cat scratches on the planet's underside, but was obviously intentional as the boundaries were too crisp to be natural. A quick terminal query reported that it was a controlled algal bloom. Their second greatest export was a modified algae.

There really wasn't enough time to make it to the surface of Planck and back before the next ship was scheduled to leave, at least not enough time to do anything meaningful. Bob wouldn't mind stocking up on a few food items for the two week trip, but he knew he'd have a longer layover a few legs further. Besides, he was itching to talk to the Chief while the exchange could be in more-or-less real time. A few commands and the connection was secured.
Chief: "Bob! How goes it? I'm glad the whale people didn't see you as fish food."
Bob: "Yeah, but I'm still wheezy and have a sore throat, sore...everything...from salt water."
Bob gave a brief but detailed account of his time with the Balaenae.

360

Chief: "Well, I hope you don't develop a fondness for breathing water. We have much less of it here on Helen."
Bob: "You're back on Helen?"
Chief: "Well, close by. I'm on Ganymede still."
Bob: "And the outbreak there?"
Chief: "You know, it's everywhere. Ganymede has a tight quarantine that seems to be holding up, but Helen is infected. I don't know if you've had time to watch much news, but the virus is spreading still, obviously, but many, many worlds have dropped their quarantine or travel restrictions. Just out of futility really. When everyone's infected, it doesn't make much sense to be too picky of one's company."
Bob: "...yeah, I guess so."
Chief: "I have some news. What kind of timeframe are you on?"
Bob: "About 45 minutes till my next jump."
Chief: "Ok. Well, I've been to Ohm and it was an interesting trip."
The Chief began to recounted his interview at Water Sprite Genomics.
Bob: "Carbuncle?"
Chief: "Carbunkle."
He then proceeded to go through the conversation with Gale Herman in detail.
Chief: "You have the schematic...or whatever it is now. You should be able to access it."
Bob scanned through his received documents and pulled up the compromised data stream. He then pondered the set of images before him.
Bob: "...it's...I dunno, it's odd. Just this, right?"
Chief: "Yep."
Bob: "Pages and pages, hundreds, of what seems like the same thing?"
Chief: "Yup."
Bob: "It almost looks like housing quarters of a ship...but there doesn't seem to be any doors or passages in or out of the quarters...at least not displayed."
Cheif: "Yeah, I was thinking the same thing."
Bob: "And the scale. If this was a ship, just with the pages we have here...it'd have to be huge."
Chief: "At least a battlecruiser, but we wouldn't know what else might be attached to it."
Bob: "It could be even larger...though we honestly don't really know what we're looking at."
Chief: "You got that right."
Bob: "...I dunno, ...there's something..."
Chief: "...?"

Bob: "...there's something about this. I almost feel like I should know what this is. Like I've seen it before, but I can't place where. ...I assume you've searched similar images?"

Chief: "Extensively. Still have people on it, but without more info there are too many things roughly similar though none that have proved useful. It is *similar* to ship barracks. It's *similar* to the coolant nacelle of a field emitter. It's *similar* to the ballast structure of those old femto-callipers. It's *similar* to the egg chambers of Lycian thunder ant hives. I could go on and on."

Bob: "Well, again, we don't have much to go on. You said this Gale Herman guy mentioned Moloch's secret lab was near a black hole."

Chief: "He did, but it's not there anymore. It was destroyed. They found it. That's where we got the schematic...or whatever that is."

Bob: "I know, I was just thinking...especially in light of the visual feed from Diophantus, you know, right before the rise of the Colossus?"

Chief: "Yeah?"

Bob: "Well, they couldn't hit his ship. Everything just whisked past it like it was slippery."

Chief: "...and?"

Bob: "Maybe the lab was near a black hole because he was designing a ship that could get considerably closer to a black hole than an average ship."

Chief: "Hmm...interesting. That would be a perfect place to hide."

Bob: "If he'd manage to make a ship that wouldn't be destroyed by the tidal gravitational forces, but instead those forces would just bend around the slippery ship, he could get considerably closer."

Chief: "Of course, if he got too close to the event horizon the time dilation would bring him back out tens of thousands of years later."

Bob: "Right, but he'd really only need to be an inch closer than our standard ships could travel to afford him absolute protection from interference. If our ships crossed that unfortunate inch, they'd get pulled in while he did not."

Chief: "Yeah, I suppose so."

Bob: "And it would provide him with a degree of invisibility as any sensor directed at the black hole would most likely not be able to return information regarding his presence. Things beamed towards a black hole tend to not return."

Chief: "That's true. So, you think he's hiding out around a black hole?"

Bob: "It's a possibility."

Chief: "So, we just need to do a thorough check of the roughly 100 million known black holes in the galaxy. I'll do it myself...I've got the afternoon free."

Bob: "Hey, I didn't say this information was practical. Surely you know me well enough to not expect anything useful coming from my mouth."

The Chief chuckled: "Well, it is interesting and does make a certain kind of sense."

Bob: "I know you and I haven't directly spoken about this, but I'm guessing we both assume Moloch made the Pixler's glass containing Harper Callus."

Chief: "The guy with the untouchable ship who made an unidentifiable virus and a indestructible monster? Yeah, I think it's a safe assumption he made the unbreakable glass."

Bob: "It's just so strange...all this showing up at once."

Chief: "Well, we're obviously dealing with some kind of genius. You know, the real mad scientist type."

Bob: "I don't know. I'm not sure about that."

Chief: "What do you mean you're not sure about that?"

Bob: "He's obviously intelligent, but those we tend to think of as the smartest of us, tend to be highly specialized. You rarely find a master theoretical physicist that is also a world renown composer...you know, things like that."

Chief: "And how do you see that fact playing out here?"

Bob: "I obviously don't know, but I'm guessing that there's one area...maybe one thing this guy figured out that led to the construction of all of this. Some common denominator that links the untouchable ship, unidentifiable virus, indestructible monster, and unbreakable glass."

Chief: "It could well be. I'm sure much more appropriately trained minds are working on this issue for us. I would even go as far to venture that these minds are *scrambling* to get the low down on these new toys."

Bob: "I don't know if that's a good thing or not. A few years from now maybe everyone will have a monster in their pocket that can destroy cities."

Chief: "Well, isn't this all just fun."

After a moment of silent thinking the Chief offered: "So what now?"

Bob: "About to start my trip to the Dandy system. About two weeks. Hey, speaking of which, they gave me a military grade stillsuit for the trip."

Chief: "Wow. Do you get to keep it? That's worth a pretty penny."

Bob: "I'm sure I don't. What do you think it's for? Are they at war?"

Chief: "I don't really know, but I doubt it. I've heard the environment there is very inhospitable."

Bob: "I've heard that too, but I don't really know in what way it's inhospitable. I suppose I'll have some time to read up on their system en route. What's next for you?"

Chief: "I'm going to stay put for now. I'm not as fond of traveling as you. Looking into all we know...that's about it."

Bob: "Well, let me know what you know when you know it."

Chief: "You do the same. Stay out of trouble."

Bob: "No promises."

Bob received docking instructions towards the tail end of the conversation with the Chief. On his way to the jump-ship, he was lost in thought about all that had been going on until that rumination was broken by a call. The call was from Abrum...of course.

Abrum appeared on the screen in what looked like a formal dining tuxedo and his hair slicked back. He was holding a duster in one hand and a worn rag in the other. Again, the backdrop revealed that he was somehow in Bob's apartment.

Abrum: "Bob, I've taken the liberty of alphabetizing your food stuffs and arranging your cookery by type and common usage. I think you'll find this system..."

Bob, interrupting: "How are you getting in my place?"

Abrum: "The door, of course."

Bob also had a passing thought, the wonder at how Abrum knew to call now. Probably just a coincidence.

Abrum: "Bob, I hear you are going to the Dandy system."

Bob: "How did you know I was..."

Abrum: "Oh, Bob, Helen is a small town and she is fond of whispering her secrets at night to those that would press their ear and heart sweetly upon her lips."

Again, he was not answering the question. Bob replied, "I have to go. I'm docking and we're about to jump."

Abrum: "If it wouldn't be too much of a bother, as I know your shoulders are already heavily burdened as is, might you enquire as to the acquisition of Demeterian marshmallow root from the local constabulary or whatever entity you might find in charge? I have heard rumor that the Dandy's marshmallow root is of a decidedly delicate nature with a ghostly sweetness that lingers eerily upon the tongue."

Bob: "I don't...I don't know Abrum...I have to go."

Abrum: "They say it has a malty edge with mahogany undertones and a crisp finish like biting into a ripe apple."

Bob: "I gotta go Abrum."

Abrum: "Farewell lonely seafarer. Though the tides may tousle thine little boat to and fro and the darkness of a night without end stretches eerily into the unknown, there, in the heavens, will always be a star to guide you home."

Somewhere toward the beginning of that recitation Bob had turned off the communique. He was about to begin his trip to the Dandy system, or at least according to the provided itinerary, this was the first ship listed on a long trip that began here in Eudoxus and ended some two weeks later at the Dandies homeworld. Here, he was to dock aboard the *Pranzo Oltranzista*, a newer, slightly sleeker looking jump-ship. There would be several jumps made by this ship, each with an hour or two layover. This would give him just enough time to make use of the jump-ship's cafeteria and get some serious sleep, of which he had been more than a little deprived.

Bob was about to travel considerably further than he ever had before and soon would find himself in the most alien of worlds.

Dream Journal:
Watcher of the Skies

We were wandering in green fields close to home. It was spring. The sky was a sky blue sky and there was life seeping up through the soil filling our lungs and hearts.
"Sweetie, come here."

Frolicking in the tall grass of the field, she was twirling and dancing to music only she could hear, a freedom the young seem to possess as the universe in which they live is one to be explored and celebrated rather than conquered.
She twirled her way to me and stopped to look upward.
I asked, "Come sit with me a moment."
"Ok, daddy."
And we sat side by side in the field then soon laid comfortably on our backs in the cool green grass.
"Sweetie, look up at the sky for a moment."
She looked, all around, eyes wide, then squinted, made a few faces.
"Just relax and calmly try to imagine the sky. Try and think about the sky and how it covers the land."

She looked, even closed her eyes a moment, then looked some more. She knew about the atmosphere, this one, others, how they covered the planets on which people lived. She was a very smart girl.
"Now try and see the blackness of space beyond the sky."
"Daddy, I can't. The sun is out. It's not nighttime silly."
She was a smart girl. And she was right, but for my purposes day makes this process easier.
Chuckling, I said, "I know sweetie. I want you to see it not with your eyes, but with your mind. Imagine it out there, beyond the sky."
Again she closed her eyes a moment, thought about it, and said, "I can see it. I can see it all around me."
"Good sweetie. Try to feel the atmosphere again. Try to get a sense of the size of it. Then feel that black space all around extending in all directions."

Her mind was beautifully active, with eyes closed and a slight furrow to her brow as is her custom in direct contemplation. The times that I managed to get a sense of it, the land, the atmosphere, the space beyond, that brief sense of if brought an acute exhilaration, like deeply breathing cool air during the hottest days of summer.

I bore witness to the moment, however brief, that it set upon her. Like she was taken aback and very curious. A moment later she popped one eye open and peeked to find me looking at her. Then opening both eyes she turned to me and said, "Daddy, everything is *so* far away from here."

She was a smart girl.

"Sweetie, I want you to do this every so often. Just when you feel like it. Every once in a while. Ok, sweetie?"

"Ok, daddy."

Chapter Twenty Six:
Symptom of the Universe

Quite out of place in an empty and unpopulated portion of the galaxy an object is drawn toward an uncertain future. If one were to be present for this objects journey, to see it as it is now, one might identify this object as a prosthetic limb...an arm specifically. It is of an old design hardly used anymore with the exception of colonies forgotten that are trudging out their lives in very much the same fashion as our ancestors. It is a metallic skeletal fragment that once possessed machinery to make the digits move, but has since been stripped of its workings. Unbelievably there still remains a portion of the forearm composed of wood. Wood, would you believe? It has been cracked, splintered, and bleached in the cold exposure to empty space, the end toward the elbow seemingly charred.

One can only imagine how such a thing has ended up floating here in the middle of nowhere. Perhaps a war-torn remnant of a battle forgotten, a ship destroyed and a fragment cast wayward toward the dark horizon...suffering argued as justice, condoned in fear, and lost to history as we are so willing to forget those horrible things we are prone to do. Despite our inability to know the specifics of the limb's origin story, it is easily and accurately assumed that it has been traveling for a *very* long time.

If one could again see the limb in detail, the metal pitted from some soupy plasmic discharge that once splattered the surroundings and, in this case, removed the body from the limb, one might notice an odd behavior of this disembodied arm. Alone and in a space with scarcely a visible star, it would be hard to find the right perspective, one that offered some object by which the relativity between itself, the observer, and the arm could be properly measured, but should such a hypothetical scenario be, it could easily be seen that the arm was accelerating. It was getting faster.

It need not be said that this is no magic limb, nor does it possess some method of propulsion. No, here, in the persistent black, far from starlight and even further from civilization, something...something dark was drawing it in. Here, it happens, it would be and remain unseen. The common term used in a variety of languages and dialects is often some variation on the word *black hole*, but a more descriptive and meaningful term might be a *hidden singularity*: forever hidden, forever singular.

It is not a lonely singularity. It is a welcoming singularity that invites all in, an offer to join and become one with all that it is and all that it might be. It offers a complete and absolute union with the unknown, and now it calls to the limb with an irresistible invitation which reads "come, let me make you whole".

At the offer the limb moves faster and faster but devoid of reference we can only see the limb in a quiet stillness. It seems not to move at all. Yet the blackness of space is separated by the blackness of the singularity, a boundary called the event horizon towards which the limb draws near. Such a beautiful term and oddly appropriate considering its age. It is a great horizon, a boundary on the periphery of all that can be between this world and that stretching beyond, beyond in all directions. But what could such a boundary truly be separating?

It is more than just an academic account of the physical ramifications of the universe, a universe so inseparable from us as to require itself as the true definition of our collective body. It is, in fact, the boundary between incompatible realities: one in which time and space behaves and the other in which it does not. That is not to say beyond the boundary exists a reality of chaos, for that dark world exists in a physics every bit as stringent as our own, only obscure and hidden from us. And this separation of realities is just that and nothing more. It separates two distinct realities, but not us from it. If the universe, as it should be, is considered our collective body...our true self...beyond the event horizon is our dark and nebulous subconscious exerting a great unseen influence, the impetus of our actions. It is there that the ground existence, the primal reality, is found. It sits in a fluidic stillness, in a screaming silence. It is something and nothing at the same time and answers the questions "Why does the universe exist? Why is there something rather than nothing?". It is because nowhere in the whole of creation is nothing to be found. It does not exist and never has. It is a word falsely constructed yet ironically perfect in its use. It is a word that means *nothing*. Here, at the boundary of incompatible realities and beyond the event horizon into the eternal and impermanent black, the question is answered. The universe exists because the opposite of *something* is not *nothing*. The opposite of *something* is *something else*.

The arm is rapidly approaching the event horizon. The erstwhile world from which it came slows and reddens in an appropriately blood-soaked hue. The universe bends and contorts, the limb along with it, and where that first finger touches the surface of the event horizon, the term is seen in its deeper meaning. As the universe bends toward the singularity, the horizon flattens out until it

370

is revealed as it truly is: a flat horizon that stretches infinitely in all directions, unbounded, separating this world from the next.

In the transition our universe becomes two-dimensional and rapidly begins to lose its former reality as it folds in on itself, every point drawing into every other point continually until there, now beyond the boundary, all points in the universe are drawn into a seeming singularity that floats ghostly on the other side. The limb, unbound by time and space and form, finds union and wholeness in a reality on the far side of everywhere and nowhere and in a future composed only of the eternal now. To this limb, that former universe from whence it came, that world we find ourselves in now, remains a distant and indecipherable black hole lost in the twilight beyond the thin and boundless extremity of that ever looming event horizon.

Chapter Twenty Seven:
The Itinerary Syndrome part 1: The Way to Demeter.

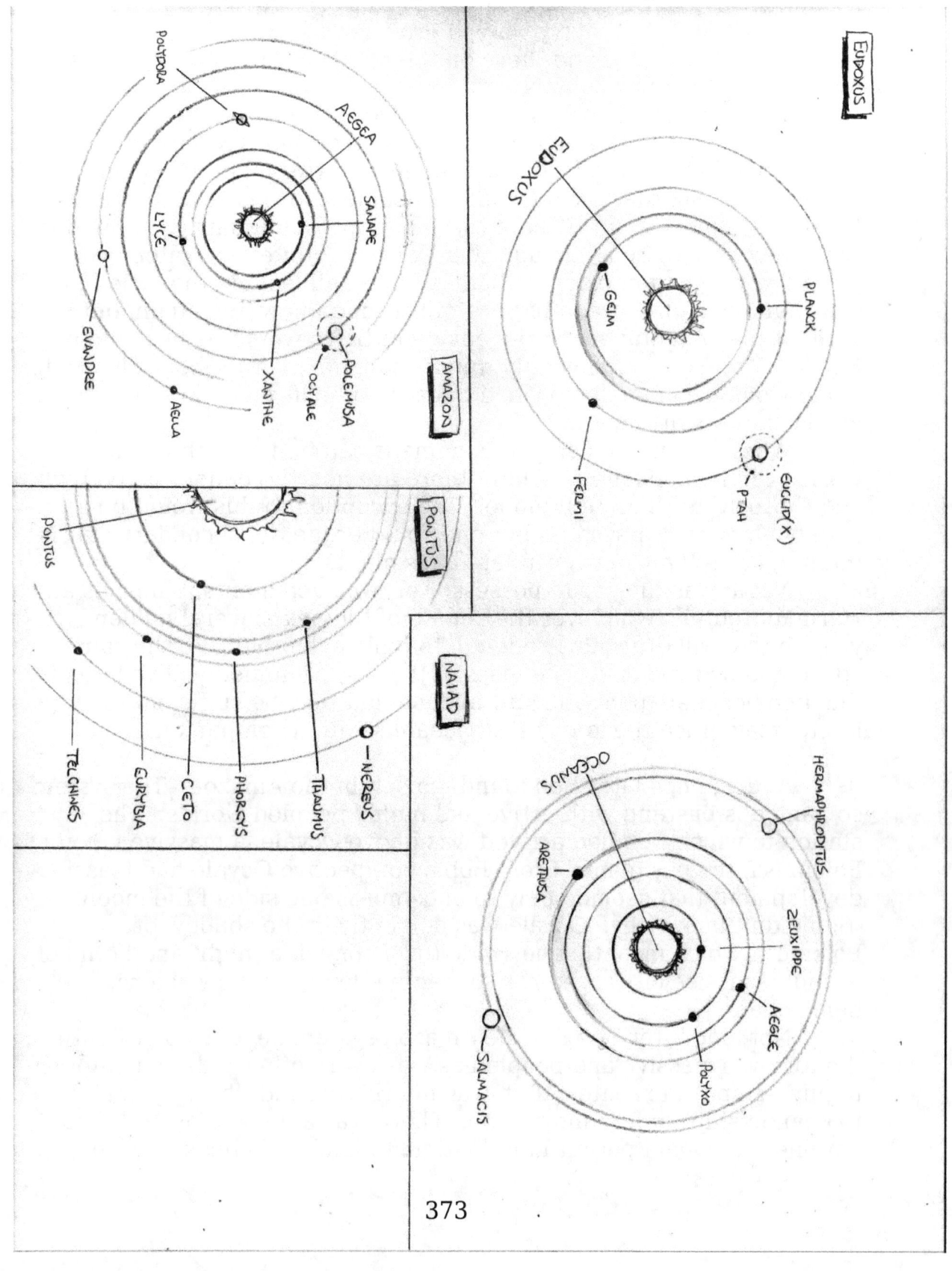

To discuss the full details of Bob's trip to Demeter, the homeworld of the Dandies, would be inordinately time consuming and render the listener inert, in a catatonic state of hyper-boredom. To avoid such unwanted injury we will provide the scaffolding of his journey touching here and there on the points of interest or distress, and there were a few such points.

Upon leaving Eudoxus in the *Pranzo Oltranzista*, Bob made a handful of jumps before reaching the Naiad system. Naiad was heavily populated with dozens of planets and two major gas giants. It's odd to think that pre-spaceflight people, those early and primitive Earthlings, knew so little about these omnipresent guardians. Ancient Earth always had Zeus, though they called it Jupiter, to watch over them drawing errant celestial bodies into itself leaving the little blue world untouched. Sure, a big one got through now and again, but without the watchful eye of the gas giant there would be little life on Earth. What squirming wiggly things managed to pull themselves into being would soon be demolished by raining hellfire...and the dance would slowly start again.

Where there are gas giants humans can find a foothold and worlds can be populated. Where there are not, the danger is too high and those systems are left alone. The exception to this would be a suitable binary star system, but one could argue the secondary star is nothing more than an over-inflated gas giant.

Naiad was the proud possessor of two such giants, Salmacis and Hermaphroditus, who, over the course of the next several million years or so, will draw close enough to pull each other into the same space and become one. The mass of the two combined will walk that fine line between giant and star and, should they be sufficient to ignite, may grace the lonely star Oceanus with a companion.

A few jumps later Bob found himself in the Amazon. The system so named is bustling with active and highly peopled worlds. The station to which Bob had arrived was above Ocyale, a massive moon of Polemusa, the gas giant. From Bob's perspective Ocyale had massive development that seemed only to encompass one side of the moon. Bob didn't know why. Ocyale was currently in the shadow of Polemusa which meant planet-wide (or moon-wide) night and lights of a single massive city arced like an eagle talon over the western hemisphere.

Not long after Bob left the Amazon system he arrived at Pontus. Pontus was massive and peopled as was every other hub that catered to jump-ship trade routes. Bob was in orbit around Phorcys and had to change ships before moving on. There was a decent layover, but not one that would permit him the time to land and check out the planet. He had to get to the next ship and wait, but...and this was a thing that did please Bob greatly...the layover provided time for several vending ships to dock in his next jump-ship and Bob could stock up once he got there. He'd been at it for days and was getting tired of the food he had available.

Leaving the *Pranzo Oltranzista* Bob headed to his next target, a dark gunmetal gray jump-ship called the *Delirium Cordia*. Once safely inside Bob hurried to the temporary docking block where the vendors had set up shop and eagerly perused the wares. He made out like a bandit. He came back with a ten pack of rice noodles, fermented garlic, river oak acorn cakes, twenty five bags of cheese pagodas, and three sticks of skewered morels. The morel was an unmatched mushroom anywhere in the galaxy and each stick had six decent sized morels delicately pan-fried in a crumb batter. They were fantastic. Bob would have brought back far more than three but they wouldn't keep and there's nothing worse than ruining a delicacy by forcing one's self to eat a pallid, runny, and bland or rancid version of the food one loves. Best to enjoy all things in the moment of creation which is and always has been the ever present now.

It would be appropriate to justify, in some small way, the reasoning behind Bob acquiring twenty five bags of cheese pagodas. Well...Pontus was, in many ways, the last system in the family of worlds where Bob had a generalized and shared familiarity. This ship, the *Delirium Cordia* was about to take Bob into an area of the galaxy known as the "Deep Central" systems. Things are different there. Cultures are different. Worlds are different. Oh no, Bob would not find any cheese pagodas in the Deep Central...not a single, solitary, cheesy pagoda.

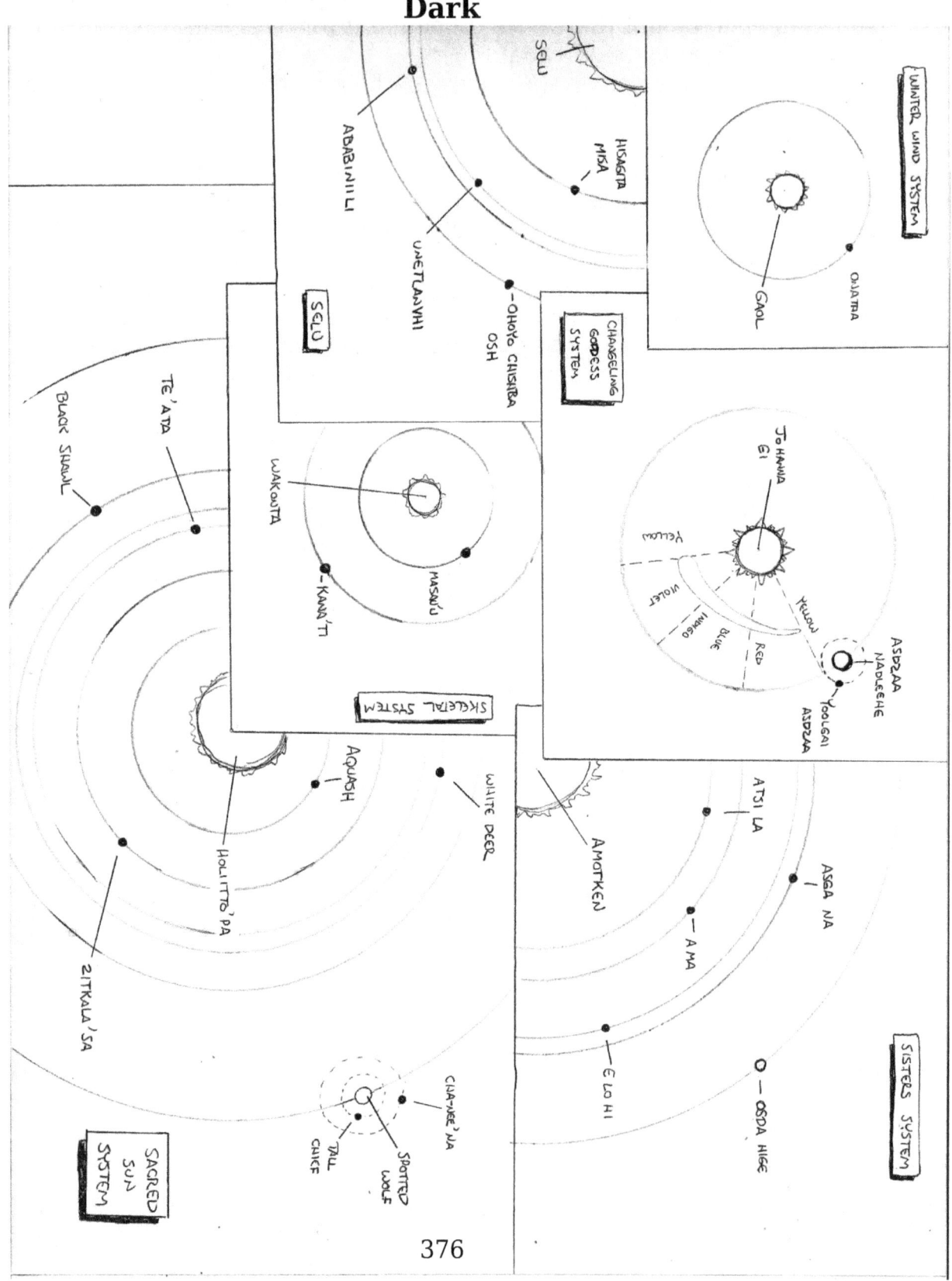

The Deep Central region was culturally very different from, honestly, the rest of the galaxy. Where most of the galaxy was partitioned in relationship to the galactic arms, the deep central was a vast and constantly expanding amorphous blob. It should be emphasized that the idea of a central authority presiding over such a vast portion of the galaxy, be it the Deep Central or the many arm divisions, is rather academic. Enforcement of law that covers potentially tens of thousands of worlds is not practical or possible and these regions are more loose associations of planetary powers that share a tacit agreement upon philosophy and governance. In a particular region one can predict the likeness of the laws one will encounter, but there are and never have been any absolutes. Therefore, it's always best when in a neighbor's home to be a courteous guest and avoid making assumptions.

Planet to planet there would be a variety of cultural differences in the Deep Central, but the obvious surface variations would be the way in which systems were named. Most systems in the galaxy were named after the primary star. Of course there are a few exceptions to this, more so towards the fuzzy boundary between arm regions and the Deep Central. However, in the Deep Central it is much more common for a system to have a name unrelated to the central star which can make travel a bit more confusing to the forgetful mariner.

Below the surface of the Deep Central systems, a less obvious variation from the arm regions has to do with governing bodies. The Deep Central systems all share a form of direct democracy where influence of opinion is guided by small chiefdoms that in and of themselves have no actual power. It is an odd combination of modern governance and ancient hierarchy. The result, some would argue, is an interstellar society guided by the will of the people. Others would argue that it is a society heavily influenced by popular opinion rather than philosophy.

The finer points of Bob's travel into the Deep Central systems took him, via the *Delirium Cordia*, first to what is known as the Winter Wind system. Though a map may give the impression of a little world all alone in orbit around a bright yellow sun, there are a dozen other planets in the system which are not suitable for habitation. These other unlabeled planets and planetoids provide invaluable resources for the well developed world Onatha.

Bob could see the highly reflective and massive cities on Onatha, seemingly composed of a singular brilliant metal, shine in the blue-white glow of Gaol, the star of the Winter Wind. The position of the jump station in orbit around Onatha, in relation to Gaol, provided this perfect picturesque moment to Bob who happened to be in the right place at the right time.

After leaving the Winter Wind system and jumping to and from about a dozen other stars, Bob and the *Delirium Cordia* made it to the Changeling Goddess system. The main inhabited world here was a massive moon known as Yoolgai Asdzaa. It was the satellite of the system's only gas giant Asdzaa Nadleehe. Bob was temporarily attached to a station in concentric orbit with the moon.

The central star, known as Johanna Ei, was a standard yellow sun, however a vast shell of gaseous material lay in between the sun and the moon. Thought to be either an ejected mass from the sun's early formation, or an ultra-massive gas giant that was torn apart by the sun's tidal forces, this gaseous shell gave the system its name. As the people of the moon Yoolgai Asdzaa went about their yearly cycle (about 13 standard years) this gaseous shell would change the appearance of the sun from yellow to orange then red followed by shades of blue, indigo and finally violet before clearing the field and returning the sun to its brilliant yellow. Bob wanted to see it, but didn't have the four to five years it would take to see the transition and unfortunately he arrived during a yellow sun. It was just a matter of being in the wrong place at the wrong time.

It was here that Bob was required to change jump-ships. He said goodbye to the *Delirium Cordia* and made his way to the opposite side of the station. On his way he saw a slue of jump-ships; the *Harrow*, the *Harvest*, the *Space Oddity*, and the *Era Vulgaris*. He, however, was to dock promptly inside the *Rain Dog*, which he did, and awaited for the next phase in this seemingly endless commute.

The *Raindog* made more jumps than Bob cared to count before arriving at the Sisters system, where he materialized in orbit around the planet Asga Na. The Sisters system was heavily populated with many developed worlds in orbit around the blue-giant sun Amotken.

This was the point in Bob's itinerary that had him actually traveling from one planet to another before getting to his next jump-ship. Bob had to travel under the power of his own little ship from the planet Asga Na to the system capital of E Lo Hi. The only reason this was even feasible had to do with the relatively close proximity of the two. Had this trip happened a year or two earlier the distance between these planets would be great enough that Bob would have to find another means to get there...which wouldn't be a big deal, but the way things have worked out he now had about an eight hour trip before him.

Besides a crippling boredom that brought about the decimation of several bags of cheese pagodas, the trip was completely uneventful. To be honest, that assessment was from Bob's perspective only as unbeknownst to him there had been one rather eventful moment somewhere towards the middle of this long transit. Between two worlds and a good distance above him, Bob had come close to a ship that he hadn't seen, nor had the ability to detect...an almond shaped vessel that was practically invisible to all but the naked eye and had Bob happen to have looked directly at it would only have found a black body against the blackness of space.

Not completely by chance as these two were entangled in the same affair to some degree, Bob had come in rather close proximity to Moloch who watched amused as they passed literally as two ships in the night. Traveling in opposite directions, Moloch slowed to have a look. He was amused at the coincidence, but knew that there would have to be some overlap of the only individual who had managed to figure out a portion of his plans. Inside the glowing white innards of his untouchable ship Moloch looked down upon a view screen with Bob's ship in sight. He knew who it was and where he was going. Slowly raising a hand toward the screen, his fingers taking the position of gun, Moloch made a childish "phew" sound as if he had fired the imaginary gun in his hand directly at Bob's ship. He then chuckled to himself and continued on, quickly leaving at a speed of which Bob's little ship could only dream. Then he was gone.

If Bob had noticed him he would have wondered why Moloch would be out in the middle of the Deep Central. Bob might have wondered if he was being followed...which was not the case. Sooner or later it would have dawned on him that the Deep Central was almost completely untouched by the virus. A man that wants to spread something to the entire galaxy will find little rest and a lot of travel, especially if he wants it to happen in a timely manner. By the time Bob arrives at the Dandies world there will already be reports of widespread infection in the Deep Central and places further.

Bob, having effortlessly made it to the station in orbit of E Lo Hi, was about to dock on a jump-ship called *Nivraym*. It was a good hour before departure and Bob was excited to see a string of merchant vessels had already attached themselves to *Nivraym*. He needed to dock quickly to maximize his browsing time. There is almost nothing better than the adventure of perusing regional delicacies.

Below is a list of the items brought into Bob's possession:
1) An odd black melon...something like a watermelon, but the inside was more like pear with a sweet astringency and slight bitterness like one might find in the pear skin itself.
2) Some kind of radish, like a Daikon, but about the size of an infant. It was reticulated and had a powerful earthiness to it, that sort of thing that tastes like dirt...but in a good way. Bob would put that in some noodle soups.
3) A corn-like grain that is kept exposed to the vacuum of space. It has the effect of freeze drying, irradiating, and in an odd way

379

somewhat cooking the grain. It is then reconstituted in a lye and salt solution, which makes it highly poisonous, before entering a bath of distilled water. Under an ebb and flow of pressure, the water filters out the poisons and the remainder is a plump grain that is then eaten as is, or made into a variety of dishes such as cornbread or salads. They call it Pashofa and the culture claims it extends back to old Earth antiquity, but this cannot be verified.

4) Something that roughly translates into bean silk. It is a protein strain that is pulled from a type of regional bean and amassed into bundles that resemble fat noodles. Used in soups and as a snack. Nutritious and chewy...and odd.

5) Flat-rock bread. A bread that is made in thin, thin layers on a hot flat rock. It is presented in rolls and has an almost paper-like texture. It tastes of fine grain and ash.

6) An assortment of regional seaweeds. Bob realized he really should have stocked up on seaweed on the Balaenae world. That would have been the place to experience some interesting sea vegetables, but there really wasn't a good opportunity and Bob had wanted to get away from there sooner rather than later (and still had an occasional cough that he blamed on the experience).

7) Staples of an average diet. Dried figs and licorice root. Several kinds of olives. Fermented garlic. Onions and regional leafy greens. Something that sounded similar to apple-cider vinegar.

8) Fruits that look like, but currently undefined, apples, pears, citrons, grapes, blueberries, lychee, strawberries, and several varieties of raisin-like things.

It was a good stash and would surely last him for a decent portion of his transit to the Dandy system.

Leaving the Sisters system Bob bounded from one system to another before having to change ships at Selu. Selu was one of the few systems in the Deep Central that actually was named after the sun. Bob arrived at an oddly flat and long station...like a scimitar curving with the orbit...around a planet known as Ohoyo Chishba Osh.

Bob, in his comparatively small transport vessel, detached from the innards of the *Nivraym* and met his next travel companion, a jump-ship known as *The Seer*. The *The Seer* was another dark gunmetal gray ship but architecturally more angular than the standard to which Bob was accustomed. It gave the ship an overall more buggy appearance. All jump-ships tended to look like giant fleas and this one appeared to have a greater, almost intentional, grasp on that insectoid quality.

After about an hour and a half wait, a loud thud announced the first jump. Yet before leaving the Selu system the jump-ship would first need to make a leap to Hisagita Misa, a nearby planet, followed by another system planet called Unetlanvhi. Though the trip was progressing as planned there's a completely psychological aspect to hopping around a single system that made one feel they weren't getting anywhere in a timely manner which was exactly how Bob was currently feeling. Attention and focus can relieve some of that antsyness but some degree is inevitable when spanning the better length of the galaxy.

Some number of thuds later and Bob was in what is known as the Skeletal system. Why it was called the Skeletal system Bob had no idea and it would have just remained another one of the many, many unmentioned systems from which Bob had jumped to and fro had it not been for the historic fact of the Skeletal system's infamous bubble gunners. The bubble gun, in common slang, is more accurately called Bolan's zip gun named after the inventor Bolan Choogle. Bolan was an escaped convict from a system in the outer SagAr arm who fled to the Deep Central to evade authorities. Bolan was the classic sociopath with a creative gift for dangerous things. Bolan established himself on Masau'u of the Skeletal system in the usual way of the outlaw: false identity, false profession, false commitment to community matters, etc. Masau'u, as much of the Deep Central can be, was welcoming to outsiders granted they accept and be part of the shared social fabric.

Through this, and in the prescribed manner of a dangerous mind, Bolan began work on a weapon employing people in a fashion that made them ignorant of the penultimate goal. The result was Bolan's zip gun and the operators of this zip gun became known as bubble gunners.

The concept is fairly simple; a plasma core attached to a modified jump engine for the purpose of striking a target light years away. The jump engine is, in a way, turned inside out, formed like a hollow tube, so that instead of transporting the bubble gun itself it merely folds the space within. When this happens in conjunction with a plasmic discharge through the hollow of the jump engine, the contained plasma, velocity intact, materializes at the desired destination.

The operators of the zip gun, the bubble gunners, were usually unskilled workers hired to push a button at the right time. They often had no idea what they were doing or what the device in which they had been stationed even was. It was a paid job, nothing more. They'd show up for work, be taken via some rogue ship with jump capabilities to an unknown location in the middle of nowhere and told what to do at what time. They might hear a rumble and see an internal flash of light, but nothing more and nothing that would make them suspect they were firing upon a helpless people three systems over. Later, the ship would return and take them back unless the situation demanded that they be abandoned to starve to death in unknown space. That situation usually involved legal issues or suspicion that made a return to the zip gun not cost effective. Yes, it turns out those involved in attacking unsuspecting worlds tend to not be very decent human beings having little qualms about the awful death of an innocent worker trying to feed his or her family or make their life a little less burdened.

Bob knew of the bubble gunners from his study of modern and historical armaments, which he found an interesting subject, but couldn't get past his disbelief in the audacity of such a thing and the sheer and sad ridiculousness of it all. We can't seem to leave each other alone...on any scale from tribes to countries to planets. Even an entire solar system with plump little worlds going about their own business couldn't be left alone. Someone, somewhere, would find the need to attack remotely...a detached violence that makes the horror of it all the easier to digest when distance offers protection and shields the eyes from suffering. It is honestly a disgusting trait of the human being and one we have never seemed to transcend.

Fortunately, Bolan's zip gun has a decent degree of inaccuracy and obviously has been uniformly banned in all regional authorities. On the agreed upon galactic list of human rights violations Bolan's zip gun falls under the subsection of banned objects along with the Annie Jump Cannon, the common death ray, and the Torquey Rectifying Jiggler which is far too horrible to describe in any detail here.

Bob, in the jump-ship *The Seer*, left the Skeletal system and made a few errant jumps before landing in what is known as the Sacred Sun system. The trip had been going fairly well up to this point...that is until Bob found himself in a dimly lit prison deep beneath the systems capital. This, which is a fairly safe supposition, will require a bit of explanation.

Bob sat quietly in the middle of the prison cell sipping a cup of hot tea from a rather nice porcelain teacup. The tea was a dark rust color and had a woody, almost fired, roundness to the taste. It was like drinking a fine mahogany. Within moments the same guard that had escorted Bob to his cell returned. She was tall with dark hair and wore a uniform that seemed, to Bob, an odd amalgam of style. The upper portion had an air of officialdom with regimented buttonry that climbed the torso and met at what appeared to be a short and stiff collar. The lower portion was a dress that fell below the knees revealing matte military-esque boots which seemed to be a reinforced cloth material hugging a rather slender foot. The guard spoke with a determined formality.

Guard: "The tea. Is it too your liking?"
Bob, a little confused: "...It is. It's very good, thank you."
Guard: "The temperature is adequate?"
Bob: "...Yes. It's fine."
Guard: "It has not become too bitter?"
Bob, wondering what the point was, offered: "...No. It's lovely, thank you."
The guard turned and disappeared down the corridor.

Bob was on his guard some due to the circumstances, but all in all his treatment had been exceptional which is a thing to be exceedingly thankful for when imprisoned in a faraway land by a culture that one knows nothing about. Bob wondered if the issue of the tea was something other than what it appeared, but it may be nothing more than a protocol of treatment for the accused. Innocent until proven guilty is not a universal guarantee and the cultures that possess this judicial golden rule tend to, at the very least, treat their accused like human beings.

And why was Bob now sitting alone in a prison cell? Bob had arrived in the Sacred Sun system at a station in orbit around a planet known as White Deer. This was the endpoint of a major trade route into the area and Bob had to catch his next jump-ship at a station in orbit of the system's gas giant, the Spotted Wolf. Easy. White Deer to Spotted Wolf. Bob would have liked to board another jump-ship and quickly go between White Deer and Spotted Wolf, but there wasn't a ship scheduled in any sort of timely manner *and* the jump-ship he needed to catch at the Spotted Wolf wouldn't be back again for several days. Both White Deer and the Spotted Wolf were major hubs in the system and heavily populated. White Deer was the endpoint of a major trade route and the Spotted Wolf was the endpoint of two other major trade routes. Being so populated and dominant in regional trade one would wonder why this particular jump-ship that Bob was after would have such an infrequent schedule. Well, Bob was not moving along any trade routes. Bob was headed into a distant and unpopulated portion of the galaxy. Not much call for travel into the middle of nowhere.

As a result, Bob had to make the trek from White Deer to the Spotted Wolf in his little ship. Not a big deal, but a good twelve hour jaunt which had given him a smidgen of time to learn about the Sacred Sun system and the planets involved.

The Sacred Sun system is considered by most to be the seat of power in the Deep Central. It is unparalleled economically and while technically not the most populated system in the Deep Central, it is the most developed...and its population is second only to one system that is suffering through severe overpopulation. Historically, as the

Sacred Sun system grew, it provided aid to surrounding systems at unprecedented levels, even to an extent that burdened its own people. The philosophy was that strength and stability only exists in any lasting form in the presence of strong neighbors. The result is a system that currently is on par with any system in the galaxy.

Somewhere, about eight hours into Bob's flight from White Deer to the Spotted Wolf, a group of official military cruisers detained Bob and his ship. They confined him to a small holding cell aboard one of the larger cruisers while personnel detailed the contents of Bob's ship. They didn't say a word to Bob about what was going on except generalities like "we'll let you know when the investigation is complete and if charges are to be filed." Bob thought it had to be a mistake or some xenophobia of outsiders that surely would resolve itself, but Bob was getting anxious that he might miss his jump-ship and be delayed considerably on an already lengthy mission.

After about an hour and a half in the cell Bob heard and felt the unmistakable thud of a jump. Bob instinctively brushed his forearm to summon terminal access, but it had been disabled...which was to be expected when detained. Bob was in the dark, but knew that they had jumped somewhere and hoped it was toward his intended destination.

Soon after, Bob stood and politely gestured to a soldier that had been sitting and looking rather bored.
Bob: "Can you tell me where we're going? I no longer have terminal access."
Soldier: "I'm not permitted to exchange information with detainees, however, you do have limited access to information via the console in the far corner."

Bob looked and said thanks but the soldier had already sat back down. There was a small console that Bob ignored assuming it was only for terminal projection, but it was, in fact, operational. Bob imagined that it was severely limited in what it would allow to be accessed and assumed it was also monitored. None of that really mattered to Bob, he just wanted to find out where they were headed. Pulling up the details Bob was hit with a sinking feeling in the pit of his stomach. They were not far from Zitkala'sa. They were heading in the wrong direction and Bob knew he would now miss his jump-ship. It was almost a certainty.

Setting his disappointment aside in the face of what seemed like the inevitable, Bob realized from his prior reading of the Sacred Sun system that Zitkala'sa was home to what is often called the "Earth Mover" project and this did pique his interest. The Earth mover is an ongoing project to build what amounts to a mammoth jump-ship designed for a specific purpose. That purpose is to encapsulate an entire planet and generate a jump field around it. Yes, the idea is to transport an entire planet. The impetus for the project is centered around old Earth and the fact that in a mere billion years or so Earth's sun will expand into a red giant and either consume the Earth or push it so far out of orbit that the planet will effectively die. The Earth mover project is the beginning of the study of planetary relocation with the idea being that a planet could be moved in a large enough jump ship. Earth is the primary focus as it is the source of all human life in the galaxy and even so terribly far away here in the Deep Central systems the people have not forgotten their heritage. In addition to Earth, and long before it would become necessary for Earth, there are a multitude of planets that are a little earlier in the queue for the chopping block. There are, in fact, thousands of worlds suitable for life but with too unstable a star to be habitable in a long term practical sense. This process might open up entire planets for colonization and offer considerable practice for a process that is in its infancy.

To say the Earth mover project is in its infancy may even be a bit premature. There are seemingly insurmountable problems that haven't been addressed yet even in theory. The idea is to build the Earth mover, which has a rough estimated time of completion in a little over a thousand years, then figure it out from there. Surely by then some of these problems will be addressable or at least a suitable workaround will be developed. One of these problems has to do with dither. Avoiding too lengthy and technical of an explanation, let us just say that dither is the small amount of vibration in the jump engine envelope generator's signal to noise ratio. The envelope is created around the jump-ship to move it temporarily out of the universe, then back in. When that envelope pops, like an oily soap bubble, there is a small amount of disturbance from the incompatible realities of a thing that is both there/not-there and in two places at once...briefly. This accounts for the characteristic "thud" of a jump being made. Not a big deal when dealing with little things like ships and people, but magnified over a large scale...that of a planet...that little added noise is calculated to cause effects that would range from widespread planetary seismic activity, unlike anything experienced in a natural setting, all the way to planetary fracture. Basically, we haven't figured out how to jump a planet without shaking it up considerably. There should, however, be a workaround in the next one thousand to one billion years.

Bob pulled up the image from the ships senors of the Earth mover. At a considerable orbit from Zitkala'sa, floating alone in space, the gleam of metal reflected the golden light of Holiitto'pa, the systems central star. So far all that can be seen is the base frame to which is attached the skeletal framework of the field generator's echo chamber and the clock-coupling manifold...basically the ships transmission, often crudely referred to as a *gearbox*. It was fascinating though. The intricate shape of the base frame with the long transmission attached to and extending beyond gave the object the appearance of a metallic violin floating errantly in dark space.

Bob was just getting to the point of wonder. He was wondering why they were in orbit and not landing on the planet surface. Maybe they do on-site trials or maybe this wasn't enough to warrant more than a detention and investigation and they were about to let him go. Bob was certain that he had every right to be there, pass through, and hadn't done a single thing wrong. It was not long after that an official, of some kind, approached Bob's holding cell and in an almost oratorical manner read the charges brought against him.
Official: "You are charged with the unlicensed possession of war paraphernalia by a civilian in neutral territory and are ordered to present defense before council in a trial of your peers."

There was a number of similar statements and through all the wordy legalese Bob managed to figure out what was going on. It was the stillsuit. The stillsuit itself was not a weapon, but it is the sort of thing that usually is only found in the hands of soldiers in the worst kinds of war. It was understandable that they would wonder why he had it. Bob didn't even know why he had it...something to do with the Dandies...so there really wasn't much he could do to explain why he was in possession of such a thing. So all he could do was accept that he was being charged with having a thing that reminded them of more dangerous things.

That's why they hadn't landed. The officials had run the details of the case and conducted the investigation at an orbiting military outpost around Zitkala'sa, but a formal trial would have to take place at the capitol, which was the planet Aquash where Bob currently found himself in a cell drinking a cup of tea.

The approach to Aquash had been odd. It's easy to get turned around in space, but he was certain from their trajectory that they should have landed on the daylight side of the planet, but everything here was dark, like a uniform twilight. However, he didn't get a chance to see much before descending into a structure that took him deep beneath the surface and landed him in this cell.

Now, waiting for who knows what, Bob sat quietly in jail. The guard returned several times to ask about the tea but offered no conversation otherwise. Bob had been there a while before someone with some actual information materialized. Her name was Mary RedCloud and she was the equivalent of a public defender. She went over the details of the case and got as much information from Bob as

386

she could. RedCloud wore an almost identical uniform to the prison guard, but it was a pine-beige color of cloth and had a formal yet less militaristic air. Her hair was long and unbound and black as night. They spoke for a considerable time, but one little portion of the conversation was particularly troubling to Bob.

Mary RedCloud: "So, you were given the stillsuit by an officially recognized entity...an entity known as the Center for Infectious Disease and Entropic Recomposition, or CIDER, headed by a Dr. Morris...for the purpose of non-military reclamation of genetic samples?"

Bob: "Yes. This mission has no affiliation with any military operation and is, in theory, for the greater good of the galaxy as a whole."

Mary RedCloud: "Well, I think this will be an easy dismissal. We just need to contact the source, this Dr. Morris, and verify proper ownership of the stillsuit and licensing for use connected to you. We'll also need to verify this information with the arms manufacturer that built the suit and make sure the path from creation to you is one straight and legal."

Bob just nodded but he knew this was not good. His mind immediately jumped back to getting this still suit. The tight ship that Dr. Morris likes to run left Bob waiting unexpectedly for the *Cell-Scape*. When the *Cell-Scape* arrived it had a huge plasma burn across the hull and Lydia was suspiciously missing an arm. It struck Bob that they had probably stolen that stillsuit and the theft did not take place non-violently. This was bad. Not only did it mean that Bob was not going to make his connecting ship, he might never be leaving this cell...unless of course this was an executable offense. Bob immediately became interested in the particulars of this planet's judicial system. But...

While this conversation had been going on something was happening. Somewhere not far from Bob, in a room black as pitch, a pair of eyes opened and peered through the dark...something stirred and in a distant indirect way became aware of Bob's presence. This was not a psychic power nor the workings of magic, no. Rather, it was that old, old spider's web of causality that when one took the time, the time to sit in the silence of the world and become sensitive to that delicate awareness, the little vibrations of that web can be felt and pondered upon. It was that vague feeling that something was going on...that instinct that something wasn't quite right. Questions were asked and soon after an order was issued for an audience with this stranger called Bob.

As Mary RedCloud was going over procedure with Bob a message came to her terminal, one urgent enough to demand her immediate attention. Looking down at her forearm and receiving the message, Mary RedCloud looked up at Bob with a great deal of concern...almost sadness...and said, "*She* wants to see you."

According to the brief explanation that Mary RedCloud offered as she anxiously gathered her things and summoned the guards, this *She* is some sort of authority, an ultimate authority not just on Aquash but for the entire system and perhaps much further. Mary said *She* has unrestricted judgment and can order the instantaneous sentencing of anyone without question, a sentence that extends to execution...or worse.

Bob would have assumed that this situation might grip him in the squeeze of a relentless panic attack, but he felt very calm. Maybe because it all seemed so unreal and he couldn't imagine he'd be facing death considering that he'd committed no crime...in his opinion.

Bob asked: "Does *She* often exercise her power of capital punishment?"

Mary RedCloud's demeanor had instantly changed. Maybe she was concerned about Bob's meeting with whoever this *She* is, or maybe this request has placed a strong suspicion on Bob and Mary is no longer assuming this is a matter of a simple misunderstanding of an innocent individual.

Mary RedCloud: "Seeing as her judgment is unquestioned and absolute there are no requirements that this information be made public. Do yourself a favor and assume the worst."

Two guards removed Bob from his cell and escorted him, along with Mary RedCloud, quickly to a lift in the central shaft of the detention area. A command at the lift console turned the display red and instantly they shot skyward with enough g-force to require a sturdy push against the momentum to avoid falling to the floor of the lift. By the force and duration, they must have been heading up a great tower, dozens of stories at least, before coming to a halt and entering a narrow docking bay housing a handful of medium sized cruisers.

The cruisers had spindly legs and seemed to grip the supports that held them in place giving them the appearance of giant bugs. As they neared, the docking bay door opened letting in a rush of clean moist air with a scent of the woods, pine and cedar perhaps. Quickly they rushed into the cruiser. One guard took helm with Mary RedCloud in the copilot position. Behind was Bob and the second guard keeping a close eye on him.

The cruiser sealed and came active. Like a scuttling spider the legs animated and hurried toward the opening. With a gripping support against the sides of the docking bay door the cruiser flung itself out with a locust like dexterity. Once airborne the abdominal portion of the cruiser, housing the pulse engines, hinged earthward while the legs straightened and angled up and back like skeletal fish fins. The descending abdomen and the rising legs gave the ship a remarkable likeness to an insect in mid-leap.

From the tower the cruiser seemed to slowly fall through the night sky which led Bob to believe they were to land somewhere on the ground nearby, but the ship merely glided to a low altitude, a few stories above ground, then maintained a steady course away from the sun.

This was the first time that Bob got a good look at his surroundings. They were definitely in a city, but it was dark and odd. The tower they left was tall and narrow composed of two intersecting rectangular blocks...like a long plus-shaped peg. The tower was black, almost as if it was made of a black stone, perhaps something similar to obsidian but not glossy...flat, non-reflective, and dark. The inner corners of the tower were slightly illuminated and one could see a few openings and catch the occasional glimpse of a window or internal light, but very little. These towers were exceptionally dark.

Looking out over the city Bob could see this same tower replicated in all directions to the horizon. Each tower separated by a good mile or so and in between...not much. Between these towers Bob could make out some wooded areas and what seemed like roads of the same black material, but nothing and no one on these "roads". Other than the black towers extending skyward there seemed to be no other structures...no buildings, no landings, no industrial structures...nothing.

Bob was surprised that it took him this long to realize the bizarre dichotomy that had thrown him for a loop when they first descended toward the detention facility on his arrival. Here it had the appearance of night, or early evening, but behind them was the sun high in the sky. Apparently on Aquash the sun has the audacity to come out at night.

Racking his brain to try and figure this out Bob first wondered if they were just at a distant orbit from the sun, but the sun didn't *look* *f*ar away and, besides, Bob had looked up some info on this system while he was being transported to the cell and Aquash is comfortably in the "goldilocks" zone so should be at or near Earth equivalence. It must be the material. Everything here seems to be made of that black stone. It probably absorbs light and is used to power everything. If it was efficient enough it could alter the appearance of daylight and everything, *everything* here is black.

Bob asked: "Mary, what is the material here...of the buildings? Is it for light absorption?"

Mary Redcloud turned to Bob and seemed perplexed: "...Well, yes...it's a material for solar absorption. It's our primary source of energy."

Bob: "And that's why it's dark in the daytime?"

Mary RedCloud, still perplexed: "I suppose I'm just used to it, but yes, it does absorb almost all ambient light...but that's only here. This is where most of our planet's energy resources are generated. Elsewhere the sun is not deprived of its daylight. But, how is it that you are interested in this? You should be preparing for *Her* audience. Any problems with your story and things will end very badly for you."

Bob: "Well, I have nothing to prepare for. I only have the story I have. I suppose if that is not adequate there isn't much I can do about it now." Mary RedCloud offered a facial expression that was halfway between skeptical and concerned...with a partial eye-roll thrown in.

Below, somewhere on the ground, Bob kept seeing something...in groups...scurrying here and there. They were moving in packs, but weren't people. Actually, Bob couldn't and hadn't seen a single person down there the entire flight. Were people only in the towers around here? After a moment Bob got a good look at the scurrying animals as a pack of them all looked at the cruiser before running off. There were wolves. Everywhere.

The cruiser approached a tower that to Bob was indistinguishable from the others. As they neared, their trajectory became a natural exponential function rising to meet the opening of the docking platform. When closing in on the opening the insect-like qualities of the cruiser reanimated. The legs came to life and gripped the opening and side of the tower as it scurried inside. As the ship passed through the opening of the tower the distended abdomen housing the engines rose flat once again and the ship scuttled a good fifteen feet in before halting. Once stopped, the legs bent, softly placing the torso on the ground, before curling upward like a dying spider.

Exiting the ship were a small group of nervous people, except for Bob who was unusually calm...even eager to see what was going to happen. The guards and Mary RedCloud didn't really know what to say. They silently gestured toward the door at the far end of the docking bay and Bob gave a little wave to the group before heading that way.

As Bob passed Mary RedCloud she spoke in a commanding but almost inaudible whisper.

Mary RedCloud: "You need to be very careful. Take this seriously and no clowning around, got it!?"

Bob gave a determined nod that did not instill Mary RedCloud with confidence.

Beyond the door was a circular passage surrounding a central lift. The lift opened as he neared it and Bob stepped inside. As he entered he scanned about for a terminal or something that he'd access to tell the lift where to go, but before he could even formulate that idea fully the doors closed and he was off. Downward, apparently. The lift was descending just short of a freefall as Bob could feel his organs floating around a bit. From the duration of the fall before the lift began to slow then stop, Bob could tell he had traveled quite far below ground, a depth at least equivalent to the height of the tower above the surface.

The lift door silently opened to a long hallway. Every surface since he had entered this tower, like the previous tower, had been composed of the same black material. The hallway was quite dark, but there was light. It was not like walking through darkness, but like a hazy twilight that persisted. It was like being in fog where everything seems foggy except the immediate surroundings but instead of fog...darkness. Everything right out of reach seemed lost in shadow but just around Bob he could see. It struck him as odd that he couldn't source the light. There seemed to be only a bubble of illumination around him and nowhere else which Bob assumed had to be a result of the black material absorbing ambient light. Wherever the light was originating, Bob was the only reflective surface for it to bounce off of which in an odd way made him the source of illumination.

During his walk down the corridor Bob was aware of two distinct sounds he couldn't quite place. One was a high pitched and intermittent electric sound...almost like an old telegraph he had once seen in action during a class on primitive tools. The other was the sound of drumming...a repetitive pattern, but one that sounded very far away...something that had to be unassociated with his current location.

Toward the end of the hallway Bob encountered a massive door. It wasn't until now that he realized how tall the passageway had been, as this door was not composed of the same black material. The great double door appeared to be wood...still black but seemingly natural like a smooth ebony. Though the wood was dark it was greatly more reflective than the black stone which made it quite visible. It almost had a dark glow about it. Etched into the wood was a figure that Bob at first didn't recognize. It covered almost the entire expanse of the door and Bob's first reaction was that it must be a character in the native language of the people here. But after a moment Bob considered that it might not be a character at all. It was something, almost familiar.

Both the drumming and the electric sound seemed louder here, but still very far way, but Bob paid this little mind and was more intrigued by the door, the wood grain, the smooth unfinished surface, and the image skillfully etched into it. "That's it." Bob thought. He recognized the figure etched into the door. It was the most minimal of marks to produce the desired symbol. It was an owl. Almost in conjunction with this realization, the doors silently opened.

As Bob set foot in the chamber he could tell by the faint echo of his steps that it was quite large and something hinted to him that it was round, though he wasn't sure why. There were two fires that burned in black braziers at either side of the chamber, but they were up high, a good twenty feet in the air, supported by a long slender column that assumedly met with the ground but Bob could only verify that they reached *toward* the ground and ended in the darkness that crawled throughout the chamber.

About the chamber too was clean air and a faint scent of moss, and though it could not be heard, there was a moisture in the air that suggested possibly a small creek ran through, though how that could be this far underground was a mystery.

Somewhere in the center Bob had a faint awareness of a person, someone, but couldn't really see them through the dark.

It wasn't until now that Bob had acquired a strong jolt of concern and he lamented that he had not begun this worry much sooner...even though it wouldn't have benefited him in any way. This setting had all the markers of some sort of spiritual practice or religion and, unlike law, was a thing that is never predictable especially when a perceived injustice has been committed like, for example, a man bringing a military grade stillsuit into peaceful territory.

She: "Sit."

The voice was that of a woman, which was to be expected, and the command demanded complicity but there was no aggression in its essence. Bob looked in the direction of the voice and could see some structure near, possibly for sitting, so he carefully wandered forward. Near the center of the chamber was a dark platform, maybe two feet off the ground...hard to see, and a figure...*She*...sat upon it. Before it was a long seat...a log actually, smooth and solid...and Bob carefully but hastily sat.

As he sat, there remained a lingering silence that left Bob feeling uncomfortable, but gave him time to see, inasmuch as he could, the image before him. She seemed to wear garments similar to those of the guards and Mary RedCloud, but the darkness made it hard to discern many details. Dark, uncut auburn hair from the crown of her head poured down over her shoulders...but hiding beyond that hair was only darkness and what seemed like eyes floating in absolute void. It was jarring, but collecting himself from the instinctive effect of the image Bob surmised that it was a face paint and one that had to be made from the same black stone that was robbing this place of light.

Through that absolute void the glimmer of white teeth emerged as *She* said, "Why have you come here?"
Bob, caught off guard: "Well...Aquash? ...It was an accident really."
She: "There are no accidents. In the entire lifespan of the universe no single snowflake has ever fallen in the wrong place."
Bob keyed into her use of the word *lifespan*. He then collected himself and in an abbreviated fashion spoke of what brought him here...the deaths, the virus, Dr. Morris, the Rapulis, the Balaenae, etc... Bob wasn't sure if it was the acoustics of the chamber or his own weariness with the same story, but it began to sound only like noise to him...his own words sounded like a murder of crows fighting over crumbs. However, *She* listened quietly and let Bob say what he wished to say. It was only after Bob's voice trailed off that *She* again spoke.
She: "Your motivation is to eliminate this virus?"
Bob: "Yes, absolutely."
She: "Disease comes and goes. Worlds end. Worlds begin. What is it you actually hope to accomplish?"
Bob: "Well, I hope to prevent the death of countless people."
She: "And once you have prevented their death, how do you intent to alleviate their suffering?"
Bob: "I...well...I don't know. I think that is beyond my abilities and job description."
She: "And what would you say are the boundaries of this plague that you fear?"
Bob: "The boundaries? ...Well, practically the entire galaxy."
She: "You are very mistaken. It is the same boundary that has always been and will always be. It is that which is in the reach of the conscious animal, where our hooked claws may puncture...not one sliver shorter nor one wound beyond."
Bob had to admit to himself that *She* was absolutely right.
She: "Would you say that you are a seeker of life or a fighter of death? Because those two objectives are not the same."
Bob: "In all honesty I would have to say that I fight death."

She: "Then perhaps you study birdsong in a collection of stuffed nightingales."

Bob had to think about that for a bit.

She: "Someday you will need to realize that life and death are unified as the breath of existence. There is not inhalation without exhalation. There is not pulse without stillness. There is not this world without that world. How do you intend to separate yourself from the eternal? Through fighting death? It can't be done."

Bob, discouraged: "...Then what am I supposed to do...Just let everyone die?"

She: "No. You continue with what you are doing, but not in the vain attempt to halt the grief of the world, but because it is in your nature to do so. Fighting death only allows death to disguise itself as life. There is a time for words and there is a time for sleep. Once you realize this you may find that your abilities could be put to better use."

Bob: "I,...I don't know how."

She: "I have a perturbed awareness of a thing hiding in the singularity of my blindspot...a thing crawling outward like a shadow that is dispelled by the direct light of attention. It is struggling into being, a drowning mass that swims wildly and frantically toward the surface."

Bob: "..."

She: "...I have this unusual feeling that there is also something...some use for you. It is on the edge of my awareness...in the periphery of shadowed consciousness...but it *is* there. Nothing is ever quite what it seems."

Bob: "I'm not often accused of having a use, but I appreciate the thought."

Her eyes closed creating only darkness where a face should be as her last words reverberated softly through the chamber.

She: "You are free to go."

Bob didn't know exactly what to think but didn't linger. He got up and quietly exited the chamber. As he walked down the hallway he could hear the ebony doors close behind him. After that he upped his step to a brisk walk as he made it to the lift then shortly back to the docking bay.

The guards and Mary RedCloud seemed quite surprised to see Bob emerge from the lift. They looked at him, then each other, then back to him. Bob didn't really know what the big deal was...nothing terribly eventful happened. Almost immediately Mary RedCloud and the guards received a message via terminal and looked up at Bob.

Mary RedCloud: "We are instructed to take you back to your ship. You will then dock with a private jump-ship that will rendezvous with your missed transport. It looks like things went well...somehow."

Bob: "Yeah, it really didn't seem like a big deal."

Mary RedCloud, almost irritated: "Regardless of how it *seemed*, it *was* a big deal."

They then all boarded the cruiser which came to life and scuttled its way out of the docking bay.

After a bit they came to a tower...the same one they had left from or a completely different one, Bob couldn't tell...and in the docking bay was his familiar ship. Bob didn't know if it had been transported there immediately after his capture, or if it had been brought there by the same jump-ship with which he was to soon dock, either way he was glad to see it.

Mary RedCloud: "You'll need to head to the coordinates soon, the window of opportunity is not large."

Bob, now with full terminal access, looked over the instructions. The jump-ship they had procured for him would take him to meet the jump-ship he had missed by being detained. This was great news and would put Bob back on course with essentially no delay. This would literally save him about a week in waiting for the next ship out and readjusting his itinerary to suit. It couldn't have worked out better.

Bob: "Thanks for your help Mary."

Mary RedCloud: "I did almost nothing, but you're welcome."

Bob: "If you meet with the one you call *She*, tell her I said thanks for getting me back on track."

Mary RedCloud looked dour: "My hope is to never meet with her, ever."

Bob nodded and waved goodbye.

Leaving the atmosphere of Aquash, Bob could clearly see the city in which he had formerly been imprisoned...briefly. It was huge, had to cover at least an eighth of the land mass, and dark enough to make it look like nothing more than a pronged black plug stuck into the side of the planet. Soon after, Bob docked in the nearby jump-ship to which he'd been assigned. It had no visible name, but information available to him via terminal stated the ship was known as the *Tamer Animal*. Within minutes of docking Bob heard the thud of a jump made and knew he was on his way.

Bob was excited to be back on track and hopefully resolve this thing...or at least his involvement in it...but he couldn't help but feel a little helpless. Bob thought it had to have been the conversation he just had. *She* said a few things he couldn't quite mull over enough. Things that seemed unimportant to the task at hand while at the same time seeming like the only aspect he'd found so far that had any substance. It was like there was something he'd been missing...like a foggy darkness in the periphery of *his* consciousness. He just couldn't discern whether *She* had put it there or whether *She* had only pointed it out. Either way, Bob couldn't help but feel he was acting out his role in a play that had already been written and performed *ad nauseam.*

...the lifespan of the universe...

...the hooked claw of the conscious animal...

...the grief of the world...

Dream Journal: Witness

I was walking down a cobblestone roadway toward some fancy pavilion. Cobblestone is irritating because it's never even; one is always jostled around trying to walk straight. I was on my way to an elaborate gala and I was more than fashionably late, in fact, I had no desire to go to this damned party but felt compelled due to some social obligation and my own vanity in not wanting to appear the wreck that in actuality I was. Like many of my dreams this one was an odd mix of time periods. In my mind it was current, but the vision of the pavilion was intricate stone architecture like one might find in those primitive pre-electric, as they once called it, dark ages that are now all but lost to history. The night illumination, sparsely along the roadway and rich in the pavilion, shone a warm and thick amber light through the glass windows of the approaching structure. It had what one might imagine was the appearance of gas lamps though hardly anyone in this day and age would have ever seen such backwards means of making light or heat.

Once inside, the party was exactly what I had expected: friendly nonsense, a cacophony of murmuring and laughing, introductions and reacquaintances, and of course, specifically in my case, the obligatory and awkward offering of condolences. It was more than uncomfortable. It was brutal. When something terrible has happened people feel compelled to address the event as the contrary might imply they are not the warm, caring individuals they want everyone to see them as but rather a cold-blooded reptile insensitive to human suffering. Whatever the impetus might actually be, I couldn't help but see it as anything more than them placating their own social burden so that they may just as quickly forget.

I had just about had my fill of forced somber expressions that moments past me lit up and exploded in joy at the sight of an old friend, coworker, or familiar face. I had it in my mind to get as far away from this place as soon as possible when I, against my will, was introduced to the event host. She was a pleasant woman of early middle age. In the noise I didn't catch her name but she seemed to know who I was. She offered no condolences which I greatly appreciated, perhaps she didn't know, yet there was something about her that seemed to engage various calming mechanisms of my brain. It was as if near her the noise was attenuated and the crowd slowed down...time slowed down. Yet this effect was far from the most unusual thing about her. This host had the most peculiar physical appearance. I couldn't quite place what it was except that her eyes were definitely much farther apart than was expected and she had such a petite nose that at times I questioned whether or not it was actually there. Something...something about her was distant, almost not human.

Sensing that I was about to leave, she took my arm and offered a single suggestion.

Host: "You should stick around. We're about to start a very special event and the prize is something that *you* in particular might find useful." She gave a little nod then casually drifted away through the crowd.

It's hard to describe, but her addressing me specifically carried with it some unspoken knowledge as if she knew me, knew my situation and burden, the trauma inescapable, and found this "special event" to be relevant. I had no idea how it could be, but my interest was piqued enough to stay a bit longer.

Shortly after, the host appeared near the main banquet table and gingerly tapped a glass with a fork to get everyone's attention.

Host: "First of all, I want to thank everyone for coming and being a part of this celebration. What do we celebrate? Life inexhaustible, for the way in, and benevolent Death, for the way out."

This was greeted by throngs of cheers from the crowd. When they were brought to attention once more:

Host, smiling sweetly: "We are now going to begin a very special event and I welcome you all to participate. It is a sort of competition, but I don't like to think there are winners and losers, I prefer to think everyone stands equally to benefit."

Someone in the crowd shouted humorously, "What's the prize?"

The Host offered an even sweeter smile: "The prize?" And as she spoke the coming sentence, through the mass of people in the pavilion, hundreds, she made direct eye contact with me.

Host: "The prize is none other than the means to unravel knots in time." She then smiled gaily at the crowd that erupted into well intentioned laughter.

I immediately thought to myself, mulling over the words "*unraveling knots in time*."

Getting the crowds attention again the host's mood turned visible darker.

Host: "But I have to warn you, and a warning you should take very seriously, the stakes of this little game are very high and it is possible there might be no... *winner*... at... all."

The crowd murmured.

Host: "We'll begin shortly. Those remaining will be considered part of the event. For the rest of you, you know what they say *you don't have to go home but you can't stay here*."

The crowd laughed.

Host: "Thanks again for coming and have a lovely evening, a lovely life, and a meaningful death."

And there was applause for the host followed by mingling as people filed out.

There was somewhere around three hundred people at the party and after the exodus there remained about a hundred or so. Workers came in and removed all the tables and chairs and waste, quite efficiently, and before long we were in a giant empty pavilion where we could now see clearly the fine wood floor extending to each corner of the open hall. Around the edges of the room were long wooden benches built into the wall and broken only by the placement of the massive pavilion doors.

Host, smiling: "Hi, thank you all for staying and being part of this very special event. You are in for a treat. If you wouldn't mind, please have a seat around the perimeter of the room and we'll get started."

Everyone sat and it struck me as quite a coincidence that sitting side by side we filled the available seating. I suppose if more had stayed they could have brought out chairs. The hostess looked around and made sure that everyone was seated and comfortable, estimating a head count, then smiled.

Host: "Ok, let's begin."

She walked to a set of large wooden double doors which opened in tandem as she pulled one wide. Before we could see what lay beyond the darkened opening, long before any sound or scent, even before light could reach us, we were greeted by what can only be described as a crippling, paralyzing wave of abject horror. Fear and terror absolute had pressed itself on our senses long before anything physical had the time to interact and in this horror we sat motionless, petrified as if made stone by a Gorgon's gaze.

Following the paralysis a hideous creature lumbered into the room. It was like a legless caterpillar or maybe more like a gargantuan maggot. Perhaps eight feet tall and a good eighteen feet long, it had a fleshy girth similar in size to a whale. It's skin was a translucent white and hazy organs could be seen beneath. It wasn't fast, but rather seemed to struggle under the bulk of its own weight as it lurched forward.

As soon as the larval creature had begun its progression a second set of doors on the opposing side of the pavilion opened and another one began lurching forward. There were two of these monsters creeping inward both getting a sense of their own surroundings.

The fear was an interesting experience on me. Recent events had deprived me, for better or worse, of the fear of death. I almost welcomed it. Yet the terror instilled by these creatures was something biological. The urge to remain petrified most likely stemmed from feeling the situation was inescapable and trying to remain as inconspicuous as possible. For me it was almost like an out of body experience, or at least some kind of dual existence. I knew I was petrified with fear, but also aware that I did not fear death. It was as if I was observing distantly my own reaction of horror and the whole process seemed more academic than experiential.

Soon, as these great larva sniffed out their surroundings, they each opened their fleshy lamprey-esque mouths and lashed some tongue-like proboscis at the crowd. The end of this proboscis was a flattened toothed appendage that was surprisingly skilled at ripping flesh from bone and though the larva themselves were slow, their tongues were quick.

Lash after lash pulled limbs off the unsuspecting crowd. The hardest to watch was the disembowelment. It was like watching an ill-mannered toddler scooping spaghetti out of a bowl with their hands and carelessly mashing the contents into their face. Eventually the larva would get ahold of a whole person or the fresh carcass of one previously dissected. Pulling the bodies into their fleshy mouth parts the muffled sound of bones crunching and crunching was almost too much to take, but the abject terror prevented anything less than quiet acceptance.

These larva were not going about this task in any sort of organized manner. They would go from one person to someone on the other side of the room. Maybe two in one area and then one on the adjacent wall. Needless to say, blood had completely covered the wooden floor of the pavilion, but that was far from the most terrible sight. As these monstrosities ate, their translucent skin became redder and redder reflecting the horror of their undigested contents. Their consumption of flesh and blood amplified their fear induced paralytic effect which is evident as this all took place upon a motionless crowd. Not one of us moved a muscle until all or part of us was forced into the mouth of the monster. Not one single solitary sound could be heard from anyone. The only sounds heard were the tearing, slurping, and munching of human flesh.

Both individuals on either side of me were taken. This gave me the direct opportunity to witness the power of the fear induced paralysis. One of the individuals, some slender mid 30's man, was grabbed around the legs and pulled into the beast's gullet feet first. It chewed like a caterpillar eating a plump leaf consuming the man legs, then thighs, then lower abdomen. He uttered not one sound. His eyes darted back and forth like a confused and frightened pup until the beast had eaten up to his mid abdomen when death made his eyes dull and motionless. As his head was the last to enter the beast's mouth a loud crack echoed as his skull was shattered spilling the contents onto the floor.

Time played enormous tricks on me during this event. The fear had stopped time coldly making these proceedings incalculable while my seeming out of body observation of these events encapsulated everything in a momentary flash. It was disorienting and I had the dizzying feeling that the universe had somehow left me and I was alone. In a way, that experience was more frightening than the monsters before me as my connection to the universe and time was all I had of her. I was connected to her still through that silvery thread of time in the only reality I've had the fortune, for better or worse, to know. I was not willing to lose that.

Somehow, in some random act of astronomical luck, I was still alive and untouched. The larva had devoured everyone in the crowd. I was the only exception. Unbelievable gore still remained covering the floor, but the larva, both a deep red, seemed satiated and sluggish.

In the interim, before the paralysis had worn off, one of the larva began lurching toward the other. As it got close it began lashing wildly at which the other recoiled. Soon the recoiling beast lurched forward and lashed several times at the attacker's mouth parts before managing to pull part of it in. It then began to devour the attacking larva. It's mouth opened like a snake unhinging its jaw and it began to swallow. The attacker struggled but the other happened to get the better of it and there wasn't much it could do now. These monsters were primarily nothing more than a mouth and a gut wrapped in gross flesh. Without a mouth to devour they were helpless.

It seemed to take forever, but eventually one had completely devoured the other. The redness of the two had darkened considerably which I had attributed to the blood inside coagulating and dying, but something else was happening. The darkening kept continuing until beneath the still ghostly white translucent skin only blackness could be seen. It was blackness wrapped in fog.

The now double sized larva was bulging and taut. It seemed about to burst and for a long while had been completely motionless. I couldn't even detect breathing and it was about then that the paralysis of fear wore off. I slowly stood and inched along the perimeter of the room not wanting to disturb or awaken this terrible thing. I thought it might be dead but wasn't intellectually curious enough...or stupid enough... to go and poke it with a stick and find out.

I made my way through a blood soaked wooden floor to the main door of the pavilion not for a moment taking my eyes off the monstrosity. Blood, discarded in such a disgraceful wastefulness, has a strange duality about it. It is at once both sticky and slippery and fills the air with a peripheral, almost undetectable, olfactory awareness of metallic astringency.

As I was about to leave I heard a low creaking sound coming from the mass of flesh in the middle of the room. The larva was arching slightly causing the creaking and what followed was a gurgling tearing sound where it had split down the middle of its back. A large black mass arose from the split, black as deep space, and I could clearly see folded and malformed wings in the mess that began to stretch skyward and uncurl.

I could do no more than walk. The paralysis had passed, but I had only partially reclaimed my faculties. So I walked. I walked out and away from the horror of that evening.

Chapter Twenty-Nine:
A Needle, A Haystack, and a Tiny Hole That Binds Them in Time:
Tomorrow is Yesterday's Day After Tomorrow.

Grains unaccounted for: Upsilon-0-Delta-00 and Majoris-Tri-010110-Sigma. That is all.

Gibbering grain 000-Psi-00-8-Lambda-Mu repeatedly sending transmission of minor variance.

Lost grain 00-Psi-0-358-13-Xi is alone and cannot find home.

The Chief sat on the bridge of a police tactical cruiser looking intently at the view screen before him. He sat with his hands together, fingers interlocked except for both pointers which were straight as a steeple and resting vertically across his mouth terminating at the philtrum, his thumbs hooked under his chin. He was in deep thought with a blank mind, both focused and lost in absent contemplation. It is a common duality experienced by those that have a tremendous amount of concerns but no solutions. Days were overlapping and folding back on themselves.

The scene before him was a fantastic sight; a swirl of energized gaseous material amid far too many stars packed into too small a space. The dominant color was a spectrum of maize to squash, but every color was present especially the deeper one peered into the distant chaos. The chief, along with a web of other ships, were at a specific location near the galactic core. By *near* it is meant they were close enough for it to be dangerous but were thousands of light years from the actual center, so to speak. In fact, they were much too far in for anyone's liking...far enough in that there were no habitable planets or civilization of any kind. One doesn't have to get too close to the galactic core before the conditions are too volatile for life. Collisions, streaming plasma, ejected matter from this star and that, and violent solar winds that creep like titanic cosmic storms easily dispelling the fragile atmosphere of any Earth-like world that in some fictitious reality found itself too close to the galactic center prevents anything but very temporary habitation. This area is the realm of titans, of great violent old stars, and even they are easily dismembered and scattered or devoured by even darker monsters. Yes, this place is not compatible with life. It reminded the Chief of a fragment stuck in the back of his mind from an archaic text he had once skimmed through ages ago, "A land so full of terrible volition was not meant for us to dwell." Yes, it was hard here to not personify the static cataclysm of these unimaginable forces.

The periodicity was 6.18 seconds and the Chief had sat in silence for well over an hour marking time in 6.18 second intervals. He had no idea what to do. The particular area of interest in the midst of this painted desert of violent flame was a small, small patch of blackness enrobed in a blinding white fire. A black hole. The Chief had taken to heart a conversation he'd previously had with Bob that echoed the words of the Chief's father...or the scanned facsimile that remained since his passing. Bob suggested that Moloch's slippery ship might be able to get closer to a black hole than standard ships and surmised that he might be hiding out around such a place. The black hole would prevent interference because if he could get a bit closer without being sucked in, then we'd have no ability to apprehend him. The gravity would also almost completely mask or diffuse any extruding transmission rendering him almost invisible. *Almost*.

Using this idea the Chief assumed that Moloch might be hiding in more or less plain sight. If he could accomplish this he wouldn't need some distant black hole in the most remote part of the galaxy, rather he'd probably choose one as close to civilization as possible making interaction with people, gather resources, and initiating the spread of the virus much easier. The Chief first began with a list of known black holes that were in a relatively close proximity to sightings and known operations of Moloch: his early lab associated with Water Sprite genomics, his military job, Diophantus, the location of the body encased in Pixler's glass, and a few areas that seemed like hubs of the viral spread. Black holes in these areas were processed into three initial categories; *most likely, less likely, and not likely*. The factors that generated these categories are unimportant but fairly obvious. Each of these categories, for each target location, produced between fifty and a hundred black holes for the *most likely* category, a hundred or more for the *less likely* category, and two hundred plus in the *not likely* category.

This was much more than the Chief's personnel could manage in any sort of timely manner, but the dire nature of the epidemic had allowed him access to practically any region's law enforcement and/or investigations bureau with the complicit consent of the scientific community's resources.

404

In any other circumstance the Chief would have lost control of this case long ago. He was, after all, merely the police Chief of a single city. However, the whole event had just snowballed out of control and taken him with it. Since he was onboard so very early in this crisis, before anyone was concerned, he had been given authority over the case from almost every system he'd encountered. Atlas didn't care and gave him the authority to investigate, Alpha Centauri followed in suit. Rho Geminorum, Pollux, Castor, and several others were all either unconcerned or in over their heads and the Chief took the lead on their investigation directing their personnel and setting forward their plans of action. It wasn't long before the Chief had become, through no desire of his own, a proxy regional administrator. It did make sense as he was at the epicenter of the investigation, but it was also a sad reminder of a galaxy that has given over to almost total automation in the execution of the law.

The result? The Chief was now being aided by an organization that he'd prefer to not have dealings with. The nearest habitable region to this portion of the galactic core is a tightly banded group of stars known as the *Outer Wall*. The Outer Wall formed from an ancient gravitational ripple emanating from the core that pushed a group of stars into an almost straight line, or shell to be more precise. For this reason, there is a boundary between the outer wall and the core that contains practically no stars. It appears as an insignificant sliver on a map and would go completely unnoticed by practically anyone except those that lived there. Regardless, the outer wall is an influential regional power representing hundreds of systems and their investigations bureau is not accustomed to taking equal footing in important matters. Politically though, due to the enormous press and widespread association of the Chief with this case, they had to work with the Chief rather than take the case and dismiss someone they considered to be a lowly police officer.

The ships that were accompanying the Chief were the agents of the Outer Wall's investigations bureau, though they preferred to appear less like a secretive organization and more like an open agency which they were not. For this reason they were named the Outer Wall Law Enforcement, or O.W.L.E. These OWLE officers peppered the space around the Chief in dark metallic ships shaped like hooked claws.

The initial investigation of the *most likely* locations turned up nothing and was quite discouraging. It took a week of hundreds of ships instructed to intently scan each black hole for a fragmentary or errant signature not compatible with a black hole emissions. The model was the information gathered from Moloch's ship during the attack on Diophantus. It was a tiny breadcrumb of information, but enough to give them something to look for.

In the second week the Chief procured more ships and began scanning the *less likely* targets. It was a difficult task. The known signature trace of Moloch's ship had to be parsed from the background noise and emissions of the black holes to be scanned. Even if they found the right one it could be easily overlooked. However, early into the week they got a lucky break when a slight irregularity showed up in the long scan of this particular black hole. And here they remained in wait of orders from the Chief staring at a violent patch of space.

6.18 seconds. Every 6.18 seconds a faint blip appeared then was gone. It was a gap in the tidal forces of the black hole, the trough beyond the crest, that let a small bit of information escape some object in orbit. 6.18 seconds. It was not a natural occurrence, that they knew, and if it was a ship it was deeper in orbit than any ship known could attain. It had to be Moloch.

What could they do? They couldn't go get him. Even getting close would insure they would be sucked into the void beyond. They didn't have weapons that could touch him and even if they did manage to destroy him it would only insure that any potential information was lost forever making the prospect of a cure a decisive impossibility. Here was nothing to be done but monitor and wait. So there the Chief sat quietly with a blank mind running a mile a minute. He wanted to run some of this by Bob but hadn't heard from him for a bit. The Chief was sure he hadn't run into any trouble...probably bored out of his mind.

OWLE officer, pensively: "...Sir, ...what should I report?"

OWLE had sent the Chief a rookie as an operations aid, or so they said. In reality, they just wanted one of their crew on board to make sure nothing was conveniently omitted from any reporting on the part of the Chief. The Chief knew this but accepted it as a gesture of kindness to ease any suspicions OWLE might have. After all, he had no reason to hide anything. Ultimately, any help was welcomed.

Chief: "Ensign...Curbs, is it?"

Ensign Curbs: "Yes, sir. Ensign Dale Curbs."

Dale Curbs was a gangly man that looked far too young and inexperienced to be involved with this objective.

Chief: "Well, damned if I know what to do. He's definitely there. I've sent the data stream to your commander a few ships over, but I imagine he's already aware."

Ensign Curbs: "...so, we can't go get him."

Chief, raising both eyebrows but remaining focused on the view screen and honestly only paying half attention: "...No. ...No one can get that close."

It was then that a console lit up and the Chief received a message he had been expecting. The Chief read it over carefully, though what it had to say was fairly direct and brief.
Chief: "Hmm...almost twenty percent."

The Chief had sent the incoming data from Moloch's ship, that small blip that showed up every 6.18 seconds, to the Hawking Center for Theoretical Physics on Poseidon. Every once in a while physicists come in handy, though their knowledge of the material world tends toward a false belief in an equal understanding of philosophy which they often use to make errant conclusions on the nature of reality.
 Along with the blip, the Chief also sent the original signal captured from the ship at Diophantus and the coordinates at which the current signal is received relative to the black hole.

The Chief was looking for two things. One of these was an estimation on just how close of an orbit Moloch's ship had to the black hole's event horizon. Moloch couldn't be too close to it or even he'd get sucked in, but an idea of his orbit might, *might* be useful. This information would provide the answer to the Chiefs second question.
 Black holes a have rather peculiar property. They tend to dilate time around them. This is actually a very common phenomenon we've all experienced, but on such a small scale as to be insignificant during a lifetime. Space-time tends to get stretched out a bit by gravity and things in and out of a particular gravitational field don't move through time at the same speed.

In Moloch's case it was, though admittedly an estimate, a difference approaching almost twenty percent. The Chief was attempting to explain this to Ensign Curbs.
Ensign Curbs: "Wait, so...like at the end of the day today, it will be like tomorrow for him?"
Chief: "No, it's a twenty percent variation. He is essentially moving twenty percent slower through time than us."
Ensign Curbs: "....so,...like,...yesterday for him is like today for us."
Chief: "No, its..."
Ensign Curbs, interrupting: "Oh, I get it. Like, day after tomorrow...for him...is our day, today."
Chief: "No, we are moving about twenty percent faster through time than he is. That's all."
Ensign Curbs: "So his tomorrow then, ...is our yesterday's day after tomorrow?"
Chief: "No, that would be the same."
Ensign Curbs: "So...yesterday for him..."

The Chief interrupted and was getting irritated: "Forget yesterday. That doesn't matter. All you need to know is that we're moving a little faster through time than him. For every eight days that pass for him, ten days pass out here."

Ensign Curbs: "So that's good then. We've got more days than him...ten to his eight."

Chief: "No. That would be good if we were in a competition with him, both trying to solve a puzzle by a specific time, then we'd have ten days to solve the puzzle to his eight, but as it is we're not in a competition with him. No, this is a bad sign. He's waiting it out. In that orbit he doesn't have to wait as long to see the effects of his efforts."

Ensign Curbs began to say something but the Chief politely made a gesture that suggested silence. The Chief then sent the findings to the other ships in the area and in a transmission to be received back on Helen's Crown. From there he returned to his mile-a-minute blank stare watching the faint blip come and go every 6.18 seconds. It was a bad sign. Moloch was waiting this thing out and the orbit and the time dilation reeked of someone eager to see the results. The Chief had the specter of a conclusion hovering closer to his awareness than it had previously been, the conclusion that we may well be too late. Maybe there was still hope for an antidote. Maybe Bob would pull everyone out of this mess.

Chapter Thirty: The Danger with Dandies

After yet another seemingly endless chain of jump-ships and three times as many jumps...at least...Bob felt the final thud of arrival and was eager to get moving. Pulling up the coordinates Bob was irked to see that they were quite a ways from the Dandy system and chose to share some of this irritation with management. Bob was on a rather small and a bit run down jump-ship called the *Stormwatch*. It was a commissioned ship as no jump-ship would have any real reason to regularly travel to the Dandy system. Summoning customer service aboard the ship, Bob decided to ask a few cranky questions.
Bob: "Yeah, ...why are we so far from the system? We're too close to make another jump, but quite a bit farther than I had anticipated."
Customer Service, in a somewhat muffled and garbled transmission:
 "If you check your map you'll see that we're very near the Orchid nebula. Thank you for choosing the *Stormwatch* for your transportation needs."
Bob, irritated: "I *have* looked at my map. I know our location."
Customer Service: "Thank you for choosing the *Stormwatch* for your transportation needs."
Bob, more irritated: "Why have we not gone further in?"
Customer Service: "We don't jump into nebula or gaseous fields of any kind. No telling what's in there. You'll need a cloud miner to get into something like that via jump. Regardless, it's much better suited for a small ship and physical transit rather than jumping. Thank you for choosing the *Stormwatch* for your transportation needs."
Irritating.

Bob looked over the most direct path through the nebula to the Dandy system. It was not direct, merely the most direct. At top speed he was a good two hours from the outer boundary of the nebula and once in couldn't maintain top speed due to a certain amount of weaving in and out and around chunks of things floating through the fog. To get to the system itself would take at least ten hours and another two to get to the planet surface. Bob left the docking bay of the *Stormwatch* and headed out promptly. He was ready to get all of this traveling over with.

Finding himself in the false emptiness of space once again, Bob had to admit that the view of the Orchid nebula was breathtaking. It seemed considerably denser than other nebula he had been near and though he couldn't see any resemblance to an orchid the color palette appeared as if the most delicate and subtle hues of paint had been recently poured into fresh milk. The interplay between the colors was unusually harmonious. Where glacial blue bled into the warm orange saffron of intermingling entities the boundary produced a radiant glowing soft whiteness from the interaction. Bob imagined if his homeworld of Zeus had been transformed to paint and some celestial brush dipped within, that this, introduced to a mammoth pacific sea floating strangely in space, would produce a similar scene. This was but one small portion of the outer boundary of the Orchid nebula. To spend a lifetime here one surely would be able to find all conceivable combinations and interactions of light and color and texture. This scene eased Bob's irritation at the distance to travel and he now looked forward to the fact that he was about to enter this cosmic painting: a natural galactic work of art.

Somewhat behind at least a portion of the nebula Bob could see a radiant arc of fire. It was a star, a very large star, that was darkened like a waning crescent moon in the night sky. The only suitable means of such an eclipse would be a rather small black hole in the foreground, visually removing all but a sliver of the stars magnitude and, as would be expected, a fainter yet still brilliant accompanying arc rose in opposition as the distorted and redirected image of the star stolen by the black hole bent wildly around its unseen bulk.

After a while at top speed Bob entered a planet-sized hole in the nebula that opened into what had the appearance of a great cosmic cavern. Inside the Orchid nebula there was no sense of dark space but rather a luminous glow of an unimaginable visual spectrum extending in all directions.

The view was so breathtaking that Bob felt distracted by the interference of his own ship. A few commands that coupled the ship's sensor array to his own terminal access allowed every surface of the small cruiser's interior to appear to be it's own display. Almost immediately the rendering protocols adjusted for the myriad angles and curves of the interior and modulated for Bob's slack-jawed swiveling head. Once the rendering stabilized it was, from Bob's perspective, as if he stood upon a small metallic oblong platform and his ship was no more. This gave him the complete freedom to look about the nebula as if he himself was floating unobstructed through the vacuum of space.

410

Concentrations of the nebula formed great tendrils of star-creating speleothem-like stalactite and stalagmite amid flows of cosmic rivers spotted with sparkling gems of incubating stars. It was impossible to not be moved by such a sight that spoke directly to the heart from the mouth of creation.

Bob's ship was adequately maneuvering around floating debris and ejected remnants of past star formation that has since become cold and dark providing an unreal contrast to the vibrancy of the inner nebula. These floating, lifeless rocks here took the form of illusory specters of the once real that, deprived of their dimensionality, had become shadows cut free from their material companions. If one was to manually pilot some craft here a collision would be unavoidable as those things not bathed in color were hard to interpret as anything other than insubstantial or immaterial.

There was a perceptual displacement that came from being inside the Orchid nebula. The human mind is not equipped to interpret cosmic distances visually. Our formation and design is solely geared toward the mechanics of terrestrial life. Even larger terrestrial distances can be misleading and confusing. Here though, the scale was cosmic and uninterpretable.

What amplified this displacement was the radiant light of the nebula. In most other grand-scale scenarios distance would yield only an increasing blackness speckled with fainter and fainter points of starlight. Here, however, the entirety of the nebula radiated light...in all directions...in a chromatic absolute saturation.

The effect on Bob was an almost flickering of conflicting perceptual data. As he traveled, the size of the Orchid nebula would at times seem like a mammoth cavern akin to something found on an Earth-like planet. At other times the nebula would seem a small, claustrophobic, prismatic burrow. Interspersed from moment to moment was the realization that the scale was cosmic, an intellectual and academic insertion that could not be sustained in the emotional centers of the mind and even easily loosed from the mind rational. Bob could unequivocally claim participation in an experience to which he had no previous reference of comparison. He was awestruck.

Near Bob, figuratively of course, to the right of his ship, was a wall of the inner nebula that had the appearance of a gargantuan tidal wave about to strike. Shades of turquoise and glowing almond streamed skyward and Bob's attention was drawn when some fantastic lightning-like discharge crawled upwards and across the surface. It had to be at least the length of several standard solar systems, the discharge itself, and with tendrils reaching to a dozen stars in the mass. In what strange world had Bob found himself?

It would be interesting to see this wonder outside the constrictions of the brief time granted unto us. To exist in a fluidic tempest of time streaming relentlessly by, this spectacle would seem as some prismatic writhing egg sac forming star after star in its belly so subtly as to be difficult to capture the instance of conception. A star would spark into being from a gentle aggregation of gaseous plasma and the eyes would be drawn to it. In the periphery elsewhere the same would happen and again draw the attention of the eye. Darting back and forth, to and fro, seeing the burst of radiant light, but never actually seeing it happen. It would be like witnessing bubbles forming within a babbling brook, one can seen the bubbles, but when they actually comes into being seems a bit of a mystery.

Fortunately for Bob, his dumbfounded state played serious tricks on his perception of time and he found himself in complete disbelief when his ship notified him of the approaching system. He had been staring at the heavens slackjawed for over ten hours and could not, *could not* believe it had been any longer that a half-hour or so. When he came to his senses he realized he was very thirsty and his eyes were dry and itchy. After a glass of water and a moment resting his eyes he accessed his trajectory to the Dandy's planet. He had a little over two hours and thought it might be a good time to read, at least a little, on the very foreign world he was about to visit.

The Children of Demeter
Compiled from the resources of the Free Galactic Library (FGL)

Though very few have ever met a Dandy and even fewer will get the chance to visit the Dandy system, the Dandies are by far the most known human variant in the galaxy. This is due to their very alien nature and appearance compared to the human standard. No educational institution could claim a proper teaching of human design without firm knowledge of the extremes that form can take. The Dandies are *the* example of this extreme.

To understand the Dandies one must understand their unique history. In the early days of jump-ship technology, which opened the galaxy to human colonization, most colonization was done gradually from point to point. From Earth human beings spread to the next nearest habitable stars, Alpha Centauri then Sirius, then gradually further (Formalhaut, Arcturus, Pollux). This spread human beings very slowly, radiating outward from the central hub of Sol. The early colonizers which eventually became the Dandies adopted a variation to the general philosophy of human dissemination. They, in part philosophy and part exploration, set out to find the most distant habitable system and from there seed the galaxy with the human form, and there they found Demeter.

The Dandies were not the only civilization to share this philosophy. For example, the Deep Central systems were seeded in just this way as were the systems of the Perseus Arm (PeAr).

However, the Dandies were the first, and both the Deep Central and PeAr seedings took place thousands of years later which may account for their significantly greater success compared to the Dandies.

The System:

To understand this absent success and to understand the Dandies as a people we must first look at the system to which they found a home.

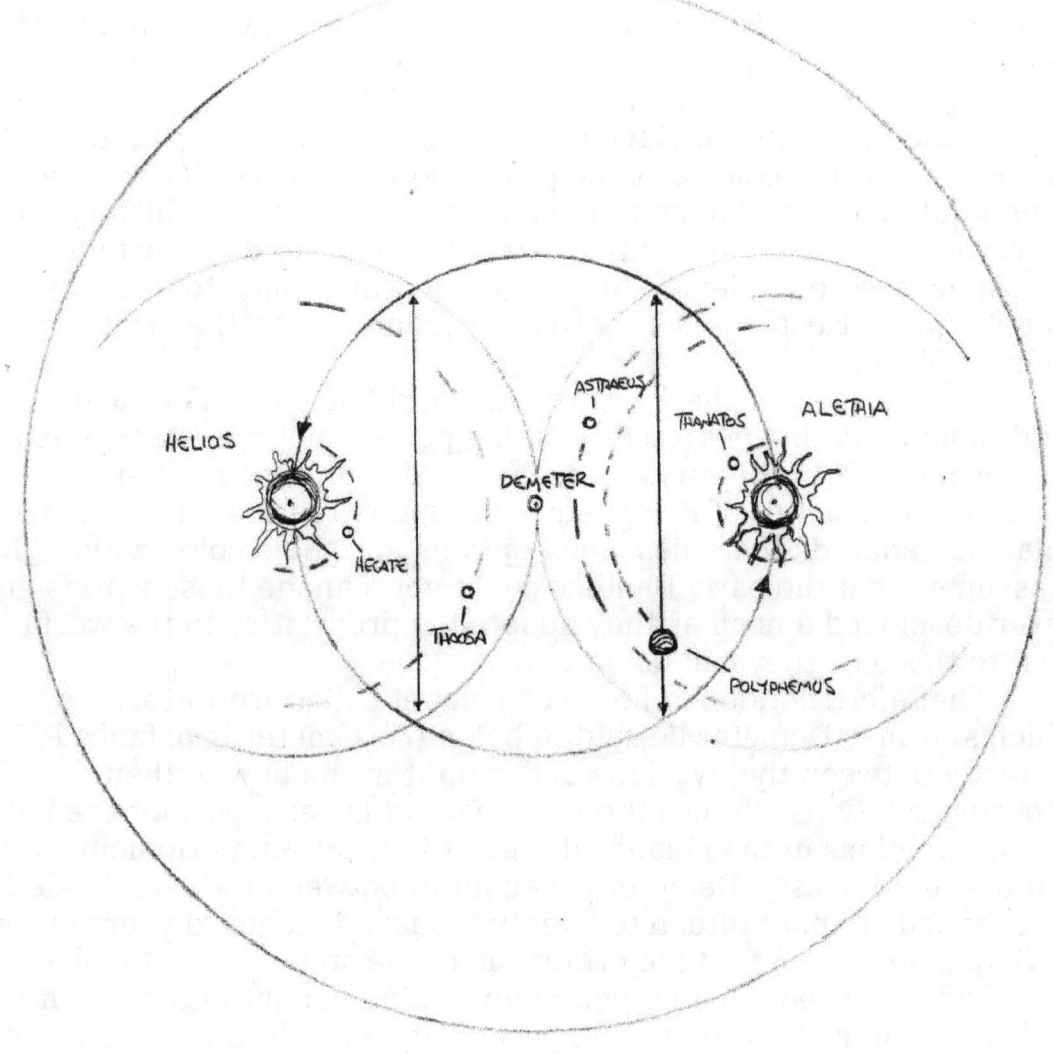

As communication with the Dandies is difficult at best, it should be noted that there are different standards for addressing the Dandy system. Often systems derive their name from the central star, yet the Dandy systems has in essence two central stars. It is common to hear people throughout the galaxy refer to the Dandy system as Helios...less common Alethia, yet the Dandies themselves often refer to their planet and the system both as Demeter. For the Dandy people the word Demeter is interchangeable with planet and system.

The formation of the Dandy system is exceptionally rare in that the two stars, **Helios** and **Alethia**, are so closely equivalent in mass, composition, and age that any variation between the two lies in a range not significantly detectable by scientific measurement. The Dandy's system is a binary star system in the most equitable sense. Whereas the vast majority of binary star systems involve a primary star and a smaller, secondary star in orbit, the Dandy's system is composed of two stars locked in a cosmic minuet. From Helios it would seem Alethia is encircling and from Alethia it would appear the Helios was encircling.

Each star has it's own family of associated planets. Helios has the hot and uninhabitable **Hecate**, too close for life to form. Also the, rather volatile **Thoosa** was once colonized by early settlers to the region but abandoned a long time ago for reasons lost to history, most likely the unpredictable nature of plate tectonics and an unstable atmosphere were to blame. Besides a handful of planetoids and sub-planet bodies, Hecate and Thoosa are predominantly the orbiting bodies of Helios.

Alethia has a similarly scorched world known as **Thanatos**. Additionally Alethia possesses a stable planet known as **Astraeus** and the gas giant **Polyphemus**. For reasons also unclear neither Astraeus nor any of the moons of Polyphemus are inhabited though by modern galactic standards there lies many options for stable colonization. It is assumed that the early Dandies could not manage these worlds and never developed a need as they adapted appropriately to the world that, to this day, they call home.

That aforementioned home is a planet called **Demeter**. To which star may Demeter be said to belong? Demeter is balanced perfectly between the two suns and caught in the flow of their opposing rotations. To use the word *perfect* is perhaps a bit dramatic as imperfections in the balance do result in a certain periodicity of capture and release. Demeter is caught in between Helios and Alethia for a period of about fifteen to twenty thousand standard years. Once it wiggles its way out it then orbits one of the stars for a little over seven standard years before yet again getting caught in the gravity well between the two stars. The periodicity is 15-20 thousand years in; 7 years out. In the years out, Demeter might orbit either of the stars. For a detailed discussion on determining which star is orbited and to obtain a calendar of Demeter's projected orbital path for the next million years, or if suffering from insomnia read "*Stochastic fluctuations in the orbital differential of Demeter*" by Tandy Fantander, FGL.

What does this mean for Demeter? It means that Demeter is a planet bathed in light from two opposing suns; a world that would be cold confined to a single sun is made warm in perpetual light. Yes, Demeter is in perpetual light as true night only comes every fifteen to twenty thousand years.

Outside of the Goldilocks zone of either sun, the combined radiant energy of the both Helios and Alethia create a pseudo habitable zone in the gravity well between. This constant warmth to which Demeter has found itself caught has produced an extraordinary evolutionary advantage so conducive to life that no equal has been found. Even life from old Earth, the world that peppered the galaxy with the thinking beast, seems improbable...a won game of astronomical chance...compared to lonely Demeter whose fortune could do nothing but insure that life would crawl undeniably from the abyssal darkness into the luminous consciousness of the infinite.

Let us not forget that Earthly claim, our ownership of the mind, as no intelligent life has been found elsewhere other than from our shared origin. What form then does this life on Demeter take? The simplest term would be *vegetal*. Demeter is the domain of every imaginable green thing that might grow. Every tree, creeping vine, moss, flower, root, shrub, tuber, fruit, seed or grain, foliage of any kind one might find anywhere in the galaxy, an equivalent can be found on Demeter with a plethora of variations found nowhere else.

Though *vegetal* is a good term to imagine the nature of Demeter, the term is rather unscientific. Demeter also possesses an astounding variety of fungi, molds, mushrooms, algae, slimes, yeasts, lichens, diatoms, and bacteria. As different scientific traditions throughout the galaxy separate life differently amongst a large number of kingdoms (those of the Sol regions, or OrCa, generally accept six kingdoms while those of NoAr use twenty-three different kingdoms, for example) it might be easiest to think of life on Demeter as life that excludes the animal kingdom. Early cataloging of Demeterian life erroneously included a small variety of insectoids, but it was quickly discovered that these lifeforms were free-floating plants, motile seeding structures, or flagellum-fungi and not, in fact, sentient.

The image of a world ripe with vegetation, green and moist, conjures thoughts of paradise and must have seemed so to the early travelers that became the Dandies. The stark reality though is something else entirely. Geological data suggests Demeter greatly predates the formation of the Earth and though specific data is lacking it is unanimously assumed throughout the scientific community that life of Demeter predates Earth life as well. Some even go as far as to suggest that life in the Milky Way was first granted to Demeter. Regardless of the speculation, Demeter has an impressive evolutionary history and had achieved a bio-stability, the point where adaptation is no longer necessary, long before there was such an animal as the human being when Earth was a lonely rock on the opposite side of the galaxy. One can imagine that a world with such a history, one that excludes the animal, would not be particularly conducive to mammalian life.

This was the case for the early settlers. The two main obstacles facing them can be grouped into two general categories: the elements and resources.

Resources:

Despite being inundated with vegetation, acquiring food proved more of a challenge than anticipated for these settlers. Though fruit on Demeter is overly abundant one can imagine that a world absent of an animal evolutionary history would have little reason to produce *edible* fruit and this is very much the case on Demeter. There are fruits that can be eaten but they tend to be rare and hard to get. Most fruits of Demeter are hard, prickly, and designed to withstand calamity. They are fruits with a designed longevity making them durable and either woody or rock hard.

Edible seeds are abundant, but quite resource dependent in collection. The unbreakable husks and dense pods that hold them resist the exposure of their precious contents. The reason for this hardiness in both fruit and seed has to do with that periodicity that faces life on Demeter. For the fifteen to twenty thousand years that Demeter is snuggly between the two suns life is warm and lush. In the seven years out Demeter becomes cold and inhospitable. The resilience of these seeds and fruits are what allows many of the vegetation to re-flower once the warmth is returned. Their tough skins protect them from the years of cold.

There are plants that produce edible seeds and fruit that are more easily accessible to the Dandies, but surprisingly few. Oddly, a large number of plant species on Demeter reproduce by means other than seeding. Many, many species on Demeter have an unbelievably complex symbiosis that is responsible for their reproduction. In fact, it is said that most of the vegetation on Demeter is more accurately understood as an interconnected, interdependent, super-organism rather than a mere collection various individual species. For this reason, growth, expansion, and reproduction are functions of the whole based on availability and need. Unlike Earth and the kin it has spawned, Demeterian life is almost absent of that competitive survival aspect. For example, it is easy to find instances of greenery growing strong in the almost absolute darkness of thick overgrowth, acquiring resources from a vast interconnected root system. That very plant on an Earth-like world would quickly die alone in the dark.

Elements:

The second general category of obstacles to early colonization has to do with the elements. Obviously an entire planet of vegetation requires an enormous water supply and Demeter is exceptionally damp. The water cycle that supports this relies on vast oceans, rivers, lakes, and streams and the efficiency to circulate this water between source and sky. This results in powerful storms with alarming regularity. It is *always* rainy season on Demeter.

In addition to weather and the difficulty of maintaining adequate shelter the primary elemental danger lies in the voraciousness of life on Demeter. Pollen and mold spore are thick in the air and contaminate every water source available. All part of the process that generates life on Demeter, where resources are adequate germination is practically instantaneous. This is partly due to the need to quickly recover from the years of dormancy during Demeter's journey out of the gravity well and into the cold, but also an after effect of the symbiotic relationship between plant species. When growth begins it gorges on the collective resources and propagates rampantly. Early settlers of Demeter constantly faced the danger of a life support breach which would result in rapid deaths due to lungs full of flowering fungi and sproutlings emerging from the warm and moist flesh of the dead.

So what were these early colonizers to do with such inhospitality? One option might be to build better, stronger structures that could partition the people from the elements, but this is an unending fight. Let us not forget the primary tenant of transmography:

When a system comes under constant need for regeneration the system must be abandoned or changed. In such situations where neither abandonment nor change are options the external should be made internal.

This is the philosophical beginning of transmogrification. This is how the Dandies became who they are to this day.

The Transmogrified Body:

There were many changes required to make a human being suitable to this environment. Perhaps the first notable difference has to do with the skin of the Dandies. They adapted their skin to take advantage of the abundant light of Demeter. This photosynthetic adaptation has provided them with a variety of rich green skin-tones. In addition to chloroplast production, the tissue structure as a whole (flesh, organ, and bone) had to be modified to resist the elements and be less appealing to foreign germination.

Even with more durable skin these early settlers were still in need of a means of preventing organic contaminants from entering their delicate lungs. This was accomplished through a complete overhaul of the mouth, face, and sinus cavity in addition to a modulated immune system. Though Dandies do have a very small, moderately functional mouth, the main facial feature one will notice is a series of horizontal slit-sieves designed to filter out the bulk of the pollen and spore found in the air. The nose was abandoned in favor of these seven to ten (depending on size) slit-sieves that allow respiration while preventing inhalation of organic contaminant. These slit-sieves run horizontally beginning approximately where the bridge of the nose once was and continuing in rows down to the chin, each running ear to ear.

It should be said that knowledge of Dandy anatomy is incomplete and the other physical differences are unclear as to purpose and are perhaps the natural ramifications that result from the necessary modifications. These include elongated limbs and extremities and an exceptionally delicate and narrowed frame. The eyes have been modified into solid black orbs in the majority and the occasional solid red orb. The reason is unknown but it is speculated that an additional eye covering may be intentional to either resist organic contaminant or to possible filter out a specific spectrum of light which may help to identify certain species of plant that would be easily confused otherwise.

However, the main non-functional difference lies in what became of the human hair. The hair of the Dandies became wiry, standing on end and universally a shade ranging from a grayish white to a true white. This is where they acquired their almost galactically agreed upon name of *Dandies* as their modifications give them a certain resemblance to the matured dandelion flower of Earth. It should be said that though one's chance of ever encountering a Dandy is exceedingly rare that it may be inappropriate to call them by their commonly used name. These distant and unique people, when properly translated, call themselves the Children of Demeter.

There are many sources in the FGL for further reading on the Dandies, but most are fictionalized accounts as actual data is sparse considering the difficulty of travel to the Dandy system, the protected status of variant worlds, and the difficulty in communication.

For further reading please see:
"Classifications of Specie, Sub-specie, and Supra-organism Co-relationships of Demeterian Flora." by Fuhd Derbis. FGL
Also re-read the popular Dandy-based children's book:
"Where is Your Home?" author unknown. FGL.
Though it was not written by a Dandy or anyone who had probably ever encountered a Dandy, it is a common children's book galaxy wide and represents the general image the populace has of the Demertarian people.

There, almost unnoticeably in the luminous distance, were the two small stars of the Dandy's system. Bob entered by means of Helios and rode the outer orbit towards his destination of Demeter.
 He passed close enough to the surprisingly large planet Thoosa to pull a decent visual. It was obvious there was and had been a great deal of volcanic activity and Thoosa appeared to have a fury that warned of getting too close, but still had a certain beauty about it, a certain untouched purity that spoke of its unexploited potential.
 In a short time Bob found himself in the gravity well between stars and was approaching a faint green dot in the distance. When Bob reached Demeter he was amazed at the sight. It was completely green. Everywhere. He didn't know exactly what he had expected, but was sure he'd see some significant bodies of water, but no, only a deep verdant green. Bob occupied a stable orbit around the planet to give himself time to scan and think and, honestly, time to collect himself. He still felt that his grip on reality had been...not shaken, but somehow transposed throughout this very different realm in which he'd somehow materialized.
 There were two peculiarities about what his scan of the surface had revealed to him. One was the absence of visible bodies of water.
 His terminal displayed a demarcation of various oceans and lakes and dominant river structures, but when he magnified the visual, even greatly, all that he saw was vegetation...green on green on endless green. Bob couldn't help but think, "Good grief! It's everywhere."
 The amount of overgrowth was mind boggling. Perhaps these bodies of water were subterranean, but they had to be fairly accessible for this amount of growth. It was more likely that there were in fact oceans and lakes and river and streams, but for every one there was thick vegetation growing right out of, and through, it. Bob thought,

419

"Imagine! Several oceans covered in growth." The lesson here was that Bob needed to avoid these places because obviously some of the seemingly solid ground was quite less so than it appeared. He couldn't afford to lose a ship out here, alone, on the odd side of the galaxy. If this ship didn't make it, Bob wouldn't be coming back either...ever.

The second oddity revealed by the scan was the absence of construction. There really weren't buildings of any sort: no cities, towns, or even something reminiscent of a village. There were no ports (air or space), no orbiting constructs, nothing. There was nothing around Bob that spoke of any kind of civilization. Where could these people be hiding? Again, Bob wondered if there was some unseen subterranean aspect that he couldn't detect, but honestly the scanners were not picking up any significant rock formations other than bedrock deep, deep below the surface vegetation and a substantial soil sheath from which life grew.

The one exception to this was an equally peculiar reading. Apparently there are seven small pyramids spaced evenly around the globe. Small as in *small*. Each pyramid probably had a square footage only a little larger than Bob's apartment...which wasn't a big apartment. Yet, the crowning jewel of this curious finding was the material that composed these small pyramids: Fermiized gold. Fermiized gold is practically indestructible and completely non-corrosive. Bob really didn't know exactly what Fermiized gold was used for, but thought it was something that physicists used in small amounts for sub-particle string extraction and dark energy experimentation, and by small amounts meaning an atom or two which even that would be used for parts. Bob had never heard of a structure built of the stuff. Seven golden pyramids spaced equally around a sphere. Why?

Considering they were the only structures to speak of, Bob decided to land near one, the one closest to his current position, but first, due to the peculiarity of this situation, he planned on trying out the stillsuit. He wasn't willing to even enter the atmosphere of this planet without being completely prepared for whatever might be down there and whatever might have prompted the gift of the suit. Something here was not what it seems.

Bob had fiddled with the headpiece of the suit days earlier when the endless boredom of travel had reach a fevered pitch and drew him to find interest in any scrap of heretofore undigested information, regardless of the information's usefulness. He had re-read the entire list of ingredients of an empty bag of cheese pagodas, had wondered what his soap was made of, and pondered the number of elm trees still on old Earth...for some reason. One could use these large expanses of time for scholarly research, or something important, but acute boredom additionally robs the mind of ambition and prefers entertainment over knowledge. In that time the headpiece of the stillsuit was a nice change. It appeared, fresh from the case, as a sort of black metallic mandible...like a shiny jawbone with a triangular brace that fit over the bridge of the nose. Once positioned it pulled itself tightly around the back of the head and drew itself from the front jaw over the top of the head to meet the connection in the back. It was a bit like pulling some vacuum sealed plastic bag over one's head, and too a little startling at first as it took the briefest second before the filters and respirator kicked in meaning there was a slight moment of darkness where breathing was not possible.

Now Bob put the headpiece back on with an intent to use it. Once the headpiece became active there was about three seconds of startup scanning where the eyes accessed information from probably a dozen or so frequency spectra, a couple of which were blindingly bright, before it returned to what one would consider the standard range of human vision. Bob was greeted from the headpiece with a warning that there was no suit attached and containment was inoperable. Once he figured out how to dismiss this warning he began to look around the ship. Apparently the suit is sensitive to eye focus and will begin to draw information on something that is given more than passing attention. He looked at his ships console and the suit told him the type of console and the model of ship to which if belonged. Looking at the view screen and seeing the image of Demeter, the suit provided him with planet, system, and galactic location data along with atmospheric composition (elevated oxygen levels obviously), temperature, and current weather conditions (excessively windy apparently). Bob looked at that empty bag of cheese pagodas which the suit identified and suggested nearby options for acquisition that displayed the two words "not available".

The headpiece also had a barely noticeable row of icons in the far periphery of vision on each side. Eye attention accessed these icons which were useful for a variety of purposes. These icons were system tools, preferences, and a visual interface for changing the visual spectrum and whatnot. One displayed a terminal console that could easily be repositioned...you know, if for some reason you need to do some desk work or detailing whilst wearing a military grade stillsuit. In these preferences Bob made sure to identify that auto-translate was on, otherwise he most certainly would be unable to communicate with the Dandies. This was the first identifying trait that made sense to Bob, but there had to be some reason other than translation to go to the trouble of getting him a military grade stillsuit. What could it be?

Now, Bob put on the suit proper. The body of the suit was a flexible black metallic chest plate attached by some sort of dense tendrils to what seemed like scapula on the back. From these structures protruded more tendrils that attached to footplates with braces that must go around the knees and a set of finger rings. When Bob attached the appropriate bits to his appropriate bits the helmet informed him that the suit was to begin "enclosure protocol" and it was best for him to stand comfortable with good posture for the next moment. In a similar fashion to the headpiece, the suit enclosed itself around him snugly. It was an odd sensation, especially on the arms. The covering had a creeping goo-like feeling that crawled and solidified around him.

Bob looked at himself in the lavatory mirror and imagined that most of those that wore these suits were probably a little less...pear shaped...and Bob didn't appreciate that when he looked in the mirror the suit informed him of his current body mass index...a stat that seemed to take precedence over the other displayed vitals. Regardless, after a moment of getting accustomed to the suit, Bob was all business and ready to get to the surface and get this job done.

Bob decided to set a course for the nearest golden pyramid away from these unseen water masses but landing a reasonable distance since he really didn't know what these pyramids were, who was really down there, and what he was getting into. Caution was called for here and Bob didn't mind a bit of a walk.

* * *

Bob found the proper window and descended into the atmosphere of Demeter. The splash of orange from a fiery entry that illuminated the viewscreen momentarily cast shades of purple across the forest green below. Unbeknownst to Bob, this descending fireball was observed from the surface. His arrival was known.

After the atmospheric breach Bob's descent was turbulent, surprisingly turbulent, which he had blamed on the weather which had been forecast as "excessively windy". The deeper he plummeted into the atmosphere the more turbulence his little ship underwent. Additionally, the viewscreen was becoming less clear. The image before him was becoming hazy and obscured. None of this particularly bothered Bob until he got an alert from the ship's console expressing that the engines were working at a compromised efficiency and the ship had taken measures to compensate. When landing on a planet one obviously uses pulse engines rather than trans-space propulsion, but still these pulse engines should be working just fine yet the drop in efficiency was a good twenty percent and dropping.

422

Trying to identify the problem Bob could find nothing more than a high particulate warning and turbulence readings. At this point Bob was close to the surface but the efficiency of the engines had dropped a little over fifty percent and they were heating up in the compensation. It most likely wouldn't be a problem if he landed quickly, but he can *not* afford to burn out these engines this far away from civilization.

Bob made a rattling and shaky touchdown and quickly checked the status of the pulse engines. They were quite hot but fine. However, the console was lit up with a slue of warnings of external readings. Some involved the ship itself, but the one that caught his attention was an atmospheric warning: "Breathability alert: Atmospheric conditions due to unidentified particulate matter not compatible with life." It was concerning. Bob scanned the atmosphere again and got a very reasonable chemical breakdown of oxygen (though high levels), nitrogen, carbon dioxide, and insubstantial trace elements. Bob said to himself, "Well, I suppose this is what the suit is for" and released the lock on the cargo door.

When the door opened a crack, Bob was greeted by the bright light of Helios followed by a powerful gust that almost knocked him down. The wind was violent and warm, the warmth he could still feel through the suit, and carried in this wind was thick powder, like a snow that was quickly filling up the main chamber of his ship.

Bob hurriedly stepped out and closed the cargo door to avoid any more of whatever that was filling his ship, though when he set foot on the ground he fell to his knees before struggling to stand upright. He staggered for a moment and wondered if the suit was heavier than it had seemed, but he was fine in the ship that maintained an artificial gravity of one Earth standard. It had to be Demeter. The gravity here was stronger than it had appeared. It was similar in size to the Earth standard, so it didn't make much sense that it would be significantly different, but what he was experiencing seemed to him almost twice that of the standard, a fact he quickly corroborated with the help of the suit.

Looking around him Bob could see endless growth in all directions and was pelted by the wind that carried a thick powder which gave his surroundings a foggy, or perhaps hazy yet iridescent glow. After his eyes adjusted a bit, he could see the powder, which lay thick on the surroundings like winter snowfall, was a yellowish green in hue. He knelt down to scoop up a handful and stared at it intently to get a reading from the suit. The suit returned with a listing of 253 varieties of unknown pollen and mold spore. Yes, without the suit filtering breathable air for him, Bob would most certainly be dead here.

Bob struggled up from kneeling in this bad case of gravity and felt compelled to get moving. Whatever was going to happen here needed to take no longer than absolute necessity dictates so Bob lumbered forward.

It was like trudging through a terrible blizzard with pollen piling up in snowdrifts at times waist high, yet it was exceptionally warm and where the pollen met the ground it formed a kind of slurry, a thick muck. There was a *lot* of moisture here and where Bob tread was muddy and sticky. Between the gravity, the wind, the piles of pollen, and the muck, travel was slow and labor intensive. Pulling a direction from the suit which outlined the structure in the distance, and of which Bob could not physically see, he headed toward the golden pyramid.

In orbit, Bob had considered this walk twenty minutes tops. In reality it looked like it was going to take a good hour and a half at least. He had to stop and rest repeatedly. The gravity made it hard to breathe and he easily wore out. Also, he had to find his way around several clumps of growth that were far too dense making his path a winding, twisty route. He had been knocked down by the wind twice and getting up from the ground was no small task.

It's often the unknown that brings a certain life to the psyche. Like a rarefied air that seems to teem with an unseen electricity. Bob had been living this deeply and in spades the past few weeks and certainly that rarefied psychic air was turned thick as a good blackstrap molasses here on Demeter. There was far too much activity and exposure for Bob to be truly aware of his surroundings. Beyond the pollen and the wind there lay endless green, twisting vine and towering tree, winding wildly into deepening shades of darkness as the density of it seemed to prevent even a solitary ray of light from escaping. This modest respite...one would even hesitate to call it a clearing...provided some small break, a minuscule fissure, between the engulfing green extending shortly from here to the encompassing and ever unreachable horizon lost in the brush. Here Bob could see the sky and the light, an obvious reason for this particular area on which to land, but the green beyond was incalculable in its enormity, even hard to acquire a sense of perspective. It was some strange parallel to the nebula enclosing this system where life had demanded itself unlimited. Bob had often felt, and just as often commented, that everything in the universe seemed to be some kind of metaphor for everything else, like some golden circle upon which each point exists only because it learned to do so from the others.

In this contemplative state Bob was completely unaware of the fact that near one of the dense overgrowths that he circumvented he had walked within a couple of feet of a watchful Dandy. The Dandy blended seamlessly with the environment and was practically indistinguishable from the surrounding wildgrowth. The Dandy, long slender limbs and deep black eyes, stood motionless except for the gradual swivel of the head as Bob passed by. The Dandy was not afraid, just curious, and did not follow.

In time Bob came into rather close proximity of the approaching pyramid, close enough to see a bit of it over the trees. This gave him a moderate sense of relief in that there was an endpoint in sight. He complemented this relief by resting near some kind of oak tree and catching his breath. After a moment of resting his eyes and slowing his breathing, which helped considerably in this heightened gravity, he notices something odd about the tree. Extending from the tree was a descending protrusion that Bob couldn't help but see as something like an arm. It, like the tree, was covered in a thick fuzzy green moss, but did seem out of place. Extending up from the arm a bit was a round protrusion that had an uncanny resemblance to a skull of some sort shortly beneath the bark of the tree. It had to be some natural formation, but the proportions were right, that is, the placement of arm to skull. Most likely Bob was experiencing pareidolia, or seeing objects in the clouds...just a simple random natural occurrence that when given to the mind is made into some familiar correlation...nothing more.

A while later Bob entered into the vicinity of the pyramid which seemed to be more of a clearing, though peppered with these rather tall and gangly, viny trees. It was here that Bob resolved the mystery of the oak tree. Before him, and not far from the pyramid, was one of these gangly, viny trees and slumped over, partial protruding from the base, was the body of a Dandy. Half of the body had been absorbed by the tree and only a portion of the upper torso and one extending arm was identifiable. Not sure what to make of this, Bob stepped away and looked around at the other trees in the area. Yes, each of them had at least one, sometimes two or three, bodies of Dandies that had been grown over by the trees. Was this was some sort of macabre land of the dead for the Dandies? Bob even wondered if they had all met a similar fate and perhaps this planet was vacant.
Pushing onward Bob couldn't help but consider these reclaimed bodies. Why had they not decayed? The parts visible often seemed unspoilt. It really didn't make any sense but he had hoped that maybe the pyramid might have some answers.

When he had come close to the pyramid Bob could see that the face facing him did have a set of airlocks and he might be able to get inside. It was a sight to see. The vibrant Fermiized gold of the pyramid was explicitly out of place against the swirling backdrop of natural color. It, especial being struck by the light of Helios, seemed to radiate light and give a fiery aura to the surrounding vegetation.

Close to the opening there was yet another gnarled and gangly tree with the body of a Dandy pulled close into its bulk. The Dandy seemed to have been sitting, but the process of absorption had pitched this body sideways. The abdomen and most of the chest was completely absorbed, but the head protruded and slumped forward. The left arm seemed to dangle free but the other appeared to reach backward and curl away into the trunk of the tree. Toward the base some angular, almost exposed root-like appendages, could be made out to be the former Dandies legs mostly absorbed.

Bob leaned in close and was amazed at the preservation of the flesh. Perhaps this process occurred considerably faster than one might assume, or there was something preventing the decay, but it was decisively unsettling. A startling bolt of fright then hit Bob and knocked him backward harshly onto his posterior. That start came from the body of the absorbed Dandy that unskillfully turned a shaky head towards Bob. This thing was alive. It turned towards Bob with the dexterity of a newborn whose meager musculature is inadequate to control their massive heads.

Bob looked at the Dandy, then looked to his surroundings to see if there was other detectable movement. It was a panic response. He was in a strange place of which he didn't know the rules. After a moment Bob carefully approached the absorbed Dandy which had returned to its motionless state. He stood and stared several minutes, then attempted to communicate with it. He said a variety of things, made a variety of sounds, and a few of these sparked a similar motion but soon Bob decided this movement seemed more reactive than intentional. Bob was unable to communicate in any acknowledgeable way and assumed it must have been a reaction to the change in light, or the vibration of his steps...something. It didn't seem aware.

This left Bob a little shaken which in turn spurred him to get into the pyramid, see what's going on, then get back to his ship as soon as possible. The opening of the pyramid was a double doored airlock which had upon the seam the indention of an elongated human hand...a Dandy hand. Bob didn't know what was inside and attempted several readings that produced nothing. The suit scanner could not penetrate the pyramid nor access anything from it. With no other option, Bob placed a hand firmly on the indentation all the while reminding himself that he was in a military-grade stillsuit so if there was something dangerous inside it would have to be *pretty* horrible to do much to him.

The opening of the doors proved to be quite anti-climactic. They slid open silently and revealed a darkened room. Inside was a fairly empty space with nothing but a solid table-sized console in the middle...probably for nothing more than terminal access. The ceiling was only about seven or eight feet meaning there could be something above, but not much considering this was not a very large pyramid.

Bob walked to the console, which seemed inoperable, and took a look at the ceiling wondering if there was some access to the upper portion. He could see none. Unknown to Bob, standing behind him in the open doorway of the pyramid stood a figure in silhouette bathed in the white light of distant Helios. The figure was that of a Dandy or, more appropriately now, one of the children of Demeter.

Chapter Thirty-one: Whom Nightshade Destroys

Nu-00-Zeta-01 errantly cycled awareness into feedback loop and closed self off from reality. Terminus initiated.

Elder grain 1-Alpha-000-0 resends transmission: temperature requirements of stasis inadequate. Requests solar occupancy.

Grain Omega-00-Tau-naught has encountered unknown phenomenon. Uncertain of what to transmit.

Bob and the Dandy stared at each other silently for what in normal social circumstances would be considered and inappropriately long period of time. The Dandy was tall, slender, and rich green with large orb-like eyes, black as night. This Dandy stood quietly looking at Bob with an occasional suspicious eye toward the surrounding interior of the pyramid. This tall green variation on the human design gave a very slow wringing of the hands as time passed.

Bob had about a dozen things going through his mind in this moment, but seemed to settle on the wringing of the hands. The Dandy didn't seem worried, or anxious…at least from what Bob could read of the facial expressions from this very different face…but rather, calm…tranquil and at ease. The Dandy was, in fact, very much at ease, the overriding emotional content experienced being curiosity. The suspicious looks around the room were just that, an unfamiliarity with being enclosed.

After another stretch of silence had passed a word was uttered.

Dandy: "Hello".

The sound of the Dandy was coming through the headpiece of Bob's stillsuit and a lit transparent icon in his lower field of vision held the indication *"translated from the Demeterian"*.

Bob: "Hi". Which the suit, as far as Bob could tell, translated his word in kind.
Another silence followed.
Bob: "My name is Bob. I was sent here to contact someone about acquiring some information."
The Dandy seemed surprised.
Dandy: "My name is Crumb."
Another silence followed.
Bob: "Hi Crumb..."
Crumb: "Hi", interrupting. The Dandy then offered a large smile that seemed exaggerated as if to make sure the gesture was understood.
Silence.
Bob: "Yeah, hi. You are a...one of the children of Demeter."
Crumb: "I am. We all are here. ...Where is your home?"
Bob: "Well, I'm from Helen's Crown."
The Dandy looked confused.
Bob: "I was born on Earth."
Surprised, the Dandy let out odd laugh-like sound.
Crumb: "Earth! You have come a long, long way."
Bob: "I have."
Still fresh on Bob's mind and somewhat troubling him, Bob addressed what he had seen outside the pyramid.
Bob: "May I ask, those people outside...they are stuck in the trees..."
Crumb, confused: "Yes, they are."
Bob: "What has happened to them?"
It took Crumb a minute to rationalize why this was confusing to Bob.
Crumb: "Oh, they are very old."
Bob: "...yes...and?"
Crumb: "Ah, I see what you are asking. Here, when we get very old, we sit peacefully and grow into Demeter."
Bob, understanding: "I see. This is the process the elderly undergo in death."
Crumb: "There is no death here, only reclamation."
Bob: "Hmm...so this is a place the children of Demeter come to be...reclaimed? Have I done something improper by coming here?"
Crumb, not exactly sure of the context: "You are welcome here."
Crumb: "Why have you come here?"

Bob explained as succinctly as he could the story of the deaths, the virus, and the madman causing it all. He then told Crumb of Dr. Morris and the efforts to combat the disease. Bob could tell the story wasn't lost on the Dandy, but some aspects of it Crumb found very strange. Towards the end of the tale Bob notice over Crumbs shoulder and out through the opening of the pyramid that there were at least a dozen other Dandies standing motionless in the clearing, all looking intently on what was going on inside.

Bob, lost in thought: "Crumb, why are there no buildings here...no structures except for these pyramids?"

Crumb had to think for a moment: "Oh, yes. Our ancestors had towers, though that was a very long time ago. We've seen images in our history."

Bob: "...right...so...why are there none now?"

It obviously didn't make much sense to Crumb, but Crumb decided on what it probably was that Bob was after in his question.

Crumb: "They are too perishable here."

Bob: "Ok..."

Back to business Bob asked, "This man, the one I explained had created the virus, could he have been here in the recent past?"

Crumb: "I believe so. We assumed you were him...but you talk much more."

Bob, thinking, *not sure exactly how to take that*, asked "When? When was he here?"

Crumb: "The crest of Polyphemus over Alethia's decline."

This was something either not translated properly or not translatable. Bob realized it did make sense that the Demeterian concept of time would be measured wholly differently considering they were trapped between two suns for a good twenty thousand years. A yearly cycle around either sun would have little meaning to them. He might could find out from research or some other means, but either way the damning factor was that Moloch had been here.

Bob: "What happened? What happened when he was here?"

Crumb: "He poked one of us."

Bob: "He *poked* one of you."

Crumb, for some reason elongating the word: "He *pooooked* one of us."

Crumb: "I can show you."

Crumb walked over to the console in the center of the pyramid near Bob. Placing a hand on the surface it lit up with a host of iconography that Crumb quickly maneuvered, much more dexterously than Bob would have assumed. Bob had to look away temporarily as the suit was trying to translate everything on the console and the doubled field of view was going to quickly give Bob a headache. In moments a virtual cube appeared over the table producing a gritty three-dimensional rendering of a Dandy sitting and looking back and forth around the room.

Crumb: "This is a rendering of the interview". Pointing, "This was the one who encountered the strange man."

Bob watched the video.

Unseen Dandy voice: "First, say who you are."

Dandy on screen: "Me? Say who I am?"

Unseen voice: "Yes, say who *you* are."

Dandy on screen: "I'm Schnitt. You know I'm Schnitt."

Unseen voice, irritated: "For the *recording* Schnitt. Not for me."

Schnitt, eyes darting around: "Where do I look?"

Unseen voice, irritated: "Here, *here*!"

Schnitt, confidently looking forward: "I am Schnitt."

Unseen voice: "Where did this happen?"

Schnitt: "Ouac forest, near the winding stair clearing."

Unseen voice: "Tell the story, tell the story."

Schnitt, contemplating: "Well, there was a guy. He was not a child of Demeter."

Unseen voice: "And how did you know this?"

Schnitt: "He was short and squatty. He wore something over him...a black clothing."

Unseen voice: "What did he do?"

Schnitt: "I looked at him but he said nothing. He has some stick...a shiny one with vines...he pointed it and I could feel my heart squeeze, then it stopped."

Unseen voice: "And why did he do this?"

Schnitt: "I don't know. I think he thought it would bring my ending."

    At this point Crumb paused the recording and asked Bob,

Crumb, curious: "Is this how it works for your people?"

Bob, confused: "How what works?"

Crumb: "If your heart stops for a while, it won't start again?"

Bob: "Well, yeah...without medical treatment."

Crumb, fascinated: "Hmm...and it must beat always? You have nothing to compensate if it stops?"

Bob: "That's the short and long of it."

Crumb: "Very interesting. And you only have one?"

Bob: "Afraid so."

Crumb stared at Bob for what seemed like a long time.

Crumb: "Let's continue." And the recording resumed.

Unseen voice: "He thought you to be dead. What did you do?"

Schnitt: "I acted in accordance to his wishes, which I thought of as only being properly polite."

Unseen voice: "Dead?"

Schnitt: "I pretended to be. ...or, I pretended to not be. What is the correct way to say?"

Unseen voice: "It doesn't matter. What did he do after?"

Schnitt, pointing to the upper shoulder: "He poked me."

Unseen voice: "He poked you?"

Schnitt: "He *pooooked* me."

Unseen voice: "With what?"
Schnitt: "I don't know. With something... and took some juices from by shoulder."
Unseen voice: "What then?"
Schnitt: "He put them in a tube and left."
Unseen voice: "When you were sent to intercept him, you brought with you moorl spore?"
Schnitt: "I did. It was everywhere."

Crumb stopped the recording and turned to the console. He then retrieved a video of the man in question leaving. It was very brief. They managed to get a grainy shot of him before he left. Crumb turned to Bob and asked: "Is this the person you are looking for?"

Bob looked carefully and though the figure was in a similar stillsuit masking any features, the little unmarked medical transport he scurried into which quickly shot into the air was the same. It was, of course, Moloch.
Bob: "I'm sure that is him."

Bob could also see from a translated timestamp on the projection that the image had been made several years ago, all of which did not bode well for stopping Moloch. Bob was a few years behind him and Moloch had seemed to account for every potentiality.
Crumb: "Was any of this helpful?"
Bob: "Well...yes and no. It was what I needed to know, but it looks like I may be too late...we all may be too late."
Crumb offered an understanding nod which Bob returned.
Bob: "Crumb, at the end of the video they mentioned something about a spore that Schnitt brought to the encounter."
Crumb: "Yes. Moorl spore."
Bob: "Right, what was that about?"
Crumb: "It gives off a unique energy signature, a special type of decay."
Bob: "What do you use it for?"
Crumb: "Tracking. We can, with enough time, tell where someone might have gone or where they might be."
Bob: "And you could tell where this man went?"
Crumb: "Well, it is difficult, it involves summing readings from nearby jump-ship activity. Where they pick up the trail can give some information on the path."
Bob: "Do you know anything about that man's whereabouts?"
Crumb: "It seems from here he went somewhere not populated. No jump-ship traffic. We got a reading several months ago that was most likely from indirect tangential detection, meaning it is likely several years old and about the time this man came to Demeter."

Bob: "What does that mean, exactly?"

Crumb: "It means we don't really know where he went, but we know a general probability of direction and distance of the reading."

Bob: "And...what does that mean...*exactly*?"

Crumb: "We believe he went from here to a planet known as the Silent World. It is a guess because there really is nothing else anywhere around there. We are about as far as thinking life can be found and this planet is a little further. I can give you the coordinates...but it is just a guess."

Bob: "I would appreciate that. Thank you."

Crumb: "Is there any other way in which we might be helpful?"

Bob explained again some details of the virus and the efforts to stop it. He then requested some biological data to have analyzed by Dr. Morris and Crumb was more than happy to accommodate. Crumb turned to the console and began scrolling through pages of data looking for the correct procedure to obtain and transport a sample. It was curious to Bob that Crumb seemed knowledgeable of the console and had a considerable amount of information, but seemed unfamiliar with it all...not sure exactly how to go about it. Bob wondered how their society was structured, what kind of education system might be in play...if any...or if knowledge of the past was passed down in an oral tradition akin to our ancient common ancestors. It seemed almost certain that the only structures survivable on the planet were in fact these seven golden pyramids and were most likely the only source of anything one might call technology.

While Crumb was fiddling with the console Bob noticed out beyond the opening of the pyramid, in that surrounding clearing, he could see seven or eight more Dandies standing motionless but all looking his direction. These were not the partially absorbed Dandies of the graveyard, but healthy, free Dandies most likely attracted by curiosity. Each was standing tall doing the same slow wringing of hands that Crumb had done when they met. At some point Crumb noticed Bob and turned to see what had caught Bob's attention. When Crumb saw the others Crumb's face wrinkled and a batting gesture was directed towards them as if to say go away. Seeing this, each Dandy slowly curled their upper torso to the left before returning upright...which must mean something...something at which Bob could only guess.

Crumb returned to the console and managed to produce a cylinder from below it, very much like the others in which Bob had acquired samples. Crumb then looked to the cylinder, then console, then cylinder, then console again. During this Bob peeked outside again and saw the same set of Dandies had moved closer to the opening of the pyramid. Bob hadn't seen any of them move, but they were markedly closer. Beyond them were more that hadn't been there shortly before. When Crumb noticed, another gesture was offered and the response was the same for the now dozen or so Dandies in the surrounding area: a bending of the torso to the left.

Crumb, reading carefully from the console, pulled a slender tube from the cylinder which was full of a powerful preservative. Turning the base of the tube caused a rather wide needle to emanate from the top. Taking the three inch needle, Crumb jabbed it deeply into the area where one might find the sternum on a standard human being. Bob wondered about it. It sure didn't seem like Crumb had any concern for puncturing an internal organ, nor did it seem like the jab was careful or calculated in any way. Regardless, a dark green goo was intermingled with the clear preservative and returned to the cylinder, which Crumb promptly handed to Bob.

As Bob took the cylinder he noticed Crumb making that same wrinkled face toward the opening of the pyramid. When Bob turned there were four Dandies just inside the opening of the pyramid and a couple of dozen beyond. Still, Bob had never actually witnessed them moving.

Crumb stood facing the others then looked to Bob.

Crumb: "Bob, this is Paert, Guba, Cage, and Olive. They are very nosy."

At the introduction each Dandy offered the widest smile available to them considering the small dimensions of their actual mouth, however, their gill-like slit-sieves made them kind of look like they were always smiling with several mouths. Bob also wondered if the word *nosy* was merely an approximation in translation from the suit, or if it was a literal translation. It would be interesting if they maintained the expression considering their people haven't had anything like a nose is tens of thousands of years.

Crumb: "Bob, I wish I could help more than only this data and goo."

Bob: "I appreciate what you have already done."

Crumb: "Bob, maybe I could tell you a story that might prove helpful. It has been helpful to us."

Bob: "...sure. I'm up for a story."

Crumb smiled: "A long time ago, when we had only been here a short time, our ancestors struggled greatly. The environment here was terribly inhospitable to them. We believe this because we have been told we were once like you and you, even with your fancy suit, would not have lasted long here without help."

Bob raised an eyebrow and nodded in agreement.

Crumb: "It was a long time before we became free and the stories of our early struggles are horrific and hard to understand. The problem here has never been the resources of life. That is to say, there is never a shortage of food or healing medicines. They grow everywhere in vast overabundance. The problems with survival here are the elements that interfere with the standard human design. You've experienced to a small degree one of these...the pollen, spore, and seeding plants of all kinds. It is quite hard to parse the air from the germ. But even overcoming this, much of the life here finds the fleshy human a perfect medium of germination, much of this life being microscopic. Death and disease were rampant. It was a constant struggle for our ancestors to fight off such a world and their fighting was woefully ill-placed. You see, this world is not like so many of the others peppering the galaxy where life grows from competition of resources. No, this is a world that very much wants to make you part of the whole. It wants for you to become one with it, a symbiotic union, but the standard human design, such as that of our ancestors, wished to cling to a form familiar to them...a false ideal of identity. It was a spiritual stepping for a missing stair, to use a phrase you might find familiar."

Bob wondered if that expression was spoken in Earth speak, but couldn't tell through the stillsuit's translation.

Crumb: "We have an old story that is a parable of our transformation. Everything changed for us when we found the creeping nightshade."

Bob: "The creeping nightshade?"

Crumb: "Yes. Our creeping nightshade is akin to your angel of death. When our ancestors had been here only a few hundred years two factors led to their near demise. One was critical overpopulation. Again, it wasn't food or medicine that overpopulation burdened; it was the mechanisms of fighting the elements that were stretched far too thin. The second factor involved the influx of foreign materials to combat these elements. For reasons we don't know, whoever and from wherever our early people were supported, ended that support. Our ancestors were abandoned and isolated."

Bob wondered if he could find out some of that information. It had to be recorded somewhere, didn't it?

Crumb: "In the isolation, overpopulation, and dwindling protection, fighting broke out. Wars began. The least likely of all worlds to experience war was embroiled in it. The common denominator to all wars, of course, is the human being."

Bob: "It does seem like a thing to which we have committed ourselves...at least as far as the hundred thousand plus years of recorded history will attest to."

Crumb: "Exactly. It was in this fighting, as the story goes, that our ancestors encountered the creeping nightshade."

Bob silently wondered.

Crumb: "The creeping nightshade was found hidden in a thicket of brambles and, for human beings, was easily identified as a bringer of death. Death radiated as some dark aura from the knotted sticky vines of the plant."

"When first found, in fear the discoverer asked, 'what are you?', at which the creeping nightshade shot a bolt of darkness, like the arcing discharge of lightning, into the head of the finder. In his head that bolt formed a thought by which the creeping nightshade could answer his question: 'I am the great gift giver. I am the bringer of death."

"Running and terrified, the finder had just enough time to make it back to camp and tell this story before he fell lifeless and still. In fear of a mysterious disease his body was taken far from camp and burned, the ashes carried further by a strong southerly wind."

"Though fear kept the bulk of them away, curiosity mused some to find and prod this creeping nightshade. Perhaps, it was thought, that they could be the controllers of death, blighting their enemies, winning their wars...and they did. If winning a war ever meant something, then perhaps it would have mattered, but the creeping nightshade had far different plans for our people."

"Where each body fell, there grew a small knotted, sticky, and tangled vine...a twisting little thorny nightshade creeping slowly upward. Soon, it was found everywhere, speaking softly into the minds of our people and they fell in frightening numbers. Emaciated, lucid, helpless, hopeless, and cold, our people fell in *frightening* numbers."

"How could one conquer such an adversary? How could we overcome the creeping nightshade? When our people encountered the nightshade some would run in fear. Running only tripped one up, got one entangled in the gnarly vine and death was the gift received. Some would embrace the nightshade. For them it was their hopeful entrance into power, to bring death to their enemies, to whomever they chose. In this sticky embrace they found they could no longer let go and their own death was the gift received. Those who fought it found it a superior opponent. Poked, pricked, and entangled on the thorny vines, they found escape by the only means available and death was their gift."

"How then, you may ask, are we here today? How did we transition beyond the time of the creeping nightshade? We found not to run, not to embrace, and not to fight it. We sat quietly in its presence. We listened when it spoke and nothing more. We found in this quietness the foundation of our being, of our consciousness, and let go of those false things to which we had clung so tightly, those false concoctions of identity. In our listening we heard, for the first time, the world now to which we did belong, a thing we had only been able to see as a mess of countless, countless particulated forms, but now could feel breathing as one breath...as our own breath...and we were inseparable from it. Yes, we rise, we fall, we rise, we fall. We listen to the nightshade when it speaks. But, for the thing we have awakened into, there is no place for death, only life endlessly renewed."

Something of this story spoke to Bob and reached a deeply thoughtful space within him.

Crumb: "Perhaps you are embroiled in a struggle with the creeping nightshade right now. I would not suggest you do anything other than what it is in your nature to do, but should you find the struggle fruitless perhaps sitting quietly in its presence and listening will grant you the transition you seek. That thing you fear may be the workings of your salvation."

Crumb: "We have an expression that I don't know how well will be translated."

Bob nodded.

Crumb: "She is darkness."

Bob: "She is darkness?"

Crumb: "Those things we fear, fear itself, the unknown and the potential within that unknown. She is darkness and is ever present. She exists within and beyond all worlds. She is all encompassing and all embracing."

Crumb: "She is darkness and without her there is no medium through which light may pass. She is darkness. The perpetual unknown against which all things known may be discerned. The boundary between here and there, this and that. She who exists in both the eternal and the everlasting in between being and non-being."

Bob was aware that for a culture such as the Dandies, for whom photosynthesis was a primary giver of life in a world bathed almost always in sunshine, the concept of light would have a powerful significances in their philosophy as would darkness.

Bob thought for a moment and offered: "It is a common thing for us to say that it is only by the background that we can comprehend the subject. It is impossible to understand light without the knowledge of its absence. It is impossible to know the self without a knowledge of the universe to which that self belongs...so these things are a continuum and so are inseparable."

Crumb, smiling: "Then you have seen her too."

Crumb, gestured to Bob's shoulder saying: "Bob, you should probably go. Demeter is already trying to reclaim you and will do the same to your ship before long."

Bob looked to his upper arm and shoulder and yes, in fact, there were little tendrils winding upward from something...or several things...germinating, interwoven in the fabric of the stillsuit.

Crumb: "Also, there is a storm coming. If you don't get out ahead of it, it is doubtful you will ever leave."

Bob, alarmed: "Oh. Ok, thank you very much for your help. I wish you all the very best."

As Bob walked toward the opening he waved politely to each of the Dandies in the pyramid. They followed him as he strode out. Yes, the wind was definitely picking up and Bob could see it carrying away strands of the Dandies hair as it blew. Bob was still tired from the heavy gravity and it was a trek to get back. He needed to leave now.

Crumb: "Bob, before you can take off your suit you'll need to decontaminate yourself and your entire ship. Otherwise it will start growing on and in you. It's not survivable."

Bob: "Uh...ok. Thanks."

Bob waved to them all and headed out as fast as he could, which was quite slow. He legged it to the edge of the clearing before he had to rest near a tall oak-like tree guarding the entrance to the thicker brush he needed to transverse. Looking back toward the pyramid and beyond Bob could see a mountainous storm cloud in the distance crawling with lightning. In front of it was a massive wall of yellowish-green dust, pollen and spore being kicked up by the weather. Turning back to the oak Bob noticed that quite high up on the trunk was another absorbed Dandy. Only the upper torso and head could be easily seen. The legs were gone and the arms seemed to reach upward into the branches. The head gently turned to make eye contact with Bob and offered a gentle smile. If Bob didn't get out soon he'd be absorbed into this place as well, though not quite as peacefully.

Bob was putting everything he had into getting back to the ship. The terrain and gravity was making this a terrible job. He was beyond exhausted and certainly had pulled and strained most of his musculature. If it wasn't for the suit keeping his shape, Bob would have probably curled up into a tight ball of cramping spastic muscles...or at least that's what he was certain of due to the strain of unexpected prolonged exercise. He wanted to take a rest but, as he kept looking back, the storm seemed to be making frightening headway. The wind was harsh enough and Bob had trouble landing the ship through the thickness of the polleny atmosphere as is. If this storm hit, it would surely either rip his little ship apart or bury it in a thick slurry of mud, pollen, and debris. Bob estimated that depth to be almost exactly six feet under. No, there was no time to rest yet.

In this area, and according to the suit, Bob felt he should surely be able to see his ship in the distance, but as of yet could not. It was then that Bob heard a crack of thunder unlike anything he'd

438

experienced before. It was loud enough that it had activated some involuntary instinct causing him to crouch down and cover his head. This seemed to happen before the sound of the thunder had made it to his awareness and left a slight split second where he was wondering why he was crouching and what was going on. The next small sliver of a second, when his mind had time to process the experience, he realize what had caused the panic and compensated by struggling to a standing position and trudging onward. The storm was close.

At the site where he landed, Bob could still not see his ship. The suit drew a nice outline of it, but it had been completely grown over and was not visible. It was a mess of tangly vines and grasses, little sproutlings, and things globby and goopy. Bob began pulling it off of the ship which would have been job enough had he not been for a considerable jog through brush and heavy gravity. He cleared enough to, in his opinion, unburden the ship but spent some time clearing absolutely everything he could from the pulse engines. It was a big mess.

While he was tending to the first engine Bob felt a smattering of raindrops that hit like descending pebbles in the strength of Demeter's gravity. He turned to see a wall of pollen that had consumed the surrounding forest and would be over him very soon. Beyond that was dark thunder clouds which had devoured the remainder of the sky.

By the time he had cleared the second pulse engine the smattering of raindrops had become a steady sprinkle. The wind was becoming fierce and the area was visually hazy from the incoming pollen storm. Bob bolted into his ship and sat at the command console. He started up the pulse engines and let them run until they had burned off the remaining contaminants and had reached an adequate efficiency for liftoff. This took more time than he had hoped.

While he waited on the engines, Bob looked around the cabin. His instinct was to get out of this uncomfortable suit but knew well to take Crumb's advice. He needed to first decontaminate his ship...which was its own problem...but couldn't worry about that now. It was just as startling inside his ship as it had been outside. There was stuff growing everywhere. Mossy, licheny, little sprouting things were all over the place. It was that brief moment when Bob left the ship that enough got in and decided to make due with what it found. The lavatory was crawling with growth, the storage had things poking out from around the edges of the door, every console held tiny white sproutlings, the vents were creeping with moss, and *stuff*...which really is the best word in this case...*stuff* was floating in the air. On the floor, a previously empty bag of cheese pagodas now

439

seemed plump with some spindly green grassy lifeform. All of this and Bob had been gone for perhaps four hours. The console displayed several warnings about air quality, contaminants, and a life-support efficiency compromise, but Bob could only focus on the pulse engines for now. They were almost there.

When the engines were barely adequate for the task, Bob commanded a liftoff and his little ship struggled upward into the stormy atmosphere. The little ship rattled and jostled, lost altitude several times but regained, and climbed enough over the treeline to head laterally and quickly away from the storm.

If one could have seen the sight from the right vantage point, it would be a marvelous intersection between colliding fronts. On one side was the wall of torrential darkness and rain the entire height of the atmosphere with the footing of a yellow-green pollen storm. In opposition to this was a cloudless blue sky footed with the rolling green of wilderness. From the darkness and into the blue a small speck, a mere insignificant dot, broke free. It was Bob's ship and the moment it hit the clear blue it climbed skyward until gone, returning to the blackness of space from whence it came. *She is darkness* and Bob was once again in her endless embrace.

***

Bob had plotted a return path and was lost in thought. His immediate problems were far from over. The ship was not livable and the little things growing everywhere were causing his life-support systems to fail. He could survive in the suit, for now, but still needed to do something quick to solve the life-support problem. The suit had about an hour of breathable air in an airless environment, but Bob was at least ten hours from exiting the nebula and when a jump-ship would show up to take him elsewhere was another unknown question. Regardless of the amount of air with which Bob could or could not make do, it wouldn't matter much if life-support shut down and things got a little chilly.

Crumb said the ship needed to be decontaminated, which was painfully obvious now, but Bob's ship lacked any such process...at least the level of decontamination required to stop Demeter from taking over his ship. This was possibly a bad situation until Bob came up with a rather simple solution: expose himself and the innards of the ship to the vacuum of space.

At this point Bob had left Demeter far behind and had passed beyond the orbital path of Thoosa. His trajectory was to angle near Helios to sling him a bit faster away, but this couldn't wait. Bob came to a full stop in the middle of nowhere and accessed some special commands at the console. First, Bob needed to disengage several locks that prevented one from opening their ship in deep space. Second, he needed to put a time limit on the process in case something went haywire. Yes, Bob would be leaving the ship and if something went wrong he wanted the ship to come and get him.

The idea was to make sure any little living thing was deprived of air, frozen solid, and irradiated fully in the light of Helios. Setting the proper protocols, Bob strapped himself to a cargo support to prevent the vacuum from hurtling him out at an unfriendly speed. The cargo door slowly opened to lessen the effect, but it still yanked him toward it, toward the outer dark.

Once the doors were fully open Bob unstrapped himself and carefully floated out. When Bob was a good hundred feet or so from the ship he stretched and relaxed into the quiet of space. It was very peaceful. It should have made him nervous, but he only felt peace and calm now. It was relaxing to go from an environment with a bad case of gravity to weightlessness and the darkness was soothing to the eyes, but it was not a desensitizing darkness as the warm glow of Helios could be seen in the distant periphery. Beyond that darkness, and when Bob's eyes became accustomed to the dark, was the prismatic glow of the surrounding nebula which seemed to spontaneously come alive. It was glorious.

Several times Bob had notice some kind of debris floating slowly by. He couldn't catch a good look, and was sure it was just the average rocky or icy space debris, but then something floating in the distance seemed to reflect a deep blue. Not an ice-blue, but almost a royal blue thick as paint. Curious. Several minutes later one floated gingerly by very close to Bob and he got a good look at it. It was some delicate little thing...like a...tendrilled, winged thing, but solid and smooth, like it was made of skin, small enough to fit in the palm of the hand.

Moments later another floated by, then another, and another. They were sparsely distributed, but everywhere. Bob reached out to allow one to gently intercept his hand and when it lightly touched, it's little wing-like tentacles grasped almost imperceptibly before releasing and floating onward. Bob's attention prompted the suit to identify the little critter as a Glaucus Galacticus.

Glaucus Galacticus
Compiled from the resources of the Free Galactic Library (FGL)

The origin of the **Glaucus Galacticus**, commonly referred to as "vacuum slug", is highly speculative. It is believed that the creature was modified from old Earth sea slugs for the purpose of terraformation, though little evidence remains in our collected history. If so, it carries the assumption that it was one of the earliest attempts at distant world terraformation and must have accompanied interstellar travelers in pre-Dandy colonization. They are found exclusively in the barren space between Thoosa and Hecate in orbit around the Dandy's sun Helios.

It is speculated that there was at one time a small planet that was deemed suitable for habitation, perhaps more so than the Dandies world Demeter, and terraformation was conducted using the modified sea slug for some unknown purpose. The terraformation may have proved more problematic than expected and the world was abandoned leaving it the domain of the modified sea slug. An early colonization attempt that was so abandoned could possibly account for the lack of information in historical records but a greater omission lies in the planet itself. It's no longer there.

Compounding speculation, it is assumed the planet was destroyed, most likely by a large asteroid. Evidence of this event can be found in the debris in orbit of Helios in what is known as the **Glaucus Galacticus band**, the orbit of the vacuum slug, where there is a mix of two distinctly different types of debris which could be attributed to a mix of planetary and extra-solar asteroid, though admittedly adequate testing of the debris has never been fully executed.

In the process of transmogrification, the art of modifying a life form for a specific purpose, much has been borrowed from one of Earth's tiniest inhabitants the Tardigrade, more commonly known as the Water Bear. The Water Bear is one of the few known life forms that can exist unharmed in the vacuum of space and for this reason there is speculation that the origin of the Water Bear is not terrestrial but perhaps a traveler from another place that found it's way to Earth upon some wayward rock in prehistory, though complete evidence for this is lacking. Regardless of the Water Bear's origin, this tough little creature has been a model for various modified species borrowing this bit and that of its genetic code.

The main purpose of imbuing modified species with such a rugged sturdiness is obviously to make them stand up to the elements they are to face and to make the process of terraformation smooth rather a than chaotic struggle in attending to the deficiencies of the species itself. With this in mind we find instilled in the Glaucus Galacticus those very sturdy traits of the Water Bear, namely a resistance to the ill effects of the vacuum of space and an immunity to radiation poisoning.

In the assumed destruction of the host world, the Glaucus Galacticus was cast hither and yon in the scattered debris of a dead planet. This most likely resulted in death of a high percentage of the vacuum slugs, but those that remained, those that had that slight variation from the norm that allowed them to survive, continued, reproduced, and thrived.

When floating detached in empty space the vacuum slug is in a state of quasi-dormancy surviving on light and radiation that is absorbed through an amplified photosynthetic process. When encountering or colliding with planetary debris the vacuum slug becomes significantly more animated (akin to that of an Earth Asteroidea, or Starfish) and uses the opportunity to dissolve and consume minerals from the debris via solvents from its cerata, or feather-like appendages. Attaching to rock also provides the hermaphroditic Glaucus Galacticus the opportunity to reproduce.

It might be assumed that once attached to debris the vacuum slug would remain indefinitely, however, for reasons not fully understood, they only remain attached temporarily for mating and consumption then release to once again float in the empty vacuum of space.

Though the numbers of vacuum slugs are great and their environment is mostly untouched, they carry a high-priority protected species status for two general reasons. One, the only location in the galaxy they exist is in this narrow band around a single star. Two, they are of a non-terminal aging status and exist in an environment that moves quite slow. This means that the Glaucus Galacticus, like a variety of old Earth Sea Urchins, does not suffer from the effects of aging. They don't die of old age. They can die of disease, but are resistant to almost all known diseases, and they can die of mutilation, but in lieu of these two factors they will live indefinitely. This may seem like a positive trait encouraging survival, but species that have no temporal urgency tend to not get into too much of a hurry about

anything. The Glaucus Galacticus, for this reason, spends up to one hundred years or more to reach maturity and may not reproduce for another fifty to seventy-five years. Things move slowly in space. So it can be seen that if a disease or predator began to ravage the vacuum slug they might not have the time to adapt or counter the stressor. For more information on the Glaucus Galacticus look for the following related articles available via the FGL.
"Glaucus Galactics: It's Genetic Transmogrificational Path and History" by Paul Papaulus.
and,
"All Things Gross and Squishy" by Maleaus Undertaught.

About three quarters of an hour later, Bob's ship slowly maneuvered into a position and collected him from space. Bob checked the status of the ship's systems and everything seemed back to normal. Most of the growth had been sucked out in the decompression and the ship purged most of the rest. Bob still had to brush some out of the lavatory and a few edges before closing the cargo doors. It wasn't that important if some remained as there was no way anything survived. Anything left would be very dead.

When Bob closed the cargo door and the cabin became habitable again, he did another series of checks, systems operations and air quality, before deciding it was in fact safe. He then resumed course and took off the stillsuit. It was a fantastic feeling to take it off. It was a little too form fitting for Bob's taste, though he had to credit it with saving his life in a couple of different scenarios.

Even though the decontamination had worked, whatever bits of material were left was giving Bob itchy eyes and a runny nose that was sneezing with an almost clockwork regularity. He had plenty of tissues, but the remnants were probably infused in the tissue as well, so he'd just have to put up with it until he could get a thorough scrubbing of the cabin done.

On the way out of the Orchid nebula, Bob was stuck between exhaustion and being lost in thought. The words of the Dandy, the creeping nightshade, intermingled with the potential fool's errand of fighting this virus put his mind in a rarefied space. And when Bob closed his eyes he kept seeing the face of the woman on Aquash, eyes floating in the dark. She had said, "*Then perhaps you study birdsong in a collection of stuffed nightingales.*"
Bob thought, "Is that what I'm doing, as she had put it trying to *halt the grief of the world*?"

Bob wasn't sure what to think and was honestly too tired to do much more. All he knew for sure was that the Dandies and their world was not what he expected and doubted that anyone really knew much about what had been going on there for the past tens of thousands of years. Though Bob would have to admit that the children's book he grew up with, that most kids have read at one time or another, did have a certain quality to which he could relate this experience.

Chapter Thirty-two:
Where is Your Home?

There was a little Dandy
in a place so unknown,
confused and concerned
lost and alone.

From where you are now,
where would you like to go?

The little Dandy said,

"A place in the trees
where my family calls home."

Here's a good map.
It contains every star,
above and below,
quite near and
quite far.

She looked at the map,
of that old Milky Way,
and found that she had
no idea to her dismay.

Let me explain
and I'll ease your upset.
We'll read this map together
and get you home yet.

Our galaxy is like an octopus
floating in space
but his arms are made of stars
and so is his face.

If you happen to know the name of the arm
that holds your precious home
you'll be on the path, in the blink of an eye,
you'll no longer be alone.

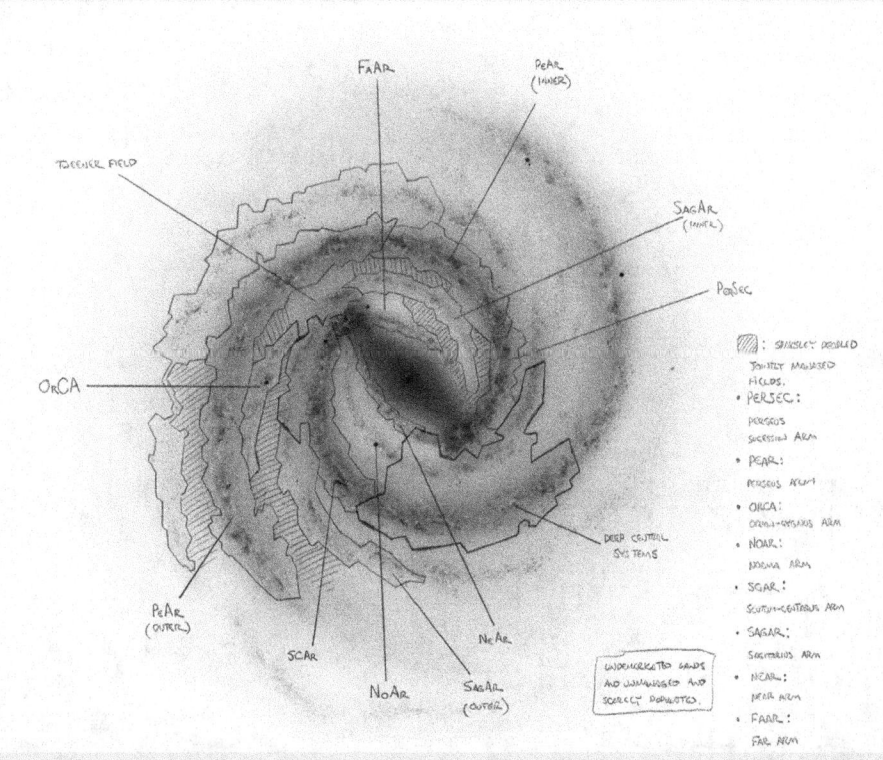

There's NoAr and OrCA
and SCAr and PeAr.
There's SagAr and PerSec
and FaAr and NeAr.

It began in OrCA,
the littlest arm,
where Earth,
warmed by Sol,
gave birth to us all.

From there we
spread quick,
one star after
another.

A little only
child
now has countless
sisters and brothers.

454

But where is your home, little Dandy?
We seemed to have forgot.
I can tell you the secret
though you may like it not.

Your home is the world,
Wherever you are.
Where you've been and will be,
You'll never stray far.

We come from a place
before space and time.
From there to each of us
one can draw a straight line.

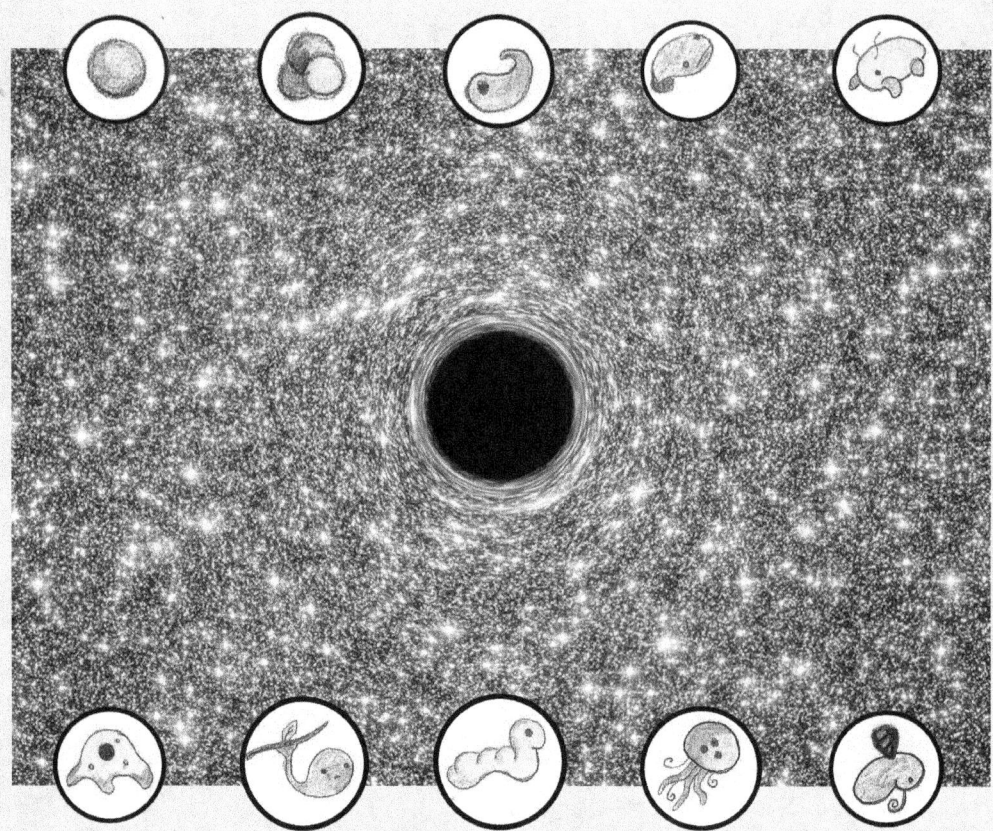

We wiggle and wobble
again and again,
and fresh new beginnings
from where we thought were loose ends.

She said,
"But how can this be?
I'm so small and
so brief."

Because, in fact,
you are the tree
though you think
you are but a leaf.

Beyond our one galaxy
are others too far to reach.
Beyond them are more
ad infinitum for each.

It all feeds into you
and through you is awake.
You are it looking back
on itself as if by mistake.

So search each star, little Dandy,
you have plenty of time.
And in the end you'll agree
your home you did find.

She said, "It all seems so sad...
...so easy to get lost.
Overwhelming and frightening.
Through endless darkness tossed."

"What about all that space?
That distance between?"

The darkness is not what it seems,
little Dandy,
The darkness is not what it seems.

fgl

a little

Galactic Book

Chapter Thirty-three: For the Galaxy is Hollow and I Have Touched the Sky

Bob had arrived at the mouth of the Orchid nebula...or that opening from which he had previously entered... and headed in the direction of the coordinates were the previous jump-ship had left him. The decontamination of his ship had been successful and he didn't have much trouble getting back aboard, though since he removed the stillsuit he has had a fairly constant fit of sneezing and the itchiest of eyes. Any bit of pollen or mold spore left in the ship was most assuredly dead, but it didn't prevent Bob from reacting to it adversely. After hours of allergy driven itchiness Bob had considered christening his little ship 'La Histamine' and knew that it would require a good detailing when he managed to get back to civilization.

Bob really didn't know what to expect now. He didn't know if the former jump-ship would show back up, or if another had been scheduled. He didn't know if he'd have to wait a long while or if they all just assumed he wouldn't make it back and had left him here to die. Bob had accomplished the tasks asked of him by C.I.D.E.R. so presumably they would want the final piece of their puzzle. Bob hoped this might solve the current galactic problem but his recent experiences and the scope of the travel itself colored existence as a thing wild and out of control. How could anything in this galaxy be tamed? Once a thing acquires a certain momentum, that momentum seems to always exist in some form or another. Bob endeavored not to succumb to pessimism and knew that long travel, and he had gone about as far as one can go, often had a corrosive effect on the spirits. Bob was more than ready to head home, but knew he had one more destination before he could begin the lengthy and tedious trip back.

It was then that from the nothingness a distant blip appeared not terribly far from his location. Scanning and bringing the image to the fore Bob could see it was the *Cell-Scape*. This gave Bob a sense of relief that a mere commissioned transit wouldn't possess. Despite the shadowy nature of their operation, Bob did feel like they knew what they were doing and they seemed fairly reliable...as far as he could tell considering he really didn't know much about what they were up to and what their organization was really about. Soon a familiar voice spoke through a sent transmission.

Lydia: "Hellooooooo. We have sent you the coordinates and docking procedures so...you know...hop to it."

461

Bob was on his way before the message completed, eager to get back to some kind of civilization. After a routine docking, scan, and sterilization protocol Bob walked eagerly from his cargo hold onto the deck of the docking bay. The sterile vibrancy of the white interior aboard the *Cell-Scape* was a perfectly jarring tripolar contrast to the environments from which he had recently come. It was a balanced trifecta between black space, prismatic nebula, and the now harsh white of the jump-ship interior. On the platform to which he had docked, there to greet him, was Lydia.

Lydia: "Welcome back, Bob." She then scrunched up her face and added, "You have definitely been on some strange planet. Your ship has a strong musty ragweed smell."

Bob, as they walked: "Yeah, it's been murdering my sinuses for hours now."

Lydia, with a smirk: "You smell like it too, but I said it was your ship so as not to be rude."

Bob: "I appreciate that. I do."

Bob was surprisingly sore. He had pulled several muscles in the mad dash to his ship under heavy gravity. It made him move with a labored lumber like an ape being prodded to walk upright.

Lydia: "It is odd isn't it, that every planet has it's own smell."

Bob: "I suppose so. And I suppose I've caught a whiff of several as of late."

During the exchange Bob notice Lydia now had an arm where one had been absent before. Oddly it was a prosthetic, mechanical arm and not a real one.

Bob: "Lydia! You've got a new arm!"

Lydia gave a sort of regal wave followed by a soft gesture as if trying to catch a distant star in her new hand.

Bob: "Why did you opt for a prosthetic and not a real one?"

Lydia: "The medical facility on our last mission only had old lady arms and I didn't fancy a single one of them...besides, in a couple of weeks we have a mission in Arete. Two of the planets in that system, Pockels and Germain have great medical facilities. For someone looking to acquire dismembered limbs, they'll have *lots*."

Bob: "Well, I'm glad you're back together."

Lydia: "Thank you, thank you."

Bob: "Ok, down to business. The stillsuit. What do you want me to do with it?"

Lydia: "Ehrrr...not much. It's best you keep it. We really don't want to have an association with it...you know...for certain *reasons*."

Bob had felt that this thing was not acquired on the up and up and wasn't really sure he wanted it either. That, though, he could sort out later.

Bob: "O...k...then...the sample..."

Lydia, extending a metallic hand: "Yes. The sample would be much appreciated."

Bob produced the cylinder and reached toward Lydia's open palm, but as she grasped he pulled it just out of her reach to which she gave a jovial angry fist gesture.

Bob: "I need to ask a favor first."

Lydia: "A *favor*...hmm...I'm afraid we're fresh out of those, but I guess it wouldn't hurt to hear what you have in mind."

Bob: "After Moloch took a sample from the Dandies, they believe they traced his following destination to a place they call the *Silent World*."

Lydia: "Hmm...haven't heard of it. Sounds boring."

Bob: "Me either, but they gave me the coordinates and I think we should check it out."

Lydia: "Well, I don't want to rain on your parade but *we* are not in the business of checking things out. You (then pointing a metallic finger into Bob's shoulder), *you* could check it out. I'm sure we could commission an appropriate travel itinerary for you, but that's about as far as it would go."

Bob: "The problem though is that a chain of commercial jump-ships wouldn't go there so one would have to be commissioned from a hub that would be ages away. It would take weeks to get there, but from here it is two jumps. *Two jumps*. We could be back on your schedule in a little over an hour."

Lydia: "I would like to help, but it's not part of the plan and things need to move along in the direction of the plan."

Bob: "Look, you really had no idea how long it would take me to get to Demeter and back. You had to account for at least a few hours, if not days, of variability. I'm just asking for a little time to check this place out. Can you at least try to run it by the big boss? There may be something there that will solve this whole problem...or even something more interesting...something that might be of interest to the good doctor. Aren't you curious?"

Lydia, looking somehow playfully frustrated: "Dr. Morris in not fond of deviations from the plan, but I will...for you...ask her."

Bob: "Hey, for all you know, this planet may be covered in dismembered arms. Right up your alley."

Lydia giggled as they walked down a corridor away from the docking bay. After a distance they stopped at a room and Lydia gestured toward the door.

Lydia: "Go in there and clean yourself up. There's a tumbler to clean your clothes too. Use it. I'll go and contact Polly Ann and see what she has to say. Don't get your hopes up."

Bob: "Tell her everything I said. Be persuasive. Remember the arms Lydia...all the arms that might just be lying around there." Bob then handed her the sample cylinder.

Lydia giggled and rolled her eyes, shutting the door on Bob which left him alone in the clean room. Yes, it would be nice to be clean again.

* * *

The steam from the bath was helping considerably with Bob's sinuses and the warmth was easing the strain on his muscles. It had been, in full disclosure, a while since he'd had a proper bath. Collecting his clothes from the machine...clean, warm, and dry...he felt more himself and a lot more at ease. Upon exiting the room, Lydia was there waiting.

Lydia: "You're a lucky, lucky fella. She said yes."

Bob, relieved: "Excellent."

Lydia: "But, there are some conditions."

Bob: "Ok?"

Lydia: "First, we'll be making two jumps. On the first jump you'll send a transmission to your Chief and request a verification that Moloch is still being monitored at the location around the black hole."

It occurred to Bob that he couldn't remember discussing Moloch's whereabouts with anyone affiliated with CIDER, and didn't think that information was currently public.

Bob: "Sure, no problem."

Lydia: "The second jump will take place a sizable distance from the location, within reach from your ship, but a good distance. Assuming we receive confirmation that Moloch is still in his assumed location, you may proceed. If confirmation is absent this side mission will be aborted. We will not run the risk of a disastrous encounter. I'm sure you understand."

Bob: "Alright. Not a problem."

Lydia: "Also, if anything goes awry, at any time, we may abandon this side mission and *you* if needs be. Returning or sending help will be solely at our discretion and should not be expected. In that eventuality you may be on your own."

Bob: "Y'all are a skittish bunch, are you not?"

Lydia, smiling: "We are baby bunnies in a land of new world vultures."

Bob: "I really think there's nothing to worry about. The Dandies tracked him there several years ago. I'm sure he's long gone, and besides, the Dandies could be completely wrong. This may all be for nothing."

Lydia: "As long as you understand our terms, we can proceed. Are we in agreement?"
Bob: "Sure. Why not."
Lydia smiled and suggested Bob head to his ship.

***

The Chief had been spending his days between monitoring the black hole and a temporary residence on a nearby system of the outer wall. Daily jump-ship commutes between the two were getting tedious and in all honesty he probably should have just returned to Helen a long time ago. This operation was really running itself and there was little to be done. However, the Chief didn't completely trust that the accompanying OWLE officers would efficiently update him in the event of a change and really, as little as was happening, this was probably more important than him sitting behind a desk on Helen's Crown even though all he had managed to accomplish was the record of an unbroken string of blips spaced in 6.18 second intervals.

Much to the Chiefs relief, he received a recorded transmission marked URGENT. It was from Bob and the Chief was rather delighted to know he was still alive though, despite the Chief's tendency towards worry, he really didn't think Bob had been up to much but routine business, probably exceptionally dull work. It must have been fascinating, the Chief thought, to visit the Dandies homeworld, and he looked forward to hearing about it, but they are not a dangerous people so surely it was a walk in the park. The Chief eagerly read over the incoming recording.

"Hiya. It's Bob. Things are good. In a hurry. Need confirmation that Moloch is still present around the black hole. Urgent. Dandy planet almost killed me. Hope to talk soon."
The Chief thought, "Hmm...wonder what that's about?" He then promptly sent the following reply.

"Glad you're not dead. Consistent signal from what is assumed to be Moloch's ship, unbroken since discovery, same location. If the Dandies almost killed you, you probably need to work out more. Looking forward to hearing from you."
The Chief was glad to hear from Bob. It was a good sign.

* * *

Back on the Cell-Scape, the first jump had sent Bob's message and the second jump received the Chief's. Bob was glad that he was so reliable and not out-of-pocket for some reason. With the conditions satisfied, and following a thorough scan from the Cell-Scape insuring there was no immediate danger, Bob left the *Cell-Scape*, disembarking for a point of light in the distance.

Bob's ship was still musty and revived the itchiness of his eyes along with an occasional sneeze. The *Cell-Scape* had kept a sizable distance giving Bob nearabouts a forty minute trip at top speed to this so-called Silent World. Bob spent the time looking for data on this place and there was none. The star had been classified remotely and an estimation of a gas-giant present, the sort of general data one can find on probably any star in the galaxy, but nothing that spoke of a civilization or even an inkling that a human being had ever set foot anywhere in the system. From Bob's current location he could identify a class G star, similar to Sol; a gas-giant, similar in size and location to Zeus; a distant smaller gas-giant, similar in size and location to Poseidon; and a smattering of planets.

When Bob reached the coordinates supplied by the Dandies and attained an orbit around this Silent World, he was at a bit of a loss for words. Bob wasn't sure what to make of it...unusual to say the least.

Here was a planet of a standard habitable size in the goldilocks zone, possessing vast oceans and a proportionally small land-mass ratio.

The air, according to Bob's scan, was breathable. None of this can be said to be odd except for the unlikeliness of what appears to be a conditioned world in an untouched portion of space. A thorough scan of the surface, however, provided the oddity that struck Bob so.

There were no structures, no signs of habitation, no signs of civilization...primitive or otherwise...yet the land-mass was covered in trees...some variation on a sycamore...which were almost perfectly arranged in a grid.

This told Bob at least one thing; someone was responsible for the manicured nature of this world. Yes, there are trees in the galaxy, a type of Sequoia, that do grow from the fallen trunk of their parent tree and tend to form straight lines, but these produce groupings of five to six trees in a line and are dependent upon the whims of the fallen tree. To get more than a dozen or so in a straight line would be an unlikely statistical anomaly. Here though, on this Silent World, were lines of trees in a more or less perfect grid extending thousands of square miles. It had to be done by people, and not just one, it would take an enormous effort to manicure a planet in this fashion. It would take a concerted effort by an entire civilization and obviously one that does not reside in this system as far a Bob could tell. So the question remains: who did this and why?

Unbeknownst to Bob, a series of events were currently taking place of which he'd soon be aware. Some hidden device, one he could not see nor detect, had become aware of his presence and communicated this information a great distance away. The order of these events transpired thusly:

In a brightly illuminated room on a rather small ship, a proximity warning had been displayed on the ships console. In the center of this room, sitting in a meandering thoughtfulness, was Moloch who allowed but one thought before action. That thought was an inquisitive "hmm."

The next event was neither a signal nor warning, but a startling absence. In his diligent monitoring of the repetitious 6.18 second blip, the Chief was jarred, almost as if struck, by the end of that signal. The 6.18 second blip was no longer there. Ordering a scan of the surrounding area produced, as thought, nothing and the Chief couldn't help but experience a gloomy foreboding at the fact that this interruption came so shortly after Bob had requested a verification of that very information. Could it be a coincidence? Either way, what did it mean?

It's difficult to describe the sinking feeling that Bob experienced at the following two events. One, a ship appeared out of nowhere extremely close to his location which Bob almost instantly identified as that of Moloch's. Two, at that instant the distant pinpoint which was the *Cell-Scape* vanished. They had fled and Bob was alone.

For a moment Bob stood very still as if somehow that might make him go unnoticed. It was a silly instinct produced of the irrationality caused by panic. Even in this potentially grim situation Bob couldn't help but almost chuckle at the ridiculousness. Turning to the console Bob could see Moloch's almond shaped ship, surprisingly visible, and for some reason appearing to slowly tumble. After a minute or two Bob received a request to open a communication channel which Bob thought it best to immediately reply. When he did before him was the image of the interior of Moloch's ship. Gravity was obviously disabled for some reason, surely intentional, and in the center of the room was Moloch, standing upright but touching no surface, the image tumbling in a fashion that made it hard to know what was happening. What Bob couldn't see was that in fact he and Moloch, in their separate ships and across a short bit of space, were standing face to face as Moloch's ship slowly tumbled around him.

Moloch, flatly: "Why have you come here?"

Bob felt, at this point, a compunction to tell the truth as lying would only insure his demise.

Bob: "Honestly, I've been trying to figure out what you've been up to."

Moloch: "To stop the coming cataclysm, I suppose."

Bob: "I suppose. At least to try."

Moloch: "It is done. There is nothing to stop. What led you here? How did you know about this place?"
Bob: "Dandies. They said you probably came here after you left Demeter."
Moloch, surprised: "How did they know that, and how do they know about this place?"
Bob: "I have no idea how they know about this place, but they traced you with some type of spore."
Moloch: "Huh. You know, I just couldn't figure out if they were intelligent or not."
Bob: "They definitely weren't what I expected. I knew nothing about them and feel that after meeting them I know even less."
Moloch: "An enigmatic bunch."
After a thoughtful silence Moloch continued.
Moloch: "Well, you can't be here. I'm afraid you'll have to leave."
Bob was surprised that this sentence implied he might survive.
Bob, with a sincere understanding: "Ok."
Moloch, seeming very calm: "Ok. Just so there are no loose ends and everything is crystal clear, you'll need to leave immediately. If you hang around I'll destroy your ship. If you attempt to land on the surface I'll destroy your ship. Non-compliance is not survivable. I'm sure you believe this threat to be factual."
Bob: "I do."
Moloch: "There is nothing down there for you. Even for what you fear, there is nothing down there. It is perhaps time to quit struggling and go home."
Bob: "Home sounds good."
Moloch: "Good."
Bob, probably against his better judgment, offered: "Well...would you like to talk...about all this, or anything?"
This took Moloch off guard a bit. He didn't know what he expected from this exchange, but it seemed a genuine offer of dialog, which it was, and not laced with deceit or scheming, which it was not.
Moloch, raising his eyebrows: "...no. I don't think so. Not now."
Bob: "Ok."
Moloch: "Ok."

With that Bob slowly headed toward the location of the now absent *Cell-Scape*. His plan would be to wait in that general area in the hopes they would return someday soon considering at Bob's top speed the nearest system from the Silent World was at least twenty some odd *years* away.

Back near the Outer Wall, several hours after the incident, the 6.18 second blip returned and the Chief was left with a terrible fear that the worst had just happened to Bob.

Bob, however, was quite calm. Sure, he was worried about being abandoned, but he survived an encounter with Moloch and more than that, he gained a certain insight into this mysterious bespectacled man. It surprised Bob that he didn't seem crazed, or like some sort of lunatic. Not that Bob was a psychoanalyst or anything remotely akin, but Moloch didn't seem like the psychopath that Bob had imagined him being. There was much more going on here than anyone was aware.

Regardless, Bob had been on one too many strenuous adventures and it had been a long time since he had rested properly. With nothing else to do and his emotional and physical reserves quite depleted, sleep would be the perfect means of passing the time waiting to be rescued.

* * *

Lydia rounded several tight corners before entering a long hallway, metallic and reflecting only white ambient light. At the far end she entered a set of airlocks that within had scanned her intently before opening into a rather round chamber the size of a small office space containing next to nothing but a central square protrusion a few feet high originating from the floor. The walls, still a gleaming metallic white, were partitioned into a variety of fixed panels suggesting a vast conspiracy of hidden mechanics beyond, though the room was unusually silent. Across from the airlock was a round opening several feet in diameter into another room beyond and straight above the central protrusion, in the ceiling, was another such round opening. The gravity had been purposefully absent in this room and Lydia, with the grace of someone who had done this very thing hundreds of times, gently kicked off of the protrusion and floated through the opening in the ceiling, just enough force to delicately stop herself with a couple of fingers in the space above.

The opening in the ceiling was about four feet in length and terminated in a small chamber above. This chamber was dark, and square. A plate of unusually dense metal slid in place effectively decapitating the smaller chamber Lydia was in from the one below. Should she have looked down at the opening it would almost seem a liquid metal had filled the portal.

Once closed another set of scans invisibly judged Lydia before bathing the room in light. Shortly after, a projection from so very far away, appeared to Lydia with the partial transparency and illumination of a wandering ghost.
Lydia: "So, can we make this quick? I'm really busy."

Dr. Polly Ann Morris: "I know you're busy, we're all busy." Then chuckling "...I'm far more busy than you."

Lydia, rolling her eyes but smirking, "All the more reason."

Polly Ann: "Ok, ok. You know why we're talking."

Lydia: "I'm fine. Everything is fine."

Polly Ann: "There is the routine psychiatric evaluation..."

Lydia, interrupting: "I can do that, but you know it's a waste of time. I am fine."

Polly Ann: "If it was anyone else working for me I'd not believe a word of it, but..."

Lydia: "But you do. You know I'm alright."

Polly Ann: "Lydia, I just worry about you. You're important to me, not just in what you do, but in who you are...as a person."

Lydia: "I know Polly. I appreciate the concern."

Polly Ann: "That mission did not go as planned."

Lydia: "No it did not. Those guys were real jerks. Would. Not. Listen. To. Reason."

Polly Ann: "Well, I bet they wish they had now."

Lydia: "The ship is being repaired faster than we had expected, maybe a day or two..."

Polly Ann, interrupting: "You know I don't care about that. Lydia, what can I do to make it up to you?"

Lydia: "Hey, you get me an arm I like and we're right as rain."

Polly Ann: "That goes without saying."

Polly Ann: "...Lydia, how did you dodge that thing?"

Lydia, summoning a deep introspection: "I dunno. The discharge was just a massive wall of plasma from where I was. I somehow kind of anticipated the blast and moved. Luck I guess...well, except for the part of me that was in it."

Polly Ann: "What was it like when it happened...your whole arm just instantly gone like that?"

Lydia: "It was strange. There was a brief flash, like a vacuum in my mind that collapsed into something hot. I could almost feel, with my missing arm, the absence...like I could feel the nothingness into which it merged. It was like touching a black hole with a phantom limb...it was a sensation that couldn't really be."

Polly Ann: "Hmm...well, when there is time, after this is all over, I want to hear everything...in person."

Lydia: "You got it."

Polly Ann stared at Lydia for a solid moment before her apparition disappeared.

Lydia left the overly secure communications chamber and got back to work.

Dream Journal 13: A Gate into the Stars

She and I followed the faint path, once worn but now covered in a dense overgrowth, toward the mountain summit. Several times she asked "Where are we going daddy?"
I would say, "We're going to the top."
She looked around, looked up and up, then said, "All the way to the top?"
I would say, "Yes, sweetie."
We packed lightly, much more lightly than should be appropriate for such a trip, but still the trip was a hard trek. Periodically she would say her legs were tired and I would say "Let's just make it a bit further, then we'll rest." Shortly after she would modify her statement and say "Daddy, my little legs are tired." She was a smart girl and knew how to choose words for maximum sympathy...at least in regards to my reactions. I would then pick her up and carry her on my shoulders for a while, usually until she got bored and felt again like scampering about.
The trek took several days. It was difficult, at least on me...she seemed to be fine. She was the happy little girl she had always been. Often she would ask, "What's at the top, Daddy?"
I would say, "A gate into the stars, sweetie."
Her: "What's it look like?"
Me: "I don't know. I've never seen it before."
Her: "If you don't know, then how will you know when we find it?"
That was a good question. She was a very smart little girl.
Me: "I think we'll know."
Her: "If you don't know what it looks like, maybe we've already found it and we can just go home."
It was a wishful sentiment but she and I both knew there was no home to return to.
She giggled and then became distracted with some beetle that scurried by which she followed for a bit.

Towards the top it was very cold. We were both wrapped in blankets which honestly were not adequate for the weather. Through craggy gray and snowcapped rock we winded and climbed to the clearing of the summit. It was as if the top of the mountain had been carved into a small circular room. A ring of protrusions, maybe eight or nine...I didn't count, encircled the center of the chamber. They looked as if large stalagmites had been leveled and scooped out to provide a place to sit, one of which was just the right size for the two of us. In the center of these rocky seats, the central point around which the room was focused, was yet another leveled stalagmite upon which was a thing hard to see.

She looked, eyes darting and blinking around the central object, and said, "Is that it?"

I replied, "That's it, sweetie."

She: "It's hard to see."

I: "It is."

She: "What is it?"

I: "It is a transition into another world."

She: "Hmm..." And she skipped around the perimeter of it several times before coming to sit with me.

She: "So...what do we do?"

I: "We sit and we wait...together."

As time streamed past us the night became bitterly cold. We, wrapped tightly together in a blanket, waited for just that...for time to stream past us. In and out of sleep, in and out of consciousness, there really was no way to tell how long it had been. At some point I jostled out of the fog, my body hardly responsive from the cold. I couldn't sense much more than a high pitched ringing and the little light that entered my failing eyes. She was pressed tightly into my side, her head at my chest. I could only see the top of her sweet head and knew she had already passed. There was a sadness in this, oh yes there was...but there was a sweetness too. The delicate ephemeral breath of a story told from beginning to end, told in completeness by which that book could be closed, set aside, contemplated, and cherished. Then a new book is opened, one in which a sweet little girl frolics through endless pages of an equally endless universe, dancing wildly as she sips the nectar from every verse. And I, soon to follow, will frantically skim the pages looking for that sweet little girl, in the desperate hope that I may, in some small way, share in the ever presence that is her.

Chapter Thirty-four: The Ultimate Commuter
and
Patterns of Farce.

Bob was jostled awake by an alarm from his ships console. He was jarred from a deep sleep, the kind of deep sleep that once interrupted brought one back into the world of the living with a strong disorientation and an absent knowledge of the where, when, and why of one's own existence. The alarm was a proximity warning of a nearby ship. Bob scrambled up and tottered over to the console to see just who was out there.

Bob: "Oh, thank goodness."

It was the *Cell-Scape*. They had come back for him.

A message containing docking instructions was received and Bob quickly complied. Back in the *Cell-Scape* Bob was once again greeted by Lydia who was as chipper as always.

Lydia: "You...", poking a metallic finger again into Bob's shoulder, "...are a lucky, lucky fella."

Bob: "I think I would be the first to agree with you."

Lydia: "Fortunately, I put in a good word for you...a real sob story about how helpless and dimwitted you were and the likeliness that you'd die of loneliness long before your supplies ran out..."

Bob: "We prefer the term half-witted."

Lydia, giggling: "Well, you're here now. I'm assuming you're done with these fun little side adventures and are ready to head home. Or, did you get a hint that there might be something of interest on the surface of a star and want to go for a little walk first?"

Bob: "Yeah, I'm done. My capacity for both excitement and boredom have been greatly exceeded. So, ...what now?"

Lydia, escorting Bob to a waiting room: "We are a few jumps away from our next target. We have business to attend to in the Minotaurus system. In orbit around planet Nambu there is a wonderful research facility...the Kabuse genome modulatory institute. We're going there. *You*...are not. From Nambu, a planet or two over, there is a fairly large port, the *Cerium* station. We've got a nice itinerary lined up for you from there."

Towards the end of Lydia's sentence Bob felt the distinctive thud of a jump being made. They were on their way.

Bob: "Thank you, Lydia. I'll be honest, I am ready to be home.   ...Uh, the tracking device that Dr. Morris shot into my chest, are y'all going to remove that?"

Lydia, smiling politely: "You mean the infectious disease monitor that is definitely *not* a tracking device? It is best you keep that with you. It would hurt more coming out than going in. Besides, don't you want us to inform you when you've contracted some terrible thing?"

Bob: "Well, I suppose that could be useful seeing as how it is an infectious disease monitor that is definitely *not* a tracking device."

Lydia gave a smile and a brief two finger salute.

Lydia: "Oh, and Dr. Morris would like to politely request a thorough detail of your little encounter that almost got you stranded in deep space."

Bob: "Yeah, sure. I'm certain it isn't pertinent to you or Dr. Morris, but no one can go near that planet. For reasons unknown Moloch has decided that travel there ends in death. Not a good idea to test him."

Lydia: "Travel there ends in death for everyone but *you* apparently."

Bob: "I think he considered it fair warning."

Lydia shrugged her shoulders.

Bob: "Hey, I assume Dr. Morris is going to let me know what comes of the collected samples and the progress on disarming the virus?"

Lydia: "I'm sure she'll let you know something at her earliest convenience. Probably. Definitely probably."

Bob passed the time resting in the waiting room until they arrived in the Minotaurus system an hour or so later. At the sound of the last jump, Lydia materialized at the door and escorted Bob to his ship.

Lydia: "Well Bob, I wish you well on your trip home. You're much more pleasant to talk to than most of the people we deal with on a regular basis. If our paths cross again I suppose I wouldn't find that too objectionable."

Bob: "Thank you, thank you. Lydia, I hope here soon you get the arm you've always wanted. Consider something unique, like one with a bunch of extra fingers...could be useful, or talons or something."

Lydia: "I've been thinking of going with a large octopus tentacle, which could be quite useful...only, it'd have to be kept moist all the time, so I'm still undecided."

Bob: "Maybe just a regular young lady arm then?"

Lydia: "Yeah, probably a boring proper arm."

Bob: "Good luck."

Lydia: "You too."

Bob returned to his ship and left the *Cell-Scape* which headed toward Nambu. Bob set a course for the *Cerium* station and left in the opposite direction. After a relatively short jaunt *Cerium* was in view. Bob didn't know anything about this system, but the station, at least, was a quite populated hub. The station itself was fairly drab: two large concentric rings attached to a central orb by seven opposing perpendicular arcing spokes. Gunmetal gray, but well lit, Bob made his way toward the station as he glanced over his itinerary.

Bob, thinking through the systems aloud: "Ok, so I'm in Minotaurus and I'm going through Arion, Laelaps, Alicorn, Chrysaor, Ladon, Asbolus, Chimera...hmm..."

Due to the *Cell-Scape's* business in Minotaurus, the most direct path back to Sol was to arc around the galactic core in opposition to the path Bob had taken to get there. One might wonder why traveling significantly above the galactic core, but more or less straight over, would not be a more direct option, but remember, the jump-ships need a solid pool of gravity in which to operate...not merely the luminous matter we're all familiar with, but the dark matter and dark energy that, unseen, glues the galaxy together. Getting too far way from those dark waters insures that once the ship leaves it doesn't return.

Bob immediately docked at the prescribed ship at the prescribed location and felt almost giddy that he was in such a place that would allow him to easily communicate abroad. Once the docking was complete he practically couldn't engage the terminal fast enough to get ahold of the Chief.

Chief: "Bob?"
Bob: "Hello, Hello, Hello."
Chief: "Goodness, it is good to hear your voice."
Bob: "I feel the same way."
Chief: "Where are you?"
Bob: "Minotaurus, *Cerium* station."
Chief: "What are you doing there?"
Bob: "Heading home."
Chief: "Excellent, excellent. You know, I had this sinking feeling that you were a goner. What happened after I sent you that message?"
Bob: "Yeah, we need to talk about that."
Bob retold the story of the encounter with Moloch in precise detail to which the Chief listened intently.
Chief: "And that was it? Nothing more?"
Bob: "Don't you think that's plenty? It was plenty for me."
Chief: "I suppose so."

Bob: "Right now, only Dr. Morris and you have knowledge of this information and I don't know exactly how to proceed."
Chief: "What do you mean?"
Bob: "Well, we need to make sure no one investigates that place. I do, for some reason, take Moloch at his word that there is nothing there for us, so...do we do nothing and assume that no one will probably travel there, or make a statement letting everyone know where it is and that they shouldn't go there?"
Chief: "I see, yeah, it could invite too much curiosity. I think the best thing to do would be for me to put in a report detailing the event and issuing a general warning and travel restrictions to unpopulated systems of the galactic rim in the vicinity of Demeter. I'll not include specific coordinates and let any entity that for some stupid reason would be traveling out there anyway contact our department for a red or green light on their desired destination. Should be easy to automate...no big deal."
Bob: "Ok. That small problem solved."
Chief: "Bob, what do *you* think is there?"
Bob: "I honestly have no idea. Like everything else with him, it just doesn't seem to make much sense."
Chief, thinking as if something wasn't right: "...wait, after I sent you the message that we were still monitoring Moloch's signal, how long after was it that you encountered Moloch?"
Bob: "Um, not long. Why?"
Chief: "Can you send me the timestamp of when you received the message from me and the ship's log from the detection of Moloch's vessel?"
Bob: "Uh..." riffling through console commands, "...yes. There."
The Chief spent several moments looking over the data again, and again.
Chief: "This doesn't make sense."
Bob: "What doesn't make sense?"
Chief: "From the time we lost the signal to your encounter, only a few minutes had passed. That's about 40 thousand... *over* 40 thousand light years in a few minutes."
Bob: "Not possible. That must not have been him you've been monitoring."
Chief: "It has to be. What else could it be? And the disappearance of the signal matches perfectly with your encounter."
Bob: "But how long did it take before the signal returned?"
Chief: "Several hours."
Bob: "See, that's about the time that distance would take for a dedicated jump-ship doing nothing but jumping and recharging...honestly, it's still faster than a standard jump-ship, but

476

he's obviously got some tech that we don't possess...but if he could do 40K in a few minutes, why would it take him hours to return?"

Chief: "Yeah, I dunno. Something's not right about it though. I'm going to run it by a few friends who might have some idea. Odd, though."

Bob: "Well, what now?"

Chief: "Bob, it's spread everywhere. Isolated peoples are still clean, but everywhere else...it's not good."

Bob: "..."

Chief: "Most populated places have even ended quarantine and instead merely placed a travel warning to those who might happen to be virus free. You know, ...in a way, it's an improvement. Travel and commerce have more or less returned to normal. Other than the knowledge that everyone has some strange bug, things aren't much different than before."

Bob: "I suppose that's a plus. You haven't happened to have heard any progress towards identifying it and developing a vaccine...or something?"

Chief: "Me? That's what I should be asking you. You're the one that's dealing with Dr. Morris, retrieving samples and whatnot. I'm guessing you know nothing either?"

Bob: "Not yet. Hopefully soon. Those Dandies are an odd sort. If any body has a chance to fight off a rogue virus, it'd be them."

Chief: "Speaking of that, you gonna tell me about that leg of the trip."

Bob: "I suppose so."

Bob relayed the entirety of the story on his trip to Demeter and transferred a detailing of that visit, ship's log, timestamps of events, etc... for the Chief to peruse through later.

Chief: "Wild. Sounds like you've had a series of close calls on this extended vacation."

Bob: "Ha...vacation."

Chief: "...Hey, send me your itinerary for your return."

Bob, riffling: "...uh, ok. Done."

The Chief read carefully in silence of a few moments.

Chief: "Interesting. Ok. I'm still roundabouts the Outer Wall, a system called Erebus, and before long you'll be a handful of systems over...what is it...Aegis."

Bob: "Yep."

Chief: "Bob, I'm heading home. There's nothing to be done here. We're monitoring a blip pertaining to a man that can't be caught. It's fruitless."

Bob: "Ok."

Chief: "I'll meet you in Aegis and we can travel back together. That is, if you don't mind some company."

Bob: "That would be fantastic."
Chief: "Good. Ok, I need to get busy tying up all the loose ends here to make it to Aegis on time. Let me know if you learn anything new."
Bob: "Sounds great. See you in Aegis."
Chief: "See you there."

Bob thought to himself, *"Wow. After all this isolation...a travel companion."* It filled Bob with a contentment that he knew existed only in this temporal immediacy, but one can only worry and dread the future so much when they have done about all they can do and the rest is up to the machinations of the universe.

Bob was walking around the interior of his current commercial jump-ship visiting attached merchants partly to replenish his empty food stocks, but also to kill time before the next jump. It's true that his ships replicator would provide him with everything he would actually need in terms of sustenance, but life doesn't exist, at least in a pleasing form, in copies and replication. It's the excitement of the genuine that fuels a consonant and harmonious solace.

It was somewhere in the noise of the crowd that Bob received a message to which he only casually attended. When he saw that it was from Dr. Morris his interest piqued and he became absorbed in the potential weight of it. The message, read-only, was as follows:
The recombinant samples have provided no modulatory or mitigating structure and/or pathway to dismantle or impair the perceived pathogen. Thank you for your service.
-Dr. Morris, Center for Infectious Disease and Entropic Recomposition
Bob: "..."
That was that...and nothing more.

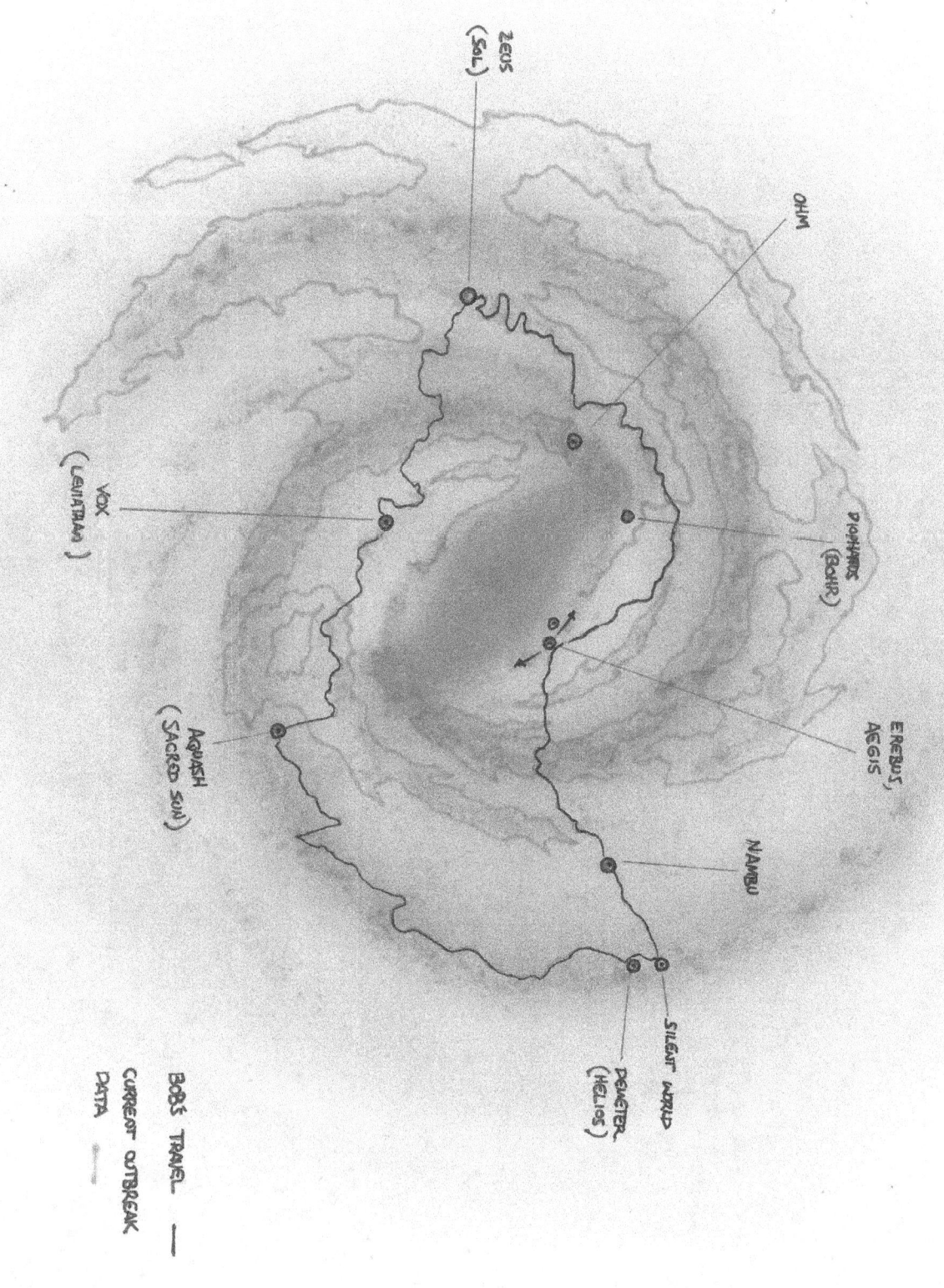

ZEUS
(SOL)

OHM

PIONEERS
(BOHR)

VOX
(LEVIATHAN)

EREBUS,
AEGIS

AQUASH
(SACRED SUN)

NAMBU

SILENT WORLD

DEMETER
(HELIOS)

BOB'S TRAVEL ——
CURRENT OUTBREAK
DATA ————

479

Chapter Thirty-Five: Return 2: Make Haste for Armageddon
and
The Two Return To Tomorrow Too!

Bob and the Chief met up in Aegis. They docked in a ship whose moniker emblazoned on the side read *Remain in Light*. Inside they met in a rather lush waiting room and greeted each other with a heartfelt embrace. Bob had sent the message as stated from Dr. Morris to the Chief several jumps ago. It painted both of their demeanors with a slightly off-white solemnness.   They spent their time avoiding talk of business and instead spoke as old friends who hadn't had a proper opportunity to catch up in a considerable while.

They had a few days of travel before them, not merely due to their distance from home, but more due to the fact that public transport spanning light years tends to take a circuitous path.

Bob: "You know, it's all very odd."

Chief: "What is?"

Bob: "A galaxy of stars, hundreds of billions, ...and so many inhabited. And beyond that countless other galaxies we'll never reach...hundreds of billions, and that's just the ones we can see...all from the great ripple that began this particular utterance of reality."

Chief: "Yep."

Bob: "And the chaos. I do recognize that, comparatively, existence is more peaceful now than it was for our ancestors, but still...chaos. And how do you stop it? It's just a little overwhelming."

Chief: "It is that."

Bob: "And imagine if in the distant future we manage to figure out how to get to another galaxy. Would we just spread further, spreading our chaos as we go? Where does it actually all stop? What is the endgame here?"

Chief: "I'm afraid I haven't an answer for you, Bob."

Bob: "There has to be a transformation. Some great transformation. Something that is not relegated to the valor of the individual, but some metamorphosis that permeates us as a people, transcending us past our pettiness and cruelty and that most developed propensity towards fear."

The Chief, nodding and considering carefully: "So...some kind of ointment or salve?"

Bob laughed.

Chief: "Hey, what's the deal with your roommate Abrum?"

Bob, intently: "He is *not* my roommate."

Chief: "I keep getting messages from him saying things like '*tell Bob that the few books he possess have been separated irrevocably from their former dust jackets and a suitable replacement is not to be found*.'"

Bob, rolling his eyes: "Yeah, I know."

Chief: "Or, this one was particularly entertaining, '*Bob must know that yonder bakery, the only such reputable establishment near our dwelling, has been offering sub-par croissants. The quality has suffered greatly and upon his return he should expect not a acceptable pastry from the aforementioned confectionery.*"

Bob: "Yeah, yeah, yeah. He's basically broken into my apartment somehow and the last I saw had covered the place in doilies."

Chief, chuckling: "I suppose you could press charges."

Bob: "He's a good guy, just...bizarre. He's like a Dandy in vintage clothing...he's kind of the embodiment and personification of an antique shop."

Chief: "Well, I'm sure he'll be happy to know you'll be home soon."

Bob rolled his eyes again.

There is a process every jump-ship must undergo routinely known in lay terms as a *complete physical*. For an onlooker foreign to the modern galaxy it would seem funny, like a comical game done for no other reason than playfulness. It involves a massive tubular structure through which the jump-ship must pass. The tube is composed of what appear to be slats running the length of the tube with an occasional ringlet holding them together. These slats happen to house great numbers of people employed in the administration of the physical, and mammoth equipment to carry out the necessary operations.

These operations include bio-scans, integrity assessments, systems checks, passenger/crew analysis, and communications ordering/detanglement, among other things. To allow each analytical body of the tubular slats full access to the jump-ship's bulk, the jump-ships must carefully transverse the tube while slowly tumbling. This tumbling is accompanied by a slow rotation around the perpendicular axis.

From a distance, seeing the long line of jump-ships wait before their slow twisty tumble through the open frame of the tube seems much like children waiting their turn on a park slide. To an outsider, one not familiar with the routine of this galaxy, it would seem a trifling nonsense. Inside, due to artificial gravity, the passengers are wholly unaware. The exception to this would be a passenger or crew member that happened to look out one of the few windows to the outside. This individual would see a bizarre twirling of a skeletal tube-like structure as if the structure itself was whirling oddly around the stationary jump-ship.

It was several jumps and several ships later, about halfway home from where Bob and the Chief joined company, that information channels erupted. Messages and communications flooded the populated portions of the galaxy as there was news that couldn't spread quickly enough. A hand had been played. Wheels where in motion. Gears were grinding. This viral invention of Moloch had indeed become active and a certain portion of the population had become sickly.

Chapter Thirty-six: Errand of Mercury

By all accounts, and the best assessment of the medical facilities galaxy wide, it appears the virus became active a little over a month ago. It was, as Moloch himself had said in the message to Diophantus and the conversation he had had with Bob in orbit of the Silent World, a *done deal*, and the realization of the true purpose of this *virus* had left the people of countless worlds slack jawed in a stumping confusion about how to proceed.

As it turns out, it wasn't exactly a virus. This accounts for the inability of medical teams, who feverishly worked on a cure, to produce results. They were, understandably, attacking the problem from an inaccessible angle. It was engineered. It was fashioned after a virus and so did spread as such, but it was a machine of unheard of complexity and researchers know now almost as little as before with the exception that the device is now producing results that can be detected.

This sickness that had affected a portion of the population was in fact morning sickness. The virus, though remaining dormant other than spreading itself, had within a month or so become alive. This activity involved attaching to an ovum at which time the virus would open or unfold in a similar fashion to a blossoming lotus. From there it would collect material, even absorbing other ovum, to construct an implantable sequence of genetic information. In this sense, the virus would be more aptly described as a sort of artificial gamete that engages in sewing together material to produce a viable zygote. This obviously affected only those of childbearing years, but seemed to have a terminal range within twenty five to forty five years of age. This is a statistical delineation of currently known impregnation but is expected to hold as numbers or reports increase. The minor variants in this age bracket are assumed due to the analysis of biological age versus actual age as the virus must only be capable of detecting the former.

The picture is clear and concerning. Almost all of those capable of birthing, within the defined age bracket, are now pregnant...but pregnant with what? Bob and the Chief, merely a few days from home, met in a private room on their current jump-ship the *Swan Dive* to discuss the recent revelation.

Chief: "Well, Bob...what...how do we even begin in talking about this?"

Bob: "I have no idea. Do we talk about the violations of individual human rights? Do we talk about the effects on entire civilizations? It's a massive web of issues."

Chief: "I mean...on the one hand...at least...   ...it's not something that's killing people."

Bob, nodding: "Yes. But the chaos that will ensue..."

Chief: "...you know we are at the whims of this lunatic...it could have been, if he so wanted it, that we were dealing with piles of bodies now...in numbers that would only grow exponentially."

Bob: "Oh yes, I am very aware that we are not in control of this situation."

Chief: "What do you think will happen now?"

Bob: "Well, I imagine that some portion of the population will willingly terminate any pregnancy not intended...and I imagine that some planetary cultures will institute a termination policy, but anything organized will begin to tread on individual rights so it will most likely be a person by person decision."

Chief: "Meaning that whatever the choices made end up being, we are still dealing with a coming massive increase in population galaxy wide...and a population of what? What exactly are we dealing with here?"

Bob: "I feel that that is too much to consider right now. It won't be long before a bio-analysis is complete and we know...more or less...what kind of life-form this guy's created for us all."

Chief: "...good point. I suppose it won't be hard to tell if it's got fangs or a tail."

Bob: "But, you know, it's just what seems like the final piece of this puzzle that doesn't clarify anything. Every step of this catastrophe makes less and less sense."

Chief: "It could be that he's just some madman with a superiority complex and wants to spread his perfection to the whole galaxy."

Bob: "You know, I suppose that's possible, but it doesn't seem like it to me. Something about him, when we spoke, seemed...troubled. And the meticulousness with which he's carried this all out seems to speak more to a purpose rather than an agenda. I think, and fear, that to him this is about some terrible dark logic rooted in a necessity."

Chief: "And there's the factor of the murders that seem to make no sense either."

Bob: "And the man forever in glass."

Chief: "Yep. *Technically* not a murder."

Bob: "Hmm...you know...this will destroy some civilizations."
Chief: "The pregnancy?"
Bob: "Absolutely. There are so many colonized worlds that most likely can't handle a massive influx of newborns. Even more developed worlds will find their resources strained in dealing with it."
Chief: "I imagine those worlds would be the first to opt for termination."
Bob: "That's problematic though. There are some peoples that have been dumped on a planet with the intent of colonizing it and have little aid. They could lack the technology, or at least in adequate numbers. And think about this; some under-developed worlds can't afford to essentially miss out on an entire generation of progeny and would need the numbers. Otherwise, their people would wither away...and that's assuming that this virus won't hang around for more than a generation...which we have no reason to assume."
Chief: "And assuming this progeny is something akin to a human being."
Bob was silent in thought.
Chief, eyebrows raised and nodding: "...it is a problem."

Chief: "To somewhat change the subject, I did get a report back from a pal of mine in the theoretical physics department last night."
Bob, curious: "About what?"
Chief: "Our little time discrepancy on your encounter with Moloch."
Bob: "Hmm...and?"
Chief: "This is basically what he thinks took place. Moments after we lost the signal from the black hole you encountered Moloch's ship almost a third of the galaxy away. Yet it took him several hours to get back."
Bob: "Right, that's what we think anyway."
Chief: "Well, we know that jump-ships need a substantial pool of dark matter and energy to operate within a usable range...essentially a pervasive gravity source...which is why we can't travel between galaxies."
Bob: "Right."
Chief: "If you remember from your studies of jump technology...'
Bob: "That was a long, long time ago."
Chief: "Me too. The basic gravitational pool in which the galaxy sits gives us a small window to get in and out of a jump...a little less than a second."
Bob: "Ok."
Chief: "What we think took place was that Moloch, in orbit of the black hole..."

Bob: "Had a considerable increase in gravity that opened the jump window a bit wider."

Chief: "Right. The intense gravity acts like a thick molasses that slows the whole process down and allows the jump window to be open longer equaling a greater distance. But here's the thing; his orbit wasn't adequate for that length of a jump. So it's believed that he must have allowed himself to fall towards the hole...probably far enough that even he couldn't escape without jumping...and that's how he made that incredible distance in almost no time."

Bob: "And also why it took him several hours to get back. Fascinating."

Chief: "The crazy thing is that for that distance, they calculated his position before the jump would need to be near or *at* the event horizon of the black hole."

Bob: "That is unbelievable."

Chief: "Right. I don't know what, exactly, to think about it."

Bob: "Well, that means in addition to having a technology that is undetectable, he also has a ship that can survive the tidal forces of a black hole near or *at* the event horizon. I...I can't even imagine how this is possible."

The Chief shrugged and they both sat in silence for a time.

Bob, as if making a sudden realization: "Irritating. So, irritating...and I'm so close to home."

Chief, concerned: "What's irritating?"

Bob: "I think...I think I'm going to need to make one more trip before we get home."

The Chief offered only a puzzled look.

Bob: "And I need to acquire a small volume of mercury."

The Chief nodded and the two immediately stood and headed toward the docking bay.

In the docking bay they made their way to the cruiser the Chief had procured for his trip to the Outer Wall. The Chief stepped in while Bob waited and shortly returned with a small glass cylinder full of a thick metallic liquid. He handed it to Bob and placed an aged and weather beaten hand on Bob's shoulder.

Chief: "I remember giving someone...I can't recall whom...an almost identical cylinder such as this not long ago."

Bob: "That's odd. I received one as a gift not long ago but inadvertently left it scattered within the debris of the previous ship I left on Boreas."

They both smiled at one another.

Chief: "I would offer to come with you but I imagine my presence wouldn't be helpful in this situation."

Bob: "Yeah. I'm going to need to go alone."

The Chief nodded.

Bob: "You can set the wheels in motion...authorization and such...and keep the area clear?"

Chief: "It'll be done long before you get there."

Bob: "Thanks. Well, I'll be home in less than a week...or not at all. Who knows?"

They shook hands...the Chief's method of offering a farewell steeped in acute seriousness...and Bob headed in the direction of his ship.

Chief: "You know, they say travel makes a wise man wiser, and a fool worse."

Bob turned and said: "I know nothing but the certainty of my ignorance. See, I can quote dusty ancient tomes too."

The Chief laughed and Bob gave a raised hand as he walked away.

***

The chain of jump-ships that took Bob to his current location spanned a little over two days, which was fortunate considering the last minute nature of his plans. Bob had passed some of this time sitting quietly trying to still his mind, but sometimes the silence and the stillness are both deafening and jarring, like trying to stay put in a universe that is thrashing about and screaming at you. Still, it had helped.

Bob was now approaching the orbit of a particular black hole. The thing about a black hole is...it isn't really very black. Well, to be precise, what might be considered the hole is absolute black, but what surrounds that is a constant stream and influx of material that is on its irrevocable path towards oblivion...or the opposite of oblivion depending upon one's philosophy. As this material accelerates towards its inevitable fate it heats up until it becomes the embodiment of radiant pearly light. This forms a rather beautiful accretion disk following the flow of the black hole's rotation. The poles of the black hole emit, perpendicular to the accretion disk, powerful streaming jets of particles that possess a similar brilliance. This is amplified by the intense gravity of the black hole that tends to bend and distort the images of distant stars about it creating a ghostly halo that seems to adjust to the position of the onlooker. These effects, or the strength of them, do depend on the age of the black hole and the distance of the hole from surrounding stars, but here, near the galactic core, the sight of this object was otherworldly. It was a black pearl entangled in divine gossamer.

Bob positioned himself in an appropriate orbit. It was not as close as he could possibly get to the black hole...he wasn't here to push any boundaries...but just close enough. He was given the data,

488

what to specifically look for, and did find the 6.18 second blip that told him Moloch was, as expected, there. Bob set up a recurring hailing frequency, not frequent enough to be annoying but enough to insure that repetition would overcome the high potential of interference, and sat back comfortably into the seat at his console. Now he would wait. He wouldn't wait long, but long enough to allow his ship to be scanned, the message of the mercury to be understood, and a decision to be made.

Not far away, surrounded by an unimaginable turbulence flowing past like an unnoticeable breeze, a bespectacled man walked casually to the console of his ship.

Moloch, thinking aloud: "Hmm...this guy again."

Moloch stood and closed his eyes in thought then placed a palm carefully over his mouth lightly grasping his jawbone.

Moloch: "Well, I suppose it wouldn't hurt to see what he wants."

With the small discrepancy in time, Bob had been waiting a little over ten minutes when his console came to life. Before him was the almond shaped ship of Moloch, this time still and difficult to see. Soon after a hail was received and Bob immediately opened the channel of communication.

Moloch, silent for a considerable moment: "...Well, what exactly can I do for you?"

Bob: "I was just wondering if you'd like to talk."

It was genuine and it took Moloch off guard yet again. Moloch was silent for a rather long time then thought to himself *"Maybe it is time. Maybe it's time to talk."*

Moloch: "Position your cargo hold in line with the bow of my ship and I'll bring you aboard."

Bob was hit with the feelings of both excitement and anxiety. He immediately complied. In position he wondered how Moloch intended their ships to connect, whether he had an unseen docking port or some means to link their cargo holds with a sufficient airlock, but then he saw something for which he hadn't prepared. The mouth of Moloch's ship was agape and there, seemingly in the vacuum of space, stood Moloch in plain clothes waving Bob over.

Moloch: "It's fine. Open your cargo door."

Bob had a brief moment of vertigo brought on by the sheer disbelief of what he was seeing. However, Bob scanned the space around the ship and did, in fact, detect breathable air.

Moloch: "Come on."

Bob read and re-read the scan and replied with a hesitant "...ok." He then held extremely tightly to the console as he activated the cargo doors, preparing for the worst. The doors opened uneventfully and outside was Moloch standing in wait, still on the open mouth of this almond shaped ship. Bob walked to the open cargo door of his ship and looked suspiciously around the empty yet breathable space beyond.

Moloch: "When you walk out don't step harshly. There's no gravity between our ships. You want to go across, not up."

Bob: "Got it."

Bob gingerly walked across and awkwardly floated the foot or two between the two ships. Moloch and Bob grasped forearms in an effort to stabilize Bob from the short burst of weightlessness and Bob felt that would do nicely as an introductory greeting between two individuals, neither of which were certain of the others motives.

Bob and Moloch walked to the interior of the ship as the mouth closed behind them. The ship then turned and headed back into a deep orbit amidst the radiant fury of the black hole.

Chapter Thirty-seven:
...and the Multitudes of Children Shall Rule.

    Bob was lead into the interior of Moloch's ship. The ship was larger than Bob's standard cruiser, but it was not a large ship by any means. The interior was a bright luminous white...paneling, console, decor...all displaying the astringency of an individual intolerant of disorder. The central portion of the interior had been set up as a small but quaint living room with a couple of nice chairs, a small lounge, and a round wooden table varnished and darkly stained. There was no real separation between this living room and the command console, but the arrangement of the furniture and the large, round rug upon which it all sat partitioned the two areas distinctly. There were three doors elsewhere, two on the starboard side most likely leading to a small sleeping quarters and lavatory, and one on the port side that most likely opened to a slender room running the length of the ship for storage and system components access.

    Moloch gestured politely for Bob to sit then approached a console to make tea. Moloch produced two cups of tea, returned to the living area, and sat comfortably across from Bob. Bob took the tea with a kind "thank you."

Moloch, calm and polite: "So, what would you like to talk about?"

Bob, thinking carefully: "Well, I suppose I have lots of questions, but I'm also more than willing to listen."

Moloch took a moment to think, slightly nodding, then added: "Why don't we hear your questions."

    Bob had been thinking frantically about how to best navigate this conversation. He felt that pressing too firmly against the heart of this would result in...something not good: an end to the conversation at best. He needed to proceed carefully and thought first addressing some of the less potentially volatile subjects was the way to begin after which he would see if he could guide the conversation toward the murders. Moloch was an engineer and engineers tend to love talking about their work so Bob chose to begin there.

Bob: "I know you've worked as an engineer for a considerable portion of your career. The technology you've produced...it's...it's fascinating. It's unbelievable."

Moloch seemed visibly more at ease with this comment and offered a genuine "Thank you."

Bob: "Would you mind talking about it a bit? The only word I can properly offer in the form of a genuine question about it is...*how*?"

Moloch: "Sure. It was really a long and slow laborious process that culminated in a sort of Pandora's box. I've been a suspension-field engineer for a long time. Theoretical mostly, and in all honesty there hasn't been much progress in that field in the past three or four hundred some odd years. The first practical suspension-field became operational thousands of years ago. It was weak but demonstrated a decreased velocity of projectiles entering the field..."

Moloch was talking like an engineer now. Bob prepared for a lengthy explanation that would invariably involve terms, formulas, and equations that were assumed to be understood by all, but were only understood by the immediate few working on the specific project in mention. That was the modus operandi of the engineer.

Moloch continued: "The housing for this field generator was the size of a large building. The secondary stage envelope generator was the size of a convoy ship and operated nominally, *nominally* at 400 femtohertz."

Bob thought, *yep, there it is.*

Moloch: "...anyway," realizing he lost himself a bit, "...even now our most powerful field-generators are not much smaller and used almost exclusively aboard large ships and *important* buildings. They are considerably more powerful, but not impenetrable. The scientific community has abandoned research in the minutia of field properties in favor of brute force. I, however, have always been much more interested in small things."

"I began prototyping smaller and smaller field-generators, initially with the intent of shielding electronic components by suspension field. My dream had been to integrate the world of quantum technologies and suspension field engineering by which quantum states could be guided or manipulated by suspension fields. The usefulness of this, ...to me anyway...seems so terribly obvious."

Bob nodded.

Moloch: "It was an ordeal, Bob. I was swimming upstream. Field engineering institutes were most often funded by military operations that wanted a force-field a bit more powerful than their enemies. Many engineers were siphoned off to weapons manufacturers and munitions companies as consultants in designing phase disruptors that would better pierce the suspension fields they themselves had previously been developing. It was an endless, though lucrative, cycle: stronger armor, sharper weapons. And keep in mind that there hasn't been a major interstellar conflict in over a thousand years. It's the war-mind of the animal brain. We have never been able to evolve past it and it's disappointing."

"As for my research, I was never taken very seriously. I just couldn't find the outlet that would let me work like I so needed. I don't like the mindset, but I do understand. Imagine if an employer is asking you to produce a much more powerful and larger shield generator and you reply with research on smaller and weaker ones. It was not conducive to employment."

Bob: "I would imagine not."

Moloch continued: "I think I would have been less disheartened if I had been ridiculed or fought against in some way. At least that would have given me something to fight for and implied I was onto something, but what I encountered my entire career was casual disinterest."

There was a long pause and Bob could see a sadness envelope Moloch.

Moloch: "...then there was...an event..."

Another long pause and Moloch seemed to stir himself from some deep place where he was on the edge of getting lost in turbulent thought.

Moloch: "...I regained a certain focus...worked tirelessly, endlessly...almost no resources meant the work was largely theoretical..."

There was another long pause, this time the look on Moloch's face was that of odd wonder, puzzled, almost detached from reality. Bob was cautiously curious.

Moloch, slightly shaking his head: "...it sometimes seems that everything, every little dark thing, falls right into place."

Moloch removed his glasses and briefly massaged both temples with one hand before continuing: "I found the ease by which the fields could be made smaller and smaller and smaller. I learned how they could be more tightly controlled, wielded with scalpel-like precision. From there it was easy to enter the quantum world and exert a quasi-control of that environment...a funneling and shaping of probability. I won't bore you with the details, but from there I could re-entangle entangled duples into triplets that were both entangled and free..."

He then proceeded to bore Bob with the details.

Moloch, fairly energized by the conversation: "...which created a cyclic and syncopated quantum inverted ringlet that both exists and ceases to exist at the same time. This is what gave me access to the foundational associated strings, but not just the functional strings, also the *potential* strings that could vary the outcome of the quantum ringlet. Which, of course, you know what that means."

Bob: "Uh..."

Moloch, too involved in the explanation to notice he lost Bob long ago: "Right: singlets, duples, triplets...all existing and/or not existing at the same time in any desired permutation."

Bob: "And...so, how did that translate into, let's say, the ship we're in?"

Moloch: "Well, on the large scale, a shield could be generated that would be practically impenetrable, which I have to admit to a certain smug satisfaction at this accomplishment in the face of those who ignored me but wanted just that...impenetrable shielding. In fact, the solidity of the shielding is not the problem. The problem is the danger of potentially shielding one's self from the continuity of reality. It would be easy to accidentally partition the contents of the field from the formal universe and in a rudimentary way cease to exist. It's like everything else, a median must be achieved."

Bob: "And that's how you can survive the tidal forces of the black hole."

Moloch: "Right, and we could get a lot closer if we felt like it, but if we get much closer we'd have to jump to get out. This is about as close as we can get and still allow the ship to leave of its own power."

Bob: "Amazing. We made the calculations on our first encounter. Spanning a third of the galaxy in an instant. It's...unbelievable."

Moloch: "Thank you, though I wouldn't say that is the safest way to travel. A small error or malfunction and I'd be in the hole rather than far away from it."

Bob, after a pause: "I...I am merely here for conversation, so please forgive me if I tread into an area off limits, but may I ask how this applies to the Colossus risen on Diophantus?"

Moloch: "Ah, I like that name. I wasn't sure what to call it, but everyone seems to have settled on Colossus and that's fine with me. Well, the real bread and butter of this discovery has little to do with large shield generators regardless of how interesting and potentially useful that may be. The strengths of this discovery lay in the ability to condition and control that quantum world. For example, imagine a shield being generated that is impenetrable and sub-atomic in size. What can be done with such a small thing? What if instead of using suspension fields to augment material components, we used suspension fields to function *as* the components themselves?"

This did strike Bob with an acute fascination.

Moloch: "Field mechanics, Bob. Devices, components, and computations composed entirely out of suspension fields."

Bob: "A sort of quasi-real device?"

Moloch: "Yes, but here's the pinnacle of that effort...or perhaps the precipice; when power is adequately supplied, the field-generator itself could be composed of suspension fields. The power supply could be composed of generated fields. It becomes an enclosed perfect circle. A device, seemingly immaterial, quasi-real, but operating in the very real world. It needs no maintenance as the components are non-material, and it acquires and/or generates its own power."

Bob considered the implications, some of which were grim.

Moloch: "This is the reality of the Colossus. The Colossus, contained entirely within that little glass jar, unseen, was my triumph in field theory. Basically a series of protocols and operational instructions, the primary being power acquisition. It absorbed energy from its surroundings. New protocols and field-constructions were opened as various levels of energy were available. After power acquisition, material acquisition was next. From little bits of dust, to larger and larger materials in the vicinity, the Colossus collected or suspended these about itself and grew. As it became larger, building sized, an analysis of surrounding material provided the Colossus with the means to generate its own power. By the time it was destroying the city it most likely had suspended several power plants within itself and had them fully operational, modified for its own purposes."

Bob: "Wow. None of us knew what to make of it."

Moloch: "Fascinating, right? It looked like a large mess. A jumble of brick and metal and dust, but it was structured on the inside. The best part is that since there are no actual material components to the Colossus, it can't really be destroyed. It can be disrupted, as you saw when it was repeatedly fired upon, but even vaporizing the entire body would merely mean it would have to start over again. To truly kill it, one would have to deprive it of any energy source for a considerable amount of time, and you'd be surprised at how little energy it takes to sustain the initial quantum protocols of the Colossus. Floating helplessly in the space between star systems would merely render it dormant as the faint light from the distant stars would keep the protocols alive."

Bob: "So...what then could stop something like that?"

Moloch: "One obviously has to build in a kill switch into the primary programming...or at least a dormancy command. In lieu of that it would continue its purpose endlessly. It *is* still there, Bob. It will come back to life if needs be."

This did visibly startle Bob who added: "...is, or was that the only one?"

Moloch: "You know Bob, I consider myself to be a reasonable man. I am not after power, but there are a few things that *need* to be. These very few things that need to be must be maintained and I think any world wishing to test those boundaries should expect the same outcome. I think that is all I would like to say about that."

Bob: "Ok. That's fair."

Moloch: "I would imagine that some of our more ambitious scientists are hypothesizing about the Colossus and the ship. I am guessing that even with a realigned effort my research is at least a hundred years ahead of the crowd. Which is probably just enough time."

Bob began to question that statement in his mind but was stalled by the overwhelming inflow of data and the knowledge that he needed to choose his questioning wisely. In the beginning of their conversation Bob had a certain fear that a misplaced word might lead to his own demise, but not now. Now there was something very familiar, very human about this discourse and that fear was gone only to be replace by the less critical concern that a misstep might end the interview.

Bob: "You don't have any concern that they might find your research? I mean, ...something like that in the hands of every planetary power would be disastrous. You have to know they are scouring the minutia of your entire life...what they can find anyway."

Moloch: "I destroyed it all, Bob." With a reassuring smile. "I destroyed every bit of it. All the research, gone. There is no evidence of my work lest what's in my own head. They will not catch up, not in time. I've made everything I need and I have no romantic or noble inclination to further the science of human beings or indulge myself in some self-serving pride. Thousands upon thousands of years, Bob, and all we make are sharper swords. It is coming to an end."

Bob thought to himself *"What end? And what about the hundred years being 'just enough time'?"*

He had to work his way toward this line of questioning, but not prematurely.

Bob issued the next question rather carefully: "So the quasi-material constructs...machines made of suspension fields...this explains your ship's shields, and the Colossus, ...did it also play a role in the puppeteering?"

Moloch was silent and looked as if the question had been disheartening. Bob knew it would be a touchy subject, but he had to somehow break the ice on the murders and the reasoning behind them.

After a long pause Moloch spoke: "You know Bob...in all honesty I hated doing that...it's...it's hard to explain. It was the intersection between necessity and opportunity and the right actor to play the role. That was the second time I had to animate a dead body. The first was someone I considered a friend...someone for which I had a genuine admiration. Brilliant scientist. I know how horrible it is. I know why it's considered a universal crime... as it should be. It was unfortunately...unavoidable."

Bob: "I thought perhaps you had used him...what was it...something Eurnum...to hire that detective to follow me."

Moloch: "I did. I don't know why. There was no conceivable means by which you could stop what was coming, but when the fate of the galaxy is at stake one is inclined to make unnecessary precautions. The unknown is always within arm's reach. Besides, it wasn't just you. I needed him for a variety of organizational purposes."

Bob planned on circling back to those 'organizational purposes' but could sense a tension rising in Moloch from this line of questioning and decided to mitigate the situation with a short, but related diversion.

Bob: "On a tangentially related note, may I show you a document we uncovered and ask you about it?"

Moloch was mildly surprised and curious about what it could possibly be: "Sure."

Bob brushed his forearm accessing the terminal prompt and the file the Chief had obtained from Moloch's old lab using the "ghosting" process that partially recovered lost data. Making the display visible to both he and Moloch, Bob flattened the image across the table revealing one of the pages of what seemed to be interconnecting rooms absent of entrances or exits.

Moloch was fascinated.

Moloch: "Huh. Where and *how* did you get this?"

Bob: "We got it from your former lab." Bob then explained what he knew of the "ghosting" process that reclaimed the data. Moloch listened intently with a strong interest.

Moloch: "That is truly fascinating. I wouldn't have thought it possible. It's skewed, and lacking any substantial detail, but that is definitely it."

Bob: "Definitely what?"

Moloch, pointing to the display: "That's it. The virus...or the thing everyone has been calling a virus. It's some of the inner chambers."

Bob: "How can that be?" Bob began flipping through page after page. "There are around six hundred pages of this?"

Moloch: "Oh, considerably more. It's around fifteen hundred chambers across thirty seven floors. That little machine had to dutifully accomplished an enormous number of tasks. See Bob, the unknown at arms length...it's right here. I had no idea that reclaiming this much lost data was even conceivably plausible. I went to great lengths to dump that data. Sure, this is nothing that could have been

497

of any use to anyone, but fascinating none the less. I'm going to have to do some research into this *ghosting* process."

Bob was reassured by what seemed like a genuine joy from Moloch at this unexpected feat of science which gave him the confidence to press a little further.

Bob: "This is very curious to me. So, the shields, the Colossus, and this virus...all built from essentially the same process...the same discovery."

Moloch: "Yes. I mentioned that it really was a Pandora's box. Here, it was an entrance into the very small realm of the universe. One might even go as far as to say that the universe exists here, this sub-surface reality, and everything else is a mere byproduct. With access to the inner workings of the quantum and sub-quantum world, limitations tend to disappear."

Bob: "This does make sense to me in a theoretical-philosophical sense, but I really can't see the mechanics of actually making something, like this virus. It's almost like a massive starship...but tiny."

Moloch: "It is like that, like a little starship. Well, the specifics are extremely complicated...complicated to the extent that only one person in the galaxy knows the particulars...but you can think of it like this: If your hands are too big to build something, what do you do? You build a machine with smaller hands to make it for you. If you want something smaller than that specific machine can make? You instead make a machine with smaller hands that is tasked with making an ever smaller machine with smaller hands. Once the boundary between the material and the immaterial is breached and one can make substantial machines out of insubstantial quanta, it becomes a simple task of nesting protocols until the desired state or *smallness* is achieved. If there had been some reason to double the capacity of the virus it really wouldn't have been significantly more difficult...more time consuming yes, difficult no."

Bob: "I assume there was a similar process involved in creating the Pixler's glass."

This shot a small jolt of discomfort into Moloch which he managed to sidestep by refocusing on the inherent science behind the question.

Moloch: "...yes. Yes, it is a similar process but one that involved a significant increase in precision. It was funny actually. All of my efforts had been focused on the few tasks before me when it just occurred to me one day that there really was no reason I couldn't fashion a bit of Pixler's glass...then I realized that there was no reason I couldn't fashion a large quantity of Pixler's glass. You see, the theory involves a membrane made material, entangled with itself..."

Bob was lost about three words into that explanation, but he offered the attention deserved and would in honesty admit he understood almost none of it if the situation required. It was a good half-hour before Moloch concluded the "simplified" version of the theory and production of his Pixler's glass.

Moloch: "...which is why the critical point of sub-strata diffusion is so delicate and almost impossible to contain. It's a lot like trying to cut one of the poles off a magnet...you really just end up with a smaller magnet. So...imagine that, but the figurative polarization has an effective, though not real, infinite value that at the same time exists in a sub-zero value-less state."

Bob: "I...I have no idea what you're talking about honestly."

Moloch gave a small chuckle: "No one really does. The way I like to think of it is, imagine a considerable volume of pudding...now imagine having to tie that pudding up with string and contain it somehow...and also the string sometimes chooses not to exist temporarily."

This got Bob thinking of pudding, which was nothing but a distraction: "Well, it sounds impossible, but I suppose that's what it took to produce it."

Moloch: "Yes, to produce a sizable quantity of Pixler's glass.

Sensing the initial hesitation in Moloch at the discussion of the glass, Bob thought it best to buffer the conversation with these, as Bob considered them, diversions which did provide valuable information but evaded the penultimate *why*. To this end Bob chose to circle around to Moloch's employment in genomics hoping it would lead, inadvertently or directly, to the murders and the man suspended in this impenetrable glass. These individuals had to fit into this story somehow.

Bob: "Your employment in genomics...I imagine the purpose of acquiring such a job had to do with the necessity of what the virus was to accomplish."

Moloch: "No, not really. Or...not at first. It was really dumb luck and myself riding the fickle winds of chance toward something that ultimately became useful. Though my passion was in field engineering, I couldn't keep a steady job as we've spoken of already. I ended up just taking what was available and it wasn't until much later that what I learned in genomics became necessary."

Bob was aware of the fact that several statements Moloch had made implied a necessity and Bob needed to soon probe exactly what this necessity might be.

Moloch: "I worked at C.I.D.E.R. for a bit."

This floored Bob and was almost unbelievable. Moloch could see Bob's jaw figuratively drop and continued.

Moloch: "I'm sure they told you nothing of that."

Bob: "They did not. They absolutely did not."
Moloch: "Everyone to them exists in a particular need-to-know state. I imagine they felt you did not need to know."
Bob: "Wow. I really wasn't expecting that. So you worked there...with all the *unclothed* people?"
Moloch, laughing: "Oh no, no. That's Dr. Morris's upper sanctum. I worked in one of the lower labs. I actually never met Dr. Morris. I had assumed the *sans* garment aspect of that lab was a rumor."
Bob: "It's real."
Moloch: "You've been there? I mean, I know you were working for them, but I didn't really know in what capacity."
Bob: "I'm not exactly sure what capacity either. They requested I collect samples for them...but you worked there?"
Moloch: "Well, I wouldn't hold it against them. They run a tight ship and other than the novelty of that fact, there was nothing else to be gained. You knew I worked at Water Sprite Genomics, which was far, far more involved than what I did for CIDER. Everything with CIDER is on lockdown. It was a lackey job. People working there, at least in the lab in which I was employed, had specific tasks but knew nothing about what component of the assumed biological structures the work pertained to...and what the primary biological structure itself was.
 And beyond that, the ultimate purpose of the project was a complete unknown. Everyone had only a fraction of one little piece of a massive puzzle. They didn't allow any option of information leakage and, though I did learn a lot there, none of what I learned was relevant to my future plans. I'm sure they knew this and felt no need to reveal anything whatsoever of their workings."
Bob: "Hmm...they do claim a certain sovereignty."
Moloch: "Which they definitely *do* have...like it or not."
        Bob nodded, and remained silent for the briefest moment. He needed to at least try to get at the purpose or reasoning behind creating the virus and felt that the answer to this was woven into the fabric of the murders...but which to address first? What angle would be least likely to end the conversation? Bob already had sensed several areas that were sore spots in the dialog and needed to dress this wound by the least abrasive means possible.
Bob: "I have to at least ask. Who, to you, was the man in the glass?"
Moloch looked visibly irritated. Shaking his head in a fashion fitting of disbelief and anger, at which Bob had a brief concern that anger was directed towards him, Moloch was quiet then uttered a partial sentence.
Moloch, still shaking his head, said quietly, "...that man..."
In the following silence Bob, uncertain of the soundness of his judgment, added to the conversation two words.

Bob: "Harper Callus."

At the sound of those words Moloch turned his head and visibly clenched his jaw, revealing the outline of the straining musculature that did so and producing the audible sound of grinding teeth. He then returned to a proper posture as if the sound of those words had produced some arthritic trauma that he had grown accustomed to bearing and shortly overcoming, at the very least in appearance.

Moloch sat now in a seemingly calm pose and stared rather blankly toward Bob. Bob could tell that Moloch was not staring at him, but rather through and beyond him. There was some calculation being made, some seriousness being thoroughly considered. The silence they both sat in had been long and awkward enough that of which even Moloch in his inexplicably compromised state had grown aware. In so he offered a polite hand gesture implying he required a minute and Bob was happy to oblige.

Inside that dark mind of Moloch was an overwhelming drama laying him longside on the edge of a jagged sword and trying it's best to pull him in two. Moloch was being torn between a thing he had no want to speak of, of which he even questioned his ability to do so, and the need to have that very story told. It was want versus need and unfortunately for an individual like Moloch who possessed a certain propensity towards the rational, he knew that necessity should always trump desire. He had lived the past years of his life on a consuming mission of necessity and this was perhaps the culmination of that need. Perhaps this was the end.

The story needed to be told. Moloch thought that Bob seemed trustworthy...at least reliable enough to carry this story elsewhere. Moloch had honestly even enjoyed their conversation. It was the first true conversation he had had in years. Moloch told himself repeatedly that it would require nothing of him but a mountain of hard words that once said need never be uttered again. It also appealed to him the idea that he could get this necessary part over with *now* and within a short span of time be done with it...at least the speaking of it...forever. Moloch's mind calmed and a decision was made.

Moloch: "Bob...she...she was a little girl."

Bob added nothing but dedicated attention.

Moloch: "That...*man* ended the life of my daughter."

This, Bob had not expected and was struck immediately by a compassionate somberness visibly altering his demeanor. Moloch noticed this alteration which he offered a silent appreciation before continuing.

Moloch: "Bob...it's so much worse than that. Please, let me tell you what he did."

501

Moloch then recounted the specifics of the events leading up to his daughter's demise. He omitted no detail and chose not to hold back on facts that would have otherwise been delivered in a method designed to soften or circumvent the true awful nature of this terrible crime. Bob had been unprepared. One summons words like *gruesome* or *grisly* or *horrid* or *perverse*, but they all seemed so inadequate. It was a story unlike anything of which Bob had ever heard or conceived and for all the word searching that flooded his mind, looking for some foundation to which this story may be attached then understood, the only descriptor that seemed even remotely appropriate was the shambling succession of letters *unspeakable*. What happened to this little girl was unspeakable and somehow, in Bob's mind, Moloch had accomplished the impossible by flawlessly executing this tale that could only be affecting him much more greatly than it had Bob who was visibly shaken.

After a protracted stunned silence.

Bob: "...I   ...I am *so* sorry. I am just *so* sorry."

Moloch nodded in appreciation.

After silence had made another space and time for the absorption of this resonant impact, Bob asked softly of the little girl that had been etched on both their minds.

Bob: "What was her name?"

Despite the horror of the tale and the visibility of Moloch's distress, it was not until this question that his eyes reddened at which he looked down to the floor as he spoke.

Moloch: "I...I can't speak her name."

He then softly shook his head.

Moloch: "I can't speak her name."

Bob didn't know what to say or do. This potentiality had not been foreseen by him. He wanted to express some deep, deep sympathy...but how? There was nothing that could be done other than sit and share in the silence between them which they both did for a considerable time.

Following this shared grieving period Moloch stood and prepared more tea as both of their cups had become cold. They sat again in silence and warmed the chill that had crawled through their hearts with the steaming tea before finally Bob spoke.

Bob, understanding now: "So the virus and the pregnancies then..."

Moloch: "Yes. It is her."

Bob nodded and began to formulate another question when Moloch continued.

Moloch, as had been his means of coping, returned to matters more technical to dispel the thick gloomy atmosphere of the conversation.

Moloch: "The replication protocol...the pregnancies...you need to know this...there is a median age bracket of individuals twenty five to forty five. The protocol is generationally isolated meaning that it won't affect those who are not currently of childbearing years."

Bob: "You mean, the people who have the virus now will not be passing the virus on to their progeny?"

Moloch: "Right. It's a one shot deal. Of course, I could change that if needs be, but I think it will be unnecessary."

Bob: "You know a good number of people will attempt to avoid giving birth."

Moloch: "I've accounted for that. I've run several statistical scenarios and the numbers are, at least for my purposes, greatly in my favor. And I am guessing those numbers will increase even more when full knowledge of the situation is available."

Bob: "You mean when people realize they have not been impregnated with something dangerous?"

Moloch: "More when they realize there is not much they can do to avoid the outcome. The only way for the currently affected group to rid themselves of the consequences is to carry one child to full term. The virus collectively monitors the host and will re-implant on termination. Of course, one could spend their life continually avoiding the outcome, as I'm sure many will, but statistically those numbers are insignificant and don't concern me."

Bob couldn't help but be overwhelmed by all of this. There were some serious issues of individual rights violations here...among other numerous issues...but perhaps not the best time to bring these issues to light.

Bob: "So the Pixler's glass then..."

Moloch: "I destroyed his blood line...to the extent that was practical anyway. I know it's horrible in that most of those people were completely innocent, but for my own purposes it had to be done. A world without that animal now replete with my daughter."

Bob: "And we know he's still alive...somehow...in the glass."

Moloch: "Oh, very much so. Suspended. Slowed. But alive. I positioned him in a place that he could look over the galaxy and see his family die while watching that same galaxy be flooded with his resurrected victim. I know it is figurative but it is one of the few thoughts that cross my mind which actually produces a certain peace. You can see why that glass must float where it does, where I want it to be. You can see why I reacted the way I did when that idiot on Diophantus took it and ignorantly refused to give it back. In all honesty I didn't want to cause that much chaos and destruction on any world, but I needed to make it known, unequivocally, that there are some things that must be. I just happen to have the fortune and luxury to insure that."

Bob nodded. As difficult as this all was, and the problems it produced, there was a relief in just being able to put the pieces together in a sensical way. Up to this point the details all seemed arbitrary and unrelated.

Moloch: "Bob, do you fancy yourself a hero?"

Bob found this question funny.

Bob: "That I do not."

Moloch gave a short laugh and nodded: "There is the aspect of what comes next, and what to do about what is coming. We may need someone to watch very carefully and adjust...to adjust themselves or even the whole galaxy to what is coming."

Bob: "I...you've kind of lost me there."

Moloch: "I'm sorry to be so vague or enigmatic, but it's that unknown we spoke of earlier. It's always there. You see Bob, we live in a time where all permutations are open to us. We can modify ourselves as needed, and not merely in a physical sense, we can produce the mentality most desired to be "functional". Eons of physio-psychological scholarship has rendered countless human profiles which are almost effortlessly reproducible.   Bob, we could remake you. We could remake you as we like. We could remake you and change your favorite color. The smallest mysteries of human design are our perfected alchemy with which to tinker. The problem is not what we can do, but what will be necessary; what will prepare us for what is out there." He points skyward with obvious intention toward the whole of eternity.

Moloch: "We have mapped the vast majority of this galaxy, encountered innumerable obstacles and oddities. We have failed. We have succeeded. Our knowledge has collectively grown beyond the capacity of any one world to possess. Regardless, we know nothing. What is out there, what is truly out there?" Again, pointing upwards.

Moloch: "What will we encounter? Every smattering of people throughout history, from tribe to galactic empire, have been certain of their omniscience, that is, of course, until their ignorance destroys them."

Bob nodded in affirmation.

Moloch: "So we can tailor humanity to our liking. So what? What will be needed? What particulars of personality or psyche will overcome the next confrontation with our own ignorance? As it turns out, with history as both teacher and physician, our strengths are often our weaknesses, our weaknesses our strengths."

Moloch paused in sweetened thoughts before continuing.

504

Moloch: "These children will be supremely varied. There is no quality they shall not possess."

"They are a new genesis, born of a great cataclysm. They will spread across the universe, coalesce like a multitude of galaxies born in the chaos of undifferentiated and uniform fire."

Moloch then looked as if there was some sad relief in his eyes, like an end of some internal struggle.

Moloch: "Bob, ...an end to the animal mind. The abandonment of conflict. A world in which a word like *injustice* carries no meaning and is seen as some artifact of primitive times...unknown and merely speculated upon."

Bob: "..."

Moloch: "This is why I have done what I have done. This is why I have placed this burden upon the galaxy."

Silence.

Moloch: "It is a pleading of forgiveness to my daughter. It is my vengeance upon this world. It is my gift to this world."

Bob after a considerable silence: "May I ask...what I might have found on the surface of the Silent World, where we first met?"

Moloch: "You would find a small unmarked monument and some ashes, nothing more."

Bob had nothing to say as there was little more that could be said.

Moloch: "Bob, I think I need some time to rest."

Bob: "Certainly, of course."

Moloch and Bob stood and headed toward the mouth of the ship.

Moloch: "Bob, let me give you something." He then walked into one of the attached rooms and returned with a small paper book.

Moloch: "It is a replication of my original. I'd like you to take it. I know it will eventually be in the possession of authorities, but promise me *you* will read it, thoroughly, before that happens."

Bob: "You have my word."

Moloch then handed Bob the small book which Bob opened to the first page that read *Dream Journal: Sea of Shadows*.

Bob closed the book and again reaffirmed: "You have my word."

Back in orbit near Bob's cruiser, the mouth of Moloch's ship opened once again to exposed space and Bob pensively walked out on the platform. After the cargo doors of this cruiser opened widely Bob turned and exchanged a heartfelt handshake with Moloch.

Moloch: "I appreciate the conversation and your understanding. Should you choose to visit again, I think I would look forward to that visit."

Bob: "I feel the same and will do just that. Farewell."

Moloch: "Farewell."

Bob returned to his ship and made his way to the nearest station. He did contact the Chief rather promptly, but had exhausted his capacity for talk and did little more than tell the Chief that they needed to speak in person. Only in person would do.

The trip back, though it took several days, seemed to pass in an instant. Bob spent his time between reliving some of the still enigmatic details of the conversation, and the reading material so generously provided by the bespectacled man. Bob kept wondering about fragments of that conversation such as "these children will be supremely varied" and "there is no quality they shall not possess". Perhaps he'd acquire some more insight into this in the future, but with certainty the galaxy itself would eventually acquire that insight. Bob also couldn't avoid a certain worry at Moloch's concern of the future. There was still an element of this that was out of even his meticulous hands.

When Bob finally laid eyes on Helen once again he was permeated with a sense of relief and upon approaching Helen's Crown the tension of a trip too long began to unwind. Bob landed at the police station as he really had nowhere else to park his ship so kindly donated by Joan of Arcturus. He then spent a considerable time talking to the Chief who was relieved to see Bob alive...again, and eager to hear the particulars of the conversation. Those details were relayed in precise totality with the exception of what actually happened to this little girl to which Bob offered only one word: *unspeakable*. The Chief was surprised at that word, especially with a knowledge of some of the cases with which Bob has had to deal, and didn't press him further.

Bob almost made it to his apartment without encountering Abrum, who emerged from the shadows and began complaining of a ventilation fan that had been, as he put it, "sending his wits and solace on extended leave." In all honesty Bob had to admit it was good to see him again. In Bob's apartment was a disastrous mélange of doily and knitted decor...the work of Abrum. One would swear this apartment was occupied by an out of work has-been from the silent era. Bob began pulling doilies from every surface before realizing that it would indeed be a time consuming job which he wasn't currently up for. Still, it was good to be back in his apartment.

Not particularly tired, Bob went for a walk wanting to feel the city to which he had for so long called home. It was night and on his walk Bob passed a group of young women on their way to a party. It must have been a costume party of sorts. There is a bit of a trick that people like to employ that involves what really amounts to an error in terminal access. It is a way in which one can make the surface of the skin itself a visual display. Here, these young women had done just that, as the young are prone to do, for the purposes of their costume party. One woman's face appeared to be missing paneling revealing some kind of clockwork beneath, which seemed to have operational moving gears. Another woman's face appeared to be glass containing a variety of exotic fish that would swim across the surface from time to time. Yet another woman's face appeared to be deep space glimmering with a sea of stars. Bob couldn't help but think of Moloch's daughter and the lost potential of what could have been.

Bob walked to a park that, especially at night, was kept exceptionally dark. Inside a dense thicket of oak trees one could find a small grove of bioluminescent maple. Bob laid upon the cool grass and looked upward to the sky and the wash of stars beyond the chartreuse glow of the surrounding trees. There he occupied his mind with events of the recent past, of the uncertain future, and in between, not much at all.

Not far away, in a stuffy office, the Chief was absorbed in the same thoughts. Further away Joan of Arcturus looks only to immediacy as the tactical mind of a general at war is want to do. Beyond her a Rapulis known as Vasks tends to his people diligently and with a smile.

Further, Colleen of the Balaenae gazes longingly at the flesh of her people's coming form while much, much further away on a darkened portion of a planet, in a dark, dark tower, in an even darker room a woman known only as *She* looks deeply into the surrounding flush and pregnant void...that blackness that permeates all things. She looks beyond the self, to a thing that is neither acute consciousness, nor undifferentiated sentience, nor darkness itself, to a thing unseen, incomprehensible, indescribable... to the essence of the eternal... of the self and of the ending of the self.

At that far end of our reach, about as far as one can go, on a richly green planet a little Dandy wanders about through the prismatic splendor amongst the still and stoic adults. There she tries to make sense of the color and the darkness until a passing breeze brings whirling seedlings which she follows as she playfully gallops into the thick of the embracing forest beyond.

Error: Grain Alpha00-Omicron-Theta-8900x10010-Tau has received invalid transmission pathway.

Error: Deepfield grain Theta-87332-Epsilon-00 transmission interrupted by invalid terminus. Sending-path transmission field occupied. Connection reset and data resent.

Error, Error: Short terminus of coupled data stream. Reflective grain Upsilon-89xx001001-Mu within single temporal opening chose to abort transmission rather than retry or fail.

Error: Depleted pathway transmission interference for grain [Omega]-00-0. Quantus became entangled upon transmission and uncoupling recovered only partial data. Request to resend. Failure to receive. Perfunctory grain Pi-00-Omicron-8-00, upon resend was unable to translate. Syntax error.

Fatal operation performed. System check of all grain fields initiating flex and purge protocol.
...   ., Quantifiable trace transmission delineated. Error persists on recheck.
...purge 1...
...purge 0...
...purge 0...
...   .
Systemic strain of quantus distilled and uncoupled from communications stream successfully.
Field adjustment implemented and permeated.
...
...*foreign hive mind detected*.

Coming Soon! Bob the Galactic Hero Book Two:

Claire and the Bookworm

Find the answers to such questions as:
Who is Claire?
Who is the Bookworm?
What came of Moloch's many children?
What has Bob been eating lately?
What are the implications of the shocking revelation
contained within the final grain transmission?
(Did you read it carefully?)
All of these questions and more answered late 2018.
Thanks for reading!

Credits.

All illustrations created by the author, Matt Vandegriff.

I develop many of my ideas from the atmosphere created by good music. To that end, I would like to recognize some of the artists that inspired me during the creation of this book.

Melt-Banana, Joanna Newsom, Captain Beyond, Captain Beefheart, Genesis (Gabriel days), Melvins, Fantomas, Swans, Guapo, Merzbow, Mr. Bungle, Pink Floyd, Mars Volta, Boredoms, Big Business, Isis (the band, not the terrible group of people), Neurosis, The Ruins, The Beatles, Koenji Hyakkei, Acid Mothers Temple, Neil Young, T-Rex, David Bowie, Jethro Tull, The Locust, The Cramps, Faun Fables, Deerhoof,
Gillian Welch, Kore Kyojinn, Mike Patton, QOTSA, SUNNO)), Tom Waits, Cream, Tomahawk, Other Lives, Talking Heads, Keiji Haino, ELO, and the Harjo Trio.

And these composers were a great inspiration as well:
Roger Reynolds, Peteris Vasks, Einojuhani Rautavaara, Kaija Saariaho, Bela Bartok, George Crumb, Arvo Part, Alfred Schnittke, Sofia Gubaidulina, John Cage, Pauline Oliveros, Iannis Xenakis, Gyorgi Ligeti, Philip Glass, Earl Kim, and Somei Satoh whose pieces "The Heavenly Spheres are Illuminated by Light" and "A Gate into the Stars" were the atmospheric inspiration behind the dream journals of the same name.

Please do yourself a favor and become familiar with all the musicians on this list.

My literary influences are too numerous to mention here, however, for this work, there is certainly an influential trifecta between the authors Frank Herbert, Haruki Murakami, and Alan Watts. And though there is no similarity in terms of writing or story, the title is a reference to Harry Harrison's "Bill the Galactic Hero", a great book and one of my dad's all time favorite Sci-fi novels.

510

And a special thanks to my mom and dad, and all of my family and friends. This book would not be possible with out them. I love you all.